KEY WEST

Four Complete Novels of
Building Community and Love

Lynn A. Coleman

BARBOUR
PUBLISHING

A Time to Embrace ©2000 by Barbour Publishing, Inc.
Lizzy's Hope ©2001 by Lynn A. Coleman
Southern Treasures ©2001 by Lynn A. Coleman
One Man's Honor ©2002 by Lynn A. Coleman

Cover image by Nancy White

ISBN 1-58660-962-9

Scripture quotations are taken from the King James Version of the Bible.

Published by Barbour Publishing, Inc., P.O. Box 719, Uhrichsville, Ohio 44683, www.barbourbooks.com.

 Member of the
Evangelical Christian
Publishers Association

Printed in the United States of America.
5 4 3

KEY WEST

LYNN A. COLEMAN lives in Miami with her husband. Together they serve the Lord in pastoral ministry and writing. They have three children and eight grandchildren. Lynn is the founder and past president of American Christian Romance Writers, Inc. Currently she serves on the advisory board. She loves hearing from her readers. Please visit her Web page at www.lynncoleman.com or E-mail her at lynn@lynncoleman.com.

A Time to Embrace

I'd like to dedicate this book to my loving parents,
Ron and Ellie Putnam.
Without them I wouldn't be here,
nor would I have had full use of their houseboat
in Key West for my research.
May I continue to be a sparkle of joy in your eyes.
All my love, Lynn

Chapter 1

Bea scanned the approaching coastline. "Dear Lord," she exclaimed, her thoughts a jumble of fear and curiosity, "this is like heaven on earth." The crystal blue sea, the lush green palm trees, flowers bright and full of color in November—could this really be possible? So unlike the waters and shoreline of the New York harbor she had left a week earlier.

Yet she wanted to cling to Richard.

As her arm encircled the four-year-old boy's shoulders, the thought of parting with him tore at her heart. Poor, sweet Richard. Now that both of his parents were dead, it was her entrusted duty to bring him to Key West to live with his uncle. She grasped the ship's rail tighter. Ellis Southard had to be the most self-centered, uncaring man she had ever known. Not that she really knew him at all, but since he had received word of his brother's death, he had done nothing but upset her and Richard's world.

"Nanna, look!" Richard tugged at her skirt. "What are those birds?"

Bea turned to look in the direction that the child pointed. A huge bird, larger than any goose she had ever seen, bobbed up and down on the waves. Its long bill stretched down from its head and nestled in its chest. "I'm not certain, Richie. Perhaps we can ask your uncle Ellis when we see him."

If she could recognize his uncle Ellis. No pictures of Ellis were to be found in the Southard's home. From what she could recall from her conversations with Elizabeth, Ellis had left home to seek his fortune when he was a mere teenaged boy. Still, she hoped he would have some family resemblance, despite the fact that he was several years younger than his brother, Richard Southard II.

Bea donned her fingerless mitts, all the rage of new fashion, then nervously tapped at the ship's railing as she surveyed the crowd now gathering to meet the ship. The long dock reached far into the harbor. Effortlessly, the captain maneuvered the vessel up to the massive wooden structure. The seamen tossed heavy lines, and the pilings creaked under the strain of capturing the great vessel and bringing it to a standstill. As the boat lunged to a halt, Bea lost her footing and mentally chided herself for not remembering to use an onboard stance—feet slightly apart—to maintain her balance.

"Nanna, where's Uncle Ellis?"

"I'm certain he is here, Richard. Calm down, child, and let us wait for the captain's orders."

"Yes, Ma'am."

Bea smiled and tousled the boy's golden blond locks. He looked like the mirror image of his mother—her dear friend. They had been neighbors, Elizabeth older by two years. But as teens, the age difference hadn't mattered. Nearly every day they spent some time together, even after Elizabeth married Richard.

He had been the man next door. Richard was twelve years older than Elizabeth, and thus never the boy next door.

Almost sensing her weakened condition would not improve, Elizabeth pleaded with Bea to come and live with her, to help care for the baby. So many years ago. So many changes.

"I love you, Richie."

"I love you, Nanna." He grabbed her by the hand and pulled her to the gangplank. "Come, let's find Uncle Ellis."

Bea's heart tightened. How could she ever give this child up? He was as much a part of her as life itself. Her father thought it time for her to marry and produce her own children. But Elizabeth had counted on her to nurture this child.

Young Richard, straining on her right hand, led her off the ship and down the dock, casting imploring looks at strangers, yet too afraid to ask.

"Let's wait on the dock, Richie. Perhaps your uncle has been detained." A stunningly handsome man with reddish-brown hair and a trim beard nodded as he passed.

Perhaps father was right, she thought fleetingly. *Perhaps I should consider a husband and marriage.* Oh, she had some offers back home. However, with her responsibilities to young Richard, she never accepted any suitors. How could she possibly fall in love and simply toss the child aside? No, she couldn't do that.

Even the boy's mother, Elizabeth, had known she was asking a lot from Bea to give up her life, her own chance at the happiness of raising her own child. But they both agreed it was best for the baby. When it became clear that Elizabeth would lose her fight to stay alive, she assured Bea that, if Richard Sr. were to ever fall in love with her, she would have her blessing.

Bea smiled, remembering the day. Richard passed as a fairly handsome man, and perhaps she would have married him for the sake of little Richard, but she didn't fancy herself falling in love with him. He seemed too concerned with work, and he had little time for Elizabeth, though he did adore her in his own way. Bea couldn't imagine him having any time for her.

All that didn't matter. He was gone now, joined in heaven with his love, leaving Bea here with their child. Young Richard was now her responsibility. And his uncle obviously cared little for his welfare, or else he would have been here waiting for the ship. They had arrived on time. Perhaps she should just march back on the ship and leave, leave with Richard, and raise him herself. Her mind made up, Bea turned Richard toward the ship, marched briskly back down the weathered dock, and up the gangplank.

Ellis visually scoured the decks of the *Justice*, unable to spot his nephew or the nanny. One thing he disliked most in people was lack of punctuality. He wondered if she had arrived at the New York harbor in time. He'd given her two weeks to pack and make her way to the city. "She certainly should have had enough time," he grumbled. He had noticed only one woman with her child on the docks. The child looked as if he could have been the right age, but his coloring seemed all wrong for a Southard. All Southards had various shades of brown hair, and only he had been blessed with blue-gray eyes. The rest of the family had brown eyes. *Always had, always would,* he reckoned.

Spying Captain Brighton by the cargo hold, he decided to inquire about two things. One, if he would be returning to New York or traveling to Cuba before returning. Two, if his nephew had actually made it on board.

"Good morning, Jed."

Jed returned a hearty handshake. " 'Morning, Ellis. How's the sponge business?"

"Doing well. Are you heading back to New York?"

"After a trip to Cuba. Have some cargo?"

"Yes, but if you're returning from Cuba before going back to New York, I'll have more."

Jed rubbed his beard. "Wasn't planning on it; let me think a spell. I'll be picking up a healthy load of sugarcane."

"I'll take any available space you can give me."

"That's the thing about sponges, they take up room but not too much weight."

"Did my nephew make it on board?"

"Handsome lad. Sure did. I saw him and his nanny on deck a few moments ago. They can't be too far."

"I must have missed them."

"They could have gone back to their cabin to get some of their bags."

"Must be it."

"This will be my last voyage for awhile. The war's over. I'm tired, planning on settling down."

"Ah, a woman?" Ellis inquired.

"Hardly! The war took a toll on me. Privateering carries no honor, now that the war is over. During the war it was necessary. Now, well. . .now, folks just take you for a common thief."

"Sorry to hear it. I know you, Jed, you're an honorable man. Besides, I hate losing one of the fastest vessels to deliver my cargo."

"Aye, but perhaps a woman wouldn't be so bad either.

"Here comes your nephew and the prettiest nanny I've ever seen."

Ellis turned. The woman and fair-haired child. How. . . ?

She was stunning—with lily-white complexion and hazel eyes. Worried eyes. Young eyes. Weren't nannies old and gray? Shouldn't they be?

"Pardon me, Captain Brighton, but we seem to have a problem."

The captain stood with the handsome stranger she had noticed earlier. Perhaps she shouldn't interrupt, but she did want another glimpse at the gentleman with such strong shoulders and distinguished face. *What's wrong with noticing a striking man?* she rationalized.

"Miss Smith, may I introduce you to Mr. Ellis Southard."

Ellis Southard? She examined him closely. He had brown hair, but redder than she expected. Perhaps the tropical sun had painted it. His eyes, oh my, they were so like little Richard's eyes—the same blue-gray, same shape, though older, more mature. More passionate. Bea swallowed.

"Forgive me, Miss Smith, I assumed you were the child's mother." Ellis bent down on one knee before the boy. "You must be Richard?"

"Yes, Sir. Are you my uncle Ellis?"

"That I am, Son, that I am."

Richard stepped out farther from behind Bea's skirt, but still clung to it. For all the child's excitement at meeting his uncle, he remained naturally afraid of a stranger. Why wouldn't he be? The poor child already had so much loss in his short life, and was now about to lose the only mother he'd known. Bea had hoped to stay on for awhile to transition the child into a relationship with his uncle, but now uncertainty loomed. The man was too dangerously appealing.

Ellis extended a hand. Richard took it. "Tell me, Son, what do you think of this tropical isle?"

Richard's other hand trembled with fear on her skirt. Bea placed her hand on his back. "Richard, perhaps your uncle Ellis knows what kind of bird that is." She pointed to the one that had caught his attention earlier.

Ellis Southard followed her lead. "It's a pelican. Did you know those particular birds can swallow fish whole?"

"Pelican?" Richard answered.

"Yes, pelican. Their beaks have a floppy pouch they fill with fish and water. When the bird closes its beak, it spits out the water and swallows the fish."

Richard's eyes bulged as he strained to watch the interesting new bird.

"I've been unable to find a nanny for the child," Ellis said, standing again and meeting Bea's eyes. "Would you be willing to stay on for a week or so, Miss Smith?"

What an answer to prayer! On the other hand, her attraction to this man scared her. "It would be my privilege, Mr. Southard."

"Excellent. If you would excuse me, I need to take care of a bit of business. Then I'll bring you and the child to my home."

The child! He can't even call Richard by his name? Bea fumed. *O Lord, this man can't possibly be meant to care for Richie. He has the compassion of a gnat!*

Rather than speak her mind, she stepped back and led Richie to the railing of the ship where he kept a vigil on the exotic bird. She could see his mind working.

She knew he hoped the bird would get hungry so he could watch it eat.

"Nanna, why can't you stay with me?"

"Because I live in New York." Of course, the idea of moving back into her family home after she'd been a nanny for four years bothered her tremendously. She loved her folks, but having tasted independence, she didn't want to go back to the waiting season of balls and having men call on her. Well, perhaps gentlemen callers wouldn't be so bad, but. . .she wanted to do things on her own. Her folks talked about having another coming-out party on her behalf since she had been kept from social events for years.

"But why?" Richard interrupted her reverie.

Bea knelt down beside Richard and pulled him into her arms. "I will visit as often as I can, Richie. I love you as if you were my own. Your uncle Ellis is family; he will take good care of you."

She prayed she wasn't lying to him. She had serious questions about the man's parenting abilities, despite his brief attempts at friendliness toward Richie. Besides, what would a single man do with a child?

Perhaps he had married. She hadn't heard news from him prior to his letter concerning the house, the lands, and arrangements for her to bring Richard to him. She supposed it amounted, in part, to what bothered her the most about him. He hadn't come to New York to take care of family business himself. Instead he barked out his orders and dictated from Key West.

His brother had been no different, telling his ailing wife he was going off to war. Then he arranged for people to run the farm and left. Well, he had spent several private days with his wife before going. And he had come back as often as possible to oversee the house, look in on his son, and do whatever he could with his few days' leave. But those times had been rare. Of course, he had come as soon as he had received word of Elizabeth's passing. Bea had even seen him weeping at her grave. He truly did love her, Bea believed. He just didn't see marriage as a partnership.

Bea's parents, on the other hand, worked hand-in-hand. True, Mother took care of most of the social activities. Nevertheless, Bea had often heard her parents discussing matters of investments together. She knew her father was a rare man. Not many took stock in a woman's opinion when it came to business. But her mother had a head for numbers. "God's special blessing," her father always said.

She kissed Richard's cheek. "Shh, my love, everything will be all right. God is watching over you and He loves you far more than I."

Richie hugged her hard and returned her kiss. Bea held back the tears burning the edge of her lids.

"Miss Smith, if you are through coddling the child, it is time to be on our way."

Bea stood up straight and eased the child down to the deck. *O Lord, please tell me this isn't a mistake. This man is insufferable.*

Chapter 2

Ellis caught Jed's chastising glance and realized he had been abrupt, possibly even rude, with Miss Smith. Quickly coming to his own defense, he rationalized how women on Key West were rare commodities, and to know he was going to have a beautiful one in his house with a tender loving touch. . .he would definitely need to be on his guard.

She nodded in his direction, her lips tight, her jaw tense. *Yes sir, this woman will definitely need to be kept at a distance.* Even angry she looked appealing. With all the men on Key West, Miss Smith would surely have more invitations to social activities than he'd had for the past year. Ellis felt oddly uncomfortable with the prospect. It might be best to have the temptation of a pretty face gone. On the other hand, the idea of another man. . . Well, he just wouldn't allow himself to follow that particular line of thinking.

"I have a carriage to bring your baggage to the house," he said, trying to ease the tension.

"Uncle Ellis, do you have a boat?"

"Yes, a small one. Did you enjoy the sail from New York, Richard?"

"Yes, Sir. I've never been on a sailboat before."

"May I suggest, on the evenings I'm able, we go for a sail and perhaps do some fishing."

"Can I, Nanna?"

"Of course, Dear. Whatever your uncle Ellis would like. He's your parent now."

Richard knitted his brows. "My daddy died in the war."

"I know, Son." Ellis was still coming to terms with his brother's death. He was amazed at how well the child was handling the tragedy.

"Did you know my daddy?"

"We were brothers. I grew up with him." Ellis looked over to Miss Smith. What had she told the lad about him? She glanced away after acknowledging she had discussed him with the child.

"Nanna told me you were my daddy's brother. I don't have a brother."

"I know, Richard," Ellis replied.

"But Billy has a brother, and his brother lives with him. How come you didn't live with my daddy?"

Ellis reached for Richard's hand, then thought better of it. He was so timid a few minutes ago. He didn't want to spook the child. "That, Son, is a very long story. Let me take you to my home and get Miss Smith out of this hot sun."

14

Richard nodded.

"Mistress Smith, my carriage is this way." Ellis thought long and hard, trying to remember the woman's first name, but for the life of him he couldn't remember. He was not a man given to forgetfulness. This was indeed something else to ponder. She seemed as beguiling as some of the stories he'd heard of sea sirens in ancient mythology.

Her thick, dark dress would be far too exhausting in this region. He hoped she had brought her summer apparel, as he had requested, along with Richard's belongings. A simple wool coat for the coldest of days in the winter was all that was needed. He reckoned she didn't have a clue what November in the Florida straits would be like. At least her hat had a wide brim and would protect her fair skin from the hot rays of the sun.

Bea followed Ellis Southard's lead. He seemed to talk with compassion to Richard, and he certainly gave him his full attention. She found this a surprising and welcome relief, compared to the way most adults generally ignored children.

The port was busy. Ships of all shapes and sizes lined the harbor. Few horses and carriages lined the streets, but activity flourished. She had tried to learn about this island, so new to the territory, but little was written. Richard Sr. had informed her of a troop of Union soldiers stationed on the island from the beginning of the Civil War, and she had seen the fort. He had wanted to be stationed here, in the hope of spending some time with his brother, but Richard had spent most of his time in Virginia and other areas of heavy fighting.

Bea wondered if Ellis was a Southern sympathizer. The war was over, but she knew so little of the man. Her mother had told her, on more than one occasion, political matters were for men and she'd best not get involved. For the most part she heeded her mother's admonition, but only due to the fact she was busy caring for a small child. At one point she had followed Elizabeth's instructions and buried the family silver in the yard. It had been passed down for several generations and no war, no matter what the issue, would take that away from the Southards. They, of course, had fed many of the troops as they worked their way south. Never had she felt her life, or little Richard's, was in danger, but it was a weary time. Reports of families being torn apart, brothers fighting against brothers, cousins against cousins—such an ugly mess.

However, Bea was convinced slavery was cruel and heartless. Now, as she looked around the island, she saw black men, white men, and Hispanics working side by side. Could this place truly be a paradise?

She fanned herself. The sun was high in the sky and she was suffocating. Why had she worn such a heavy dress today? The first several days at sea were cold. Very cold. But the last two days, the temperatures had been warming. Now, the intense heat of the bright afternoon sun against the perfect sky of blue made her thirsty and a bit weak.

She needed to get out of these warm clothes. "Pardon me, Mr. Southard. How far must we travel until we reach your home?"

"Not far at all. The island is quite small. You could walk to my home in a few minutes' time."

Walk? The idea worried her. "I thought you said you had a carriage?"

"I did, and I do. As soon as we arrive at my home I'll show you the guest house. You'll be staying in the cottage, and Richard will be staying with me in the main house."

The guest house? She wouldn't be sleeping next to Richard? What if he cried out for her in the middle of the night? Of course he hadn't done that for a long time, not since he was sick the last time, but still. . . .

"Miss Smith, I don't believe it is proper for a man to have a single woman in his home without staff who also live in the home."

"Oh." Bea blushed. He did have a point. But she was the child's nanny. Wasn't that considered staff?

"Since you're no longer the child's nanny, I think it improper."

Could he read her mind? Bea nodded and bit back her counter-argument. As far as she was concerned, she was more than a nanny to Richard. But he was right. Her time of releasing and letting the child go had come. "A time to embrace and a time to refrain from embracing," Ecclesiastes 3:5, came to mind. Wasn't that the Scripture the Lord had been working on her heart for months now? Bea let out a deep breath and stepped up into the carriage while Ellis stowed their baggage.

The carriage moved slowly from the docks. The variety of trees, flowers, and unfamiliar sights took Bea's mind off her present discomfort. Farther in from the shore were more trees and a gentle breeze. Mixed with the shade, they eased her discomfort.

The house, a two-story wooden structure with shutters, stood proudly within a tropical garden. Fruit trees of every imaginable kind lined the yard. In the rear of the yard stood a cute cottage, looking to Bea for all the world as if a ship were buried in the earth from the deck down. The cottage gave the appearance of a ship's cabin, perhaps the captain's quarters.

Ellis jumped down and helped Bea to the ground. His firm hands on her waist as he guided her down the long step from the carriage gave her reason to catch his eyes, blue-gray and as deep as the northern seas.

He released her the instant her feet were on the ground. Her sides ached for his touch. Bea shook her head slightly, fussing with herself to take a logical approach to all this. She suddenly felt faint from the heat. She'd been to sea for days, perhaps her equilibrium was off. The sight of a handsome face certainly couldn't account for it, especially since the man was so impersonal and seemed to care only for the harsh reality of profit-making.

"The guest cottage was a ship's cabin. The former owner of this property, Captain Curtis, salvaged it and turned it into this cottage."

"It's quite unique." The place really was charming, she had to admit. But she was still agitated over Ellis's comment at the boat about her coddling Richard. *Perhaps feminine words and gestures are not endearing to the gentleman,* she thought, fighting back the sarcasm.

"I trust you will find everything you need. Dinner is served at five—you'll join us for meals."

Was that an order? Bea fought down her defensive posture and thanked him. He pointed out the outdoor water closet and other necessities for her comfort. Richard pouted. "I want to stay with Nanna."

"Richie, your uncle Ellis has a room just for you in his big house." Bea stroked his blond hair and smiled.

"Son." Ellis knelt down beside the child. He'd done that before. Maybe he did have a heart of compassion for the lad. "If after seeing your new room you still wish to spend the night out here in the cottage, it will be all right. Miss Smith will be close by. In fact, you can look out your window and see her cottage."

"Really?" Richard's eyes implored his uncle's. Two pairs of similar eyes searched each other. Bea turned. She couldn't allow Richard to see her pain.

"Naturally. Shall I show you your new room so that Miss Smith can have some privacy and gain some comfort from this heat?"

Richard propelled himself from the cottage. *He has only just met his uncle,* Bea lamented silently, *and is already willing to leave me, even forgetting to say good-bye.* Tears edged her eyes. No, she wouldn't cry. Not now. Not yet. Later, perhaps. When no one would know.

⚓

The memory of Miss Smith's delicate waist in his hands to aid her descent from his carriage had reinforced his decision to put her in the guest house. Face-to-face, day in, day out with a beautiful woman, together with the present shortage of women on the island, would press any sane man to his limits. He couldn't fault little Richie for wanting to stay close to her. Who wouldn't?

He mounted the porch stairs of his newly acquired home two at a time. "Come on, Richard, let me show you to your brand-new room." Curious in Miss Smith's presence, he'd felt the need to be formal, dignified, quite the opposite of his normal boisterous self. He reached down and scooped Richard up, placing him on his shoulders. "So tell me, Son. Does your Nanna have a first name?"

"Nanna!"

Of course. Wasn't his own mother always "Mom"? Ellis chuckled. "I guess I should say, what do other people call Miss Smith?"

"Bea."

Bea. Beatrice. That's it! How could he have forgotten? After all, that was his maternal grandmother's name.

"So, do you like fishing, Richard?"

Ellis could feel the child nod against the back of his head and neck. "Here we are, Son, do you like it?" Together they surveyed the room's single oak-framed bed, an old sea captain's chest he had purchased for the child's toys, and a small chest of drawers he had acquired from a recent wrecking expedition. A small bamboo fishing pole leaned up against the chest of drawers, just the right size for a young boy. One of the things Ellis enjoyed about Key West was the variety of items that came to port. Wrecking, or rather ship salvaging, had been the island's primary income before the war, as ships from around the world ran aground off the various coral reefs.

He settled Richard down to the floor and watched as the lad soaked up his surroundings. His eyes focused on the fishing pole.

"For me?"

"For you. I thought perhaps we could go fishing together. Would you like that?"

Richard nodded his head and tentatively reached for the pole.

"Go ahead, pick it up." Ellis sat on the bed. "How does it feel in your hands?"

Richard worked his tongue between his teeth as he held the pole in his hands, his eyes wide with excitement. Ellis breathed a sigh of relief. He didn't know anything about raising kids but figured he'd focus on things he had enjoyed doing when he was a boy.

His only problem would be caring for the child when he was at work. He had been prone to spend long days away from the house, sunup to sundown. With young Richard now depending on him, he would have to adjust his schedule. But he would need to work, and he would need a nanny to watch over the lad.

His mind raced back to the beautiful woman in his guest house. He hoped she was well. She had looked completely exhausted from the heat. He made a mental note to talk with Cook and have some lemonade taken over to her. She would need to drink a lot to become acclimated to this climate.

"Uncle Ellis? Can Nanna go fishing with us?"

"If she would like." He hadn't known many women from New York who liked to fish. Here in Key West it wasn't unusual, but someone from New York. . .well, he'd never seen it. "Have you been fishing before?"

Richard nodded his head. It seemed he didn't speak often. Ellis wondered if it was just shyness.

"Who took you fishing? Your daddy?"

"Nanna. Daddy was at war." Richard placed the pole back where he had found it.

She took the boy fishing? *Hmm, maybe she doesn't coddle the child after all.* "Did she teach you to bait a hook?"

"Nanna does that. She says it's hard to get the worm to stay on the hook."

Ellis grinned. The image of the fair-skinned, very proper young woman wrapping a worm on a hook intrigued him.

"Well, let me introduce you to Cook."

"Cook?"

"She's someone I hired to prepare meals and do some cleaning for me."

Richard knitted his eyebrows together. "Nanna cooks."

"Come on, I'll introduce you."

Ellis scooped the child into his arms and had him ride on his hip. A pleasing sense of comfort seemed to wrap the inside of his body even as little Richard's small frame wrapped the outside. He hoped and prayed it brought comfort to Richard as well.

"Good afternoon, Cook. How are you today?"

"Fine, Mr. Ellis. Would this be young Master Southard I've been hearin' about?"

"That's right. Richard, this is Cook. Cook, this is Richard, my nephew."

"Fine lookin' young lad. He has your eyes, Mr. Ellis. But his hair is much fairer than yours."

"My mommy had blond hair," Richard stated proudly. "Nanna says I have her hair."

"Nanna?" Cook inquired.

"Nanna is his term for his nanny. She's in the guest house. Would you be so kind as to run over and give her some of your fine lemonade?"

"No, Sir, but I'll give her some limeade."

Ellis chuckled. "Whatever you think best, Cook." He turned to Richard, still in his arms. "Richard, do you wish to explore the house or help me with your baggage?"

"Can I explore?"

"Sure can. I haven't explored it all yet. If you find anything of interest, let me know." Ellis watched the boy run out of the kitchen and down the hall.

Cook's broad smile disappeared from her dark, round face. "Now, why is the boy's nanny out all alone in the guest house?" she demanded, planting her strong hands on ample hips, her full figure going rigid.

"Because you won't move into my house. How's a man to keep up with proper etiquette if he has a single woman living with him?"

"Fiddlesticks, ain't no high society image here to maintain. What's the real reason? I fixed up the spare room, just like you asked."

Chapter 3

Ellis shifted nervously. He'd never been able to keep Cook from prying. The woman was incredible. He couldn't imagine her children ever getting away with anything. "Once you meet her, you'll understand."

"Ah, so she struck your fancy."

Ellis blushed. A retreat was his only option, before she learned more than he had a mind to let her know. "Please, take her some limeade." He turned around and quickly made his exit. Two steps out of the room, he heard Cook chuckling under her breath.

🌴

Inventory ledgers, exporting records—all needed posting. Ellis tried for the fifteenth time to concentrate on the books before him. He dabbed the pen in the inkwell one more time. He had planned the day off, giving himself and his nephew time to get acquainted. He hadn't planned on his nephew's nanny creating within him a driving force to flee back to work at the docks.

Maybe that isn't a bad idea. Ellis pushed back his chair and walked over to the window facing the small cottage. His hands clasped behind his back, he stood there, staring absentmindedly. A moment later Cook scurried toward the cottage with a tray and a pitcher of limeade. He watched as the door opened, but Miss Smith remained in the shadows as Cook entered the cottage. Disappointed, he turned around and faced the room.

Why was he disappointed?

Breaking his reverie, Richard's scream assaulted his ears. "Uncle Ellis!"

He bolted out of his office down the hall toward the direction of the scream. His heart racing, blood pumping, he found the lad, perfectly well, standing in the parlor.

"Richard, what on earth is the matter?" Ellis barely held back from exploding.

"Nothing."

"Nothing? You scream like that for nothing?"

"I just called you."

Ellis searched the boy's eyes. He truly was puzzled over his uncle's reaction. Was it possible that all boys yelled like that? *Well, not in my house.*

"I thought you were hurt, Son. Sit down, please."

Richard sat on the tall, straight-back sofa. "If you need me, come find me. Don't yell."

Holding back tears, Richard nodded his head.

Ellis calmed himself down and sat beside the boy, wrapping his arm around him. "What was it you called me for?"

Richard pointed to the stereoscope on the table.

Seeing the object, Ellis said, "Would you like to look at some pictures?" Against his arm, he felt Richard trembling with fear. Ellis scooped the boy up and placed him on his lap. "I'm sorry, Richard. I didn't mean to scare you."

Richard wound his soft-skinned arms up around his uncle's neck. His blond curls buried deep into Ellis's chest. Overcome with compassion, Ellis kissed the top of Richard's head and held him tight.

Bea liked Cook. At first she figured the woman for a slave, but soon her forward mannerisms revealed that wasn't the case. Whomever this woman was, she wasn't a pawn to someone else's wishes.

The limeade was refreshing, not as sweet as lemonade, yet the sour of the limes seemed a bit more gentle than that of lemons. Cook told her the limes had grown on a tree on Ellis Southard's property.

The shade of the trees around the cottage helped ease the summer-like temperatures. A gentle breeze blew through the windows. Bea loved the cottage. It was small, but wonderfully decorated, just like a captain's quarters on a ship. The wood paneling, the berth that held the bed, everything was so similar to that of the *Justice* where she had been the guest of Captain Brighton for meals during her trip from New York.

Cook's words brought her back to the present. "Your bed is made. Now remember what ol' Cook says and don't do too much today or tomorrow. Your body needs to adjust to this heat."

"Yes. Thank you."

"Dinner will be served at five. I leave to be with my family by six."

"I understand."

And Bea understood more than Cook realized. In New York the servants were ordered about. Their personal lives had no bearing on the time they were to devote to the family for whom they were employed. Their wealthy employers seldom gave thought to the possibility that their servants' families might have needs too. Here was another reason to be grateful for her parents' example. They were sensitive to their servants' needs. But in Cook's case, she seemed to be the one giving the orders. Bea grinned.

"What be on your mind, Child?" Cook inquired.

"Oh, nothing."

"The devil be in you! Don't go lying to me. You had a thought, and a funny one at that."

"I like you, Cook. You know your mind."

" 'Tis true, but I've been known to speak when I should have kept my mouth shut. The Good Lord knows He has a problem with me in regards to that." Cook slowly wagged her head. "It's not like I don't try. Well, perhaps I don't. Guess I'm getting set in my ways.

"Now, stay in your chemise in the house and drink lots of fluids. Just for a day or two. You may not think it proper, but child, forget propriety. You need to become acclimated."

"Thank you, Cook. I can get over the immodesty as long as I'm sure no one will come knocking at my door."

"Other than the child, I don't expect you to have visitors. I'll see you for dinner. . ."

"At five," they said in unison and chuckled.

Bea lay down after Cook left. She was exhausted. The heat had worn her out. Without Cook's help, she'd still be laced in a corset. Learning that they were rarely worn down here helped in her decision to leave it off for a couple of days. She took another sip of the cool limeade and rolled over for a nap.

The pounding on her door woke her. "Nanna! Nanna!" Bea fumbled for her housecoat and came to the door.

"Hi, Richie, what's the matter?"

"Cook says it is time for dinner."

"Oh. Thanks. Tell Cook I'll be right over." Richard ran off, and Bea closed the door behind him. She fumbled to put on one of her light cotton dresses. Fortunately, she had packed a couple.

She found the house's decor tasteful, yet it had some of the strangest items she'd ever seen. The table and chairs in the dining area were of a French style, and the hutch, more of a Spanish design. Oddly enough, the eclectic blend worked. Bea wondered who had decorated the house. She'd never known a man to bother with such things.

"Miss Smith." Ellis held a chair out for her to be seated.

The trestle table was set with fine china and well-polished silver. The stemware was crystal, with flowers delicately etched on each goblet. Ellis Southard apparently had made his fortune.

"Thank you, Mr. Southard."

Ellis nodded and took his place at the head of the table.

"Can I show Nanna my room after dinner?" Richard asked.

Bea watched Ellis from the corner of her eye, sitting up straight, careful not to show too much interest. After all, the man already thought she pampered the child.

"Yes, you may, Son."

Bea was pleased to see admiration in Richard's eyes for his uncle. Perhaps he had taken some interest in the child.

Cook served the dinner and sat with them at the table. It seemed odd to Bea, yet, on the other hand, perhaps it explained the familiarity with which she spoke of Ellis Southard.

"Shall we pray?" Ellis offered a brief prayer of thanksgiving.

At least he prayed over his meal, she thought. Was it possible he was a Bible-believing Christian? That would answer at least one of her prayers for Richard and his future life with his uncle.

"Cook and I often eat together, Miss Smith. She's been invited to move in and live here, but she prefers her own small cottage with relatives cluttering up the place." Ellis forked another morsel of fish.

Can the man read my mind? Bea scrutinized Ellis's blue-gray eyes, catching the hint of a smile within them. Her heart warmed a bit.

"Mr. Southard, you know that isn't the way of it. I'm the elder of the family and they expect me to keep the order."

"Now, Cook, your son is old enough to be the elder. You just like telling folks what they ought to do."

Bea found the playful bantering comforting and informative.

"Nanna," Richard broke in, "Uncle Ellis bought me a fishing pole and he said we could go fishing."

"That's wonderful, Richie."

"Richie?" Ellis whispered the question.

"I'm sorry. Richard," Bea corrected herself. She needed to remember this man was very formal.

"Richie seems a fine name for the boy," Cook muttered, and played with a morsel of fish on her plate.

"Nanna always calls me Richie."

"Enough," Ellis snapped.

Bea fought back a surge of anger. She did not intend to have this child raised by a brute. She saw no cause for him to bellow.

Ellis continued. "If you wish to be called 'Richie' by Miss Smith that is fine."

Cook quickly finished her meal. Bea hustled down the rest of her dinner in silence. No sense lingering and possibly angering Mr. Southard again. Richard excused himself from the table as soon as he swallowed his last bite. He walked around and stood by Bea's side.

"Nanna, can I show you my room now?"

"Yes, I would like that."

Bea couldn't retreat up the stairs fast enough. Richard slipped his tiny hand in hers. She cherished his touch, and her heart tightened again. How could she possibly live without him?

Richie's quarters seemed to shout out "boy's room." Intrigued by the fact that Ellis had managed to acquire a few toys, she found herself suddenly wobbly and confused. Perhaps it was the heat? She sat down on the bed and patted it. "Richie, bring me a book and I'll read to you."

He grabbed one of his favorites. "Nanna, I want to sleep with you tonight."

Bea kissed the top of his head. "Oh, Richie, you'll be fine in your new room. Didn't your uncle Ellis say you can look over to my cottage from your window?"

"Yes."

"I've got an idea. What if I place a candle in my window for you to see? Then you'll know I'm there."

Richard simply nodded.

"I love you, Richie."

"I love you, Nanna." He turned in her arms and embraced her hard. He was scared. This would be the first night he didn't have her close by his side. She held him tight. It would be the first night in four years she wouldn't be close to his side either. *O Lord, thanks for this time of embracing.* She swallowed her tears, not allowing them to flow.

"Nanna?"

"Yes, Richard."

"Can you sing 'In Peace' for me?"

"Sure, honey." And Bea began to sing the familiar Bible verse she had turned into a lullaby so many years before.

> "In peace I will both lie down and sleep.
> For thou alone, O Lord,
> makest me to dwell in safety.
> Psalms four: eight."

Ellis stood just outside Richard's doorway, his heart heavy like a sack of salt. Compassion for this woman and his nephew overwhelmed him. How could he separate them? They truly loved and cared for one another. *She's the only mother the boy has ever known,* he realized. Elizabeth died when Richard was barely one. So much death for such a small child.

He shouldn't have snapped at the dinner table. His words with Cook after they departed were not pleasant. She chastised him for his behavior. How could he explain that he was still having a hard time dealing with the loss of his brother? They had been close as children and had corresponded constantly as adults. He knew Richard's intimate thoughts about war and the massive destruction of humanity he had seen. He knew how such things had grieved his brother.

He also knew that Richard had a problem being home alone with his son—that he saw his beloved wife etched in his features—that each glance brought back the painful memory of her death and rekindled his guilt for having gone to fight the accursed war. Ellis knew all the secret thoughts of a man unable to cope with his wife's death. His brother had even been tempted to just leave the child in his nanny's care and head for the western frontier. And yet there were other times when responsibility and duty were paramount in his brother's life. He had planned to train young

Richard to run the farm, teach him business and how to turn a profit.

Ellis eventually concluded that war played havoc with a man's mind. He wished never to partake in such an event. He had been in Key West when Florida seceded from the Union and when the Union soldiers took over Fort Zachary Taylor. The captain ordered all those sympathetic with the South off the island, and the rest were given the option to stay on the island and not fight. Thankfully, few left the island before the orders to leave were rescinded.

Ellis never had to fight. He'd never been forced to take sides. Now that the war was over, the island was beginning to recover financially from its losses.

The beauty of Bea's voice lulled him away from his thoughts as he watched her caress the gentle blond strands of Richard's hair. He longed for a woman to stroke him with such a loving caress.

How long had it been? Ten? No, fifteen years since he walked away from Heather, her father, and his shotgun. They had been foolish young people who thought they were in love, only to discover it was simply infatuation. Had it been love, he would have returned for her when he was older and brought her to live with him. Instead, once out of her sight, her memory, their "love" had grown cold.

No, he was not a man to be trusted with a beautiful woman. He groaned inwardly and left them to their own loving union.

Chapter 4

The warm glow of morning sunlight lapped the palm fronds outside her window as a rooster crowed. Bea ached to be with Richard. This was the first time since his birth she hadn't been at his side, the first morning she wasn't in the kitchen making breakfast for him. She felt useless. She snuggled back under the sheet, having discarded the other bedcovers within minutes of retiring last evening. The small nub of a candle remained on her windowsill. She'd let it burn far longer than needed, just in case Richie would call out for her.

Needed her? She snickered. "He's adjusting just fine with his uncle, Lord. I'm the one who is having a hard time with it. Perhaps I should return home."

She waited for some earth-shattering revelation to bellow from the heavens. At this point she'd even settle for that still small voice spoken of in the Bible. Something, anything. She needed advice, direction. Her world was collapsing and the only verse of Scripture that seemed to placate her was Ecclesiastes 3:5, "A time to embrace. . ."

Disgusted with her self-remorse, Bea flung the sheet off and sprang out of bed. The room spun. She sat back down on the bed, clasping the edge of the mattress for balance. Her body trembled uncontrollably. Her hands felt clammy. What was happening to her? She closed her eyes. Her head began to pound.

She'd lived through hot weather before. Cook said to stay in her chemise and she had. So why was she so unsteady on her feet?

Beatrice's shaky hand grasped the water glass beside her bed and slowly lifted it to her mouth. Snow hadn't fallen yet back home in upstate New York, but she knew the pond was icing over. In a week's time she'd gone from freezing temperatures to sweltering heat. She dipped her handkerchief in the basin and dampened her brow.

Perhaps she should remain in bed. Bea eased her body slowly back upon the mattress. "O Lord, help me, I'm so dizzy and weak," she mumbled in prayer, then closed her eyes and collapsed into the cool darkness of her mind.

Ellis couldn't get over Richard's constant chattering. Questions, he had a million of them. Carefully, he answered them one at a time. Richard was a handsome child, and his eyes were so penetrating. When those eyes looked at him, Ellis felt as if they pierced his soul.

"Uncle Ellis?"

"Yes, Richard?" Ellis scooped another section of passion fruit from its yellow rind.

Richard held up his half-section of the fruit and asked, "What's this called?"

"They call it passion fruit. Some, I've heard, call it grapefruit."

"That's silly."

"Why?"

"Because it doesn't look like a grape, and it's much bigger."

Ellis chuckled. "I suppose you're right, Son."

"Uncle Ellis?"

"Yes, Richard."

"How come Nanna isn't having breakfast with us?"

"I don't know. Perhaps she overslept this morning."

"But Nanna always is up before I am."

It was odd that Beatrice hadn't come over for breakfast. He had told her the precise time for meals, and she was expected to join them. "Possibly she's tired from the heat."

"How come it's so hot here?" Richard asked, working his spoon back and forth until the fruit spit at him.

"Because this part of the earth is closer to the sun."

"How come?"

"I don't know, other than that's the way the Good Lord made it."

"Oh." Richard popped a seed out of his fruit.

"Uncle Ellis?"

Ellis didn't think he'd ever heard his named called out as many times as this lad had called him in the past hour. "What is it, Son?"

He held up the large seed. "If I plant this seed will it grow?"

"I reckon so. Would you like to do that?"

Richard's blue eyes sparkled with excitement. "Can I?"

"Sure, but we need to let the seed dry for a day or two first."

"We had to do that with the corn.

"Uncle Ellis, did you live at my daddy's farm when you were a boy?"

"I sure did. Even helped plant some corn."

"How come I never saw you?"

Out of the mouths of innocent children, Ellis inwardly lamented. "I was busy here with my sponge business."

"How do you grow sponges? Do you plant seeds like corn?"

If he answered that question, he'd be late for certain. Ellis wiped his mouth with a cloth napkin. "Richard, I'd love to tell you all about sponge-fishing, but if I don't get to work, my men will not go to work, and work is what pays to put the food on the table and roof over our heads. So maybe we can revisit this later?"

"All right." Richard grabbed his napkin, wiped his mouth and hands, and promptly stood. "Where do we go to work?"

The boy intended to go to work with him. Ellis took in a deep breath. He needed a break. But he wanted to be accessible for the child.

"Richard," Cook called. "I need you to go and visit your Nanna."

Ellis didn't pass up the opportunity. "Would you look after Nanna today? I'm sure she's having trouble with this heat. You'd be a big help to me if you kept an eye on her."

"All right." Richard scurried out of the dining hall, his feet pattering down the hall.

"Thanks, Cook." Ellis turned to her and smiled.

"The boy is most curious, I'd say. But he's a smart one. Truth be told, I'm worried about Miss Smith. She should have been up here by now. I haven't seen any movement in the house. I'm a bit concerned."

"She'll need your care today. Can you handle the child as well?"

Cook raised her hands to her ample hips. "Now who do you think cared for my young 'uns?"

Ellis held back a grin. He'd known she'd rise to the challenge. But if he had asked her straight out, she would have given him an hour-long lecture about how she wasn't "hired to be no nanny."

"Now, you take that smirk right off your face. I know what you be thinkin'. Besides, I like the gal."

Ellis chuckled and left before anyone could cause him further delay. He was already a half-hour late, though he'd still arrive before his men.

☙

"Nanna! Nanna!"

Bea heard the pounding at her door. She even heard Richie calling her. Yet try as she might, she couldn't roll her body out of bed. Every time she tossed herself over to her side she became dizzy. Her voice was weak.

"Richie," she breathed. Could he hear her? *O God, help me.*

☙

"Uncle Ellis, help!" His nephew's scream reached his ears just as he rounded the gate. "Help!"

Beatrice. . .Miss Smith. . .trouble. Ellis turned back and ran toward the cottage.

Richard stood outside the door, crying. "Help, Uncle Ellis, Nanna won't come."

Ellis lifted the iron latch and flung open the door. He rushed toward the bedroom and found Beatrice wrapped in her bed-sheet. "Richard, go get Cook."

"Is she all right?"

"She will be, Son. Please, go get Cook."

Thankfully, Richard didn't have any more questions. Beatrice was as red as a cooked lobster, and he knew what that meant. She needed to be cooled down and quickly. He reached for a rag in the basin. The water was warm. He dampened it anyway and applied it to her forehead.

The cistern will be the best place for her, he thought, his mind racing. *It should be full this time of year.* Ellis scooped her up and carried her out to the backyard, to the large coral trough protected by a weathered shed. He'd often thought the cistern was far too big, but today it would prove its worth. He set her on the top step, her feet dangling in the pool of water. He held her in his left arm and reached into the pool to dampen the rag again. This time it would be more refreshing.

Gently he applied the cool cloth over her face and neck, her arms and legs, carefully avoiding her torso.

Cook burst into the shed, huffing and gasping for breath. "Mr. Ellis, what's the matter with the poor child?"

"I'm no doctor, but I'd say she has a serious case of heatstroke. Cool her down, Cook. Keep her cool. I'll fetch the doctor."

"I'll take care of the child," she replied, immediately taking Beatrice from Ellis, cradling her like a mother with child.

Richard stood next to Cook trembling, tears streaming down his face. "Is Nanna going to die?" he asked.

"No, Son. She's going to be just fine." Ellis knelt beside him and held his hands. *So much death in this little one's life, Lord. Please make his Nanna all right*, he silently prayed. "Would you help Cook keep Nanna wet?"

Frightened eyes stared inquiringly into his uncle's.

"She'll be fine, Richard, trust me."

Richard nodded.

Cook continued to pour the water over Beatrice's lethargic body.

"Can you help her, Son?"

"Yes."

"Good. Strip down to your shorts and stand in the water next to Cook. Keep pouring water on her. I'll get the doctor."

Richard began stripping off his clothes. Ellis figured the water would help the child as well. While he didn't appear to be having any trouble with the heat, he might later. A good dip in the cool cistern would be helpful for him. Ellis headed for town, thanking God for living in such a small community with the doctor a few blocks away.

⚓

"Miss Smith."

Someone was calling her, but who? The gentle lull of a woman's voice continued to penetrate her muddled thoughts.

"Come on, Child, I know you can hear me."

"Nanna!" Richie cried.

Richard, crying. Beatrice opened her eyes wide and tried to bolt upright. Water? She was in a tub? With Richard? And. . .and. . .Cook? What was going on here?

Cook's warm chocolate face broke into a grin, and her eyes sparkled. "Glad

29

to see you're feeling better."

"Where am I? What's going on?"

"A touch of the heat. Didn't drink enough, I reckon."

"Nanna!" Richie exclaimed and jumped on her. The boy was soaking wet, she quickly realized, and in this. . .this huge tub.

Bea embraced Richard. "Where am I? Where are we?"

"This here be a cistern. Folks on the island have them all over. We collect the water during the rainy season and have it for the dry season. When the troops came to the island in the twenties, folks realized they wouldn't have enough fresh water in the wells. So they built these. Come in pretty handy."

Handy—the water was downright wonderful. Beatrice gathered in her surroundings. She was sitting on a white coral step at a rectangular pool of water with walls of coral as well. A small wooden roof with short sides stood over the area with a hatch-like opening at the peak of the roof. She cupped a handful of the refreshing water and sipped. It was cool and very energizing.

"Drink slowly. Your body has had quite a shock."

"How'd I get here?"

"Mr. Southard brought you."

Bea's cheeks flamed. She was in her undergarments. "Oh my," she gasped.

"Don't be fussing about modesty now, child. He had you wrapped in a bedsheet. I took that off."

"Oh."

"Mr. Southard is a perfect gentleman. He's gone to fetch the doctor. I reckon he'll be here shortly."

"Doctor? What happened?"

"Near as I can figure, you passed out from the heat. Your skin was bright red when I first came on you."

Bea looked at her arms. They were pink, but certainly not red.

"Your color's almost back to normal," Cook said.

Richie sat on the step beside Beatrice. "Isn't this great?" Richie wiggled his toes in the water.

Bea reached out to him, found she was still dizzy, and put her hand back down on the steps to steady herself.

"Now don't you go moving too quickly, Miss."

"I can't believe how shaky I am."

"Comes with the heat, if you don't take care of yourself. Now sit back and enjoy the water." Cook rose from her step and sat down on the top stair.

"Nanna, do you think Uncle Ellis will let me go swimming in here?"

"I doubt your uncle will want you swimming in here, Child," Cook answered. "We've got a big ocean out there, plenty of water for a boy to go swimming if'n he has a mind to."

"Can I go swimming in the ocean, Nanna?"

"Give your Nanna some time to rest."

Richard's shoulders sagged. "All right."

Bea couldn't possibly keep Richard's questions straight in her mind. It took all of her energy just to try to stay awake.

⚓

"She's in the cistern, Doc." Ellis pointed to the backyard shed covering the cistern.

"Quick reasoning, Ellis," Dr. Hanson replied.

"Cook and my nephew are back there with her. Unless you think you need me, I think for propriety's sake I best stay out front."

"I understand."

"Thanks, Doc. Send the boy to me. I'll take him with me to work."

"Sure." Doc Hanson headed to the backyard.

Ellis paced his front yard, picking up some fallen palm fronds and tossing them in a pile. A house, a yard, a child—all brought more burdens, and more responsibility into his life. Not to mention a guest who had almost died. A pain shot through Ellis's chest. She had such lily-white skin, made even more beautiful by the few freckles dotting her cheeks. The woman weighed next to nothing in his arms. She didn't have the strength to even protest. Never in a million years would he forget her lifeless form draped across his arms. Why hadn't he checked on her sooner, when she hadn't appeared for breakfast?

Ellis kicked a coral rock out of his path. Life sure had changed in a little over a month. Then, he had been a man of no worries. Oh, perhaps a few regarding the success of his business, but then he only had himself to provide for. His bank account grew. He had more than he needed.

He had sunk a tremendous portion of his savings into this old house—a house he had purchased upon learning he was to raise his brother's son. Oh, how the tables had turned.

He had hired Cook to fix his dinner and clean his rented room in town. The owner of the boardinghouse, Ana White, could no longer care for her boarders in that fashion, so he found Cook. In the end, Cook worked for just about everyone in the house, including Ana. She was quite a woman for her age.

He was thankful she had come to work for him here. But he knew she still wandered over to the boardinghouse and took care of a few folks there as well.

"Uncle Ellis."

Ellis spun around to see the child, dripping wet, his rumpled clothes in his arms and fear knotting his forehead.

"How is she, Son?"

"She's awake."

"Good."

"Do I have to go with you?"

How could he take the child away? "Not if you don't want to. But I thought we could walk down to the dock, speak to my workers, and come right back."

"Really?" Richard's eyes widened. A curl of a smile edged on the side of his mouth.

"Sure. Do you want to come with me or stay?"

Richard turned and looked back at the cistern. "Will she be all right?"

"Yes, Son. Cook and the doctor can handle things from here. But I'm sure you helped a great deal."

Richard puffed out his chest. "I did like you said. I got her real wet."

Ellis chuckled. "Good, Son, real good."

Chapter 5

Ellis worked out the tension in his back, then walked hand in hand with Richard toward his dock. The sun was bright, the sky a vivid blue, a few clouds lining the horizon. "Richard." Ellis pointed to his right. "See those tall clouds that look like a top?"

"Uh-huh."

"Those are funnel clouds. The air is swirling around real fast."

"Really? How does it work?"

"Hmmm, tell you what. When we get to my office I'll show you how the wind spins and the cloud is formed." The ploy worked; the boy seemed to have taken his mind off his nanny. On the other hand, Ellis found himself wondering how she was doing—if they had her out of the cistern yet and back in her cottage. He'd have moved her into the house to care for her, but the cottage was actually a tad cooler than his home.

"Uncle Ellis?"

"Yes, Son."

"Did you make this dock?"

"No, I bought it from the man who built it."

"How come it's so long? New York had little docks."

The child was amazing, noticing little things like that. "In New York harbor the water becomes deep quickly. In Key West, you have to go out a long way from shore before the water gets deep, so the dock goes out to the deep water to enable the ships to come up to them."

"Oh." Richard pointed toward the mounds of sponges drying on his dock. "What are those?"

"Sponges. They grow in the ocean. My men take small boats out and dive into the water to bring up the sponges."

"Can you teach me how to swim?"

"Sure."

"Nanna plays in the pond with me at the farm. But I don't think she knows how to swim."

"Hmmm, it's possible. Growing up on the farm, I learned to swim in the pond. Is that where Nanna took you to play?"

"Yes, by the big rock."

Ellis smiled. How many leaps had he taken off that rock into the cool, crisp water below? He couldn't possibly count. "The water in Key West is much

33

warmer than back home."

"That's 'cause we are closer to the sun, right?"

Ellis grinned broadly. Richard was a very bright boy indeed. He walked his nephew to the end of his pier where he had a small building which housed his office and tools for the men. Inside he showed him the sharp knives the sponge fishermen used for tools, and the nets they tied to their waists. Some of the men preferred an odd scissors-shaped tool to the knife, depending on which method the man had been taught.

"Uncle Ellis, what's this?" Richard pointed to a long pole with a two-pronged iron hook.

"That's for hooking the sponges from inside the boat."

"Do you go sponge-fishing too?"

"Sometimes, but not too often. Most of the time I have to work in the office here, or with the sponges after they've been harvested.

"Go take a whiff of that pile of sponges over there."

Richard scurried over. He wrinkled his face and looked back at Ellis. "They stink like dead fish."

Ellis chuckled.

Bea raised her head off the soft, down-feather pillow. She inhaled the freshness of the clean white sheets Cook had remade her bed with. "Cook, what were you and the doctor whispering about before he left?"

"Not worth repeatin'. He was just making sure I knew how to care for ya. I'll be spending the night with ya too."

"I'm fine," Beatrice protested.

"Land sakes, Child, you are exhausted from that heat. I've got to make sure you drink enough fluids."

"But you have a family."

"True, but the doc, he's a-sending a message to my house. My children are all grown with children of their own. They feed themselves now, since I cook dinner for Mr. Ellis, and they insists I eat with him."

"I don't mean to pry, but were you a slave?"

"No, Ma'am. My family was set free when I was no higher than your knee. There's always been good pay for honest work for Bahamians on Key West. So my husband, George, brought us here right after we married. We bought our own home after a few years, and though things been tough at times, we've had a good life here on the island."

"What about the war?"

"Truth be told, the island wasn't much a part of the war. Granted, some of the folks who were wreckers suffered hard times when they weren't allowed to do no salvaging. And, what with the navy being here, there weren't quite so many wrecks."

"Tell me about this island of Key West. Where'd it get its name?"

"Original name was Cayo Hueso. That's Spanish for 'Island of Bones.' Folks say, for a long time the island was just a watering hole for sailors. Belonged to Cuba back then. Eventually, the king of Spain gave it to a man for faithful service. That fella, in turn, sold it to four businessmen from Connecticut. And they was the ones that started building a town here. Soon after, the navy put up a base. But 'twas the wrecking industry what brought a lot of money to the island." Cook leaned back and gave a low laugh, slapping her hands on her broad lap. "Listen to me rattle on."

"No, I'm interested, really."

Cook set her ample figure down on a rocker beside Bea's bed. "I can tell a tale or two about this here island. It's very different from the Bahamas, but I'm most comfortable here."

Beatrice's eyes were getting heavy. "Were there pirates living here?"

"Sure. Still are."

Beatrice pulled the sheet up to her chin.

Cook's robust laughter filled the room. "Most of 'em are retired. They made their money. Now they've settled down, got married, had kids. Got respectable, you might say."

"Really?" The word slipped past Bea's lips before she could catch herself.

"Wreckers salvaged whatever was worth taking from ships. Story goes, years ago, before the law came to the island, some folks would put a light out on the water to confuse the sailors so they'd run their ships aground on the reefs."

"No."

"Don't know if it be true or not. Just know that's what some say, is all. But it woke you up, didn't it?"

Bea chuckled. "Yes."

"Good, you need to stay alert, keep drinking. Rest will come later. But the doctor wants you awake for a mite longer before you sleep again."

"All right. Perhaps you can tell me some more tales of Key West."

"Why don't you tell me something about yourself?"

"Like what?"

"Why are you a nanny at such a young age?"

"Oh, well, that's easy. My best friend was Elizabeth Southard, Richard's mother. She had a terrible time when she was with child. We weren't even sure she was going to pull through. Elizabeth decided she needed some help, and she didn't want just anyone. Richard's family was gone, so they were alone on the farm. And she, being so weak. . .well, she asked me."

"You was a good friend." Cook tapped Bea's hand and proceeded to dip a cloth in the bowl of water. "Go on, I'll keep you cool while you tell me more."

"At first I was supposed to help only until shortly after Richard was born. But Elizabeth never fully recovered. So she asked me to stay. My parents weren't too happy. They'd had my coming-out party just before Elizabeth turned ill. Nevertheless, they understood the closeness between us, and knew that, if it were me who was so desperately ill, Elizabeth would have constantly been at my side.

"Elizabeth worsened after Richard was born. She developed a cough and never shook it." A tear edged her eye. "A year after Richard's birth, she passed on. But not before begging me to stay and continue to watch over Richard. Not that she had to beg me for anything regarding that little one."

"He's a charmer," Cook agreed. "You should have seen him this morning. Had his uncle tied up in knots just trying to figure out where all the boy's questions came from."

Bea laughed, her parched lips feeling brittle. She reached for a glass of Cook's refreshing limeade, noticing her hand still shook, though it was much stronger than earlier this morning. "I can't believe I fainted."

"Praise be to the Almighty! If little Richard hadn't come to check on you right away, you would have been far worse."

"He was so frightened."

"That he was, Child. But the Good Lord was with us, and you're going to be fine. You should have seen him pouring the water on you. He just kept doing what his uncle Ellis told him to do. You've raised a fine lad there, Miss. You should be proud."

"Don't know that I've done all that much, really. Just loved him as if he were my own."

"It shows, Child. It shows." Cook finished applying the damp cloth to Bea's limbs and sat back down on the wooden chair beside the bed. She brushed the gray hair, streaked with black, off her face. "Tell me where the child's father was during all these years."

"The war."

"How could I forget that? Mr. Ellis sure was broken up by his brother's death. I never seen a grown man so close to someone so far away."

"Close? Elizabeth never even spoke of him."

"I've been carin' for Mr. Ellis for a number of years now. He been receivin' a letter from his brother at least once a month."

"Even during the war?"

"Truly a miracle, I say. Yes'm, he managed to get some mail out with a Captain Brighton. Seems the captain was working for the North, privateering. 'Course, you talk with a Southern sympathizer, they'd call him an outright pirate."

Bea chuckled. "I guess it all depends on which side of the war you're on." So, the *Justice*'s captain was a pirate or a privateer. Interesting.

"You speak a lot of truth there, Child.

"You mentioned your 'coming-out party.' Is that when your family says you're now ready for courtin' and marriage?"

Bea felt her cheeks heat up and she weakly answered, "Yes."

"I'm sure you left a few men lamentin' your status as a nanny."

"I wasn't one to seek the attention of a man. Never cared to, really. I suppose I never found one that was interesting enough." Bea placed her empty glass back on the nightstand.

"Uncle Ellis, who buys the sponges?" Richard asked, squatting on a tall chair beside him at his desk. Mounds of paperwork needed going over. But his mind was yet again on a hazel-eyed sea siren. His thoughts lingered on whether or not she'd survive this heat. He felt certain he had caught her before she became critical. The cistern was a true blessing from God. But he was still worried for the sake of the child. How would Richard handle losing another person close to him? Ellis shuddered and rubbed the gooseflesh off his arms.

"Uncle Ellis, can we go see Nanna now?"

Ellis plopped down his pencil. "Sure, Son. I was just thinking about her myself."

Richard's bright blue eyes smiled as he jumped off the tall chair he had been perched on. "I'm ready."

"Great, give me a minute to put these books together so I can take them home."

"Why do you write in your books? Nanna said I mustn't write in my books."

"Your Nanna is right. But these are special books for keeping track of a business's money. How much a business spends, how much it makes."

"How much money do you have, Uncle Ellis?"

"Enough." Ellis placed his large masculine hands on top of Richard's head and ruffled his curls, just like he had seen Miss Smith do on more than one occasion.

Richard smiled. "Nanna says I have a lot of money too."

"She did, did she?" What was this woman telling this child? Why would a boy need to worry himself about money at his age? He would need to have a word with Miss Smith when she was feeling better. At least one word.

Richard nodded. "Nanna said when my mommy died she had money put in a special place for me when I became a man."

"I see."

"Nanna said it was to buy my own farm, or go places, or whatever I want."

"That is a special gift, Son."

"Nanna says a wise man thinks before he spends his money."

Maybe he wouldn't need to speak with the woman after all.

"Nanna says some men spend their money on silly things."

"I see."

"Nanna says wise money is like planting corn. If you plant it right it grows and makes more."

"Your Nanna is a pretty smart woman."

"Nanna says Grandpa Smith taught her about wise money."

"I see," he said for the third time. And perhaps he was beginning to see more than he ever expected. As the child's nanny, she was responsible for his schooling, and she knew that Richard's job would be caring for the farm one day. Maybe she wasn't as overprotective as he'd suspected.

"Uncle Ellis?"

"Yes, Son?" Ellis scooped the child into his arms, figuring they would make it home faster if he carried him. The child was a wonder, his mind so quick with facts and details. He soaked up knowledge like his sponges soaked up water. He was a remarkable lad who had a remarkable teacher. Ellis pondered the possibility of asking a certain Miss Beatrice Smith to stay on as the child's nanny. Of course, he'd probably have to offer her holidays to visit with her family in New York. . . . Still, the idea was plausible.

"Who taught you about money?"

"My dad and your father."

"Was my daddy wise with money?"

"Yes."

Richard nodded. A somber expression creased his delicate face. "I miss my daddy."

Ellis swallowed back a gasp. He hadn't expected Richard to be so honest with his emotions.

Ellis paused in the street. He lowered the child down and knelt before him, face-to-face. "I do too, Son. I do too."

Chapter 6

N anna!" Richard cried from the doorway of her cottage.

"Come in here, Richie, I'm lying down."

"All right."

The old wooden rocking chair creaked as Cook eased herself up. "I'm going to speak with Mr. Ellis, Miss. I'll be back in a minute."

Beatrice nodded. Richard stood by her bed. She tapped the covers. "Come on up."

He climbed up and sat beside her. Bea wrapped her arm lovingly around him. "Are you okay?" he asked.

"I'll be fine. I feel silly for not drinking as much as I should have for this heat."

"Uncle Ellis said you'd be all right."

"I'll need to stay in bed the rest of the day, but perhaps tomorrow we can get to your lessons."

"Nanna, I can play tomorrow so you can rest more."

Bea chuckled. "I'll see that your lessons are fun. Tell me, did you go to work with your uncle Ellis?"

Enthusiastically he nodded his head. "He fishes for sponges and they stink like dead fish. Uncle Ellis says he washes them so they don't smell."

"Interesting." *Sponges and the other natural wonders this island brings will make exciting lessons for Richard and myself,* Bea thought. Then she remembered she wouldn't be teaching Richard for much longer. Bea fought back her discouragement and tried concentrating on what Richard was telling her. Something about Ellis writing in his books.

". . .Uncle Ellis says he writes his money in a book."

"You mean keeps track of his money in his books. That's good, he uses his money like a good farmer."

"I told him about corn money."

"You did?"

"Uh-huh."

Bea smiled. The man probably thought she was a fool for putting money in the terms of seeds, but it seemed like the best way to explain it to a four year old.

Cook walked in with a broad smile. "Richard, I think you need to let your Nanna rest. You best go with your uncle now."

Richard nodded and slid off the bed. " 'Bye, Nanna. I'll come later."

" 'Bye, Richie. You mind your uncle, and I'll be up tomorrow."

"All right." He ran from the room.

"Now, I say you close those heavy eyes of yours and get some rest. I'll wake you later for some more to drink and maybe a light broth." Cook applied the damp cloth over her body again.

Bea struggled to keep her eyes open. Perhaps she should rest for a moment. Slowly she let them close, the burning at the back of her lids finding relief. So tired, so exhausted, she needed sleep. . . .

Bea awoke to Cook's delicate touch.

"Good morning, Child. You slept well."

"I feel better, but still weak."

"You'll be that way for most of the day. You rest and start getting some good food into your body. Hopefully, you'll be feeling better by evening."

Beatrice grasped Cook's soft, leathered hands. "Thank you." No other words fit. She was deeply indebted to this woman, this stranger who no longer seemed a stranger, but a friend.

"You're welcome. Don't you be carryin' on about how much I did. Just watched over you is all. Any good Christian woman would have."

"I don't know what I would have done without you."

"You would have been stuck with Mr. Ellis pacing all night and young Richard wanting to sleep with you to make sure you were all right."

She grinned at the image of Richie cradled beside her in bed. They had shared many lonely nights that way. However, she couldn't quite figure why Mr. Ellis, as Cook called him, would be pacing the floor on account of her. As far as he was concerned, she was an over-protective nursemaid who would need to return home on the first possible ship. Her grin slipped into a rigid slim line.

"Did you sleep at all, Cook?"

"Some. I'm fine, Child. But if you be fine, I'm going to the house to fix up some breakfast. What would you like?"

"Nothing. I still don't feel like eating."

"Hurumph. You'll be eating something. I'll make it light. Lay back down; I'll return shortly."

"Thank you." Bea watched Cook waddle out of her room. There would be no denying that woman. If she brought you something to eat, you'd better eat it. Cook's ways brought back memories of an old school matron, Miss Arno. The woman was not one to trifle with. She bellowed orders and you followed, or you were left cleaning boards, desks, floors, windows, anything the woman could think of. Bea shook her head and attempted to get up.

Slowly she draped her feet over the side of the bed. She waited for the dizziness to return. Thank the good Lord there was none. Feeling a bit more sure of herself, she eased her feet to the floor and continued holding the edge of the mattress. Carefully she straightened up. Her legs wobbled, her body felt exhausted.

Should she dare take a couple steps to sit in the old wooden rocker?

Tentatively she lifted her right foot and slid it forward. Then her left. Yes, she could make it. She would just need to be careful. Easing herself into the rocker, she clasped her hands in her lap and proceeded with her morning prayers. She had a lot to be thankful for this morning, and a lot to petition the Lord about as well.

As always, Richard was in the forefront of all her prayers. "Father God, You know my heart, You know my love for this child. If there is any way I could remain on as his nanny, I'd appreciate it. But I do trust him into Your hands and Your protection for him. You are the Creator, and You do know what's best for him. I'm trying to refrain from embracing, to let go and trust him to You, removing myself. But it is difficult, Father. I love him so."

Ellis groaned as he dragged his body out of bed. He'd been up most of the night. Finally, Cook had told him not to come back to the cottage again; she needed some rest too. Then, the nagging torment that he was ultimately responsible for the nanny's condition kept his eyes from closing while his feet wore out the floorboards. She was doing well, fortunately. She would recover. But he couldn't forgive himself for having been so insensitive. He had a pretty clear understanding of the amount of undergarments a woman wore up north, and this heat was not fit for a lady of such refinement. Many of the wives of the local residents refused to live here year-round because of the heat. But that number was changing as the women developed a taste for Spanish clothing, a far more agreeable attire for this climate.

A disheveled face in the mirror stared back at him, his eyes bloodshot from the lack of sleep. His beard needed a good trimming and brushing. He worked the stray hairs with his hand into a some semblance of order. Hoping the water would revive him, he rinsed his face one more time.

Ellis worked his way down the stairs to make breakfast for everyone, feeling it was the least he could do. Cook needed some rest too, having been up most of the night herself. Of course, some of that was due to his wandering over there half a dozen times to check on Miss Smith's condition.

"What are you doing here?" he barked, seeing Cook busy at the stove.

"I'm fixin' breakfast."

"You should be with Miss Smith, Cook. I'll fix breakfast."

"Don't you be bellowing at me, Sir. Beatrice is fine. I appreciate your offer to make the morning meal, but. . ."

"Sorry, Cook," Ellis apologized.

"The lady needs something she can get down, not your idea of a breakfast," Cook teased.

Ellis raised a hand to his chest, feigning injury. *"Moi?"*

"Don't be using no fancy talk. You know you can't cook, that's why you hired me."

"I must have been out of my mind," Ellis mumbled. He truly loved Cook. She kept him in order. But, at times, the woman had an attitude which could make a man's toes curl.

"Probably so, but the good Lord knew you needed me in your life," Cook admonished.

Ellis chuckled. "You're quite a handful, Cook. How did your husband manage?"

"Quite well, thank you," she winked in reply. "Mr. Ellis," Cook lowered her voice, "Bea is going to be fine. She had a good night. She looks well this morning. Another day of rest and she'll be fit as an oyster in its shell."

"Thanks for all your help, Cook. I don't know what I would have done."

"Found some other lady to take care of her, I'm certain. But God doesn't put people in the wrong place at the wrong time. Remember that, Mr. Ellis. She's not here by mistake."

"But. . ."

"But nothin'. God knows, God controls, if you let Him."

Duly admonished, Ellis left the breakfast preparations in the capable hands of Cook. She was right as always. If he genuinely trusted God, he shouldn't have been so worried and shouldn't have been so riddled with guilt. God had placed Beatrice Smith in the position of caring for his nephew, and He knew that they would be coming to live with him in these tropical temperatures. So why was he still blaming himself?

Because if he hadn't commited that act in the past, he would have gone home and picked up his nephew. But fear of entering his hometown, the threat of arrest, the threat of disgracing the family name and losing the farm. . .he simply couldn't risk it. So, was it ultimately still his fault that Beatrice Smith was sick?

Ellis worked the tension out of the back of his neck. "Perhaps not," he spoke to his empty office. But, just maybe, he was still responsible.

"Uncle Ellis, can I go see Nanna now?" Richard yelled down the hall.

When was that child going to learn not to yell? Ellis took a deep breath. Now was not the time to chastise him. He stepped into the hall just as Richard rounded the corner at a run to head into his office.

"Ugh!" Ellis groaned.

"Sorry. Can I?" Richard implored sheepishly.

"Yes, go right in and see how she's doing. Tell her Cook will bring breakfast shortly."

"All right." Richard turned to walk away, then paused, looking over his shoulder, and said, "Good morning, Uncle Ellis."

Ellis broke into a wide grin. " 'Morning, Son. Now shoo." At that, the boy was off, running down the hall, slipping on one small carpet but handling the corner without falling. *Did I run that much when I was a boy?* He had no memory of it. He ran outside, of course, but in the house? Nah, he couldn't have. His mother would have tanned his hide. Come to think of it. . .Ellis rubbed his backside. . .maybe she had.

Bea heard the patter of Richard's feet long before she heard him call, preceded by the slam of the screen door.

"Nanna."

"Come in, Richard. I'm in my room." She straightened the sheet modestly over herself.

"Hi. Uncle Ellis said I could come over."

"I'm glad you came."

"Are you better?"

"Yes, thanks."

"Are you allowed to sit in a chair?"

"I believe so, why do you ask?"

"'Cause yesterday you had to stay in bed. Doctor said so."

"True, but I can sit up for awhile now. Would you like me to read you a story?" Richard nodded his head.

"Do you want to pick out a book or should I?"

"Can we do the story after breakfast?"

"Sure."

"Cook's making bacon." Richard's eyes sparkled.

"We can read after you have your bacon." As much as Bea enjoyed bacon, she couldn't imagine eating something so greasy at the moment. She silently prayed Cook would not ask her to.

"Nanna?"

"Yes, Richie."

He placed his small hands on his hips and stood with his feet slightly apart. "Are you drinking?"

Bea couldn't help but giggle. "Yes, Son. I'm drinking my juice."

He shook his finger. "Cook said you need to keep drinking or you'll get sick."

"I know. I'll be careful, I promise."

Richard gave one swift nod of the head and relaxed his stance. If Cook was having this effect on the child already, Ellis Southard would have his hands full raising the boy. "Do you think you better go back to the house for your breakfast? I think I can smell the bacon now."

Richard sniffed the air. His smile blossomed. "I'll be back, Nanna," he said, then spun around and ran out the door.

The boy was always running. Beatrice wondered if his father had been a runner as well, or his uncle.

His uncle. The image of the man brought a shiver down her spine. He was so handsome, and she was so infuriatingly attracted to him. Maybe she shouldn't ask to stay on as the child's nanny. She probably should go home and do as the

Lord says, "refrain from embracing," to let little Richard go on to be the man he was meant to become. Staying in Key West would mean staying next to temptation, and Bea wasn't all that sure she could handle it.

It would be different, she thought, if she had fancied herself interested in some boys when she was younger. But they were just silly creatures, boys were. They often would start behaving like roosters near a hen house trying to get a woman's attention. Such silliness did not endear her to the male part of the species. Grown men, however, like her father, were acceptable. They either outgrew this boyish behavior or, like her father, had not been given to such childishness. She wondered if she dared ask. Her brother hadn't been one given to such nonsense until Abigail Wilson moved into town. Around her, he degenerated into "one of the roosters."

Bea tossed her head from side to side. Young boys like Richard didn't seem to have this problem. She wondered if it had anything to do with coming of age. Perhaps she would never know. She certainly wouldn't be around when young Richard would be turning sixteen.

A rap sounded at her door. "Miss Smith."

Bea flushed. She was naked. . .well, maybe not naked exactly, but close enough. "Mr. Southard, I'm not presentable. Please do not come in."

"I. . .I. . .mean you no disrespect, Ma'am. I just wanted to let you know that I'm going to work now. Cook will be here and calling on you often. Richard will be in Cook's care, but I've given him permission to visit you as often as you wish today."

"Thank you, Sir. I'm certain I'll be about tomorrow."

"Take the time to recover, Miss Smith. We don't want a repeat of yesterday." His words were almost kind, but there was a slight edge of anger in them too, she suspected.

"I'm drinking regularly and getting my rest, thank you." Regular enough that she thought she could float away if she didn't stop soon.

"Fine," he coughed. "Good day, Miss Smith."

"Good day, Sir."

She wondered again if Ellis Southard truly was as cold as he appeared. What had Cook said earlier? That he would have kept her up all night with his pacing? Was he truly concerned about her? If so, he was a kind man with a cold exterior, Bea noted to herself. That was it. A man with a tender heart, who hid it well, she reasoned.

"Miss Bea," Cook called as she entered the house. "I've got some tea and some white rice for you."

"Rice?"

"Best thing to keep you from dehydrating. Problem some folks have with a new area is the water isn't the same as back home. They, hmm, well, they. . ."

"I understand." And Bea had. The Key West water was already having that "cleansing" effect on her body.

44

"Black tea, white rice, best medicine there is for diarrhea."

"Thanks, I think." Was there anything her body would get used to about this area? Maybe it didn't matter. Fact was, she wouldn't be staying all that long. But she wanted to be her best for the last days she spent with Richard. "Father, God, please help me get well and stay well," she moaned.

Chapter 7

The next morning Bea woke to the gentle lull of exotic birdsong outside her window. She quietly watched them flit from branch to branch, their vivid colors as beautiful and enchanting as they were different from their cousins in the North. This truly felt as if she were in a whole new world.

Today, perhaps, she could explore this tropical wonder. But would Cook allow her the pleasure? On the other hand, would her body survive it? "What could it hurt, Lord, to walk a few blocks to the center of town?" Without waiting for an answer, her thoughts skipped ahead to the quaint stores filled with merchandise to explore.

Even Ellis Southard's sponge business was so uniquely Caribbean, she reflected, as she climbed out of bed to get ready for the day. She picked up the personal sponge Cook had given her for bathing. After the very first use her skin had felt smoother, cleaner, and softer than she remembered it feeling in years.

Working into the most lightweight outfit she could find, she thought about purchasing some of the Spanish-style skirts and blouses like the ones Cook wore. They looked so comfortable.

Although she wouldn't purchase many. The island clothing would be totally unacceptable back home. There a woman was to always be properly dressed. And while Cook quite naturally wore this new casual apparel, Bea was certain the women of her social class never would, even in these tropical temperatures.

Fortunately, no one here knew of Bea's northern social status, so no heads would turn when and if she wore those outfits. What mattered was to stay covered and cool and to avoid another touch of heatstroke. In her few remaining days with Richard, she wanted to be fit and able to enjoy the merriment and wonder of seeing this place for the first time.

Perhaps she was a bit jealous of the time Ellis played with Richard each evening before he went to bed. She'd heard them laughing and longed to be in the middle of such joyous activity. Each night she had lit the candle in her window for Richard, although Cook had been the keeper of the flame in her weakened state.

She watched from behind her closed screen door as Ellis Southard marched proudly off to work. His broad shoulders straight and firm, he walked with confidence but didn't strut with arrogance. His beard seemed shorter, more groomed this morning; its red highlights seemed to beam his contentment with life and his job.

"Snap out of it, Woman," Bea chastised herself. "Why am I longing so much for this man, a stranger?" She prayed with her head bent low. "We've spoken maybe ten minutes in the three days I've been here. Well, perhaps a few more than ten. But it's been nothing, Lord. I barely know him and yet I'm attracted to him. Why? It must be the heat. Help me keep my mind together, Lord. Don't allow me to turn into some silly, swooning female."

Now what was it she had been thinking before she saw Ellis. . .Mr. Southard. . . she amended. "Ah yes, shopping." Bea opened the screen door and headed toward the main house. It was her first time in the house since falling ill. Cook had brought all her meals to the cottage, with Richard's help, of course. She smiled at the thought. He was so proud, being able to help care for her. Bea's eyes started to water. "How am I going to leave this child, Lord?" she whispered.

⚓

"Come on, men, let's get out there before the day is half over," Ellis hollered at his crew lounging on wood blocks and crates scattered around the dock. A few groaned, but all got up and shuffled over to the small boats that would sail out to fetch the sponges. The nets empty, a couple men per boat, he had a good business.

" 'Morning, Ellis, I see your crew has expanded." Ellis turned to see Marc Dabny approach, wearing his usual Union blue army slacks, though he had retired from the military right after the war to live on the island. His premature balding head glistened in the morning sunlight.

" 'Morning, Marc. What can I do for you?"

"Heard your nephew's come to live with you." Marc stopped his approach a couple feet away from Ellis.

"That's right, he's a great kid."

Marc looked down at his feet and cleared his throat. "Heard his nanny came with him too."

Ellis examined the man more closely. What was he after?

"Yes," he admitted.

"I was wondering if I could. . .well, if I could come and call upon the lady."

What? How dare the man!

On the other hand, Marc had been raised to seek out the gal's father to request permission to court. But he wasn't Beatrice's father, wasn't even close. Still, Beatrice was a guest in his home, and he supposed folks naturally assumed she was now working for him as the child's nanny. But he certainly didn't want to declare open hunting season for Beatrice Smith.

"Marc, the lady's been ill. Stricken with a bad case of heatstroke. By the time she's strong again, I imagine she'll be on a ship heading north."

"She won't be staying?"

"No, Sir." He handled that well, he thought. Didn't lie, but didn't make her available either. "And given the severity of her heatstroke, I imagine she's anxious to leave this place."

"Heard she was a looker. And I've been wanting to settle down now since the war is over. You know, get married and have a handful of kids. Besides, havin' a woman who's pleasant to look at wouldn't be a bad way to spend the rest of your life." Marc winked.

Ellis's stomach flip-flopped. The man wasn't looking for a companion. He was looking for a nursemaid plus a few wifely benefits. That certainly didn't describe Beatrice Smith, who was excellent with children and had a sharp mind. She needed a man with whom she could have a relationship, not be some prize—used whenever the prizewinner suited.

"Afraid that wouldn't be Miss Smith. I believe she has family waiting on her back home." That was also not untrue, but he really hadn't talked with her about it, just assumed. In fact, he knew next to nothing about Beatrice Smith and her family. Everything he knew was through the eyes of his nephew—his love for her, and the things she'd taught him. No, he really didn't know the woman at all.

"Well, I figured I should ask you first. Didn't know if you had other plans for the lady. Didn't want to ask the lady and upset you."

"I appreciate it, Marc, but like I say, she's not staying."

"Mind if I try and persuade her anyway?"

The man deserved some credit for his persistence.

Besides, do I really have the right to say who could or could not court Miss Smith? Ellis felt like he ought to, but knew he didn't. "I don't suppose I could stop you from approaching her, but please give her another day to recover. I was quite concerned at first that she wouldn't even make it."

"Thank you. I come from a long line of Dabnys who've been known to have a way with women. So don't be too surprised if the lady decides to stay right here in Key West."

No matter what Marc Dabny thought about his family heritage, Ellis couldn't see Beatrice Smith on this man's arm. On the other hand, not being a woman himself, he didn't have a clue as to what a lady would find appealing.

"I won't be keeping you from your work, just felt I ought to speak with you first. I know we don't run on pomp and circumstance down here, but since you and I both hail from the North, I thought I'd better ask."

"I appreciate it. Have a good day, Marc."

"Adios," Marc answered in Spanish. The blend of Spanish and English added to the island's uniqueness.

Ellis worked his shoulders in circles trying to ease the tension that had stiffened his back.

Four days. The woman had been here for only four days and the vultures were already swarming. Ellis shook his head as he walked to his office. Of course, given Miss Beatrice Smith's beauty, it was a wonder no one had approached him days ago. Maybe the fact that she was so ill had made it through the island gossip chain and had kept the pursuers at bay. In any case, she was fair game for the men of Key West, and he had no right to do anything about it.

Frustrated, he absentmindedly worried his lower lip. Why did the thought bother him? Wasn't it possible that some man on Key West might be Beatrice Smith's future husband? She certainly would make a man a good wife and mother, or at least it appeared that way. But the very idea of Marc Dabny pursuing her made him tense. Marc seemed like a decent enough sort on the surface. He was respectable and followed his orders. He wouldn't make a bad husband, Ellis supposed. But then again, Marc wasn't looking for a woman who would challenge him as a man; he was looking for someone to clean his house, cook his food, and bear his children.

Ellis rubbed his temples. This was going nowhere. He wasn't Beatrice Smith's keeper. The woman could court anyone she had a mind to. It wasn't his concern. His concern was providing for his nephew and bringing him up in a manner that would have made the boy's father proud. And to do that he needed to get to work and stop this lollygagging.

"Nanna, are you all right?" Richard questioned.

Bea's legs shook. Her arms felt prickly, as if being stabbed with lots of tiny needles all at once. "I feel a bit weak."

Richard ran to the house they were in front of and banged on the door. An older woman with graying hair came to the door. "May I help you?"

"Nanna doesn't feel well. Can she sit down?"

"Oh, gracious, bring her here, Child."

Bea didn't know whether to be proud or embarrassed by Richard's actions. They hadn't gone a quarter of a mile, but she had apparently gone too far. Richard helped her up the stairs onto the woman's porch.

"Sit in the rocker, dear, I'll fetch you some water."

"Thank you." Beatrice sat down on the wooden rocker facing the street. A small front porch with a wooden floor and white painted handrail stretched across the front of the house. A couple steps and you were to the door.

"Nanna, I'll get Uncle Ellis."

The last thing she needed was to have Ellis Southard come to her rescue. "I'll be fine. No sense worrying your uncle."

"What about Cook? She's closer." Richard's worried eyes pleaded with her to let him help.

"Come here, Richie." She scooped him up and placed him on her lap. She worked his wonderful blond curls from his face with her right hand. "I'm fine, really. I just wasn't up for this yet."

"Nanna, I don't want you to be sick."

"I'm getting better. I just have to be patient and wait for my body to recover a bit more."

"All right." Richard snuggled his head into her chest.

Bea looked up at the sound of the screen door swinging on old hinges to see the elderly woman coming out with a tall glass of lemonade. "Here you go, Miss," she said, steadying herself with her free hand on the back of Bea's chair.

Bea clasped her fingers around the glass. "Thank you." Carefully she brought it to her lips and sipped. How perfectly embarrassing to weaken in such a short amount of time. At mid-morning, the full intensity of the heat wouldn't peak for two to three hours yet.

Bea's hostess sat down in the wicker chair to her left. "My name is Vivian. You're new here, aren't you, dear?"

Bea nodded her head.

"Nanna and I came from New York on a big ship. We're living with my uncle Ellis."

"With those steel-blue eyes, I should have noticed you were Mr. Southard's nephew."

Richard looked at Bea in bewilderment.

"Miss. . .I'm afraid I don't know your last name." Bea flushed.

"Sorry, its Matlin. Mrs. Joseph Matlin."

Bea nodded. "Richard, Mrs. Matlin noticed your eyes have the same coloring as your uncle Ellis's."

"Oh. That's because my daddy and uncle Ellis are brothers."

Vivian chuckled. "That's generally how it works, Son. Can I give you something to drink, and a sweet biscuit perhaps?"

"Can I, Nanna?"

"Sure." Vivian took Richard by the hand and led him into her home. A cool breeze blew across the porch, and Bea laid her head back on the chair and closed her eyes to let the refreshing air sweep across her face. Cook had warned her to be careful, and a race to the corner of the street had clearly exceeded her limits.

She could still feel the pulse in her legs, beat after beat, protesting her stupidity. She hadn't exerted herself that much, having let Richard win. Yet she had done far more than her body could apparently handle. *How long does it take to recover from heatstroke?*

Vivian came back out with a small china plate, with Richard in tow. "Would you like one, dear?"

Bea wasn't really hungry, but the biscuits did smell good. "Thank you. I'm sorry to impose upon you in such a way."

"It's no trouble at all, dear." Vivian sat back down on the chair opposite Beatrice and straightened her apron. "All I know is that you serve as Richard Southard's nanny. I don't know your name, dear."

"Forgive me. . .Beatrice Smith. . .heatstroke seems to be affecting me in more ways than one."

"I know what you mean, Beatrice. May I call you Beatrice?"

"Bea is fine. Have you ever suffered with this ailment?" Bea wiped the crumbs from her lap.

"Years ago, when I first came here. Came about the same time of year as you. The first week was very difficult."

"A whole week? I'll be on a ship back to New York by the end of a week. I do want to take in some of the sights prior to my departure." *Maybe the good Lord just doesn't want me in this climate and I shouldn't get comfortable here.* Another lesson in learning to refrain from embracing, embracing a new way of life, a new culture, a new environment. It wasn't her time, and she just needed to accept the fact that she was to return home to New York.

At the end of the workday Ellis returned home for his evening meal and found the house quiet.

"Hello? Anyone home?" Not a sound. *That's odd,* he thought and proceeded to clean up and change from his work clothes into something casual. From his bedroom window he could see Cook, Richard, and Miss Smith sitting under the shade of the large banyan tree. Even from this distance Beatrice seemed pale, weak, and sorrowful. The woman was so vulnerable, so frail, and yet showed a remarkable ability to hold her own in adversity. Could this change in her demeanor be from the heatstroke?

Ellis slipped his arms into the sleeves of a cool cotton shirt, buttoning it as he made his way down the hall to the stairs and out through the kitchen to the back door. "I wondered where all of you were."

"Uncle Ellis!" Richard declared, jumping up from his spot and scampering over to him. Ellis smiled. *Well, the boy runs outside as well as inside,* he mused.

"Just takin' in the cool night air," Cook said. "The butcher got some fresh beef from Cuba, so we're having steak tonight. You're cooking on the outside grill," Cook teased, and sat farther back in her chair, putting her feet up on the one abandoned by Richard.

Fresh beef was a rarity on the island, and he'd given Cook a standing order that anytime there was a shipment she should purchase some.

"I see." Ellis hoisted Richard up on his shoulders. "Come on, Son. It's our night to cook for the ladies."

At the back of the yard he lifted Richard off his shoulders and placed him on the ground beside him. In the sheltered work area, he loaded the brick grill with small chunks of wood for the fire.

Young Richard grabbed a bucket filled with blocks of hickory wood soaking in water. "Cook said you use these."

"Thanks. Do you know why?"

His blond curls swung with the swift movement of his head going up and down. "It's smelly wood."

Ellis chuckled. "Yes, you could say that. This hickory gives the food a great outdoors cooking taste." Ellis continued to pile the wood into the grill, then lit the kindling. Flames climbed the small pile.

Richard clapped his hands.

Ellis bowed. "Thank you." Richard stood proud, encircling his right arm around Ellis's left leg. A storm of emotions caught in Ellis's throat. How could a child love so easily, so unconditionally?

"Uncle Ellis?"

Ellis poked the burning embers with an iron rod and placed a couple of water-soaked hickory chunks on the pile.

"Yes, Richard?"

"How come Nanna couldn't race me to the corner?"

Chapter 8

What?" Ellis's own voice echoed back at him off the shelter's tin roof. *Is that why she appeared so pale, so lethargic?*

Richard instantly released his clasp of Ellis's leg.

Ellis struggled to quell his uncharacteristic temper. "I'm sorry, I didn't mean to bellow. But I want to know what happened."

"Nanna doesn't yell," Richard whined.

"Son. . ." How could he explain this? It wasn't normal for him to yell either. He loved Richard and he was happy—no, honored to raise his brother's son. However, something—or rather someone—was getting the better of him. The constant fighting with himself not to think of a certain hazel-eyed nanny was wearing him down.

Ellis took a deep breath and went down to one knee, capturing the small boy's upper arms in his hands. "Normally, I don't yell either. I didn't mean to be so loud. Maybe I'm not used to having a lot of folks around me when I'm at home. Be patient with me, Son. I promise to try and not yell so often."

Richard scrunched his eyebrows together. "All right, Uncle Ellis. Nanna said some folks yell."

"Well, normally I don't. But I will try to be more careful. Deal?"

"Deal." Ellis held his hand out and Richard slipped his tiny hand into his. Such a good boy. A bright boy. And that was due to his nanny. His brother, if truth be told, had little to do with the raising of his own son.

"So tell me, why was Nanna racing you?"

"I asked her to."

"I see," he responded, carefully modulating his tone of voice. He could see the boy felt terribly guilty. "Then what happened, Richard?"

"I won. But Nanna didn't feel so good. We stopped at Mrs. Vivian's house. She gave me cookies. Nanna sat and had some lemonade."

So, Miss Smith overexerted herself. Hadn't the doctor given her firm orders to stay down, relax? Not only did she not stay down, she actually raced the child. And what's a woman doing racing a small boy down the street anyway? Ellis fought to keep his resurgent anger from surfacing again. "Richard, I think your Nanna needs to rest some more."

"I know. Nanna said we can't go shopping or exploring."

"Right, not for awhile."

"Nanna said she may never be able to."

What nonsense is this woman feeding the child? "I'm sure you'll be able to, real soon."

"Nanna said when she gets better, she'd be going home to New York."

So the woman doesn't want to stay in the area. Well, no sense asking her to stay on. He'd just have to find a nanny somewhere on the island. Until then, he would have to alter his work schedule, take the lad to work with him whenever possible. Take him fishing on the dock even. Yup, he'd better start doing what he needed to do to take care of his nephew. It was apparent Miss Smith was breaking her ties with Richard and would be traveling home on the next ship.

The back of Ellis's neck tightened from the tension. He would do what was necessary for Richard. He didn't regret that. But the boy loved and depended on Miss Smith in more ways than she obviously knew. Here she was ready to release Richard into his care with barely a moment's thought. Maybe Beatrice Smith wasn't the kind of person he had been building her to be in his mind. Maybe raising Richard had just been a matter of duty, of patronage to an old friend.

Ellis massaged the back of his neck with his right hand and sighed. *Guess it was good I hadn't offered her a permanent position as Richard's nanny.*

If looks could kill. . .

Beatrice swallowed hard and broke her gaze from Ellis's, who stood just outside the shelter glaring at her. What was he thinking? Those bluish-gray eyes of his, so dark beneath a deeply furrowed brow, bore into her. She had heard his outburst. Richard must have told him about their excursion.

"Excuse me, Cook. I believe I need to lie down. I don't think I'm up for dinner tonight."

"Nonsense, Child. You need to eat." Cook crossed her hefty arms across her rounded stomach.

Beatrice lifted herself up off the chair. "Perhaps Richard could bring a little something later." She closed her eyes and rubbed her temples for emphasis. "I feel a headache coming on."

"Uh-huh." Cook eyed her cautiously.

"I just need to lie down. I'll be fine." She didn't want to overemphasize her physical weakness. Truth was, a tension-filled headache was coming on, but more out of fear of dealing with Ellis Southard, who already thought her a coddling nanny. Now he was certain to think her a fool as well. Why on earth had she agreed to race Richard today anyway?

"Mr. Ellis, he cooks a great steak. Can't say I enjoy anything else the man puts his hand to, food-wise that is. But outside on the grill—umm-hmm, the man can cook."

"I'm quite certain he can, but I really must go lie down now."

"Sure, you go run along now. Just remember to stop running sometime."

Bea squinted hard at Cook. Was she implying something here? Sure, she was old enough not to be running down a street after a child like that, but. . .did she mean something else? Beatrice turned and headed toward her cottage. Whatever the old woman meant, she wasn't going to wait around to find out. She'd seen enough of Cook to know she was able to read her thoughts. A wise woman, her father would have said. A nosy one, her aunt Tilly would have said. In either case, Bea wasn't about to stick around to confirm Cook's suspicions that she might be running from Ellis Southard.

She opened the screen door and entered her cottage, letting the door slam behind her. It wasn't quite as cool as being outdoors under the banyan tree, but it was far cooler than earlier this afternoon. *Thank You, Lord, for this cool breeze tonight,* Bea silently prayed as she headed to the quiet sanctuary of her room.

Her bed, still rumpled from an earlier nap after her failed excursion with Richard, lay convictingly before her. Never would she have left a bed in that state back home.

Bea sighed and worked the wrinkles out of the bedding before collapsing on the rocker beside the bed. "O Lord, how long before I return home? I thought I would be happy with a few extra days with Richard. Instead I've gotten sick and I am miserable, Lord. I tried, Father, today I really tried to explain to him why I had to go home. I believe he understood. But I saw the pain in his eyes. Or was it fear, Father God? Please be with Richard; give him strength and bless his relationship with his uncle. Make it strong; give him the father he's never had. Amen."

Bea wiped tears off her cheeks with a delicate hand-laced handkerchief Elizabeth had made for her years ago. Embroidered on one corner were small purple violets, Bea's favorite flower. Bea sighed. "I've been a good mother to the child, just like you asked, Lizzy. But it hurts so much to let him go. I understand now why you held on so long, just one more day, one more hour to touch, to love that precious little boy. I grieve to be parting with him, but I know it is right, and I can't possibly live in this area with his uncle. I don't know if you ever met the man, Lizzy, but he is quite different from your Richard. Sometimes he terrifies me."

Bea stopped, realizing she'd been rambling aloud. It gave her some relief to think her dear friend was looking down from heaven, yet she knew that only God could answer her pain, that only He could give peace to the heart-wrenching grief she was going through. She needed to return home. She needed to return soon. Why wait until she was recovered? The ship would be sailing into a colder climate. Wouldn't that be better for her?

She lifted herself from the rocker, went to her garment bag, and pulled out a sheet of stationery. At the small desk in the farthest corner of the room she penned a letter to Mr. Ellis Southard.

☙

"Are they done yet?" Richard asked for the third time.

"Just about, Son. Why don't you go tell Nanna her steak is ready?"

"All right." Richard ran off toward the cottage. Ellis had seen her leave, wondered if she was all right, but figured Cook would have alerted him to any problem.

It was odd how old Cook sat relaxed in the chair with her feet up. Eyeing her from a distance, he realized she was slowing down. Not that he'd ever say anything to her about it. But he would like to see her do less walking and live with him. Her family could manage just fine without her. Probably should too. The woman gave far too much to folks. She needed to slow down. Relax. Enjoy. . .

"Uncle Ellis!" Richard yelled.

Ellis smiled. At least outside it wasn't quite as piercing as in the house. He looked in the boy's direction but didn't answer.

"Nanna says she's not feeling up to dinner."

"Not up to dinner?" he mumbled.

"Cook?" he called as he brought the plates piled with mouth-watering steaks to the small table at her side.

"She said she needed to rest."

"Do you think she's all right?"

"I believe so. Think it's more her pride than heat."

"Ahh." Ellis would let that issue alone. He wasn't going to be baited by Cook into doing something he shouldn't. Like offering her the opportunity to stay on as Richard's nanny.

A quiet meal was eaten. Ellis grinned, reflecting. His father often said a quiet table meant the meal was exquisite. A small dinner plate was prepared for Miss Smith. Cook cleaned up, Richard delivered the meal, and Ellis retreated to his study.

The old wood floorboards shined from Cook's excellent housekeeping. She once told him it didn't need much fussin' 'cause he mostly sat in his chair at the desk. That had been true enough, but he'd begun pacing in recent days. Pacing and bellowing. "What a combination," he groaned.

"Uncle Ellis?"

A somber child stood in front of him.

"Yes, Richard."

"Nanna said to give you this."

Ellis reached for the thin piece of paper crumpled between the boy's chubby fingers. "Thank you, Son."

Not wanting to open the letter and be distracted from his nephew, he placed it in his trousers pocket. Whatever Miss Smith had to say could wait. The time before Richard went to bed was their private time, and Ellis cherished it.

"Would you like me to read a story for you tonight?" Ellis asked, combing the blond curls from Richard's face.

Richard beamed. "Can we play checkers?"

"Checkers it is. You get the pieces, I'll clear the table."

Richard scurried off.

Ellis lifted some papers he had brought home from his office and placed them on his desk.

"Good night, Mr. Ellis. Remember, I'll be comin' after breakfast tomorrow." How could he forget? But he had. "Thanks for the reminder."

"You might ask Miss Smith to fix the morning meal," Cook suggested.

"I'll manage." After all, he would have to once Beatrice Smith moved back home. Until he found a suitable nanny or nurse, he would need to fend for himself and Richard.

"Oh, and one more thing, Mr. Ellis. I think the nanny is feeling somewhat useless," she added, tilting her head toward the cottage.

"Useless? What are you talking about, Cook?"

"I don't rightly know, but something is wrong with the dear gal. And I'm certain it isn't the heat."

Ellis snorted. "You call running wise?"

"That's nothing. I mean, yes, she shouldn't have pushed herself that way. But, well. . .I can't put my finger on it. But I knows something else is wandering around in that pretty little head."

Ellis shifted uneasily from one foot to the other. "She told Richard she was going home today."

"Mercy, no." Cook placed a hand over her heart.

"Afraid so. I'll talk with you tomorrow about this. Right now I don't want Richard hearing us."

"I can't figure what's going on. I knows she wants to be here with the child," Cook mumbled as she left the room.

Had Ellis heard her right? Beatrice Smith wants to be here? But why would she tell Richard. . . ? Ellis dropped his hand into his pocket that held her letter.

" 'Bye, Cook," Richard called out. Ellis heard the pattering of his shoes on the hardwood floors and released the letter back into his pocket.

"I got it, Uncle Ellis."

"Excellent." Ellis rubbed his hands together. "Tonight I'm certain I'm going to win."

"I don't think so." Richard giggled. "You're worse than Nanna."

Ellis chuckled. Guess he needs to work on his losing skills some. "I wouldn't be too confident there. I was practicing today."

"You were?"

"Yup, an old sea captain showed me some pointers."

Richard's eyes widened. When was the time to start winning, Ellis wondered, in order to challenge the child more? There was so much he still needed to learn about raising a boy.

O Lord, he said inwardly, *help me to know what's best.*

Ellis placed a white ivory checker in one hand and a black ivory checker in the other. He'd received the game as a gift from an old sailor who had carved it from whales' teeth. The board was of finely polished wood, with the black squares painted on. He put his hands behind his back, placing both checkers in his right hand. "Pick one."

Richard tapped his left arm. Ellis swung it around revealing his empty hand. Richard tapped the other and Ellis swung it around, after dropping the checkers in a back pocket, and revealed it was empty also.

"Hey!" Richard placed his hands on his hips. "That's not how you do it, Uncle Ellis."

"It's not?" he asked, feigning innocence. Ellis scratched his head. "I know I put them in my hand. . ."

Richard chuckled. "Where are they?"

"I don't know." Ellis winked.

"Yes, you do, you're trying to trick me."

"Am I? I know I put them in my hands; you saw me." Ellis turned around for effect and pretended to look for the missing checkers. Soon Richard was beside him searching.

"Where are they?" Richard asked.

"I don't know."

"Uncle Ellis, you're trying to trick me," Richard accused, his laughter growing louder by the moment.

Ellis roared in full-belly laughter, lunging across the table to tickle the boy.

Laughter floated on the evening wind through Bea's cottage window, as it had every previous night. How could such a joyous sound be so heart-wrenching? How come she wasn't happy with the joy Richard had found with his uncle? How could she be so jealous? So self-centered? Bea wept into her pillow. "Father God, I'm so terribly selfish."

Chapter 9

Ellis sat on the edge of his bed, the room dark, the house quiet. The gentle glow of candlelight beckoned his attention to the cottage below where Bea still placed the candle in her window for the boy. Ellis grinned briefly before pursing his lips in reflection. How could she truly love the child if she was so anxious to leave? Remembering the note, he reached into his pocket and pulled out what she had penned for him earlier.

Ellis lit the flame of his oil lamp beside the bed. The onion skin paper crinkled as he unfolded it. His eyes focused on the words flowing across the page in exquisite penmanship.

> Dear Mr. Southard,
>
> Would you be so kind as to procure my departure as soon as possible? I feel the trip home would do no further harm to my health in as much as Key West's climate is not agreeable at all.
>
> I love Richard dearly and ask only to be able to correspond with him. I hope you will find that acceptable. In time, I imagine Richard will have only vague memories of me. But I suppose that is how it should be.
>
> Sincerely,
> Beatrice Smith

Ellis's hand trembled. She did love the child, there was no question. But why couldn't she wait and give her body a chance to adjust to this area? *Why is she in such a hurry to return home, Lord? I don't understand.*

A whispered thought flickered past his ears. "Perhaps you should ask."

Should he? The hour was late. Was it proper to call on someone this late? To call on a single woman?

But she isn't just a single woman. She is the child's nanny. *And this is a matter that concerns the child,* he argued with himself. Didn't he, as Richard's guardian, have the right to ask his nanny questions, no matter what the hour? Was there some law that forbade such things? He couldn't think of one.

Ellis turned down the lamp and headed out of his room. He straightened his shirt, removed some of the creases from his trousers, and headed down the stairs toward the front door, stopping to listen for Richard. He was sound asleep. He could leave him for a moment, he decided. Besides, the boy's bedroom window was open, and he was confident he could hear the child from the cottage.

A few long strides and he was at her door. He raised his hand to knock. Then he lowered it.

He raised his hand again, but stopped short of tapping on the doorjamb.

He stepped back. Perhaps this should wait until morning.

He stood there undecided. Perhaps not. He stepped forward again.

Ellis muttered under his breath and rapped on the door. It protested in its frame, and instantly he regretted having knocked so hard.

"Hello?" a weak voice called from the bedroom.

"Miss Smith, I'm sorry to call on you so late. May I have a word with you?" *A bit formal, perhaps, but it got the point across.*

"Mr. Southard, did you receive my letter?" she asked, peering around her partially opened door.

She had taken her hair down for the evening, its silken strands cascading over her shoulders. Ellis swallowed and cleared his throat. "Yes. Can we talk?"

"All right."

Her chocolate curls enhanced her delicate features. Ellis caught himself sniffing her hair as he followed her into the living room. Perhaps it was a mistake to have come in the evening. His palms beaded with sweat. He rubbed them dry with his fingers, only to find they immediately started to perspire again. He sat in the single chair in the living room, leaving her the sofa.

"Is there a reason you need to return home so quickly?" he asked. *Remain on the subject. . .you can get yourself through this.*

"No, nothing of a pressing nature."

"Then why can't you remain a little longer? You should be feeling much better soon. Running was definitely not a wise undertaking, but it presents only a momentary setback."

"Is there a problem with procuring my return voyage?"

"No. I. . .I. . ."

⚓

Beatrice searched his blue-gray eyes. He seemed strangely vulnerable, and yet so formal.

"Richard. . ."

"Is something wrong with Richard?" Bea jumped up from the sofa.

"I'm sorry. No, he's fine. I'm just concerned that your immediate departure would be terribly hard on the child."

"I spoke with him this afternoon. He seemed to understand my need to return home."

"Understand, yes. But is he ready to break his emotional connection with you?"

"I don't believe I've coddled the child as much as you think."

"Coddled? What are you talking about?"

"Coddling. The first day we met, you said I coddled the child."

Ellis stood up and approached her. "I may have said that, but I've come to see you have not coddled the boy at all. I've never met a woman who could bait a hook. And to hear Richard say it, you're the best there is." Ellis winked.

Beatrice lowered her gaze and nervously rubbed her fingertips. "It took some practice."

"I can imagine. All the girls back home would scream and run away from me. Of course, I was threatening them with a fierce and mighty 'worm.' "

Bea giggled. "I can see Richard doing that one day."

Ellis chuckled. "Boys—we are different."

She sighed and relaxed. "I truly love him, and will miss him greatly, but my time in his life has come to an end."

"That may be, Miss Smith, but don't you see—a few more days or weeks won't hurt you, and those same days will help him tremendously."

"Perhaps. I just don't know how long I can survive in this heat."

"You're looking much better, and doing better. Granted, your little morning escapade was a supreme act of foolishness."

This man is some charmer. "Thanks."

"I'm sorry, I'm not your father. I have no right scolding you. But you do see the foolishness, don't you?"

"Of course I do. I saw it when I nearly passed out on Front Street. I thought I could handle the short distance. Richard and I did a lot of racing back home."

Ellis bobbed his head.

"I suppose you think a lady shouldn't do such things."

"Now don't go putting words into my mouth, Miss Smith." Ellis shook a finger in the air. "I've never seen a woman running before, that's all."

"I reckon. But you grew up on Richard's family farmstead. You know there are no children around for miles. The boy needed a playmate, as well as a mother, father, nurse, teacher, and whatever else needed doing at the time."

"True. I always had my brother Richard to play with. Granted, he was older, but it was still someone."

Bea sat back down on the sofa and Richard returned to his chair.

"Miss Smith, please tell me you'll stay for a few more days, perhaps a week or so."

"I would love to explore this island some. I've been trapped in this yard for days, and while you do have a charming yard and beautiful garden, I would like to see more."

Ellis grinned. "I understand. But. . ."

Bea watched his hesitancy, his hands folding and unfolding. "I need you to be spending your free time with the boy. I don't think courting would be proper."

"Courting? What on earth are you talking about?" She watched his eyes focus on his lap. Was he considering asking her to court him? Couldn't be, he'd hardly even looked at her since her arrival.

"Sorry. I had a gentleman caller today who asked for my permission to seek the pleasure of your company."

"He asked you?" She huffed. How dare the man. She wasn't Ellis Southard's ward. She wasn't anyone's ward. She had a free mind and a bright one at that, and she would determine whom she would or would not court.

"Now before you get yourself worked into a tizzy, let me explain that Mr. Dabny comes from the North. Where, as you probably know, in good society a man comes to the father before approaching the woman."

How could she possibly forget? She was born and bred in that society, and while Ellis Southard didn't have an inkling of her true social status, she shouldn't have been so offended.

"I see," she said, her voice controlled.

"I let Marc know he would have to ask you himself."

Well, that ended any lingering doubt she might have had that Ellis's intentions were to court her. No, while she had noticed how handsome Ellis was, obviously he didn't have any attraction toward her. On the other hand, hadn't she caught him staring at her when she first greeted him at the door?

Ellis appeared to be awaiting her answer. What was his question. . . ?

"Thank you."

"You're welcome." Ellis shifted in his chair and pulled at his collar with his right forefinger. "Do you agree you shouldn't be socializing?"

"Mr. Southard, whether I do or do not accept Mr. Dabny's offer has little or nothing to do with my care of Richard. Wouldn't you agree that once you are home for the evening, my time is my own?"

Ellis squirmed. "I reckon."

Bea smiled. "Then if I should accept an invitation from Mr. Dabny or anyone else, it would be when my duties as Richard's nanny are over for the day."

She couldn't believe her own ears. Was she really telling this man she was going to get on with her life, begin socializing again? Allow for the possibility of a courtship? A prickly feeling climbed her spine.

"Very well, Miss Smith." Ellis lifted himself from the chair.

She'd done it again. The man became an instant board around her. Straight, rigid, and totally unfeeling. "Why do you do that?"

"Do what?"

"Put up a wall of defense around me. Just when I think we are beginning to talk like normal people, you pull back into. . .into. . .a plank. Stiff, unbending, un—"

Fire ignited in Ellis's eyes. He closed them, and when he lifted his lids again his eyes were stone cold, dark, and piercing. "Good night, Miss Smith."

For a moment she thought she had reached him. But it was gone in a flash. With long strides to her door he made a hasty retreat. If the man had any appreciation for her as a woman, he sure kept it well hidden. No, she could never stay in Key West. Living under the same roof with a man she found so attractive she lost sleep over, yet who seemed almost repulsed by her, would be nerve-racking, to say the least. Still, he wasn't truly heartless. He had spoken words of appreciation for the fact that she would even bait a hook for the sake of his nephew. "I'm so confused," she huffed.

Ellis stomped back up to the house. How could she be so casual about courting? And why did he feel like a child caught with his hand in the cookie jar? Fact was, he would like to explore the option of courting the woman, but he was too afraid of himself, of his responses, of her beauty.

Ellis groaned. "Heather, I'm so sorry." His past, his mistake, would continue to haunt him when in the presence of someone as tempting as Beatrice Smith. Her beauty was only part of the attraction. Her strong, determined spirit. Her ability to reason. Her way with Richard. These traits and so many more formed the foundation of his attraction. An attraction he could never act upon.

No, he was not a man to be trusted.

Chapter 10

Beatrice saw nothing of Ellis Southard the following day. He even missed his evening meal with the family. "Is he still angry, Lord? And what is he so angry about, anyway?" she rambled in prayer, pacing the small cottage floor from the front room into her bedroom. "I only agreed it was my business if and when I accepted anyone's invitation."

Marc Dabny had been a perfect gentleman, but she had turned him down. For a moment she considered accepting his invitation just to get a rise out of Ellis Southard. But she saw the intensity of Mr. Dabny's interest as a wife-hunter, and she would not be the woman to break the man's heart. Better to leave a man before he's attached, she felt. Not to mention his intentions were totally self-motivated and had little to do with "love."

Given Ellis's recent behavior, all signs seemed to indicate that he was avoiding her. She'd never been so offensive to another individual and that bothered her. Of course, the other side of this meant that, by his absence, she wouldn't be led down the wrong path of temptation.

To Ellis's credit, he did manage to make time for Richard that evening. As she stayed within the confines of her cottage, laughter drifted across the yard once again, creating within her a longing to be in the middle of such joyous activity.

The candle on the windowsill remained unlit, as per young Richard's instructions. He had proclaimed during dinner that he was a big boy now and didn't need it. The unlit candle was now a solemn, cold reminder of her time to release Richard and give him to his uncle and new life.

"Nanna!" she heard Richard call. Bea raced to the window which faced Richard's room, lifted the screen in its wooden track, and waved. A wide smile filled his face, his small arms wiggling back and forth. Bea could see Ellis's strong arm wrapped around Richard's small waist. A proud smile softened Ellis's otherwise rigid stance.

"Good night, Nanna. I love you."

"Good night, Richard. I love you too." With all the energy she could muster, she stepped back from the window and lowered the screen. Mosquitoes thrived on this island, in numbers she'd never seen before. Grateful for the mosquito netting draped around her bed, she checked its corners again to make certain it hung properly, then prepared for bed.

Sitting in front of the vanity, Bea let down her hair. As a child she had worn it loose. After her coming-out party she had taken to wearing it up in public, wrapped into a tight bun and generally hidden beneath a hat or scarf, in keeping with proper etiquette. A nightly custom of a hundred strokes kept her thick curls from snarling in her sleep. She loved the feel of her hair on her shoulders and back, sometimes feeling a little ashamed of her own vanity. She'd known many women who would curse their hair, wearing it in all kinds of unnatural styles, and fuss and fume when it didn't do what they wanted.

Her hair brushed, she sat down to read before retiring for the night. Lost in her loneliness, the comfort of her nightly ritual had a hollow feel.

⚓

"Uncle Ellis?" Richard looked up from his pillow.

"Yes, Richard." Ellis sat down on the edge of Richard's bed.

"Is Nanna going to always sleep over there?"

How could he tell the boy she would be leaving soon? Granted, Miss Smith had prepared him for her departure, but. . .

"No."

"Can she move into the big house?"

"I don't think so, Son. She'll be going back to New York."

"Will you be going to New York too?"

Ugh, Ellis inwardly groaned. For a child he sure did ask difficult questions. "Richard, it's late, and you need to get your sleep. Remember, we're going fishing in the morning."

Richard nodded his head and wiggled himself under the covers.

"Is Nanna coming fishing?"

"No, Son. Not tomorrow."

"When?" Richard lifted his head up off the pillow.

"I don't know. When she's well enough. Now, let's say your prayers."

"Yes, sir." Richard lay back down and clasped his tiny fingers together. "Dear Jesus, tell Mommy and Daddy I miss them. Help Nanna be happy again. And bless Uncle Ellis and Cook. Amen."

"Amen," Ellis echoed.

Help Nanna be happy again? Was she upset with the boy? he wondered. Truth be told, he had avoided her today. Was she still upset regarding their conversation last night? Did she regret her decision to postpone her departure even for a few days?

Ellis kissed Richard on the forehead. "Good night, Richard."

"Good night, Uncle Ellis."

Ellis closed the door to the child's room and headed down the stairs to his study. Invoices needed posting. Jedidiah Brighton had managed to load additional sponges to carry to New York. Pleased with the sales and the plentiful supply of natural sponges on the various reefs around the small island, his business would continue to grow. The Bahamian men he hired were naturals in the water and excellent sponge fishermen.

A parrot cawed, and Ellis looked out the window. The sky, a blanket of dark

velvet with a silver pearl nestled on it, created a wonderful backdrop for his tropical garden. He lowered his glance to the cabin in his backyard. Scratching his
beard, he wondered if it was wrong to separate the nanny from the boy. Should he
offer her a permanent position to stay in Key West? He had assumed from the
start she would want to get back to her life in New York. From their conversation
last night, he finally understood that Richard was her life. She had poured her
heart and soul into the child. And his brother had spoken highly of her compe-
tency. Maybe he should ask her to stay in charge of the boy's care.

Ellis leaned his chair back on its two hind legs and plopped his feet on his
desk, a bad habit he never saw the need to break. Maybe he should pray about this.
He'd been praying about how to be a good father to Richard, and reading every
verse in Scripture he could find about children and disciplining them. But had he
actually asked God if Miss Smith should remain on for a time as his nephew's
nanny? Or was he simply allowing her to leave because of his attraction to her, not
wanting to fight with temptation? Not wanting to deal with his past, his. . .

Yes, prayer was most definitely in order.

The next morning, Bea woke early and hurriedly dressed. She knew of Ellis's
and Richard's fishing plans. She'd hoped for an invitation. Oddly enough, she'd
gotten used to the sport. She'd done it simply to do "manly" things with
Richard, and much to her surprise found she actually enjoyed it. The peaceful
ripple of the water allowed one to think and pray. She'd never fished in an ocean
before. In fact, until she boarded the *Justice* in New York harbor to come to Key
West, she'd never even seen an ocean. The vast water contrasted dramatically
with the mountain springs that fed the various farms she'd lived on in upstate
New York. The smell of salt permeated the air. Low tide. . .well, low tide left
something to be desired.

The movement of the water was different as well. In the springs it flowed in
one constant direction; the ocean flowed in different directions depending on the
tides. And the gentle roll of the surf as it lapped the shore was just as captivating
as the constant movement of the water rushing downstream. While she found the
two types of water very different, they both had the same soothing effect on her—
gratitude to her heavenly Father. It gave her something to remind her of home.

Late last evening she had penned a letter to her parents, hoping there would
be a boat heading to New York so she could hand it to the captain. She tapped
her pocket in her long apron-covered shirt to be certain it was still there. . . .
Perhaps the *Justice* would be coming back from Cuba soon, and she could send it
that way.

The large front door opened and out stepped Richard with his pole in hand,
immediately followed by Ellis Southard. Richard's bright smile filled his face.
Ellis's eyes sparkled as he watched his nephew maneuver the fishing pole down
the front steps.

Perhaps I shouldn't. . . Bea stepped forward from the trees' shadows. "Good morning, gentlemen."

"Nanna! Are you going fishing?" Richard ran up to her.

She glanced over to Ellis. His eyes no longer sparkled. He didn't want her along. "No, I have a letter I need to post."

Richard pouted. "Why don't you want to come fishing with me?"

I do, Child, I really do, she wanted to say but held back her emotions and her tongue.

"If you would like to come with us, Miss Smith," Ellis paused, "you are welcome."

"I would enjoy it, but I wouldn't want to intrude."

Ellis grinned and then sobered. "Come along then, and be quick about it."

Bea tucked the letter back into the apron over her skirt and placed her hands on her hips. "Ready when you are, Sir."

"Yeah! Nanna's coming." Richard pranced up and down.

Looking over at Ellis Southard, she noticed he stiffened and shut down his emotions. Why did the man keep doing that? Bea rolled the tension out of her shoulders. She didn't understand him, but she would have to accept the discomfort of the day. After all, she had wormed herself a place in this little fishing expedition. "Let's go."

Ellis bolted ahead and walked a brisk pace through the streets to the harbor and down one of the large wooden docks that reached far into the ocean. Lined with sponges, nets, and a variety of ropes in different widths and sizes, she surmised that the dock belonged to Ellis and his sponging company. Afraid to ask, she held her tongue.

She worked up a sweat just keeping pace with Ellis Southard. Even Richard seemed a bit tired from the walk. She slowed her pace. She wasn't going to fall victim to heat exertion again. Little Richard's legs took three steps for every one of Ellis's.

As Bea and Richard started walking on the wooden planks, Ellis stood at the end of the pier. He turned to face her and muttered something to himself, muffled by the expansive ocean. Bea and Richard continued to plod on down the dock. Bea decided a word with Ellis Southard about his careless behavior was in order. But she would wait so that little Richard wouldn't be privy to their conversation.

Bea sat on the edge of the dock beside Richard and dangled her legs over the water. "It's a pleasant morning, Richard, don't you think?"

"Yup." Richard's head turned as he scanned the horizon.

"Nanna, see those clouds?"

Bea looked to where he pointed and nodded.

"Uncle Ellis says they are spinning around like a top."

She looked over to the horizon. Half a dozen small funnel clouds stood up from the sea. "Really?"

"Yup. And you see those clouds over there?" Richard pointed straight in front of them.

Bea nodded again.

"Those are new clouds being made."

"Do you know how clouds are made?" Bea inquired.

"Yup, Uncle Ellis says the sun makes the water hot and it 'vaporates, and when it gets high in the sky, it turns white and becomes a cloud."

"I see." For a four year old he really had quite an acute mind. Pleased and impressed that Ellis could talk with Richard in a way he could understand, she decided to acknowledge those things when she confronted him.

Beatrice Smith's presence this morning annoyed Ellis. She'd known he planned to take Richard fishing. And she obviously made herself available to come with them. Was he jealous of Richard's affection for her, or fighting his own attraction? He wasn't certain. Last night, in his stocking feet, he had buffed the floor to a high gloss from his continuous pacing. Successfully, he had resisted the urge to go to her cottage and speak to her, wanting, longing, to come up with any excuse just to see her smiling face.

Richard had thrived from Beatrice Smith's care. In his opinion, his brother had made a terrible error in judgment. How a man could avoid his own child because the mother died was beyond him. He understood his brother's deep love for his wife, but wasn't young Richard a part of her that continued to live?

Maybe he should let Beatrice and Richard return to the farm. But his brother's wishes were most emphatic that Ellis raise his son if anything should happen to him. And dealing with his own past would be at stake if he returned to New York, having been warned never to step foot again in the state, or Heather's father would press charges. He knew from Richard's letters that Heather had married. Perhaps enough time had passed.

"Nanna, Nanna, help!" Richard cried with excitement.

"Hold on tight, Richie."

Bea stood behind the boy, allowing him to work the fish and bring it in. Ellis smiled. Anxious to help, and yet proud to watch, he stationed himself beside the child.

Instinctively, they both reached for the line to help pull in the fish. Their hands grazed each other's, and Bea abruptly pulled hers away. Ellis held the line and pulled the fish up on the dock.

"It's blue and green!" proclaimed Richard.

"It's a snapper. Good eating, I think you'll like this fish," Ellis offered.

Richard jumped up and down around the fish. "Can I eat it for breakfast?"

Ellis placed his foot gently on the fish to keep it from flapping itself back into the water. "I imagine Cook would be happy to prepare it for you."

"Nanna can do it. Can't you, Nanna?"

Bea smiled and nodded her head.

"I'm sure she can, but Cook gets fussy about who she lets in her kitchen."

"Oh." Richard held Bea's hand. "Nanna, is it okay if Cook does it?"

"Yes, it's like Daisy in New York. She prefers to do all the cooking."

"Yeah, but not the fish. You had to clean the fish."

"I remember." Bea smiled. "That's a mighty fine catch, Richie."

She even cleans fish. Of course, if she wasn't too weak to put a worm on a hook, it only stood to reason she was capable of cleaning a fish too. Even though Beatrice informed him she was the child's playmate, father, mother, nanny, etc., the other night, he realized he was just getting a glimmer of the real person. Beatrice Smith certainly was a unique woman. Aside from Cook, he had never met such a bold woman. But, Cook was another kind altogether.

"Can you remove the hook or should I?" Ellis asked.

"Nanna does that."

"Nanna." Ellis motioned her to take her place in the tradition of Richard's fishing. "Be aware of the spines on the dorsal fin."

Bea simply nodded and knelt on her skirt and gracefully removed the hook from the fish. "Looks like you shall have a big breakfast this morning, Richard."

Richard beamed. His smile ran from one side of his face to the next. Ellis loved the boy. He would be staying with him whether in New York or here, it didn't matter.

Bea placed the fish in the small bucket Ellis brought. The tropical fish flapped and fluttered, slapping the sides of the bucket with its tail.

"Can we go home now, Uncle Ellis?"

Ellis searched Bea's eyes for an answer to his silent, "Why?"

"Once Richard catches a fish, his only interest is his tummy." Bea chuckled.

Ellis smiled. "Sure, Son. I'm quite certain Cook will be happy to see your breakfast."

"Come on, Nanna. Let's get a head start on Uncle Ellis," Richard called out as he started down the pier toward shore.

Bea turned and whispered to Ellis. "Sir, you might want to remember, small boys have small legs and can't keep the pace of a full-grown man."

Ellis nodded and went in the opposite direction to pick up his pole and tackle. Bea carried the bucket and Richard's pole. The boy was determined to beat his uncle Ellis home.

Ellis sidled up beside her, tenderly removing the bucket from her hand. "Thank you for your admonition. However, Richard will need to learn to take care of his pole and catch."

"Generally he does. I believe he wishes to show you how much of a man he really is."

"A man, huh? He needs to enjoy being a boy longer. There's plenty of time for being a man."

"Perhaps, but he's had more losses than most my age. He's had to grow up fast. All of this," Bea spanned the area around them with her outstretched hand, "is an adventure. Soon he will need to mourn the loss of his father, his home and. . .me."

Chapter 11

Cook smothered Richard with praises for his fine catch and breakfast. After a simple fare of fresh poached eggs with toast, freshly squeezed orange juice, and Richard's catch of the day, Ellis slipped off to work with a single salutation.

If Bea wasn't careful, she would soon start daydreaming about Ellis. He was such an interesting character, with a kind and gentle side full of passion and warmth, as she'd witnessed in his interchanges with Richard. But there was this other darker side of him that held everyone at bay. His emotions seemed to run hot and cold. She had been too forward the other evening, addressing him on this part of his personality.

"What be on your pretty mind, Miss Bea?" Cook inquired as she helped her out of her corset at the end of another long day.

"Nothing."

"I don't know what it is with you young folks, always carrying on and saying nothing is on your mind when it's obvious there is plenty happenin' up there."

"I'm sorry, I'm not used to sharing my personal thoughts."

"I reckon it should be me apologizing for prying where I shouldn't be. Some say I have a problem with that. On the other hand, I tend to believe it's my duty to get beyond the surface and sink right down to the heart of the matter. You wouldn't be thinking about when you leave Master Richard, would you now?"

"Truth be told, it has been on my mind. But no, that wasn't what I was pondering. How well do you know Mr. Southard?"

"I suppose I've known him longer than most. He wasn't much of a man when he landed on this here rock. At the time he come, let me think, I believe it was 1850 or '51—sometime thereabouts—there weren't too many folks living here. I heard say there was around a thousand. Personally I never had a mind to count 'em."

"He's been here that long?"

"Wet behind the ears and carrying a heap of trouble on his back. He never did say what he was running from, but he's made his peace with it. At least I think he has."

Bea's curiosity rose a notch. Why had he left New York? If she recalled correctly, he was seventeen at the time. In all her talks with Elizabeth she'd never really been curious as to why he left. It simply hadn't seemed all that important.

"He seems to have a good heart."

"I see, you're worried about him being a good man to raise the child."

Bea nodded.

"There's few men with as fine a moral character as Mr. Southard. He works hard, cares for those around him, treats people fairly. He'll do right by the boy."

Bea's heart tightened. Soon she would be leaving Richard. And oddly enough, he would go on and hardly remember her, and yet, he had profoundly affected her for the rest of her life. "Cook, do you know if the *Justice* has come back from Cuba?"

"Come and gone. Why do you ask?" Cook was folding her corset and placing it on the chair beside the chest of drawers.

"I thought perhaps I should seek transport back home."

"But Mr. Ellis hasn't hired a nanny yet."

"I know but. . ."

"Ahh, I understand, Child. Your heart is breaking."

Gentle tears rolled out of her eyes. "Yes. It's so hard, Cook. I love Richard as if he were my own. But I have no rights to him. And Ellis is. . .well, he is his uncle." Bea sniffed and immediately she found herself engulfed in Cook's soft, loving arms.

"There, there, child. Trust the good Lord; He knows what is best."

"I'm trying, and He's been trying to teach me Ecclesiastes 3:5, 'a time for embracing, and a time to refrain from embracing.'"

"Personally I don't know what Mr. Ellis's problem is with having you continue on as the child's nanny, but I reckon men don't have an eye for maternal love."

"Cook, I. . .well, I am not a normal nanny. I was Richard's mother's best friend. I come from high society. I gave it all up just to help my friend. And now I love Richard not because he is Elizabeth's son, but because he has become so dear to me. He's as close as the air I breathe."

"I'm not surprised about your status in society, but what does that matter? You love the child, the child loves you. That should be the end of it."

"But it's not, and we both know Mr. Southard is not happy with me."

"Does he know? Your status, I mean."

"I can't imagine he does. I've not told him. Besides, I was eight when he left, and it's as you say, it doesn't matter."

"Maybe. If the man knew what you've given up for the child, perhaps he might think differently about you," Cook huffed. "I tell you, the man hasn't been right since you arrived. If I didn't know better, I'd think he fancies you."

"What? You can't be serious. He can barely stand to be in the same room with me."

"Precisely my point."

"Cook, you've been out in the sun too long. He can't possibly. . ." Bea couldn't even continue the thought. There was no way on God's green earth that Ellis Southard was attracted to her. However, if the tables were turned she would have to admit she was mighty attracted to him.

"Think what you will, Child, you might be right. I'm just an old woman who's lived too long."

"Nonsense."

Cook smiled. "I must be leaving your wonderful company, Miss Bea. My family needs me. They just love to tell me how their days went and to hear about mine. I must tell you, you coming from New York has made for some delightful stories these many days."

"Oh my." Bea blushed.

Cook hugged her again. "Trust the Lord, Child. He knows the desires of your heart."

Bea felt the heat on her cheeks deepen. God truly did know all her desires, which included the temptation that one Mr. Ellis Southard had caused since her arrival on Key West.

Ellis's ears still rang from the chastisement Cook gave him for not allowing Beatrice Smith to stay on as Richard's nanny. She had a point. Several in fact. And he had considered the idea. He just didn't know if it was the wisest thing for him to do. He couldn't deny his attraction to her. Yet, he knew better than to act on such impulses. Could he possibly allow her to live in his home and not react to her presence? Ellis paced his office floor.

A dim light still burned in Bea's cottage. Bea's cottage? When had he given her possession of the place? Beatrice Smith was like that. Whatever she touched, wherever she went was illuminated by her presence. She was an incredible woman. But he was a man not to be trusted around women.

Key West had been a perfect place to settle. So few women, so few temptations. It was easy to get lost in his work here and avoid the fairer sex. As the years passed and more women moved to the island, he had remained in control. He'd even escorted a few of the ladies to church and social functions from time to time, and had become the perfect gentleman.

Ellis snickered. Heather O'Donald and her father would never believe that.

What if Bea remained in the cottage? He could remodel the place to suit her needs. She probably came from a home about that size before she became Richard's nanny. Ellis scratched his beard and gently stroked it back in place with long, thoughtful strokes. He peeked out the window. A single lamp glowed. If he was going to ask her to stay on, he'd better do it now before reason won over.

Ellis's steps were fluid and fast as he made his way out of the house to the captain's quarters cabin. Taking a deep breath, he lifted his hand and paused. Should he? He held his knuckles suspended in the air. Perhaps he should pray about this, consider all the ramifications of how this woman would bring him to the brink of his self-control.

He turned around and stepped away. Only to be halted by Cook's words.

"What are you afraid of?"

What indeed? Cook didn't know. No one knew. Well, Heather O'Donald and her father did. But his brother, the only other person who knew, was gone. A gentle voice whispered in his head. "It's been fifteen years."

Ellis knocked the doorjamb with his knuckle.

"Who is it?" Bea asked behind the still closed door.

"Miss Smith, it is me, Ellis. May I have a word with you?"

Bea slowly opened the door.

Ellis took in a sharp breath. She was lovely. She looked like a young girl rather than a grown woman with her long brown hair curled in spirals, cascading over her shoulders and framing her lily white neck. He swallowed and cleared his throat to speak. He'd seen her with her hair down before, but now the stark difference in their ages was once again made apparent. "May I come in?"

"Yes." Bea stepped back and allowed him to enter.

Ellis began to pace.

"What's the matter, Mr. Southard? Is Richard okay?"

"He's fine. Sorry. I. . .well I. . .I wanted to ask you something."

"Please sit, you're making me nervous," Bea pleaded.

"Sorry." Richard sat on the sofa. Bea sat a respectable distance away from him.

"I don't know how to say this other than to state my business straight out. Do you have obligations in New York?"

"No. Not really. Why do you ask?"

"What do you mean 'not really'?"

She hesitated, took in a deep breath, then looked him straight in his eyes. His heart stopped beating from the deep scrutiny he felt coming from her hazel-eyed gaze.

"My family wishes to have another coming-out party for me upon my return."

"Coming-out?"

"Mr. Southard, I come from a family such as your own. I took the job as Richard's nanny because of my deep love for Elizabeth. We all assumed she would get better shortly after she gave birth, but that simply wasn't the case. As you are well aware."

"You did all of that for the love of a friend?"

Bea nodded.

"I am in awe of you, Miss Smith. There are few who would sacrifice so much for the love of another."

"Thank you, but it hasn't been a sacrifice."

Ellis looked around the cottage. Such humble furnishings, and she was accustomed to the finer things in life, yet not once did she complain or voice her disapproval. Nor had she informed him who she was and his obligations to arrange proper housing for her stay.

"I am sorry, Miss Smith, if I had known. . ."

"Nonsense, I didn't need to tell you. I wanted to be with Richard, he's. . .he's special."

"He's more than special to you. You love him as if he were your own."

Bea looked away and whispered, "Yes."

"I came to ask you to stay on as his nanny, but I can't do that now. Knowing who you are, I can't ask you to give up your life again for Richard."

"I would love to stay on as Richard's nanny. Wealth isn't that important to me. Mind you, I'm not saying I don't appreciate some of the finer things. But Richard is of far more importance than wealth to me. I would be honored to stay on as his nanny."

"I can't allow you. It just wouldn't be right."

"Who is to know? If I don't care, why should you?" Bea reached over and touched his arm. "Ellis, please let me stay."

Bea was trembling from her contact with Ellis. "I've prayed, I've asked God for a way for me to continue to be a part of Richard's life. In six years he will be ten and I will still be young enough to marry."

"Beatrice. . .Bea. . .I—I just wouldn't feel right. You should be marrying a man and raising your own children."

"I don't want that as much as I want to be with Richard. Can't you understand? I love him that much." Bea swallowed back the tears that threatened to fall.

Ellis took her hand from his arm and held it tenderly within his own callused palm, massaging the tops of her fingers with the ball of his thumb. He glanced into her eyes and raised her chin with his left forefinger.

Bea's heart hammered in her chest. She was drawn to this man in a way she couldn't put into words.

Ellis touched the ringlets of her hair. "You're an incredibly beautiful woman, Bea."

Bea blushed. His eyes filled with passion. The realization excited her and frightened her at the same time. She removed her hand from his and rose from the sofa.

Ellis followed and stood behind her. "I'm sorry for being so forward, Beatrice. Please forgive me."

Bea nodded. She didn't trust herself to speak.

He placed his hands on her shoulders. "I would like to get to know you. May I call again tomorrow evening? After Richard is in bed."

"Yes," she whispered, her voice shaky, her body protesting. A driving need to turn to him and bury herself in his embrace threatened any sense of decency and proper behavior she had ever been taught.

He stepped back and removed his hands from her shoulders. As if instantly chilled, she shivered. What was the matter with her?

She turned to the gentle click of her door being shut. He was gone now. The cottage seemed darker. Lonelier. A somber air filled the empty space.

O Lord, what has come over me? Over us? She truly would have to admit Ellis's eyes spoke of his untold desire. She wondered if her own eyes revealed the same passion.

Chapter 12

All the next day, Ellis found himself as edgy as a land crab in search of shelter and protection. He had almost lost his self-control last night. He prayed long into the night, thanking the Lord for stepping in and pulling them apart at the moment He had. Granted, Bea had possessed the wisdom and strength to break the connection that drew them to each other. Bea had found the resolve to step away from him and their passion. And yes, she had the same desires as he.

What was it about him and his desires which brought a woman to a point of forgetting all propriety? He must be some kind of beast or animal, unable to control his desires.

On the other hand, they needed to talk. A physical attraction between them could not be denied. But could they live so close to one another and not succumb to temptation? Ellis was quite certain he would not stand the test. He hadn't in the past. What gave him a chance of withstanding it in the present? Especially since his desires for Beatrice far outweighed any desires he ever had for Heather.

Cook was exceptionally cold to him this morning. He didn't have the strength to tell her he had gone to ask Bea to stay on, only to find out that he couldn't allow her to take the position due to her social standing.

He felt grateful his parents were no longer alive. They would not be shamed once again by his actions. They had never known exactly what he had done, but they understood from Richard, Ellis had no choice but to leave, for the family's honor.

"Honor," Ellis sighed. "Father God, why did You do this to me? Why bring a woman into my path that I can never have? If we should ever marry, she would be a social outcast for marrying the likes of me. It wouldn't be fair to her, Lord. I couldn't put her through that."

"Through what?" Bea asked.

"Bea." Ellis fought every muscle in his body to stay in place. "Miss Smith, I was unaware of your presence."

"Apparently, and you do that quite well. How long have you been practicing the cold, standoffish man?"

"Long enough."

"Ellis, something happened between us last night. Don't you think we ought to talk about it?"

Ellis turned and faced the window looking over the gardens. "I was forward last evening, Miss Smith. It will never happen again."

"Oh, so if I came over to you right now and placed my fingers upon your chest, you would not respond?"

"Don't!"

"Don't what, Ellis? Admit that I'm attracted to you?" He heard the shuffle of her dress behind him.

"Yes. . .no. Bea, we can't."

"We can't, or you won't?" She placed her hand upon his left shoulder.

"I won't."

"Why?" she whispered.

"I am not an honorable man." Ellis walked away from her grasp.

"What?" Confusion knitted the features of her pretty face.

The sun was setting and the pinks and purples of the sunlight set a rose-colored haze across the garden.

"I have a past I'm ashamed of, Bea. I can never return to New York."

Never return to New York? What kind of crime had he committed? Is that why he left town and never returned so many years before?

"Fine. Be that way. I can't force you to explain. However, I think you're afraid. I certainly am. What we saw in each other's eyes last night was. . .was. . .well, I don't know what it was. But I know one thing, it scared the life out of me."

Bea retreated from Ellis's study. It had been a forward move to approach him in the house rather than to wait for him to come to her cottage later. But it seemed safer to speak with him there, while Cook was still in the house and with Richard running around.

She found Richard playing in his room. She now knew she couldn't stay, even if Ellis offered her the position. Whatever was going on between the two of them was unstoppable if she remained. And Bea wasn't all that certain she wanted to find out what it was. She had been known to speak her mind occasionally, but she prided herself on her ability to remain in control. Last night she was not in control. And neither was Ellis. If they had kissed at that moment it would have been. . . Bea shook the thought right out of her mind. She would not allow herself to ponder such things again.

All night she had tossed and turned, hoping that she and Ellis might have a future together. And that, through their union, the three of them would become a family. And Richard would legally become her son. *Such foolish thoughts,* she chided herself. Ellis had no intentions of giving into his feelings. Instead he erected a stone wall around himself that she was too afraid to climb.

"Richie."

"Yes, Nanna."

"I want you to know I love you very much." She fought for control of her emotions and continued. "I will always love you."

"I love you too, Nanna."

She balled her hands into fists and released them, working out her tension. "Like I mentioned the other day, I'm going home, Richie."

"Home? To my New York house?"

"No, to my parents' New York house. You remember visiting my parents' house, don't you?"

"Yes. But, Nanna, I want you to stay."

"I'd love to, but I can't. Your uncle Ellis loves you very much, and he will take good care of you. Perhaps when you are older and a man yourself you could come for a visit and see me in New York."

"I'll visit you, Nanna." Richard grabbed her legs through the loose-fitting Spanish-style skirt she had purchased the other day.

Bea pulled him up in her arms and hugged him hard, groaning and giving him a great big bear hug. "I don't know exactly when I'll be leaving. I have to wait for a ship. Hopefully, I'll have a few days to spend with you before I go."

"Can we go fishing?"

She grasped him more firmly. His bright blue-gray eyes darted back and forth imploring her to say yes. How could she not? "Sure, how about tomorrow morning?"

"Yippee."

Bea smiled. A child could shift his or her emotions as easily as the wind. One minute, sad about her leaving. The next, excited to go fishing. She set him back down on the floor. "I'll see you tomorrow morning. Good night, Richie."

" 'Night, Nanna." Richie continued to play with his blocks on the floor, his face intense as he worked on his next masterpiece.

Bea slipped into the hallway and tentatively approached the staircase. This was now the second time she broached the subject of her leaving to Richard, and it was getting easier, for him and for her. Perhaps she would be able to get over the tremendous loss in time.

At the foot of the stairs the darkened silhouette of Ellis Southard stood, waiting, his stance rigid, even more than before, if that were possible. Bea took in a deep breath and descended the stairs. "Good evening, Mr. Southard."

How could she be so casual? Ellis reached out to her and pulled her toward him. Fear blazed in her eyes. He paused, then released her. "Good night, Miss Smith."

The stunned woman stood in front of him. He stepped back. Timidly she reached her hand toward his forearm, but before it connected she pulled it back.

"I'm taking Richard fishing in the morning. Then I'll begin searching for a ship to make my departure. I think it would be best."

Ellis didn't want her to leave, but he didn't trust himself around her. The temptation he had felt with Heather was nothing compared to the pull of this woman. Unable to speak, he simply nodded his assent.

She turned and walked out the front door. She would be out of his life soon.

The temptation would be gone. He could get back to living his quiet life. Ellis eased out a pent-up breath.

"Uncle Ellis," Richard hollered from up the stairs. Perhaps his life wouldn't be all that quiet. He mounted the stairs two at a time and hurried to the child.

Bea set out for town after cleaning up from her morning fishing expedition with Richard. Unlike the time before, Ellis had not joined them. There must be a ship going to New York. She fortified her resolve to go back home.

Most ships passed through the Key West seaport as they worked their way from the states to the Caribbean or vice versa. Disappointed to find all the ships sailing in the wrong direction, Bea headed toward a small shop she had passed earlier. Purchasing some gifts for her family might help her to focus on New York rather than on what she was leaving behind. A few more days on Key West would give her a few more days with Richard. Granted, the tension between Ellis and herself would probably mount, but. . .

Bea's heart caught in her chest. She saw Ellis working on his dock. He appeared to be washing the sponges. His well-groomed beard glistened in the sunlight. Its red highlights made him even more striking. Bea fought the urge to walk up to him. Again last night he had almost kissed her. Frightened by such raw emotion, she had pulled away from him. Yet, she couldn't stop thinking about what it would be like to kiss—and be kissed—by such a powerful man.

She walked into the small shop featuring handmade crafts from the area residents. There were figurines made from shells, carved coconut husks and a variety of other strange items.

"May I help you?" a medium-height, fortyish woman asked.

"I'm just browsing, thank you." Bea glanced at the shell figurines.

"Take all the time you'd like. My name is Peg; I own this little shop."

"Did you make these?" Bea pointed to the shell critters.

"Actually, those are made by someone else. My hobbies are over there." She motioned to the side wall where various cloth items lined the shelves.

Bea worked her way over. There were linen tablecloths with finely embroidered flowers on the corners, some matching napkins, napkin ring holders, and a variety of rag dolls. "These are wonderful."

"Thank you. I opened the shop during the war. I found the soldiers loved to purchase items to send home to their mothers, wives, and sisters. The island has a certain uniqueness, being so far south. And people seem to like to buy trinkets for loved ones when they travel."

Bea chuckled. "That's why I'm browsing."

"Where are you from, and how long are you here?" Peg sat down behind the counter and brushed back her long blond bangs.

"Came from New York. I'll be returning home as soon as I procure passage."

"New York, as in the city?"

"Oh no, I'm from way upstate, near the Canadian boarder. I brought Richard to his uncle Ellis."

"The nanny. I should have realized. Heard you had a bout with heatstroke."

Did everyone know her business? "Yes. Didn't know if I was going to make it at one point. The doctor said it was because I'm used to the very cold temperatures up North, in contrast to the heat here."

"Happens to a lot of folks—no shame in it. Has Mr. Southard found a new nanny for the child?"

"I don't believe he has, but Richard is a good boy. It shouldn't be difficult."

Peg laughed. "This is Ellis Southard we're talking about, right?"

Bea knitted her eyebrows. "Yes."

"You should have seen his list. The woman had to be a saint and fifty years old at least, according to what he put together. Of course, most of the young gals here were hoping to get the job in order to hook the man. He's just not interested in marriage. And it ain't from a lack of some gals trying, let me tell you."

Bea blushed.

"Sorry, I shouldn't be so forward. Comes from living here so long. People just learn to let their mouths flap a bit. Never did gossip much at home, but here. . . well, it's the favorite pastime."

"I understand."

"So, I take it Mr. Southard isn't interested in keeping you on as the child's nanny."

"I have responsibilities back home. My family is planning another coming-out party."

"Coming-out party! You best set yourself down, dear. We've got plenty to discuss." Peg beamed and pointed to a stool.

⚓

Ellis worked his shoulders back, easing out the tension. He watched Beatrice make her way around to the various docks and ships. He supposed he could have told her there were none immediately heading to New York, but he wondered if she would have believed him.

She looked wonderful this morning in her Spanish skirt and blouse. The style of clothing fit her and her more aggressive personality. He wondered what some of the high society ladies back home would think if they saw her dressed in such a casual style. "Probably collapse," Ellis chuckled.

She had slipped into Peg Martin's gift shop and seemed to be spending quite a bit of time inside. Peg was a great gal, but she could rattle on so. He wondered if he should go over to the store and rescue Bea from Peg's assault of questions.

" 'Morning, Ellis." Marc Dabny headed toward him.

" 'Morning."

"Heard the lady was leaving the island soon."

"Appears so."

"I asked her if she would like to go to dinner with me one night, but she let me know she would be leaving and was in no position to begin a relationship."

"Sounds wise." She'd given Ellis just the opposite impression. He reminded himself he wasn't interested in pursuing a relationship. She was leaving.

"She's quite a looker." Marc whistled.

"I guess. So tell me, what brings you over this morning, Marc?" He must have spent too much time in the sun; his head was pink from an obvious sunburn, Ellis observed. Why a man with so little hair on his head didn't wear a hat baffled him.

"Oh, right. I was wondering if you had room for a partner."

"Partner?"

"Yeah, I've got some money set aside and I think your business is going to be growing. I also have a couple ideas about expanding your market."

"Haven't given any thought to expanding." In fact, he was beginning to think about closing down the business and returning home to New York to raise Richard on the family farm. "Maybe we should talk, Marc."

Marc rubbed his hands together. "Great. With my investment we could hire a few more men, buy a few more boats, and begin shipping the sponges into other cities besides New York."

"I'm listening." And Ellis seriously was. If Marc bought into the business, maybe Ellis could return home and still maintain his business here in Key West.

"As you know, the railroad is expanding across the western frontier. And I was thinking, if we took the sponges to the cities where people connect with the trains, we would see the sponges move out West as well."

"Interesting. Do you have contacts in some of these cities?"

"Some. Men I served with in the war. But I could make a trip north, make some contacts, and line up initial sales."

Marc was a go-getter, and he seemed to have an eye for business. "Marc, I would need to see your books and how well you manage your assets before I agree."

"And I would like a look at yours as well."

"That's fair. All right, why don't you come over this evening and we'll discuss business in a more formal manner. I'd want a lawyer to draw up any agreement."

"Naturally."

"I must tell you, I might be interested in having someone else run the business so I can return to New York for awhile and take care of the farm."

"Either way, you stay and run it or I stay, doesn't much matter. I'll be over after dinner tonight."

"I'll have my books ready," Ellis said and took a step back toward his work. Marc waved his salutation and left.

Should he move back to New York? Should he raise Richard there? Or should he just stay put and enjoy his life here? So many questions. So many changes in such a short span of time. Ellis sat on the edge of the dock and prayed. "Father, I'm confused. I see advantages to Marc coming on as a partner, but I want to be wise. I want to honor Richard's request to raise his son, and I know he wanted the boy to enjoy growing up on the farm. But can I really return home? And what about this attraction to Beatrice Smith? If I return to New York won't she be there also?" Ellis groaned.

He sprang up, peeled off his shirt, shoes, and socks, and jumped into the ocean. A long hard swim was in order. He needed some physical exercise. He needed to relax.

"Goodness, you did all that for a friend?" Peg asked.

"Yes, and I'd do it again." Bea sipped a cup of tea Peg had given her.

"That kind of friendship is hard to find. I'm pleased to know you, Bea."

Bea dabbed her mouth with the cloth napkin. "Thanks, I'm sure many folks would do what I did."

"I wouldn't be so sure."

"We have a dinner at the Presbyterian church tonight. Would you like to come?"

"Goodness, what time?"

"Six."

Ellis usually returned home at five. "Sure, I'd love to. Thanks."

"Tell you what, I'll have my brother, Danny, come by your place and escort you to the church."

"If you tell me where it is, I think I can manage it." Bea shifted on the stool.

Peg waved her hand with a quick flick of the wrist. "Nonsense, a woman should have an escort. You know that."

"But I thought such things weren't followed down here."

"True enough, but once the sun goes down and the sailors start to drinking, it's just wise to have a man escort you." Peg tapped her hand onto Bea's.

"I see your point. I'm staying in the cottage in back of Ellis Southard's home."

"The cottage?"

"Don't ask," Bea sighed.

Peg laughed. "Guess it has to do with you not being over fifty, right?"

"Possibly. . .I really don't know. But it is the cutest little cottage. I love it." Bea smiled. "I better get going. Cook will have my hide if I don't return soon. Thanks for the tea and the conversation." Bea slipped off the stool.

" 'Welcome. Next time I'll let you buy something." Peg winked.

Bea giggled and walked out the door. She glanced over at Ellis's dock and saw him jump in the ocean, half naked.

"Oh my!" she exclaimed and turned her head. Her face flushed. She quickened her pace. *Lying in a snow bank might be the best thing at the moment*, she thought. Snow was not to be found in Key West and likely never would be. Bea opened the fan she had brought with her and fanned herself as she walked up Front Street back to Ellis Southard's home.

Chapter 13

Ellis couldn't believe it. The first evening he was home for dinner in two nights and Beatrice Smith had accepted an invitation to dine at the Presbyterian church. Seeing Peg Martin's brother, Dan, come to escort Bea had him speculating that Peg might have other intentions besides dinner. Pacing back and forth down the hall, stroking his beard, he wondered why the thought bothered him so.

While Richard slept peacefully upstairs, Marc had come and gone, scrutinizing Ellis's books and finding them in order, just as Ellis had found Marc's. It seemed plausible that the two could become partners. Marc's bid to purchase half of the business was a fair market value. But before he moved on with this merger, Ellis wanted and needed references. Truth be told, harvesting and exporting sponges was the furthest thing from his mind.

Listening, waiting for Beatrice's return, drove him into a frenzy of worry. The late hour, along with his inability to go searching for her without waking up the child, left him feeling helpless. The rich mahogany grandfather's clock chimed once, noting it was half past the hour of ten. Perhaps he should wake the boy? He placed his foot on the first step, and then heard laughter. Ellis paused.

Yes, it was definitely laughter, feminine laughter. He eased his foot off the step and sauntered over to the front door. Leaning around the doorjamb, he could see the young couple. Beatrice removed her hand from Dan's arm. They were talking; she was smiling, a friendly banter exchanged between them.

Dan bowed slightly and kissed the top of her hand. Fire blazed up Ellis's spine. How dare he be so forward? And yet, Dan was being the perfect gentleman.

Ellis waited for Dan to leave before he opened the door.

"Hello, Ellis." Bea smiled.

Had she seen him behind the door? "I was wondering if we could talk?"

"I think that would be nice. Shall I come into the big house and we can share a cup of tea?"

"Sure." Ellis slipped back into the house and raised the lights. The warm glow pushed aside some of his earlier dark emotions.

Bea slipped through the open door, the swish of her skirt alerting him to her nearness. He turned. She was beautiful.

"You waited up for me?" she asked and walked past him toward the kitchen.

"Yes. We need to talk."

"Yes, we do." She placed the full teakettle on the lit stove, then she moved swiftly to the cabinet where the cups were stored, removing two with their saucers. She must have spent more time with Cook than he imagined.

"I had an offer today to buy into my sponge business."

She paused for a moment and asked, "Was it a good offer?" She went back to her work.

"Respectable."

"Do you know and trust the man enough to join in a partnership with him?"

"Marc seems responsible."

"Marc Dabny?" She turned from the counter and faced him.

"Yes."

"And this is the same man that—"

"Yes." Ellis cut her off. He didn't want to be keelhauled all over again for that one.

"And you trust him?" She raised her cinnamon brown eyebrows.

"At this point. Is there something I don't know about him that you would question my judgment so?"

"Seems to me a couple days ago the man was hunting for a wife. Not an ordinary wife, a slave, with a pretty figure, mind you."

"He told you that?"

"Not in so many words, but yes, it was clear to me what the man's intentions were. If a man can treat a woman like that, what kind of a man would he be as a business partner? Would he want you to slave and do all the work while he sat back and enjoyed your profits?"

"I hadn't thought about that." Truth was he hadn't had much room for any thought which didn't revolve around her.

Bea poured the boiling water into the teapot and let it steep. "Why did he want to buy into your business, Ellis?"

"He said he saw room for expansion, and I think he has some valid ideas." There. He wasn't a total idiot when it came to business.

"Well, I don't know the first thing about your business and where it may or may not be expanded. Truth is, I've never heard of a sponge business before. But you seem to be doing well. Would this expansion need the help of another owner?"

"Possibly, possibly not."

Bea set the teapot on a tray with the cups. "Shall we sit in the living room or would you prefer to sit at the table?"

"Living room is fine." Ellis scooped up the tray and led the way.

Bea followed Ellis, noticing how his strong shoulders pressed his white cotton shirt. The man was in excellent shape.

Ellis poured her a cup.

Bea sat on the sofa in front of the cup of tea he had placed on the Queen

Anne mahogany table. She smoothed her skirt and waited for Ellis to pour his own tea and sit down. He sat beside her on the sofa. "What do you want to talk about, Ellis?"

"Are you aware of the hour?"

"Yes, and you and I both know you don't want to talk with me about the time I've returned home."

Ellis tugged at his collar and nodded. He stood up and began to pace. *At least he is working out his thoughts,* she mused.

"Richard said you would be joining us tomorrow morning."

"Yes. After you so wonderfully put it back in my lap."

"What?"

"Richie said that you said to go ask me about fishing with the two of you."

"Oh. Well, I didn't know what to tell the boy, and I certainly wasn't going to be answering for you."

"Thank you."

"Bea, this is crazy. I'm so full of wild emotions I don't know what to think or do. Let alone make sense of anything."

"And you think I understand these emotions?"

He sat down beside her on the sofa. The warmth of him so close to her sent a warm glow radiating within her. *O Lord, help me now,* she silently pleaded.

"Ellis, tell me what happened." Without thought, she reached over and touched his sun-darkened hand, tenderly stroking it.

"I'll tell you, but please do not pass judgment on my family for my actions. They were mine and mine alone."

"Very well."

And Ellis began. He told her about Heather, their whirlwind romance, and about the night they stole a passionate kiss. How her hands went beneath his shirt, and how he was driven by desire to go beyond where a gentleman should. And about her father, finding them locked in each other's embrace, and his warning for Ellis to get out of town or he would ruin the reputation of the Southard family name.

"So, you created a stone wall and kept women at bay for all these years?"

"It was the only way. I was so out of control that night."

"I see. And it was all you, right?"

"Of course. I was the one who initiated the kiss."

Bea smiled. "Ellis, in my opinion, unless you force yourself upon us, by and large, women are the ones who send out the signals about wanting or not wanting to be kissed."

"But what about the other night? You and I both know we could have been lost in our passions."

"True, but we weren't. At the right moment, wisdom prevailed and we stopped. Emphasis on the word 'we,' Ellis. You and I both stopped.

"Can I ask you something even more personal?"

Ellis chuckled. "I don't think anything is more personal than what I just admitted to you about myself."

"Were you used to women putting their hands under your shirt?"

His eyebrows arched up into his forehead. "No, it was a completely new experience."

"Did you direct Heather's hands to go there?"

"No." He knitted his eyebrows together.

"Do you see my point yet?" Bea stroked her thumb over Ellis's firm grip.

"I'm not sure. Are you suggesting Heather was the more aggressive person?"

"Yes."

"But I didn't do anything to stop her. She was a sweet, innocent girl before I kissed her."

"Had you kissed many women before Heather?"

"No."

Bea knew Heather O'Donald's reputation, and obviously Ellis didn't. While still a young girl, Bea had heard the whispered news of Heather O'Donald's hurried wedding and soon-delivered first child. And this occurred a year after Ellis left. Obviously, Ellis never knew, or if he did, he probably blamed himself for that as well.

She reached up and stroked his bearded jaw. "Ellis, was it Heather O'Donald, by chance?"

"Yes. But for her sake, please don't repeat any of this."

"I won't. But what I'm going to tell you isn't pretty, and I'll be as gentle as I can. Heather O'Donald married quickly, a year after you left the area, and had a child six months later." Ellis lowered his head and wagged it back and forth.

"It's not your fault."

"Of course it is. Don't you see? If I hadn't kissed her so passionately, she never would have known. . ."

Bea took both of her hands and placed them on his face and lifted it to look at her. "Ellis, I think you were the innocent one. True, you had desires, and perhaps you would have acted upon them. But Heather had desires too. She was bold, far bolder than you. Don't you see?"

"Maybe, but I'm the man. . ."

Bea chuckled. "And only men sin, right?"

He narrowed his gaze.

"Ellis, I always found that when two people sin, both are guilty. God will forgive you, and you can ask Him to forgive Heather. The hardest part is for you to forgive yourself."

"How did you become such a wise woman at such a young age?"

"I'm not. But I do pay attention, and I think what you and I are fighting is an attraction far deeper than your lustful moment with Heather."

Ellis pulled back from Bea's loving embrace. Her words made perfect sense. Had Heather already been exposed to such passions? He thought back on their few dates. She had been the aggressor. She seemed to. . . Ellis cleared his throat. "So, do you think you can trust me with these intense passions?"

Bea turned her head then looked back at him. "Can you trust me?" Her faint blush accented her beauty.

Ellis sat in the chair opposite the sofa. "You're an incredible woman, Beatrice Smith. Not only are you beautiful enough to take my breath away, your mind is quick, and you get to the heart of the matter with a forward resolve I've never seen before."

"Thank you—I think."

Ellis chuckled. "My words were meant as a compliment. Unlike Marc, I would never want a servant for a wife. I would want a companion, someone who would challenge me, someone with whom I could share my deepest thoughts and concerns. Someone I could trust with my heart."

"Is that a proposal?"

Ellis gulped.

Not giving him a chance to respond, she quipped, "And you say that I'm honest. I've never met a man like you, Ellis. And I must tell you, I like what I see."

Ellis grinned. Was she admitting she found him handsome? "What do we do now?"

"I have no idea." Bea lifted her teacup. It shook in her hand and she immediately nested in back on the saucer.

"You're afraid to be with me, aren't you?"

"Yes. . .no. It's not what you're thinking."

"Explain." Ellis lowered his chin onto his clasped hands with his elbows supported by the arms of the chair.

"Yes, I'm afraid of the attraction between us. No, I'm not afraid of you and your past. You were a boy bursting to be a man. I've heard that it is a difficult time for all young men."

Ellis's cheeks flamed. "It can be."

"I found out today that no ships will be leaving for New York for awhile."

"I know."

"You knew?" She knitted her eyebrows.

"I know the comings and goings of ships. It's all a part of my business. I need to find ships to carry my cargo."

"Oh, right. Well, I was going to say, why don't we slowly see what develops between us? You know, spend some time, talking like this."

Ellis smiled. "Yes, I think that would be in order. Shall I come to your cottage tomorrow night after Richard's gone to bed?"

"Why don't we start with some time in public?"

"In public? You want me to court you?"

Bea chuckled. "Is that a problem?"

"No, but—"

"But, since the woman is right here in my backyard, why do I need to fuss over her, right?"

She could be forward. He amended his words. "I didn't mean it that way. If you want me to court you, I'll do it." Ellis squirmed, working the tension out of his back.

"No, you don't have to court me. I was merely trying to suggest we spend time together. Like meal time, playing with Richard after dinner, those times. You've been avoiding coming home at dinner since the other night in the cottage."

"Work kept—"

"Ellis!"

"Oh, all right, yes. I was thinking up work that needed doing so I didn't have to face you. Better?"

Bea smiled. "Much."

"Oh, you can have a nasty side, I see," Ellis teased.

"Nasty? Me. . . ? Now, Ellis, whatever gave you that idea?" She winked.

Just what had he gotten himself into? Ellis's fingers tightened around the arms of the chair.

Chapter 14

Ellis lay in bed as the sun rose. The bright orange glow cast stark shadows over the room. He rubbed his face. "I can't believe I admitted everything to Beatrice last night," he groaned. Granted, she was easy to talk with, but. . . "Marriage? Did I really propose marriage?

"Lord, I'm certain I didn't. I was just saying if I was to marry. That isn't asking a woman, is it? Do I want to. . .to. . . I can't say it, Lord. The very thought sends shivers of fear up my spine. Although the conversations would be lively with Miss Smith."

Ellis pulled the covers off and sat up, swinging his feet over the edge. He stood and stretched his sore muscles. His bed looked like a battlefield. And a battle of emotions had been waged all night. Did he want to pursue a relationship with Miss Smith, or not? One thing was certain. It would solve the need for a nanny. And Beatrice does love the child. *She isn't an unpleasant woman for a man to get saddled with. . .if a man must be saddled,* he reasoned.

But a wife wasn't a saddle. She was to be cherished, loved, honored, and adored. Could he truly do those things with regard to Beatrice Smith? "I don't know, Lord. I'm so confused. And what's this sixth sense You've given her about Marc? Is there something I don't see?" Ellis paced back and forth in his room.

The gentle knock on his door stopped him mid-stride. "Who is it?"

"Me, Uncle Ellis."

"Come in, Son."

The door creaked open slowly. "Cook says to come to breakfast."

Ellis smiled, confident Cook would pronounce it as an order. "Tell her I'll be right down. I need to shave."

"Shave? You taking off your beard?" Richard questioned, his eyes opened wide, waiting for an answer.

"I may have a beard, Son. But I do still shave." Ellis pointed to the various places on his face and neck where he did shave. "Plus, I have to keep it trim."

"My daddy didn't wear a beard, just a 'stache."

Ellis grinned. "A 'stache, huh? Do you think I should take off my beard?"

"No, you look like Uncle Ellis with a beard."

Ellis chuckled. Children's logic could be so profound. "You better go tell Cook I'll be right down or she'll have both our hides."

Richard ran out of the room as if lightning would strike. Ellis grinned. The woman did have a way of putting fear into a person. He looked into the mirror.

Would Bea prefer no beard? Ellis tried to imagine what his face would look like without it. He'd grown the beard when he was twenty and had never once shaved it off. He remembered her loving touch on his beard last night, cupping his face in her tender hands. Such compassion. Such honesty. No, he'd leave his beard. She certainly didn't seem to have a problem with it.

Ellis finished getting ready for the day and worked his way down the stairs. The lilt of Bea's laughter floated into the hall. He paused, enjoying its merriment, then continued on to the dining room. "Good morning, everyone." He caught a glimpse of Bea, and she flushed slightly. Goodness, she was beautiful in the morning. He sat down at the head of the table. Cook was in the kitchen. Richard was buttering his biscuit. Ellis caught Bea's glance and mouthed the words, "You're beautiful."

A deep crimson blush painted her high cheekbones. Ellis smiled and released his gaze. While questions abounded in her absence, in her presence all arguments, fears, and worries dissolved. For the first time in fifteen years he truly felt forgiven for his past, and he owed his inner release to this incredible woman. If only he had learned that lesson before his parents had passed. He would have gone home for a visit. Heather's family's threats were meaningless in the scope of her wedding a year later.

A peace settled within him regarding his parents. They were in heaven. They would know the truth, and one day he would meet them again.

"Uncle Ellis, where are we fishing today?"

"I thought we might go for a sail and fish for some deepwater fish, like king-fish." Ellis picked up the fork with his right hand.

"Fishing on a boat?" Richard bounced up and down with excitement on his chair.

"Yes, we have to sail out quite a distance before we can fish. Would you like that?"

Richard bobbed his head up and down with such vigor, his entire body shook.

"Miss Smith, do you think you can handle the sun for an entire day?" Ellis asked, scooping another forkful of eggs.

"I'm not sure. I've been feeling stronger." Bea's voice seemed uncertain. Was she afraid of being on a boat? No, that couldn't be. . .she had sailed here from New York. Was she afraid of being alone with him for an entire day? But Richard would be with them, he reasoned.

Ellis dabbed his mouth with his napkin, then spread it over his lap again. "There's a small cabin on the boat where you can get some shade."

"I know you didn't ask my advice," Cook interrupted, "but I think a full day's sail might be a bit much for the lady." Cook sat herself down at the table.

"You think so, Cook?" Bea asked, fussing the edge of her napkin with her fingertips.

"I'd be waiting a bit more if it was myself." Cook lowered her head, clasped her hands, and silently prayed over her breakfast.

"I think I'll take Cook's advice and stay here. I'm sorry, Richard, but I won't be fishing with you today."

Ellis straightened in his chair. "We don't need to go deep-sea fishing. We could still use the boat and fish around the island."

"No, thank you. You and Richard go ahead. I'll browse some more through town. I barely scratched the surface yesterday."

Richard tattled. "Nanna didn't like the big waves on the boat from New York."

Ellis searched Bea's eyes. "Were you seasick?" he asked.

"A little," Bea admitted.

"Land sakes, child. No wonder the heat got you so bad." Cook tossed her head from side to side and ate some of her eggs.

"Did that matter?" Bea asked.

Ellis couldn't believe his ears. *Did it matter?* he grumbled to himself. "Of course it mattered. You were already a bit dehydrated from the seasickness. No wonder you were hit so hard. I want you to stay home today, and don't be spending too much time in town. We don't want you having a relapse."

"Is that an order or concern?" she rebuffed.

"Ew-wee, I'm not touching that one." Cook giggled and stood up, removing her plate from the table.

"Concern." Ellis held back his temper.

Richard's head bobbed back and forth between the two of them, then settled on Bea to wait for her response.

"Then I'll not be upset with your concern. And I'll do as you recommend."

Ellis reached over and cupped her hand under his own. "I am concerned, Bea," he whispered.

"Thank you."

Richard knitted his eyebrows together. Bea removed her hand from Richie's prying eyes. He was trying to figure out what had just happened, and Bea suspected Cook knew exactly what was going on between Ellis and her. "Richie, finish your breakfast so you can go fishing and sailing with your uncle."

"All right." He stabbed his fork into some eggs and gulped them down.

Ellis and she had agreed to take things one step at a time, but he had thrown her with his comment about how beautiful she was. On the other hand, she couldn't help but notice how handsome he was this morning, as well. They would have to decide fast if they were, or were not, going to court. She wasn't sure she could take too much of this.

"All done," Richard proclaimed, and took his empty plate to the kitchen.

"I'm sorry, Ellis," she whispered. "I should have known you were speaking with concern, not orders. I have a tendency to dislike being ordered about."

Ellis grinned. "I'm rather accustomed to women like that. I'll be more careful how I word my thoughts in the future."

"Can I have another offer for a gentle sail around the island?" Bea allowed her hand to travel in Ellis's direction.

He picked up on her cue and cupped her hand again. She breathed in deeply. His warmth and strength blended with his tenderness and found expression in the simple gesture. *Amazing,* she mused.

His voice lowered. "You feel it too?"

She nodded.

"We'll talk some more tonight." Ellis looked back to the kitchen. Cook seemed to have given Richard a chore. "Thank you for last night. I feel so at peace with my past."

"You're welcome."

He squeezed her hand slightly. "Later," he whispered.

Bea nodded and removed her hand. As much as she didn't want to, she knew she had to. Richard was bound to come racing through those doors any minute.

As if on cue, the door banged open. "Uncle Ellis?"

"Yes, Richard." Ellis winked at Bea.

"Cook says I need sailing clothes. What are they?"

"You'll need some oilcloth clothes to protect you from the rain. But we'll be okay today. Just gather a set of warm pants, a shirt, and a sweater or winter coat."

"It's too hot."

"It's in case of a storm on the water, Richard. You need to be prepared."

A storm? Could they run into a storm? Bea implored Ellis's gaze for some assurance.

"Truth be told, there aren't many storms down here in the winter months. Hurricane season is over."

"Hurricanes?"

Ellis chuckled. "An ugly Nor'easter—but these come from the south."

"Oh."

"Go get your change of clothes, Richard. We need to get going if we're going deep-sea fishing."

Richard scurried off.

"Is he safe out there?" Bea asked in Richard's absence.

"He'll be fine."

Bea tried not to worry. She didn't know anything about sailing. Her first sail was on the *Justice.*

"Trust me." Ellis now stood beside her and placed his hand on her shoulder. "We'll be fine."

Bea nodded.

She watched Ellis retreat from the dining room. Bea gathered up the few remaining dishes to take to the kitchen. Cook's remaining in the kitchen meant she was deliberately giving the two of them some privacy. But Cook being Cook, she would have plenty of questions when Bea entered the kitchen. Bea took in a deep breath and pushed the kitchen door open with her hip.

"Here's the rest of the dishes, Cook."

"Thank you. Put 'em by the sink."

"May I help?" Bea offered.

"I'd be a fool to turn down a good offer. Water's hot, you can start washing."

And Bea went straight to work.

"Nanna," Richard yelled.

"In the kitchen," she called back.

" 'Bye. Uncle Ellis said we'd be gone until supper."

Bea wrapped her damp arms around Richard and gave him a great big bear hug and groaned, "Have fun, Richie."

Richard ran out of the kitchen and grasped his uncle's hand.

"He sure took to his uncle," Cook said.

"There seems to be a connection." Bea went back to the dishes.

"Seems to be one between Mr. Ellis and you too."

Ugh, here it comes. Bea continued to scrub. What could she say?

"I told the man to make peace with you, I didn't tell him to. . ."

Bea rewashed the plate for the second time. "Oh, for pity's sakes, Cook. We're just. . ."

"Just?"

"Oh, all right, we're attracted to each other."

"If you don't mind me saying so, I knew it." Cook's grin slipped up to her eyes, causing them to sparkle.

"What?"

Cook laughed. "I could tell the first time I saw you. You were smitten by Mr. Ellis. Thing is, I've seen that in other young ladies before. But I must say, you're the first one to ever have him return the interest."

"We're going to take it slow. Be friends. See if anything develops."

Cook continued to laugh as she cleaned her counter. "I say you'll be married before the end of the month."

The woman was crazy. The end of the month was next week. There was no way she and Ellis would. . .well, maybe it was possible. A flicker of desire stirred in Beatrice. She thanked the Lord she wasn't facing Cook and closed her eyes to calm her emotions.

"Do you love him?" Cook tenderly asked. Having come up beside her, she placed her firm hands on Bea's shoulders.

Bea turned and faced her. "I don't know. I can't say what it is I'm feeling for him."

"Give it time, Child. Give it time."

"I don't know what to do, Cook. I'm supposed to go home in a few days. I can't very well stay here in his house or even his cottage if we're courting. It wouldn't be right. And yet, I don't have a job to support myself and stay on the island. I have some funds saved, but they're back home in a bank."

"Like I said, give it time. The good Lord understands all your needs, desires, and confusion. He'll help you out."

Bea sighed. "I was up most of the night praying. I've never been so attracted to a man, and yet is that grounds to get married?"

Cook's eyebrows went up. "He asked you?"

"Well, no, not exactly, but the subject did come up."

"Land sakes, he's hit worse than I thought." Cook slipped her arm around Bea's back and led her to a chair at the kitchen table. "Mr. Ellis has been asking me to move in ever since he bought this place. Guess maybe the time's come."

"What about your family?" Bea asked.

"They could use my room for some of those young 'uns who's growing up. I'll start moving my things in today."

"Don't you think we ought to approach Ellis about this?"

"Fiddlesticks. I won't let silly town gossip compromise him or you. I'll move in, and you stay in the cottage."

Bea giggled. "That's an order, isn't it?"

"Yup, and I'll be watching you two. Don't you worry yourself none. With me and the good Lord, you'll be behaving yourselves."

Bea laughed and threw her arms around Cook. "Thank you. You don't know how much your being here will help."

"I believe I do, Child. I was young once too."

Bea flushed.

Cook roared with laughter. "I say, you young folks have a terrible time realizing us older ones were ever your age."

"With you around, Cook, I don't think I'll be forgetting it."

"Good. Well, if I'm moving in today, you'll be giving me a hand."

Bea gave a mock salute. "Aye, aye, Captain."

Chapter 15

I like the waves, Uncle Ellis," Richard hollered, standing on the bench of the sailboat.

"Richard, get down, now!" Ellis roared. The surf rocked the boat and battered the hull as it crashed down on the waves.

Richard slipped back down on the bench. "But it's fun standing up," he pouted.

"It may be fun, Son, but it is dangerous. If you're going to sail with me, you have to obey the rules."

"Yes, Sir. I'm sorry." Richard lowered his head and looked at his dangling feet.

"Thank you. Now, it's time to go back home. The sun is low on the horizon."

"But I didn't catch a big one, like you."

"Next time." If there was a next time. He had had no idea how hard it would be to keep a four year old contained on a boat. And it wasn't that big a boat. Yet he still managed to get into everything. Ellis's nerves were shot. Not with the child, but with the fear that something might happen to him. He would take him again only if he brought Bea along. She could help watch Richard.

Ellis turned the bow toward Key West and began the long sail back to the island.

"Richard, cast your rod. Let's see if you catch anything on the way home."

His head bobbed up and down as he picked up his rod and placed it over the side, letting the line go out farther and farther.

"That's enough, Son."

Richard secured his rod and placed it in the mounts Ellis had put into the boat long ago. Richard lay back on the bench and watched the top of the rod to see if he snagged a fish.

"Uncle Ellis?"

"What, Son?"

"Do you like Nanna?"

Oh dear, the child had caught him placing his hand upon Bea's. "Yes, she's a nice lady." There. *That's honest, and not too leading.* He hoped.

Placing his hands behind his head, Richard leaned back and said, "Are you going to marry Nanna?"

Ellis held back an audible groan. "I don't know. Why do you ask, Son?"

"Billy's mommy and daddy hold hands, and they're married."

"Holding hands doesn't mean a man and woman are married."

"Oh." Richard sat up. "What makes a man and woman married?"

"First, they have to love each other."

"Do you love Nanna?"

Ellis closed his eyes and whispered a silent prayer for guidance. "I don't know. Nanna and I just met. We need to get to know one another. Love has to develop, it doesn't just happen overnight." While he had felt an instant attraction to Bea the first time he met her, he wouldn't call such an attraction love. On the other hand, his feelings for her today were far stronger and closer to love than attraction.

"So if a man and woman love each other, they're married?"

"No, they have to decide they want to get married."

Richard knitted his eyebrows.

Ellis continued. "A man and a woman have to go to a preacher to 'get' married. When they do that the preacher declares them married, and they kiss."

"Have you kissed Nanna?"

The sudden intense heat on Ellis's cheeks made him acutely aware he was blushing. "No, Son. I haven't."

"I love you, Uncle Ellis. And I love Nanna. If you get married, we'll be a family, like Billy's."

Ellis couldn't respond. The child longed for a family like his friend's back home. A part of Ellis would love to jump in and marry Bea just to give the child some security. But marriage was far too serious a venture to jump into for the wrong reasons. What would happen after Richard was grown? Would they separate, no longer needing to be together, or would they slowly grow in love with each other? No, Ellis resolved. The child needed stability, and he wasn't going to jump into a marriage unless love, friendship, and honesty were a part of it right from the very start.

"Richie, look—a porpoise jumping in the waves." Ellis pointed to the gray bottle-nosed dolphin near the bow of the boat. "They're swimming with us."

"Wow." Richie leaned over the side. Ellis grabbed the boy by his britches and held him fast. *Thank You, Lord, for dolphins.*

Bea couldn't believe the pack of children gathered at Cook's home. It was a simple home, clean and well-kept. Several bedrooms ran along the left side of the house, while a large living area, dining area, and small kitchen ran along the right side. Little brown children of all shapes and sizes looked at Bea. *No wonder Cook runs things with a firm hand.*

"Grandma, can I have your room?" a young girl with braided hair pleaded.

"It'll be up to your parents. But you can't move in until I move my things to Mr. Ellis's house."

The young girl nodded and walked off.

"That's Darlene. She's the oldest of my son George's children. That's Ben, he's eight, and my daughter Lizzy's oldest." Cook pointed to a thin boy with a wide grin.

"How many live here?" Bea questioned.

"Let me see. . . .George, his wife and their three children, Lizzy and her four children. Lizzy's husband died fighting in the war. And myself, so I guess that makes eleven."

More than seven children filled the house. Bea slowly scanned and counted the children. Cook laughed. "Kids from around the island come here for Lizzy to teach 'em some math and reading."

"Oh."

"We try to pass on to the children things they'll need in the future." Cook walked down the hall to the back bedroom.

"I might have some books Lizzy could use," Bea volunteered. "I bought them for Richard."

"That'd be nice, Dear. Let's get to packing my clothes. We've got a heap of work to do."

"Grandma, can I help?" Ben asked.

"Sure can. I'll be needing your strong arms to help me carry some of my things to Mr. Southard's house."

"Mother, are you certain?" the tall, thin, elegant woman asked.

"Quite. Lizzy, you know I'll still be over here pestering you. Don't you worry none."

Lizzy laughed. "I'm sure."

"Forgive me my manners. Bea, this is my daughter, Lizzy. Lizzy, this is Bea Smith."

"Hello." Bea reached out to shake Lizzy's hand.

Hesitantly Lizzy reached hers out. When Bea gave her a firm handshake, Lizzy smiled. "A white woman who's not afraid. I like you."

Bea laughed. "Your mom's a gem, but I'm sure you know that."

"She certainly can be. Other times she can be a real nag. Don't try and keep a secret from her."

Bea continued in her laughter. "I've already discovered that."

The three women wrapped some of Cook's clothes into a quilt. With the three of them it didn't take long to pack everything. Soon Bea found herself and Cook unpacking everything in Cook's new room.

"Sure takes longer to unpack," Bea commented, placing a dress on a hanger in Cook's closet.

"Mr. Ellis will sure be surprised." Cook giggled. "He'll think I got a touch of the heat."

Bea laughed. Having Cook around would be a blessing in more ways than one. "I like your family."

"Lizzy seemed impressed with you. You being from the North you might not be aware, but a lot of white folks don't touch colored folks."

"Oh, I'm aware. I'm afraid that's a problem in the North as well. Even with the war being fought."

"Sin is a pretty hard thing to rid from a man's heart," Cook wisely proposed.

"You know, I hadn't thought it was sin, just man being foolish and proud in ways he ought not. But you're right, it is sin. The Bible does say we're all from Adam and Eve, so we all have the same parents." Bea folded the quilt and placed it at the foot of the four-poster bed.

"I believe it's goin' ta take people some time to change, but one day I think most folks will realize that, like President Lincoln said at the Gettysburg Address, 'all men are created equal.'"

"It was a sad day when he was shot," Bea whispered. It had been seven months since the president's assassination.

"That be true, a lot of people still mourn his death." Cook paused and took a deep breath.

Three chimes rang out from the grandfather clock down the hall. "Goodness, Child. I better be fixin' dinner."

"You don't think they'll catch anything?"

"Oh, I reckon they'll catch some. But Mr. Ellis likes more than fish for his supper. I may just fix him some black beans and rice. I canned up some beans this summer."

"I don't believe I've ever had black beans."

"Ewww, Child, are you in for a treat. Could you fetch me a few tangerines for a sauce for the fish? If'n I know Mr. Ellis, he's caught some kingfish, and he loves this tangerine sauce I make as a marinade for the fish."

"Sounds wonderful. How many?" Bea headed for the door.

"Fetch me a half a dozen," Cook said, brushing the dust off her hands.

⚓

The evening breeze brought the sailboat gently into the harbor. Richard was asleep. The porpoises had followed the boat, playing for at least an hour before turning back to the sea. Ellis loved hearing Richard's laughter. And he enjoyed the contentment on the child's face as he slept. The sailboat slowly slid into place alongside the dock. Ellis captured a piling and held the boat fast while he draped a line around it.

In short order he lowered the sails, wrapped the mainsail around the boom, and put the jib into a sack, tossing it through the hold into the bow.

Should I wake the child or let him sleep?

"Richard." He sat down on the bench beside the small boy. "Wake up, Son." Richard groaned and rolled to his side.

Ellis smiled. The ocean had a way of relaxing a person. Often he would end up taking a nap after a good sail. He hoisted Richard up and held him firmly, the boy's head resting on his shoulder. Ellis kissed him tenderly on his soft curls. It was hard to believe how much love he had for this child in only a few short days.

With his free hand, he lifted the fish for the evening's dinner. Taking a giant step from the boat's deck to the dock, he steadied his feet on land once again.

Ellis soon found himself a bit winded as he carried the child the entire distance to the house.

Bea greeted him at the door. A warmth spiraled down his back to the tip of his toes. She was a welcome sight to return home to. "Hi." He smiled.

"Hi. Is Richie all right?" Bea tenderly touched Richard's back.

"Fine, just exhausted and relaxed." Ellis handed her the fish. "Take these, and I'll put him to bed."

"All right. Don't forget to remove his shoes."

"Yes, Ma'am." Ellis winked.

"Sorry—habit." Bea grabbed the fish.

"By the way, I look forward to our time alone tonight," Ellis whispered.

A soft pink rose on Bea's cheeks. "We have a lot to talk about. Come to the kitchen after you put Richard down on his bed and wash up."

Something in the tone of her voice made him question what else had transpired today. He wasn't certain what it meant. "All right," Ellis said with apprehension.

Slowly he worked his way up the stairs, skipping his normal pattern of taking two steps at a time. He didn't want to jostle Richard and possibly wake him up.

Ellis tenderly placed Richard on his bed, pulled off his shoes, and unbuttoned the top button of his shirt. Richard stirred slightly and rolled himself into a curled position. Silently Ellis departed.

In his room he made quick work of changing his shirt and washing the fishy smell from his hands. He sniffed his clean hands, but a pungent odor still remained. His nose crinkled. A desire to smell fresh and clean for Bea encouraged a second washing.

Downstairs he found Bea and Cook working side by side. " 'Evening, ladies."

" 'Evenin', Mr. Ellis." Cook continued to fillet the fish. "I've done what you asked me to do."

"And what is that, Cook?" Ellis leaned against the counter.

"I've moved in."

"What? I mean, that's wonderful. But what brought the sudden change?" Ellis looked at Bea. Bea's face crimsoned.

Ellis shifted his gaze back to Cook.

"Miss Smith and I were talkin'—"

"And?" Ellis cut her off.

"I'll be gettin' to it, now hold on." Cook smiled. "As I said, we were talkin', and we decided it would be best for you to have me in the house."

"I see." Ellis looked at Bea.

"Ellis, you aren't truly upset about this, are you?" Bea implored.

"No, I've been asking Cook to move in with me ever since I bought the house. Far too much room here for one man, and her home could use another open bed." Ellis smoothed his beard. "I'm just surprised."

But why was he surprised, really? Cook could get anything out of anyone. And he had openly touched Bea's hand this morning.

"Do you need me to haul over your belongings, Cook?"

"No, Sir, we moved 'most everything this afternoon. I don't see no need to take my linens, fine china, and stuff. The family will need it, and you have plenty here."

"True. But I would've moved your belongings." Ellis pushed himself away from the counter and sauntered over to the table where he saw the kingfish fillets marinating in Cook's tangerine sauce. "My favorite, thanks."

"You're welcome." Cook smiled.

Bea remained quiet and continued to work. Besides the need to report on his conversation with Richard, they needed to discuss her conversation with Cook.

Ellis rubbed his hands together and asked, "What can I do to help?"

⚓

Bea sat pensively still throughout dinner. She wasn't certain how to read Ellis. He seemed glad that Cook had moved in, but it appeared as if he had something on his mind. He left obvious holes in his description of the fishing excursion with Richard.

Richard woke as everyone was finishing up their meal. Bea sat with Richie as Cook and Ellis went off for an inspection of Cook's new room.

"Nanna, you should have seen 'em. They jump in the waves and swim really fast," Richie excitedly explained about the porpoises. "Uncle Ellis says they breathe air like we do. They have a hole on top of their heads and everything."

"Wow, you had quite a trip." Bea smiled.

"I didn't catch any fish, but Uncle Ellis said sometimes deep-sea fishing is like that." Richard scooped another forkful of his fish dinner. "Isn't this good, Nanna?"

"Yes. Now don't talk with your mouth full, please."

"Sorry," he mumbled through a mouthful of fish.

Bea stifled a chuckle, especially when Richard took up the linen napkin and wiped his mouth, trying to be so grown up.

"Nanna, do you like Uncle Ellis?"

Oh dear, nothing like the direct approach. "Yes."

"Are you going to marry him?"

Bea shifted nervously in her seat. *This isn't conversation for a four year old.* "I don't know if I like him that way yet."

"What way?"

Bea eased out a pensive breath. "Richie, there are many kinds of love. For example, I love you and I love my parents, but it's not the same kind of love a man and woman need to share to get married."

"When will you know?"

Bea smiled. "I don't know. I suppose when the Lord tells me so."

"Is that when you'll go to church and get married?"

Church? Getting married? What was going on in this little one's mind? "Where are all these questions coming from, Richie?"

"I saw you hold hands with Uncle Ellis, and Billy's parents hold hands."

"I see. Do I hold hands with you?"

Richie nodded.

"Are we going to get married?"

Richie's eyebrows knitted.

"Do you see, Richie? Not everyone who holds hands is getting married."

"Oh. But Uncle Ellis said he likes you."

So, he had spoken with Ellis about this too. "Richie, am I good about doing what's best for you?"

"Uh-huh."

"Then trust me to take care of marriage and other grown-up kinds of things."

"All right." Richie went back to eating his supper. The child was far too observant.

A warm feeling of being watched flowed over the back of her neck. She turned and saw Ellis's handsome figure casually leaning against the doorjamb. A mischievous smile and a wink sent her heart racing in anticipation of their evening's conversation. A lot had transpired since last night, and her desire to get to know him had increased a hundredfold. Was it possible to fall in love at the mere sight of a man?

Bea broke her gaze and fixed it back on Richie, who was finishing his rice and beans. "After you're done, Richie, do you want to play a game, perhaps checkers?"

"I beat Uncle Ellis."

"Oh really? Perhaps I'll challenge him to a game later." Bea turned to Ellis, softly lowered her eyelids, and slowly opened them. Flirting. At her age. She could hardly believe it, and yet it felt so right.

Ellis cleared his throat and slipped into the darkened hallway.

Chapter 16

Is he asleep?" Bea asked as Ellis descended the stairs.

"Soon. He's exhausted. Three checker games plus all those questions would wear anyone out. Have you encouraged him to ask so many questions?" Ellis sat on the chair opposite the sofa.

"He seemed to come by his curiosity naturally. I was going to ask if you or your brother were inquisitive children."

"Not that I'm aware, but I've been gaining a new perspective since Richard moved in here. I used to think I was a well-behaved child, but as I've questioned some of Richard's behavior, I remember being scolded in some of the same ways." Ellis reclined in the chair, stretched his legs, and crossed them at the ankles.

"Richie seemed to have had the 'love and marriage' question discussion with you earlier," Bea started.

"I think sitting on a hundred tacks would have been easier than dealing with his questions. By the way, you handled it better than I."

Bea laughed. "I've had a bit more experience. I found you don't have to give all the details to the innocent questions he's asking."

"I've got so much to learn." Ellis wrung his hands. "I thought I handled it well, but we ended up talking about church weddings, and other unnecessary details."

"Speaking of church, are we going in the morning?" Bea intended to go to the Presbyterian church with her newfound friends, if Ellis wasn't planning to attend a morning service.

"I was planning on going. Would you like to accompany us?"

"As in a date?" Bea teased.

"You realize things are happening fast between us," Ellis said.

"Things will slow down now that we have admitted to each other what we're feeling." Bea hoped her words were true. She certainly hadn't told him all of her thoughts, and suspected he hadn't told her all of his.

"Maybe." Ellis sat up straight in the chair. "Is Cook intending to be our chaperone?"

"In a manner of speaking, yes. Ellis, I couldn't have stayed in the cottage if we do start courting. It wouldn't be right. And gossip spreads faster on this island than a hailstorm covers the cornfields back home."

Ellis laughed. "That's true enough. I'm glad she moved in. I planned to have her stop coming for breakfast if she didn't. I didn't want her walking the streets before dawn. The island is pretty safe, but we get all kinds of ships in port from time to time, so you never know what sort of sailors will come ashore."

"You've a good heart, Ellis."

"Thank you. Yours isn't so bad either. I've never known Cook to let anyone into her kitchen, and yet you seem so at home there."

Bea enjoyed working in the kitchen, and Cook was fun to work with. "I like her. She's unique."

Ellis roared. "That she is. So, how long did it take for Cook to get the details from last night out of you?"

Bea felt the heat rise on her cheeks. "Maybe five minutes."

⚓

"She's slipping."

"I heard that, Mr. Ellis," Cook called from down the hall.

"Then come and join us so you can hear it all without straining." Ellis stood to await Cook's entrance into the room. He leaned over to Bea and whispered, "I want her to feel comfortable in my home."

Bea nodded.

Ellis pulled away quickly. The smell of lilac in her hair, so soft, so feminine, stirred a desire to kiss her behind her right ear. Thankfully, he constrained himself before he acted on his impulses.

"Are you certain, Mr. Ellis?" Cook slowly entered the room.

"Cook. . .Francine. . .this is your home now. You're always welcome."

Ellis watched Cook's imploring gaze. "Come, sit beside Bea. You've worked hard today." He held her by the hand and led her to the sofa.

"Good thing Master Richard be in bed; he'd have us married." Cook giggled.

The room erupted in laughter. The rest of the evening was spent enjoying each other's company—getting to know one another. At ten, Bea stood.

"I don't know when I've enjoyed myself more. It's been a wonderful night, but I must get some rest." Bea bid the others a good night.

"Land sakes, I don't believe the hour. I would have been in bed for an hour if I was home." Cook lifted her ample body off the sofa.

Ellis rose. "May I escort you to your door, Bea?"

"That would be nice, thank you."

"I'll see you young folks in the morning. Behave yourselves." Cook winked and headed down the hall to her room.

Ellis wrapped his arm around Bea's narrow waist. It felt right. Bea leaned into his shoulder and sighed.

I could grow accustomed to this, Ellis thought. *Quite accustomed.*

"Take me home, Ellis, before I fall asleep standing up," Bea whispered.

Ellis squeezed her tightly and led her through the front door, down the steps, and to her front door. "I would like to court you, Bea. May I?"

"Will courting be enough? It seems so shallow to what we are already experiencing."

"Perhaps, but you deserve to be treated like a lady. I'll speak with Cook to arrange an evening when I can take you out on the town and she can watch Richard." Ellis didn't release his grasp of her waist. She turned in his arm to face him.

"I'd like to go out with you." Bea's smile affected him so that his own smile swelled. "You're an incredible woman, Beatrice Smith. I think I'm falling in love with you."

"Oh, Ellis." Bea buried her head in his chest.

Ellis wrapped her tenderly in his arms.

"How can this be happening so quickly?" Bea mumbled into his thick cotton shirt.

"I don't have a clue, Darling. But I'm not inclined to fight it any longer, are you?"

"No. I'm scared."

"Me too."

Ellis held her as she trembled in his arms. How is it that love, if this was love, could be so frightening? Was it merely the fact he was ready to throw all his plans aside to pursue a relationship with a person he barely knew? Yes, that's what terrified him so. The thought of being with Beatrice the rest of his life wasn't scary, that was comforting. Yet the ramifications of it were a bit daunting.

Bea placed her hands on his chest and pushed herself back from his grasp. "I should go to bed."

"Good night, Bea." Ellis lifted her right hand and placed a gentle kiss upon it.

"Sleep well, Ellis." Bea gently removed her hand from his embrace and reached for the latch. But Ellis was faster. His hands already set on the latch, he opened the door for her. Reluctantly, she placed one foot in front of the other and entered her darkened cabin.

The door closed behind her. She listened as Ellis's footsteps disappeared into the distance.

"Father, I think I love him. How is it possible?" she called out to God. Not bothering to light her lanterns, she made her way in the dark to her room. "And how can I feel so differently about him than when I first met him a little over a week ago? I don't know how, Lord, but I do. And I know I'm wanting to be with him night and day, wrapped in his arms. Is love like this possible?"

Bea readied herself for sleep. She lit the lamp beside her bed and opened her Bible. In spite of the late hour, she needed to go to bed with the Word of the Lord on her mind. She absentmindedly opened the Bible, and it opened to Ecclesiastes 3:5: "A time to embrace and a time to refrain from embracing." Had her time for embracing come? Was Ellis the man God had chosen for her life partner?

The Lord's day had come, and church with Ellis and Richard gave Bea a hope that maybe they would become a family. The afternoon was spent reading and playing with Richard. Cook spent the day with her family, so Bea prepared the evening meal. It was the first full meal she had made since her departure from the Southard farmstead. A roasted chicken with cornbread stuffing, mashed potatoes, and carrots rounded out the fare.

Cook returned soon after they finished their dinner. "Smells good in here, Child."

"Thank you. How was your visit home?"

"Just fine. The older girls were given my room. They had to show me. They were so excited." Cook grinned.

"Do you miss them?" Bea asked, with her arms up to the elbows in dishwater.

"Sure enough do, but this is best. Now they can come and visit me. I told 'em all about sitting in Mr. Ellis's fancy parlor last night, and they can't wait to come see it."

"I'm sure Ellis won't mind." Bea reached for another plate and placed it in the hot soapy water.

"He's the one who told me to invite 'em. Fact is, he wants them here for dinner on Tuesday."

"Tuesday? The whole family?" Bea wondered where they would put everyone.

Cook chuckled. "The whole family. He said he was going to do a barbecue, and you know what that means."

"He's cooking?"

"Yes'm, for the whole lot of 'em. I thought Lizzy was going to fall off her chair when I made the announcement."

Bea laughed.

"I'm used to Mr. Ellis cooking for me a time or two, but my family, well, let's just say it'll be a new experience."

"I can imagine." Bea wondered what was going on in Lizzy's mind.

"How was church?" Cook asked, putting on her apron.

"It was fine. Cook, I can handle the dishes. You relax."

"I'm sure you can, but my family waited on me hand and foot like I was the Queen Mother. I need to do something useful today or I think I'll burst."

Bea removed her hands from the water and stepped back from the sink. "I never liked doing dishes." Bea dried off her hands.

Cook chuckled and plunged her hands into the soapy water. "I think we're going to get along real fine, Miss Smith, real fine."

And Bea could picture herself as the woman of this household working alongside Cook. It was a pleasant picture. Her heart warmed, her lips turning up in a smile.

🌴

Ellis caught a glimpse of Bea working in the kitchen with Cook. She fit right in, and she looked mighty pretty today. Her hair was up in a bun, but she allowed a few wisps of hair to come down in ringlets alongside her cheeks. One day he was going to run his fingers through that wonderful crown she wore.

"Uncle Ellis?" Richard tugged on his pant leg.

Ellis turned to see the imploring gaze of his nephew, who jumped up and down, wiggling like he had to go to the bathroom.

"Is there a problem, Richard?"

"There's a monster in the outhouse."

"A monster?"

Richard nodded and continued the wiggling.

"Let's go check it out." Ellis grabbed a lantern. He'd found large geckos in the outhouse before. To a four year old, a two-to three-foot gecko could be pretty scary. On the other hand, he was proud that Richard hadn't yelled upon first spotting the creature.

Richard's grasp of Ellis's hand tightened the closer they came to the outhouse. "Stand behind me, Son." Ellis waited until Richard was behind him before he pulled the door open. The bright flash of light caused the gecko to scurry away.

"What was that?" Richard cried.

"A gecko, an overgrown lizard." Ellis encouraged the child to make use of the outhouse. "I'll wait for you."

Richard nodded and stepped inside. Moments later the door swung open and Richard reappeared.

"Uncle Ellis?"

"Yes, Son?"

"Do guckos hurt people?"

"Geckos," he corrected. "And no, they don't. Some folks keep them as pets, others eat 'em."

Richard's eyes grew wide. "They eat 'em?"

"Uh-huh." Ellis grinned. "Some say it tastes like chicken."

"Chicken? That's silly. It didn't have feathers."

Ellis grabbed the boy and tossed him into the air. "That's right, Son, they don't have feathers."

Ellis removed the lantern he had hung on the hook to the left of the door. He couldn't imagine what Bea would have done if she had seen the gecko. Most women would scream, but he'd seen enough of Beatrice to doubt what her immediate response would have been.

"Come on, Son. Let's go play a game of checkers before you go to bed."

"I'll beat you." Richard beamed.

Maybe it was time for Ellis to win a game. He placed Richard on his shoulders and ran to the front of the house, bouncing and jumping. Richard squealed with laughter. Ellis loved children, and he wondered what it would be like to have some of his own. An image of Bea swollen with child burned a desire within him. *Could it be possible, Lord?*

Ellis watched as Bea descended the stairs, having put Richard to bed for the evening. Pleasure radiated from her. "Thank you, Ellis. It meant a lot to me to be able to put him down for the night."

"I know. I cherish my time with him also." He patted the sofa for her to sit down beside him. "Cook's retired early tonight."

"Then maybe I should sit on the chair," Bea suggested, and paused in the center of the room.

"I promise to be the perfect gentleman," Ellis implored. He wanted her close tonight. So much had developed between them in such a short span of time. "Please."

"Ellis." Bea sat down beside him. "Don't you understand? I want this too much."

"Trust me, Bea. I'll be strong for the both of us."

She sat back and he placed his left arm around her shoulders, encouraging her to rest her head on his shoulder. He breathed in the sweet gentle scent of lilac.

"I enjoyed the message from Pastor Williams today. Can you believe he has all those children?"

Ellis chuckled. "Eight is a handful. Do you want children?"

"Yes. I don't think I'd want eight, though." Bea folded her hands in her lap.

"I'm not sure I want eight either, but I'd like a few. How many do you want?" Ellis raised his hand and captured a ringlet of hair which rested on her cheek. Chocolate silk best described the sensation.

"Truthfully, I'll take as many as the Lord gives. But I think four is a good number."

"Hmm, four, huh?" Ellis whispered.

Bea lifted her head from his shoulder and looked into his blue-gray eyes. They were dark, yet as open and revealing as his soul. "Ellis, what's behind these questions?"

"If you and I should decide to. . .uh, hmm. . .tie the knot, I thought maybe we ought to find out how we feel about children, raising them, our goals, desires, plans, and all that sort of stuff. Like what Pastor Williams spoke about this morning, being prepared in season and out of season."

Bea sat up straight and grasped his hand. "I love children, as you can tell. I believe in being firm with discipline, but I also believe a child should have time to play, enjoy life.

"And you?"

"The same. What about planning for their futures?" Ellis moved his thumbs gently over her fingers.

"I think children should decide their careers. My parents encouraged me in some of my talents even though they're traditionally more male."

"Such as?"

"I have a mind for numbers, business. Father allowed me to learn some of his business and keeping records and such. He said any man would be proud to have a wife who could keep a budget. Truthfully, the skill was handy with your brother being off to war."

"I can well imagine." Ellis shifted and faced her. "Why is it that the more I get to know you, the more I like who you are, Beatrice?"

"Probably because it is the same with me. I thought you were an uncaring, rigid man the first day I met you." Bea paused. Seeing he wasn't offended, she continued. "I soon learned that it was me who you were rigid around. Little did I know you were fighting the same attraction I was."

"And we fought it so well," Ellis chuckled.

Bea struggled for neutral territory. "So we're agreed on children, what about foods?"

Chapter 17

Monday came and went with an odd sensation of normalcy. Tuesday, Bea found herself immersed in the preparations for the barbecue for Cook's family. "Where are we going to get all the tables and chairs?" Bea inquired of Cook. "I can't believe he invited his crew and their families too."

"I think Mr. Ellis has done freed his heart." Cook laughed.

"Well, I think he's lost his head," Bea proclaimed.

"Same thing." Cook waddled over to the stove. As she lifted the lid, steam billowed into the air.

"What did you call that again? Yucka?"

Cook wagged her head. "No, Dear. Yucca. It's a root like your potatoes, but we serve it the Cuban way with a garlic sauce poured on top." A fresh aroma of garlic permeated the room as Cook opened the lid of a small pot on the stove.

The food, the trees, everything is so different here—even the fruit, Bea reflected. She loved the passion fruit Cook had been serving for breakfast, but had been avoiding it for fear there was something to its name. "I thought Ellis was going to be doing all the cooking?" Bea pushed back a stray wisp of her hair.

"He's paying and he's doing the barbecue. The men don't think in terms of the whole meal. Unless of course it's missing on his plate."

Bea laughed. "I'm just grateful that the other families are bringing some side dishes as well. We should've started cooking a week ago for such a big crowd." Bea shaped the bread dough into rolls and placed them on the baking pan. She wiped the sweat from her brow. "I can see why the original owners put a kitchen outside— it gets downright exhausting in here."

Cook's worried gaze searched her own eyes.

"I'm fine," Bea responded.

"Nonsense, Child. Drink some water."

Obediently, Bea downed a glass of water and poured herself another to slowly sip.

"We'll have some time after the food is ready to freshen up. I want you to strip right down and cool yourself off, you hear me?" Cook wagged her finger.

"Yes, Ma'am."

"Don't need you getting all faint, no siree," Cook mumbled.

"I'm fine, Cook, really." A simple nod of Cook's head for a response was all that Bea received. She was fine. She caught a glimpse of herself in the glass, her color normal. Sweating was natural from the heat, she reminded herself. Cook was just being overly cautious.

Bea finished shaping the rolls and placed a clean cloth over them to let them rise. Wiping her hands on her apron, she began rolling piecrusts, placing them in the tins. "Where'd you get all these pie tins?" Bea asked.

"Oh, I asked around. A few from my home, and Mrs. Matlin, you remember her?"

"Yes." How could she forget the woman and the tender mercy she'd shown to her last week when she had pushed herself too soon after being sick?

"Oh, by the way, she'll be joining us too."

Bea threw up her hands. "Is there anyone on the island not coming?"

"Not used to crowds, are you, Dear?"

"No."

"Well, here on the island things kinda have a way of growing like this." Cook lifted the large pot of boiling yucca from the stove and brought it to the sink.

"I see." Bea encouraged the pie dough into a circle.

"You'll get used to it. Island folk, we all know each other, and depend on each other. It's a matter of survival. Nowadays, it doesn't seem as much so. But wait 'til we have a storm. Then you'll see how we all pull together."

Like a real community, Bea mused. Being so far out with Richard's homestead, she hadn't been a part of a community for a long time.

"Don't be surprised if'n you see some folks here that we didn't invite. They'll be bringing some of their own food."

Bea closed her eyes and rubbed her palms on her shirt. To go to someone's house uninvited broke all the rules of social graces. Bea couldn't imagine such an impropriety. "What's Ellis doing out there?"

"Roasting the pig. He started it last night."

Ellis turned the pig on the spit once more. He still had enough time to run to town and order the fresh fish. One of his men was bringing conch chowder. At last count, he figured there would be close to thirty coming to dinner. But he'd been to enough occasions on the island to know that number could double in an hour.

He locked the spit in place and hurried to town. Across the street was a teenaged boy he knew. "Hey, Brian, do you have a minute?"

"Sure, what do you need, Mr. Southard?"

The lean boy with a crop of long, black hair walked across the street.

"Can you run an errand for me?"

"Sure."

"Could you fetch a twenty-five-pound bag of rice and a mess of fresh vegetables from the store and bring them to my house?"

"It'd be my pleasure." The lad smiled. "Party?"

Ellis chuckled. "Yup. Wanna come?"

"Sure."

"Tell you what, if you can get your mom to cook a couple pies and a mess of that rice for me, your whole family is invited. I'm roasting a pig, picking up a mess of fresh fish and possibly some steaks if the butcher has some."

"I'll let Mom know."

Ellis handed Brian some money and proceeded to the docks. He spoke with a couple of the local fishermen. After he had purchased some fresh fish, he noticed Gerry Halstead cleaning his boat.

" 'Morning, Gerry. How's the fishing?"

" 'Mornin'." Gerry removed his glove to shake Ellis's hand.

"Looks like a good catch. Is it taken?" Ellis peered into a basket crawling with lobsters.

"Not yet, you buying?"

"I'll take the lot. How much?"

"I was hoping to make ten dollars." Gerry raked his thinning brown hair.

"Ten it is." Ellis pealed off a ten-dollar bill. "Here you go."

"Wow, thanks." Gerry lifted the basket of lobsters. "You throwing a party?"

"Sure enough. Wanna come?" Ellis invited.

Gerry chuckled. "I'm afraid I wouldn't have any lobsters to bring."

"Not a problem. Bring a salad, rice and beans, or something to drink."

"All right, what time?"

"Six, my place. If you recall, I bought the Captain Curtis house."

"I'll be there. Thanks. What's the special occasion? Getting hitched to that pretty nanny?"

Ellis's cheeks burned. "No. It started as a meal for Cook's family. It's kinda grown."

"That tends to happen around here. I'll get the wife to cook up something. See you at six."

"*Adios.*" Ellis waved and headed home. The fish purchased and several more families invited, he needed to stop by the church next and get some tables and chairs. Naturally, Pastor Williams and his family would be coming. Ellis laughed and quickened his pace toward the church.

"You what?" Bea couldn't believe her ears. "You've invited more?"

Ellis chuckled and pulled her into his embrace. "Shh, Dear, it's going to be all right. Trust me."

A shiver slithered down her spine from Ellis's warm breath on her ear. "Ellis, we don't have food for fifty people."

"Sure we do. And other folks are bringing stuff too."

"I've never given a party like this." And never would she plan one this way either. Her mother had taught her well. Occasions of this magnitude took months of planning.

"It's the island way. Trust me." Ellis's firm hand rested on the back of her neck. His thumb slowly worked its way across her cheek. Bea's knees started to tremble. He held her steady. "Do you trust me, Bea?" he whispered in her ear.

What could she do? He exuded confidence, and in his arms she did believe him. It made no logical sense, but she did trust him to pull this party off. "We'll need to make some more. . ." She was at a loss as to what to make. "Something."

"Shh, come here, Honey." Ellis led her to the parlor. "Sit down."

Ellis knelt before her. His blue-gray eyes steeled with confidence. "I've been out of proper society for a long time. But I do recall some things, and I know my mother would be in a tizzy if a party this size was suddenly thrust upon her. So I understand your fears. But, Darling, on the island things are done differently. You don't need to make any more food. There's plenty coming. Pastor Williams is bringing the tables and chairs. . . ."

"Pastor Williams is coming?" Bea was in shock. The house wasn't ready for a visit from the clergy. "Oh my. We need to get the house ready."

"No, we don't. Bea, look at me." He gently took her chin in his hand and nudged it so it was face-to-face with his. Bea quieted her soul and concentrated on the handsome man before her. His thumb touched her lips. "Oh, Ellis."

Ellis leaned into her and lifted slightly, kissing her forehead. Bea's eyes closed and soaked in the nearness, the soft touch of his lips upon her forehead. His whispered words brought her back to reality.

"We have an audience."

Bea's cheeks flamed. Ellis leaned away from her.

"Excuse me, Mr. Ellis, Miss Bea. Brian Fairfield is here." Cook departed after her announcement. Ellis stood up and went to the front hall. Bea could hear his conversation. "Thank you, Brian, you did great. Bring them to the kitchen for Cook."

"Yes, Sir. Oh, Mom said we'd be coming, and she's fixing a few pies and the Spanish rice."

"Great. Pastor Williams will be here shortly with the tables and chairs. Do you think you can lend him a hand?"

"Certainly, Mr. Southard."

Bea clasped her hands, closed her eyes, and silently prayed. *Father, give me understanding regarding this "party," and give me strength regarding Ellis and my attraction to him.*

⚓

Lord, the woman is incredible. Thank You for putting her in my path, Ellis silently prayed, walking back into the parlor. "Bea," he whispered. "I'm sorry, I shouldn't have been so forward. You were so worked up about the party I didn't know what else to do."

Her eyes fluttered open. "So, you get me flustered in another way?"

"No, the kiss was an impulse and for that I apologize."

Bea smiled. "You're forgiven."

"Good. Now I want you to go to your cottage. Relax. Take a nap, perhaps, and freshen up for this evening."

She narrowed her gaze. "Mr. Southard, are you suggesting I'm not presentable?"

Ellis prayed she was teasing. "Precisely," he teased back.

Bea's mouth gaped open.

"I can tease too, my dear." Ellis grinned. "Besides, would I have kissed you if I found you so unattractive?"

"You did miss," she coyly replied, and rose from the sofa.

"Touché." Whatever possessed him to think he could battle wits with this woman? "If you'll excuse me, Beautiful, the swine needs turning."

Bea laughed and headed toward the kitchen. "Bea, your cottage is that way." Ellis pointed to the front door.

"But. . ."

"But, nothing. I want you well tonight. Now go." He smiled to tame the intensity of his order.

She mocked a salute. "Aye, Captain."

Ellis groaned inwardly. He'd done it again. Delegating—giving orders and expecting them to be followed—came with being the boss. Bea, however, was not his employee.

Once outside, he turned the pig, added some wood to the fire, and began raking the lawn free of debris. Folks would begin arriving in a couple of hours. Pastor Williams pulled in with his wagon loaded with tables and chairs. The fishermen delivered their fish. The house was alive with activity. Every so often he saw Bea peeking out a window. *This isn't right,* he chided himself and dropped his rake. A few long strides and he was rounding the corner of Bea's cottage. "Bea!" he hollered.

"Ellis, don't come in!" Bea cried out.

"I won't. Forgive me. If you want to help or even be a part of greeting everyone, please come out."

"In a minute," Bea whispered behind the closed door. "Ellis, would you send Cook over please?"

"Are you all right?"

"I'm fine, I just need a woman's assistance."

Of course, a corset. Personally he'd prefer the woman to not be so tied up, but this being a social occasion, and Beatrice wanting to impress, he understood her need. "I'll fetch her. And, Honey, I'm sorry, I didn't mean to order you."

"I understand, Ellis, and I did need the rest, but I like being in the midst of things. It's been driving me crazy sitting in this cottage."

Ellis chuckled. "I want you in the midst of things," he mumbled.

"What? Speak up, Ellis, I can't hear you through the door."

"Never mind, I'll tell you later."

Bea heard the gravel under Ellis's feet protest his weight as he walked away from her cottage. "Did he say what I think I heard, Lord?" Bea moved to her bedroom in the back of the cottage. On the bed she had laid out her lilac summer dress with a white laced collar and pearl buttons down the bodice. The skirt of the dress gathered at the waist and descended into a V shape in the front.

The door creaked open and Cook called out, "It's me, Bea, what do you need me for?"

"My corset."

Cook entered the bedroom. "The light one, I hope. Goodness, Child, that is a pretty dress."

"Thank you and, yes, the light one. I want to be comfortable."

"Turn around," Cook ordered.

Bea turned. "How's it going in the kitchen?"

"All done, just been cleaning up. Gonna wash and change after I get you hooked up here." Cook groaned straining at the laces.

"Ouch, that's tight enough. I'm not that vain." Bea giggled.

"Sorry. Want me to help you slip the dress over your head?"

"Yes, thanks."

"I used a slip-knot. Just pull your right-hand string and it should unfasten. If not, holler and I'll come over."

Bea reached back and found the right-hand string Cook mentioned. Soon they had her dress slipped over her head and flowing down to the floor.

"Mercy, Child, you are beautiful. Mr. Ellis gonna have a time keeping his mind on his company and not on you." Cook grinned.

"I hope so." Bea winked.

"You know, with Pastor Williams coming over tonight, we could make this into a wedding."

"Hush. We're not ready," Bea admonished.

"Don't take much more than what I saw in the living room. Admit it, Child, you love him."

"Cook, I think I do, but how can you love someone so quickly?"

"It's a mystery, but some folks just get hit like that. George and I did. Once I met him, my heart was aflutter. I couldn't think of anything but George. Of course, my parents had a thing to say about that, but in the end we were married inside a year."

"A year?" Bea didn't think she could wait that long. On the other hand, a year's formal engagement period would be expected back home.

"Yes'm. 'Course, George was away most of that year. If'n he was at home, I imagine we would have been married much sooner."

Bea felt her cheeks flush.

"Truth, is all. Of course, we never told the children that until they were older, much older." Cook winked.

Bea reached out and hugged Cook. "Thank you, Francine, you're a good friend."

"I'm honored to be yours, Miss Bea." Cook patted Bea on her back. "Do you need help with your hair?"

"No, thank you. Ellis likes it down, but that's not really proper, so I thought I'd put it in a French braid."

"Sounds beautiful. Well, if'n you don't need me, I best get cleaned up. I smell like fish. You wouldn't believe how much Mr. Ellis bought."

Bea closed her eyes and let out a small sigh. "No, I'm sure I wouldn't."

Cook departed and Bea sat down at her vanity. She took down her tight bun and began combing out her hundred strokes.

A sudden knock and crash at her front door startled her.

Chapter 18

N anna!" Richard cried with excitement.

"Richard, you frightened me." Bea placed her brush down on the vanity.

"Sorry." Richard jumped up on her bed and bounced. "I'm so excited. Uncle Ellis said everybody is coming."

Bea chuckled. "I can see you're excited. What have you been doing? You're filthy."

"Helping."

"Helping with what, dirt?"

"No, silly, raking the leaves and broken trees and stuff."

"Oh." Bea smiled. "I'm sure you've been a big help."

"Uncle Ellis said I needed to get washed up."

Oh dear, Bea had forgotten about getting Richard ready first. Dirt would attach to this dress like a moth to a light. "Can you wash up by yourself?"

Richie nodded his head.

"You wash up, and I'll help you put on your Sunday clothes."

"Can I play in them?"

"Of course not," Bea lightly scolded. "You know that."

"I wanna play the games with the other kids. Can I wear something else?"

Naturally he would want to play.

"Of course." Bea wondered if she had made the wrong choice in her dress.

"Richard," Ellis called from outside Bea's door. "I told you to go clean up."

"Nanna always helps me," Richard called back.

When Richie came barreling in, Bea had completed twenty brush strokes on her hair. "Ellis, you may come in."

The door creaked open. "Richard, go to the house, Son. I. . .I'll. . . Bea, you're beautiful," Ellis proclaimed.

"Thank you. Richie, you go on. I'll be right up there to help you pick out your clothes," Bea encouraged.

"I can do it, if I can wear play clothes."

The boy was growing up, Bea thought with a smile. "All right."

Richard slipped off the bed, leaving a streak of dirt behind him. "I'll see you at the big house, Uncle Ellis."

Ellis stood there motionless, speechless. "Please stand up," he finally spoke.

Bea trembled and stood. "Do you approve?"

"Goodness, do you have to ask? I've never seen anyone as beautiful."

Heat fused with joy and painted a faint blush on her cheeks.

"Thank you."

The intensity of his attraction forced her to restrain an urge to jump into his arms. She needed to break the tension between them. "You're a handsome man, Ellis Southard, but I've seen you look much better." She winked.

Ellis looked at his blackened hands. Amused by her ability to understate the obvious, he smiled. "I'm in need of a good scrubbing."

"At the very least."

"I. . .I need to go. If I don't, I'll soil that dress." A desire to wrap her in his arms fought to have its way. Ellis thought of the Lord and how He would behave given this situation, and swallowed hard, silently thanking God for His grace.

Bea giggled. "You do and you'll not hear the end of it."

"Later, my love." Ellis wiggled his reddish brown eyebrows and turned to leave. A faint whisper tickled his ears. "I'm looking forward to it."

"I heard that, Beatrice Smith. You're a siren for certain, here to test me."

His hand reached the latch of her front door.

"Or vice versa," she replied.

He didn't have time for this playful banter, although he fought a tremendous desire to continue it. As if working his way through a thick marsh, he pushed himself toward the house. Guests would be arriving shortly.

Mounting the stairs two at a time, he arrived at his room in short order. He grimaced at the sight of his filthy face in the mirror. Sweat mingled with black soil and small bits of decaying leaves plastered his face and beard. Looking at the amount of dirt in his hair and on his body, Ellis slipped on a robe and headed for the outside shower, an ingenious contraption of a fifty-gallon barrel with a spigot. When one pulled on the string attached to the spigot, water sprayed down on him.

Showered and dressed, Ellis entered the parlor. Bea stood at the far wall examining a hand-painted vase from the Far East. "Am I more presentable now, Miss Smith?"

Bea turned with the grace of a dove floating on the wind. Scanning him from head to toe, she spoke. "Mr. Southard, you are most handsome indeed."

Ellis stepped farther into the room. "Come here, Love."

Bea placed the vase back on the shelf and walked toward him with elegant poise.

"Your hair, it's beautiful. What style is this?"

"It's a French braid. I know you like my hair worn down, yet a woman should always wear it up. So this braid allows it to be tied neatly in the back."

"Bea, you're incredible. . . ." Ellis reached for her delicate fingers. She slipped her hands into his. "I. . ."

"Uncle Ellis!" Richard yelled. "They're here."

"Later, my love," Ellis whispered in her ear. Then he took in a deep breath and released her.

He turned toward the doorway and marched to the front door. Pulling it open, he greeted everyone. "Welcome, come on in." Members of Cook's family started pouring in. As the door was about to close, another group, and then another, entered as well. The house was soon brimming with people.

Ellis encouraged the men to join him outside at the pit. The ladies began carrying out the food to the tables in the backyard. The children followed Richard as he first showed them his room, then the various nooks and crannies of the house.

Bea mingled well, Ellis noted. She spoke with loving grace. Constantly throughout the evening he watched her. Occasionally he would catch her watching him. All different ages and races mingled together, the house and yard overflowing with people.

Key West is a good place to raise a child, Ellis decided. *But what about the homestead—my brother's wishes? I must make a decision regarding that property someday,* he mused. *But today is not that day.*

Pastor Williams, in his black and white preacher's suit, walked up to him with a hand outstretched. "Quite a feast, Ellis. Thank you for inviting us."

"My pleasure, Pastor. Thank you for the use of the tables and chairs."

"They're always available. So, tell me about this Miss Smith. . .will she be staying on?"

"That's hard to say, Pastor." How could he admit his feelings for Bea when they hadn't yet discussed them?

"Does she have a commitment back North?" Pastor Williams inquired, searching Ellis for an answer.

"No, but I can't ask her to stay on as the child's nanny."

Pastor Williams lowered his voice. "Why not?"

Ellis looked at Bea. Pastor Williams caught his glance. "I see." Pastor Williams smiled. "If you don't mind me making a suggestion, totally unasked for, I wouldn't let that one slip from my hands, if I were you." Pastor Williams slapped Ellis on the back. "God's blessings, Son. You're going to need it."

Ellis swore he heard the pastor chuckling under his breath as he walked away. Was it that obvious? Heat blazed on his high cheekbones.

" 'Evening, Ellis." Marc Dabny sidled up beside him, his swollen belly lined with a gold chain. "Quite a crowd here tonight. Anything special going on?"

"Just invited a few friends, and it kinda grew." Ellis smiled, grateful for the distraction.

Marc whistled for Lizzy, Cook's daughter, as she walked past. "Hey, get me a drink."

Lizzy turned to face Marc, but held her tongue.

"She's a guest, Marc. You can get your own drink, like everyone else here." Ellis held back his emotions.

"Excuse me?" Marc confronted Ellis face-to-face. "I can understand you throwing a party for your workers, but to consider them guests. . . Are you daft?"

"Forgive my friend, Lizzy. He seems to have forgotten his manners." Ellis stood toe-to-toe with Marc, towering over the balding man. "Lizzy is my guest. Her mother works for me, but she is not my employee. May I suggest you apologize?"

"You're daft, I'm not apologizing to no n. . ."

Ellis grabbed Marc by the collar and lifted him to his toes. "Not in my house. No one, not anyone, uses that word in my house. Do you understand, Marc?"

Marc's bulging eyes blazed with anger as he nodded his assent.

Ellis eased him back to the ground. "I believe our business partnership will not be pursued, Mr. Dabny."

"You'd throw away a solid offer for the likes. . ."

Ellis knitted his eyebrows.

". . .for. . ."

Ellis leaned closer and set his jaw.

". . .those. . .those. . .people?" Marc spat on the ground.

"Any day. I believe you've worn out your welcome, Mr. Dabny. Have a good evening." Ellis turned his back to Marc and stepped back into the crowd which had gathered behind him.

Marc spat at Ellis's feet. "You're a fool, Ellis Southard, an absolute fool."

Ellis refused to bait the man, but simply ignored him and walked up to Lizzy. "My apologies, Lizzy." He reached for her hand and bowed. "You're welcome in my home anytime."

Bea watched as Lizzy's eyes pooled with tears. Bea's own eyes threatened to stream. She bit the inside of her cheek to hold back the tears. Ellis had handled Marc with absolute authority. She was so proud of him. By the looks of the folks gathered around him, they were proud of him as well.

Bea worked her way to one of the tables. On its far corner a lantern glowed. She sat down and waited. She'd been on her feet all evening greeting folks, learning people's names and their relationship to Ellis. She rubbed the back of her calves. She hadn't been in high heels since she arrived, apart from the short outing to church the other day.

"Care if I sit down?" Mrs. Williams, the pastor's wife, asked, holding a bald baby with a toothless grin.

"Of course not." Bea placed her hands in front of her on the table.

"Are your feet hurting?"

"I'm afraid so. I haven't been in high heels much."

"Hardly wear them myself. Can't go chasing eight children in high heels." Mrs. Williams bounced the little one on her lap.

"I can't imagine. Chasing one child keeps me busy."

Mrs. Williams chuckled.

"Will you be staying, Beatrice?"

Bea didn't know what to say. To respond that she had fallen madly in love with Ellis and prayed she would be staying at his side forever was not an option. "I'm waiting on a ship bound for New York."

"So, Mr. Southard doesn't want to hire you on as Richard's nanny? Or do you have obligations back home?"

"Truth be told, I have no obligations. But Mr. Southard doesn't believe he can hire me to stay on as Richard's nanny."

Mrs. Williams's pleasant face contorted with confusion.

"It's complicated."

Mrs. Williams's brown eyes softened. "I'm sorry, I didn't mean to pry."

"It's hard to explain. Ellis—I mean Mr. Southard—learned of my social status and he feels it is improper for me to continue on, especially since he is quite capable of hiring someone."

"That doesn't sound like the man who just. . ." Mrs. Williams caught herself and stopped. "I'm sorry, I have a tendency to rattle off my thoughts before thinking them through."

"Mrs. Williams. . ."

"Edith, please."

"All right. Edith. Please don't think poorly of Mr. Southard. In our community back home I already created quite a scandal by staying on as Richard's nanny. But over time, many came to realize I deeply loved Richard's mother and would honor my commitment to her."

"There seems to be a lot in that pretty head of yours, Dear. Is it your prayer to stay with Richard?"

Bea placed her hands in her lap.

Edith's black hair sparkled from the light—or was it tears threading her eyelids? Bea wasn't certain. The baby cooed at a moth flying around the lantern.

Edith reached her hand and placed it upon Bea's. "The Lord will give you the desires of your heart. Trust Him."

Bea nodded her head, afraid to speak. The desires of her heart had shifted drastically since the day she first arrived on the island. No longer did she simply want to not separate from Richard. Now, she no longer wanted to part from the man who had captured her heart.

She glanced up and saw Ellis saying good night to a few families with younger children. He lifted a small child and tossed him in the air. *He's so good with children, Lord.*

"There's something more than your social status keeping you from being Richard's nanny," Edith whispered.

Bea nodded. She couldn't deny it any longer. Of course Cook knew, but was

Ellis ready to have the town, the pastor and his wife, know of their budding relationship? "Please don't think poorly of Ellis, Mrs. . . .I mean, Edith. Cook has moved into the house, and I am remaining in the cottage."

"I do not thinking badly of you or Ellis. Go with your heart, Dear. Trust God to work out the details."

"Thank you."

"Forgive me for leaving so, but I'll never get these children to bed if I don't start rounding them up now." Edith smiled. "Good night, Beatrice. It's a pleasure meeting you. I'll be praying."

Bea started to get up.

"No, Dear, sit. . .relax. You've done enough."

"Good night, Edith, and thank you."

"You're welcome. Stop by the parsonage anytime if you need to talk or just want to visit." Edith slipped back into the darkness, calling her children.

A parade of lanterns exited Ellis's home and worked their way down the street. *What a truly different place this is, Lord,* she pondered.

🌴

Ellis said good-bye to Pastor Williams and his family. Some of Cook's family members were helping with the cleanup. Most folks were gone, and Bea sat alone at a table. He longed to be next to her. But one person after another kept them apart.

Ellis looked to the right and left. No one. He grinned and hurried over to Bea's table. "Finally, we can be together." He sat down beside her. Tears edged her eyelids. "Bea, have you been crying?"

She smiled and shook her head, no.

Ellis brushed his thumb up to her eye. A tiny droplet of water sat on his thumb. "Then what's this?"

"I've been holding them back," she whispered.

"What's the matter?"

"Nothing."

"Nothing?" Do women cry at nothing? He thought back to his mother. There were a few times when he found her with tears in her eyes.

Ellis scooted closer on the wooden bench and leaned toward her ear. "I've longed to be this close to you all night."

"Oh, Ellis." Bea reached her arms around his shoulders.

Ellis completed their embrace, pulling her closer.

"I'm so proud of you, the way you stood up to Mr. Dabny tonight."

Ellis squeezed her gently. "Thank you. The man is a. . .I won't say it."

Bea giggled. "I think I know what you were going to say."

"Hmm, you're dangerous, do you know that?"

"Me, dangerous?" She pulled back and looked him straight in the eye. "You, Sir, with your gallant behavior. . . And tonight—this entire evening—I can't believe you pulled it off with no planning. It was just like you said it would be. Folks brought plenty of food. Everyone enjoyed themselves. I'm amazed, Mr. Southard, truly amazed."

"Amazed enough to. . ." Ellis trailed her lips with his thumb.

Bea's eyes closed in anticipation.

Did he dare? If he kissed her there would be no turning back. He wouldn't be able to let her leave. Everything shouted she was the one for him. His soulmate, his gift from God. But for so long he had given up on the possibility of having a wife, a woman who could love him, accept him, forgive him.

But how could he resist her? No, he would not resist. "I love you, Bea," he whispered before her velvet lips touched his.

She kissed him back. He tightened his hold of her. She tightened her hold on him.

Time dissolved into a blanket of tranquillity. Slowly he pulled away. He opened his eyes. A blush, the shade of a pale pink rose, accented her delicate nose.

Bea's eyes fluttered open. They were wide with passion and honesty. "I love you, Ellis." Her fingers trailed his swollen lips.

Ellis felt a tug on his pant leg. "Uncle Ellis, are you and Nanna married now?"

Ellis groaned.

Bea coughed out, "No."

"But Uncle Ellis said that when you kissed you were married!" Richard whined.

"Richard, I said after the pastor says the man and woman are married they can kiss."

"And you were kissing."

"Honey, your uncle Ellis and I were kissing, but we aren't married. We like each other," Bea pleaded. *How do you make a four year old understand?*

"But. . . ," Richard pouted, "don't you have to marry Nanna now?"

Ellis left her side and squatted next to Richard. "Son, a man has to ask a woman first if she would like to be his wife."

"Did you ask her?" Richard held his mouth firm.

"No, Son."

"Are you gonna?" Richard folded his arms over his chest.

"I'm thinking about it." Ellis squirmed.

Bea smiled. Was he really? She'd been thinking about it forever, or so it seemed. And yet it had only been a little over a week.

"Then ask her."

"Richie. . . ," Bea admonished. She hoped Ellis wouldn't think she put Richard up to such nonsense.

"I might just do that, Son." Ellis turned to Bea.

"Ellis, you don't have to do this." Bea squirmed on the bench. Was he really going to ask her? Now? Here? In Richard's presence?

Ellis smiled a wicked grin and took her by the hand. "If I ask you, Bea, it's because I want to do this, not because of Richard's pleading."

"Oh, my!" Bea needed a cool cloth, her cheeks were on fire.

"Beatrice Smith, you are the most incredible woman I've ever known. First, you've raised my nephew through all sorts of perils, and all because of a love for a friend. Second, you showed me how to release myself from my past and to allow God's forgiveness in my life. Third, you're profoundly beautiful inside and out, and I would deeply be honored if you would consent to become my wife."

Bea trembled. Her hands shook as they nested inside of Ellis's larger ones and she noticed his were trembling too.

"Are you married now?" Richard said impatiently.

"No, Son. You have to let the woman answer first."

"Oh. Answer, Nanna."

Bea chuckled. This had to be a first, being coached by a four year old for a proposal of marriage. "I'm going to answer your uncle Ellis."

"When?" Richard placed his hands on his hips and tapped his foot.

Ellis bit his lips. Bea did the same and composed herself. "As soon as someone stops interrupting me."

"Me?" Richard asked.

Bea nodded. "Yes, you. Now hush for a minute."

"Ellis, I love you with all my heart and soul, and I would be truly honored to be your wife."

"Is that a 'yes'?" Richard asked.

Bea and Ellis roared in laughter. Ellis composed himself first. "Yes, Son, that was a yes."

"Yippee! Nanna has married Uncle Ellis!" Richie ran into the house screaming.

"Are you certain, Ellis?"

Ellis climbed up off the ground, brushing the sand off his pant knee. He sat down beside her on the bench again. "Quite, my love." He reached his arm across her shoulders. "I wasn't going to ask you so soon, or with an audience, but I was going to ask."

Bea combed his beard with her fingers. Soft warmth coiled around her fingertips.

"Would you be needing a year's engagement period before we marry?" Ellis asked.

"Not if I can help it," Bea blurted out.

"Good, I was hoping you wouldn't want to wait. How's next week?"

Bea chuckled. "Too soon. Although Cook said we'd be married by the end of next week."

"I always did like Cook." Ellis nuzzled into her neck.

"Ellis, could we wait until my parents can come, or reply if they can't?"

"Of course. I don't want to wait forever, but I'll wait as long as it takes."

Bea wrapped her arms around his neck and gave him a quick kiss.

"Now you two better stop that. Unless what the boy said is true and you're already married." Cook chuckled.

"Oh dear." Bea blushed. "He said that?"

"Yup, the entire house knows you were kissin' and are married."

Bea groaned.

"Well, he got part of it right. We're getting married, Cook. Bea's honored me by saying she'd be my wife."

"Well, praise the good Lord in heaven. It's about time the two of you got it straight."

Bea and Ellis chuckled.

"Suppose we ought to go in the house and correct the rumors our son has been spreading?" Ellis asked.

"Our son," she whispered. *Our son.* Richard would finally be her son.

"Yes, our son." Ellis squeezed her gently.

"I suppose so." Bea hated the thought of being out of Ellis's arms. Perhaps her parents would understand if she were to just write them and tell them her happy news.

No, she reasoned. They'd be fit to be tied. She and Ellis would have to wait. And waiting wouldn't be such a bad thing. They still needed to get to know one another better.

Ellis stood and held his hand out for her to grasp. He curled her arm into the crook of his elbow and he led her to the house. "Come on, Cook, they're your family. Help us straighten this mess out."

Cook chuckled. "You has got yourselves into this mess, you can get yourselves out. I'm goin' to enjoy watching ya."

Epilogue

Three months later

"Mom, help me?" Bea pleaded. "I'm so nervous I can't clasp this pearl necklace."

"Relax, Bea." Joanna Smith eased the necklace from her daughter's hands.

"I can't believe my wedding day is finally here." Bea looked at the high-collared, French-laced wedding gown that she, her mother, Cook, and Lizzy had sewn. Every day and evening for the past month, they had worked on the gown, the train, the headpiece, Lizzy's gown, Cook's dress, and her mom's dress. Bea often thought Ellis had it easy. He simply went into town and hired a tailor.

She put her hair in a French braid, interwoven with pearls.

Joanna's eyes teared. "You're so beautiful, Bea."

"Thanks, Mom. I hope Ellis is pleased."

Lizzy laughed. "The man would have to be dead not to notice how beautiful you are." Bea smiled at the woman who had quickly become her closest friend.

"Thank you, Lizzy."

Although Lizzy still mourned her husband's death, she was free from the anger toward the white man who had killed him. Prejudice still existed in the world, even on Key West, but Bea and Lizzy learned the only way to battle it was one person at a time. And to hate an entire race because of the actions of others was foolishness to God.

A gentle knock on the door caused Bea to stiffen.

Her mother opened the door and smiled. "You're looking mighty handsome today, Dear."

Bea watched her father enter the room, his sideburns laced with gray, his mustache completely gray, and his receding hairline glowing with maturity. His eyes sparkled. "You're beautiful, Beatrice. Almost as pretty as your mother."

"Thanks, Daddy."

"Are you ready?"

"Yes." Bea stepped forward and captured her father's elbow. It was firm and comforting. Today she needed his confidence.

"Thank you for coming, Dad."

"I wouldn't have missed this for the world. Come on, Precious, let's go meet your groom."

Bea took in a deep breath and stepped to the edge of the doorway.

The music began. Ellis stepped out with Pastor Williams and Richard. Richard looked so handsome in his junior-sized black tails with a white shirt and black bow tie. Beatrice didn't know he had Richard fitted; it was one of many surprises he had planned for her today.

Ellis watched as Lizzy came down the aisle, followed by Ruth Williams, Pastor Williams' four-year-old daughter. She tossed the flower petals in front of her with precision, stopping to make certain the area was properly covered before moving on. Ellis grinned and spied Pastor Williams enjoying his daughter's performance.

The music shifted and the congregation stood. Ellis watched as Bea's father rounded the corner and a billow of white followed. His heart raced, his palms instantly dampened. "O Lord, she's beautiful," he whispered.

Richard tugged on Ellis's pant leg. "Nanna's pretty."

Ellis smiled. "Yes, she is."

It had taken awhile, but Richard finally understood that marriage was more than kissing and holding hands, that it was a pledge between a man and a woman with God and others watching.

Bea was so close he wanted to reach out and take her hand. Instead, Ellis held himself back and waited for the pastor's cue.

"And who gives this woman to be married to this man?"

"Her mother and I do," Jamison Smith answered in a strained voice.

Ellis reached out his hand to his bride. Jamison slipped her hand into his. Ellis's strong hand encircled hers. They turned and faced Pastor Williams.

"Dearly beloved. . ." Pastor Williams continued with the service. When he reached the pronouncement that they were husband and wife, he proclaimed, "You may now kiss the bride."

Ellis lifted her veil and cherished the sweet kiss of his new wife, then felt the all too familiar tug on his pant leg. "Are we married now?" Richard asked.

Bea and Ellis started to bubble with giggles. Soon the entire congregation was laughing.

"Yes, Richie, Bea and I are married," Ellis replied.

"Yippee!" Richard screamed, then cupped his mouth with his hands. "I'm sorry." He stood up straight and placed his hands by his side.

Bea smiled. "It's okay, Son. We're a family now; you can relax."

Bea embraced her new husband and was reminded of Ecclesiastes 3:5 once again. Her time of embracing had come. She held Ellis even tighter.

Lizzy's Hope

I'd like to dedicate this book my son,
Timothy Daniel Coleman,
God's promise to me fulfilled.
May the Lord continue to bless you and your wife
as you continue to build your relationship together.

Chapter 1

Key West, 1866

E venin'. Miz Lizzy?"

A massive chest caught Lizzy's gaze as she opened the door. Slowly, she raised her head. A large, dark man with mahogany eyes and squared shoulders towered over her. She tightened her grasp around the glass doorknob.

"Yes, may I help you?"

His shoulders eased. His rigid stance softened. "Mr. Ellis sent me here."

In turn, she loosened her grip of the knob.

"Come in," she offered with a smile.

Ellis Southard, a local businessman, had become more than her mother's employer. He and his new wife, Bea, had become some of her closest friends.

"Thank ye, Ma'am." He lifted his straw hat from the top of his head and stooped to enter through the doorway.

"Take a seat, Mr. . . . ?" She hesitated, realizing she'd forgotten to ask the man his name.

"Name's Mo."

The large rattan chair creaked as his huge body mass eased down. It wasn't that he was a heavy man. Lizzy doubted there was an ounce of fat on him. His broad shoulders were well rounded with thick muscles. His hands were massive, and yet also agile, she noticed, as he curled the edges of his Bahamian hat.

"So, what does Mr. Ellis have need of?" She sat on the sofa opposite Mo's chair.

"No, Ma'am, Mr. Ellis don't need nothin'. I's afraid I misled ye."

Her eyes caught the glimmer where his wrists were marred with encircling dark scars. Lizzy scanned the house to catch sight of someone, anyone, she could call if necessary. She had lived with her brother George and his family since her husband, Ben, had gone off to fight in the war. When Ben had died, her stay with her brother and his family had become permanent.

"Mr. Ellis sed ye might be able to help me. It be embarrassin' to ask, bein' a grown man and all." The hat in his hands twisted into unnatural shapes. "Mr. Ellis, he figures ye understand. And bein' that yer helpin' the young 'uns, ye be understandin' why I, uh, need this help." His shoulders slumped. His eyes looked down at his feet.

"Relax, Mo." She'd seen folks like this far too often. If her suspicions were

131

correct, he didn't know how to read or write. "If Mr. Ellis sent you here, I guess he figures I might be able to help you."

He stopped fumbling with his hat, leaned forward, and lowered his voice. "I cain't read or write."

"And Mr. Ellis thought I might be able to teach you?"

"Yes'm. He be showin' me some letters and makin' me practice 'em, but he ain't got no times for me." He pulled out a crumpled piece of paper and handed it to her. A series of As and Bs lined the page. "At least not 'nuff so's I can learn faster. I wanna learn."

She examined the letters more closely. He had a steady hand, but the deep impressions on the paper showed he worked with intensity.

"I can pay ye. I know ye teach the young 'uns, and I's a working man. I can come after work or on the Lord's day. Don't seem right to have schoolin' on the Lord's day—but if'n it's all the time ye can give me, I be a-willin'."

She could give him a couple evenings a week, and the extra income would help. She loved her brother George and his family, but she desperately needed a place of her own. Of course, a widow with four children finding earning enough for the family would be quite an undertaking, but it was her secret dream and hope.

"Which evenings would you be free, Mo?"

"Whatever be best fer ye." Mo settled into the high back of the rattan chair, resting his hat on his left knee.

Lizzy clicked her right first fingernail on the arm of the sofa. She usually went to church with her mother and the children on Wednesdays, and on Fridays her mother often came by. "My best nights would be Tuesdays and Thursdays. How about around seven?"

"Seven's fine, Ma'am. Would I be needin' to buy anything?"

"Some paper, a pen, and some ink would be helpful."

Mo nodded his head. "I can git them, Ma'am."

"Momma." A whine broke through the hushed atmosphere. "Benjamin's picking on me." Sarah came running into the room.

"Excuse me, Mo." Lizzy removed herself from the sofa and pulled her daughter by the hand toward the back door. "Benjamin Joseph Hunte, what have you been doing to your sister?"

Her slender son shrugged his shoulders. "Nothing."

"Whatever 'nothing' is, you'd better behave. I have company in the front room, and I don't need you children making a fuss." Lizzy leaned over to Sarah. "Now, you go play, and don't you start picking on Benjamin either."

"Yes, Ma'am." Sarah's braided pigtails bobbed with her nod of agreement.

"Good. Now go play." Lizzy tapped her daughter's backside as she jumped down the stairs.

Lizzy walked through the kitchen and back to the front room. "I'm sorry about that."

"No trouble. I best git goin'. Shall I come tomorrow night, it bein' Tuesday and all?"

"Sure, Mo, tomorrow will be fine."

He rose from the chair and again Lizzy was struck by his size. "Thank ye kindly, Ma'am. I do appreciate ye takin' on the likes of me."

"Don't think of it. I've taught a few adults how to read and write. There's no shame in it."

Mo nodded and bent his head to exit the door. For a man so tall, he certainly seemed gentle. Lizzy couldn't help but notice the scars on his wrists. . .former slave, she imagined. Her jaw tightened and her fists curled, nails biting into her palms. She took in a deep breath, counted to three, and eased it out slowly. She had lost her husband in the war against such things. Ben's parents had been slaves too, but they had won their freedom in the Bahamas. Lizzy's parents never were slaves, so she hadn't known the pain, fear, and anger firsthand. But she'd seen enough over the years, and the very idea of someone owning another human being made her skin crawl. When would she be free of this anger? She didn't hate like she used to, but she still burned with fury when she saw someone like Mo, scarred and illiterate because some slave owner thought the color of one's skin determined his or her intelligence.

"Jesus, thank You for letting me grow up here. Help me deal better with the pain of the injustice." She mumbled her prayer and returned to the kitchen. "Dinnertime is coming, and ten people with hungry bellies will be wanting to be fed. So you better get your mind to your work, Lizzy," she chided herself as she went to the sink to clean her hands.

🌴

Mo placed the hat back on his head and ambled out of Lizzy Hunte's front yard. Palm trees lined the road heading inland toward his own place. A smile spread from ear to ear. "I be a learnin' man in no time at all. Thank Ye, Lord."

Mo looked back at the house, now distant. "She be a fine woman, that Lizzy Hunte." Her home was a simple but serviceable structure, he noticed, with a coral foundation, clapboard siding, and a pitched roof. Why anyone would need a pitched roof in Key West didn't make sense to him. Pitched roofs were for snow and ice-bound houses. Word was, the first owners of the island came from the North.

Mo thought back on his previous visit with Ellis Southard in his home where he'd met Lizzy Hunte's mother, Cook. *She be a fireball*, he thought, remembering how she had stood her ground. And yet Lizzy seemed not to have that same self-assurance her mother possessed. *'Course, losin' a husband and havin' four young 'uns to raise probably factored in on that.*

Lizzy had taken a quick glance at his wrists. Not much a man could do to hide 'em, especially down in this heat. Mo slowed his step and wiped his brow. The sun beat down on the pulverized coral streets, and a fine white dust filled the air around him. He glanced to the west and could see the sun lowering on the horizon. So different from the cotton fields back in Alabama. The blue, flat surface of the water turned to crimson red, then caught the streaks of the last rays of the setting sun before it slipped quietly below the horizon.

Yup, this place sure was different than the plantation. His mind flashed back to the sweet smile on Lizzy's face when he'd mentioned Ellis Southard. His name relaxed her. *She feared me, though,* Mo realized with a sigh. Seemed most folks he met feared him. Sometimes being built like an ox didn't come in handy.

Of course, he was used to it. Folks just had a problem with someone as tall as himself. He'd yet to meet a doorway he could go through without bending. A knot tightened in his stomach. That wasn't exactly correct. The Southern mansion his master had owned had a door he could have walked through. Two his size could have walked through it shoulder to shoulder.

His mind darkened. The past, the beatings—all of it swirled in confusion and anger. He'd escaped eight years ago and still the memories haunted him.

"Evenin', Mo." James Earl waved from his porch.

"Evenin', James."

"Been out walkin'?"

"Some." James was a kindly old man. His graying hair and eyebrows accented the wrinkles that lined his face.

"Wouldn't be courtin' now, would ya?"

Mo chuckled. "No, Suh. I's not ready to find me a woman." He wanted to know how to read and write first. He knew he'd have to sign a marriage license if he were ever to marry, and without being able to read the license, he didn't trust anyone. He could be signing on as someone's servant and never have a clue until they came to get him for work. *No siree, I'm not signin' no papers until I knows how to read and write.*

"Seems to me you're old enough, and you've got a good job." James tapped his pipe on his porch railing.

"Thirty years ain't that old."

James rapped his hand on his knee and let out a guffaw. "Son, you've been old enough for a decade."

Mo thought back. "I fell in love once."

"What happened?"

Mo sat on the step of James's house, removed his hat, and worked the brim with his hands. "My master decided to bed her, just to show me who wuz in charge."

James got up and settled beside Mo on the steps. "I'm sorry, Son. I earned my freedom when I was a young man. How'd you earn yours?"

"Escaped! After my master took Caron, she didn't want no part of me. I was just so mad that I up and run to freedom. When the war came, I signed up. They promised freedom for every Negro man who fought fer the Union Army fer a year and wages after that. So I fought."

James placed a hand on Mo's shoulder.

"I never did see Caron again or the plantation. I heard the South ransacked the house and took most of the food, but I never saw it to knows if'n it be true or not."

"How long were you on the run?"

"Three years. Kinda hard to hide, being as tall as I am. But I worked my way west for a spell, then went north. I had a mean master. Some folks didn't have it quite so bad. But I did. Truth be told, I think my master wuz afraid of me, so he set out to try and scare me every chance he git. I stood head and shoulders over the man."

James chuckled. "You're a big one. How tall are ya?"

"The army said six foot, nine inches. But them trousers they gave me were still a couple inches too short. So I guess I be closer to seven feet."

James let out a slow whistle. "And how big was your master?"

Mo's chest rumbled with laughter. "Tiny little man, maybe five foot seven."

"No wonder he was afraid of you. You could have crushed him with one hand."

"Oh no, I couldn't do that. As bad as the man wuz, I couldn't of killed him. Ain't right to take a man's life, no matter how bad that man is to ye. Not to say I didn't think it a time or two, but no, God wouldn't be pleased. War's different. But I never git used to seein' a man fall because of my own hands. I took more prisoners than a lot of men. Most were so full of anger they didn't mind killin' off every Reb they came in contact with. Just ain't right."

"You're a wise man, Mo. Not too many understand and accept God's forgiveness."

"I wouldn't say I's all that wise, just tryin' to live by the Good Book."

"Was that Mo Greene I saw leaving here, Lizzy?" George asked as he came into the kitchen and washed his hands.

"Yes."

George dried his hands. "Is love in the air?"

"Goodness, no, George. He's needing someone to teach him how to read and write. And don't you be spreading that around either."

"My lips are sealed. He's a good man, Lizzy."

"How do you know him? He seemed nice."

"Met him at Ellis's dock a time or two." George leaned over the simmering pot. "Dinner smells great; what are we having tonight?"

"Chicken and dumplings, just like the ones Mom used to make." Lizzy grinned.

"Now, Sis, you're a fine cook and all, but no one can make them like Mom," George teased.

"Perhaps you better tell me that after you've eaten. I think I figured out her secret ingredient." In fact, she'd finally gotten her mother to tell her the truth for the entire recipe. The secret ingredient was a spice in the biscuits, or rather, the right combination of spices. Lizzy grinned.

"Did I miss something?" George lifted the pot lid.

"Momma, Ben's pickin' on me again," Sarah whined.

"Did not."

"Were too." Sarah stomped her foot.

"Nah-uh, you were foolish enough to go fetch it," Benjamin defended.

Lizzy looked at Sarah's legs full of muck and mud, and some scratches from briars, no doubt. "Sarah, get yourself outside and cleaned up right now."

Lizzy placed her hands on her hips, then turned toward her son and watched his grin instantly dissolve. "And you, Benjamin Joseph, what do you have to say for yourself?"

"Aww, Ma, it's her fault. She kept daring me."

"And you, being the older, don't have enough sense not to let your sister's teasing get the best of you?" She tapped her foot for emphasis.

"I'm sorry." He bent his head low and looked at his bare toes.

"How's a mother supposed to make a living knowing she can't leave her young 'uns at home without them getting into trouble?"

"I'm sorry."

"I've got work tomorrow cleaning for Mr. Sanchez. How am I to go and not concern myself with you misbehaving?"

"It won't happen again, Mom."

"You're right it won't, and you'll be painting the chicken coop tomorrow for your uncle George just to remind you not to get all caught up with your sister's teasing."

"But, Ma, that ain't fair."

"Isn't, not ain't."

"But it isn't fair, Ma. Sarah ought to have to do something too."

"I'm the parent, I'll decide who gets what punishment. And you're right, life isn't fair. Never has been, never will be."

Benjamin held his tongue. She could see his little mind working. As for Sarah, she'd have to think up a real good punishment for her. Not only was she teasing Benjamin but tattling as well, exonerating herself in the process, or so she thought.

George's wife, Clarissa, walked in with her three children. "Smells great, Lizzy." Clarissa gazed back and forth between Benjamin and Lizzy, then over to George, who nodded.

"Thank you, Clarissa. Dinner's done cooking when everyone's ready to come to the table." Lizzy went to lift the large pot from the stove.

George called the household to the table. The family of three adults and seven children sat down to pray. Lizzy examined each of their faces. So many people under such a small roof. Perhaps tutoring Mo was the answer to her prayers?

Chapter 2

Lizzy snuggled under the covers and rolled to her side. She had another fifteen minutes of rest before she had to get up, and she was bound and determined to get it. Division of the household duties worked well: Clarissa made breakfasts and lunches, Lizzy cooked the dinners. That allowed her the opportunity to teach the children while preparing dinner. She punched her feather pillow and snuggled in deeper.

Olivia's little hands and feet cuddled up next to her. She never knew her father. In fact, she wasn't sure Benjamin had even known he had a second daughter when he died. Lizzy took comfort in knowing Ben could look down from heaven and see their little true blessing. She rolled over and caressed Olivia's cherub cheeks. " 'Morning."

" 'Morning, Momma."

"Did you sleep well?"

"Yes, Ma'am. Can I go to work with you?"

Lizzy lifted her head off the pillow. "No, Darling, you know I can't take you to work with me."

"I know." Olivia's large oval eyes looked into her own. "Momma, why do you have to work?"

Rip my heart out, Child. Out of all her children, she thought Olivia at least would be used to her working. "Honey, you know I have to."

"I know, it's just that I don't want you to. Sarah says that before Daddy went off to war you stayed home and took care of her and Ben."

Ah, Sarah again. Perhaps the punishment for teasing Ben yesterday might not have been tough enough. "True, but I still worked, Dear. I used to do some people's mending to earn a few extra dollars."

"Momma, why'd God invent dollars?"

Lizzy chuckled. "Actually, God didn't invent money, man did."

"Well, if God didn't, why do we have to have 'em?"

"Them, not ' 'em,' " she corrected.

"Them?"

"Liv, I don't know if there is an easy answer to that one. I do know that it's the easiest way to get what you need. For example, we don't live on a farm and don't have enough room to have a herd of cattle so we can have the hides to make shoes. So with money I can buy the shoes from someone who makes them, and he can buy more leather to make more shoes."

"But wouldn't it be better if we didn't need money and everyone just gave everyone what they needed?"

"Now, Girl, that's heaven, and we don't live there yet." Lizzy sat up in the bed.

Olivia's white cotton chemise accented her creamy chestnut skin, and her bright hazel eyes sparkled. "Daddy's in heaven, right, Momma?"

"Right, Sweetheart."

"Then Daddy doesn't need money, right, Momma?"

"Right." Lizzy slipped on a cotton robe she kept on the bedpost and cinched it at the waist.

"But we still do, right, Momma?"

"Right." How Lizzy wished she could stay at home with her children. God saw fit to take Benjamin, though, and somehow He was going to be providing for her and the children. She just hadn't figured out exactly how yet. Her mother helped with bills, since she earned a good living and had few expenses. But Lizzy wasn't fond of charity; family made it easier. From as far back as she could remember this house had been always filled with someone from some-place—generally the Bahamas, where her parents came from. Her mother had moved out seven or eight months ago and moved into Ellis Southard's house. That gave the house a little break, allowing the older children to share their grandmother's room.

In all fairness, it wasn't hard living with George and Clarissa, and Lizzy always felt useful. She couldn't charge the parents who allowed their children to be schooled; it didn't seem right. Few of the families had any real extra. Of course they often would share some extra fish, lobster, or fruits and vegetables they harvested. Thank the good Lord there was never a lack on their table.

She was also thankful she could teach the children and didn't have to keep it a secret, the way folks had to on the plantations before the war. Of course, black children weren't allowed to go to the island academy. On the other hand, lots of families taught their children in their homes. Some said the children concentrated better at home. Others said it was better to have professional learning. In either event, Lizzy was the teacher for any of the island children who came by. Often it was difficult because the children were not consistent. But the need for an education, the need to learn to read and write, was growing like rapid fire among her people. And that was another sign of the changes that had started since the end of the war.

"Momma?"

Olivia's sweet voice brought her out of her reverie. "Yes?"

"Will I ever go to work with you?"

"Not likely, but I might be able to let you visit Grandma one day while I'm working."

"So I can play with Richie?" Olivia's curls bounced up and down. She always enjoyed playing with Bea's nephew.

"Of course. Now go get dressed."

"Thank you, Momma."

"You're welcome, Sweetheart." Now if only her mother was as excited about the prospect as Olivia. Lizzy chuckled. Her mother loved children but ruled them with an iron hand. Although in recent days Lizzy had noticed that her mother was letting the grandchildren get away with more, and she was definitely feeding them more cookies.

Lizzy shook off the image of her mother and joined the family in the kitchen. Her nose caught the scent of the bacon before her ears heard it sizzling on the griddle.

Mo scanned the horizon. The ocean had a slight chop, but not enough to prevent the men from gathering their sponges today. Mr. Southard had told Mo that if he learned to read and write he'd be able to promote him to foreman over the divers. He'd always wanted to learn to read and write, but the job promotion reignited the old dream. And for the first time in his life he believed it could be possible. On the plantation he hadn't been allowed. Now. . .well, now things were different. Mo grinned and aligned his face with the sun. "Thank Ye, Lord," he said for the millionth time since Lizzy Hunte had agreed to teach him.

"Good morning, Mo, how are you?" Ellis Southard walked up behind him on the dock.

"Fine, Suh. Feelin' mighty fine."

"Did you speak with Lizzy?" Ellis grinned and surveyed the dock with a watchful eye.

"That I did, Suh, and she be agreein' to teach me."

"Wonderful. I figured she would."

"Mr. Ellis, would it be a problem if while I'm sponging if'n I could be pickin' up some conchs to sell? I wanna pay Miz Lizzy fer the lessons, and the extra will come in handy if I goin' to be learnin' a couple days a week."

"Sure, just as long as you keep your quota of sponges up, I don't have a problem with it." Ellis bent down to pick up one of the long hooked poles they used to gather the sponges.

"I checked 'em all before ye came." Mo pointed to the far end of the line of equipment. "That one I's thinkin' we need to replace. Depends on whether or not the man has a light hand, I suppose."

"If you think it's weak, I'll purchase another. Let's see if we can brace it in the meantime."

Long poles were not something you could harvest from the island. Ellis would need to order them. *And that's why I be needin' to read and write. A foreman cain't order if'n he cain't read an invoice.*

Ellis sat down on his haunches and examined the pole, then grabbed it with both hands and bent it over his knee. "Good call, Mo. The grain's ready to snap."

Mo nodded his head. He liked Ellis Southard; he was the kind of human being one could appreciate. Rumor had it he once stood up to a man who insulted one of his black guests. Mo hadn't been on the island when that happened, but from what he knew of Ellis Southard, he could see him doing it.

Ellis interrupted his thoughts. "Can you get me a couple of shunts and some sturdy twine?"

"Yes, Suh." Mo ambled into the small building at the end of the dock. Inside was an assortment of sponging equipment and a small desk where Ellis worked on his paperwork. Mo found himself looking at the papers and even recognized his name, Mo, in a couple of places. There were numbers but he couldn't make any sense out of what they meant. He only knew that Ellis Southard paid him well and paid him fairly from week to week. Most weeks it was the same pay, but once in awhile he'd get more if he worked an extra day, and occasionally he'd get less if the day was too bad and they couldn't go out. On the other hand, Ellis was good about allowing a man to go out for a second haul, if the time and weather permitted it, to make up for the lost day. "Yes, Suh, he be a right good boss. Thank Ye, Lord."

Mo picked up a couple small strips of wood and a ball of twine. "Here ye go, Mr. Southard."

"Thanks." Ellis worked the shunts around the weakened area of the pole and fastened them to it with the twine. He wrapped the twine tightly and evenly around the area.

"Fine job."

Ellis nodded.

The other men started to arrive for their day of work. Most were reliable, but once in awhile you got one or two who wouldn't make it because they spent the night drinking. Each man took his small skiff, loaded up his poles, knives, and nets, and set out. Mo was always the last to leave, making sure everyone had what he needed.

"Mo, I'd like to have you stay at the dock today. You'll get the same pay, but I need some help washing and drying the sponges."

"Yes, Suh. Whatever ye need."

Mo worked long and hard in the hot sun. One thing about diving for the sponges was that being in the water cooled him down some. Unfortunately, the water in the South was nothing like he'd experienced in the North. He'd taken baths cooler than that ocean some days. Even during the winter, he'd learned that the waters didn't chill much. Often they were warmer than the air.

By lunch the entire dock was covered with sponges drying in the hot, tropical sun. "Mr. Ellis, what do ye wanna do with those sponges still in the vat?"

"They'll have to continue to soak for another day or so—no other place to set them out to dry."

"What about the roof of the shed? We could put up a net around the edge so as they won't be blowin' away. Seems a shame to let that space go to waste," Mo suggested.

Ellis scratched his beard. "Good idea, Mo."

As the divers came in with their day's haul, Ellis and Mo were putting on the finishing touches of the net wall around the perimeter of the shed's roof. Mo continued working on the roof while Ellis helped the men put the new sponges in the soaking vats. Mo covered half the roof with the sponges in need of drying. Tomorrow the other half could be set up. Stretching his back, Mo worked the kinks out and proceeded down the ladder.

"Mr. Ellis, may I take a skiff out?"

"Day's done, Mo. What do you need it for?"

Mo shuffled his feet. "I want to try and git a few conchs to sell."

"I'm sorry. I forgot you mentioned that earlier." Ellis reached into his pocket and pulled out a couple silver dollars. "Here, take this as a bonus for your suggestion for drying the sponges on the roof."

"No need, Suh."

Ellis reached for his hand and placed the coins in Mo's palm. "Mo, take it with my appreciation."

"Thank ye, Suh. I don't knows what to say."

"Thank you is just fine. Learn lots tonight. I'm looking forward to training you to be my foreman."

Mo nodded his head and headed down the dock toward his home. A small room in a boardinghouse served his needs, though there were times when he'd wished for a bit more elbow room.

Mo turned a corner off Front Street. A sharp pain to the back of his head sent a flash of bright light across his vision before everything went pitch black.

⚓

The children cleaned up the kitchen and dishes from the evening meal as a part of their chores while Lizzy went through her limited supply of materials under her bed. She pulled out some basic charts for writing letters. Tonight she'd concentrate on the letter C and have Mo hear several words that began with A, B, and C. *That should keep the man busy enough for one night,* she hoped. Especially when she taught him that C had two sounds, not just one. Lizzy pictured him trying to keep C straight once they hit K and S.

"Momma, can George Jr. and I go outside to play?" Benjamin hollered from somewhere behind her.

"Sure, for a little while."

"Thanks, Ma."

"Momma," Sarah called.

"Yes, Sarah."

"Can I go outside and play too?"

Lizzy got to her feet after replacing the supplies under the bed. "Yes." If she was going to have a moment's peace she needed reinforcements from George and Clarissa.

"George, Clarissa?" She wandered to the back bedroom, their private sanctuary.

George popped his head out the door. "What do you need, Sis?"

"Mo's coming for his first lesson today and it appears that the children need lots of attention."

George held up his hand. "Say no more. Come on, Honey, let's take the young 'uns outside for a spell."

"Wonderful idea, George," Clarissa called from behind him. "Don't worry none, Lizzy. We'll keep 'em out of your hair."

"Thanks. He's real nervous."

"We understand."

Lizzy looked at the clock. *Fifteen minutes, great.* She put a bucket of water on the stove so everyone could wash up with warm water when they returned from outside. In the dining area she set out the alphabet cards, a slate, and some chalk. She also placed a dog-eared homemade book on the table. She'd drawn and painted items for each letter, and each letter had its own page. For years she'd used it, and it continued to be one of her best teaching aids for the children.

She glanced at the clock again. Seven o'clock. He hadn't seemed like the kind of man who would be late. Then again, everyone on Key West went by a different kind of clock, called island time. Some said it came from the Spanish, some said it just came from the heat. Everything slowed down a pace or two, especially during the height of the day.

Lizzy went to the back door and watched George wrestle the older children. Perhaps she should have put on two buckets of water, she mused. Clarissa had the younger ones engaged in a story. She caught another glimpse of the clock. Maybe he forgot? Or maybe he just decided he was too embarrassed to show his ignorance when it came to book learning? She'd wait a few more minutes.

George had two boys holding onto his legs as he attempted to walk across the yard. George grunted. The boys laughed and sat on top of his feet.

"Mr. Mo not coming?" Vanessa, her niece, whispered from a chair in the kitchen.

"He should be here shortly. Something could have delayed him. What are you doing in the corner?"

"Reading. I didn't want to go outside and get dirty again." Vanessa scrunched up her nose and placed her hands on the book she was reading.

"What are you reading?"

"Little Briar Rose."

The front door rattled in its hinges. "Coming!" Lizzy called.

"Must be Mr. Mo," Vanessa offered and lowered her gaze back to the book in her lap.

"I imagine so. Enjoy your stories." Lizzy rushed to the front door and pulled it open. A scream tore from her throat. "Help!"

Chapter 3

Help me, please." Mo's hoarse whisper sent chills down Lizzy's spine. She leapt out and grabbed him. A crimson red trail covered the back of his head and neck.

"What?" George came running up huffing and puffing. "Let me help you." George sidled up and placed Mo's left arm across his shoulders.

"Let's bring him over there to sit down." Hearing Clarissa and the children gasp, Lizzy handed out orders. "Clarissa, get me a sharp needle and thread. Vanessa, some clean rags. Ben, get some of the hot water from the stove."

George and Lizzy set Mo on the chair. "What happened?" they asked in unison.

"I wuz headin' home from work and someone hit me from behind."

"Hard," George added.

Lizzy worked her fingers around the wound, examining it.

"I don't recall much of anythin' else, 'cept comin' to. I knew y'all be spectin' me so's I came here. Sorry."

"Don't be apologizing. Let's see how much damage they did." Lizzy carefully blotted the area with a cloth Vanessa brought. His short nappy hair was scarlet. "There's a cut about an inch long, not too deep. I'll need to clean it out."

"I appreciate ye helping. A man cain't do much fer himself workin' behind his eyes." Mo's head nodded forward.

Is he going to lose consciousness again? "George Jr., would you bring a glass of water for Mr. Mo?"

"Yes, Ma'am." Lizzy heard his footsteps heading into the kitchen.

"Thank you." Lizzy looked at her brother. "Did you see anyone?"

"No, Ma'am."

She saw the inside of Mo's pockets were hanging out. "Have any money on you?"

Mo fumbled for his pant pockets. "Appears to be missin'."

George interrupted. "Was it a lot?"

"Had a couple silver dollars."

"I'll get the sheriff," George offered.

"Don't think it will help. Feller hit me before I saw anythin'."

"Perhaps so, but the officials need to know this has happened." George headed for the door.

"Someone must have seen Mr. Ellis payin' me," Mo mumbled.

Lizzy placed her hand on his shoulder. "Shh, relax. Let George fetch the sheriff."

Clarissa returned with the needle and thread, and soon the children brought her the various items she'd requested. Everyone huddled around Mo and stared.

Olivia's gaze widened. "Is he going to die, Momma?"

Goodness, the children didn't need to see this, and they certainly didn't need to see her stitching up the man. "No, Darling. There's only a small cut on his head. Head wounds just bleed a lot." Granted there was more blood than normal, and he probably had a concussion too, but if he could make it here, she was sure he would be fine.

Lizzy fixed her attention on Clarissa. Soon their eyes met, and Lizzy motioned for her to corral the children and bring them to the other room.

"Come on, children. I think your aunt Lizzy has everything under control. Why don't we go clean up and get ready for bed?"

Lizzy cleaned the blood off the back of Mo's neck and shoulders, sopping up as much as possible from his hair. "Are you okay, Mo? Any dizziness?"

"I's a bit unsteady on my feet, but I be all right."

"I need to stitch up that wound."

"Let me show ye a trick I learned in the army. Helps with the stitchin'. I'll need a lit candle and the needle."

She placed a dry rag against the wound and encouraged him to hold it there. "I'll be right back." Lizzy wondered what a candle could be used for, but he seemed to know what he wanted. Being in the army, she reckoned, more than one man needed some stitching from time to time.

She returned and lit the candle, placing it on the small tea table in front of the sofa. He picked up the needle and heated it until it was red hot. He used the wooden spool and pushed the needle's head down on it in a rolling manner. The needle now had a slight hook shape to it.

"With head wounds the bone of the skull is close to the surface. So's this here needle will cut into the skin but will start coming back sooner. Just hook the other side of the torn skin and it will come out."

Lizzy nodded. It seemed to make sense, but she'd never worked with a hooked needle before. "I'll do my best. This will hurt."

"I trust ye."

Mo's hands clasped the arms of the chair after she threaded the needle. "Don't fret, Mo. I need to shave off some of your hair around the wound first. Don't want hair in the wound."

Mo nodded and released his grip on the chair.

He heard Lizzy coming even before he could see her. In her hand she held a straight-edge razor. "I'll be careful."

Mo grinned. "I's not worried about ye. Ye have a gentle touch, unlike some."

Lizzy knitted her eyebrows but refrained from asking her obvious question. He respected that. She had no idea about the scars on his back or the events that led up to getting them. Thank the good Lord she was raised in a place like this, where she was never owned, never treated like. . . Mo shook his head. No Suh, he wasn't going to think about those things again.

"I'm sorry, did I hurt you?"

"Huh?" Mo hadn't felt a thing. What did she mean?

"You shook your head just as I was about to shave near the wound."

"Sorry, I's wasn't payin' attention. I keep it still fer now on."

"First lesson, Mo. Don't say I's, simply say I. You'll find I'm a stickler for proper grammar."

"I don't understand whatcha talkin' 'bout, but I will do as ye say. At least try."

Lizzy's smile lit up the room; her bright white teeth were like a fine string of pearls on a wonderful sea of amber gold. But even her smile couldn't dull the pain. His head throbbed. Whoever had whacked him had hit him real good. The sun was setting when he'd come to, so he must have been out awhile.

"Mo, I'm going to start stitching now."

Lizzy's words snapped him back to the present. "Go ahead." Mo braced for the pain, knowing it couldn't be much worse.

"This works great." Lizzy tugged away at his flesh. Her gentle fingers contradicted the pain. A mixture of warmth from a woman's loving touch and a desire to scream caused him to curl his lips and hold them shut.

"Two more, Mo, and I'll be through."

He lifted a hand and waved off the comment, certain if he spoke he would have been less than a man, and moaned.

"I'm tying the last one, Mo."

He released his hold of the chair, then worked his fingers to bring the blood back into them.

"Momma, Aunt Clarissa said to give Mr. Mo this." Sarah brought in a tall glass of limeade.

Mo reached out for the glass. "Thank ye, Miss."

"Tell Aunt Clarissa Mo's all stitched up."

"Okay, Momma. Are you feeling better, Mr. Mo?" Sarah whispered.

"Some. I think a night of rest will fix me up real good."

Sarah nodded and walked into the kitchen.

"Let me look at your eyes, Mo." Lizzy waited for him to turn and look at her.

"I's, I mean, I am fine, Miss Lizzy—just feel like a mule kicked me in the head."

Lizzy chuckled, then sobered. "At least a mule you know how to watch out for. Do you think whoever did this was after your money?"

"Don't know. Coulda been, I suppose, hard to say. Coulda been they's were hard up fer a drink."

"Maybe. Still seems odd for a man to knock out the likes of you." Lizzy flushed. "I mean with you being as tall as you are and all."

Mo grinned and gently tapped the top of her hand. "I know what ye mean. Probably why they hit me from behind."

George came running through the door. "Sheriff is on his way."

Sweat poured down the back of George's neck and stained the collar and armpits of his shirt. "You should not have run," Lizzy commented.

"A man needs his exercise, especially after wrestling the youngsters in the backyard. Didn't know I was that out of shape. Getting old, I suppose." George sat down on the sofa.

Clarissa came in with a glass of water. "The children are ready for bed, but I told them they could read or practice their schooling for a bit before they go to sleep." She sat down beside her husband and handed him the water, then leaned toward everyone and whispered, "I'm willing to bet they're all by the door trying to listen in."

Lizzy smiled. "I wouldn't put it past them. Once the sheriff comes and goes we'll let them out."

"After the sheriff comes, I better git to my place," Mo said. "No sense in tryin' to learn with this here headache."

The screen door rattled in its hinges as a loud knock hit the door.

"Come in," Lizzy, George, and Clarissa called out.

"Mr. Ellis!" Their voices sounded in unison as they jumped up from their seats.

"Sit down. Mo, what happened?" Ellis came up beside him.

"Someone hit me."

"Took his money too," George added.

"Did you see anyone?"

"No, Suh. They's come at me from behind."

"How bad's the injury?" Ellis asked and sat on the stool by the rattan chair.

Lizzy spoke. "Cut's about an inch long, took five stitches. I could see the skull. They hit him pretty hard."

Ellis nodded.

The door banged again, but this time it opened immediately.

"Mr. Ellis, ya walk like there's a fire." Cook placed her hands on her ample hips.

"I'm sorry, Cook. I didn't know you were coming too."

"Course not, ya ran out of that house like the good Lord Himself had hit ya with a bolt of lightning." Cook chuckled and hugged her daughter.

"Hi, Mom." Lizzy was a taller, thinner version of her mother. They shared the same almond shaped eyes, although Lizzy's were hazel and Cook's brown. It was obvious to Mo where Lizzy got her beauty.

"Now who be foolhardy enough to mess with the likes of you, Mr. Greene?" Cook addressed him. He had to grin; she was a take-charge kind of woman. He'd met her on more than one occasion, and he honestly liked the woman.

"Appears they weren't just fools, since they's hit me from behind."

"Chickens."

"Grandma!" The seven children couldn't contain themselves any longer and ran into the front room. Mo knew he was the reason for all this bustle in the house tonight. He imagined something was always keeping this house hopping like a brown lizard in search of a warm rock.

The door rattled again. Mo got up and met a man he assumed was the sheriff. "Mo?" the man asked.

"Yes, Suh. Let's take this outside and I tell ye what happened." The sheriff stepped back into the front yard and Mo followed. He turned back when he heard the door open. Mr. Ellis and George came out to join them.

"Tell me what happened." The sheriff's voice was firm.

⚓

"All right, children, that's enough excitement for one day. Let's get to bed and don't forget to say your prayers." Lizzy shooed the children off to bed. She busied herself with helping the younger ones brush their teeth and hair. Being naturally curious, she wanted to be out front and hear what the sheriff would do, if anything.

'Course he always has been fair to the Negroes on the island, she reminded herself. *Why is it still so difficult to trust a white man after all this time?* Perhaps she'd never openly trust anyone, but she was willing to work on it and allow folks the benefit of the doubt. Her friendship with Bea Southard had helped tremendously in that regard. But sometimes she wished she could be more like Bea, less assuming of the bad and more accepting of the good, until the person proved himself unworthy.

She returned to the front room to see her mother listening at the doorway. Lizzy chuckled. "Hear anything, Mom?"

Francine jumped. "I didn't hear ya come in."

"No, that's quite obvious."

"Oh, don't ya go fussing with me, you wanna know just as much as I do."

"True, but it doesn't make it right, and I'm not the one hovering at the door."

"Humph." Her mother came and joined her on the sofa. "So, you're going to teach Mo?"

"Yes, I'm hoping the extra income will be enough for me to get a place of my own for myself and the children."

Lizzy felt her muscles relax as her mother placed a warm wrinkled hand on her knee. "Getting crowded?"

Lizzy chuckled. "Getting? You made your escape."

"True, but I didn't bring any young 'uns with me." Francine smiled.

"Be happy to share some," Lizzy teased.

Clarissa walked in and added, "Me too."

Francine roared with laughter. "No, thank ya. I've raised mine, now it's your turn to raise yours. I'll just spoil 'em rotten for ya."

"Thanks, Mom," Lizzy responded.

"How much money did they get?" Clarissa steered the conversation back to what was on all of their hearts.

"He said a couple silver dollars."

"Mr. Ellis mentioned something to Bea about him givin' Mo a couple silver pieces earlier in the day," Francine put in. "Something about him earning a bonus."

Ellis Southard was a kind man, but Lizzy hadn't heard of him being free with money. He'd always seemed mighty conservative in that regard, so if he gave Mo that kind of a bonus, whatever Mo had done for Mr. Ellis must have been worth the pay.

"Can I get you something to drink, Mom?" Lizzy offered.

"No, thank you, I'm fine."

"How's Bea doing?"

"She's been sick in the mornings, but she feels better around the middle of the day."

"When's the baby due?" Clarissa asked.

"She's figuring he'll come around Christmas," Francine offered. "You should see Mr. Ellis parading around the house proud as can be."

Lizzy chuckled. "I remember Ben when he first learned I was in the motherly way. Never saw that man smile more."

Clarissa grinned. "George was the same way."

"Ahh," Francine said. "But my George, he's got ya'll beat. When he found out I was a carryin' his young 'uns he ran to the paper to place an announcement. The editor congratulated him but let him know as gently as possible that ya don't place a birth announcement before the baby is born. When George stood up in church the next Sunday, I was about ready to crawl under the pew. I was so scared he'd tell everyone."

"What's so funny?" George asked, coming inside.

"We're just talking about your father, Dear." Francine got up from her seat. "Guess it's time I headed home. Good night all."

Ellis paused. "Mo, would you like me to walk you home?"

"No, Suh, I be fine." Mo hesitated at the door. "Thank ye fer speakin' on my behalf with the sheriff."

"I figured it wouldn't hurt to add my character reference for you. Not that it was necessary. Sheriff already seemed to know who you were."

"Appears so." Mo slumped his shoulders.

"You're a big man, Mo Greene, and dark. Some folks just get nervous," Lizzy suggested.

"I knows, but I'm glad the sheriff, he knows I always kept to myself." Mo's legs wobbled and he grabbed the doorknob for support.

"Mo, sit down before you go banging up the front side of your skull," Lizzy demanded.

Ellis helped him to the sofa. "Maybe I should call the doctor."

"No, I's fine, Mr. Ellis. I been hit harder. Just need to rest 'tis all."

"You can spend the night on the sofa," Lizzy offered.

"I's, I mean, I don't wanna impose on ye none."

"It's no imposition, right, George, Clarissa?"

"Nope, none at all."

Ellis headed back to the door. "I'm going to take Cook home, then I'll stop over to Mo's place and pick him up some clean clothes." Ellis left before Mo could respond.

George cleared his throat. "It's late. I've got to go to work early, so I'll say good night, unless you need something, Lizzy."

"I'm fine. I can handle getting Mr. Greene settled. You two get some sleep. It's been a mighty full day."

"Night, Mo. I'll say a prayer for you." Clarissa joined hands with her husband and walked down the hall to their room.

"Did you eat, Mo?"

" 'Fraid not. Could. . ." He paused. "I trouble ye for some hot tea?"

"No trouble at all. I'll even bring you some leftover lobster and shrimp casserole I made."

"Thank ye, I'm too hungry to play humble and turn ye down tonight." Mo grinned. He was a large but gentle man. Lizzy headed into the kitchen and placed the kettle on the stove to heat up some water for tea. She watched his hands, how he'd played his fingers along the edge of his hat a few days ago, how he caressed his fingers over a book when he thought she wasn't looking. She wondered how it would feel to have his fingers caress her cheek with the same wonder and adoration. . . . *Oh my, what brought that crazy thought into my head?* Lizzy fanned herself, waving off her wayward thoughts.

"Lizzy?" Mo whispered.

Chapter 4

Mo walked up beside Lizzy and placed his hand on her shoulder. She jumped.

"I didn't mean to scare ye. I's sorry."

"Sorry, I was daydreaming. You just startled me." Lizzy wiped her hands on a towel.

"I wuz looking fer. . .the. . ." Mo tucked his hands in his pockets, looked down, and shuffled his feet.

"Ahh, it's in the backyard, to the left."

"Thank ye."

She placed a bowl, a loaf of bread, some jam, and a spoon on the table. Before Mo came back from the outhouse, Ellis Southard had brought a bundle of his clothes. When Lizzy returned to the kitchen and didn't find Mo, she opened the back door to see if he was in trouble. She certainly hoped not. She always figured herself to be a strong woman, but helping the man to a chair earlier this evening showed her just how weak she was. The door on the outhouse creaked open and she eased out a pent-up breath. *Thank You, Lord,* she silently prayed.

"Come in and sit down. Your dinner is all fixed for you."

"Thank ye, Miz Lizzy, I don't know how to be repayin' ye fer all yer kindness."

"Nonsense, it's nothing any good Christian wouldn't have done." Lizzy sat across from him at the small oak table.

"All the same, ye don't know me, not really, and you've opened yer home to me. I appreciate it." Mo grinned and bowed his head for a silent prayer.

"If I'm not being nosy, how badly does the loss of the silver dollars affect you?"

"A week's worth of lessons, I'm afraid." Mo forked up a large chunk of lobster. "This is mighty fine vittles. Thank ye."

"Vittles?"

"Food. Sorry, an expression I picked up from some fellers headin' west."

"Just how much of this country have you seen?" Lizzy loved the thought of traveling. So many ships from so many countries passed through Key West harbor. They gave her wanderlust.

"A fair amount. I wuz running fer a long time. Didn't wanna stay too long in one place. As ye notice I's. . .I," he corrected himself, "ain't exactly able to blend into a crowd."

"I suppose that would be true. You escaped?"

151

"Yes'm. I could take the beatin's, I just couldn't take. . ." Mo let his words trail off.

"Sorry, I didn't mean to upset you. I've seen slavery, but not as severe as I've heard stories about. I'm one of the fortunate few who was never owned by anyone."

"When you're young it's easier. Once you're older and understand not every man is owned. . .well, gits a bit hard to live with. One of the hardest things about accepting Christ as my Lord was the verses the preacher would say about being a slave for Christ. And if you're a slave, to stay put and show your faith. I failed the good Lord on that one. But I know He ain't holdin' it against me." Mo pushed his plate away from him and patted his stomach. "Thank ye. That be a fine meal."

"You're welcome." Lizzy found herself warming to the man's compliment. "I better get some linens for you to sleep on. I've set a pot on the stove for you to wash with. There's soap and a rag by the sink, and this towel hanging over the chair is for you to dry yourself."

"Thank ye."

Lizzy made a hasty retreat. Caring for a man would crumble the wall she'd built around her heart. *You're just reacting to the injustice,* she decided, attempting to fortify herself. Although she had to admit his dark molasses eyes drew her attention, like the sunlight kissing the ocean. She fought to keep herself firmly planted on solid ground.

Mo woke early, his head still pounding. Restless, he got up and folded the linens and placed them on the sofa. He tiptoed out of the house, praying he wouldn't wake anyone. Dawn lingered on the eastern horizon as he headed for the waterfront and Ellis Southard's wharf. If he caught the tide just right he'd be able to catch some snappers for breakfast, a small payment for the kindness of Lizzy's family.

Pulling in half a dozen fish, he set his poles back in the small cubby that Ellis provided him. Roosters still crowed in the distance as he ambled back up the streets toward Lizzy's home. Mo squinted, shielding his eyes from the direct assault of the bright morning sun's rays. Soon he found himself back at Lizzy's home, gently knocking on the front door.

Lizzy opened the door and smiled. "Mo. I was wondering where you wandered off to."

"Done me some fishin'. Thought youse folks might like some fresh fish fer breakfast."

"Thank you, Mo, but that wasn't necessary."

"Seems little enough to say 'thank ye,' but I'd appreciate yer takin' these."

Lizzy reached out and took the string of fish.

Mo tipped his hat. "I best be goin' now. I need to git myself to work."

Lizzy's soft satin touch on his arm sent a ripple of warmth through his body. He'd be needing to guard himself against such foolish desires. After all, Lizzy was educated; he was not.

She saw him glance down at her hand on his dark arm, her amber skin's creamy perfection against his scarred body. Yes, he could not let his wayward thoughts travel far. Everything inside him shouted how wrong he was for her, how there could be no future in any thoughts or desires of a romantic nature. He looked into her eyes, eyes that sparkled green and gray this morning. He loved her eyes, always changing, never the same.

"Mo, don't dive today. An infection might settle in the wound. You can't mess with head wounds. They're just too close to the brain."

"I's a-hopin' Mr. Ellis. . ."

"I hope," she corrected.

"I hope Mr. Ellis will have some dock work for me, or I might not be able to start my classes fer another week."

"I'll pray for you, Mo," Lizzy offered.

Mo blinked at the gentle words. No one had ever offered to pray for him since he left his mother and escaped from the plantation. He suspected his mother was still praying for him, and it warmed him during some of his darkest moments.

"Would you like to stay for breakfast?"

"No, thank ye. Old James Earl, he likes having me come fer morning breakfast. I suspect he likes the company."

"I understand. Have a good day, Mo. I'll see you when you're ready to resume your lessons."

Mo tipped his hat and exited the small but comfortable home. For a house of ten people it didn't seem overcrowded. There was love in that home, and for the first time in many years he truly missed his home on the plantation. He missed his mother, his brothers and sisters. What were their lives like now?

Lizzy's next few mornings at work were busy. Mr. Sanchez was away on business in Cuba, and Mrs. Sanchez had her scrubbing every closet and airing every room for a good spring cleaning. Lizzy could understand why Mrs. Sanchez waited for Mr. Sanchez to go out of town.

Mo hadn't come by for two days since his accident. The stolen money must have really put a hole in his pocket, she surmised.

Of course today was Friday and payday. Perhaps he would feel free to come and learn tonight, she hoped. For some reason she wanted to help Mo, wanted him to be able to read and write. To be able to get a higher position working for Mr. Ellis could only be a good thing, she reasoned.

"Momma?"

"Yes, Olivia."

"Is Mr. Mo coming to learn tonight?"

"I don't know, Sweetheart. I hope so."

Olivia played with a folded piece of paper in her hands.

"What do you have there?"

"Something."

"And 'something' is?"

"A present." She turned her chin down to her chest and drew a circle on the floor with her big toe.

"And can I ask who the present is for?" Lizzy continued.

"Mr. Mo."

"Oh." She hadn't talked much with the children about Mo or his accident, but obviously it left an impression on her delicate little water lily. Of all her children, Olivia had the lightest skin and the same sharp nose and features as herself.

William came running in through the front door all huffing and puffing. "William, what's the matter?" Lizzy asked.

"I won," William gasped.

"You won what?"

"A race with Mr. Mo."

Mo was running? Didn't the man know he'd cause blood to rush to that head wound? "Where did you meet Mr. Mo?"

"Down by the salt farms."

"And what on earth were you doing down there?" Lizzy placed her hands on her hips.

"I was looking for work."

"Work! William, what on earth are you talking about? A five-year-old boy doesn't go looking for work."

"But Ben said if we all got a job we could get our own house."

"Benjamin!" Lizzy hollered. *If that boy doesn't stop trying to be the man of the house, I'm going to. . .okay, maybe I wouldn't go that far. But goodness, Lord, do something about that child.*

Mo rapped on the door. "Come in, Mo. I'll be right with you," Lizzy answered, then turned to shout, "Benjamin Joseph Hunte, where are you?"

"Here, Momma. What's the matter?"

"Did you tell William to get a job?"

"Wellll." Benjamin pushed his hands down into his pants pockets. "Sort of."

"What do you mean by 'sort of'? And if you're all fired up about earning money, why aren't you out looking for a job?"

Benjamin looked shocked.

"Exactly. If you're going to be asking your brother and sisters to go to work, you've got to be willing to do it as well. And since you're the oldest, I'll be expecting you to work twice as many hours and bring home twice as much pay."

"But, Ma," Ben whined.

"Well?"

"But what about playing?"

"Oh, a man can't be playing. He has to work. And since you're all fired up about working, I guess you want to be the man. And if you're going to be the man, you best be getting a good job and working the kind of hours your uncle George puts in every day, leaving the house first thing in the morning and not getting home until supper time."

His wide brown eyes widened even further as he gulped down her words.

"I expect you to have a job by the time we finish supper. Go on, shoo! Go find a job so you can pay for all of us to have our own home, and I won't have to work for Mr. Sanchez and can just stay here and take care of the house and the other children's learning. Go on now." Lizzy waved her hands toward the door.

Slowly he walked to the front door.

"Go on, you've got ten minutes. Better hurry."

"Ten minutes, Mom? I can't get a job in ten minutes."

"You can't get a job anywhere. You're too young. And your foolish words had your five-year-old brother down by the salt farms. Now go to your room and think about what you did and what it is to be an adult. We'll discuss the matter later."

"Yes, Ma'am." Benjamin quickened his pace and headed into his room.

Mo thought how wonderfully wise Lizzy was. On the other hand, he also envied the boy's life. He'd started working on the plantation by the time he was four. Play was done quietly and away from the master's view.

"Hi," Mo offered, when she came into the room wagging her head from side to side.

"I swear that boy comes up with more brilliant ideas than God has stars in the night sky."

"He's creative."

Lizzy chuckled. "Thanks for bringing William home. I didn't even know he was gone."

"Just happened to be in the right place at the right time, I suppose." Mo reached into his pocket and pulled out a nickel. "Apparently he'd worked fer awhile before I found him. The owner of the farm wanted him to have this. Says he gathered a couple pounds of salt. He also sed when he's older to send him to the farm and he'll hire him on the spot."

Lizzy chuckled and took the five-cent piece from Mo. "Thanks. I'm sure he'll enjoy buying some candy with this."

"Would ye be able to teach me this evening after yer dinner?"

"Of course. How's your head?"

"No more headaches, thank the good Lord. But I needs to rise slowly or it causes some pain."

"Did Mr. Ellis have work for you?"

"Some, but I fished fer the sponges from the boat, just didn't dive in after any."

Lizzy nodded.

Mo tucked his hat back on his head. "I'll see ye later then."

"All right, and thanks again." Lizzy followed him to the door. "Would you like to have dinner with us?"

"I's wouldn't wanna be any trouble."

"No imposition. I'm making conch chowder and fritters."

"Mmm. You're sure I won't be a bother?"

Lizzy reached out and touched his arm. "Mo, it's the least I can do after you rescued William."

For some strange reason he'd hoped she would say she enjoyed his company— of course, she hadn't really experienced his company before this. He'd only come briefly to ask her to teach him, and then he arrived battered and in need of some help. The memory of her hands touching him, like now. . .so soft and light. . . satiny. . . Mo cleared his throat. "Anyone would have helped."

"Perhaps, but not anyone did, and God obviously put you in the right place at the right time for a reason. Now, I know you mustn't get a home-cooked meal all that often, so let me treat you."

Mo grinned. "Home-cooked would be mighty nice, thank ye, Miss Lizzy."

"You're welcome. You can make yourself at home in the living room, or you can return in forty-five minutes." Lizzy headed into the kitchen.

"If'n ye don't mind, I'd like to return. I's got some errands."

"Okay, see you later."

Mo waved good-bye and headed for home. He needed to bathe. Salt water and sweat didn't make a man smell fresh. *Now why am I's so concerned about how I smell?*

Chapter 5

Later that evening, with the house quiet, Lizzy sat beside Mo at the table. Hunched over, he practiced penning the letter C. "That looks great, Mo. Now here is the hard part about the letter C. It has two sounds. One sound is like another letter, the letter K. For example, words like cap, cake, cookie—all start with the letter C but have the harder sound."

Mo nodded.

"The other sound of the letter C is like the letter S, but often that is when C is in the middle of the word, not the beginning."

"If'n youse says so. I's don't know what those other letters even look like."

Lizzy penned a copy of the letters K and S for Mo, pointing to which was which. "Now think of the hard sound for the letter C. What words have you heard that use that sound?"

"Cake. . .cookie. . . ," he repeated. "Conch?"

"Good! Conch does begin with the letter C." And on and on they went, discussing various words that began with C. Then Lizzy moved on to the letter D.

As they discussed the sound of D and the various other letters, he asked, "Does Daniel begin with D?"

"Yes, Daniel begins with D. And the second letter is A, which you've already learned."

Mo's face lit up.

"Why do you ask, Mo?"

" 'Cause that be my name. My real name. Everyone calls me Mo, so I go by it. But the name me mother called me wuz Daniel."

"How'd you ever get a nickname like Mo if your name is Daniel?" Lizzy asked.

" 'Tis my own fault, I suppose. When I's. . .I mean, I signed up to fight I wuz asked to make my mark. And not wantin' to appear like I didn't know how to write, I put two letters that I seen together and figured they would sound like Mo."

Lizzy giggled. "You'll have to tell me more. How'd you know the letter M?"

"From signs on stores. And I knew the stores were markets or mercantiles. So I figured it be an M sound. The O come from no trespassin' signs. And I figured if thar could be a small word like no, why couldn't thar be a small word like Mo?"

"Well, you figured correctly, Daniel. Would it be all right if I call you Daniel?"

"I be honored, Miz Lizzy. I's not been called Daniel fer five years. Sounds mighty fine coming from ye."

Lizzy fought down a slight blush. "Would you like to see your full name written out?"

"Yes'm."

"This will be your homework, practicing your first name."

"All right."

Lizzy watched as Mo, correction, Daniel, saw his name unfold before him. Like a child caught in the wonder of a bee gathering honey from a flower, Daniel savored every pen stroke. Then she handed him the pen. "Here, you try once."

The only trouble he had was with the letter E, which she had noticed many folks seemed to find troublesome when beginning to write.

"Excellent, Daniel," she praised.

"I thank ye kindly, Miz Lizzy. I can almost feel it in my bones. I'm goin' to learn to read. I be educated."

Lizzy grinned. "Yes, you will. But remember, you already have a lot of learning in you. This is just one area that you've never been allowed to develop."

"I best be goin'. I need to git up early tomorrow."

"Good night, Daniel."

"Good night, Miz Lizzy. I see ye tomorrow, if'n that's all right."

"Tomorrow's fine." She hadn't been planning on teaching him tomorrow, but it would work out just fine.

"Who's Daniel?" George called from the den.

Mo couldn't believe his good fortune. In the past few weeks he'd learned all the letters of the alphabet, his numbers, and how to write his own name. He was beginning to read some of the earlier readers, but he wasn't as confident in reading out loud as he was in writing on paper. Mr. Ellis was genuinely pleased with his progress and began to explain the various ledgers and books he kept. Mr. Ellis's books weren't as easy as Miz Lizzy's. . .*but them be the kind I really need to learn*, he reminded himself.

"Course, Miz Lizzy's purdier to look at." Mo grinned as he said the words out loud. "On the other hand, she has four children." Mo felt his grin slip. What was a man to do? How was he supposed to court a woman with a ready-made family? And would she even be interested in having a man around? On the other hand, she did seem to smile when he walked in the room. *'Course, she's probably just thinkin' how fast I'm learnin'*.

Mo kicked a chunk of coral on the path between his home and James Earl's. The elderly gentleman had been pleased to hear that Mo was learning to read and write. James hadn't learned much, but he knew some.

" 'Morning, James," Mo called as he opened the screen door.

No response.

Mo paused and listened.

Then he went to the back of the cottage and looked out in the yard. Not seeing his friend, he called again, "James?"

No response. Mo headed to the back door and called again.

Still no answer. Mo's heart hammered in his chest. He turned the knob and entered the kitchen. The scent of death crossed his nostrils. "No, Lord," Mo moaned and ran to James's bedroom.

The old man's still body lay sprawled on the bed, semi-covered by a clean white sheet. His skin was ashen. Mo stepped forward and cradled the cold, lifeless hand of his friend. A salty tear burned a blazing trail down his cheek. James Earl was gone. A man who had become like a father to him.

Mo never knew his own father. He'd died the winter Mo turned two. James's wife had passed on many years ago, and they had never been blessed with children. So Mo always figured he and James were good for each other.

Friendship demanded that Mo do his duty to see James buried next to his wife. He set to washing and dressing his old friend, then got the undertaker. He'd planned a morning lesson with Lizzy, but now he penned a quick, clumsy note and paid a boy a nickel to deliver it. His words were simple: "No Come, Daniel." He figured he could explain later, but he hoped it would be enough for her to understand.

"Rev, I needs your help," Mo told the pastor while gulping in some air.

"What can I do for you, Mo?"

"James Earl is dead. I found him this mornin' in his bed. I cleaned and dressed him, and the undertaker is coming by. But I need ye to come to the house and see if he left any important papers."

"I reckon I could do that." The preacher set his wide-brimmed white hat on his head and followed Mo.

"How'd you know James Earl, Mo?"

"I been seein' him every mornin' since I first came to Key West. He is a kind old man and needed some company."

"True, James hasn't been able to get about much anymore. I'm glad he had a friend in you."

In truth, Mo was the man who was blessed to have a friend like James, but he wasn't so sure the pastor would understand if he shared his thoughts.

At James Earl's they found the undertaker arriving with his horse-drawn hearse. Mo fought the images of the past, of watching folks carrying the dead to a small section of the master's land. The women wailing. . .the men somber during their funeral march. . .battlefield images of men being buried with no one to mourn.

Mo left the pastor to speak with the undertaker and went into James Earl's home one more time. What should he do with James's personal effects? Who would you send them to when there wasn't any family? James had to have a brother or sister, some kind of family somewhere. They'd want to know. They'd need to know. Mo searched through a small desk in the front sitting room. A few old letters and a note with "Daniel" written on it, but Mo couldn't figure out the writing on the inside. He hadn't learned to read this style of lettering yet. Mo tucked the letter in his pocket. Mr. Ellis or Lizzy could read it for him.

"Mo," the preacher called as he walked in.

"In here, Pastor. Just goin' through his desk, seein' if'n I can find some letters from family."

The pastor picked up a folded paper with fancy lettering on top. "This is his will, Mo."

Mo's hand stopped digging through the drawers. "That'll be telling us who to notify, right, Pastor?"

"Yes, it should." The pastor unfastened the fresh white papers that crinkled when opened. "I, James Earl," he read, "being of sound mind, do hereby give all my worldly possessions to Mr. Daniel Greene of Key West, Florida." The pastor paused. "I don't know a Daniel Greene. Is he a relative of yours, Mo?"

Mo wanted to stick his finger in his ear to clear it. He couldn't believe what he just heard. James gave him all his earthly possessions? Why? The pastor's dark eyes darted back and forth catching Mo's attention. "Sorry, what did ye say?"

"I was wondering if you know this Daniel Greene."

"That would be me, Suh."

"Pardon me?"

"My name is Daniel, Daniel Greene. I've been goin' by Mo fer many years, but my given name is Daniel."

"Well then, it appears that James has left you all his worldly possessions."

"I knows not what to say. I knows not what I will do with James's possessions. I only have a small room."

The pastor scanned the document further, then chuckled. "Mo, I'm not sure how to tell you this—but James owns this house and the land it sits on. This paper says you now own it."

"James owns this house? I cain't believe it. James wuz a poor man, just like me. He didn't have nothing fancy, nothing. . .he owns the house?" Mo collapsed in the maple chair.

"He did. Now it's yours."

"He never told me. Ye certain?"

⚓

Lizzy smiled at the young boy with a missing front tooth. "Can I help you?"

"Mr. Mo said to give ya this." He thrust a piece of crumpled paper toward her. "Thank you."

"Bye." The boy waved and jumped off the steps, landing with both feet on the ground in a squatting position. He jumped up and ran off.

Places to go and things to do, she mused. Lizzy opened the crumpled note. The message was simple, and she certainly understood its meaning. She smiled at how well Daniel had constructed his letters. She glanced at the note again. What could be keeping him away this morning? After they'd begun lessons a few weeks ago, he'd never missed a session.

Perhaps Mr. Ellis had some additional work for him, she decided. With her morning plans changed, she had a few free hours to herself. George and Clarissa had taken the children for a morning fishing trip.

Lizzy felt so out of place in her family's home. *A few hours to myself and I can't enjoy it. I need my own home.* "Lord, I still feel like I'm intruding on George and Clarissa. It was easier when Momma lived here, seemed more like her home then." Today, she just didn't feel a part of the place.

"I'll go visit Momma and Bea. Haven't seen them in ages," she told the Lord, and headed out the door.

As she walked down the street and headed toward Front Street, a horse-drawn hearse passed. Lizzy crushed her hands to her sides. A part of her could never accept that her husband was buried in some unmarked grave. And yet that was reality. Death with no grave to mourn at left her feeling incomplete. Graves certainly served a purpose. She didn't see herself going to her husband's grave on a regular basis. But once in awhile, when she was feeling blue, it might have been a place where her soul could sit and reflect on the love they had, on the lives they had brought into the world, and somehow rejoice that God was in control.

Lizzy entered the Southards' property but faltered as she was heading for the front door. Mr. Ellis had bought this place nearly a year ago, and he had hired her mother to work full-time for him. Mr. Sanchez required Lizzy to enter through the servant's door in the rear. She raised her hand and knocked on the solid oak door.

"Lizzy. Come in, come in." Bea smiled. "It's so good to see you."

Lizzy stepped into her friend's open arms and hugged her. "How are you feeling?"

"Better. I'm still getting sick in the mornings, but just a little."

"I remember with Benjamin I was up night and day. . . . Can't believe I actually wanted another child after I went through the first."

Bea laughed. "Let me get through this one before we talk about another."

"Lizzy?" Her mother came out of the kitchen, wiping her hands on a dishtowel.

"Hi, Mom. How are you?"

"Fine, is everything all right?"

"Nothing is wrong. Mo couldn't come this morning for his lesson, and the children have gone off with George and Clarissa. I thought I'd share a cup of tea with you two, if it's all right?"

"Of course." Francine headed back to the kitchen. "I'll go put on the kettle."

"Come, sit in the parlor with me." Bea led her to the front sitting room and sat on the sofa beside her. "So, tell me about teaching Mo."

"He's a fast learner."

"Ellis said he's grasping things very quickly," Bea added.

"He is. I don't think I've ever had an adult more interested. So how's Richie?"

"He's fine. He and Ellis went for a sail. I was invited, but the very idea of riding up and down on those waves. . ." Bea placed a hand on her stomach.

Lizzy laughed. "No need to explain."

Francine came into the parlor with a tray of fresh biscuits and a silver bowl with guava jelly. "A morning for girl talk." Francine beamed. "I love it."

Lizzy smiled. She loved it too. It had been ages since she was free from the children, work, or other responsibilities. The ladies chatted for awhile, and finally Lizzy shared her heart. "I just feel I need my own place."

Bea patted the top of Lizzy's hand. "I think I understand."

"Makes sense, but how ya going to afford it?" Francine asked.

"I make a fair pay cleaning for the Sanchezes, and I've been saving. But I honestly don't know how I'm going to manage it. Ben was a good man, but he didn't own any property, and he certainly didn't know how to save for the future. Not that he had all that much time to save."

"I could probably help you with some money to buy a place," Bea offered.

"Oh no, I couldn't do that. It wouldn't be right. And I figure if I can't afford to rent a home what makes me think I can afford to keep one up?"

"Well, the offer still stands if something comes up."

"Thank you, it's a very generous offer." Lizzy still had to fight the lines in her mind between white and black—what white folks did or didn't do. Her friendship with Bea had been slowly dissolving those images. Granted, there were many a folk out there that fit her previous image. But she was beginning to see that not everything was black and white—literally.

"What ya need is a man." Francine placed her china teacup in the saucer.

"I don't think I'll ever be ready for another man."

"Nonsense. You're young, healthy, and attractive. Any man would be proud to have you as a wife."

"I'm also the mother of four children. Not any man could take on that kind of responsibility. Not to mention, I'm not sure I'd want to be married and birthing more babies."

Bea chuckled. "I'm beginning to understand that."

Francine's chest bounced up and down with laughter. "You might have a point there. But a good man. . ."

"Mother, please. I'm really not ready to think of another man. Just this morning, on my way here, a hearse passed. I. . .I, well, I just felt the grief all over again. I loved Ben. I miss him." Salty tears burned at the edges of her eyes.

Chapter 6

Mo held the legal document in his hands. It just didn't seem right for him to be owning James Earl's property. On the other hand, it didn't seem right to turn down a man's final request. What was he to do? He didn't need a house. A small room suited him just fine. *A house? What's a man like me to do with a house?* Mo tossed his head from side to side.

He needed to put this will in a safe place. But where should he put it? Some folks might not believe he had inherited the property.

The pastor had left after making arrangements for the funeral service that evening. He also promised to spread the word. Mo figured he should probably be telling folks about James, but who should he tell? Who knew him? James hadn't talked about many folks here on the island. He talked some about his wife, but mostly he had listened to Mo talk about his life, his job, and his past. James's sympathetic ear had brought some healing to Mo's memories of the plantation and the beast who had called himself his master.

Mo got up and began to pace. The house had small doorways, he noted, as he bent down to enter from one room to the next. "If'n I am goin' to be living here, Lord, I need to fix them doors."

Mo stepped out the back door and looked around the yard, taking a mental inventory of what was there and what wasn't. He latched the back door from inside and exited by the front.

"Mr. Ellis can help me. He has one of them fancy safes for his house. Lord, I's not sure why Youse decided to take James at this time, and I's not sure why he gave me his home, but I ask Ye to help me be worthy of such a gift."

Mo knocked on the front door of Ellis Southard's home. " 'Mornin', Cook. Is Mr. Ellis here?"

"I'm afraid not, Mo. What's the matter?"

"I's needin' a favor. I can come back."

Cook grasped his arm as he turned. "Mo, Miss Bea is here. Can she help ya?"

"What can I do for you, Mo?" Bea asked, entering the front hall.

"I need a safe place to keep this." He handed her the will.

"What on earth? Mo, why do you have this man's will?" Bea asked.

"James Earl passed last night. I visit him every mornin' and, well, I found him. The pastor, he found this here will and, well, he said I needed to put it in a safe place. I knows Mr. Ellis has that fancy wall safe and thought he might be able to keep it for me for a spell."

163

"I'm sure he wouldn't mind. I'm sorry to hear about your friend." Bea reached out and placed a gentle hand on his forearm.

"Thank ye, Mrs. Southard. I appreciate that."

Mo's eyes caught the slight figure of someone else in the hallway. His gaze set on Lizzy's lovely face. "Miz Lizzy," he said softly and smiled.

"Daniel, did I hear correctly that James Earl died last night?" Lizzy asked, stepping closer to him. Her movements were as graceful as a dove's.

Mo shook off his wayward thoughts. "'T's. . ."

"I'm," she corrected.

Mo's jaw tightened. "I'm afraid so."

"I'm sorry to hear that. I know you spent a fair amount of time with him. Was he sick?"

"No, that's the surprise of it. He wuz talkin' last night about all his grand plans for the future." Mo looked down at his sandaled feet. "It wuz a shock."

"Come on in and sit a spell. Tell us what needs doin' and we'll be happy to lend a hand. Won't we, Lizzy?" Her mother ushered Daniel toward the front room.

"Of course."

"I already arranged the funeral service tonight, and he be buried tomorrow after the morning service. Too hot to wait until Monday."

Francine nodded her head.

Bea offered to put James Earl's will on her husband's desk until he got home and could put it in the safe. They talked about the meal they should fix for folks and decided to meet in James Earl's home. Lizzy offered to go to James's home and check out his pots and pans so they'd know what they needed. Soon she and Mo were headed out the door.

"Thank ye for the help, Miz Lizzy. I don't knows what I do without youse and Cook's help."

"You're welcome and we're glad to help. Another correction in your speaking. . ." Lizzy paused; she didn't want to overstep her teaching role in Mo's life. "The word is know, not knows. A nose is what you have on your face, and they're spelled differently."

Mo gave a stilted nod.

Lizzy reached out and touched his huge forearm. It was solid, proving his strength equaled his size. Daniel stopped and placed his hand over hers.

"I didn't mean to correct you at Mr. Ellis's, Daniel. I'm sorry about that."

"I appreciate the help, but in front of others ain't helpful, it's, it's. . ."

"Insulting. I know. I'm very sorry. My mother and Bea are the two closest people I have in my life. I don't think of them as public. But they aren't your family."

"No, they ain't, and, yes, it bothered me."

"Daniel, I am sorry. I promise not to do it again."

He caressed the top of her hand with his thumb. Her lighter skin against his darker complexion sent a bolt of awareness that he was a man and she was a woman, singeing her fingertips. Lizzy lifted her hand from his arm.

"I forgive ye," he whispered.

"Daniel, if you don't mind me asking, how'd you get those scars on your wrists?"

He stepped forward and they resumed their walk toward James Earl's home.

"I wuz put in irons on several occasions when I wuz a young man."

"Why?"

"Many reasons, I suppose. Mostly, my master wuz afraid of me. And he wuz afraid I'd run away. Funny thing is, them chains actually made me stronger. They be a bit heavy."

Lizzy considered the irony—the very item a man used to keep another man weak had actually strengthened him. "Was it hard?"

"I seen worse but, yes, after I turned fifteen it wuz much worse."

Daniel unlocked the front door. For an old man, James Earl kept a pretty clean house, Lizzy mused. "Show me the kitchen."

"Back here."

She watched Mo duck going through each doorway. *How tall is he?* Lizzy found a few small pans but nothing that would allow them to fix food for a crowd. "I'll need to bring some pots and pans over."

"I can help."

"Thank you, I might take you up on it. Daniel, who's paying for James's funeral?"

"I am, but don't go tellin' no one. It ain't something a man should speak about."

"You can afford it?"

"I have some money set aside. Been savin' for awhile."

"Saving for what?" she asked and sat in the caned chair next to the small kitchen table.

Daniel pulled up another and sat beside her.

"Don't rightly know, really. My momma told me to save as much money as I could. So I save. I suppose it will come in handy if I ever git married."

"Have you found someone?" Lizzy didn't know why she was asking. Perhaps all that marrying talk that Bea, her mother, and she were engaged in earlier.

"No, I cain't say that I has."

Lizzy found herself relieved that no one special was in Daniel's life. Not that she wanted to be the someone special. But somehow she was pleased to know there was no one.

She looked around the room, needing to change the subject. It was her own fault for bringing up such silly conversation. "This is a nice place. Who do you suppose owns it?"

"I do."

"What?" Lizzy peered into his midnight eyes. Oh, a woman could get lost in those eyes.

"James left it to me in his will."

"That's quite a gift."

"I don't know what I be doin' with a house."

Lizzy wanted to scream, *You could give it to me!* But that hardly seemed right or fair. "How many rooms does it have?"

"I don't know. Never counted."

"You could rent rooms, earn a little extra income."

"Perhaps. I don't fancy doin' other people's laundry. Where I rent, they wash my sheets once a week."

"Must be nice." Lizzy chuckled. "I do more laundry than any woman ought to. Four children of my own and their linens, plus my own, keep me hopping. Of course, Clarissa and I do everyone's together—goes faster with the two of us."

"You have a nice home, Lizzy."

"It belongs to my mother. But she's going to give it to George. I don't fit there, Daniel. I need my own place. A place to raise my family. I just can't afford it yet."

"On the plantation we would have as many as ten to a house as small as this room. That's needin' your own place."

"You know how to humble a gal." Was she just being selfish? She knew plenty of folks who had it worse off than she. She shared a room with her girls, the boys shared a room with George Jr., and George and Clarissa had their own room. Their daughters had her mother's old room.

"Miz Lizzy. . ."

"Just 'Lizzy' is fine."

Mo nodded. "Lizzy, would ye do me another favor?"

"Sure, if I can."

Mo reached into his pocket and pulled out an envelope. "James left this for me, next to the will. I wuz wonderin' if'n ye could read it."

"Sure."

"I tried, but he wrote different letters than ye taught me."

Lizzy opened her hand, palm side up, to receive the letter. After opening it, she commented, "Cursive. That's the type of lettering this is. What I'm teaching you is printing, and it's the style of letters for books, newspapers, and such. Cursive is what folks write letters to each other with."

"Why?"

Lizzy chuckled. "I don't know."

Mo wagged his head. "So many things don't make sense to me."

"You're not alone on that score." The handwriting was poor but legible. Lizzy cleared her throat and began to read.

Dear Daniel,
If you're reading this then I'm dead. Don't grieve, Son.

Lizzy paused. "James Earl was your father?"

"No. He just sort of adopted me."

"Oh, sorry." Lizzy continued.

I'm giving you the house in hopes you can use it one day to raise a family. As you know, my Emma and I, we didn't have no children. And I don't have no kin. No real kin. My father was white, my mother one of his slaves. When I grew to be a man, my father bought me this house and asked me never to return to the Bahamas. I was an embarrassment, you might say. He gave me and my mother our freedom and I stole my wife from him. To give you this house is to break the bondage of the past. A free man, with a free house. Find a wife, Mo, and fill the house with children. Don't mourn too long. I'm an old man. And I had a good life. Now, I'm joined with Emma again.

Your friend,
James

Lizzy wiped a tear from her eye. "He was a good friend, Daniel."

Mo fought the tightness in his throat. "Yes, he wuz." *But why didn't he tell me about his past? Why the big secret?* Even in the letter, James never revealed the man's name.

Lizzy folded the letter and placed it back in the envelope. "Here, you'll want to keep this."

Mo's hand trembled as he reached out for the letter. Lizzy grasped his hand with both of hers. He stood, pulling her up with him and embraced her. He needed to connect with someone. He needed her friendship, her warmth, her love.

Chapter 7

The weekend passed quickly. James Earl's funeral service and burial had taken up Lizzy's free time. She was happy to help, though, and so were others, once they learned of James Earl's death. For an old man, he had many acquaintances but few who were close friends.

The next few weeks went by uneventfully. On more than one occasion, Lizzy found herself thinking about James Earl's home and just how large it was. It had three bedrooms, a sitting room, a dining room, and a kitchen. She had to fight envying Daniel's possessions.

More and more women were warming up to Daniel on Sunday mornings at church. Her feelings of jealousy were another sin she had to fight. After all, she wasn't in love with Daniel, and she certainly wasn't looking to be falling in love with him—or anyone.

And just when she thought she had handed her sins to God, she remembered the embrace she had shared with Daniel in James Earl's kitchen. To be wrapped in Daniel's strong and protective arms would get any woman weak in the knees.

Lizzy brushed off her thoughts and continued to do the Sanchez's laundry. She'd taken home some of Mr. Sanchez's white shirts that needed ironing.

"Momma," William yelled, as he ran into the room.

"William, lower your voice. You're not outside. There's no need for yelling in the house."

"Yes, Ma'am." William lowered his head. The poor boy had such a thin body and such large hands and feet. She knew one day he'd be tall, possibly as tall as Daniel. *No*, she thought, *no one was as tall as Daniel!*

"Now, what's the matter?"

"Nothin'."

Lizzy blew out an exasperated breath. "Then what on earth were you yelling for?"

"Oh, Mr. Mo is coming with a wooden crate in his arms, and he says it's full of surprises."

What could he possibly be bringing over here? She placed the iron on the stove and reached the front room as Daniel entered carrying the wooden crate.

"Evenin', all. I'm come bearin' gifts."

"What's this?" Lizzy pointed to the crate.

"I wuz doin' some cleanin' in James's house and found some things I cain't use and thought the children might enjoy."

A circle of enraptured children gathered around Mo, each trying to sneak a peek at the items in the crate, and each trying to be patient and wait. Lizzy chuckled seeing young Henry, George's youngest, reaching out for the crate.

Daniel sat down on the sofa and placed the crate in front of him. "Now, let's see." He slowly lifted the cloth hiding the contents, building the children's curiosity.

"Vanessa." He reached his hand in, then pulled it out, continuing to explain. "I found this here book and thought ye might be interested in it. I think thar are some of the stories ye like readin' in thar."

"Oh, Mr. Mo, thank you." Vanessa cradled the book close to her chest and then she reached over and gave him a hug.

"Now, let's see, what have I got here?"

Lizzy smiled, watching the children lean slightly forward.

"Well, the next gift is for a man, and since none of ye fit that yet, I guess I better pass it over." Daniel winked at Lizzy.

She placed her hand over her grin so the children wouldn't see her laughing at them. All four boys' smiles slipped. Daniel continued, "Of course, someday some of ye will become men."

Benjamin straightened to his full height, followed by George, then Henry. William, who didn't understand, tried to peer inside the crate.

"I reckon since Ben is the oldest. . ."

"But I'm only a month younger than him," George protested.

Daniel scratched his chin. "Hmm, well, we might have a problem here. 'Cept that I know one of you loves the ocean and being on boats."

"That be Ben. I can't swim." George slumped his shoulders.

"All right then, Ben, this here gift is for ye. It's a sextant, and the sailors use it to navigate their ships."

"Oh boy, Ma, look!" Benjamin brought his prize over to her for closer examination.

"It's wonderful, Ben. Don't you think you ought to thank Mr. Greene?"

"Sorry. Thank you, Sir." Ben went over and shook Daniel's hand. Lizzy grinned. He was trying to be such a man. But Daniel didn't settle for that and pulled the boy to him, giving him a big bear hug.

"Now, George, I do has something fer ye."

Daniel again fished through the crate. Lizzy noticed he pulled out a strange figurine. "James told me this is a soldier from the Far East. He said these soldiers were called samurai and were the best soldiers in their country. He also said this type of porcelain came from Japan as well. I don't know much about Japan 'cept what James said, and he didn't know much but the soldier was a man of honor, truthful, and a protector. Would ye like it?" Daniel gently handed the fine porcelain piece to George. "Be careful; it's very delicate," Daniel warned. "It's the kind of thing that best goes on a shelf where one looks at it and imagines."

George's hands trembled as they cupped to receive his new treasure. Lizzy made a mental note to learn what she could about Japan and add it to the child's lessons.

"Now, Sarah, I'm afraid James—not being a lady—didn't leave much to choose from, but I did find some things that belonged to James's wife, Emma. What I have here is a fine bone china teacup with a matching dish. They's come from England, and when I saw the purty flowers on it, I thought of ye."

"Oh, thank you, Mr. Mo, it's beautiful." Sarah hugged Daniel and kissed him on the cheek.

Daniel gave William a spin-top and Henry some glass marbles. And for Olivia he'd found a small, handmade doll with black button eyes. Each child thanked him and ran off to play with the new gifts.

"That was very special, Daniel. Thank you." Lizzy smiled.

"You're welcome. I don't have use fer those things and I figured the young 'uns would enjoy 'em."

"You truly made their day."

Daniel bent down and reached into the crate. "I want ye to have this, Lizzy."

"Oh my, Daniel, it's beautiful." Lizzy held up a glass vase.

"When I saw it, I thought of ye. The colors are so rich and they change in the light. They remind me of yer eyes."

Lizzy blushed. "Thank you."

For the past few weeks she'd been fighting her growing attraction to Daniel. His kind and gentle way was wearing down her resolve not to get involved with another man. What frustrated her were times like this when he'd compliment her but wouldn't go further. *Does he care for me as a man cares for a woman? Or is he just being his typical, kind self?* Lizzy fought down her frustrations and asked, "Can I get you a drink?"

"No, thank ye. I need to get back to cleaning."

"I understand. Are you all moved in and settled?"

"I guess. I don't have much. I'm still havin' trouble livin' in James's home. Somehow it still doesn't feel right."

Lizzy reached out and placed her hand on his forearm. "It'll get better in time."

"I reckon youse is right."

Daniel moved, breaking her connection with him. He bent down and lifted the near-empty crate. "Oh, I almost forgot. Give these to George and Clarissa."

He handed her a linen tablecloth and a spy glass.

"You're sure you don't want these things?"

"Nah, don't have use fer 'em. Someone else should have the pleasure. Good day, Lizzy."

"Good-bye, Daniel." Lizzy found herself wanting to leap in his arms the way

Olivia had and snuggle into his chest. To be wrapped in his arms again. . . She stopped her thoughts abruptly, brushed the heat from her face, and said, "God bless you, Daniel."

🏝

Mo cradled the crate under one arm. He'd come bearing gifts just so he could get a glimpse of Lizzy. Why hadn't he accepted her invitation for a cold drink? Why couldn't he admit to her that he enjoyed her company? Why couldn't he allow himself to forget the past, the pain?

"Caron," he moaned. Had she really loved him? Or had she just seen him as a good man to have as a husband? He'd never know. He'd never return to the plantation to find out. She'd made her choice, and her choice wasn't him.

"Could Lizzy be interested in me as a man, Lord? I saw her blush. Can I be a good father to four children? I never had a father. . . . I'm not sure what a man should do. Ahh, these be just silly thoughts, Lord. Sorry to bother Ye."

Mo decided to work in the yard. He needed good hard physical labor. He wanted to put in a small garden in the back for vegetables. Flowers would be pretty for the front, but those were extra. Food would be best. It was getting to the hottest months, so he didn't know which foods to plant; he'd have to ask around. One thing he enjoyed about Mr. Ellis's home was the various fruit trees. Mo thought he'd like to plant banana, passion fruit, and coconut palm trees first. He worked hard, digging and hoeing, getting the small patch of earth ready for some planting.

🏝

Days later he found himself back at Lizzy's for his scheduled lesson. Reading children's books had a way of humbling a man, but he began to feel good about what he was accomplishing.

"Excellent, Daniel. You're really catching on quickly."

Mo's heart thumped in his chest. It meant more to him to make her proud than it did to actually have achieved anything in his reading and writing. "Thank ye."

"Daniel." She reached across the table and picked up a small leather-bound book. "I'd like to give you this."

He reached for the thick book and read the words. "A Bible?"

"It's a gift."

The dim light of the lamp darkened her hazel eyes. Their twinkling green rays captivated him.

"Daniel, I have other books to share with you. The works of former slaves like yourself. Frederick Douglass and William Wells Brown. But when I was reading over them they just didn't seem like the right pieces of literature to learn to begin reading. I mean, they bring the anger out in me; I can't imagine them not bringing the anger and memories out in you."

He glanced down at the Holy Word in his hand. His fingers followed the leather binding of the book, its ribbed edges and fine gold leaf lettering, worn over the years, but sparkling as if they were fresh golden hay glistening in the sun. His own book. His first book.

Lizzy continued, "I also have some older books written by black authors—poetry from Phillis Wheatley and Jupiter Hammon. But poetry is harder to comprehend. That's why I settled on God's Word. It'll be difficult in some places, but the truth will also minister to you as well."

His voice caught. "Thank ye, Lizzy."

"You're welcome. Take it home. Read what you can, and we'll discuss it next time."

He stood up, still stunned by the thoughtfulness of the gift. *My own Bible.*

She took back the Bible for a moment and opened it a few pages from the beginning. "Start reading here."

"G-E-N. . . ," he began to spell out the larger word on the top of the page.

"Genesis," she supplied.

Mo smiled and repeated. "Genesis. Thank ye, Lizzy."

"In the beginning," he continued to read out loud. He paused and looked at the pleasure in her eyes. "Ye is a fine teacher, Lizzy."

She placed her hand lightly on his. "You're a fine student, Daniel. I've not had a finer."

Daniel felt his chest swell with pride. He never considered himself a vain man, but when Lizzy complimented him, he felt an overwhelming need to do even better the next time. "I must be going. Mr. Ellis needs me before the sun rises tomorrow."

She led him to the door. "Good night, Daniel."

"Good night, Lizzy." He fought off the desire to kiss her on the cheek, to thank her for such a generous gift. He knew his feelings for her were developing beyond simple friendship, and he didn't trust his reasons for wanting to kiss her. He stepped into the cool dark air and waved.

Daniel gazed into the night sky of black velvet peppered with sparkling white stars. A ring of midnight blue encircled the moon. "Oh, Lord, Ye be a mighty fine painter tonight."

Chapter 8

Lizzy cuddled up beside Sarah as the gentle pink and purple hues of predawn sunlight filtered through her screened window. She brushed the soft curls away from her daughter's face. Sarah stirred in her arms. Her eyes slowly fluttered open. " 'Morning, Momma."

"Good morning, Sweetheart."

"Do I hafta stay with Aunt Clarissa today?"

"You know you do. What's the matter?"

"Nothing. It's just that I'd like to spend more time with you. Vanessa just reads all day, and Liv plays with Henry and William. Ben and George are always off doing boy stuff like catching lizards and snakes. Aunt Clarissa is all right, but she's got to work in the kitchen and around the house. A girl can only spend so long in the kitchen."

Lizzy suppressed a giggle. Her poor daughter didn't know the half of how long a woman actually spends in the kitchen. "I see—so you're by yourself most of the time."

Sarah nodded. She was Lizzy's quieter child. If any child could really be described as quiet, Sarah fit the bill. Lizzy sighed. "As much as I'd love to bring you with me to work, I'm afraid I simply can't do it. Mr. Sanchez has rules."

"I know, Momma, I just wished you didn't have to work. Liv doesn't like it either."

"And neither do I. But the good Lord decided I needed a job to help take care of you since your daddy passed. So I should do it the best I can."

Sarah snuggled closer. "Why did Daddy have to die?"

"I don't know, Child. I really don't know." Lizzy felt her stomach tighten. She wished she had the answers. Truth be told, she was still working on finding them for herself. She pulled Sarah close to her heart. "I love you, Princess."

"I love you too, Momma."

"I miss you too," Lizzy sympathized.

Sarah's head nodded up and down on her chest.

Oh, Lord, I know You have a plan, but I'm fresh out of answers. I wish I understood why You took Benjamin when You did. I know it was a bullet that killed him, and war is something You don't cotton to, but—leaving me with four young 'uns. . . It just doesn't seem fair.

"Momma, what are we studying today when you come home from work?" Sarah pushed away from her mother's chest and looked at her from deep toffee eyes, her father's eyes.

Lizzy closed her eyes for a moment and pictured Ben and how proud he had been to go and fight for the cause. The war was won and now she could teach her children to read and write and not be afraid of being arrested. *You helped do that, Ben.* She whispered a prayer of thanks.

She opened her eyes and met her daughter's imploring gaze. "I think today we'll take a picnic and play at the beach."

"No schoolin'?" Sarah bounced up in the bed.

Lizzy chuckled. "No schooling."

Sarah embraced her with a big hug. Her bouncing woke Olivia. In moments Lizzy found herself being danced around by two gentle sprites, happy with life, happy to be alive.

Taking in a deep breath and letting it out slowly, she recommitted herself to moving forward with her life. For the sake of the children, for the sake of the cause. Her children would be smarter than her; her grandchildren would be even more educated. In the end, she believed, a Negro would have as much education as a white person and the freedom to rejoice in it.

Mo dove into the crystal blue water. Everything on and around Key West seemed cleaner, purer, so incredibly different than plantation life. The muddy brown water of the Mississippi with its swirling eddies were like the pits of despair, nothing like the transparent blue seas of the tropical island. The fish in their brilliant colors danced in the sea, unlike the dark brown and black bottom-feeding catfish of the Mississippi. Even the birds here wore vivid colors of reds, yellows, and greens, while on the plantation he had seen only brown barn swallows. . . . He reached for the sponge with his left hand, lifted it slightly, and cut it from the coral reef with the knife in his right.

He rarely dove in and cut the sponges now, but the need to enjoy the warm water and the beauty of God's creation drove him through its cleansing waves. With enough air in his lungs, he cut additional sponges. A strong kick of his legs brought his head through the surface of the water. He gulped in some fresh air and dove again, filling the net hitched to his waist with sponges. The net full, he swam up to the skiff and climbed aboard.

Once in port, he unloaded the boat and set the sponges in the fresh water vat.

"Good haul, Mo." Ellis slapped him on the back.

"Thank ye, Suh."

"Did you want to go over the ledgers again this afternoon?"

If Ellis was asking if he wanted to, as in really looking forward to getting into his books, the answer was no. "Sure," Mo said.

Ellis chuckled. "Such enthusiasm."

"I's not sure I'll ever understand dem books."

"You will. You already recognize all the words on the columns."

"Yes, Suh, but I'm thinkin' my mind ain't made for addin' and subtractin'."

He'd been trying to learn Ellis's books for months now. *It sure didn't take this long to learn to read from Miss Lizzy.*

Ellis roared with laughter. "Come on."

Mo put his shirt back on and headed into the small building at the end of the wharf. Ellis stood in the center with his hands on his hips. "You know, I think I'm going to build another building at the end of the dock on shore. We need more room."

"Want me and the men to help build it?"

"Possibly." Ellis scratched his beard. "Need to think on it for a bit."

Mo placed the ledger on top of the small desk.

"How's the house coming along?" Ellis moved to the desk, sat on the stool beside it, and grabbed a pen.

"Fine, fine. Most of the extra things a man don't need I've given away. The garden is in; top soil ain't too thick."

"It isn't like the North." Ellis placed his hand on a set of figures.

"Mr. Mo! Mr. Mo!" Benjamin came running up the dock.

"Benjamin?" Trailing behind him was George. "What's the matter?"

"I'm not sure. Momma came home in tears. I've never seen her this way. Uncle George and Aunt Clarissa went to Key Visca. They won't be back 'til tomorrow. I didn't know who else to come to, 'cept you and Mr. Ellis." Benjamin nodded toward Ellis as he stepped out of the shed.

"May I leave, Mr. Ellis?" Mo turned to his boss.

"Please—find out what's wrong. Have one of the boys come back and tell me if everything is all right."

Mo nodded and made it to shore in a dozen large steps.

"Wait for me," Benjamin cried.

Daniel stopped. *Lord, I don't know what's wrong with Lizzy, but please help me to be able to help her.*

🛉

Lizzy locked her bedroom door and flung herself on the bed. Tears burned her cheeks. "How dare he!" she fumed. She threw a pillow across the room, hitting a picture frame so that it hung crooked on the wall.

"Momma, are you all right?" Sarah knocked on the door.

"I'm fine, Honey. I just need to be alone for a few minutes." She knew she wasn't convincing anyone, least of all her children, who knew her better than anyone else. How could she hide this evil from them? How could she provide for them? She couldn't go back to work. *Not now. Not there.*

Lizzy's heart wrenched deep inside. She cradled another pillow to her chest. What was she going to do?

Certainly not what Mr. Sanchez wants, she determined, bolstering her resolve. But how could she go back to that house, knowing what he wanted, knowing she was putting her very virtue at risk. He'd nearly assaulted her this morning.

Her mind flashed back to his hot breath on her neck, his arms. . . Shaking her head to remove the images, she tightened her grasp around the pillow. Olivia's pillow. Her daughter's pure scent filled her nostrils. She breathed in deeply, holding in the memory of her daughter, her innocence. Her sweet daughter.

"Oh, God, help me. Why? Why? Why did he have to do this?" She curled up into a ball.

Mo entered the house and found the group of children huddled around Lizzy's bedroom door.

"Mr. Mo," Sarah sniffled, wiping a tear from her eye.

"Is she in there?" Of course she was in there. He needed to help the children calm down. He needed to calm down. "Tell me what happened."

Olivia ran to him and hugged his legs. He leaned down and picked her up. "She's goin' to be okay." He prayed his words were true. "Come on, children, let's do something special for yer Momma."

"What?" William whispered. His thin little limbs shook with fear.

"I say we make a fancy dinner for her and set the table up real special like."

"How?" George Jr. asked.

"By picking some flowers to put on the table. William, ye and Henry are in charge of gettin' the flowers. Ben, ye and George can go to town and git me some things for supper." Mo reached into his pocket and pulled out some coins. "Vanessa, ye and Sarah can help in the kitchen."

"You know how to cook?" Sarah knitted her eyebrows.

"Not like yer mother, but I can do a fair job."

Olivia clung to his neck. "Liv, you'll set the table. Let's see, what should we have fer supper?" He tapped his foot and looked up at the ceiling, then peeked a glance at the children. It was working; he was getting their attention on him and less on Lizzy.

"I know." He squatted down to meet the children's gazes. "Word is, a new shipment of beef came in from Cuba today. Why don't we fetch some?"

The children all nodded their heads. "Okay, boys, you're in charge of getting the meat. Girls, put on some rice and beans. William, Henry, don't forget the flowers."

They all ran to their appointed tasks.

After a few minutes Olivia slid out of his arms and began putting the plates on the table. Holding a plate in two hands, she looked up. "Momma was going to take us on a picnic today."

"I'm sure she'll take ye another day."

Olivia placed the plate down and put her hands on her hips. She sucked in her lower lip and wrinkled her forehead, lifting one eyebrow. "I think you're right." She removed her hands from her hips and stepped to the sideboard to retrieve another plate. "I don't like it when mommas are sick."

"I don't like it either, Sweetheart. Why don't I go and see if yer ma needs anythin'?"

"I think that be good, Mr. Mo." Olivia put another plate on the table. A grin inched up his cheek.

Mo slipped down the hall and tapped the bedroom door with his knuckle.

He paused and listened. He waited.

No response.

He tapped again a little louder. Again he waited.

Again no response.

He tapped again and spoke softly, "Lizzy, it's me, Daniel."

He heard her moan. His stomach twisted inside. Should he open the door? Should he give her more time?

"Lizzy, may I come in?" He heard the bed creak.

Chapter 9

Oh, Lord, I can't face Daniel. Not now, not like this. Please, send him away.

"Lizzy, speak to me or I'm gonna open this door."

She heard him check the doorknob.

"Lizzy, I'll break down the door. Speak to me." His voice became firmer, more determined.

She closed her eyes and pictured him standing on the other side of the door. A smile touched her lips at the thought of him shifting his huge frame against her door. She couldn't picture anything withstanding a direct assault from Daniel.

"Lizzy?" His voice raised another notch. "Last warning."

"Daniel, no. I'm fine."

"Ye ain't fine. But I'll not push ye fer more. I'm just letting ye know that in about an hour the children are putting together a dinner fer ye. Something special. Will ye be ready to come out by then?"

"I–I. . . ," she whispered.

"Lizzy?"

She heard him grumble and stomp off. Lizzy took in a deep breath. At least she didn't have to face him right now. What should she tell him? She curled back into the fetal position on the bed, hugging Olivia's pillow again. Her thoughts drifted to Sarah. Was it just this morning when she awoke with no fears, enjoying her daughter, the day, life?

The distant sound of scraping metal tickled her ears. What was that? What were they doing out there? Lizzy sat up on the bed just as her bedroom door opened.

"Lizzy?" Mo stood in her doorway.

She flung Sarah's pillow at him. He simply stood there, not catching it, not picking it up. Nothing.

"What happened, Lizzy? Are ye all right?" he asked.

Lizzy could feel her entire body begin to shake.

In one large step Mo had crossed the room from the door to her bedside. He picked her up in his arms and cradled her. She wrapped her arms around his neck and cried into his shoulder.

He sat on the bed, still holding her in his arms, and rocked her. Setting her on his lap, he raised a hand and brushed the tears from her face. "No one. . ." His voice faltered. "No one. . .took liberties with ye?" he asked.

She shook her head no. But could she tell him that Mr. Sanchez had wanted to?

He rocked her some more. She felt like a child again, sitting in her father's lap. All the comfort, love, and security her father had for her she felt coming from Daniel.

She heard Benjamin yell, "Mr. Mo, we got some beef."

"Bring it to the kitchen," Mo called back to them. "I don't want to leave ye like this, Lizzy," he whispered against her arm.

"I'll be all right." She sniffed.

"Ye take some more time to yourself. The children and I have everything under control. If ye come to dinner, it'll mean a lot to the children. But if'n ye can't, I can explain it to them. I'll have the older ones take care of the younger ones with regard to getting them ready for bed after dinner. But after those young 'uns are settled, youse and me is goin' to have a talk. I don't know what happened, but I'm fightin' all sorts of horrible images in my mind. I told Olivia ye probably didn't feel well. They need answers, Lizzy. They're scared. I'll help, but they need their mother to tell them everythin' is goin' to be all right."

"I'll come out for dinner."

"Good." Daniel lifted her up off his lap and placed her on the bed.

He lifted me like I was no more than a ten-pound sack of flour, she mused. She reached for his arm. "Thank you."

He took her hand in his and tenderly kissed it. "You're welcome."

He released her hand, cherishing the tender trail her fingers left as they pulled away from his. *Goodness, Lord, I'm gettin' mighty strong feelin's fer this woman. I just don't know if I can be a father to four children. And no man ought to awaken desire in a woman if'n he cain't take on her young 'uns as his own.* Daniel closed the door behind him. He found the older boys were sitting in the living room.

Benjamin had his arms crossed and his hands hitched up under his armpits. *The poor fellow probably doesn't know what to do with himself.*

"How is she?" Ben asked.

"Better. She asked fer a few more minutes." Daniel came over and placed a hand on the boy's shoulder. "She's goin' to be just fine."

"What happened?" Ben pushed.

"I don't know, but I suspect someone said somethin' to hurt her feelings."

George jumped up. "Who? I'll go take care of 'em."

He couldn't fault the boy for having the same feelings as himself. "Ye set yourself right down in that chair. I knows your mom and dad didn't teach you to fight first."

George hung his head. "No, Sir," he mumbled.

"Look, boys, ye bein' the oldest boys, I'm goin' to need yer help. I ain't never had no young 'uns, and I'm not sure what to do, so can ye help me?" Both boys stood taller, puffed out their chests, and gave him a nod. "Why don't ye see if Olivia needs any more help settin' the table."

They scurried off and Daniel glanced at Lizzy's door. Tonight ought to be a good test as to whether or not he could take on the responsibility of another man's children. It wasn't that he didn't love children or that he didn't already feel a bond to Lizzy's children. He just wasn't sure what a man should do to help raise a child. Being a slave took away your rights to your children. You could be sold, or your children sold, with no say in the matter. *We was property, Lord. Just plain old property. At times we didn't even feel human.* Mo fought the bile rising in his stomach. "Chattel, Lord, nothing but chattel," he muttered out loud.

"What's chattel, Mo?" William asked, as he entered the house carrying an array of bright red, orange, and yellow flowers.

"It's the name for what the white slave owners call their slaves. It means property."

"What's property?" William stood beside him.

Daniel squatted down beside the boy and placed his hand on the boy's shoulder. His innocent brown eyes bore into him. A free child. A boy that will never know slavery. *Thank Ye, Lord, fer that.*

"Property is something ye own. Like yer shoes and clothes."

"So being a slave means someone owns you?"

"Yes." Daniel's throat tightened.

"My daddy went to fight to free the slaves."

"Your daddy wuz a brave man."

William nodded. "Mr. Mo, why do you have scars on your wrists?"

The boy didn't know half of his scars. Mo had caught a glimpse of his own back once in a mirror and winced at the sight. "I wuz in chains from time to time as a slave."

"Why?"

"Mostly 'cause my master seemed mighty afraid of me."

"Why?"

Daniel chuckled. "Well, 'cause I'm a big man, and I'm a very dark man."

"But you don't scare me," William protested.

"Thank ye, Son." Mo rubbed the top of William's head. "We best put dem flowers in some water or they won't be lookin' so nice for yer momma."

"Mr. Mo," Vanessa called.

Maybe tonight's more of a warnin' that I cain't handle a pack of young 'uns. Mo rose from his squatting position and headed into the kitchen.

"I'm not sure how you want to cook this meat." Vanessa spread her hand over a large hunk of red and white marbled beef.

"George, where did the butcher say this here meat came from?" Mo asked.

George peeked around the corner. "Said it was from the rump. Called it a rump roast."

"Thanks." Daniel looked over the thick hunk of beef. It was too late to cook it in an oven, or even on a spit over an open fire. "Let me have the knife." He reached his hand out and she placed a large knife with a wooden handle in his hand.

"Let's make steaks. I'll cut up the meat and ye can fry 'em in the pan."

"All right. Should I season it?" Vanessa asked.

"Yes. Salt, pepper, and sauteed onions and garlic, if ye have some."

"I can cut up some green onions," Sarah offered.

"Sounds wonderful." Mo sliced the beef into inch-thick slabs. "These leftover pieces can be put into a pot for some soup tomorrow." Mo gathered a small pile of ends and tips of the meat. "Or they can be dried."

"I'll ask Aunt Lizzy after she comes out." Vanessa placed her tiny hand on his. "Is she okay?"

"Yes, she'll be fine."

Vanessa nodded her head and went right to work frying up the steaks.

"Smells delicious." Lizzy entered the kitchen and winked at him. "Daniel, you didn't tell me you knew how to work in a kitchen."

"Been on my own for a few years. A man learns to cook or he starves."

Lizzy chuckled. "You ought to get yourself a wife."

Mo felt his face grow warm. He was thankful that his skin's dark tones would not reveal too much.

"Momma, I cut the onions," Sarah boasted.

"And you did a mighty fine job too." Lizzy hugged her daughter.

"Are you feeling better, Momma?"

Daniel watched the interchange between mother and daughter. *Lizzy's a good mother*, he silently praised.

"Yes, Sweetheart. I'm much better now."

"What happened?"

"Someone said some bad things to me."

"I'm sorry, Momma. Jesus says we're not to say bad things. Maybe the bad person doesn't know Jesus."

"You may be right, Child."

"Aunt Lizzy, I'm frying steaks." Vanessa smiled.

"I thought I smelled something wonderful. Where'd we get the beef?"

George and Benjamin walked in. "We got it."

Lizzy caught Daniel's gaze and mouthed a silent thank you. He smiled back. "Fine shoppers, these boys. Came home with a rump roast."

"Rump, huh?" Lizzy giggled.

"Well, it sounds a lot better than buttocks." Daniel grinned. It was wonderful seeing the tension ease. In the corner of Lizzy's eyes he saw the strain. She was putting up an excellent front, a front for her children. Tonight would take all of his self-control, he knew. Once she told him what he suspected, he would need every ounce of his strength to keep himself planted in the room and not find the person, probably a man, who had mistreated her.

"Eww," Henry groaned. "I ain't eating somebody's buttocks."

"Nope, you'll be eating steak."

"Oh, okay. Who said it was buttocks?" The room erupted into laughter.

Lizzy watched Daniel as he worked with the children. They all seemed genuinely enamored with him. He sat on the chair and allowed them to climb on him or huddle close to him. Dinner had been wonderful. The children had gone out of their way to be perfect ladies and gentlemen. Lizzy sighed. Daniel and the children in the chair were living shadows of what her life would have been like if Ben hadn't been killed in the war.

She knew Mr. Sanchez would never have made his rude suggestion if Ben hadn't died. Lizzy felt her blood rise a notch. She didn't want to tell Daniel, and yet she figured he probably guessed what must have happened.

Lizzy recalled being in Daniel's tender embrace. So gentle, so kind, so. . .loving? Daniel? She shook the thought off. He'd have been that way with anyone. Wouldn't he?

She snatched a glimpse of his mahogany eyes, his rugged chin, and wonderfully full lips. Lips? What on earth was she doing looking at his lips? She dropped her gaze immediately.

The hour was late and she needed to put the children to bed. On the other hand, if she put them to bed, she'd have to discuss the day's events with Daniel. But she'd put off sending them to bed long enough. "It's that time."

"Oh, Momma," four of them whined. The other three simply moaned, "Do we hafta?"

"Yes. Now, go get yourselves ready and I'll be in to say your prayers with each of you. Scoot."

"Good night, Mr. Mo." Olivia reached up and hugged him, giving him a kiss on the cheek.

"Good night, Mr. Mo," the chorus chimed in. Each gave him a hug and kiss. She watched his eyes pool with unshed tears. For a tree-trunk of a man, he had the most tender heart she'd ever seen.

"Good night, young 'uns. Ye did a mighty fine job tonight. I'm mighty proud of y'all."

They each beamed from his praise.

"Momma, can Mr. Mo say our prayers with us?" William asked.

Lizzy glanced back at Daniel. "Would you like to?"

"I'd be honored."

"Mine too?" A chorus then ensued: "Me. . . Me. . . Me!"

Lizzy chuckled. "All right, if Mr. Mo is up for it."

Daniel grinned. "I think y'all is just tryin' to stay up a few extra minutes. But I'll come and listen to yer prayers. Shoo now."

The seven all ran to their rooms. Lizzy could hear them tossing their shoes and clothing off. "Thank you, Daniel."

"You're welcome. Why don't ye fix us some tea or hot cocoa while I git the little ones settled."

"Sure. You don't have to stay. I'm fine." She hoped he'd take the hint.

His eyes burrowed deep into her soul. "No, I don't think ye be fine yet. We need to talk, Lizzy. Ye need to tell someone."

"But. . ."

"Shh." He stepped up beside her and cradled her in his arms. Her defenses vanished. He was such a kind man. He'd understand. She hoped.

When Daniel released her, her knees wobbled. Maybe she did need his strength tonight. Maybe she should go see her mother. She'd know what to do. Perhaps Daniel would stay while the children slept so she could visit her mom.

Lizzy curled her lower lip and nibbled it. *Well, Lizzy old girl, you best be making the man some tea unless you're wanting to impose upon him some more.*

Mechanically, she worked her way around the kitchen. Water, tea kettle, stove, fire. . . She reminded herself what to do at each step. Then she stared off into space. Another kitchen came into focus.

Mr. Sanchez entered the room as she worked with Mrs. Sanchez's dress, pressing it, getting every wrinkle out.

"Lizzy, I know you're finding it hard to make ends meet."

A surge of joy entered her. Perhaps the Sanchezes knew of another family who needed some extra help around the house. "Yes."

"Well, I have a proposition for you." His smile tightened. His gaze shifted down from her face to her bosom. Oh, God, no, please, stop him, Lord, *she silently prayed. She grasped the iron more tightly as she counted the steps to the back door.*

"Don't be frightened. I'm just offering you some extra income to be my mistress."

"No!" she protested.

"I won't hurt you, Lizzy. A man needs. . ."

"Lizzy?" Daniel's voice drew her from the memory. "Lizzy, are ye all right?"

"Oh, Daniel." She fell into his arms. "It was horrible. I said no. I told him no, several times."

"Did he take advantage of ye?"

"No, he just spoke such vile things. Things private between a husband and wife. I–I. . ."

"Who was it, Lizzy? I'll take care of him. He won't be sayin' anythin' like that to ye again," Daniel fumed.

Chapter 10

Daniel held Lizzy in his arms with all the tenderness he could muster. A part of him wanted to strike out so badly he could taste the coppery scent of blood. "Who, Lizzy?"

"No, Daniel. You can't; you'll be arrested."

"So, he wasn't Negro."

She tossed her head back and forth, saying "no" into his chest. He caressed her hair. It felt like fine wool already spun and ready for making a soft sweater.

"Who, Lizzy? He cain't get away with this."

"He didn't touch me. He tried but. . ."

The angry flames of justice burned more deeply in his chest. "Who, Lizzy?"

"No, Daniel. You'll be arrested. I can't allow that. I'm all right. He didn't touch me."

"No. It ain't right. A man should not take such liberties with a woman. Ye a free woman, not some slave given to her master's whims. I won't stand fer it. Tell me who, Lizzy."

Lizzy clutched his shirt. Her hot tears fell on his chest.

He cradled her more gently. "Shh. I won't push ye any further, Lizzy."

"Thank you, Daniel."

The tea kettle whistled.

"Come, let's have something to drink." He led her to the table. Somehow he needed to get her to talk with him. To confide in him. But pushing her obviously wouldn't work. *Help me, Lord.*

Lizzy left his arms and wrapped a cloth around the handle of the kettle. She poured the hot water into the earthen mugs and set some tea leaves on top.

Daniel rubbed the day-old growth on his chin. By this time of night he usually shaved if he was going to be seeing folks in the evening. "If I promise not to beat the man mere inches from his life, will ye tell me who it is?"

"Daniel." She placed her hand on his. He grasped it, her long, delicate fingers such a contrast to his own thick ones.

"It's just not right, Lizzy."

"No, it's not. But what can we do about it? Folks just think because of the color of our skin. . ."

"No, Lizzy, that's not true. It's taken me a lot of years to realize that, but I've seen good men and bad men, and they come in all colors."

"I suppose you're right. But. . ."

"Ye think he made the proposition just because ye were a Negro?"

"I don't know." She grasped her mug and spooned in some raw sugarcane. He did likewise. "Maybe he just thought I'd be easy."

"Maybe. But why do ye think that?"

" 'Cause he knows I need the money."

"He was offerin' to pay ye to, to. . ."

"Yes," she whispered.

Daniel clamped his jaw shut. What he was about to say wasn't pleasant, and he wasn't so sure he could keep the volume down so as not to wake the children. He contained his reactions and looked more closely at Lizzy. "Oh, Lizzy." He was beside her in seconds. The woman was trembling. "I promise not to hurt the man, and I'm sorry I'm more caught up in my own anger than seein' yer pain. Forgive me."

Hot tears flowed down her cheeks. She couldn't believe Daniel was asking for forgiveness. He'd been a perfect gentleman. "Oh, Daniel, you've done nothing to be forgiven for."

"I put myself before ye. Ain't Christian."

She looped her arms around his strong and massive neck. He pulled her up and cradled her in his arms. She held him tighter. "I was going to ask you to stay with the children while I ran to see my mother."

"I don't want ye out on the streets like this, Lizzy. It ain't safe."

Lizzy swallowed. He was probably right.

"Lizzy, wuz it your boss, Mr. Sanchez?"

She tried to hide her reaction.

"I thought as much." He carried her into the living room and placed her on the sofa. "I'll walk ye to and from work. He'll see me and he won't try anythin' with ye."

"I can't ask you to do that."

"I cain't see ye goin' back to his house. He'll keep comin' and askin'. Can ye find another job?"

"No, I haven't been successful. The island's income hasn't been all that high since the beginning of the war. Not too many folks can afford to pay for extra staff."

"I don't like it, Lizzy. I'll need to come with ye. He won't touch ye, once he sees me."

Lizzy grasped his hands. "No, Daniel, he'll have you arrested. It's as you say—he'd be terrified of you. He'd find a reason to get you in trouble."

"Ye cain't arrest a man for nothin'."

"No, but I wouldn't put it past him to make up lies and say you did something you didn't do." As fair as the sheriff had been to Negroes, she still didn't trust him not to believe the opinion of another person over a black person. No, she couldn't put Daniel in harm's way just to protect her virtue.

"Then ye cain't return to work."

"I need the income."

"God will provide another job. Ye cain't go back."

"I have no choice, Daniel."

"Elizabeth Hunte, ye do have a choice. Youse a free woman; ye ain't a slave." If she wasn't going to allow him to walk her to and from work, then he'd have to see that she didn't go back to the job. He needed to protect her. He understood her need to provide for her family. In fact, it was one of the things that made her so special to him. *Yes, Lord, she is special to me*, he silently admitted.

Fresh tears streamed down her face.

"I knows what it's like to have no choice. But ye do, and God will provide."

"What do I tell Mrs. Sanchez? I—I just don't know what to do."

Daniel reached over and wrapped a protective arm around her shoulders. *She's so fragile, Lord. I needs to say the right thing. Help me.* "Lizzy, I can help with yer expenses until ye find a new job."

"I couldn't take your money, Daniel."

"Sure ye could. I don't need what I used to since James gave me his house."

"No, Daniel, it wouldn't be right."

It wasn't fair. No man should take advantage of a woman. He was fighting the urge to pay a midnight visit to Mr. Manuel Sanchez, but he'd given his word to Lizzy that he wouldn't beat the man. On the other hand, she probably was right that if Sanchez saw him, he'd call the sheriff and claim Mo had come looking for him. And what was Mo's connection to Lizzy other than friendship? It wasn't like he was her husband, and. . . "Lizzy, I've got it. Ye and I need to git married. Mr. Sanchez wouldn't dare lay a hand on ye if'n he knows ye is married to me. And the sheriff wouldn't be blaming a man fer protecting his wife."

"Marry you?"

"Yeah. Look, I have a big house, more room than a single man needs. I can provide fer ye and the children, Lizzy."

Lizzy pushed herself away from him. Her gaze locked with his. "You're asking me to marry you for my honor?"

"Yes. I guess I am." Did she not want to be married to a man such as himself? Perhaps his lack of education was a problem. "It wouldn't have to be a real marriage. I could be your husband in name only. You'd be protected."

"Let me get this straight. You're not offering me marriage out of love, just offering marriage for protection?"

"Yes." Daniel looked at her. *I'm missing something here. She's looking mighty angry, Lord.*

"No, Daniel. I can't marry you for that." Lizzy got up and walked across the room. "Daniel, I've had a long, hard day. Please don't take this the wrong way, but would you please leave?" Her voice was tight.

He rose from the sofa. "I'm sorry to have offended ye, Lizzy. I should have known." Silently he left her house.

Outside, he hurried off her property and ran toward the ocean. "Oh, God, I said it all wrong. I wuz just tryin' to help." He ripped off his shirt and flung his shoes down to the sand. He needed to work off his anger, his frustration. He dove into the ocean and began to swim. Long, hard thrusts with his powerful arms and mighty kicks with his legs pulled him farther and farther from shore. Swimming at night in the tropics wasn't the wisest of choices, but he almost wished a barracuda would come after him so he could rip it apart with his bare hands.

Lizzy gripped her sides. Not only had Mr. Sanchez propositioned her, but Daniel had decided to marry her, not out of love or romance, but just as an excuse to give him the right to walk her to work. Lizzy paced the front room back and forth. Each step brought renewed anger. She needed to talk with her mother, to someone, anyone. No, that wasn't true. She had talked with Daniel, and it only made her more upset than if she'd kept what had happened to herself. She was such a fool. *A man just doesn't understand, Lord.*

She looked out her side window to see if her neighbors still had a light on. A warm glow emanated from the back bedroom. *They're down for the night, but they aren't asleep yet.* Lizzy hurried over to their house and feverishly knocked on their door.

"Lizzy, what's the matter?" Mabel Jones clutched her nightclothes shut under her chin.

"I need a favor. I have to run and see my mother about something. Could you sit with the children? George and Clarissa are away."

"Of course. Let me get my robe and I'll come right over."

"Thank you." Lizzy hurried back home. With seven kids it was always possible to have at least one wake up in the middle of the night.

Soon Mabel knocked on her front door.

"Thanks so much for coming."

"Are you sure you're all right?"

"Fine." Lizzy looked away from Mabel's imploring gaze. "I just need to speak with my mother."

Mabel reached out and touched her shoulder. "Lizzy, I don't know what happened, but your young 'uns were all upset about your coming home crying. When I saw Mo Greene come over I figured you'd be all right. He didn't hurt you, did he?"

"Oh, goodness, no. Daniel's as gentle as a lamb."

"Daniel?" Mabel's puzzled look spoke volumes.

"Sorry. Mo's given name is Daniel. I've found it fits him better than Mo. So I tend to call him Daniel."

Mabel nodded. "You go speak with your momma. If anyone can help you see straight it's Francine. God's given her a mighty fine gift to look right to the heart of a matter."

"Thanks for understanding. I'll be back as soon as I can. You can lay down on George and Clarissa's bed if you get tired," Lizzy offered.

"I might just do that. Now run along, Child, and be careful."

"I will, thanks."

Lizzy sprinted toward Ellis Southard's home. *Father, keep Mom awake for me. I need her, Lord.* She rounded the corner and saw a lamp burning in the front parlor. Relief washed over her.

She lightly knocked on the large oak door. Bea answered it. "Lizzy, what's the matter?"

"I need to speak with my mother," she explained, holding back her tears.

"Come in, come in. Are you all right?"

Lizzy nodded.

Bea wrapped her arm around Lizzy and led her to the front sitting room. "You sit down and I'll get Cook."

Bea walked down the hall toward Lizzy's mother's room. Lizzy could hear mumbling, followed by, "Lizzy?"

Without taking the time to put on a robe, her mother entered the sitting room in her nightclothes. "What's the matter to bring you out so late at night?"

"Oh, Mom." Fresh tears trailed down her cheeks. Francine came up beside her on the sofa and enveloped her with her ample arms. Bea brought in her mother's robe and whispered something about tea.

"Tell me what happened, Dear." Francine stood and put on her robe.

"Oh, Mom, it was horrible. Mr. Sanchez wanted to hire me to be his mistress. I've never felt so, so sick in all my life. I've been working for them for years and he's never even looked at me in such a way. It just doesn't make sense."

"Of course it makes sense. 'Tis rude and unforgivable, but it makes sense. You're a widow, Lizzy. A beautiful widow. Men get to thinkin' you're lonely and will be easy."

"Easy!" Lizzy huffed. "If I'd done half the things my mind wanted to do to him, he would have no question I am not easy."

Francine chuckled. "No, I imagine not. Being propositioned comes with being a widow, I'm afraid. Men—not all, but some men—are full of sin, and they gets themselves in such bad ways they can't think straight."

"After Daddy died, did, did. . ."

"Of course, I had offers. Didn't have a mind to take anyone up on them. Those kind of men don't appeal to me. Besides, I'm older. I had far more years with George than you had with Ben."

"What am I going to do? I'm afraid to go back to work. Daniel said I shouldn't."

Francine raised her eyebrows.

"The children ran and got him when I came home crying."

"And Mr. Ellis ain't come home yet, had dinner and meetings in town this evenin' or else he would have told me and I would have come over. Curious, the children didn't fetch me."

"Actually, I believe they tried, but you weren't home."

"Must have been when I was in town doing some shopping. In fact, I thought I saw George and Benjamin buying some meat at the butcher's."

"Yeah, Daniel had the kids make me a special dinner. Vanessa fried up some steaks."

"Sounds nice. So is Daniel with the children now?"

Bea brought in a teapot and cups. "I won't intrude, but I thought you might like a cup of tea. And this."

Bea handed her a fine white handkerchief.

"Thanks. You can stay."

"Oh, good. Otherwise, I'd have to pump your mother full of questions after you left." Bea settled on a chair opposite the sofa.

Lizzy chuckled and quickly recounted Mr. Sanchez's vile offer.

"Mo knows?" her mother asked.

"Yes, but only after I made him promise not to kill the man. I don't want him being arrested trying to protect my honor. In fact, he wanted to walk me to work to put the fear of God into Mr. Sanchez."

"Sounds like a wise idea." Francine picked up her cup of tea.

"No, Mother, I can't let him do that. Mr. Sanchez might make up something so Daniel would end up in jail."

"Hmm, you might be right there."

"How could he?" Bea asked.

Lizzy looked at her mother. She loved Bea, but sometimes she didn't have a clue what it was like to be living in this world with dark skin. Bea didn't see skin color, and Lizzy cherished that about her.

"Because he's a very dark Negro. If Mr. Sanchez was afraid enough of him, he might lie."

"But Mo can tell the sheriff the truth." Bea knitted her eyebrows. Then slowly raised them. "Oh, you mean. . ."

"Exactly."

"Oh." Bea bobbed her head up and down, finally comprehending.

"After I told Daniel no, he insisted I not go back to work. Jobs are hard to come by. I can't just leave it."

"But you're not safe there, Lizzy," Bea gasped.

"No, I suppose I'm not. But I don't know what to do." A nervous giggle slipped out of her throat. "Daniel decided the next best thing was for me to marry him. Can you believe that?"

Chapter 11

Back on shore, Mo lay on the beach and looked up at the stars. He was free, as free as the stars in the sky. But what was he free to do? He couldn't protect a woman for fear he'd be arrested. "It ain't right, Lord."

His mind shifted to messages he'd heard preached before, like when Stephen was stoned to death simply for telling others about Jesus. "Should I risk bein' arrested and confront Mr. Sanchez? Lord, I don't knows what to do. And why'd I make Lizzy mad all over again by askin' her to marry me? I have a home, plenty of room, and I think she likes me well enough. Am I so worthless that someone as pretty and wise as Lizzy couldn't find me worthy?"

Mo pulled in a deep breath that filled his lungs, raising his chest to its full size. "Ye know, Lord, being a big man has its problems. I've been whipped, beaten, and given up for dead a few times just 'cause of my size."

He scanned the sky to where a sliver of the moon pointed down to the sea. Following the direction of the moon's light, he looked over the inky black ocean. The horizon merged into the night. He knew the ocean carried on for miles, but the blanket of darkness hid the majestic wonder of the crystal blue sea. "Sure does look different from this morning, Lord."

Was it only this morning when he'd swum in the ocean without a care in the world? "Lord, I know Lizzy don't want me to walk her to work, but I hafta. I cain't let her go unprotected."

The muscles on his back tightened. His hand clenched. He wasn't about to let another woman whom he cared about get mistreated by someone. Not now. Not with him being a free man and able to stop it.

Mo brushed the sand from his body and picked up his shirt and shoes. He'd need to get to bed if he was going to wake up bright and early tomorrow morning. "First, Mr. Ellis will need to know I'm comin' into work late," he mumbled to himself. He walked past Lizzy's home. The house stood quiet. A dim light shown through the front window. He wanted to see her again, to try to explain why he'd offered marriage. But tomorrow morning would be soon enough. She needed more time to relax. Truth was, he knew he needed more time too. "She's a stubborn woman, Lord. Purty, but stubborn."

At his home, he lit a lamp in the kitchen, then headed outside to wash the salt from his body. After he dried himself off and headed into the house, he heard a noise in his bedroom. Mo reached for the large cast iron frying pan from the top of the stove and stealthily headed into the back room. He took a step, then stopped to listen, shifting his weight to his right foot.

The room was silent.

He moved forward again, shifting his weight to his left foot, and paused.

He heard a strangled cough.

"Who's in here?" he demanded.

⚓

"Mo asked ye to marry him?" Francine slapped her knee and smiled. "That's wonderful, Dear. But I wasn't aware that the two of you had taken a shine to each other."

"There's no shine, Mom. The man offered marriage for protection. Protection!" Her voice raised. "Can you imagine the gall?"

Bea giggled. "Some have married for less."

"I can't do it. It's just not right."

"Look at me, Child," Francine demanded. "Do you love him?"

"No. It's like I said, we're friends. At least, I think we're friends." Lizzy focused on her hands, folding and refolding the handkerchief.

"Ahh, but I'm thinkin' you've been thinkin' more about him," her mother pushed.

Lizzy felt the heat rise on her cheeks.

"Is it true, Lizzy? Have you started to have feelings for Mo?" Bea asked.

"No," she protested. "Oh, I don't know. I was looking at his lips tonight," she mumbled. Her cheeks flamed even brighter.

"So, you're more upset with Mo because he's offering marriage and isn't feelin' the same way about you." Francine crossed her arms over her ample chest and began to chuckle. "You do care for him, Lizzy. I can see it."

"I care, but I don't know if I love him. I'm just starting to have feelings for him. A woman shouldn't marry a man if she doesn't have feelings for him," she argued, defending her position and looking toward Bea for some help.

Bea raised her hands in surrender. "I'm not getting in the middle of Cook's matchmaking."

Lizzy groaned. "What a friend you are."

Bea chuckled. Francine put her hand on Lizzy's. "Tell me what interests you about Daniel."

"He's so incredibly gentle. He's huge, goodness, the man's as big as a house. In fact, he has to duck down before entering a room. Well, some rooms. But still, in spite of his size, I've watched him be so tender with the children. It's absolutely amazing. And I can't believe how fast he's learning what I teach him. He's a man of character, and yet he's so mysterious. For example, those scars on his wrists, how'd he get them? He said he was put in chains a time or two, but he never elaborates."

"The scars on his wrists are nothing compared to his back," Bea murmured. "He's had a very hard life, I'm afraid."

"His back?" Francine and Lizzy echoed.

"Yes, I saw a glimpse of it once when I went to the dock to speak with Ellis one day. Mo had his shirt off, just coming in from harvesting. . . . I could see he'd been whipped and whipped often. Deep dark lines crisscross his back. It's a horrible sight." Bea's body shook from the memory.

"I never knew," Lizzy mumbled. A tear for Daniel and the pain he'd suffered under the hand of slavery burned a solitary path down her cheek.

" 'Tis no justice for what's been taken from a man, but we can thank the good Lord he's free now." Francine grasped her daughter's hand tighter. "Lizzy, if you love him, marry him. He'll come around."

"Personally, I don't see Mo offering marriage just to protect you. I can't imagine he doesn't have feelings for you too," Bea offered.

"Really? He's never said or showed it."

"Oh? Didn't you say the man had the young 'uns prepare a special meal for you?" Francine reminded her.

Bea giggled.

"What?" Lizzy asked.

"I was just thinking, wouldn't it be fun to be a fly on the wall if you decide to tell Mo yes." Bea moved closer, leaning into them. "And to be there the day he discovers his true feelings for you. The man will be busting at the seams."

"Do you really think I should take him up on his offer to marry?"

"Sure, if ya love him," her mother responded. "The kids seem to like him."

"Like. . .enraptured is more like it. You should have seen them tonight. All seven of them huddled around and on him in the chair, each taking a turn reading to him."

"Ahh, I see you've got it bad for him," Francine teased. "So, what did you see in his lips?"

Mo raised the frying pan, waiting for a response. He heard another sniffle. "Who's in here? Speak up before I blast ye."

"Mr. Mo, don't shoot. It's me, Benjamin."

"Benjamin, what are ye doing here at this time of night?" Mo lowered the frying pan.

"I heard you talking. . .talking with Momma."

"What did ye hear, Boy?"

"I heard Mr. Sanchez was mean to Momma and made her cry."

Thankfully the child didn't understand exactly what Mr. Sanchez had done.

"I want to kill him, Mo. I want to kill him real bad. He made Momma so afraid she can't go back to work."

Mo cradled the boy in his arms. "I know, Son, I knows the feeling. Yer momma is okay, though; he didn't hurt her."

"But it ain't right," Ben protested.

"No, it ain't. Neither is yer sneaking out in the middle of the night."

192

"I know. But I can sneak in before Momma hears me."

Mo brightened the lamp in the kitchen.

"I'm the man of the house now. Well, when Uncle George ain't there," the boy amended. "I need to protect my momma."

"I'll protect yer momma," Mo said firmly. "Ye can help by watching over the other children."

"I've heard her crying, Mr. Mo. It's been real hard for Ma since Daddy died."

"I'm sorry, Son." What else could he say? He knew it had to be hard on a widow with four children. She was fortunate to have family to help her. "Would ye like something to drink?"

Benjamin nodded yes.

Mo went to the cupboard and pulled out a lemon and some sugar.

"Mr. Mo, did you mean what you said when you asked my momma to marry you?"

He heard that? Another knot tightened Mo's already tense stomach. "Yes, but she turned me down."

"Why?"

"I guess 'cause marrying me ain't something she ever thought about." Mo fumbled through the drawer looking for the juicer.

"Why'd you ask her?"

"I thought if we was married she wouldn't be having no more trouble from Mr. Sanchez."

Ben curled his lower lip and nibbled it. Mo stifled a grin. It was the same nervous habit he'd seen Lizzy do so many times.

"I still want to beat him up." Benjamin pounded the table with his fist.

"Son, yer old enough to know right from wrong. But are ye old enough to learn to trust God with vengeance?"

"Huh?"

"A man's a real man when he can take the garbage of this world and trust God to change it in the end. I'm not sayin' I don't want to hurt Mr. Sanchez myself, but as a Christian, I hafta trust God. Only God can git back at men like Mr. Sanchez."

"How can God get back at someone who doesn't know Him?"

"I's cain't say whether Mr. Sanchez knows God or not. And I cain't say I'd hold my fist back if I wuz to see him right this very minute. Which is why I'm home and not in front of his house. But I do know that when the time comes, if'n I've given my anger over to God, I'll be able not to harm the man."

"If you hit him, you'd knock him over."

Mo chuckled. "Yer probably right. But when a man's been given more strength, God asks him to be more careful with it."

"I don't get it, Mr. Mo. You was a slave. Don't you hate men like Mr. Sanchez?"

"No, not really. I suppose some days I do. But most days I don't. I hate the sin. I hate the things my master did to me and to others around me. But I learned somethin' watchin' people die at my feet day in and day out in war. Life is special. Everyone deserves it; just not everyone appreciates it."

"Huh?"

"It's like this, Ben. Remember when ye wuz tellin' William he had to get a job?"

Ben looked down at his feet. "Yes, Sir."

"Well, ye weren't doin' somethin' God would be proud of now, were ye?"

"No, Sir," he mumbled.

"But ye learned from your mistake. Ye haven't tried it again, have ye?"

"No." Ben's head darted up and caught Mo's gaze.

"I didn't think so. See, some men don't learn from their sins; they just keep doin' 'em again and again. Like my master, fer example. He used to whip me over and over again. He was so afraid of me he just keep whippin' me. In his mind, he thought it wuz keeping me submissive.

"But I didn't submit, at least not the ways he thought I did. A slave doesn't know where to go, where to run to. He knows he needs to, and I knew I needed to, in order to save my life. But I wuz afraid to run. Afraid to be caught and have my foot half chopped off, or worse. My master, he wuz a mean one.

"But in order for him to really own me, he had to own my soul. And I never gave him my soul. When he beat me, I just concentrated on God, on my freedom in heaven one day, and took the pain. My master couldn't touch my soul. He tried. He tried mighty hard to break me. But he couldn't."

"Are those marks on your back from the whippings?" Ben asked.

Mo had forgotten he hadn't put his shirt back on when he came in from bathing. "Yes. I'm sorry ye saw them."

"Do they hurt?"

"No, they're just like any other scar ye can git from scraping yer knee on the ground. The pain is temporary. The scar's permanent and so is the memory."

Mo finished squeezing the lemon for Ben's drink. He added some water and sugar and swirled it together, then handed the glass to the boy.

"Thanks. So what can we do about Mr. Sanchez?" Ben asked, taking a healthy sip.

"Nothin'."

"Nothing? I've got to do something," Ben protested.

"No, Son, ye don't. It's up to yer mother. I'll walk her to work. That should stop Mr. Sanchez."

"But Momma said no."

"True, but I don't give in that easily." Mo winked. "I want ye to promise me you'll let me handle Mr. Sanchez and your mom about this. She be real embarrassed if she knew ye knew."

Ben curled his lower lip again. "All right."

"Good. Now ye best finish that drink and get on home before yer mother has yer hide fer sneakin' out like this."

"Will ya tell her?"

"Not if I don't have to."

"Thanks, Mo. And thanks for being a friend. Momma shoulda taken you up on your marriage offer, but I think I know why she didn't."

"Oh?"

"Lips. I can't believe I let that slip, Lord." The heat of embarrassment still lingered on her face, while she tried to brush away the teasing thought that perhaps she should take Daniel up on his offer. *He does have a home with plenty of room.* She and the children would be very comfortable there, and he was the kind of man a woman could fall in love with.

Bea's comments about the scars on his back made her pause. How much did she really know about Daniel? And was it enough to marry him?

No, they were strangers, friends who had talked a few times, barely sharing their innermost thoughts. He'd shared very little about his life, and yet on a couple of occasions she had shared her heart.

Bea's words upon their parting tonight rang once again in her ears: "Perhaps the scars on his back reach all the way to his heart and he's afraid to open himself up."

"Lord, does Daniel have deep scars on his heart?" *Of course he does. He was a slave,* she chided herself, but then she shook her head. *You're making a mighty assumption here. Why must everyone who was a slave have deep heartaches?*

"You know, Jesus, I can't picture it any other way. I can't imagine a person being owned by someone and treated like nothing more than a cow or a chicken, not having anger and bitterness. Isn't that why Ben went off to fight? To free them? To stop the injustice of it all?" She'd read Frederick Douglass's *My Bondage and My Freedom* several times. Anger and bile rose in the pit of her stomach as she'd read the accounts of how he'd been raised as a slave. She could barely imagine what it would be like to be taken from your mother, near birth, and to have family members who meant nothing to you because you were never around them, or to be property, fit to be sold at the whims of a master. "Yes, that's why Ben went off to fight, Lord, and gave his life to free men and women locked in such bondage."

Lizzy passed the street toward Daniel's home and hesitated. Should she go tell him she'd be accepting his proposal? No, she wasn't settled on that. In some strange way, though, his proposal made sense. It seemed like the answer to her problems and prayers. And Daniel was right: If he were her husband he wouldn't be arrested for protecting his wife. But would she need to work? Could Daniel provide enough for her and her four children?

Her head throbbed. "Lord, I'm so confused."

Lizzy looked up at the stars and saw order in the heavens. She sighed. "Lord, put order back into my life, please."

Chapter 12

Lizzy groaned as the children asked for their breakfast. "In a minute," she muttered, pulling the pillow up over her head. What a night. She'd hardly slept. And when she finally had fallen asleep—sometime around three, she guessed—she tossed and turned.

"Maaa," Sarah whined. "I'm hungry."

Where were those sweet little angels who had made dinner for her last night?

"Did Ben get the eggs?"

"He's still sleeping," Sarah pouted.

Ben sleeping? That wasn't like him. Lizzy threw off the covers and headed straight for Benjamin's room. His cherub face smiled in his sleep. *At least someone's content in this house,* she mused. She brushed her fingers across his cheek. His temperature was normal, his coloring fine. *He's just tired, I guess.*

The other six were in various stages of dress—some in their sleepwear, some in their underwear, and Vanessa, as always, was up and dressed with her nose in a book. "That girl sure loves to read, Lord," Lizzy muttered.

"George, would you go collect the eggs this morning?"

"Why can't Ben do it?" he whined.

Lizzy put her hands to her face and rubbed it, raking her fingers through her hair. She didn't need whiny children, not today. "George!" she snapped, raising her voice. The boy ran out the door without another question asked. The rest of the children stood at attention. Even Vanessa pulled herself away from the book. "Get dressed, all of you. Vanessa, start cooking some oatmeal or cornmeal, whichever you prefer."

Lizzy headed into her room and freshened herself for the morning. It would be nice to have a day with no children, to get away like George and Clarissa. George and Clarissa would watch the children; they owed her that much for the times she watched theirs. But who would she go with?

An image of Daniel popped into her head. The thought of his rich mahogany eyes, black coffee hair, and deep walnut skin made Lizzy sigh. "You're right, Mother. I have got it bad."

How can a woman fall so deeply for a man who doesn't have the slightest romantic desires for her? "I'm in a sad state, Lord."

Dressed, hair in place, she went to the kitchen where George put down a basket of fresh eggs. "Thank you, George."

"You're welcome, Aunt Lizzy." He lowered his voice and leaned toward her.

"Are you feeling better today?"

"Yes." She placed a hand on his shoulder. "Thanks for asking."

He nodded and headed for his room.

A knock at the front door made Vanessa holler, "I'll get it."

Lizzy dried off her hands and went to see who was there. " 'Morning, Mabel. Did you sleep well?"

"Yes, thanks. I'm here to watch the children so you can go to work."

Oh dear, in all her running around she hadn't told Mabel. . . "I'm sorry, I'm not going to work this morning."

"Is anyone sick?"

"No. Something came up."

Mabel looked puzzled, but she nodded and smiled. "Well, it's a fine day to not go to work."

"Thank you," Lizzy silently mouthed.

"So, what's burning in the kitchen?"

"Oh no." Lizzy went running back. The frying pan with the eggs was on fire. She pulled out a lid and plopped it on the frying pan. "Great, just great," Lizzy hissed.

"Lizzy, why don't I finish fixin' breakfast for the children? You go visit your mother or spend some quiet time at the beach."

"Are you sure?" Lizzy prayed Mabel wouldn't back down on her offer.

"Yes, I was planning on watching them. So take advantage of your day off." Mabel winked.

The children all watched with interest. They knew their mother wasn't completely back to her old self yet. "I think I'll take you up on your kind offer then."

"Wonderful. Be gone, Child. I can handle it from here."

Lizzy grabbed her purse, said good-bye to her children, except for the still-sleeping Ben, and headed out the door. She hadn't gotten far when she spotted Daniel.

"Lizzy, if ye insist on goin' to work, I'm walkin' ye."

She sucked in a deep breath and grabbed her courage with both hands. "Daniel, I'm happy to see you. We need to talk."

His dark coffee eyebrows raised.

"I've been thinking about your proposal."

"I'm sorry, I didn't mean to offend ye by it. I just figured it might be a good answer to yer problem. I knows I'm not much of a man to be marryin'. . ."

"Daniel Greene, I don't ever want to hear another word like that coming from my husband's mouth. You're a wonderful man, and any woman would be proud to have you as a husband."

His mouth hung open.

"Yes, you heard me right. I'm planning on marrying you. Now, when would you like to do this?"

"Lizzy, are ye sure?" Daniel couldn't believe his ears. She was going to marry him, but why? Benjamin had made it perfectly clear that a woman like his mother wanted romance. And he just wasn't the romantic type.

"Yes. I thought about it long and hard last night. If you're willing to take on a wife with four children, I'd be a fool not to accept your generous offer."

Mo rubbed his face, then moved his hand to the back of his neck. He didn't remember being this nervous when he'd proposed marriage to Caron. "I'm willin'. I can provide fer ye and the children. I wouldn't want ye to go back to work."

"Are you sure?"

"I make good pay workin' fer Mr. Ellis. Yes, I can provide."

"If you don't want me to work, I won't work."

Lizzy looped her arm around his elbow. It felt wonderful to be so close to her. Could he keep his promise to have a marriage in name only? The heavenly scent of vanilla and. . .and. . . Mo sniffed. "Did you burn something this mornin'?"

"Uh, yeah." She looked toward the ground. "I normally don't burn the eggs." Daniel chuckled. "Lizzy, I knows ye can cook. So, why'd ye burn the eggs?"

"Just that kind of a morning, I guess." She shifted her weight and looked up. Her hazel eyes, even more green today, shimmered in the sunlight. "Daniel, when do you want to get married?"

Today, he thought. "Are ye sure, Lizzy? Absolutely sure?"

"Yes. Oh, I know we don't know each other very well, but I think we can make a good marriage, Daniel. I'm not fooling myself. I know there's no romance between us. But you're a good man, and I'd be honored to have a man like you as my husband."

"Really?" He couldn't believe his ears. Here she was praising him again. Didn't she know he had been found unworthy by Caron? No, she didn't know anything about Caron, or anything about his life on the plantation.

"Yes. Are you having second thoughts, Daniel?"

He could feel her tremble against his arm. "No. Why don't we do it right now?"

"Now? Don't you want a wedding party?"

"I'm not one for crowds. I like small, quiet things."

Lizzy giggled. "Then you'd better reconsider. Because with my family, nothing will ever be small."

He couldn't see himself rejoicing with a bunch of people about getting married with Lizzy. Not under these circumstances. If they had fallen in love. . . If they had gotten together like most men and women. . .then perhaps a large party would be in order. How could he make her understand? He knew it had to be embarrassing to marry him like this. Benjamin told him his father had brought his mother flowers often. He'd given her frequent kisses. *Kisses.* He wasn't sure she'd accept a kiss from him. The idea of kissing Lizzy stirred a desire so deep he feared it. No, this was a marriage of convenience. But maybe in time. . . "Lizzy, I think we should get married right away, today in fact. Then plan a party for sometime in the future."

He wouldn't trust Mr. Sanchez for one moment, knowing his intentions toward her. No, the sooner they got married the better.

"All right, if that's what you'd like, Daniel."

"I think it best, Lizzy. Later we can celebrate. Now we need to make ye safe."

She stiffened in his arms.

"Let's go tell Mr. Sanchez ye won't be workin' fer them no more."

"I don't know if I can face him."

"That's all right. I'm yer husband; I can face him. Come on, Lizzy, show me which house is theirs."

He could feel her fear as she slowed her pace the closer they got to the house. "Ye stay here, Lizzy." He left her at the curb. "I'll be just a moment."

He pounded on the door. A Hispanic gentleman with black hair and a thin mustache opened the door. "May I help you?"

Daniel smiled. "Are ye Mr. Sanchez?"

"Yes. What can I do for you?"

"I'm Lizzy's husband."

The man instantly paled. "I've come to let ye know she won't be working fer ye no more." Daniel lowered his voice and leaned over the man. "And I don't ever want to hear that ye even looked at my wife again."

"Manuel, who's at the door?"

"Lizzy's husband; she's not going to be working for us any longer." Then he spoke Spanish to his wife, and Mo simply left him. It didn't matter what he told his wife. Mo knew he'd never lay a hand on Lizzy.

"What did he say?" Lizzy asked.

"Not a word, Dear. His tanned complexion paled to the color of buttermilk." Daniel winked.

"Thank you, Daniel. I just didn't know how to confront him."

"I'm certain he won't be botherin' ye again."

Daniel paused in the street facing town. "Since we're so close to the church, let's go see the pastor. I don't have a ring fer ye, Lizzy, but I'll get ye one."

"You don't have to."

"I want to. When the time is right, I'll get one. Right now, let's go make ye my wife and not make a liar out of myself. I introduced myself to Mr. Sanchez as yer husband."

"We wouldn't want to make you out to be a liar, now, would we?" She grinned.

"I'm afraid after the preacher marries us I have to go to work. I told Mr. Ellis I'd be late, but he's expectin' me by now. I'll be home a little late making up for lost time. I'll help ye move yer belongings over to my place in the evening."

⚓

"You may kiss your bride." Daniel stiffened, and Lizzie winced. Was he afraid to kiss her?

He bent down and brushed her lips ever so gently. *Oh, Daniel, we've got so much to learn as a married couple.* They walked hand in hand down to the waterfront and to Mr. Ellis's dock.

"I'll be home around six, Lizzy."

"I'll be waiting." Lizzy headed on back to her house. She had to pack—and she needed help. She rushed to her mother's.

"You did what?" Francine planted her hands on her hips. "Goodness, Child, I suggested you get married, but I didn't think you'd go and do it the next morning."

"I know. I didn't know what to say to Daniel. He wanted to get married right away. I was afraid if I said I wanted to wait a week or two until we could make a dress, plan a party, or something, that he'd think I didn't want him. Mom, he doesn't believe he's worthy of a wife."

"You've got your work cut out for you. But I'll come help you pack."

"Thanks, Mom. I'll see you at the house. I have to tell the children. I hope they understand."

Francine tossed her head from side to side. "You'll make them understand. It might take some time, but they'll get there."

"I'm most concerned with Benjamin. He remembers his father more than the others."

"Ben's a good boy. He'll come around."

"I hope you're right."

"I know I am. He comes from good stock." She winked.

Bea walked into the kitchen. "Did I hear right—you married Mo this morning?"

Chapter 13

"Foolish, huh?" Lizzy worked the linen napkin in her hands.

"Not necessarily, if you love him," Bea countered.

"Oh, I do. I don't love him like I loved Ben, but I do care for him."

"What's done is done. We should get to it, Child," her mother intoned. "Packing for five will take some doin'. Would you mind, Bea, if'n I help my daughter?"

"Of course not, as long as I get to help too. I'll bring Richie along to help as well."

"Help what?" Richie bounced into the room, his golden curls bouncing along with him.

"Help Miss Lizzy move her stuff to her new home."

"All right! Does that mean I can play with Henry and William today?"

Bea chuckled. "Yes, Dear."

"Thanks, Nanna! I'll go put on my play clothes."

Lizzy giggled. "He's still so cute. What are you ever going to do when this little one comes along?"

"Count on him being the big brother. He's become quite a little man around the house."

Richie shouted from down the hall, "Can I bring my checkers?"

"Sure." She turned back to the other two women. "Well, I better change into a dress I can work in as well. Richie and I will join you at your place as soon as possible. I'll hitch up the horse to the wagon. That'll make things go faster."

"Thank you, Bea. I really appreciate your willingness to help."

"Come on, Lizzy, let's get a move on. The day is slipping away." Francine took her apron off and draped it on the kitchen chair.

Lizzy dropped the linen napkin she'd been wringing in her hands. She was more nervous than she thought. Following her mother out the door, she asked, "How should I tell the children?"

"Straight out. Ain't nothin' they can do about it now."

"Do you think they'll be upset?"

"Not if you put it in a positive light. For example, if you tell them they'll be getting new rooms and moving in with Mo, they might get all excited before they realize what it means that you've gone off and married him."

"Do you think I should have waited?"

"Yes. But God will work it out. It's as I told you last night, you both have feelings for the other—ye just haven't opened up and talked with each other about 'em."

"I do believe he'll be a good husband and father to the children."

"That's what counts. Honey, look. You're a grown woman. You know what it means to be married, and by them bags under your eyes, I'd say you didn't sleep much last night thinking about this."

"True."

"So, if you believe it's the right thing for you and Daniel to get married, then I'll respect your decision. Actually, I don't doubt the marriage part, just the timing. As a mother, I guess, I think you should have waited a few months, talked about your feelings, then decided. But. . ."

"But it's done now," Lizzy said with a smile.

"Yeah. Honey, I love you, and I'll support you in any way I can. You know that."

"Would you spend the night with the children? George and Clarissa are due back this evening but. . ."

"No need to explain. A wedding night should be private."

"Thanks, Mom. It's as you say—Daniel and I have a lot to talk about."

"Hmm, I was thinking about something other than talking. . . . But you're right, the children don't need to be interrupting your private conversations tonight."

Oh dear, sharing Daniel's bed. . . Lizzy started to tremble.

"What's the matter?" Francine halted in the road.

"I just realized about, about. . ."

Francine swung her head back and roared with laughter. "You've been a widow too long. Come on, Child. We've got a marriage bed to make up as well as getting your belongings over to Mo's."

A marriage bed. Yes, she could make up the marriage bed, arrange the room, and even fix an intimate dinner for two tonight. It could be her wedding gift to her husband.

Husband. Daniel Greene was her husband. *Oh, Lord, help me be a good wife for him.*

Ellis rubbed his beard. "You married her, just like that?"

"Yeah." Mo beamed.

"Goodness, Man, don't you know a woman likes to be wooed?"

"I guess I don't." Mo slumped his shoulders. "Have I done it all wrong?"

Ellis chuckled and slapped a hand on his back. "Mo, if she married you, just like that, I'd say she cares for you. And that's all that matters."

Should he tell Ellis that the marriage was really for her protection? That they were man and wife in name only? On the other hand, being married to Lizzy and keeping his end of the bargain of remaining "in name only" was going to be the most difficult test he'd ever encountered in his life. Even the whippings he'd endured as a slave would be nothing to living day and night beside that won-derful lady and not holding her, kissing her.

Oh, that kiss. . . Her lips were so soft.

"Mo, are you all right?" Ellis asked.

"I'm fine. I'm just realizing what I done."

Ellis roared with laughter. "Trust me, Mo, there's far more reality coming in the next few weeks. But, let me tell you, being married to a special woman is well worth anything you lose as a single man. In fact, there really isn't anything I miss about being single."

"That part ain't a problem. I didn't go out much anyway."

"Then what's the matter?"

"I–I'd rather not say."

"Fair enough. So, did you buy her a ring? Or get her a wedding gift?"

"No. Was I suppose to git her a gift?"

"You don't have to, but it's a nice gesture. I bought Bea a pearl necklace. She gave me this pocket knife." He pulled a knife out of his trousers. "Bea knew I was always looking for one, so she bought it. She had it engraved too."

"I wouldn't know what to git Lizzy. Pearls would look mighty purty on her."

"Yes, Lizzy's a fine looking woman."

"She takes my breath away sometimes."

"Glad to hear it. A man ought to feel that way about his wife. Well, come on, we've got some work to do. Why don't you leave early and fetch something from Peg Martin's store before you go home?"

Mo had been to the store a couple of times. Peg had some fine lace and linen table things. Would that make a good wedding gift for Lizzy? Jewelry sounded better, but he'd need to buy the wedding ring before he could buy her a necklace. Yes, he could provide for her and her children, but he'd have to be careful with his expenses. Very careful.

The day lingered on. Washing the sponges was boring, but at least here he didn't mess up the paperwork. Initially, Ellis had him working on the ledgers. After Mo's third mistake, Ellis sent him to work on washing the sponges. "I can see your mind is on other things today," Ellis had said with an understanding laugh.

Mo pushed the dry sponges down into the vat. Once they soaked up the fresh water, he leaned his weight on them to squeeze out the water, then released them to fill up again. The monotonous job gave him time to think. *What can I get Lizzy for a wedding present?*

He pushed the sponges down into the vat again. A sharp pain ripped across his palm. When he pulled his left hand out of the vat, he found it covered with blood. "What on earth?" He looked down in the vat. His hand stung. "Mr. Ellis!" he hollered.

Ellis Southard came running out of the storeroom. "What's the matter. . . ?"

His gaze was fixed on Mo's hand. "What happened?"

"I don't know. I wuz cleanin' the sponges and somethin' sharp cut open my hand."

Ellis reached for his hand. "Let me look at it." Carefully, he looked over the wound. "There's too much blood. We need to wash your hand, and I think you're going to need stitches."

Mo sat down on the edge of the vat. Carefully, he fingered through the sponges until he found the sharp object. He fished it out and discovered a sponge had grown around a rusty knife. Using his knees to hold the sponge, he ripped it open with his good hand and pulled out the blade.

"Where did that come from?" Ellis asked, carrying a jug of water.

"Inside this here sponge. The thing just grew around it."

"Wonderful." Ellis shook his head. "Here, hold out your left hand so I can pour some water on it. With all that rust, we're going to need to flush this wound real good."

Mo gritted his teeth. The pain was intense, but he'd experienced worse. He knew about treating wounds, though he'd never had one from a rusty knife before. He'd known some men to die from getting cut with rusty objects. Even from stepping on a rusty nail. A cold shiver slid up his spine. He couldn't die, not when he'd just gotten married. What would happen to Lizzy?

Ben grinned. "You married Mr. Mo?"

"Yes." What was going on in this boy's head? She had been certain he'd have the most trouble with the idea of her marrying Daniel, since he had the best memory of his father. Instead, he looked downright pleased.

"Good. When do we move into his house?"

Lizzy scratched her head. She wanted to clean out her ears. She couldn't possibly be hearing right. "Uhh, Grandma and I are here to start packing our stuff."

"I'll get George to help me pack mine and William's things." Ben turned around, his shoulders squared, and left to find the others.

Francine chuckled. "Not what you expected."

"Not in the least. Something isn't right."

"Maybe you're not giving the boy enough credit. He's getting to that age where he thinks he's all grown up."

"Yeah, I know."

"Could also be the young 'uns took a shine to Mo."

"Apparently. Mom, he didn't even flinch. He just took the information as a matter of fact. I'm not ready for this." Lizzy snickered.

"No parent is. We just do the best we can and pray we survive it. This is the good part, the confident part. Then comes the I-don't-have-a-clue-but-I'm-not-listening-to-you part. Them days are hard. You were the toughest of my children."

Lizzy wanted to protest. She'd seen George give their mother a lot more grief during his teen years than she ever did. Her memory was that she had been their easy child. But then again, her memory was biased. *Guess I'll be asking Mom more questions in the days to come.*

"Let's get packing. Bea should be here pretty soon." Francine rolled up her sleeves and headed for Lizzy's room.

"Wasn't it only a year ago we were doing the same for you, Mother?"

"Just about. A little over a year since I moved in with the Southards."

"Do you miss your own house?"

"Oh, maybe sometimes. But then I get to thinking about how many of you live here. I like my nice quiet room all to myself—and the fact that there's only one child under foot instead of seven."

Lizzy giggled. "Not for long." Lizzy reached under the bed and pulled out the crate where she kept her extra bed linens. Since moving into her mother's house, she'd been sleeping with her daughters in one double bed.

"True, but I can't imagine the Southards wanting seven children."

Bea walked into the room. "Oh, Cook, didn't we tell you, Ellis decided to have a dozen?"

"Dozen? You best have a talk with that man. Or is he planning on birthing half of them himself?" The room erupted with laughter.

Lizzy moved to the dresser and began to remove some of the girls' clothing.

"Where do you want me?" Bea asked.

Lizzy looked at the dresser drawers. "You know, this would probably be the best job for you since it's all got to go. I do want to leave an outfit for the girls to dress in tomorrow."

"Great, I can handle this." Bea stepped up to the dresser.

"I'm going to go to the kitchen and take some of my pots and pans. I wouldn't take them, but Mo has next to nothing in his kitchen."

"George and Clarissa will understand." Francine opened the closet. "Is everything in here yours?"

"I think so. I'm sure you'll be able to tell, Mom."

Francine nodded. Lizzy left and headed to the kitchen.

"Momma," Sarah whined, "Ben says you're married to Mr. Mo and that we'll be moving to his house."

Oh, dear. She knew she should have gathered them all together before she told one of them. Unfortunately, Ben had been the only one in the house. The rest had gone over to Mabel's, but now they were back.

Lizzy sat in a chair. "Come here, Honey."

Sarah inched toward her with her lower lip puffed out.

"Here, sit on my lap." Lizzy patted her legs and her daughter plopped down. "The answer to your question is yes."

"Why?"

Why indeed? The children had no understanding of the events that had transpired yesterday. Was it only yesterday? Lizzy could feel the weariness start to overtake her body. Her arms felt heavy and her eyelids felt worse. "It's hard to say in one word. But I like Mr. Mo, and he asked me."

"But don't people marry because they love each other?"

"Oh, I love Mr. Mo." It's just a different kind of love from what her daughter was picturing. She was old enough to see how George and Clarissa responded to each other. The kissing, the holding hands—none of these she'd seen her mother do with Daniel. She certainly could understand her daughter's confusion.

"Don't you like Daniel?"

"I like him, but I don't know about him being my daddy."

"Daniel will never replace your father. But I think he'll make a great second daddy, since yours went to heaven."

"Will I have my own bed, or will I have to share it with you and Mr. Mo? He's really big, and Olivia and I already take up a lot of room in the bed."

Lizzy stifled a chuckle. "No, Honey. You and Olivia will be sharing your own bed in your own room."

"Where you going to sleep, Momma?"

"With Daniel, in another room. Like Uncle George and Aunt Clarissa."

"Oh. Then it's okay if you marry Mr. Mo."

"Thank you, Dear." She wasn't about to point out to her daughter that the deed was already done. But it was nice to have two of her children's blessings. Now to hear from William and Olivia.

"Grandma is here with Mrs. Bea, packing in our room. Would you like to give them a hand?"

Sarah nodded and wiggled off her lap. Lizzy got up and started working her way through the cupboards. From what she could recall of James Earl's kitchen, she would need quite a few of her pots and pans. She did have a crate or two in the back shed with some of her belongings that had not been needed in her mother's house.

"Momma," called William, as he and Olivia scrambled into the kitchen with Mabel following close behind. "You married Mr. Mo?"

"Yup."

"Yipee!" William hooted.

Olivia popped her thumb in her mouth and sidled up beside her mother. Lizzy hadn't seen her suck her thumb in several months. "Liv, what's the matter?"

"Are you still going to be my momma?" Olivia mumbled around her thumb.

Chapter 14

If you keep this clean, Mo, you shouldn't get lockjaw," Doc Hanson said, as he finished stitching up the injured hand and then wrapped the wound with white gauze. "Here, take this home with you and change the bandage tomorrow."

With his good hand, Mo reached out and took the rolled bundle of gauze. "Thank ye, Doc. What do I owes ye?"

"Nothing," Ellis chimed in. "You were injured working for me, so it's my responsibility to pay for your medical."

Ellis forked over a couple of bills to the doctor. Mo fought with his pride, but he was grateful that Ellis was paying. He wouldn't have gone to the doctor if it hadn't been for Ellis, though he was glad he had after he saw the doctor fish out bits of shell and sand from deep inside the wound. Not many doctors recognized the need to make sure wounds were cleansed well.

Mo was relieved. Facing the possibility of death on his wedding day didn't set well with him. Although the idea of not being able to work for a week right after he'd taken on the expenses of a wife and four children made him concerned in a whole new way.

The hand bandaged and the doctor paid, he and Ellis left the doctor's office and headed back toward the dock. "Don't know what you can do for me with that hand, Mo."

"I know, Suh. I'd be willin' to work one-handed."

"No, you heard what the doc said about infection. You'll need to keep it clean, Mo. And this job is anything but a clean job."

"I know." A week without pay. He had some savings, but that was for a rainy day. And what about buying Lizzy a wedding gift? This day sure had been an expensive one. First a couple bucks to the preacher for the wedding, now the loss of work, and the wedding gift. Could he really afford a gift at this time? On the other hand, his rainy-day fund hadn't been dipped into, except for James's funeral.

Ellis reached into his pocket and pulled out his wallet. "Here, Mo." He handed him some bills. "This is your pay for the week."

"But I's didn't work fer it."

"True, but like I said in the doctor's office, you were injured on the job. I don't want to lose you. If you were one of my other divers, I might only give him a couple of days' pay. But with you, well, you deserve it. Some of the others we can't count on. You've seen that."

"Yes, Suh." Mo covered the bills in his hand, clenching his fist, then shoved them into his pocket. He looked around the area to see if anyone had seen him putting away the money. He wasn't about to get his head banged again. The sheriff had a suspect and he was keeping an eye on him, but the sheriff couldn't prove anything yet. The fellow had some money that same day and had gotten himself rather drunk that evening, but that was circumstantial evidence.

"Also, when you have time to count the money, you'll find your pay is doubled," Ellis went on. "Since you're doing so well with the reading and writing, I'm hiring you on as my foreman."

"But I still don't understand yer books," Mo protested, reaching back into his pocket to give back some of the money.

"Tomorrow I want you to come to work and take the ledger home with you. See if Lizzy can understand them, and see if she can help you understand them better than I."

Mo nodded. He certainly did learn faster with Lizzy as his teacher. No offense to Mr. Ellis, but he sure did make things confusing.

Ellis chuckled. "Your face reveals a lot, Mo. I can see you agree Lizzy might be a better teacher."

Mo grinned. "Well. . ."

The two were still laughing when they stepped into Southern Treasures. " 'Morning, Peg," Ellis said as he entered.

" 'Morning, Ellis, Mo. What can I do for you?"

"Good morning, Miz Martin. I'm wondering if ye might have some of that fancy lace work ye do?"

Peg Martin's fair face beamed. "Sure do. It's over to the right."

"Thank ye." Mo headed toward the area she pointed out. He had in mind to get Lizzy a linen tablecloth with a lace border. But his eyes caught a cloth with embroidered flowers.

"Mo, I'll see you tomorrow." Ellis waved and headed out the door.

"Ellis tells me you went and got yourself married, Mo."

"Yes'm. Lizzy Hunte."

"Congratulations. Lizzy's a fine woman."

"Thank ye."

"Can I help you?" Peg stepped closer to him. For a single woman, she'd always seemed very sure of herself. And she was one of the few folks who hadn't been intimidated by his size the first time she met him.

"I want to give Lizzy a special gift. I have a couple pearls I've collected from some oysters, but I knows it would cost too much for me to have 'em put in some purty setting."

"Wish I could help you, Mo. But my handcrafting is limited to embroidery and such."

He had figured as much. "I like this cloth, here. What kind of flowers are these?" The bright purple flowers with a tiny center of yellow seemed to be salt and peppered around the border of the cloth.

"Those are African violets."

"I like the deep purple." And he'd love to see Lizzy in a dress made from the same rich color.

"I have matching napkins that go with that cloth. You're in luck—I just finished the last one this morning, shortly before you came in."

Tablecloth and napkins. Could he afford both? His countenance brightened as he remembered his pay had just doubled. "How many napkins?"

"A set of eight. Should be enough for you, Lizzy, and the four children."

"Thanks, I think I'll buy them."

"Wonderful. Can I wrap it up for you?"

Mo wondered if wrapping a gift was necessary.

"I received this beautiful paper in the other day, and I'd love to dress this gift up for your bride. No charge, Mo. It'll be my wedding gift to you."

"Thank ye. I think Lizzy would like a fancy wrapped present."

Peg pushed her blond hair behind her shoulders. "As a woman, I know she will."

Ahh, that was the problem. As a man he didn't know what a woman liked. Yes, Peg Martin would be quite helpful in the decisions he'd make in terms of gifts.

Peg bent and picked up the tablecloth and brought it over to the counter. "You know, Mo, if you have some pearls you want put in a setting you might want to talk with the jeweler."

"I don't think I can afford that right now."

"Oh, I understand. On the other hand, you might want to talk with him anyway. He might be willing to buy those pearls."

"Not sure I trust the man—don't know him."

Peg knitted her eyebrows and glanced up at him. Then a realization crossed her face. "If you trust me, I'd be happy to ask him what the value of the pearls are. Personally, I've never done business with the man, but I haven't heard folks complaining about him either."

Mo scratched his chin with his good hand. His left hand was beginning to throb. "I might take ye up on that. I need to get Lizzy a weddin' ring. Maybe he'll barter for some pearls."

"Might be a good idea. So, where'd you get these pearls?"

"I've been collecting some oysters when I'm harvesting the sponges. Since I've been working for Mr. Ellis, I've found three."

"Wow, maybe I should start oystering." Peg smiled and continued to place the tablecloth and napkins in the fancy paper.

"I found a rose-colored one and two white ones."

"Rose one would be worth more." She folded the paper over the bundle and held it together with a thin string. Then she grabbed a pale pink ribbon woven into a ribbon of lace.

"Yer making this look mighty purty. Thank ye, Miz Peg."

"You're welcome. Would you like me to go with you to the jeweler's now?"

"I don't have the pearls on me. I keep 'em in a safe place."

"Wise. I heard you had a run-in awhile back."

Mo rubbed the back of his head. "Afraid so."

"So what say you, yes or no to my accompanying you to the jewelers?"

"All right. Can we leave Lizzy's gift here? I wouldn't want to soil it."

"Sure." Peg escorted him out of the shop, pulled a key she had hid around her neck, and locked the store. "So, when did you and Lizzy start having feelings for one another?"

☙

Lizzy stood in Daniel's kitchen, wondering where she should begin. Her head was pounding. The lack of sleep and the long morning of packing and unpacking had left her even more exhausted. Ben should be here shortly, she hoped. She'd sent him to the docks to see if he could buy some fresh fish or lobster for the special dinner she planned for Daniel tonight. It was the least she could do. "But what besides fish can I feed the man?" she mumbled.

Again she opened the cupboard that contained a few food items. Some dry beans, rice, flour, and some brown sugar. He had a few spices, but nothing compared to her cupboard back at her house.

"This is your house, Lizzy old girl, you best get used to it." She amused herself, speaking like her mother. Her mother and Bea had left about a half hour earlier. "Mangoes. That's it! I'll get some fresh mangoes from the Southards' tree."

She removed her apron, straightened her dress, and headed out the door as Bea drove up with her carriage. "Bea, what on earth are you doing back here?"

"Cook and I decided you needed some basics for the kitchen. Have you had a look at that man's shelves?"

Lizzy giggled. "Yeah, I was coming to your place to get some fresh mangoes. I'm hoping Ben can come back with some fresh fish or lobster."

"Sounds delicious. Well," Bea reached over and pulled a box from the seat next to her, "I've got some mangoes here, some limes, and a couple of canned vegetables your mother and I put up."

"Thank you."

"I also put in some dried herbs that I grew this winter." Bea handed the box over. "You know, I'm still not used to saying that. Up North you can't plant anything in the winter. And yet, down here, it's better for a lot of the crops to be planted and harvested in the winter months."

Lizzy smiled. "For me, the idea of only being able to plant four months out of the year sounds really strange."

"I guess it's all a matter of perspective, huh?" Bea got down from the wagon. "I also had a set of dishes that I was given as a wedding present. I've never used them. Ellis had such a full house before I married him. Anyway, I figured you could make better use of them than just sitting in my closet."

"I can't take your wedding present."

"Sure you can. It's from a distant cousin who will never come down here. And even if Grettel does come, I know she won't be offended."

Bea started to lift the box of dishes. "Let me get that. You carry this one," Lizzy offered.

Bea pondered the idea for a moment then, looking at her blossoming tummy, readily agreed. "I keep forgetting."

"Soon there'll be no forgetting."

"So I hear."

Ben came running up. "Mom, Mr. Mo had an accident."

Lizzy felt her knees go weak. "What happened?"

"Mr. Ellis said he was washing the sponges and one of them had a knife inside it."

"What?"

"A rusty old knife. The sponge just grew around it." Ben leaned over and placed his hands on his knees while he caught his breath.

"Mercy, is he all right?"

"Mr. Ellis says his hand is cut up, but he should be okay."

"Where is he?"

"Don't know. He wasn't working for Mr. Ellis when I got there. He said Mr. Mo can't work for a week, or until his hand heals."

Oh dear, no work for a week. Can Mo afford that and us? "What should I do?"

"Not a thing. Wait for him to come home and he'll tell you all about it. Then you two can decide what to do. Obviously, he went to Doc Hansen," Bea said confidently, placing a loving hand on her shoulder.

"Yup, Mr. Ellis went with him. Said he was stitched up with fifteen stitches."

Didn't the man have enough scars on his body already? *Lord, what's happening here?*

"Come on, Lizzy, let's get these things settled in the kitchen." Bea turned to Ben. "What did you get from the fisherman?"

"Oh, a couple of lobsters."

"Great." Bea headed into the house, and Ben trailed after her. Lizzy stared at the crate of dishes wrapped with straw and brown paper. She thought of Daniel, the cut on his hand, rusty nails, and the loss of her young brother some twenty years ago because he had stepped on a nail. A shiver slithered down her spine. "No, Lord, please. . . No."

Chapter 15

Thank ye." Mo extended his hand to Nathaniel Farris, the owner of the jewelry store.

Nathaniel grasped his hand firmly and shook it. "Pleasure doing business with you, Mo."

Peg Martin, having come in with him, no doubt helped with the warm reception he'd gotten from Mr. Farris. "Thanks, Peg."

"Pleasure, Mo. Now take that ring home to your pretty new wife, and I'm sure Mr. Farris will be happy to see you in the morning." Peg smiled.

"I appreciate this, Mr. Farris."

"Well, as I said earlier, if you have a pink pearl it will more than cover the cost of the ring. But if it's not of the right value, I'm sure the other two pearls will more than compensate."

"I've got to get back to my store, Mo." Peg stepped toward the door.

"I'll come with ye to pick up Lizzy's gift."

The jeweler handed Mo a small box, which he slipped into his pocket. Maybe this day wasn't going to be as expensive as he'd thought. Peg's fingers seemed a bit thicker than Lizzy's, so they had found a ring that was just a bit too tight for her. He hoped he wouldn't have to bring it back, but Mr. Farris said it wouldn't be a problem either way.

"Thanks, Miz Peg. I don't think he would have given me the ring today without yer say so."

"Ah, it's nothing. Happy to help."

Peg went to unlock the door to the store and stopped. "It's not locked, Mo. I swear I locked it."

"You did, I saw ye. Let me go in first."

Mo grabbed the doorknob and stepped inside the store. His gift for Lizzy sat on the counter. He listened. Hearing nothing, he stepped deeper inside. A floorboard creaked, and it wasn't one under his foot.

"Call the sheriff, Miz Martin," Mo hollered, and blocked the front door.

A thin man with a scraggly beard stood up from behind the counter. He cocked a crooked smile. "Ain't took nothin'."

"Good, but ye can tell the sheriff, not me."

"I think I'll just be leavin' before the sheriff gets here." He stepped from behind the counter.

"I don't think so."

"Who's goin' to stop me, you?"

"Appears so." Mo inhaled deeply, crossing his arms in front of his chest.

"I knocked ya down before, big boy. I can do it again."

Then Mo saw a thick hickory club behind the man's back.

"Ye may have hit me once when I wasn't lookin', but today is a different day. And I don't make the same mistake twice." Mo knit his eyebrows and peered down at the dirty, disheveled man. The muscle of his jaw tightened. He opened and closed his hands in front of the man, letting him get a good inspection of his size and strength.

The thief pulled the stick from around his back and raised it shoulder length, holding it with both hands. "This here is none of your concern. Back off."

"Oh, I think this is my concern. Come on, give me a chance to pay ye back for the clunk on my head," Mo dared the weak man.

Seeing Mo's determination, the man paled.

Mo dared him again. "Come on."

The man dropped the club to the floor.

"Wise man. I'm sure ye heard the stories about Samson in the Bible and his bein' able to kill a lion with his bare hands. Well, if you've been around here long, you'll have heard I did near the same one night when a black panther came after me."

The man fell to his knees and raised his hands. "Don't hurt me," he pleaded.

"Move aside, Mo. I'll take it from here." The sheriff came in and placed handcuffs on the sniffling man.

"Ye best tell the sheriff what you used that club for before," Mo advised.

The man cackled. "No proof. Why hang myself?"

Mo stared at him long and hard. "Sheriff, did ye hear the story about the panther?"

"Sure did. Ellis Southard told me." The sheriff winked. The fact was it was just a story. Something someone made up.

"And can ye believe this here fella doesn't want to tell ye he's the one that hit me over the head a couple months back? Amazing." Mo wagged his head back and forth to exaggerate his feigned astonishment and took a threatening step closer.

The man gave a whimper of fear. "Oh, all right. I knocked him out and took his silver pieces."

"Thought so," the sheriff said grimly. "I was just waiting for you to make your next move, Joe Everly. For future reference, after you get out of my jail you best move on. This island is small and folks around here know everything about everyone. You won't be getting away with your shenanigans around here." The sheriff pushed Mr. Joe Everly out the door. Then he turned back to Mo. "What I hear true about a new bride?"

"Yes, Suh." Mo grinned.

"Congratulations."

Peg's voice wavered next to him. "Thanks, Mo. I hate to think what would have happened to me if you weren't here."

The lobster tails were prepared and ready for cooking; the rice and beans simmered in a pot. A fruit and nut salad with the mangoes, chopped almonds, and lime juice rounded out the meal. Lizzy wiped the sweat from her brow. She wondered what was keeping Daniel in town and fought the dark thoughts that something bad had happened to him.

She was exhausted. She needed a few minutes of sleep before Daniel came home. But first she needed to freshen up. If Daniel should come home before she awoke, she didn't want him to see her in this state.

The china pitcher and basin on the commode provided welcome relief. Either Bea or her mother had filled it and placed small hand towels and wash rags in the drawer. Lizzy stripped and washed herself. She took from the closet a fresh cotton blouse with puffy short sleeves and a laced neckline. The next item was a long Spanish-style skirt that gathered at the waist, and seemed the perfect attire in which to greet her new husband.

Dressed, she slipped back into the kitchen, stirred the black beans, removed the rice from the heat, and placed it on the side of the stove where it would stay warm but not cook further. Lizzy didn't want the first meal she made as Mrs. Daniel Greene to be a disaster. She tossed the fruit salad, blending its juices, and glanced at the table.

She'd set it with the new dishes Bea had given her, and with some silverware she'd found in Daniel's kitchen. A small Mason jar was filled with bright red and pink hibiscus. Lizzy smiled. "Oh, Daniel, I hope you're pleased."

She scurried off to the bedroom and lay down on the bed. Soon he'd be home, and they needed to talk. Her eyes closed. Sleep overtook her weary body immediately.

"Lizzy."

Someone was calling her. She rolled over and snuggled deeper into her pillow. "Lizzy."

Daniel! She sprang from the bed, straightened her hair and clothing, then walked into the kitchen. He stood staring at the table.

"Hello, Daniel."

"Ye did all this?" He pointed to the table, then around to the stove.

"Yes. I wanted to make you a special dinner."

"Smells great." He looked down at his soiled clothing. "I'm not fit for such a feast."

She saw the bandage on his hand. "Ben said you were injured."

He held up his hand. "Yeah, a sponge grew around a knife. Doc said I should be all right."

Under his other arm she saw a fancy, wrapped package.

"Where's the children?" he asked.

"Home. I mean, home at their old home. My mother is watching them until George and Clarissa get settled in from their trip." She looked down at her bare toes. "I wanted to give us some privacy."

Daniel came up beside her. "Oh, Lizzy girl, ye didn't have to do that. But I'll cherish the night alone with ye. I suspect we won't have many of those until the young 'uns are grown and married."

Lizzy smiled. "I suspect you're right."

"Here, I bought ye something. A weddin' gift."

"Oh, Daniel, you didn't have to do that."

"We had a rushed weddin'. Thar's a bunch of things we haven't done or discussed, but I've been told a man gives his wife a gift. So I went and got ye a little something. When I saw it, I thought of ye."

"May I open it now?"

"Yes."

Lizzy sat down on a chair at the table for two she'd fussed over earlier. She pulled the lace bow and it opened, revealing the hand-embroidered napkins. "They're beautiful."

"I think the purple is the perfect color for ye. Peg says they are African violets."

She placed the bundle at her place setting and jumped up into her husband's arms. She leaned up on her toes and threw her arms around his neck. "Bend down, Daniel. I can't kiss you."

Daniel bent down and she placed a gentle kiss on his lips. He scooped her up in his arms and held her tightly. "Lizzy, I know I said we would have this marriage be in name only. But. . ."

She cut him off. "Daniel Greene, I did not marry you and not expect to do my wifely duty. A marriage is a marriage, and I aim to make this as good of a marriage as I possibly can."

"Ye mean it?"

"Yes."

He brought her gently to the ground. "I'm glad. Cause after that kiss in front of the preacher I was thinkin'. . . Well, ye don't want to know what I was thinkin'."

Lizzy chuckled. "I think I can imagine."

"Let me clean up. I got dried blood on my pants. Then I have to tell ye about my day."

"Sure. I'll cook the lobster tails while you're changing."

Mo stepped into the bedroom. "Woman, how did ye get all of this done in just a few hours?" he called.

"I had help. My mother and Bea gave me a hand."

"Lizzy girl, yer amazing."

Father, God, thank Ye for Lizzy. Thank Ye that she wants to make this a real marriage. Help me be the kind of husband she needs, Daniel silently prayed.

He glanced at the bed. It had fancy white pillowcases with embroidered flowers on them and a white spread over the mattress that spoke volumes of just how feminine this woman he married was. Could he possibly be sensitive enough for her?

"When I wuz at Southern Treasures I stopped a man from robbing it."

"What?"

Daniel scrubbed his chest and under his arms.

Lizzy came up behind him—and gasped when she saw his naked back.

Daniel turned. "I'm sorry."

"Sorry? What are you sorry for? Goodness, Daniel, who whipped you like that?"

"My master. He wuz a short and very insecure man. He thought the best way to keep me in submission wuz to keep whippin' me."

Lizzy came up beside him and lightly touched the scars. He saw tears fill her eyes.

"Each stripe on my back made me more determined to leave the plantation, but I never had enough confidence that I could do it."

She traced a scar that ran diagonally across his back. He felt the warmth of her feather-like touch.

"How often did he beat you?"

"I don't know."

"I'm sorry you had to live that way, Daniel."

He put down the washcloth and lifted her to the bed. Then he knelt down beside her. "Lizzy, it's a horrible life, no question about it. In fact, youse almost don't even feel like yer alive. Ye have no say about what ye can do. You're treated like chattel. In fact, you're called that by yer white masters. But God's showed me that He goes to the darkest pit and gives His love to everyone."

She placed her hands in his and gently touched his fingers.

"I knows ye were born free, but was someone in yer family a slave?"

"Yes. I've heard stories. But I've never seen a man so badly beaten like you were."

"Thar's more, and someday I'll tell ye. But tonight is a night for celebratin'. If ye don't mind, I'd like to talk about my life as a slave another time. I'd rather concentrate on being a free man tonight, and on all the blessings God has given me."

Lizzy smiled. "You're right. There'll be plenty of days to talk about both our pasts. I'd like to tell you about Ben sometime. I think you would have liked him."

Daniel smiled. Ben was a part of her past, just as Caron and slavery were a part of his. Yes, he'd like to know about Ben, but not tonight. He already knew from Ben's son that they had had a happy marriage. How could he compete?

"So, what were you saying about Peg Martin's store?"

"Oh, well, I got yer gift from her store and we left the store for a bit. When we's came back the door had been unlocked, and so I went in. Thar wuz this man. . ." He told her the entire story.

"I'm glad the man who attacked you is behind bars. I hope he stays there. We don't need folks like that on Key West."

"Nope."

"But what's this about the panther and Samson?"

"Awhile back, before I came to ye fer lessons, someone tried to blame me fer some other trouble in town. Pretty soon a rumor wuz spread that I'd taken a black panther and killed it with my bare hands. Ain't true, but it has kept people from challengin' me to a fight every time I turn around. I've kinda adopted the story."

Lizzy chuckled. "Don't you think your size is enough?"

"It's because of my size that I'm always bein' challenged."

"I suppose. I never understood that about men."

"Me neither, just part of being a man, I guess."

The sound of water hissing as it hit the hot stove made Lizzy jump up from the bed. "I forgot the lobsters."

Mo got up off his knee and went to the closet. Inside, he found Lizzy's dresses hanging next to his trousers. He grinned. "Guess I'm really married, Lord."

Chapter 16

Lizzy caressed Daniel's chest as she nuzzled in closer. "Good morning," she whispered. She caught a glimpse of the sparkling gold band on her hand. Daniel had given it to her last night. Moment by moment she was falling deeper in love with this man. Perhaps it wouldn't take too long before they really knew and understood each other.

" 'Mornin', Mrs. Greene." Her heart soared. He wrapped his arm around her. "What would ye like to do today?"

His bandaged hand came up and caressed her cheek. Her eyes caught a glimpse of the bloodstained bandage. She bolted up in bed. "Daniel, you were bleeding."

He lifted his palm to get a better glimpse of it. "I guess I wuz."

"Didn't the doctor say we needed to change the bandage?"

"Yes."

"Come on." Lizzy slid out of bed and pushed her hair behind her shoulders, then grabbed her robe hanging on the back of the door. "Where's the gauze that Dr. Hanson gave you?"

Daniel sat up in bed and lifted his knees, resting his elbows on them. "Uh, I don't know. Wait, let me think. My pants, in one of the pockets."

Lizzy grabbed the pitcher. "I'll fetch some fresh water and a pair of scissors. You can fetch the gauze."

A cock crowed in the distance. *The sun's up, so the birds must have overslept. Just like yourself, Lizzy, old girl.* It had been natural staying so long in bed, with Daniel not needing to go to work. They had talked and talked until the wee hours of the morning. A bond developed last night, a bond that would create the foundation for their marriage. *Forgive me, Ben. I may learn to love him with the same fiery passion I felt for you.* Lizzy jumped, startled at herself for thinking of Ben now. On the other hand, wouldn't it be natural? Ben was the only other man she'd ever loved.

She fished a pair of scissors from a kitchen drawer and pumped the water into the pitcher. Quickly she walked back to their bedroom. "Daniel, I've got the. . ." Her voice caught in her throat. The scars on his back reminded her of his past. Of the life he'd been forced to live. She swallowed down the raw emotions of anger and the bile of bitterness. This was what Ben fought for after all.

"Ye will get used to it." He turned and he reached for his shirt.

"I suppose, but it just makes me more determined."

"Determined to what?" he asked and sat down on the edge of the bed, holding out his injured hand.

"Oh, I don't know."

"Why don't we just keep working where God's put us? Thar young 'uns here that need your teaching. If ye wasn't here to teach them, who would? We have to raise the children to become educated, to learn a trade, to make a life for themselves and their families." Daniel reached out and lifted her chin. "Lizzy, I don't run away from a fight, but this one is a big 'un, and we's need to do what we can where we can."

"I suppose you're right."

"I knows I am. At one point I'd thought of usin' this here house as a school fer Negroes and to set ye up as the teacher. We can still open the house, but with us married we'll also be needin' the rooms fer the children."

"You thought about setting up a school?"

"Yes'm. Ye taught me so much. I'm still learnin', but my eyes are open. I can see signs and know what they say. Or, at least sound them out. Takes me a bit, but I'm gettin' thar." He locked his brilliant mahogany eyes with hers; their red hues sparkled with his fiery belief in education. "Ye have a very important role on Key West, Lizzy. Ye can read; ye can teach. God's given ye a gift."

Unable to speak, she lowered her glance to his injured hand. "Let me cut off this soiled bandage." He held out his hand. She snipped the edges and worked the bandage open, down the side of his hand. "Oh, my," she gasped. "How big was that knife?"

"Six-inch blade."

Blood had dried on the edges of the wound, though the gauze had soaked up most of it. "You can still move your fingers?"

Daniel demonstrated, lightly brushing her arm with his fingers.

Lizzy swallowed. "I guess so."

Daniel chuckled. "Yer a fine woman, Elizabeth Hunte Greene, and Caron pales in comparison to ye."

"Caron? Who's Caron?"

🌴

Oh no, this wasn't how he'd planned to tell Lizzy about Caron. "She wuz the woman I wuz engaged to."

"What happened?" Lizzy's nimble fingers cleansed around the wound, her touch so gentle, the warmth of her breath so personal. *Goodness, Lord, she's beautiful.*

"I wuz twenty-two, and we wuz all set to get married, when my master discovered how set I wuz on her. That's when he. . ." Daniel coughed to clear his thickening throat. "When he bedded her."

"Oh, Daniel, how horrible. She must have died."

"No. The worst part of it wuz, she preferred what the master offered over me. That wuz why I ran. I had nothin' left at the plantation. And to see Caron day and night, and knowin'. . . Well, a man can't live with himself under that kind of circumstance."

"I can understand that."

"It's not all Caron's fault. The best jobs, so's to speak, for a female slave wuz to be taken in like that. And she didn't know there wuz any life other than the life of the plantation. Which is no life at all. It's hard comin' from a plantation to livin' on yer own. Yer confused, lost, and alone. Some days ye even wonder if'n ye should go back."

He and Lizzy continued to talk about his days on the run, his time in the service of the Union Army, and the various changes he went through realizing what freedom meant to him. Even today he still worried that someone might snatch him and tell him the government had changed its mind about freeing the slaves.

"Hey, Mom, Mr. Mo, are you in here?" Benjamin called from the front door.

"Oh, goodness, I'm not dressed yet." Lizzy clutched her robe and got up off the bed where they had been talking.

"Ye got yer nightgown and robe on. Hasn't yer young 'uns seen ye in that before?"

"Yes, but. . .well, it's so late in the day." A dusky pink rose on her delicate cheeks.

"I'm in my room," Lizzy called out.

Her room. Mo certainly did enjoy hearing that.

Ben stood at the doorway. "Oh, what a cut." Benjamin's brown eyes rounded to the size of saucers.

Mo looked down at his hand. The knife had cut clear across his palm.

"Does it hurt?" Ben asked.

"Some, not too much. Son, yer mother and I needs to dress. Would ye excuse us?"

"Sure, the others will be here shortly. I ran ahead." Ben puffed up his chest.

"Why don't ye go help Olivia? Her little legs must be tired by now."

Ben nodded, and Mo closed the door. Lizzy hastily bandaged his hand.

"You handled him like an experienced father. I'm proud of you." Lizzy draped her arms around his neck.

"Didn't ye say yer mother was watchin' 'em last night?"

"Yes. Depending on when George and Clarissa got home, she might have stayed the night."

Mo lifted her off the floor and held her close to his chest. "Then I suggest ye get dressed," he said with a wink, "or else your mother might find you in your night clothes."

He watched her blush deepen. She gave him a quick peck on the lips and wiggled down from his arms.

"You'll be wanting to get some clothes on too." She patted his backside and headed for the dresser.

Mo chuckled. Life with Lizzy was already bringing more joy and excitement into his life than he'd had since he moved to Key West eight months ago.

As he had suspected, Cook came in with all four children, saying they'd been up since the crack of dawn wanting to come to their new house. She'd held them off as long as she could. After talking a few moments longer, she left, going on to work at Ellis Southard's home.

The children were all lighthearted. He'd never seen them this talkative before, and before long his head pounded with each syllable they spoke. "Lizzy, I have to run into town for a couple errands. Do ye need anythin'?" He needed a little peace and quiet.

"I could use some fresh fruits and vegetables, and whatever meat you'd like for dinner tonight."

"Done. I'll bring them home with me." He reached for her hand and squeezed it slightly. They'd agreed to limit their physical expressions of affection in front of the children for awhile to let them adjust to their mother being married. His first test of holding back and already he wanted to flunk. But Lizzy was counting on him. He wouldn't fail her. He wouldn't fail her children. "Be home as soon as I can." He winked, and his heart overflowed with joy when he saw the sparkle in her eyes.

"Can I come, Mr. Mo?" William asked.

He looked to Lizzy to see if she had any problem with it. Seeing none, he agreed.

"Yippee!" William jumped up and down.

"You'll have to behave," Mo cautioned.

William grew somber and promised, "I will." Reaching up, he took Mo's hand. He had a son, two sons, he realized. *Goodness, life can change mighty fast.* He knew he could never replace the boy's real father, but he could try to be a good example. The problem was that he didn't have a clue.

"Mr. Mo?" William spoke as they walked on the crushed coral path toward town.

"Yes, William?"

"Is Momma going to have a baby?"

"Where'd you hear a fool thing like that?" Lizzy stood stunned at Sarah's question.

"Jimmie Joe says the only reason people get married quickly is 'cause they're going to have a baby."

"Well, Jimmie's wrong." Lizzy wiped her brow. "I'm not having a baby."

"I knew it wasn't so. You won't have a baby, will you, Momma?"

"Oh, Sweetheart, I don't know. That's up to the good Lord and His timing. I'm not planning on having a baby any time soon." Did she even want another child? Still, the idea of having a child born out of her and Daniel's love. . .

"Momma?" Sarah pouted.

"What?"

"You weren't listening to me. I asked if I could give Jimmie Joe a fat lip."

"No. You know I don't cotton to fighting."

Sarah crossed her arms across her chest. "But he said. . ."

"It doesn't matter what he said. It isn't true, and in time the truth will come out. In the meantime, the question is, would Jesus give someone a fat lip because they asked if His momma was having a baby?"

"No."

"Well, then that's your answer to how you should behave." Lizzy began washing the inside of the cupboards. She knew Mo had cleaned the place after James Earl passed on, but apparently cleaning the inside of cupboards wasn't included in his idea of cleaning.

"All right, Momma, but I'd rather give him a fat lip."

"Just see that you don't. That's the real test."

Sarah nodded and headed up the stairs.

A baby! Where'd Jimmie Joe hear a fool thing like that? Probably from his mother. Lizzy sighed. By now all of Key West no doubt believed she and Daniel were expecting. She worried her lower lip. People probably thought they'd been courting for ages, seeing how he came to her house every other night for lessons. "Oh well, ain't much you can do to get a conch back in its shell once it's out."

"What conch?" Ben asked with a mouth full of banana.

"Just rumors."

"Oh, you mean the one about you havin' a baby?" Ben laughed. "Can't believe how silly children can be."

Lizzy eyed her oldest son cautiously. Being all of eight years and a man of the world, she didn't think he even knew how babies were born. She hadn't explained it to him yet.

"And how silly is that?" Did she dare ask?

"Come on, Mom, I'm not a baby. I know where babies come from."

"Well, I suppose you do." What he knew, he hadn't learned from her or her brother, so what exactly he knew could prove interesting. "But why don't you tell me what you've heard?"

Ben rolled his eyes. "You know, you have to kiss under the moonlight. A full moon."

"Ah, I forgot that was a part of it." Lizzy smiled.

"Well, I know you've never kissed Mr. Mo. So I know you're not going to have a baby. Even if you did kiss him yesterday 'cause you got married." Ben wiped his mouth. The very obvious fact that he found kissing girls to be distasteful was something Lizzy found reassuring. "That wasn't a full moon last night."

"Well, kissing has something to do with having a baby, but there's more to it. When you're older I'll have Mr. Mo fill you in on the man's part."

"No thanks. I think Uncle George and Aunt Clarissa kiss all the time, but they're careful about the full moon. So if you start kissing Mr. Mo, watch out for the full moon, Mom."

"Thanks for the warning, Son." Lizzy wasn't going to argue the point, and she certainly didn't want to fill the young man in on the facts of life before he was old enough to understand.

"You're welcome. I like my new room."

"I'm glad."

Lizzy wrung out the rag and wiped the shelves in the cabinet one last time. "There, those are done. Ben, will you chop me some kindling?"

"Sure." He tossed the banana peel over his shoulder and it landed in the trashcan.

No sooner was he out the back door than William came running in through the front door. "Momma, we're home."

A smile rose on her face. The children loved their new home. Or at least loved the adventure of having a new home.

"William, you best go up to your room and settle your things," Lizzy suggested.

"Aw, Ma," William whined.

"Do as yer mother says," Daniel commanded with his deep, rich voice and gentle approach.

"Yes, Sir."

Lizzy blinked. "What did you do with the boy while you were in town?"

"We came to an understandin'." Daniel winked.

"Oh, I'm all ears."

"Later, Darlin'. We've got company comin'."

"What?"

"Yer brother and his family are on their way. I saw them when we came up the walkway. We're about three minutes ahead of them."

"Oh."

Daniel walked up beside her and whispered, "There's some rumors."

"Sarah informed me."

Daniel nodded. "I'm sorry, Lizzy. I guess we should have waited awhile. I just didn't want ye vulnerable to that—that horrible excuse for a man, Sanchez."

"Hello!" Clarissa called as she pulled the screen door open. "Lizzy, we go away for one day and the whole world changes. What on earth happened?"

Daniel draped his arm across her shoulders. "We got married."

Clarissa rolled her eyes. "No foolin'. So when did you two fall in love?"

Chapter 17

Daniel and George grilled the fish outside while Clarissa and Lizzy put together some rice, biscuits, and a fresh salad. Daniel's little vegetable garden was a godsend. Unexpected guests for dinner strained the amount of fish he'd brought home, but everyone had a piece, and the rest of the meal was rounded out with the various items the ladies had prepared.

"I thought they'd never leave," Daniel mumbled at the evening's end.

"Me too. I love them and they needed to find out what had happened between us. But I'm glad to be alone now."

"You didn't tell them the full truth?" Daniel whispered, not wanting the children to hear him.

"No, I suppose I didn't. But I don't want everyone to know either."

"I'll not say a word, Lizzy." He stepped up behind her and wrapped his arms around her. He'd been waiting all day for an opportunity to embrace her, to feel her soft skin against his.

Lizzy sighed and nuzzled into his chest.

"The children seem to like their new home."

"Yes. And it's time for them to be settled in their new beds. Care to lend a hand?"

"Tell me what I need to do," Daniel offered.

"It's easy. Make sure they wash and are dressed for bed. William has to be encouraged to change his undergarments."

Daniel chuckled. "I think that's a male thing. I remember my momma givin' me a tongue lashin' when she found out I hadn't changed mine for a week. I's about William's age at the time."

"I was, not I's."

"Sorry. I'm getting better, but I've been speaking that way for near thirty years."

"I know, and you're doing wonderfully. Do you mind my correcting you?"

"No, just keep doing it in private. Public, I do mind. But we've been over that before."

"Momma," Sarah whined. "Olivia keeps putting her doll on my pillow."

"It begins," Lizzy whispered into Daniel's ear. He'd released her when Sarah had whined, and now she ached to be back in his arms. How could a person fall so deeply in love in such a short time? Was it love? Or was she just so lonely after not having had a husband around for nearly five years? In either case, Daniel's arms were a place of solace.

After the children were settled, Lizzy sat down at the table with Daniel as he pored over the bookwork Mr. Ellis had given him earlier.

"I just don't understand this. Mr. Ellis has explained it a million times, but it just don't make sense."

"Show me what you know." Lizzy examined the ledger, noting the various columns and figures below each one and beside each name.

"This here is a list of the men who work for Mr. Ellis." He pointed to the column to the left-hand side. "And this here column is where the number of sponges gathered that day is recorded."

Lizzy nodded.

"This is the total of sponges for the week."

He was doing fine so far.

"I just don't understand how he gets the figures in this column."

The payment column for the men, she noted. "How does Mr. Ellis pay the men?"

"By how many sponges he harvests."

"Okay, so how much is that?"

"Some are paid a nickel per sponge, others are paid up to a dime. Depends on how long they been working for him."

"That's recorded in this column, right?"

Daniel nodded.

"So, Toby brought in one hundred and twenty-five sponges this week."

Daniel nodded again.

Lizzy continued, "And he gets paid a nickel per sponge."

Daniel knitted his eyebrows and nodded again.

"So he earned six dollars and twenty-five cents."

"How'd ye do that so fast? Yer just like Mr. Ellis. I'm still counting."

"Daniel, do you know how to multiply numbers?"

"What's multiply?"

"It's a way to figure numbers faster than adding every time. First I'll show you a trick for all the men who are earning a dime a sponge. Then I'll explain it for you. If you add a zero after the number of the amount of sponges a man brought in, like Micah's two hundred and thirty here, he earned twenty-three dollars."

"How'd ye do that?" Daniel's eyes rounded with excitement.

"Well, if you have ten bananas and bought another ten how many would you have?"

"Twenty."

"Right, so you could say you had two sets of ten bananas. That's multiplying. Tens and ones are easy. Anything multiplied by one is the same number. Anything multiplied by ten adds a zero. Then we start multiplying by twos, threes. . ." Lizzy went on to explain how to multiply and show Daniel that basically he just had to memorize the multiplication chart, which she proceeded to draw out for him.

"Lizzy, this is amazing. It will save a bundle of time figurin' the men's wages."

She kissed him on the cheek. "Good. Do you mind if we go to bed now? The children will be up early and I've been dragging all day."

Daniel closed the books and got up from the table.

"Thank you, Lizzy. I don't know why Mr. Ellis never told me about multiplying."

"Probably because he didn't realize you've been adding all the time."

"Guess so." Daniel looked down into her eyes. His unspoken request caused her heart to hammer in her chest. She placed her hand into his and followed her husband into their bedroom. Daniel closed the door and locked it shut before he lifted her into his arms. "Oh, Lizzy. . ."

Mo woke feeling on top of the world. He'd gotten up before Lizzy had stirred. He could still feel the pleasure of her full lips on his. They reminded him of sweet plums in both color and taste. Daniel groaned and went to work. He couldn't wait to use the multiplication chart Lizzy had drawn for him last night.

A few men had gathered on the dock. "Mornin', Toby."

" 'Morning, Mo. How's married life?"

"Wonderful." Mo beamed.

Toby chuckled. "What about having those four young 'uns under foot?"

"They's good young 'uns, well behaved. Lizzy's done a fine job raisin' 'em."

"Glad you're happy. Me, I like being single." Toby grinned. His dark skin glistened in the sunlight. His yellowing teeth, minus a couple, peeked through his smile.

"Don't think I'll miss being single." Mo reached over and grabbed some nets with his good hand. "Better get out there, time's a wastin'," he encouraged Toby.

"Whatever. I bring in my share."

Daniel remembered that Toby's share was typically far less than that of most of the other men. And he could see why Mr. Ellis kept him at the lower pay rate. Often there were days when Toby didn't even bother to come to work. "Ye might try doin' a little more spongin' than sleepin' in yer boat."

Toby looked over at Daniel and narrowed his gaze. "What?"

"I've seen yer skiff just floatin' and ye layin' in it more than once. You'd earn more if ye worked more."

"I earn enough."

Daniel couldn't imagine how. Of course, Toby had the kind of life he'd never been inclined toward. "Yer choice." He glanced past Toby. " 'Mornin', Mr. Ellis." Mo watched Toby lighten a shade of brown.

" 'Morning, Mr. Ellis," Toby coughed out.

" 'Morning, Toby." Ellis stepped up to Mo. "I didn't expect you to make it this morning."

"I'm feeling fine. Need to keep the hand clean, but I'm in good shape otherwise."

"Just the same, after you get the men off, you can go home with the books. I don't need them done until tomorrow."

"Lizzy showed me how to multiply last night."

"You didn't know? I'm sorry, I just assumed. . ." Ellis's words trailed off.

"It's all right. She showed me. And I think I can get the hang of it now. She wrote me a multiplication chart but says I have to memorize it."

Ellis chuckled. "She is a good teacher."

Mo laughed. "Yes, Suh, she is."

Day after day, week after week, Mo found himself coming to work with more joy than he'd known in a lifetime. How could one woman change a man's life so much? They'd been married a month now. The stitches were out and he was back to work full time. Every evening he'd come home to a clean house, a table full of food, and an increasing wonder at just how amazing God was to have given him such a gift.

They talked and talked every evening. He was surprised to find he had stuff to talk about. He'd always been a quiet man, didn't give much time to chewing the fat with others; with Lizzy, though, he couldn't stop himself. He found he wanted to share his day, and she wanted to know. "Amazin', Lord."

Mo dove into the crystal waters once again. His skiff was fully loaded, but he wanted to fill the net one more time. He pulled and cut the sponges and moved on to the next one, leaving the smaller ones to continue to grow for harvesting another day.

Breaking the surface for air, he sucked in a deep breath and went down again. Tropical fish swam up beside him. He delighted in their vivid blues and reds, so unlike the black and brown catfish he'd catch from the river up North. Catfish did make some good eating, even though they were such an ugly fish.

Ye know, Lord, I'm still amazed that Lizzy finds me desirable. I'm not a handsome man. And the scars. . .well, they don't improve my image none.

Mo kicked back to the surface. He had a good haul for the day. The sun was getting halfway between the high point and the horizon. He'd have enough time to go over the books again. He'd memorized the multiplication chart, and that was a blessing.

Once back in the boat, the wind shifted direction. Mo looked up to the sky and then froze. A funnel cloud was forming to his left.

Lizzy beat the rug again and more dust formed a cloud around her. The house was shaping up nicely. She'd even had enough time to do some planting in Daniel's garden. The kids seemed to enjoy their new home, but they did miss their cousins. Today she'd let them go to George's for the afternoon and dinner.

Tonight she planned an intimate dinner for two.

Lizzy wagged her head. She and Daniel had been married for a month, and she found herself falling more and more in love with him. And yet she was more and more afraid to admit it. Telling Daniel she loved him seemed somehow to lessen her love for Ben. She knew in her head Ben would be pleased that she'd found someone to spend her days with, that he'd be happy for her and the children. But the reality was she was beginning to feel more and more disloyal to her original marriage vows. She'd pray every day, reminding herself that their vows were meant to last only until death. But she couldn't release herself from those vows.

Lizzy reached out and whacked the rug yet again. Working on the rug helped work through her confused emotions.

"Trying to kill it?" Bea called out.

"More like using it for target practice," Lizzy quipped.

"Uh-oh. What's wrong? Which one of your little ones is in trouble now?"

"No one. Nothing's wrong."

"Come on, something's bothering you. Spill it."

Lizzy smiled. Bea coming by was an answer to prayer. She needed someone to talk with, and her mother wasn't the one right now. "I'm feeling disloyal to Ben because I'm falling in love with Daniel."

"Oh." Bea stepped up beside her. "Come on in the house and pour us some limeade. I need to get off my feet for a spell."

"I could use the break." Lizzy leaned the broom up against the hanging rug and led Bea into the house.

Lizzy went to the sink and pumped out some fresh water to rinse herself off before serving up the refreshing drink.

"So, how bad is the ghost of Ben?" Bea asked, easing her swollen body into a chair.

"Not too bad, but I almost called Daniel 'Ben' at a very inappropriate time," Lizzy confessed.

"Oh dear. That wouldn't encourage a new husband to hear his wife calling out her previous husband's name."

"No, and Daniel's so vulnerable. I can't make that mistake. He's such a tender-hearted man."

"You really do love him, don't you?"

"I suppose I do. I just can't tell him. I wouldn't want him to feel I was pressuring him into loving me."

"Excuse me? You're married."

"Yes, but. . ."

"But you didn't marry him for love?"

"Right."

"Do you think he doesn't love you?"

"I honestly don't know. There are moments when he looks at me and I get so weak in the knees. I'd swear he believes I'm the best thing in his life. But then there are moments when we don't connect. He's had such a different life, such a hard life. So many people have hurt him in the past. And not all of them used a whip. I can't hurt him. I just can't."

"You think by telling Daniel you have these thoughts of Ben he'll be hurt?"

"Yes. I can't apologize for my life with Ben. I loved Ben with all the passion two people can enjoy. But with Daniel it's different."

"Because?"

"Well, for one thing, I didn't fall in love with him the first moment I saw him. In fact, I was frightened by him. He's so big."

Bea giggled. "He is a giant. But you got past that."

"Of course, or I'd never have started teaching him."

"Hmm, are you still teaching him?"

"Yes."

"Is it necessary?" Bea took a sip of her drink.

"He has so much to learn. He's doing wonderfully but. . ."

Bea cut her off. "Lizzy, he's your husband. Did you teach Ben?"

"No, he could read. At least, I thought he could read." Lizzy rubbed the back of her neck. "You know, I never got one letter from Ben once he went off to war. I figured it was a problem with the mail. But he never read to the children. He'd sit and listen and encourage them in their lessons, but he. . . Do you suppose Ben just hid it from me?"

"It's possible. I've seen many folk who pretended to know how to read when in fact they couldn't."

"But. . .why should I stop teaching Daniel? He's so anxious to learn."

"I'm not saying you shouldn't answer questions he might have. I'm just saying that a man needs to feel he's the head of the household, and with you being in command of the teaching, well, he might not feel that way. On the other hand, you also may not see him as head, like Ben was."

"I wouldn't. . .I don't think. . .I mean. . . Oh goodness. Do you think that's the problem? By not giving Daniel his rightful place as head of the household I keep putting Ben back in it?"

"Might be some of it. The other fact is simpler—Ben was your husband. You loved him. War took him away from you. Daniel will understand that. I think you should talk with him about it."

"I can't, Bea. He'll be so hurt. He'll feel like I don't love him."

"He probably already feels that. You said you can't tell him you love him. Which means you haven't said it, right?"

Lizzy hung her head. "No, I haven't told him I love him."

"Why not?"

"I don't know. I suppose because I feel I'm being disloyal to Ben. But I guess that really isn't the whole problem. I don't know if he loves me. I'm afraid to be vulnerable, to open my heart and have the man not respond the same way."

"That's the real problem. You don't trust Mo."

"I do. He's wonderful to me and the children."

"Nope, sorry. You don't. If you did you'd open your heart and tell him how you feel."

Chapter 18

Mo rowed in as fast as he could. Funnel clouds on the ocean weren't that unusual, but gray ones were. By the time he reached the dock, he found Ellis already battening down the hatches, netting the sponges, and tying them down to the pilings—anything to save them from the fierce wind that appeared to be coming fast.

"Good haul, Mo."

"Thanks. I think I beached it high enough off the shore line."

Ellis glanced at the shore. "Should be safe."

"I covered the skiff with the netting. Shouldn't lose the sponges unless we lose the skiff." Mo grabbed some nets and climbed up on top of the shed to gather the sponges there. "Do ye want me to slack the lines on your boat, Mr. Ellis?"

"If you get to it before me, sure."

Slack lines would give the boat the ability to ride the waves without being pulled back by the dock it was anchored to. Mo finished gathering the sponges on the roof and hustled down the ladder. "What should I tie these to?"

"Anything. After the storm they'll need to be cleaned and dried again. I just don't want to lose them."

Mo nodded and tied the netted sponges between two pilings, fishing a rope through the opened ends of the net so the sponges wouldn't be blown out of his hammock-like storage spot. Pulling in Ellis Southard's personal sailboat, he jumped on board and moved it between the dock and a couple of posts that stood loosely in the harbor. The lines set, he pulled the boat back toward the dock. Mo spanned the three-foot gap, thankful he had long legs. The outer poles would keep the boat from hitting the dock. The ties to the dock would keep the boat from hitting the outer poles, and all four should keep it from being torn out to sea or dumped up on shore. In the end it would depend on the size of the storm.

"Mo!" Ellis hollered. "I can't get these ropes free."

"If ye can't, the storm probably can't either," Mo quipped as he went to help Ellis.

Ellis Southard was a relatively strong man, but there had been more than one occasion where Mo's strength had come in mighty handy. Day by day he was feeling more useful, a needed part of a community, something he'd never felt before in his life.

The two men continued to work. Other men brought in their skiffs loaded with sponges. They pulled each boat up on shore and turned them over, leaving the sponges inside the skiffs.

"Do ye think it's a hurricane?" Mo asked as they looked at the darkening horizon.

"Not likely—too early in the season. Probably just a good storm."

"If'n ye don't need me any longer, I'd like to get home and take care of the house."

"We're set here. Go home, Mo. And thanks." The other men had left as soon as they had their skiffs up on shore. No one bothered to count each man's haul. And Mo figured some of the men might claim to have brought in more than they actually had, but there wasn't much he could do about that.

"See ye tomorrow." Mo headed toward shore.

"If the storm passes—if not stay home with your new bride." Ellis grinned.

Mo found himself grinning as well at the prospect. Life with Lizzy had become so special.

His smile slipped. The love he felt for her was so deep and so real it scared him. He wanted to tell her how he felt; he longed to tell her. But they hadn't gotten married because of love. A mutual respect for one another, yes—but not love. Could he risk his fragile marriage with a declaration of love? Mo quickened his pace toward home.

The wind whipped at his shirt. The air held an unusual warmth, and its smell was peculiar. He'd never seen a storm quite like this before. He broke into a run. He'd have to hurry to get the house's windows boarded up. Thankfully, he'd fixed the shutters last week. The cistern was clean, and the drainage tubes from the roof he'd cleaned last month. He'd plug the opening to the cistern for the first few minutes of rain. Then he'd open it so clean, fresh water would fill it. He'd hoped to enlarge the cistern with Lizzy and the children living with him, but he hadn't gotten up the extra funds for such a large project. For James Earl the small cistern would have served him quite well. For a family of six, it wouldn't be enough during the dry season. Luckily, they were just beginning the rainy season. He had time to build a larger cistern.

Mo found Lizzy outside, closing the shutters over the windows. "Where's the children?"

"They went to my brother's for the afternoon and dinner. I think they may end up spending the night, from the looks of this storm."

"I hope so. I wouldn't want to see them out in this. Do ye need me to go runnin' over there and tell them to stay put?"

"No, I need you to help me. I'm afraid I didn't see this storm coming until a few moments ago."

Mo reached up beside his wife and clasped the shutter she was struggling with. "Go inside. I'll take care of these."

"I'm glad you're home."

Her eyes were red from tears. He reached out and cupped her face. "Lizzy?"

"Not now, Daniel. Later, after we've got the house ready for the storm."

"All right." His heart twisted in his chest. Something had hurt her. Could it be those silly rumors about her expecting? Somehow he didn't suspect that was the case. Lizzy didn't appear to be the kind of woman who would be hurt by idle chatter. No, something else was wrong. The question was if he was man enough to handle it.

He hit the wall of the house with his fist. "God, give me strength. I don't know what I'll do if Lizzy tells me our marriage is a mistake."

Lizzy washed her face one more time. Why was she still crying? Bea left hours ago. The reality was she was afraid. Afraid of the truth. Afraid to completely trust her husband. Bea had nailed the problem on the head. She needed to confess her fears and concerns about Ben, about her near slips at calling Daniel by Ben's name. If she wanted God to be the center of their marriage, she needed to be honest and open with Daniel.

But was he ready for that kind of a relationship? He kept so many things to himself. Oh, sure, they talked most evenings. But so many times he avoided the deep secrets of his past, which in turn had her keeping her memories of Ben and their marriage to herself as well. He hadn't said another word about Caron, what she was like, how hurt he was. Could they really build a marriage on so many hidden secrets, hidden hurts? Could they ever open up completely and become that threefold cord the Bible spoke about?

Perhaps in time. She shouldn't push it. Not now. The marriage was too fragile.

Lizzy finished arranging the table for their dinner. The romantic dinner she'd planned would be lost to the storm and her worries about their marriage. How could she hide this from Daniel? He'd already seen she'd been crying.

She wrung the linen napkin in her hands. The longing to tell Daniel her feelings was so strong she wondered if the good Lord was trying to squeeze it out of her.

The front door opened and closed with a bang. "Sorry," Daniel offered, as he headed down the hall toward her. He leaned down and gave her a quick peck on the lips. "I need to wash up." He glanced at the table. "What's this?"

"A romantic dinner for two." She winked.

"Then why the tears?" He stumbled over to the sink and pulled off his shirt.

Lizzy walked up to him and traced the lines on his back. "These," she mumbled. She felt his muscles stiffen under her fingertips.

"What about 'em?" He continued to pump the water into the sink.

"Daniel, I need to talk about your past. I need to talk about my past. I know you married me for my protection, but I believe God doesn't want us to have a marriage in name only. He wants to draw us close to each other. I. . .I. . ." She fought the fiery blaze of salty tears filling her eyes. "I just think we need to talk."

"Haven't we been doing that? I told ye where those scars came from," he huffed.

"Forget it, you're right. I shouldn't have brought it up." She pulled her hand away from his back. He stomped into their room and closed the door.

Why, oh why, had she listened to Bea? She should have kept her mouth shut, should have kept to her resolve that now wasn't the time or the place, that their marriage was too young for this kind of deep conversation.

Lizzy could hold back the tears no longer. The walls of the kitchen seemed to be closing in on her, and she pushed herself out the door into the back yard. "Why didn't I keep my mouth shut, Lord? I knew he wasn't ready to open up." She fought the wind and walked around the back yard. Her skirt whipped past her, creating a sail. The dark gray sky sizzled with lightning.

Mo kicked the chair. Why had he spoken so harshly to Lizzy? She only wanted to get closer. Didn't he want that? Didn't he hope and pray she would come to love him in the same way he'd come to love her? "So why am I pushing her away, Lord?"

Mo fumbled with the buttons on a fresh, clean shirt. *A romantic dinner—she planned a romantic dinner, and instead we're having our first fight. You messed up big time, old boy.* He stared at the dark reflection of himself. The years had taken their toll. He wasn't the same handsome lad of his youth. His body was scarred; his heart was scarred—and yet Lizzy had still married him. She even honored the commitment of intimacy between a husband and wife. How could she possibly. . . Mo rubbed his hands over his face. Echoes of Caron's flattering words pulled him back to his past.

> *"Danny, you're so handsome, all the girls envy me."*
> *He caressed her cheek.*
> *"Mother says we can marry next month."*
> *"I's happy about that."*
> *"The master, he wants to see me tomorrow. Do you think he'll make me a house slave?"*
> *Daniel didn't think that was his intention at all. He'd watched the master watching him and Caron for weeks now. No, his intent for Caron was far worse. "Don't go, Caron."*
> *"You know I can't disobey the master." Caron sat in his lap.*
> *He wanted to make her his wife right then and there, but a Christian man was to wait and honor the Lord. "Please, Caron, don't go."*
> *"Don't be silly, the master probably heard about our wedding and wants to congratulate us."*
> *"If'n that's so, then how's come he didn't ask to see me too?"*
> *Caron shrugged her shoulders.*

"Please, Caron. Don't go."
"You know I can't disobey the master. I ain't 'bout to be whipped like you."

And that was the truth of it. Caron was a good slave, always doing what was expected of her. She never complained, not even once. He, on the other hand. . . Well, he had a mind of his own sometimes, and that just seemed to get him in more and more trouble.

Mo blinked and came back to the present, to the man in the mirror, no longer a slave, no longer bound to a woman who found. . . No, he wouldn't think about that again. It was over, done with.

"Lizzy?" he called. Hearing no answer, he opened the door.

"Lizzy?" he called again.

No answer.

He stepped into the kitchen. She wasn't there. The room was dark. The storm was upon them. His palms started to sweat. Sulfur filled his nostrils as he lit the candle on the table and the oil lamp on the wall.

"Lizzy, where are ye?"

The back door banged in its casing. He caught a glimpse of her in the back yard, bent over, holding her sides. Mo's heart twisted in his chest. He'd hurt her. He'd hurt her bad.

Mo ran to the door and stepped out. "Lizzy!" he hollered against the wind. Bits of sand and coral stung his face and chest. He needed to get her inside. Mo stepped closer, holding onto the railing. The wind sucked his breath away.

"Lizzy!" He leapt from the stairs, sprinting across the yard. He pulled her up from the ground. Tears streamed down her face. "Oh, Baby, I'm sorry." He held her as tightly to his chest as he could without breaking her ribs. How could he have been such a fool? How could he have hurt someone so precious to him? How could he. . . ?

Lizzy collapsed in his arms. "Lizzy!"

Chapter 19

Lizzy darling, please wake up." Mo laid her on their bed. He had examined her for cuts and bruises and found none. *Why has she fainted, Lord? Please, show me what to do.*

She groaned.

"Lizzy, wake up, Girl." Mo brushed her lips with his own. "I'm sorry, Honey, I didn't mean to get so upset." Her eyelids flickered open and closed. "Come on, Darlin'. Come back to me."

She opened her hazel eyes, her pupils dilated and unfocused. "That's it, Honey, wake up."

"What?" A hoarse whisper escaped her throat.

"Ye fainted in my arms, Honey." He pushed a few strands of wayward hair from her mocha cheeks. "Are ye feelin' sick?"

"I haven't eaten much today."

"Can I get ye somethin'?" He eased off their bed.

"No, stay, Daniel. We need to talk."

"All right. I'm sorry about earlier. You're right, I've kept some of the darkest parts of my past hidden from ye. I don't want your head soiled with such horrible memories."

"And I've hidden things from you," she confessed.

"Ben?"

A gentle, rosy blush painted across her cheeks. "Yes. I loved him, Daniel. I—I. . ."

"Of course ye loved him. That doesn't bother me."

"Really?"

"Of course not. You married him for love. I could never take that place in your heart."

"That's the problem, Daniel, you are."

"What are ye sayin'?" He lay down beside her and cradled her in his arms.

"I've fallen in love with you, Daniel Greene. I know you didn't marry me for love, and I don't expect you to love me the way I love you. . ."

"Hold it right there, Woman. Ye love me?"

Tears filled her eyes. "Yes, I'm sorry."

"Silly woman. Don't ye be sorry for loving me. I just can't believe ye can. I'm not worthy of your love."

Lizzy propped herself up on one elbow. "Daniel, I don't ever want to hear you say that. You are the most tenderhearted man I know. You've won my heart, pure and simple. God's blessed me by giving me a man like you as my husband. Don't ever put yourself down again."

She loves me, Lord. His heart raced with joy—and fear.

"Honey," she continued, "your body may have scars, and I suspect your heart has some too, but they are nothing compared to the beautiful man you are. You're a wonderful husband, a good provider. Ben had trouble providing for his family. He had a bit too much of the wandering spirit in him. Don't get me wrong, he was a good man, but he'd start thinking about things, and before I knew it, he'd be out there plotting and planning. When news of the war came I knew he'd go. It fit in with his desire to free the slaves. He'd read *My Bondage, My Freedom*, or rather, he'd listened while I read. . . ."

"Ben didn't know how to read?"

"Well, I always thought he did, but since I've been working with you, and since there's been some time since I've been with Ben, I'm starting to see that he may not have known how to read. Or if he did, it wasn't very well. He always said, 'I love to hear you read; it's like the gentle call of an evening bird song'—or some other romantic thing. To make a long answer short, no, I don't think he knew how."

"For some reason, I always figured Ben was the perfect husband and an educated man."

"He was smart, don't get me wrong. But he was far from the perfect husband. Personally, I don't think there is a perfect husband, just a husband that's perfect for a particular wife."

"Do ye think I'm perfect for ye?" Mo leaned over and kissed the nape of her neck.

Lizzy groaned. "Yes."

"Great, because I love ye and I can't believe God's blessed me so much with such a wonderful gift as ye."

"You love me?"

"With all my heart, Lizzy. I have for a very long time. I've just been afraid to tell ye."

"Me too."

"There's something else you're keepin' from me."

"What?"

"Ye haven't been eating right lately."

"No, I've been so worked up about Ben and feeling I've been betraying my wedding vows, my stomach's just been a bundle of nerves."

Mo traced his finger down her side and placed his hand lovingly on her stomach. "Oh, I thought maybe. . ."

Lizzy's eyes opened wide. "Do you want a child?"

"If'n the good Lord gives us one, I'd be happy, yes. But with ye having four already, I'd understand if ye don't want another."

Lizzy rolled to her side and snuggled up to Daniel. "I've just been so emotional lately. I almost called you 'Ben' when, when. . .well, you know. And it shocked me."

Daniel chuckled. "Ye have called me 'Ben,' Darlin', and never knew it. I wasn't offended. I felt somehow connected to ye on a deeper level. Does that make sense?"

"I did?"

"Yes."

"I didn't mean to. I'm sorry."

"Forgiven. Tell me about Ben, how you fell in love."

"Do you really want to know this?"

"Yes. He's a part of ye, Lizzy. That will never change. Your relationship with Ben helped mold ye into the woman I fell in love with. Now I might be jealous that he's the one that gave ye those four wonderful children, but I'll never be jealous that ye had a good relationship with your husband."

"Well, he didn't look a thing like you."

Mo chuckled and listened to his wife's heart. She told him how she fell in love with Ben the first moment she'd laid eyes on him, how they had a whirlwind courtship and married as soon as her mother and father had allowed it. She explained how Ben had two passions in his life and how she shared the same passions. One was her and the children, the other was justice for Negroes. And while they talked the wind howled and whistled through the shutters.

Lizzy couldn't get over the fact that Daniel loved her. Of course, he had treated her as someone special all along, but he'd never proclaimed his love before. But today, lying on their bed together, he'd confessed his love half a dozen times.

"I love ye, Honey, but I'm starvin'. Do we have anythin' to eat?"

"Oh no." Lizzy jumped from the bed. "I had a special dinner warming in the oven."

"Let's hope the fires burned down before the food burned up."

Lizzy ran to the oven and opened the door. A charred layer crusted the pastry she had laid over the meat pie.

"Hmm, a little on the done side," Daniel teased.

"Slightly. We can take off the top layer of pastry and see if the insides are fine."

"You're a wonderful cook, Lizzy. I'm sure if this isn't okay we can find something else."

She nodded and took a fork and lifted the black crust off the meat pie. Sniffing the pie, she smiled. "I think it's okay."

"I'll get some crackers from the cupboard to take the place of the crust."

Crackers sounded wonderful. Her nerves had worked havoc on her system. Even after not eating all day, she had little desire to fill her stomach. Just one sniff of the pie and she felt her stomach roll.

"Lizzy?"

"Hmm?"

"Are ye sure you're all right?"

"My stomach isn't feeling too good. I really got myself worked up over nothing. I'm sorry."

"Think nothin' of it, Girl. I love ye, ye loves me. Life is great."

Lizzy smiled. Yes, life was good. Now if she could only get her raw emotions to calm down and realize what her brain and heart already knew. She and Daniel would have a good marriage. They would build a good home for themselves and the children.

Lizzy poked at the meat pie, eating a couple chunks of potato and some crackers and water. She didn't dare put anything more in her stomach. Maybe she'd caught a bug.

"Ye don't look well, Lizzy. Are ye sure you're all right?"

"I was just thinking maybe I'm coming down with something."

"A couple of the men haven't come in this week because they weren't well. It's possible you've caught somethin'."

"If you don't mind, I think I'll go to bed." Lizzy pushed the chair from the table.

"I'll clean up. Ye go lie down. I'll be in shortly."

Lizzy felt dizzy again and grasped the table.

"Whoa, come on, Girl. I'll carry you in."

"I can walk," she protested, as she wrapped her arms around his neck.

"Yeah, but this is much nicer." Daniel wiggled his eyebrows, and Lizzy felt the tingles all the way down to her toes. God had really blessed her by giving her this kind and gentle man. *Thank You, Lord,* she praised as she snuggled her head onto Daniel's shoulder.

⚓

After a good night's rest, Lizzy welcomed the morning. The storm had passed, and the birds were singing as light filtered its way between the cracks of the shutters. Lizzy watched the dust particles dance in the sunlight. They were so carefree and light, exactly the way she felt this morning after confessing her heart to Daniel. He loved her as much as she loved him; could life be any better?

" 'Morning, Lover." He reached for her and pulled her back to bed.

Lizzy giggled. "Daniel, you've got to go to work."

Daniel groaned. "Don't remind me. The way that wind howled last night, I'll be cleanin' up that dock for days." He snuggled up beside her. "Besides, the rooster hasn't crowed yet."

"He's probably still in hiding."

"Let's stay in bed and hide too." Daniel tickled her sides.

Lizzy squirmed away.

Daniel sat up in bed. "Glad you're feeling better."

"Nothing a good night's rest didn't cure."

"Good. Can ye cook me up a hearty breakfast before I go to work?"

She fetched her robe. "Sure. Eggs and bacon?"

"To start."

"Daniel Greene, you eat more than the whole lot of us and you haven't got an ounce of fat on you. Where do you put it all?"

They enjoyed their playful banter all through breakfast and then said their morning prayers together.

"Lizzy, I'll open the shutters and then go to work. I don't want ye up on a ladder after ye fainted yesterday."

"I'm fine."

"Maybe so, but I don't want nothin' to happen to ye. I'll take care of the shutters."

"Thank you." It was nice having someone who cared about her who didn't just need her, like the children needed her to look after them constantly.

She wondered how the children had fared through the storm.

Daniel opened the door. "Oh, no."

"What's the matter?"

"We've got someone's battered boat in our front lawn."

"What?" Lizzy ran to the front door. Sure enough, a capsized boat lay dry-docked on their lawn. "Oh my. I didn't realize the storm was so bad." Fear rose in her heart. "Do you think the children are all right?"

"Get dressed. I'll go with ye."

Please, God, keep them safe. She knew it was too late for that kind of a prayer, but still she had no idea the storm had been that intense. The bright azure sky didn't show any signs of last night's raging storm.

Daniel wrapped his protective hand around hers. "I'm sure they're all right, Honey. They would have sent someone over if there was a problem."

"I'm sure you're right but. . ."

Daniel squeezed her hand. "I understand."

They walked as fast as her legs would take them. Daniel's gait was much longer than her own. He piled up the distance in one step that would take her two to three. She could tell he was worried about the children despite his reassuring words. *He really loves the children, Lord. Thank You.*

They rounded the corner. Palm trees were down; palm fronds littered the street.

"Late last night I heard what sounded like a train outside our house. I'd say we had a small twister touch down not too far from us."

"God kept us safe."

"Amen to that." He released her hand and put a protective arm across her shoulder. "Ye slept soundly last night."

"My heart relaxed."

His broad smile warmed her. "Mine too. I love ye, Lizzy. I want the children to know I love them too."

"I think they already know."

"I suppose but I wanna tell them. And I wanna tell them how much I love ye."

"Oh, Daniel. Go slow. They'll need time to adjust."

"If ye say so. But I think they already know." Daniel winked.

"Momma." William came running toward them as they neared George and Clarissa's house. "Did you see the storm?"

"Some. Is everyone all right?"

William nodded his head so hard it looked like it could fall off. "The roof came off."

Cold fingers of fear gripped at her spine. "And everyone is fine?"

"Yeah, happened when we were sleeping. It's only part of the roof, Momma."

"Momma." Olivia came running. "Daddy, I missed you."

Daddy? When had Olivia started calling Daniel "Daddy"?

"We missed ye too, Sweetheart." Daniel got down on one knee, and Olivia jumped into his arms.

"Momma, Mr. Mo, we were just getting ready to head over to the house," Ben offered. "We lost the front corner of the roof. Uncle George says he can fix it."

"Let me go give Uncle George a hand." Mo placed Olivia in Lizzy's arms and headed toward the house. Lizzy couldn't help but smile.

"You love him, don't you?" Ben asked.

"Yes, Son. I do."

"Good. He's a good man, Mom. I think Daddy is happy for us."

"I think he is too." She brushed her son's short, nappy hair and pulled him to her side. "I'm so glad you're all safe."

"Uncle George says a twister touched down."

"Daniel thought the same. We have a boat in the front yard."

"I want to see it," Ben clamored.

"You will. Where's Sarah?"

"In the house or out back. She's looking for Kitty."

"Kitty?"

"A kitten. Mrs. Jones's cat had kittens about the time we moved to Mr. Mo's." In the distance she heard Sarah calling, "Kitty-kitty!"

Lizzy walked toward the house. "How bad is it?"

George stood on the roof with his hands on his hips. "It's repairable."

Daniel stood on the ladder. "I'll lend ye a hand, George. I'll run to town, tell Mr. Ellis, and come on back."

"Thanks. Buildings and I don't get along so well. I can make it so it won't leak, but it won't look pretty."

241

Daniel chuckled. "I don't knows how purty I'll make it, but it won't look too bad."

"I saw some of your handiwork at your place, Mo. You can come build at mine any time."

A terrible shriek came from the back yard.

Chapter 20

"Sarah?" Lizzy ran to the back of the house. Daniel jumped off the ladder, forgetting to climb down first. Everyone followed the terrible cries of Lizzy's seven-year-old daughter.

George called down from the roof. "She looks just fine from here."

In the middle of the yard, sitting on the ground, Lizzy found Sarah sobbing. Lizzy's heart raced. She tried to control her emotions. *Speak calmly,* she reminded herself. "What's the matter, Sweetheart?"

Slowly Lizzy slid to the ground. Something was in her daughter's lap.

"Kitty's dead." Sarah sniffed.

"Oh, Sweetheart, I'm so sorry."

Daniel sat down beside them. "Are ye sure, Sarah?"

"Kitty's not moving." She wiped her nose with her sleeve.

"Can I see Kitty?" Daniel asked, reaching his hand out ever so slowly.

"Why'd she hafta die, Momma? Why?"

"I don't know, Sweetheart."

"But it's not fair."

How could she deny that? Death was a part of life, but it was a part of the sinful life that we now live on this earth. Death wasn't supposed to happen. And yet it did.

"Sarah," Daniel whispered, "sometimes bad things happen to good people. And sometimes bad things happen to innocent kittens. But God uses these bad things to make us stronger. Look at my wrist, Sarah. What do ye see?"

"Scars." She lifted her gaze to Daniel's. He'd gotten her attention.

Give him the right words, Lord, Lizzy prayed.

"And do ye know how I got these scars?"

Sarah nodded her head, yes. "Because you were a slave?"

"Right. But are thar any shackles on my arms now?"

"No." Sarah knitted her eyebrows.

"That's because God took somethin' bad and turned it around. I'm sorry Kitty is dead. But one day, and it may take quite a few days, you'll only have good memories of Kitty, of all the times ye played with her, petted her."

"Do you still remember the bad things that happened to you as a slave?"

"Yes. But the pain is getting less. Look at what the good Lord has given me, and other people like us. The war is over; the slaves are free. And God's given me a special family that loves me and that I love. My heart hurts because your heart hurts, but I know together we can get over this pain."

Sarah opened her hands. The small animal lay in her skirt. "Mr. Mo, can I call you Daddy?"

"Of course ye can, Sweetheart."

"Momma, is it okay to call Mr. Mo 'Daddy'?"

"Yes," Lizzy croaked out. Her emotions were running amok again. The salt of her tears burned the edges of her eyelids. God was taking the bad in their lives and making it right again.

"May I take care of Kitty, Sarah?" Daniel asked.

"Yes."

Tenderly Daniel's large dark hands lifted the white and black spotted kitten from Sarah's skirt. It fit completely in the palm of his hand. "Shall we bury her?"

Sarah nodded.

Lizzy went to the storage shed and pulled out a shovel. The children all gathered around Daniel. With very slow and careful movements he wrapped the kitten in his handkerchief and laid it on the ground. Then he took the shovel from Lizzy and proceeded to dig the hole. The solemn assembly watched with calm patience. How could one man engage seven children so much that they didn't move a muscle? *Oh, Lord, he's such a good father. Thank You.*

Lizzy stepped back to the shade of the house. The horror of Sarah's scream and the fact that she'd been so sick the day before had left her weak.

"Are you all right, Lizzy?" Clarissa whispered.

"I'm getting over a bug. I'll be fine."

"Can I get you a cup of tea?"

"Thanks, that would be wonderful."

Clarissa darted into the house. Lizzy sat on the back step and watched Daniel carefully place the wrapped animal into the bottom of the pit he'd just dug. Gently, he placed the first shovel of dirt onto the poor little creature. Sarah sniffled. Soon, each of the children were wiping their eyes. Ben and George Jr. pretended not to shed any tears.

Daniel clasped his hands and bowed his head. All seven children bowed their heads as well.

"Father, God, Ye give life to everythin' that lives. So we give Kitty back to Ye. Help these young 'uns to get over the pain. In Jesus' name. Amen."

All seven mumbled, "Amen."

Lizzy found herself saying amen as well. But to hear George's "Amen!" from the roof startled her. Not only had Daniel captured the children's and her attention, but he'd also captured George's.

"He's a keeper, Lizzy," George said, staring down at her.

"Yeah, I know."

"Young 'uns, I hafta go to work, but I'll be back soon. Will ye help while I'm gone?" Daniel asked.

They all nodded their agreement.

"Lizzy, walk with me partway?"

"Sure."

Clarissa handed Lizzy a cup of iced tea. "Take this with you."

"Thanks."

Daniel escorted her out of the yard and down the street before he began to speak. "I hope I did good with the children."

"You were marvelous."

"Do you mind the children calling me 'Daddy'?"

"No. I'm glad the girls want to call you 'Daddy.' I'm sure the boys will soon."

"I'm honored." Daniel pulled her closer to him. The warmth of his chest deepened the closeness she felt for him. "I can't tell ye how proud it made me feel."

Lizzy stopped and Daniel turned to face her. "I'm especially glad for Olivia. She never knew her father. She never called anyone 'Daddy' before."

"God has blessed me."

"No, Daniel. God has blessed us."

A quirk of a smile slipped up the right side of his face. "I love ye, Lizzy."

"I love you too."

"I've got to go. Ellis will git a-worryin'. I'll git back to your brother's as soon as I'm able."

"I may take the kids home, have them change their clothes, and come back."

"Whatever ye think is best. That roof won't be fixed by the end of the day. I can get it right, but it won't be waterproof tonight. It'll take some materials George doesn't have and, I suspect, will be in short supply if this storm hit many homes."

"You might be right. Should I prepare dinner for everyone at our house? Get the little ones out from under foot?"

"Might be a good idea. Make a large pot of that fish chowder. Have the boys go fishin'. Gotta be some good fishin' right now."

"All right." Lizzy didn't want to release him. She wanted to spend the rest of the day in his arms.

He stepped back.

She leaned into him.

He stepped back again.

She let him slip from her grasp.

"I'll see ye soon, Honey," he whispered, before his lips captured hers.

And then the cool breeze that swept past her lips made her aware that she was still standing in the middle of the road with her eyes closed. She opened them to find Daniel walking toward town. "I'll miss you," she whispered.

He turned and waved. Had he heard her?

⚓

" 'Morning, Mr. Ellis," Mo called from the edge of the street.

" 'Morning, Mo. It's not too bad, considering."

Mo surveyed the damage. Seaweed lined the shore and lay in heaps on the dock. The netted sponges appeared to be all in their places. "Looks pretty easy to clean up."

"How'd your home survive?"

"Just fine. Someone's boat capsized on my front lawn, though."

Ellis shook his head in wonder. "And you're several blocks from the shore."

"I think it may have been in someone's yard. It didn't appear to have anythin' growin' on the hull."

"You're probably right." Ellis leaned down and pulled the lines to his sailboat. "How'd she fare?"

"She looks fine. Need to bail her out, though. She's riding low in the water."

"I'll stay and lend ye a hand, but I was wonderin' if'n I could help my brother-in-law. He lost part of his roof last night."

Ellis paused and dropped the line. "Is everyone all right?"

"They're all fine. Kinda scary. The children were there for the afternoon and ended up stayin' the night."

"I'm glad everyone's okay. Can I lend a hand?"

"We're needing to replace the front corner of the roof. I know I can get most of that done with what George has around his house. But new shingles will be in high demand."

"I'll run into town and see what I can find. You go, take care of your family. This can wait until tomorrow. We'll need to wash all the sponges again before we can dry them."

"Thank ye, Mr. Ellis. I appreciate it."

"No problem. Cook would have my hide if I didn't let you go."

Mo chuckled. "I imagine she would. Everythin' all right at your house?"

"Yes. I had a tree lose a good sized branch, but it missed the house. Knocked over a bird feeder I put in last month—but that's nothing."

"Sounds like the good Lord spared us from anythin' major."

"So far. I haven't heard from too many folks, but things are looking pretty good." Ellis headed down the dock with Mo before turning off to town. "I'll see you in a bit, Mo."

Mo headed home and gathered his tools and a couple of two-by-eights he had been saving to help with the roof of the new cistern he planned on building. With the boards over his right shoulder and his toolbox in his left hand, he headed back to George and Clarissa's home.

His joy overflowed when he saw Lizzy and the children heading toward him. "Hi."

"Mr. Mo, can I help you?" Ben asked.

"Honestly, I need ye to help your momma. We've got shutters that need opening and I don't want her goin' up the ladder. She wasn't feeling very good yesterday."

"You're sick, Ma?" Ben asked.

"I'm feeling better, Dear."

"Can I count on ye, Son?" He eyed Ben, man to man, or rather, father to son. Ben puffed up his chest. "Yes, Sir."

"Thank ye. Your mom might need some other help. There's a boat in our front lawn—no telling how bad the back yard is."

Actually he knew and it wasn't too bad, just debris from downed tree branches and palm fronds. But he didn't want to be looking out for Ben with so little time to do a major repair job on George's roof.

"Can I help Momma?" William asked.

"I'm sure ye can, Son. Your momma is goin' to need all your help."

William beamed.

Mo turned to his wife. "You're looking pale, Lizzy. Are ye okay?"

"I'm fine, just tired."

"Ben, when you're finished helpin' your momma, get George Jr. and catch us a bundle of fish for dinner."

"Yes, Sir."

Lizzy grabbed her stomach.

"Lizzy?"

"I'm fine. Just the thought of cleaning fish made my stomach queasy."

"Can ye clean a fish, Ben?"

"Yeah, not as good as you. But I can do it."

"Okay, ye clean the fish. Sarah, ye help your ma in the kitchen. Liv, ye make sure Momma lies down. And, William, your job will be to clean up the back yard."

All four nodded their heads.

"Lizzy, lie down. I don't want ye gettin' worse."

"I'll try."

He narrowed his gaze, givin' her fair warning he wanted to see that she had lain down. She looked to the ground and slowly raised her gaze. Mo chuckled. "Lizzy, you're a beautiful woman and I love ye, but I need to get to work. Behave for your momma, children."

Olivia waved. "Bye, Daddy."

"Bye, Sweetheart."

Sarah hugged his leg and William hugged the other. *Goodness, Lord, it's hard to leave these people.* It was a good thing he went to work every morning before they woke up. "Love ye all, bye." He stepped forward, the children released him, and he willed himself to go help his brother-in-law, though every last muscle demanded that he turn around and help his family. Yes, *his* family. *Thank Ye, Lord. I'm so blessed.*

Ben worked hard doing his man-sized job. Lizzy was thankful Daniel had taken the time to give each of the children an assignment. As much as she didn't want to admit it, she was starting to feel poorly again. She lay down on her bed, and Sarah stood guard. "Can I get you some water, Momma?"

"No, Sweetheart. I'm fine. I'm just going to rest a bit."

"All right. Olivia and I will do the dishes."

She'd forgotten that they'd just run out of the house this morning without taking care of any of the chores. Lizzy rolled over. She needed to rest. Her eyes flickered shut. Peace swept over her. She went to sleep hearing the girls pump the water.

"You young 'uns go clean up now. I'll take care of your momma." Lizzy woke to the distinct sound of her mother's voice. Or had she been dreaming, as often happened when she wasn't feeling well and wanting her mother to come and take care of her? A silly notion, since she was all grown up, but one that would slip in her subconscious once in awhile.

"Mom?"

"Land sakes, Child. What's the matter?" Francine towered over her.

"Just a stomach bug. Has me dizzy and my stomach is uneasy."

"Hmm. What did you have to eat today?"

"A slice of toast and a cup of tea."

"How long have ye been feeling this way, Child?"

"A couple days. Not too long."

"Elizabeth Hunte Greene." Francine placed her hands on her ample hips. "Think, Child, when was your last. . ."

"No, I can't be."

"Well, you've been married a month."

Lizzy's eyes widened. Could she be expecting? She placed her hand on her stomach.

Francine chuckled. "I'm going to be a grandma again."

"It could be a bug."

"And a conch can live outside its shell." Francine wagged her head. "I'll fetch you some crackers and make some tea. You stay down. I'll take care of the family."

Lizzy groaned. Pregnant? Shouldn't she and Daniel have more time together before they brought a baby into the world? On the other hand, this way there would only be five years' difference between the baby and Olivia. *A baby? Diapers.* Lizzy rolled over. *Okay, let's think this through.* When was her last cycle? Two weeks before she got married. Which meant she could be close to four weeks pregnant. How was she going to tell Daniel?

No, Daniel said he'd love to have a child. Apparently she didn't have much say in the matter.

A baby. . . Oh no, Lord, the rumors. People are going to think. . . No, I don't need to worry about what people think. I know, Daniel knows, and You know we weren't in the family way before we were married.

Her mother brought in a cup of tea and a plate of crackers. "Eat what you can, Dear. You need to get something down."

"What am I going to tell Daniel?"

Francine chuckled. "The truth."

"Of course I'll tell him the truth. I meant, how am I going to *tell* Daniel."

"Does he not want children?" Her mother sat down on the bed beside her.

"He does. I'm the one that wasn't sure about having any more. I have four already."

"I know, which surprises me why you didn't figure this out for yourself."

"I just wasn't thinking, I guess."

Francine roared. "Something like that. Tell me, Sweetheart, do you love him?"

"More and more each day, Mom. He's so incredibly gentle and kind."

"He's got a good heart." Francine tapped her gently on her shoulder.

"Yeah."

Francine went to the kitchen. Lizzy heard Ben and George come in with the fish. Her mother complimented them on the fine job they'd done cleaning them. Lizzy decided to stay in her room a bit longer.

"Momma, are you feeling better?" Olivia asked.

"Some, Sweetheart. Thank you."

"Daddy said to let you sleep."

"Daddy's here?"

"He's out back with Uncle George."

Lizzy leapt out of bed, then realized she shouldn't make quick moves. The smell of fish bubbling in the pot. . .the fast movement. . . She held her stomach.

She fought her body's responses and headed into the kitchen to find her way to the back door. "Daniel, are you finished?"

"Roof's done. Mr. Ellis came by and several of the neighbors and lent a hand. It's shingled and everythin'."

"Wonderful. Are you busy?" Lizzy held the doorjamb for extra support.

"I'll be in in a second, Honey."

"Smells great, Cook. Where's my wife?" Daniel asked as he kicked off the dirt from his boots on the threshold.

"In your room." Francine gave him a strange smile.

"Lizzy?" Mo stuck his head in the doorway.

"Sit down, Daniel. We need to talk."

"What's the matter? Are ye okay?"

"Oh, I'll be fine."

"Then what's the matter?" Daniel eased down beside her. Her eyes sparkled, but her hands wrung the quilt as if it were her worst enemy's neck.

"I figured out why I'm not feeling well."

"And?" He reached out and placed his hand on top of hers. His heart sank, but no matter what was wrong, they would handle this together.

"I'm going to have a baby."

"A baby!" he boomed.

Lizzy nodded.

"Yahoo, Lizzy girl, you've made me the happiest man alive."

"Really?"

"Really." Daniel placed a hand on his wife's flat stomach. "There's a little one growin' inside of ye. I can't be more pleased and more amazed at God's good grace."

A smile lifted Lizzy's deep plum lips. "A few short months ago I prayed for a home, a place of my own for myself and the children. I can't believe God's filled His promise to me from Romans 15:13: 'Now the God of hope fill you with all joy and peace in believing, that ye may abound in hope, through the power of the Holy Ghost.' My hope was a home. Not only did God give me a home, but He gave me a new husband and another child born out of love. I love you, Daniel Greene."

"And I love ye, Lizzy girl. A father. I'm going to be a father! I can't believe it." Daniel threaded his fingers around Lizzy's. "A few months ago I only hoped for a peace from the past, to be able to feel like I was worth somethin'. God has filled us to overflowin'."

🌴

Lizzy looked over and saw their bedroom doorway filled with ten faces, all smiling, all staring.

"You're going to have a baby, Momma?" Olivia asked.

"Yes, Sweetheart."

"And I'll be her big sister?" Olivia continued.

"Yes." Lizzy nibbled her lower lip. "But the baby could be a brother."

Ben crossed his arms. "You kissed Mr. Mo, didn't you?"

Lizzy chuckled. "Yes, Son."

"Under the moon." Ben shook his head. "I told ya that's how you get babies," he lectured.

The house erupted in laughter. God had filled their house with joy. The past would leave its mark, like the scars on Daniel's wrists and back, but the heart could still find the peace, the hope, and the joy of the Lord.

Southern
Treasures

To my church family.
May God continue to bless us as we work together to bring God's love
to various cultures and people in Miami, Florida, and beyond.
I love you all and thank you for your faithful prayer support.

Chapter 1

Key West, 1868

Ship's a-comin'!"

Peg heard the bustle of folks outside her storefront window. When a ship came to port, everyone tended to notice. She slid the needle into the white linen cloth and placed it on the counter. Holly leaves and red berries gave the napkin the Christmas flavor she missed. Stretching her back, she stepped up to the bay window overlooking Key West harbor. She loved her little shop and the view.

A two-masted schooner with a black hull and white trim pulled up to the long dock. It still amazed her how shallow the waters were around the island, so unlike the waters around Savannah. Out of habit, she looked toward the stern of the boat to see the name of the vessel and its point of origin. Even after all these years, she still feared running into people she had known back home.

The Patriot, out of Boston, Massachusetts. A smile creased her face. She watched as the men secured the lines, then helped the passengers off the ship. Peg giggled, watching them regain their legs as they waddled down the pier.

Nathaniel Farris bounced down the gangplank from the boat. Peg waved. Nathaniel turned in the direction of Peg's store and also waved. She knew he couldn't see her, but she also knew he was well aware of her practice of watching the ships unload.

Ellis Southard marched up the pier, shook hands with Nathaniel, and proceeded to make his way onboard the ship. Peg stepped back from the window. Ellis always made a point to get to know the captains of the various ships. His business depended upon reliable export of his sponges.

"Anyone interesting?"

Peg jumped and turned around to meet her customer, Vivian Matlin. "Good morning, Vivian. How are you today?"

"Fine, fine. Tell me—did anyone interesting arrive? I can't see as far as I used to." The gray haired woman came up close to the counter.

Peg glanced back out the window. A stately man, with dark hair and silver sideburns, braced himself against the piling, allowing his body the time it needed to adjust to solid ground.

"Well, Nathaniel Farris returned from his latest trip."

"He's such a fine jeweler. Can't believe he escorts some of his jewelry to New

York, though. You'd think he'd trust someone else to do that."

"Ah, but that's because of a sweet little woman who also lives in New York," Peg confided.

"You don't say," Vivian grinned. "Tell me more."

Peg smiled. She knew more details than the rest of the island residents. Nathaniel had proposed marriage to Julie this trip. He'd made her the most beautiful engagement ring Peg had ever seen. And by the smile on his face Peg could tell that Julie had accepted. "You'll have to ask Nate."

"Oh, it's Nate now. Come on, Peg. First you tell me there's a special woman in New York, now you're calling Nathaniel Farris by a nickname. You're trying to confuse an old woman, aren't you?"

Peg chuckled. "Possibly."

"Oh, phooey. You used to be the best source of island gossip. What's come over you?" Vivian pushed.

"Conviction, I guess. It finally occurred to me that if I didn't want my secrets talked about on the streets, I shouldn't be talking about others."

"Oh, well, that's a low blow." Vivian smiled. "But you're right. It's hard when it's the island's favorite pastime."

"Yes, I know." Peg went to the counter and pulled a package out from underneath. "Here you go, Vivian."

"I'm so excited. May I open it and see?"

"Of course."

"You do such marvelous work. My granddaughter will be so surprised to get this for Christmas." Vivian delicately lifted the fancy box covered with a printed fabric and lined with lace. The box alone was quite a gift. But Vivian had insisted that, for her first Christmas as a wife, her granddaughter needed to have something very special.

"Oh my, Peg. This is wonderful." Vivian's voice caught in her throat. "Even in my younger days, when my eyes were good and my fingers nimble, I couldn't have done something as lovely as this."

"Trisha deserves it." Peg beamed. She loved when people were genuinely pleased with her work. The store carried crafts from a variety of island residents, but the thrill of a special sale like this—or the linen napkins she had been embroidering earlier for Bea Southard—made her feel useful.

Vivian's blue-veined hands pulled out the lady's blouse Peg had transformed. A fine lace border lined the collar and cuffs. Delicate tea roses traced the tips of the collar, and a small bouquet draped high over the left breast. A ring of tiny tea roses encircled each buttonhole and cufflink. It wasn't Peg's normal fare, which amounted primarily to making napkins and linen tablecloths, but Vivian was a good customer, and she had purchased the blouse. Peg praised the Lord she had been able to fulfill Vivian's desire.

Vivian gently placed the garment back in the box. Her hands shook with emotion. "It's beautiful. Thank you."

"You're welcome. I enjoyed it." And she truly had. The money she would make from the sale wouldn't come close to compensating her for the hours she'd spent on it, but that didn't matter, not really. "Charity begins at home," she recalled her grandmother saying on more than one occasion.

Vivian fished through her drawstring purse. "I can't believe this is only costing me a dollar. You're sure that's enough?"

No, but that's not the point, she reminded herself. "Yes." After all, hadn't Vivian helped her get this business off the ground during the war? Hadn't she been the one to help drum up the local residents to come into the store? Vivian Matlin, advertiser extraordinaire. She was the best advertising Peg's store, Southern Treasures, ever had.

Nathaniel Farris walked in. His broad grin spoke volumes. "Looks like it went well, Nathaniel."

His grin slipped. "In one way, yes, in another, no."

"Oh?"

⚓

Matt scanned the tropical island while regaining his land legs. The captain had warned him to expect a certain amount of unsteadiness. The trip from Savannah seemed short enough, but he'd watched the folks struggle down the dock. Pride dictated some decorum. If he were going to establish a business office in Key West, he didn't want the locals' first impression to be that of an unstable man.

Thankfully, he'd convinced Micah to join him during his Christmas break from school. Micah was the real reason he'd come to Key West. Granted, the business would prosper in this strategic location, but Micah's future—and his past—quite possibly rested upon this small, remote island.

Matt eased out a pent-up breath.

Today is not the day to be dwelling on that, Lord. Lead me to the right location and the right individuals for this business, Matt silently prayed. He lifted his brown derby, wiped the headband with his handkerchief, and placed it back upon his head.

"May I help ya, Sir?" a gangly Negro boy asked with a smile as bright as the sunshine.

"I've rented a room from a Mr. Isaac Salinger. Are you familiar with this man?"

"I know where he lives. Would you like me to show the way?"

The boy was probably trying to earn a coin or two, what with Christmas coming on. Matt was confident he could find the place with the help of the instructions on the letter in his pocket, but he had to smile at the lad's entrepreneurial spirit. "That would be most agreeable. Shall we wait for my luggage?"

"Momma won't worry none if I'm a few minutes late. I can wait."

"What's your name, Lad?"

"Ben. Benjamin Hunte."

"Well, Ben, it's a pleasure to meet you."

The boy nodded and leaned toward him. In a hushed voiced he added, "If you don't mind me saying so, Sir, you need to get in the shade. Dem dark clothes in this heat isn't wise. Unless, of course, you're used to it."

Considering the trickle of sweat running down the back of his neck, he figured the boy made sense. Savannah was hot in the summer, although it cooled down some in the winter. "You might be right." Matt scanned the shoreline. There were a few palm trees, but not much shade. "Where do you suggest I wait?"

"That cluster of palm trees might help some, but if'n you have a light shirt on under your overcoat, take the coat off."

The lad had a thin cotton shirt with short sleeves and a pair of light cotton trousers hanging loosely on him, with the cuffs rolled up to just below the knees. A pair of sandals adorned his feet. Matt's long jacket, vest, and wool pants contrasted like night and day. Matt removed his jacket and draped it over his arm. "Is this better?"

The boy tossed his head from side to side. "Not much, but you'll get used to it, if'n you're going to be here for awhile."

"I'm hoping to." At least as long as it took to explore the possibility of setting up his business here.

"Hey, Ben. What are you doing down here?" A full-bearded gentlemen in his thirties approached from the ship. Matt had seen him board the ship shortly after it docked.

"Mr. Ellis, I'm helping him—" The boy pointed in his direction. "He needs to find Mr. Salinger's place."

"I see. And does your momma know you're down here?"

"No, Sir."

"What about Mo?"

"I saw Dad a few minutes ago. He knows." The boy puffed out his chest.

The stranger extended his hand. "Name's Ellis Southard. Ben here is the oldest son of my foreman."

That explains the man's familiarity with the child but—"Pleasure to meet you, Mr. Southard." Matt extended his hand and exchanged a short, courteous handshake with Ellis Southard. He always believed you could tell a lot about a person by his or her handshake. This one was firm and straight to business. "My name is Matthew Bower. I'm looking into using Key West as a possible location for my export business."

"It's a busy port. What do you export?"

"Cotton. I'm based in Savannah, but the war was hard on my industry."

"On a lot of men's, I'm afraid. I'm not sure how a cotton export would work for you here, but if I can help, just let me know. I deal in sponges. It's a natural product for the area, and the demand for them is growing."

"Interesting. I export from Georgia, as well as the Louisiana and Alabama areas, so it seemed logical to see if Key West would give me an advantage over waiting for the cotton to sail up to Savannah."

"Makes sense." Ellis Southard nodded slightly. "I hate to run, but I'm on a tight schedule. Ben here will show you where to go. See that dock over there?" He pointed to a dock to the left of where they stood. It was long, and loaded with brown and yellow balls, obviously sponges. "That's my dock. Come on over after you're settled in. I can give you a general idea of the time schedule of the ships."

"Thank you. That's very kind of you."

"Just being neighborly." Ellis Southard waved and headed down the dock toward shore.

"Friendly."

"Most folks know everyone here," Ben offered.

Matt hadn't realized he'd spoken out loud. "Appears so. Your father works for Mr. Southard?"

"Mo is my second dad. My father, he died in the war."

"I'm sorry to hear that, Son." And he truly was. He lost a brother to that war. And he'd been fighting his personal politics on the subject ever since.

Finally, his trunk was lowered and brought off the ship by some seamen. "Can you bring it to the end of the dock?" he asked them.

"For two bits." One sailor cocked a grin.

"One."

The two grumbled and carried the trunk to the end of the dock. He'd need to rent a wagon or something to bring his trunk to Isaac Salinger's.

The boy tugged on his shirtsleeve. "I can get a wheelbarrow."

"Thanks. I think that would be a good idea."

Ben ran off like lightning was licking at his feet. Matt ambled down the dock. The two crewmen walked up to him and held out their palms. He tossed them a silver dollar and figured they could work out splitting it between them. He sat down on his trunk and visually examined the local businesses. The harbor seemed lined with boats and warehouses. Tucked in among them, he noticed a store.

A store? Sure enough, in the heart of a trading port was some sort of ladies' store. He could barely make out the sign. S O U T H, *Southern*, T R E A S, *Treasures*, Southern Treasures? What kind of a business was that?

Matt heard the sound of iron hitting rock and turned to see Ben pushing a wheelbarrow just about as big as himself down the street. Matt rushed over to relieve the boy. "Where'd you get this?"

"Mr. Ellis."

Either Ellis Southard was quite important to Key West, or he was just a very friendly man. On the other hand, Ben's stepfather was the foreman of Ellis Southard's business. "Tell Mr. Ellis I said thank you when you return it for me."

Ben nodded and stood back while Matt lifted his trunk onto the wheelbarrow.

"What's that store over there?" he asked the boy.

"Southern Treasures."

"What kind of a store is it?"

"Mostly ladies' things. My dad bought my mom some fancy napkins and a tablecloth from there for her as a wedding present."

"Oh. Are there other stores in town?"

"Sure. But Miss Martin, she owns Southern Treasures. She likes being on the water."

"Martin?"

"Yes, Peg Martin."

Peg Martin! Margaret Martin—Lord, it can't be that easy to find this woman, can it?

Chapter 2

Peg slipped the hard-earned dollar into the cash drawer. In reality it was a tenth, a tithe, of what she should have charged. But a gentle breeze of pleasure calmed her. It was right to do unto others as she would like them to do for her.

When Vivian exited the building, Peg returned her gaze to Nathaniel. "What happened?"

"She turned me down."

"Is that woman out of her mind?" Peg placed her hands on her hips. "Did you show her the ring?"

"Never got a chance." Nathaniel's shoulders slumped.

"Well, you best set yourself right down and tell me what happened. Start from the beginning." Peg settled on a stool behind the counter as Nathaniel sat on a stool opposite her in front of the counter.

"Not much to tell," he said, folding and unfolding his hands. "I came calling, and she seemed distant. Not like any time prior. It was all so strange."

"Did you ask her to marry you?"

"No, not really. I asked her to go out to dinner with me, and she said she was busy."

"That doesn't seem like the woman you described before."

"That's my point. She was different. She avoided my touch. It was all rather bizarre." Nathaniel looked up and caught her eyes. "She wouldn't even look at me."

"Did you speak with her father, mother, anyone?"

"No one was talking. Her father suggested I return home. Nothing for me in New York."

"Ouch." Peg reached over and placed her hand on top of his. "Nate, something isn't adding up. Pray about it, and write her some letters. See if she starts warming up."

"I don't know, Peg. It seemed so final."

Peg cared for Nate, not in a romantic way, but he was a good and honest man. She wanted to storm up to New York and demand to know what happened. On the other hand, she thought of two possible answers right off. One, the woman had fallen in love with another. Two, she had been violated. Her own past made her sensitive to these kinds of reactions—the family's shame, the woman not wanting to touch or even look at Nathaniel. But she could be all wrong, and she didn't want to pollute Nathaniel's mind with such horrific facts of life. It was probably none of her business, but she would be penning a letter off to Julie Adams as soon as Nathaniel left the store.

"Do you love her, Nate?"

"You know I do."

"Then fight for her. Write to her. Keep writing until you feel nothing for her. Or until the Lord tells you it's hopeless."

"Do you think she'll even read my letters?"

"Maybe not at first, but give her time. Something must have happened." Peg clamped her jaw shut. She wasn't going to say another word.

Nathaniel pulled out the ring. "I was thinking of giving this to my best friend."

Peg stared at the small jewel case.

"On the trip home. I did a lot of thinking." He rolled the box between his long, slender fingers. "You and I get along so well, I was—"

"No," Peg said with a bit too much force. Nate jumped and blinked. "Sorry. I like you, Nate, but not as a woman should love a man she marries."

"Yes, I feel the same way about you. You're more like my older sister."

"Older, huh? Thanks."

Nate chuckled. "Sorry."

It was true, though: She was getting on in years. At thirty-eight, she was an old maid, but she wanted it that way. It was her destined lot, her payment for her past mistakes. "Now you know it's not polite to tease a woman about her age."

"I was going to say, before you interrupted me," he winked, "that, unlike Mo and Lizzy, I don't see us getting married as friends. I was just feeling low."

"And this is to make me feel better—picking on my age?" Peg teased.

Nate fumbled for his words. "Oh. . .I mean. . .well. . .oh, just pull the conch out of my mouth. Maybe I'm not designed for romancing a woman."

Peg chuckled. "Your approach could use some work."

She glanced back at the ship. Most of the passengers were off. The distinguished looking gentleman had taken off his jacket and was talking with Benjamin Hunte. "Did you mingle with the passengers?" she asked Nathaniel.

"Some, why do you ask?"

"Just curious. Who's that man speaking with Ben Hunte?"

He glanced out the window. "That's Matt Bower, a businessman from Savannah."

"Savannah?" Peg felt the room sway. She took in a deep breath, eased it out slowly, closed her eyes, and sucked in another breath.

Calm yourself. There've been others from Savannah. Never, not even once in the twenty years she'd been on Key West, had anyone ever addressed her past. Of course, she kept a low profile. Most folks didn't even know she came from Savannah. Not that she kept it a secret, but she didn't go reminding everyone every time she turned around either.

She opened her eyes and focused on the two blurred images of Nathaniel in front of her. His hands were now holding hers. "Are you all right?"

"Fine, must be the heat." She pulled her right hand from his grasp and fanned herself to hide her duplicity. *Get control. It's been twenty years.*

"Shall I get you some iced tea or something?"

"I'm fine. I have some water in the back room. If you'll excuse me, I'll go fetch some."

"Sure, I need to get to my store anyway." Nathaniel slipped off his stool. "Peg?"

She turned and faced him.

"Thanks. I appreciate your friendship."

"You're welcome. I'm sure it will work out." She smiled. At least, she hoped she was smiling.

In the back room, a narrow storage space that followed the backside of the building, she chipped some ice from the icebox and poured herself a glass of water. "Lord, I know I should be over this, please give me strength."

"Hello? Anyone in here?" a male voice called out from the storefront.

Peg straightened her skirt and exited the back room. "May I help—" Her voice caught. Her throat constricted.

Sweat beaded on her forehead.

Her hands turned to ice.

The room darkened.

Prickles traveled up her skin as the past slammed into the present.

The room spun.

Darkness. . .escape. . .

Matt caught the delicate blond in his arms before her head hit the floor. *Does she know who I am, Lord? How could she?* He pulled a decorative pillow down from the shelves and placed it under her head.

"What happened to Miss Martin?" Ben leaned over her.

"Not sure. Do you have a doctor on the island?"

Ben nodded.

"Would you please go get him?"

"Be right back." Ben ran from the store.

Matt released her and folded her arms across her belly. He eyed a small pitcher in the back room she'd just exited. Had the heat overtaken her? It was warm, but it didn't seem that hot. And if she lived here all the time, why would this moderate heat bother her?

He fetched the pitcher and a small towel that hung on a post beside the ice box. *Ice box.* He opened it, chipped off some ice, and wrapped it in the towel.

Beside her again, he gently dabbed her face with the cool cloth. *Father, she's beautiful. Of course, she would be.*

She groaned.

261

Her eyes fluttered open and closed.

Blue, of course.

"Hello." He waited.

Her eyes darted back and forth.

"You fainted. Here, drink some of this." Matt lifted her head and placed the glass to her soft pink lips.

Her gaze focused. "Who are you?"

"Matthew Bower. But most folks just call me Matt."

"Do I know you?"

"No, Miss Martin, we just met."

She took another sip. "I'm sorry. I don't know what came over me."

"Doc Hansen is on his way," Ben huffed from the doorway.

"Thank you, Ben."

"You're welcome, Sir."

Ben sat beside Peg Martin, who was now sitting on the floor. Matt realized he was still holding her head for support.

"Are you all right, Miss Martin?" Ben asked.

"I'll be fine, Ben. Thanks."

"Ain't nothing. Just came in to show Mr. Bower your store."

She looked into Matt's eyes again, seeking an answer to her question. *No, you don't know me,* he realized, *but I certainly know you and all about your past.* He glanced down to her ring finger. Her hands were slender and lightly bronzed from living on this island. But her ring finger was empty, and she was still going by her maiden name. Could she be the one? How many Margaret Martins could there be on such a small island? "The boy said you sold fine linens in here."

"You're looking for linens?" She knitted her eyebrows.

She'd caught him at his deception. "Truth be told, Ma'am, I was simply admiring a storefront in the middle of an export harbor. I myself am in the export business."

"I see."

"Peg?" a voice from behind queried. Doc Hansen, Matt presumed. "Ben said you fell."

"Mr. Bower says I fainted."

"Did you eat this morning?" The doctor began his examination. Matt got up and turned his back to give her privacy. There was no question in his mind; she was the one. The one he'd been searching for since he learned the truth. *The truth. . . God help me, I don't know if I can do it, Lord. I certainly just can't—*

"Dr. Hansen, I'm staying at Isaac Salinger's place. If you'll be needing anything from me, I'll be there." Without turning around, he added, "I hope you're feeling better, Miss Martin. Good day."

Matt flew out of the store faster than a goose flying south for the winter. Whatever possessed him to go into that store the first moment he came into town?

He kicked a sun-bleached hunk of coral out of his path. Picking up the ends of the wheelbarrow, he said to Ben, "Suppose you show me where Mr. Isaac Salinger lives before anyone else passes out from this heat."

"I never known Miss Martin to faint like that. She's been here forever."

Matt stole a glance back at Southern Treasures. It was a quaint store, he had to admit. Seemed to fit her delicate beauty. He wasn't a connoisseur of fancy lady things, but he'd bought Esther a few niceties in his day.

Esther. What would she say if she knew? Would she bury the secret like Dr. Baker had? Or would she be as compelled as he had been to find Margaret Martin and tell her the truth?

Matt raked his hand through his damp hair. It *was* hot today. Perhaps Miss Martin was simply stricken by the heat after all.

No, there was a look in her eyes when he walked in the store. As if she knew—but how could she?

Chapter 3

Three weeks," Peg mumbled and went back to her work. It had been three weeks since she'd made a perfect fool of herself fainting in front of Matthew Bower. The man seemed perfectly harmless, but she still couldn't face him. If she saw him coming down the street, she'd hurry off in another direction just to avoid him. Daniel, her brother, had even had some business with Matt. He seemed normal enough, yet there was something about him that unnerved her. The worst part was that she couldn't figure out why.

Peg stitched the final blue heron on the baby blanket for Bea and Ellis Southard's boy. He looked just like his father with his brown hair and blue-gray eyes. Southard eyes, Peg decided. Their nephew, Richie, had the same blue-gray eyes. The same shade of blue she'd used to embroider the heron.

The bell over the door jingled. Peg looked up with a smile, then dropped it immediately. Her hands gripped the blanket.

"Good morning, Miss Martin." Matthew Bower stood tall with his handsome jet-black hair and green eyes. The silver streaks on his sideburns made him look even more refined, if that were possible.

Peg swallowed. "Good morning, Mr. Bower. How may I help you?"

"You can tell me how you are. I've been concerned, but every time I've seen you in town you've run in the opposite direction."

He'd seen her. Heat assaulted her cheeks as strong as the hot sun at noon bore down on the small tropical isle. "I'm sorry. I'm rather embarrassed by my behavior the other day."

"For pity sakes, Ma'am, whatever for? You simply fell victim to this heat. I'm still adjusting to it. I certainly understand why things slow down in the middle of the day and don't really resume until midafternoon." He stepped closer to the counter. "I met your brother, Daniel. Nice fella. Pretty wife too."

"Carmen, she's a sweetheart. Perfect wife for Daniel."

"So it seems." He surveyed the various shelves of the store. "I haven't been in here since I first arrived. If you don't mind, I'd like to browse."

"Help yourself. You'll find we have a variety of items. Several island folks make them, and I sell them."

"Your brother seems to think rather highly of your skills." Matthew's hand traced the stitching she'd done on a placemat. Did he know what work was hers? How could he? *Lord, what is going on with me?*

"Your brother says you also hail from Savannah. That's where I'm from."

"Yes," she croaked out. Did he know her shame? Did he know Billy? *And why did Daniel open his big mouth? Okay, Daniel doesn't usually have a big mouth, but this time. . .*

"I'm looking into Key West as a port for my exporting business. I distribute cotton to South America and Europe."

Why is he giving me all this information?

"Savannah's a good harbor, but I'm not the only distributor there. I'm looking to expand my business and speed up the delivery time by working from here."

"We certainly have enough boats passing through," Peg said lamely. What else could she say? She didn't know why the man was here; she couldn't help her attraction to him, and yet she was terrified by him. All of which were silly reasons. After all, she was a grown woman, completely in control of her life and her destiny. She was right with God, and she'd made her peace with the past. She had a good life. So why was Matthew Bower so unsettling?

"That's what attracts me to Key West." Matthew stepped farther away, examining the next shelf over. In front of him stood items carved from coral rock. He lifted one and examined it closely. "These are quite good."

"Carlos Mendez makes them. It's a hard stone to work with."

"I can see that." Matthew placed the item back on the shelf. "Do you miss Savannah?"

"At first I suppose I did, but now I wouldn't know what to do with myself there."

"Have you ever spent any time in New York?"

"No."

"Fascinating place, but far too busy for myself." He moved over to the far wall where some of her lace work and linens were. "Ben said you made some linens for his mother."

"Mo bought them as a wedding gift."

"Right, he mentioned that. Fine boy."

"Yes, he is." What was this man fishing for?

"Miss Martin, let me be honest with you. I'm a widower. My wife passed away two years ago. I have a son named Micah. We were never blessed with any other children. I'm a decent man, make a fair wage for my labors, and I was wondering if you'd do me the honor of your company for dinner this evening."

"What?" Peg nearly fell off her stool.

"I find you an attractive woman, but that isn't what interests me. The fact that you passed out at the very sight of me—well, that can make a man be fascinated with a woman. Granted, I'm certain it wasn't my stunning looks that made you swoon."

"You look fine." Had she really let that slip out? Judging from the smile upon his face, she had. Her face reheated for the second time in a few short minutes.

"Ah, so it's not the hideous growth on my back that caused you to pass out," he chuckled.

Peg couldn't help but laugh. The man had to be the most handsome man she'd seen in a long time. Plenty of men passed through Key West, but none distinguished themselves quite like Matthew. "I don't keep company with men."

"You. . .your brother did tell me that. I forgot. Forgive me, Ma'am. I was so taken in by your beauty, I simply forgot myself." He bowed and grinned.

"What are you after, Mr. Bower?"

"A chance to become friends. If anything else develops we'll leave it in the Lord's hands, but I'm simply reaching out as a friend. Most folks are paired up here."

That was true enough. The seamen that came to port weren't the kind to settle down, but most other folks married young. Peg fanned herself. How did he do it? She was so flustered just being in the man's presence.

"I've been here for ten minutes, and you haven't passed out or run in the other direction. I'm making progress, I see." Matthew flashed his handsome, twisted grin, and Peg felt gooseflesh rise on her body all the way down to her toes. No one had ever affected her like that. Well, no one since Billy, she amended.

Peg chuckled. "You're positively incorrigible."

"Another one of my endearing qualities. Although Esther did find it annoying a time or two."

"Was Esther your wife?" She was interested; she couldn't help herself.

"Yes, we were married for twenty years. A good marriage. We had our ups and downs, but God was good, and we worked through most things."

"What happened? If you don't mind me asking." Peg placed the blanket on the counter.

Matthew edged closer and reached out to touch the embroidered heron. "You do marvelous work, Miss Martin. I've never seen anything finer. May I see the other side?"

"No, it isn't as pretty because there is a lining to cover it."

"Ah, much like ourselves, hey?"

Peg shielded her eyes. How could he know this about her? She was a fairly decent looking woman, although age was taking its toll. But on the inside she was still a mess. A scarred mess from the bad choices she'd made years ago. No one knew. Only her parents, and they were gone, and her brother, Daniel. No one else.

"Sorry, didn't mean to be so personal. It's just how I see myself. I have a great facade, but some of my inner thoughts, my secrets, need to remain hidden from anyone else's eyes."

"Did you know my family in Savannah?" Peg pushed.

"No, I'm afraid I didn't. It's a fairly good-sized city and, unless your father was in the same line of work as myself, I can't imagine our paths crossing."

"Dad was a fisherman."

"That explains your love for the water."

"How did you know?" she asked a little too quickly, amazed that for the second time she'd spoken her thoughts rather than kept them to herself.

"The view. You're the only residential business on the harbor. Everything else is commercial."

"I got the place during the war. A wrecker was calling it quits."

"A wrecker?"

"Oh, that's the name they gave the folks who salvaged the goods from sinking ships. The reefs around the island fool quite a few sailors. It was a great business until the war. Then the soldiers stopped it. Of course, the increase of naval vessels in the area stopped a lot of the groundings, and the light stations helped as well."

"So wreckers were pirates?"

"Goodness, no. It was very legal. They recovered material from the boats and were paid by the company that owned it, or their insurance company, or by the folks who bought it. Either way, a judge had to decide who got which wrecking permit. Mostly it was done in order, but from time to time a man would come in with a sighting and simply stake the claim. In other words, it was salvaging."

"Ah. I think I understand now. So, what do you say about having dinner with me?"

"Like I said before, I don't—"

"Keep company with men. I know. I just thought once you got to know me a bit you might change your mind. Besides, I'm not really looking for a romantic dinner for two, just someone to have some conversation with. Do you go out to dinner with friends?"

"Sometimes."

"Well, don't I deserve your friendship after I saved your life?"

"My life?" Peg wagged her head in disbelief.

"Ah, but, Ma'am, I caught your head in my hands mere seconds before it came crashing down on this hard floor." He winked.

"You *are* incorrigible." Peg smiled in spite of herself.

"I try. Please say you'll do me the honor of eating dinner with me. It's so boring to eat alone."

"I'm really sorry, but I've already made plans for the evening."

"Fair enough. But be advised, I shall return, and I will ask again." He nodded slightly, then winked before turning around and exiting the store.

"Thank You, Lord, for dinner plans." She didn't know how she could have turned down Matthew's request. He had a way about him that just. . .just what? Made her feel so on edge she felt like she was going to explode? That her past could come crashing down around her heels at any time? Or was it more simple than that? Was he awakening in her desires she thought long ago buried? She closed her eyes and breathed in deeply. That was probably the case. He represented a threat to all the decisions she'd made in her life. Decisions that had kept her well for many years. Decisions that kept her alone and never quite forgiven.

Oh sure, she knew God's grace covered the multitude of her past sins and present ones. But she couldn't forgive herself. Not now, not ever. She'd made foolish choices. Costly choices, and they had long-term consequences.

"Enough," she fumed. "I buried the past with You, Lord. Please take this guilt away. I can't deal with it any longer." Her son was dead, and it was all her fault.

Peg locked the door to the shop and slipped into the narrow back room where she knelt down in front of an old wooden chair and cried. Cried for her past. Cried for her son. Cried for the life she'd lost. "Oh, God, it still hurts after all these years. Why? How much longer do I have to wait for healing?"

🌴

Came on a little strong there, didn't you, Bower? Perhaps he should have tried a less forward approach. But it did demonstrate one thing. She might not be the same Margaret Martin he was looking for. *Who are you kidding, Bower? She's the one. There's no question, and you know it.*

Matthew walked up to a palm tree and leaned against it. He was due at the Southards' dinner party in half an hour. He'd hoped to bring Peg with him, but she'd refused just like Daniel said she would.

Did her past dictate her current choices? Obviously. *Twenty years, Lord. Hasn't the woman learned to cope with it by now?* He sighed. *Lord, I've only known for a couple months, and I'm barely coping with it. What will she do once she learns the truth? Maybe I shouldn't tell her.*

Matt headed toward the shoreline. Mounds of black eelgrass lined the shore. White puffs of churned-up sea foam draped the edges of the grass. Black and white, side by side, each contrasting the other, each having a part in the beauty of the ocean. They told a symbolic story that made him smile. Black stripes of sin cover us, but the white cleansing foam of Jesus washes the many sins of our lives and pulls them out to sea to be buried in the sea of God's forgetfulness.

Okay, Lord, I get Your point. I'll wait, but give me the words when the time comes. I can't imagine how this truth will rip apart this woman's heart. It's ripping mine. Matthew bent down and pulled up a handful of the eelgrass and tossed it in the ocean. *Help me get close to her, Lord. She needs a friend. Of course, when I tell her what I know, she'll not want to talk with me again.*

He rinsed his hands in the water and walked down the shore. Ellis Southard's house was down this way and up a few blocks. The long walk would do him some good, Matt reasoned.

"Hey, Mr. Bower."

Matt turned to see Ben waving. He appeared to be walking with his entire family. Mo Greene stood head and shoulders above any man he'd ever known, but the few times Matt had met him he seemed to have a gentle spirit. "Hi, Ben, Mo."

"Ya comin' to Mr. Ellis's for dinner?"

"Sure am. Are you?" Matt headed toward the family.

Mo extended his hand. "You're welcome to walk with us. Matt Bower, this be my beautiful wife, Lizzy."

"Pleasure to meet you, Ma'am."

"Nice to meet you too, Mr. Bower. Ben's told us so much about you."

Matt grinned. He'd hired the boy a few times over the past couple of weeks since arriving at the island.

"And these are our young 'uns. Ben you know. This here is Sarah, William, and Olivia."

"Pleasure meeting all of you."

"Do you really sell cotton that slaves picked for you?" Sarah knitted her eyebrows and crossed her arms over her chest.

"Since slavery is against the law, I don't suppose I do. But I did when it wasn't against the law."

"Sarah," Lizzy chastised.

"It's all right, Ma'am. It's an honest question. Don't know many men who didn't make a living using slaves in the South. I won't go talking politics, but I honestly never saw it as folks from the North did prior to the war. War makes a man think, some good thoughts, some bad. In the end, I surmised the Bible says a man shouldn't own another man. So I realize we were wrong. I'm afraid it doesn't change the way things were, but I feel I've wrestled with it and come to an understanding of my sin in this area. Can you share the table with a man who owned slaves?" Matt asked.

He watched Mo put a hand around his wife's shoulders. "Ye bein' honest, I suppose we can accept your word for how you were and how you feel now."

"Thank you. Did it take you long to feel a whole man, Mo?"

"Took some time. How'd you know?"

"The scars on your wrist are a dead giveaway, but I've read some of the abolitionists' works."

Lizzy relaxed her shoulders. "Who have you read?"

"Frederick Douglass, mostly."

The small parade made their way toward Ellis Southard's home. "Lizzy has me reading some of his work now," Mo said. "He explains it well."

"I was afraid you'd say that." Matt's lips twisted ruefully.

Mo slapped him on the back. "I think I like you, Mr. Bower, even if you owned slaves."

"Did you beat your slaves like Daddy's master?" Olivia looked horrified.

"No. I never beat another man nor did I order any beatings. But I did have men who worked for me that did. Once I found out, I fired them and hired others." Matt's stomach tightened. It was hard facing his past. He'd owned slaves. At the time, he didn't even have an inclination that it was wrong. It was so socially acceptable. Slowly, he was beginning to learn that what might be acceptable to men wasn't necessarily acceptable to God. These Negroes had every right to hate him.

He represented all the heartaches their people had gone through, and yet they were willing to share a table with him.

"You didn't tell me you owned slaves." Ben sidled up beside him and whispered.

"I'm sorry. You didn't ask. Does that mean you don't want to work for me anymore?"

"Hard to say. My father died fighting people like you."

Matt nodded. "I lost a brother, a father, and a dozen cousins to that war too, some on both sides."

"Some slave owners fought for the Union army?"

"Yes, families were torn apart. Some may never recover because of their pride."

"Which side did your brother fight for?"

"The South."

"Oh." Ben slumped his shoulders.

"Like I said before, Ben. I can't change the past. I can only choose to learn from it and move forward."

Ben paused in the road and scrutinized him. He bit his lower lip, then spoke. "You've been fair to me. I guess I can still work for ya—if'n Mo and Momma don't mind."

Matt sighed. Judging from how uncomfortable he was at this very moment, how much more discomfort would Peg Martin feel when he told her why he'd come to Key West?

Chapter 4

Peg washed the tears from her face and changed her dress. Tonight she would be having dinner with the Southards, and she didn't need to look like something just washed up on shore. She slipped the baby blanket into a cloth sack she had made for Bea for carrying diapers and a change of clothes for the baby. The same blue heron she'd put on the blanket also stood proudly on the sack. It could also make a handy bag once the child was old enough to carry things to the shore or whatever, she mused.

Peg nibbled her lower lip. Perhaps it was making these items for little James that had bought back those memories—not the fact that a handsome stranger from Savannah, Georgia, had been paying her some attention. How could he know her shame? It wasn't at all logical.

Peg slipped the blanket into the sack and pulled the drawstring closed. She took in a deep breath, straightened her skirt, and marched toward the Southards'. Tonight was for rejoicing, rejoicing in God's grace and His gift to the Southard family.

Peg smiled at the sound of the muted voices drifting from the house. Ellis had a penchant for doing things on a large scale. A small dinner party would turn up half the town, if Bea didn't put her foot down. Peg chuckled under her breath. Who could have stopped him? He was so proud, holding this first party to announce their new son. He'd been beaming since the day he discovered Bea was with child.

" 'Evening, Miss Peg." Richie bounced out from behind the railing of the porch.

" 'Evening, Richie."

"Is that for James?" he asked. His blue-gray eyes sparkled with excitement. "It is."

"Nanna is going to love that. Did you make it?"

"Yes."

Richie nodded his head up and down and placed his hands behind his back, then looked down at his feet.

"Has James received a lot of presents?"

"Nanna says for a little while folks will be giving James lots of presents. Then, after awhile, it will only be on his birthday, like me."

"I see. So, this little item I have in my purse—you would like me to wait to give it to you on your birthday?"

Richie's grin beamed. "You brought me a present? Yippee! Can I open it?"

"You'd better ask Nanna or Uncle Ellis."

Richie ran off hollering, "Nanna, Uncle Ellis."

Peg reached the front door, chuckling to herself, and knocked. Bea had told her often how she couldn't keep the boy still. Thankfully, most of the time he didn't run in the house.

"Peg, I'm so glad you came." Bea hugged her friend. The deep shadows under her eyes revealed volumes. "Come in, come in and join the crowd."

"Ellis got carried away again, I see."

"I don't think Cook or I could have held him down on this one. But he promised me that I was free to escape into our room if the evening wore on too long."

"Good, you look as though you could use some rest."

"James was up half the night. He's a good baby but. . ." Her words trailed off.

Peg picked them up. "But you won't mind when he's sleeping through the night."

"Exactly."

"I've missed you. I haven't been to town for ages." Bea draped a hand around Peg's waist.

"The shop's been busy. I meant to come before now. I just haven't had the time." Peg walked in step with her friend. "Oh, I made a little something for you— and James, of course."

Peg handed her the gift. "It's beautiful. And the heron is the same color as Ellis and Richie's eyes. How'd you do that?"

"A special blend of thread."

"You're so creative, Peg. This is wonderful."

Bea took the gift and showed it to Cook, who fingered the fine work with knowing hands. Her deep brown skin accented the white linen. "Mighty fine work, Miz Peg," Cook offered. "My eyes are getting too dim to do fancy work like this."

Peg was flattered, but she knew Cook could still weave a needle as fast as the best of them. Peg had sat in on several quilting sessions where folks were making quilts and linens for the displaced slaves. Lizzy, Cook's daughter, had begun the project shortly after she married Mo Greene.

The sack passed from woman to woman, and praises mingled with statements on how they were going to do more shopping at Southern Treasures and save themselves some time. She wouldn't mind the additional business, but Peg knew they were just being nice. Most folks didn't have the kind of money to buy too many of her gifts. She tried to keep costs down, but they were labor-intensive projects.

Peg whispered into Bea's ear. "When you get the sack back, you might want to look inside."

Bea smiled. "I did. It's wonderful."

"Now, where's this handsome son Ellis has been bragging about?" Peg scanned the room.

"Upstairs taking a nap. Come on. I need to check on him anyway."

The two women headed up the stairs. "Oh, I brought a little something for Richie," Peg offered as they stepped into the hallway on the second floor.

"Is that what he was hollering about?"

"Afraid so. I hope he's not disappointed. It's just some penny candy and a top."

"He'll love it."

Bea opened the bedroom door. Inside, the white bassinet was covered with fine white mosquito netting. Bugs were a problem on the island but manageable. Bea lifted a finger to her lips. "Shh," she whispered.

Peg nodded and stepped lightly on her toes, avoiding the click her heels would make on the hardwood flooring.

James's toothless grin looked up at them.

"Guess he wasn't asleep." Bea fussed with the netting and retrieved her son.

Peg's heart tightened. "He's beautiful."

"I'm kind of partial." Bea smiled. "Would you like to hold him?"

"May I?"

"Of course. He'll be asking for his supper shortly. Let me run downstairs and tell Ellis I'll be feeding James."

Peg sat down on the rocker and cradled her arms to receive the tiny infant. Bea scurried out of the room. Tears nipped at Peg's eyes as she fought to hold them back. "My, my, James, aren't you a handsome lad."

The baby cooed.

Peg removed the hoods from the baby's hands and caressed the tiny fingers. He wrapped his fingers around her much larger one and held on tight.

He turned his head toward her breast. Peg lifted him higher. "Your mommy will be here shortly." She caressed his soft cheek and kissed him tenderly on his forehead.

"You look so much like I pictured my own son." A tear slipped past her eyelids and ran down her cheek.

"Peg?" Bea whispered and closed the door. "You have a son?"

⚓

Matt couldn't believe the crowd in Ellis Southard's home. It appeared to be just about everyone who lived on the island. They all mingled—white, black, Hispanic—everyone together in one room. Since the war began, he'd been trying to understand how folks could look at others without considering race and equality. Yet here on a tiny, remote island in the middle of nowhere, the people had figured it out. Matt held his glass and saluted the heavens. *I finally got it, Lord. Thanks.*

Mo Greene walked up to him. The pure size of the former slave could make a man quake in his boots. Matt squared his footing. "Quite a crowd."

"Mr. Ellis doesn't hold back when he celebrates," Mo agreed.

"I can see that."

"I wanted to apologize for Sarah's behavior earlier."

"Nothing to apologize for, Mo. She spoke from her heart."

"The young 'uns have been born free. They don't know what it's like to speak only when spoken to, to not look a white man in the eye."

Matt noticed Mo had no trouble looking him in the eye. "You escaped, didn't you?"

"Yes, Sir."

Matt nodded his head. "Those wrists tell a story, Mo. I'm sorry you were locked in chains."

"The chains weren't nothin' compared to the beatin's."

"I'm sorry, Mo." What else could he say? It wasn't his fault, and yet, by not resisting the inhumanity of slavery, by owning his own slaves even though he'd paid them well, much to the annoyance of his business associates, he had been just as guilty as the men who used the whip.

"You understand, don't you?" Mo placed a hand on Matt's shoulder. Their eyes connected. Volumes of words were shouted between them, though not one was spoken. Mo tapped his hand on Matt's shoulder. "I'm pleased to know you, Mr. Bower."

Matt's voice caught. "Pleasure is all mine." Matt internally winced at the choice of social formalities he'd used. For it certainly wasn't pleasure that stirred in his gut. Acknowledging one's sins was never a pleasurable experience. However, God's grace covered those sins and brought about a cleansing so deep it washed him from head to toe. Matt couldn't wait to have some quiet time with the Lord.

Mo chuckled. "It's hard gettin' used to livin' a new kind of life, but I think you're gettin' there."

Am I that transparent, Lord?

"I'll leave ye to your thoughts." Mo left him standing there in the corner of the room, looking out the picture window to the back gardens of Ellis Southard's property. People were even out there mingling. Just how many folks had Ellis Southard invited?

"Matt. Glad you could make it." Ellis Southard walked into the dining room.

"Thank you for the invitation." Matt raised his glass of limeade.

"You're welcome. I wanted to hear more about the plans for your business." Ellis grabbed a sandwich from the table and walked up beside him.

"Not much to it. I've decided to relocate. Savannah was devastated by the war, although it is rebuilding. I thought if I could cut down on my expenses and speed up the delivery time by having the cotton arrive here rather than in Savannah, I might be able to still turn a profit."

"So you'd be needing a warehouse, some place close to the harbor."

"That I would. I'm afraid the property is pretty locked up. Most folks who own waterfront property have been making a profit and have no intentions of selling."

"True. But the wrecking business isn't what it used to be before the war, so there may be some property up for a decent price."

"Perhaps." Matt raised his glass to his lips. Maybe exporting was still out of the question. It had been his business before the war, and he'd done well. But with the boycott of Southern goods to the North, and the pirating of ships bound for Europe, he'd barely made anything during the war. Not to mention the fact that Confederate money wasn't worth the paper it had been printed on. "My understanding is that Key West remained under Union control throughout the war."

"Your understanding is correct. The men and women who sided with the South were allowed to leave. Some did. But not too long after that order had been given, it was rescinded. Folks somehow lived harmoniously during the war. That isn't to say a few arguments didn't get passed between the best of friends, but there was no blood shed, and for that I'm grateful."

Ellis Southard was an interesting man. Word on the street was he paid Mo more than most folks earned. And yet his business continued to grow. How could he afford such benevolence?

"So, where's this strapping young man you said was your son?" Matt recalled his own pride and joy at bringing Micah home for the first time.

"His mother is feeding him. Bea said she'd bring him down shortly after he's through." Ellis beamed.

"Children are a blessing from the Lord."

"Amen. You said you have a son?"

"Micah, yes. He makes this father proud."

"I know what you mean. Richie, my nephew, is such a fine young boy. Bea did an excellent job raising him," he added. "My brother and his wife both died, leaving Richie to my care. I know he's not my son, in terms of biology, but I still feel the same pride for him as I do for James. And at the same time, I have the same awareness of what an awesome responsibility God has given me to raise these boys."

"I hear you. I felt similar about raising Micah. He's twenty now and continuing his education, but he plans on coming here to spend his Christmas holiday with me."

"I look forward to meeting him."

"Ellis," a female voice called.

"Excuse me."

Ellis left, leaving Matt back to his own thoughts. He too felt that same awesome responsibility to raise Micah. Now, he realized, due to someone else's sin, he might lose what he thought was as much a part of him as life itself. Matt fisted his left hand, then flexed his fingers. *God, I don't think I can carry this yoke.*

Chapter 5

P eg, what happened to your baby?" Bea asked.

Peg's tears burned a path down her cheek. "Bea, I–I. . ."

Bea sat down beside her and placed an arm lovingly around her shoulders. "I'm sorry, I didn't mean to pry. I just never knew."

"No one does. Well, except my family." Peg sniffled and handed the tiny infant back to his mother. For twenty years she'd kept this secret, and now it was out. Peg closed her eyes and took in a deep breath, then slowly eased it out. Peg's heart tightened again as she watched little James suckle at his mother's breast.

"My child died at birth. I–I never knew him."

"Oh, Peg, how horrible for you. What about your husband?"

Peg twisted the handkerchief in her hands and turned away. How could she admit to her friend what kind of woman she had been?

Bea placed her hand on Peg's. "I understand."

"I'm glad you do; I certainly don't. I wasn't raised that way. I still can't believe I let Billy. . . Well, it was my fault just as much as it was his." Peg got up and started to pace. "We were engaged. Not that it matters any. The minute he found out I was with child he snuck out of town.

"My family had me stay with some relatives once I began to show, but no one could have guessed I would have lost the baby. Dan and I moved to Key West right afterwards. I thought I'd buried my past. But this new stranger to the island, Matthew Bower, something about him—I don't know, I can't put my finger on it— but his being here is bringing it all back. Like my entire shame will be brought to the surface. For twenty years no one has known.

"Just look at me rattling off my tongue with you now about it. I've never said a word to anyone. I barely even talked with Daniel. God took my son because of my sin."

"You can't believe that!"

Peg sat back down beside Bea. "Honestly, I don't know what to believe anymore. I had dinner with gentlemen a few times after we arrived, but I figured it was best to keep men at a distance. I don't trust myself."

"Peg, you're not the same naïve girl from the past. I don't think it would happen again."

"I don't know. I don't even want to find out. It's best to remain single. Doesn't Paul say something in the Bible about it being a noble calling?"

"Sort of. But still, God is a God of grace. He died for our sins. He doesn't continue to condemn us over and over again."

"I figure God's allowed me to have a peaceful life, a good business. That's His grace for me."

"I'm not going to argue as to whether or not it is God's will for you to remain single or not. I simply couldn't answer that. But Peg, you can't believe God took your son because you sinned. You're not the first to have a child out of wedlock, and you won't be the last, I'm sorry to say."

"Maybe you're right. I guess it really has nothing to do with Matthew Bower being from Savannah. Maybe it has to do with the fact that it's the twentieth anniversary of my son's birth and death. He cried so loudly when he was born. It was so hard to believe he lost his life mere moments later. I don't know what I would have done if not for the love of my family."

"God would have gotten you through it. What day was he born?"

"November twenty-eighth at six o'clock in the morning. It was a long night. I started labor early the afternoon before." Peg went on to explain the long labor, the need to be at the doctor's home, and the doctor's face when he told her the news. "He just confirmed what everyone's opinion was about a single girl having a child. Granted, it was a mistake, and I shouldn't have allowed myself to get into such a predicament in the first place, but—"

"But one sinner was condemning another."

"Right. I know I was wrong, but to have people condemning me on top of my own condemnation. . . It was a horrible time. That's why Daniel suggested we move here. A new place, a fresh start. No one would know. No one would care."

"So what does Matt Bower have to do with all of this?"

"Nothing, other than the fact that he hails from Savannah. I've avoided contact with folks from Savannah. Didn't want word to get out."

"Peg, my lips are sealed. I won't tell a soul. It's a matter between you and the Lord. But I'm here if you ever want to talk about it. Especially with the birth date coming up in a couple weeks."

"Those are my hardest days. Every year I relive what might have been. I know God has forgiven me, but I can't forgive myself."

"You must. You need to be free of the past." Bea squeezed her hand. "Twenty years is a long time."

"I know. I can't believe I told you everything."

Bea smiled. "Guess it's because you trusted me."

"Nah, it's because you caught me with my guard down."

Bea chuckled. "Probably."

Peg sniffed and dabbed her nose with her handkerchief.

James finished his dinner, and Bea handed him over to Peg to burp him. The tiny infant seemed so strong in her arms. She placed the cloth over her shoulder and lightly began to tap the baby's back.

"What would you do if the Lord placed a man into your life, Peg?" Bea asked, making herself presentable.

"Thankfully, I don't have to wonder about that. I know He won't. I've accepted the fact that I'm to remain single."

"Hmm, I wonder." Bea's eyes sparkled with mischievous intent.

Matt placed his empty glass on a tray and headed for the door. He'd spent enough time at Ellis Southard's to be able to leave yet still be socially appropriate.

"Mr. Bower," Nathaniel Farris called out to him.

Not quite fast enough. He sighed and put the social smile back up on his face. "Mr. Farris, how nice to see you."

"Pleasure's all mine. I heard you were looking to buy some waterfront property."

Word certainly does travel quickly on this small island. "Yes, do you know of some?"

"Not really. Jefferson Scott has a piece that he might be willing to rent. Don't believe he has a mind to sell. At least not yet."

"I see. And where might Mr. Scott's property be?"

"Do you know where Southern Treasures is located?"

Matt nodded his head.

"The dock behind the storefront. Actually, he owns the building the store is in also."

Of all the property on this little berg, it had to be Peg Martin's. "I thought Peg Martin owned it."

"The store, yes, but the building, no. Of course, she's a great tenant, and that added income would be helpful for launching a new business."

"True." But Matt needed more than just a pier, he needed a building for storage of the goods between shipments. And he'd been inside that storefront more than once; it was too small for what he needed. Of course, he could build a second and possibly a third floor. Matt scratched his five o'clock shadow. "Where might I find this Jefferson Scott? And speaking of buildings, who owns yours?" Matt added.

Nathaniel paled. "You wouldn't be—"

Matt chuckled. "No, it's too small, and too far from the harbor. I heard folks saying you might be asking Peg Martin for her hand in marriage."

"What?" Nathaniel swayed his head from side to side. "This island's grapevine can kill a man."

"Interesting term to use regarding marriage." Matt toyed with him. All the same, it was interesting he would mention Peg Martin's property if he were going to ask for her hand in marriage. Perhaps he hoped to keep his wife at home. Not that Matt could blame him; Esther had stayed at home raising Micah. But she had worked in her own way, arranging their social calendar, hosting dinner parties and endless other social occasions that helped a man's business grow and succeed.

"Peg Martin is a dear friend, but there is no truth to the rumor." Nathaniel looked uncomfortable.

"Ah, I see." And he did. Rumors and rumor mills abounded in small towns, and in large ones, for that matter. If he didn't know that to be true, then why had he kept his intent for coming to Key West such a secret? Because he knew how gossip spread. And no matter what the doctor had done of his own free will, Matt knew he'd have to live in the shadows of that doctor's decision for the rest of his life. Folks were bound to talk once the truth was told. And Micah might never have a future here as a result. Perhaps Matt should reconsider. After all, no one knew except himself.

Peg washed her face and dabbed it dry with a hand towel. Bea had left her alone in the nursery to collect her thoughts. In some small way, she felt better to have someone know her secret. *Would she tell?* Peg nibbled her lower lip. *No, not Bea. Someone else, possibly, but never Bea.*

Straightening her hair in the mirror, she practiced a smile. It looked fake, but she had no choice. Half the town was here, or so it seemed. Maybe she could sneak out while Bea and Ellis were showing off James. She clutched her drawstring purse and forced herself to leave the quiet walls of the nursery.

Laughter filled the air. Peg clutched the railing. No, she chided herself, they weren't laughing at her. She stepped down another stair.

Ellis's voice boomed above the rest, and the house went silent. Folks looked toward the dinning room where Bea stood beside her husband. The happy couple. Had it only been a couple years since Bea arrived at Key West?

Peg's eyes drifted over the crowd. Folks were paired off. Mo and Lizzy stood proudly in a corner. Lizzy's swollen belly spoke of the love and new life she and Mo had. Toward the back wall and close to the front door stood Matthew Bower. He looked as out of place as she felt.

His eyes glanced up the stairway and locked with her own.

Peg's palms began to sweat. She rolled her shoulders back and took another step down.

Matt gave her a solitary nod and broke their gaze. He focused on Ellis.

Peg tried to hear the words, but they were muffled by her own inner thoughts and turmoil. She fought off her fear and took another step down, one step closer to the front door. Did she really want to walk past Matthew Bower? Her hand tightened again on the railing.

The crowd erupted into laughter and cheers. James started to cry, and Bea jiggled her son on her shoulder. The room calmed and folks resumed their conversations with each other in hushed and whispered tones.

Cook stood proudly at the bottom of the stairs as Peg stepped down the remaining steps. "Cook, please tell Miz Bea I've an order I just have to finish, and thank her for the kind invitation."

"Certainly. Are ya feelin' all right, Child?"

"Fine. Just exhausted getting ready for Christmas orders."

"I imagine so. I'll give Miz Bea the message."

"Thank you, Cook." Peg sidestepped to the front door.

"Allow me." Matt Bower opened the door for her and bowed slightly. *A gentleman—what's a man like that doing in Key West?*

"May I escort you home or to your business?" Matt asked.

No, she wanted to scream. Didn't he know he was the source of her discomfort? Of course not, he didn't have a speck of knowledge. And yet there was something in his vivid green eyes. "Home," she answered.

He held out his elbow for her to slip her hand within its crook. His arm seemed strong and firm below the layers of his clothing. She clasped tighter.

Matt placed his hand upon hers and patted it. "Your honor is safe with me, Miss Martin."

Honor? He had no idea how little she actually had. Peg bit her inner cheek and nodded her agreement to his escort. They stepped down the stairs and walked out the small driveway to Front Street.

"Nathaniel Farris mentioned that Jefferson Scott might be interested in selling his waterfront property."

Peg stopped, pulling Matt Bower to a halt. "You're going to buy my building?"

Chapter 6

"I need a pier, but the building is too small for my purposes," Matt told her.

Peg stayed firmly planted. Matt tried to move her forward, but she resisted his gentle encouragement.

"Why are you doing this to me?"

Her golden hair glittered in the lamplight. "I'm not doing anything to you, as you say. I'm simply looking for a place where I can conduct my business. Your building quite possibly may be the answer to my prayers."

"But. . ."

"Look, you have a quaint business. But I need a place to store and distribute my goods from. Personally, the property is too small for my needs, but perhaps I could build upon it."

"You'd tear it down?"

"Progress, Miss Martin, progress. You must think in those terms."

"Progress? You can't be serious. I've been in that location for seven years. I'm bringing in a fair salary for my work."

"I don't doubt that. You've some fine merchandise. But my business would employ folks from the town. Yours simply gives them some extra pocket change every once in awhile. Besides, you don't need to be located on the waterfront, whereas it is essential for my business to be located there. You could move yours further up Duval Street, no harm done. Mine couldn't be anywhere else."

"Is this why you came into my store earlier today? Did you ask me to go out with you simply to tell me of your grand plans to ruin my business?"

"What was in the limeade you were drinking? I'm simply letting you know I will be speaking with Jefferson Scott on the morrow. I certainly didn't want you to assume I would go behind your back regarding the property."

She bent her head down. "I'm sorry," she mumbled.

Matt calmed his inner thoughts. Knowing the truth didn't set a man free; it bound him tighter than a bale of cotton. "Apology accepted. And I apologize for any offense I might have caused you. I must say, we have quite a way with each other. The first moment you see me you faint, and now—"

"Correction, it wasn't the first time. I noticed you after you departed the ship."

Matt grinned. "Ah, it must have been my captivating good looks. It causes all the women's heads to turn."

She shot him a sideways glance, and he chuckled. She giggled and recaptured his arm. "It must have been."

"But, Madam, you must not swoon at my feet. For, alas, my heart belongs to another."

Peg released his arm.

"I'm a widower, Peg," he explained. "I still love my wife. We had many cherished years together."

Peg recaptured his offered elbow. "Yes, you mentioned that earlier."

"So you see, your honor is safe with me." Matt flashed his million-dollar grin. Getting to know this woman would take all the understanding he could muster. Esther had easy been to read. Or so he'd thought. She did manage to keep her illness hidden from him for a year. Looking back now, he saw how she hid the truth from him.

"I have no doubt you are a gentleman, Mr. Bower."

"Tell me about your island." Matt hoped if her tongue loosened about something simple, that might help build a bridge to one day allow them to. . . To what? What did he hope to accomplish by telling this woman anything? He fought the tension rising in his spine.

"There's not too much to tell. The island was first a part of Cuba and thus a part of Spain. It was a gift to Juan Pablo Salas as a thanksgiving for his services. He immediately sold the place to Mr. Simoneton from Connecticut. Prior to that it was a watering hole for ships passing through the region. I've been told it's on some of the oldest maps of the area. Today, cisterns are a major part of most households, but back then there was fresh water on the island. The government is involved with removing the salt out of the water for fresh drinking water. But it's a costly task. Thankfully, there is a good rainy season, and the cisterns hold us well."

"How many folks would you say now live on the island?"

"Around four thousand. Back in the thirties John Audubon was here, painting and drawing the birds and animals of the island."

"Were you here then? You must have been a child."

Peg's lips curled upward into a delicate smile. "No, my brother and I arrived about twenty years ago."

"Esther and I arrived in Savannah about that time. I was bringing my wife home from the North where I attended business school. My father, a true Southern gentleman, couldn't believe I'd educate myself in the North. But he loved Esther and decided, if for nothing else, my education in the North brought him a fine daughter-in-law."

"If I'm not imposing, what happened to Esther?" she asked with tender compassion.

"She had an illness that caused her great pain. The doctor said he'd seen it before, but there was nothing to cure her. It was as if her insides were dying before they should. Unfortunately, the pain became so great that her medicine took control of her body. Her last months were exhausting, and with the war in full swing, little could be done. Her suffering tested my faith in a merciful God in ways I never dreamed possible."

Peg tightened her grip of his arm. "I'm sorry. Losing someone close to you is a terrible pain."

Matt tapped the top of her hand. "But the good Lord gets us through it."

"Yes, yes, He does," she whispered.

Matt stopped at the end of Front Street. "Where do we go from here?"

"Oh, sorry. I wasn't paying attention. I live up Duval a couple of blocks. My brother and I purchased the home shortly after we arrived on the island. I have a small apartment, and he and his new wife live in the main part of the house. Carmen was a widow with three young children when Daniel met her."

"A brave man to take on an entire family."

"Seems to be a lot of that going around after the war. So many families left without husbands and fathers."

"True. War rips at the very heart of a family. I lost my father and brother during the war. Thankfully, my son was spared. By the time he was old enough to fight, the war was ending. At least it had ended in Savannah."

"I understand the North took Fort Pulaski in 1862? How did that affect the city?"

"Just about ruined us. My business, by virtue of its trade, was perhaps one of the hardest hit. Shipping cotton became a primary target of the North. They didn't want us earning money to reinforce the troops with supplies."

Peg nodded soberly. "We were spared bloodshed on the island. As soon as word got out that Florida was seceding from the Union, Captain J. M. Brannan marched on Fort Zachary Taylor and took possession of it for the North. He actually sent for reinforcements before he marched. So it wasn't long before additional troops from the North came here."

Peg halted. "This is my home. Thank you for the escort. It wasn't necessary, but it was nice to get to know you a bit."

"Pleasure was all mine. I'd love to visit with you again, if you don't find that being too forward." Peg Martin was easy to talk with. Perhaps he could establish a relationship with her of some sort that would help him build up to telling her why he'd really come to this remote island. Of course, there might be no need to tell her at all. It might simply not matter.

Who are you fooling? He, more than anyone, knew the importance of the information he had. She would want to know. She had a right to know. *Didn't she?*

"Good night, fair lady, may your dreams be blessings from our heavenly Father, gifts of mercy, peace, and joy." Matt kissed the top of her hand and departed.

Why on earth did you do that, Bower? Now the woman will never want to see you again. She'll be certain you're after a romantic relationship. Was he? No, he had been a happily married man. One only finds true love once in his lifetime, and Esther was that love. But the golden image of Margaret Martin fused in his mind as he watched the silver moon edge past the palm trees that lined the road. Was he ready for another relationship? No, he couldn't be. Esther had only been gone for a little over two years. And what about Micah? What would he say?

"Micah, I miss you, Son," he whispered into the night air.

Peg unlocked the door to her small apartment. A part of her missed the full use of the house, but it had been practical for Daniel and Carmen to have the majority of the dwelling. She often wondered if Daniel had put off marriage because of her and her past. Just how many lives does one sin affect? Peg closed her eyes and blinked back the tears. No, she wouldn't cry again. After all, she'd opened her heart to Bea—wasn't that enough?

Peg filled a kettle with water and placed it on the stove. Lighting a small fire, she got comfortable for the evening.

Matthew Bower seemed like a fine man. She looked down at her right hand where he had kissed it. She'd been kissed many times in formal greetings, but never had she experienced the warmth that traveled up her arm as his lips touched her skin. Now, Peg fought off a chill that ran through her body.

Oh, admit it—he's handsome and nice, and you're attracted to him. She heard the water boiling in the kettle and poured a cup into an old mug she'd had for years. She dropped in a pinch of English breakfast tea leaves, her favorite, and brought the mug to the living room, where she lit a small oil lamp and fished out some needlework from her bag beside her chair.

Needlework by day and night. "You really should get out and enjoy life, Peg," she said out loud. "And speaking to yourself is a sure sign of senility." Perhaps being social with Matthew Bower wasn't such a bad idea after all.

Peg picked up her tea and sipped it slowly. Had she really not accepted God's grace and forgiveness for her past sins, as Bea had indicated earlier?

She scanned the solitary apartment. Bare walls, no paintings of family members or loved ones. Nothing more than a few hangings she had made to try to brighten up the place in a small way. The muffled laughter from the rooms next door revealed her empty life tonight. Life had moved on without her. She'd kept herself on the sidelines, refusing to accept that life could be different, that God's forgiveness covered a multitude of sins, including hers.

"Lord, I don't understand why Matthew Bower affects me so. Why am I so afraid of him and yet feel so comfortable with him? How can life be so confusing? Neither one of us is looking for a relationship, a romance. You know I could never have another romance with a man. But I would like to establish a friendship with him, if that is all right. He seems like a fair man, an honest man. Oh, but don't let him buy my building. I couldn't possibly afford to rent a store in town."

Peg finished off her prayer time with a few moments of reading God's Word. By the time her tea was finished and her daily readings were done, it was time for bed. For the first time in days she felt peace. Real peace. A God-given peace that allowed her spirit to calm.

A few days later, the sun shone brightly through her sheer white curtains, greeting her with a kiss of sunshine. Life was good. The anniversary of her son's birth weighed less upon her shoulders as the fateful day approached. Opening her heart to Bea had been a wonderful release, a reminder that not all condemn, and that some even show compassion when others stumble.

She was spending less and less time with Daniel and Carmen, having resolved they needed their own private time to build their new family. But each day she'd run into Matt Bower. Their friendship grew slowly, very slowly. He still set her on edge when he was around. It didn't make sense—the man was a perfect gentleman. Yet possibly that was the problem. He seemed almost too perfect, although he did admit to his own shortcomings, like being unaware of his wife's illness for nearly a year.

Micah, she learned, was his son. *There couldn't be a prouder father,* she thought. He positively beamed when he spoke of the boy. But he wasn't a boy any longer; he was a man, twenty years of age. *Could it be that I'm jealous of Matt and his relationship with his son simply because his son is nearly the same age as mine would have been?*

Peg dusted the ceramic pottery Gus Witchell had made for the shop. Matt was right; her trinkets did bring in pennies compared to what a thriving business could do for several families on the island. *Should I consider relocating?*

"Penny for your thoughts?" Nathaniel stepped up to her.

"I've got to get that bell back up on the door," Peg teased.

"Why'd you take it down?"

"To polish it. But I never got around to putting it back up. So, what can I do for you today, Nate?"

He fished an envelope from his pocket. "I received a letter from Julie."

"What did it say?" Peg made herself comfortable on a stool behind the counter.

"She apologized for not spending an evening with me and said she felt unworthy of becoming my wife."

"Did she tell you why?"

"No, not really, just words. . .like she wasn't the same woman I once knew. It's all very strange."

Peg nibbled her lower lip. Should she tell him what she suspected? "Nate, have you ever known a woman who was, was. . ." How could she put this tenderly? "Who'd fallen prey to a man's unwanted advances?"

Nathaniel's eyebrows came together and creased his forehead. "No, I suppose I never have. Are you saying. . . ?"

"I'm not saying anything except that I am seeing signs of a woman who may have been attacked."

Nathaniel crumpled the letter in his hand. Red infused his pale features. Peg leaned over and placed her hand upon his. "Nate, if she's feeling unworthy, perhaps something happened to her. Women feel an incredible shame when something like this happens."

He grabbed her hand and held it tightly. "If that be the case, I have some rather unholy thoughts toward the man who, who. . ."

"That's natural too. Pray, and write Julie again. Tell her that no matter what has happened you still love her and want her to be your wife."

"Why would her family not allow me to see her if that were the case?"

"Some families feel ashamed. In some cases, they believe their daughter or sister allowed it to happen. If she were a victim of an unthinkable act, they may not believe she was totally innocent."

"That's ludicrous."

"No, that's shame and guilt. A father feels he should have protected his daughter more. A mother feels she should have been more watchful. And on and on it goes. Some families work through it. Some kick the daughter out and turn her to the streets. I suspect since she's still with her family, they will work it out. But you and I both know your social standing in New York, and her family may assume that your family would not accept tainted goods."

"Hogwash! My family would never even need to know."

"Nathaniel, write her again. Tell her your heart. Give her a chance to heal. I may be all wrong. Possibly nothing has happened. But if something has, I know you're a man with a tender heart and would want to help Julie heal."

"You're a good friend, Peg. How did you acquire such wisdom?"

Because I've been there. "Just watched and listened over the years. You hear all sorts of problems. It's nothing more than any other lady would have told you."

"Perhaps."

"Go write another letter. Give her time to respond and see what she says. If she still loves you, then I suspect she'll come around."

"I should have just brought her with me when I came. Forget the formal ideas of a year's engagement and such. None of this would have happened," he mumbled.

"Now don't you go blaming yourself for what might or might not have happened. You'll be no use to her or yourself."

Peg got up from the stool and came around the counter. She wrapped her arms around Nathaniel and embraced him.

"Thanks, Peg."

"Excuse me," said a voice from the door. "I'm sorry to interrupt."

Chapter 7

Peg rolled her eyes at Vivian's grin. It would take hours to convince her that nothing was happening between her and Nathaniel.

"I'd better get back to work. Thanks, Peg. I really appreciate your help," Nate said.

"You're welcome." Peg hustled behind the counter. Why had she felt the need to embrace Nate in the first place? Her foolish actions would have the grapevines humming the rest of the day.

"So, what can I do for you today, Vivian?"

"Nothing really. I just came to browse. I've done my Christmas shopping." Vivian came up to the counter and leaned toward her. "I thought you and Nathaniel were just friends."

"We are. I was just consoling the man."

"Consoling? What is going on?"

"Vivian, you know I can't tell you."

"Oh, phooey. You really are becoming quite a stick in the mud, Peg."

"Just call me 'Stick,' " Peg teased and picked up some needlepoint she was working on.

Vivian pulled up another stool. "Seriously, Peg, there's nothing going on between you two?"

"Nothing."

"What about the new man in town, Matt Bower? Folks are saying he's been beating a path to your shop nearly every day." Vivian wiggled her eyebrows.

"Matt is also a friend. He's from Savannah, where Daniel and I came from."

"Oh, so you're old family friends?"

"No, just have the same area in our backgrounds."

Vivian's shoulders slumped. "Hrumph. Isn't there anything exciting going on?"

Peg wondered if some harmless gossip might be in order to occupy the island's time on someone besides herself. "Heard little James Southard is cooing. Ellis seems certain he's saying Dada."

Vivian chuckled. "He's quite proud. You should see little Richie. You'd think he was just as responsible for the baby as his father."

"Oh? Tell me."

Vivian rattled on about Richie and the many errands he was taking to make certain James was being cared for properly, and how Cook and Bea had to do some creative thinking to keep the boy occupied. But Vivian was only momentarily distracted. "So there's nothing to the rumor that you and Nathaniel are getting married?"

"For the last time, Vivian, no."

Vivian waved her hands. "All right, all right. I can take a hint. It's just that he made this beautiful engagement ring. . . ."

"Yes, I know. It is beautiful. The woman he gives it to will know she is loved."

"True. I rather like Nathaniel's way of setting a ring. Nothing overdone, just simply stated, showing the jewels in the best lighting."

Peg pulled the thread through the cloth and tied off the end. "He is quite good."

"I shouldn't keep you, but I was curious."

Peg chuckled. "I could tell."

"Two men wooing you at the same time makes for quite the conversation, Dear."

"Vivian!" Peg groaned.

"Just teasing you. Have a wonderful day. Fancy that, here comes Mr. Bower."

Peg rolled her eyes. She definitely had become the subject of many conversations on the island of late.

"Good morning, Miss Martin. How are you today?" Matt said, removing his derby and holding the door open for Vivian to exit the building.

I'd be better if you and Nathaniel didn't visit quite so often. Peg plopped her work on the counter. "So, what brings you this morning?"

Matt closed the door behind him and stepped farther into the store. "I've secured some property for my business."

"That's—" Peg's heart leapt in her chest as she caught Matt's somber expression. His green eyes darted back and forth. "You didn't?"

"I'm sorry, Peg. I had to. It was the only waterfront property available."

Peg looked around the full store. To move everything, the shelving, the inventory. . . The mere thought of it sent dread into the marrow of her bones. "How soon do I need to move?" she mumbled.

"January. I couldn't put you out just before Christmas."

"Thanks, I think."

"Peg." Matt stepped up beside her. "I really tried to find something else."

"I know." She stepped back. Her mind raced for an alternative location.

"I promise I'll help you pack and do whatever I can to help you set up a new store," he offered.

Like come up with the money? she wanted to scream. "I appreciate the offer. I don't even know where I'll begin."

"Micah's arriving just before Christmas. I'm certain he'll give a hand as well."

"Look, Matt, the island is a great place to get folks to help. I appreciate your offer, but seriously, I don't need it. When the time comes, I'll have more help than I can handle." She turned and marched back behind the counter.

Matt nodded and retreated to the front door. He looked at the slate that told folks she'd be closed on the twenty-eighth of November. "What's this?"

"Oh, nothing, just a personal day. Every so often a person needs to take one." She wasn't about to tell him the importance of that date and what it meant to her.

"Good day, Miss Martin."

"Good day, Mr. Bower." Their fragile relationship had reverted to formal greetings. She had to move. She definitely didn't like the month of November. Nope, nothing good ever happened in November. At least not to her.

You handled that well, Bower. Matt stomped toward town. *And to bring up the notice on her door. You know perfectly well what that day represents, and you're keeping that information from her,* Matt scolded himself. If he kept this up there would be no living with himself.

But what kind of life would. . .

Nope, he couldn't think about that. Too much uncertainty remained. If he started to think in those terms he'd never be able to simply leave the past in the past. He'd have to reveal the truth. But was he man enough to face it once it was revealed? With each passing moment, he was becoming less and less sure of himself.

Enough rambling about things not yet an issue. You've got work to do. Ordering lumber, setting up a construction crew. . . Letters needed to be written. The next few days would keep him hopping. If he was to open his business in Key West by February, he didn't have time for idle thoughts or worries from the past.

"Good morning, William." Matt beamed as he walked into the man's office. "I might have some work for you."

William rolled the edges of his mustache and said, "I heard you bought Jefferson Scott's waterfront property."

Matt chuckled and sat down on the oak chair. "You heard correctly." *I'm glad I told Peg immediately. Nothing is a secret for long on this island.*

"So, what can I help you with?" William pulled out a fresh sheet of paper and a pen.

Matt liked a man always ready for business.

The two men spoke for an hour, talking about materials needed, where to order from, how much from Cuba and how much from the North. All in all, William Horton gave solid advice, and Matt felt certain he would prove to be a valuable asset.

"Heard you were courtin' Miss Martin." William beamed, his handlebar mustache riding up his full cheeks.

"Now that rumor isn't true. Peg has simply been a good friend. But after I bought the place out from under her, I'm not so sure she'll be appreciating my friendship."

"Peg's a great gal. She'll get over it. She's always been a loner. Never spent any time with any fella that I'm aware of. Terrible shame for someone as pretty as her to not have an interest in men."

Apparently that hadn't always been the case, Matt mused.

"She does have a fine store," William said out loud. "I know my wife will be sad to see it close."

"I hope she'll be able to relocate further in town."

"Hmm." William rolled his mustache between his thumb and forefinger. "You know, there might just be the perfect place for her on Duval Street. A block east of the church. It's small but can't be smaller than the size of the place she has now."

"Really? Tell me more."

William scribbled a name and address on a piece of paper. "Here. See John Dixon, that's his address. I believe he owns the place." William handed the torn sheet of paper to Matt.

"Thank you. I hate to have her relocate, but it was the only property that would meet my needs."

"Does appear that way. Let me get on these orders. There's a ship heading to Cuba with the evening tide. I'll get your order out on that ship."

"Wonderful. Thank you again, William." Matthew extended his hand.

William grasped it firmly. "Pleasure's all mine. I hope your business will help our community. It appears like it might be able to."

Matt grinned. In Savannah, his business was like so many others. Here in Key West it would be one of a kind. Yes, God was with him, and he could make this work.

⚓

Peg grasped the side of the counter. *Of all the days. . .* She broke her train of thought. Wallowing in self-pity wouldn't help matters. She'd seen the inevitable. There wasn't another piece of property on Key West that would suit Matthew Bower's needs apart from the one she rented.

But today of all days! Why today, Lord? Why?

Peg let out a pent-up breath and decided to close the shop early. She'd need to find a new place to rent, and she had no spare time unless she closed the shop.

The island, with its large wooden structures around the harbor, seemingly would have lots of available space. But the fact of the matter was that many of the spaces had been owned and operated for years by the same businessmen. Hotels seemed to take up a large section of Greene and Front Streets.

Maybe she should just close up shop and do piecework for folks. They certainly knew where she lived, and she wouldn't have to pay rent for a shop that way. After all, the house was bought and paid for, and it wasn't that far up Duval.

Peg grabbed the accounting books. In order to decide, she would need to look the books over. She'd need to figure her profit, then decide what she truly had available for additional rent.

Lots of math, lots of homework. Numbers had never given her a problem, but to be working such detailed work the eve of her son's birth and death. . . Peg closed her eyes and fought back the painful memories.

November 28 was the one day she allowed herself to grieve. A solemn day. A day to reflect on the past, the present, and the future. Apparently not this year, though. *Future, huh? You've kept yourself from any future, Peg old girl, admit it. And now you're standing two years shy of forty, and you're wondering why.*

Peg lifted the ledgers and turned the sign that said to all the world CLOSED.

Her hand trembled. *One day that might be forever.* Her heart tightened in her chest. She fought the bile in her stomach toward one Matthew Bower. "Why did he have to come to Key West, Lord? Isn't there another place he could set up his business?"

Chapter 8

Carmen greeted Peg with a curious stare. "What's the matter?"

"Matt Bower bought the property."

"Oh dear." Carmen put down the broom. Her wonderfully tanned complexion and dark black hair glistened in the tropical heat. "What are you going to do?"

"I don't know. I brought home the books and thought I'd see if I should even bother with a new storefront, or try and do piecemeal work from my apartment. I've certainly established a clientele."

"True." Carmen brightened. "That's a wonderful idea."

Peg continued toward her private entrance into the house. Her sister-in-law followed. "Peg, Daniel told me about tomorrow."

"What?"

"Shh, I love you. I wouldn't say a word to anyone."

But why would he tell her?

Because she's his wife, Peg reasoned. Not that it made her comfortable with the notion that one more person knew her past. In a matter of two weeks, two additional people knew. Peg hung her head in shame and closed her eyes, fighting back the raw emotions.

"If it's any consolation, I nagged him for the answer. Once he finally told me, I was ashamed that I had pushed him. I'm sorry, Peg. I promise no one will know from my lips."

Peg simply nodded her head. What could she say? Her nostrils flared; her breathing deepened. When she saw Daniel she would give him a piece of her mind. Not that it mattered any. He'd held her secret for twenty years. She supposed a good marriage was based on openness and honesty. But why did it have to be openness about her life?

Carmen placed her hand upon Peg's shoulder. "For what it's worth, I understand your pain. I lost a child at birth," she whispered.

Peg opened her eyes and looked into the dark brown eyes of her sister-in-law. She saw the sorrow, the understanding, the pain. Without another word, the two women embraced.

Carmen pulled back and wiped the tears from her eyes with a delicate handkerchief Peg had embroidered for her as a birthday gift. "You're welcome to spend the day with me tomorrow."

"Thanks, but I generally spend the day alone."

"*Sí*. I understand."

"Thank you."

Carmen left the apartment shortly after, and Peg changed into her casual clothing. She had the ledgers spread across the table, along with other scraps of paper, ready to work the figures. The question was should she take some time and walk the streets looking for vacant storefronts, then work on the books. A gentle knock on her door gave her a momentary reprieve from making the decision.

Daniel stood outside the door. His sandy brown hair shadowed his eyes. "Danny." Peg couldn't keep her hurt and anger from her voice.

"I'm sorry, Peg." Daniel hung his head.

"I can't believe you said anything. Why?" Peg placed her hands on her hips, blocking the entrance to her rooms.

"I don't know. May I come in? Please," he pleaded.

Peg stepped back and relaxed her hands at her sides.

"Thank you. I truly am sorry. I know I probably should never have said a word to Carmen. It's just so hard not telling her everything about me. I love her, Peg. She's such a part of me. I can't bear the thought of keeping things between us. And November twenty-eighth had come between us. I hope you don't hate me."

"No, I don't hate you. I'm disappointed, but I don't hate. How could I hate you, Daniel? Without you, I never would have made it those first couple of years."

Daniel cocked a half a grin up the right side of his face. "And you've been an equal blessing to me. I don't think staying in Savannah I would have grown as much. I would have followed in Father's footsteps and never been allowed to be myself, to follow my dreams, not his, you know?"

Peg grinned. "Yes, I know. It's hard to believe they are gone."

"I know. When I went home to settle their accounts, it was hard selling everything Father had worked so hard for. And yet, there was nothing there for you or me. I just wished we could have convinced them to move to Key West." Daniel sat down on the sofa.

"Me too." Her father had been a hard man. A man of the sea, who'd lived through more storms than he could count. To have him and their mother die from an accident on shore seemed so strange. They had managed to visit Key West a couple of times over the years, but their visits were far too few and far too short. On the other hand, Peg realized she could have gone home and visited also. But she could never face the folks back home. Her mother swore no one knew, but she didn't trust Billy and what he might have said before he left town.

"Peg, Carmen won't say anything."

"I know. It's a hard year, Daniel. I don't know why, but it is. Last year seemed so serene. I thought I was getting used to it. But this year. . ."

"What do you think is different?" Daniel folded his arms across his chest.

"Mother and Father being gone, I suppose."

"Hmm, I suppose that's possible. Oh, is it true that Matthew Bower bought your place?"

"Yup. Right out from under me."

"I'm sure he didn't buy it intentionally to hurt you."

Peg nibbled her lower lip. "Maybe not, but it sure feels that way. I brought the books home to go over them."

"Carmen said you might work from the house. Personally, I think that's a great idea. You don't have any extra financial needs. We've done well over the years. You could even retire, and you'd still be taken care of."

"We don't have that much money, Danny."

"Okay, I'd still have to work. But we've invested well. My biggest mistake was not buying Jefferson's property years ago. Then you wouldn't be in the place you're in right now."

Peg grinned. "At the time, Jefferson wanted far more than it was worth. I imagine he's come down a few dollars."

"Oh, I imagine so. Word is, Matthew Bower is quite a businessman. He's fair, honest, and he can barter with the best of 'em." Daniel grinned.

"He's a smooth talker, that's for sure." Peg rubbed the ever-growing stiffness in the back of her neck.

"And tell me, is the word on the street correct that you and he are engaged?"

"What?"

"Just fooling with ya. Nothing's been said for a week now. I think folks were hoping for a romance, but they've seen you're just not interested." Daniel eased himself deeper into the sofa.

"I've spouted off more Scripture verses from Paul talking about the nobleness of remaining single in the past couple of weeks. Folks ought to be getting the idea." Peg finally sat down on the overstuffed chair in her sitting room.

"What are your plans for tomorrow?" he asked.

"The same. I'll find a nice quiet beach and pour out my soul to God. I have a feeling I'll be doing a lot more pouring this year."

Daniel reached over and placed his hand around hers. "When are you going to forgive yourself?"

"I'm working on it. It's hard. I still can't shake the thought that if I hadn't sinned, my baby would have been alive."

"If you hadn't sinned there wouldn't have been a child and I doubt there ever would have been one with Billy. I don't think the man ever would have married you, and I don't think he would have made you a good husband if he had."

"Daniel, please. It wasn't just Billy's fault."

"I know that. But," he hesitated. "Peg, I heard some things about Billy when I returned home. He was hung for murder, Peg. He—"

"Murder?" Peg's breath caught in her throat.

"I double-checked. Apparently, he returned to Savannah back in 1850, just about two years after we left. Anyway, seems he got into a drunken brawl with someone. Before the dust cleared, Billy was standing over the man with a smoking pistol in his hand. He didn't deny killing the man. Word is, he never said he was sorry for it. He stood proud of himself and his actions in front of the hangman's noose."

"Don't you think if he and I had. . .waited, his life would have been different?" Peg felt tears sting her lids.

"I don't think so, Peg. There were other things I heard about Billy when you and he were engaged. Remember, we talked about those before."

And she did remember. But she never wanted to see how bad Billy really was. He'd always been sweet to her. Of course, his being sweet had caused her to sin. It was one of the things that kept her leery of smooth talkers. Smooth talkers like Matthew Bower.

No wonder she was fearful of the man. She realized she had kept Matt at a safe distance because he was like Billy, not in looks, but in his manner with women.

"Peg, it's been twenty years. You need to forgive yourself," Daniel whispered, breaking her thoughts.

"I know. I'm trying."

"Are you? Why take the day off? Why allow even one day to have a foothold over you?"

"I have to. It helps. It truly does allow me to be at peace the rest of the year. This year is just different."

"All right, Sis, I won't push you. I'll support you in any decision you make."

"Thanks. Now go home to your wife and children. I've got work to do."

"Yes, Ma'am." Daniel saluted.

"Hey, just remember, I'm the older sibling."

"Oh, like I could forget it, with you holding rank over me all these years," Daniel teased back.

She couldn't ask for a better brother. He'd supported her when no one else did, even her parents. Peg closed down the old images of anguish and pain her parents had levied against her all those many years ago. Tonight she had more important things to do. One of which included a quick walk through town to see what was and wasn't available for possible rent.

She left the house in her sandals, a light cotton skirt and blouse. She held her hair back with a leather barrette and a small stick. It was easier to manage this way and didn't take a lot of time to fashion.

The three-story buildings that lined Front Street were large, wooden clapboard structures scattered between homes and offices that belonged to lawyers and other businessmen. *When did the island change so?* Peg wondered. Oh, she knew new businesses and buildings had gone up, but had she sheltered herself so much she'd become unaware of the changes on the island? Granted, all her free time was spent working or at church, and at work she stayed inside the store. Her chest heaved with the awareness that life was indeed passing her by.

"Peg? Peg Martin?"

Peg turned to the unfamiliar voice.

"Mr. Bower, a pleasure to meet you. The island's been buzzing about this new business you're planning on starting here. Can't say I blame them. New industry is what we need here."

Matt had to grin at the older gentleman with white hair and a roughly shaved face. In the man's wrinkles, longer nubs remained from a less than close shave.

"Afraid I don't have any waterfront property for you." John Dixon grinned.

Matt smiled. "Not here for that. I bought Jefferson Scott's place this morning."

"You don't say. What will become of Peg Martin?"

Twist the knife deeper. "Well, Sir, that's why I'm here. William Horton mentioned you might have a place in your room facing Duval Street."

John scratched his scruffy chin. "Hmm, I suppose I do. What do you have in mind?"

"I was wondering if you might be willing to rent the place to Miss Martin. Seems a shame such a sweet little business like hers would need to go under just because I'm bringing in another."

"You don't sound like no sharp-nosed businessman I ever heard about." John gave him a sideways glance.

"That may be so, but I don't like the idea of making folks angry with me for no real reason. I had some time on my hands, and William did mention your place." There, he'd let the old gent gnaw on that for a bit.

"Makes sense. Well, I ain't been planning on renting the room, but if'n you wanna see it, I don't mind showing you."

Matt waited as John rose slowly from his chair. For an old man, he seemed pretty agile in spite of the gnarled hands and bent spine. Matt guessed the man to be close to eighty.

"These old bones slow down if'n I don't keep 'em moving." John led the way to a side room of his house. It had a private entrance and large bay windows on either side of the door. The room, a large rectangle, perhaps twenty feet wide and about fourteen feet deep, lay before him. It had a nice hardwood floor and plenty of room for Peg to put her shelves.

"What would you want to rent it for?"

"Can't say that I know. I don't need much, but I don't believe in giving something for nothing either. Do you know what she was paying Jefferson for his place?"

"Can't say that I do. Would you be willing to give her the same price?"

"If'n Jefferson will verify that's the price he charged her, I don't see why not. I've just been using it for storage. The kids don't visit too much. Don't need a lot of space."

"How many children do you have?" *Pleasant conversation wouldn't hurt,* Matt thought.

"Five. I have seventeen grandchildren and half a dozen great-grandchildren, at last count. Most have moved to the mainland. My youngest daughter, she's in her fifties, she lives here on the island with her husband. Other than a handful here, the rest are spread out. I live for the letters. They all write me."

"That's wonderful. I have a son, and this is the first time I've spent any real time away from him. He attends the university, but he comes home on weekends and such."

"I remember my wife when the first ones moved away. She flopped around like a flounder."

"Micah didn't go to the university until after his mother passed away. We couldn't see giving her more pain."

"Sorry to hear you lost your wife. Hard to lose someone so close to you. Worst part was losing a child, though. Ain't natural, you know?"

"Right." Matt scanned the room again. "May I invite Miss Martin to come and pay you a visit?"

"She's welcome. Might be fun having folks coming and going all the time." John grinned. He hiked up his suspenders and led them back to the main part of his house.

Matt exchanged a firm handshake and headed back toward Peg Martin's home. He grinned, seeing how short a distance she would have to walk each morning to go to work. Two and a half blocks.

He rapped on the door. Paused. No answer.

He knocked again. Paused. Again no answer. He turned down the pathway leading away from the house.

"Who are you?"

Chapter 9

P eg turned. How did she know this person? Or better yet, how did this person know her?

"Don't recognize me, huh?"

Dark chestnut hair turned up neatly in a bun framed her face. A thin nose, with a slight crook in the middle of it, set the woman apart from others.

"I'm afraid I don't."

"Must be 'cause I was around seven the last time you saw me."

Peg knitted her eyebrows. Who was this strange woman staring her down? "I'm sorry, but I don't recognize you."

"Not a problem. Jasmine Seymore."

Jasmine Seymore. Peg rolled the name around. It seemed somewhat familiar.

"I used to play with Elsie Beasley."

"Ah, I remember now." Elsie was the little girl she cared for when she first arrived on the island.

"How have you been?" Jasmine asked.

"Just fine. Yourself?"

"Good. The folks moved to Mobile when I was seven. This is my first trip back to the island."

"What brought you back?"

"Memories, mostly. My husband decided the best way to have me stop talking about this place was to bring me here for a visit. So here I am. Do you know what happened with Elsie?"

"She and her family moved to St. Augustine years ago."

"Oh." Jasmine was noticeably disappointed.

"Where are you staying?"

"A hotel down Front Street."

"Wonderful." Peg didn't want to seem rude, but the sun was setting. "I have a store, Southern Treasures, on the harbor. Come on over and visit sometime. I'm afraid I need to get going."

"Great, I'll try to come by your place." Jasmine waved good-bye and headed toward her hotel.

Twenty years and I see someone from way back then. Amazing! Lord, what are You trying to get me to realize here?" Peg hurried home, making a mental note of every possible storefront. She couldn't believe how many places were vacant. Maybe she could afford renting some place else after all.

As she approached her house she heard her niece yell, "Who are you?" Peg picked up her pace. Mariella's tone conveyed caution. The island was basically a safe place, but she didn't want her niece in any danger.

She rounded the corner to see Matthew Bower holding his hands out to his sides, showing he wasn't a threat. Mariella, on the other hand, held a pole in her hands and was ready to swing. "Mariella, it's all right. He's a friend."

Mariella relaxed her aggressive stance. "He says he was looking for you."

"Yes, I imagine he is. You go on home now. I'm sure your mother must have dinner ready."

"All right. Sorry, Mister." Mariella tossed her weapon into the hedges that lined the front of the house.

"Sorry about that. I've never seen her so aggressive."

Matt chuckled. "No harm done. I'm glad you came home, though. I had some interesting news I wanted to share with you."

Hadn't he *shared* enough news today? "Come on in. I'll fetch you a glass of iced tea."

"Thanks. I could use something. I've been out in this heat most of the afternoon." Matt fanned himself with his hat.

Peg led him into her apartment. Having decided earlier why this man seemed such a threat to her, she felt she could guard against it. "Make yourself comfortable while I get us something to drink."

Matt nodded and chose the overstuffed chair. Which, she decided, was a noble thing, leaving the sofa and the rocker for herself to choose from. Billy would have chosen the sofa and encouraged her to sit beside him. She made quick work of their drinks and carried them out to the sitting room. "So, what brought you here this evening?"

He took the glass she offered him and gulped a healthy portion before answering. "I think I found a storefront for you."

"What?" She raised her voice in disbelief. *What is this man trying to prove?*

"I was placing an order with William Horton and we got to talking about Southern Treasures and how you'd have to relocate, and he mentioned John Dixon might have a room suitable for you."

"John? He doesn't have a storefront."

"Yes and no. He has a grand room on the side of his house that faces Duval Street. It has its own entrance and two bay windows on either side of the door. Actually, I think it's quite nice. It has more room than your present storefront, and it's not too far from your home."

"But it's so far out of town. One of the things that has helped my business prosper has been the sales from travelers who depart from the various ships. They spend some time in port and end up buying some trinkets for loved ones. No one would make their way up Duval Street just to buy something."

"I hadn't thought of that. I'm sorry. John said he'd rent the place at the same price you were paying Jefferson, if Jefferson would verify that's what you have been paying him."

Peg chuckled. "Sounds like John. He's a cautious old man. Wise, though."

"I know I've sprung this on you, and I'm not trying to control your life or your decisions, but you might want to look at the place. It really has some potential. You may miss out on the tourist traffic, but from what I hear, the ladies of the island will be disappointed to see your store go. I feel badly for purchasing the building your store is located in, and I wanted to help."

"Would you consider selling your property?" Peg teased.

Matt's eyebrows rose and he clamped his mouth shut. Peg snickered at his expression. "Dan and I had considered buying the property years ago, but Jefferson was asking too much for it."

"Oh."

"I didn't know he was seriously considering selling the place until you mentioned it on our way back from the Southards' that evening. By then it was too late to put in a bid. Not to mention, it seemed somewhat unethical bidding on a piece of property you were going to bid on."

"That's just business. You should have." He reclined back in the chair.

"But if I had, you would have paid more."

"True." Matt sipped his tea. "Thanks for not bidding. It took some work to get the man down to a fair price."

"I imagine it did." Jefferson Scott could be one of the most stubborn individuals she'd ever known. But he'd been a good landlord and hadn't raised the rent on her over the entire seven years she had been there. Of course, he knew she wouldn't have been able to afford more rent and would have moved out. Which, in the end, would have caused him to lose even that small bit of income.

"There are a lot of vacant storefronts. I was out looking."

"Perhaps John Dixon's place isn't the answer for you then." Matt swirled the ice in his glass. "I haven't eaten this evening. Would you care to join the enemy for dinner tonight?"

"You're not my enemy, Matt."

"I'm glad to hear that, but the offer for dinner still stands. I'd love to have some company tonight."

He seemed almost melancholy, as if he were terribly lonely. Indeed, he appeared as she felt on this the eve of her son's birth and death. "You know, I think it would be nice to have dinner with you. I'm facing a mountain of book work and would love to put that off."

"Book work? I'm rather handy with figures. Could I help?"

"No, it isn't necessary. I'm just trying to decide what I can and cannot afford with regard to other rental options."

"I see. Well, if after dinner you'd like a hand, I'm more than happy to lend it."

"Thanks. Let me change, and I'll be right with you."

"Peg, you look fine. You don't need to go fancy yourself up. Our options for dinner establishments are limited."

"True. I suppose I could go in this." Peg stood and examined her skirt for wrinkles.

"We're simply going out as friends."

"Have you heard the recent gossip?" Peg teased.

"No, I don't believe I have. What's on the grapevine now?"

"Oh, something about us getting engaged. Of course, they have me engaged to Nate as well." Peg gathered their empty glasses and brought them into the kitchen.

"Hmm, definitely don't dress up then. We wouldn't want them having us married and on our honeymoon." Matt chuckled.

"You do understand small town gossip."

"Definitely. It was disturbing at first, but I think I'm reasonably comfortable with it now."

Peg chuckled.

She found she rather enjoyed Matt's presence. Whatever problems or tension that existed between them seemed to have diminished. Could the solution to her worries have been as easy as finally recognizing his likeness to Billy? She didn't want to give it any further thought right now. Instead, she found herself relaxing and enjoying Matt's stories about his son and wife.

"So, tell me what brought you to Key West?" Matt asked.

"Ah, well, a fresh start mostly. My father was a fisherman. A proud fisherman. Daniel enjoys the ocean, but he's never gotten used to the churning of the sea. He didn't want to follow in our father's footsteps, so we came here for a new start."

"Hmm. My father was the same way concerning the family business. I did go into it, but not until after I went away for my university training. Being forty-five, I now understand my father's desires. When I was eighteen, and full of myself and my own dreams, I didn't understand the man."

"I suppose some of that was true for Danny as well. He had a good mind for business, but Daddy didn't see that. He only saw honest pay for honest work. He wasn't too sure about investments and such. Thankfully, my father allowed us to leave."

Matt pushed back his chair from the table and folded his hands across his stomach. "So, you left your home for your brother?"

"Somewhat. I had my reasons for wanting to live someplace else as well. But at least here Daniel could develop in business. And he has. He helped the wreckers market their sales, and we invested in some real estate. Nothing much, but it's been profitable."

"So, why did you open Southern Treasures?"

Peg eased back in her chair, rather pleased with how easily the words had fallen from her lips about their reasons for coming to Key West. Of course, she and Daniel had rehearsed them so many times. It wasn't like they were lying, since there was truth to the matter. It just wasn't the whole truth. "Probably because, as I've gotten older, simply making money wasn't as satisfying. With the embroidery I see a finished product. I see the joy it brings on people's faces. It's a more personal business. Does that make sense?"

"Yes, I understand that completely. My business is export. No faces, no personal connection. My personal connection comes with my employees. The work I do provides jobs for them and a real income for their families. If I'm lax, then I have to lay folks off. If I work hard, then they have a decent income throughout the entire year."

"Does it bother you that so many people are depending upon you?"

"Actually, no. At first, when I was a young man, it did. So many days I wanted to simply kick off my shoes and stay home with my family. But duty would nip at my conscience, and I'd kiss my wife good-bye and head for work, all the time wanting to be at home, relaxing and enjoying life."

"Didn't you take off a day or two a week?"

"Oh, sure. Sundays, of course. And an occasional Saturday. But, more often than not, I ended up working some portion of that day. The hardest time was when my wife was dying. I hated to go to work, and yet I needed to for my own sanity, to think about something other than the pain Esther was enduring." Matt clamped his jaw tight and closed his eyes.

Without thinking, Peg reached over and placed her hand upon his forearm. "I'm sorry."

Matt's eyes shot open. The sudden movement made Peg jump and remove her hand. How could she have been so forward—so foolish?

🌴

Matt couldn't believe she had reached over and touched him. She knew the rumors that would buzz, but for a moment, he had allowed her tender touch to do exactly as she intended, soothe his weary soul. For two years he had chastised himself for seeking relief from feeling his wife's pain.

Esther had understood his need to go to work, but she also wanted him next to her. She cherished his touch. It calmed her. He knew it. She knew it. But still he went to work faithfully every day. He was such a cad.

"I'm sorry," Peg whispered.

"No, it's all right. I was thinking of the gossips." *Good cover,* he mumbled to himself.

"I doubt it, but I'll let you have that to save face."

She has you pegged, old boy. He grinned. "Perhaps we best not talk about it."

"Perhaps." Peg dabbed her lips with the white linen napkin. "I think it is about time for me to be getting home, or I'll never get that paperwork done."

"I'd be more than willing to give you a hand."

"What, and incite the gossips all the more by coming late in the evening into my home?" She fanned herself like a proper Southern lady. "My dear Mr. Bower, what would people say?"

He held his hands up. "I surrender."

Peg grinned and acknowledged his assent with a single nod of her head. He escorted her home and left her.

What was he thinking, trying to take on this woman? *A woman so capable of deceit.* He thought back over the story she had told him. He could see the logic in Daniel Martin needing to find his own way in the world. But he knew the truth, the full truth. She hid it, and hid it well, he mused.

When he reached the small cottage he had recently secured for his dwelling, he was greeted with a letter tacked to the door. A letter from Micah. Matt ripped the sealing wax and rushed inside to light an oil lamp. Tomorrow was Micah's birthday, and he so much wanted to be with his son.

His son—how could he live with himself knowing Micah wasn't really his son? He had to get up the nerve to. . . No, it was best this way. To tell Micah would be to shatter his world. To tell Peg Martin would be to shatter her world. The best alternative was to keep the secret hidden. *Why had Dr. Baker found it necessary to tell the truth on his deathbed?* Matt raked his hands through his hair.

He needed to tell Peg. It simply wasn't fair to her. But how does a man go about saying, "You know that illegitimate child you had twenty years ago? Well, he's alive and well. Apparently, he didn't die at birth as the doctor had told you. Apparently, he switched the baby with another patient's dead infant. My wife's own dead child."

Who in the world would believe him? Doctors didn't do that. It was unethical.

But old Dr. Baker seemed to think it was ethical. Perhaps not, though, since he had needed to confess the truth before he met his Maker.

"Lord, why did he have to tell me? Micah and I would have gone along just fine not knowing the truth. We would have continued our comfortable life. Now I'm faced with hiding the truth or exposing it. How do You think the people on this island would react knowing Peg Martin had an illegitimate son? That he'd been taken away from her at birth and given to another couple. It just doesn't seem fair."

Matt closed down his emotions and focused on the now crumpled letter in front of him.

Dear Dad,

I'm fine and looking forward to our time together in Key West. I still can't imagine why you are locating the business down there, but your reasoning always seems to make good business sense. The office here is holding up without you. I'm working when I'm not in classes. My final exams will put a strain on my ability to do well for the business.

I've met a charming young lady here in Savannah. She's a delightful creature, has the same blue eyes and wavy blond hair as myself. Her real father has a past the family would not be proud of. But, Father, her heart is as pure as any I've ever seen.

I suppose I sound like a love-sick puppy, but truthfully I'm not. I'm still praying about whether this is the woman the Lord has put in my path for love or for a mutual friendship. We met at a corner restaurant where I've been taking my meals. We have so many similar interests, and yet we have our differences. I don't know, Father. I am looking forward to discussing this matter with you when I reach Key West. Oh, before I forget, her name is Anna Ingles.

Thank you for the wonderful gift for my birthday, early of course. It's hard to believe we are apart on this day. Mother always made it such a special day for us. I still miss her terribly, but it's getting easier.

> *All my love,*
> *your son Micah*

Matt's hands trembled. His heart pounded in his chest. His son was considering marriage. *Is he old enough for that? Am I old enough for that?*

Chapter 10

"November twenty-eighth." Peg groaned and pulled the pillow over her head. Sleeping the day away sounded good. She flipped her body around to the other side of her bed, closed her eyes, and prayed the day would just pass. All night she had dreamed about giving birth and hearing her son's first cry. His only cry. The doctor had pulled him out of the room before she had a chance to look at him.

Someone was pounding on her front door. Peg pulled the pillow off her head to be certain. Yup, someone was knocking. Peg plopped the pillow back over her head. Nope, she wasn't fit to deal with people today. The house could be burning down and she wouldn't move.

Peg paused, lifted the pillow just in case, and made certain there was no smell of smoke in the air. Sensing none, she groaned and pulled the pillow over her head once again.

Muffled sounds of someone calling her name between the heavy banging fluttered to her brain. Someone wanted her attention and wanted it badly.

"Nope. It's my day. I don't care who it is or why they've come, I'm not answering the door, Lord. Not today."

"Peg," a female voice called to her.

Peg lifted the pillow. The voice was far too clear. Had the person walked around her house to her bedroom window?

"Peg," the voice called again, but from the wrong direction.

She turned and faced her bedroom door.

"Bea?"

"It's about time you surfaced," Bea chided.

"What are you doing here?"

"I'm here about a friend, a dear friend."

"What?"

"You silly. You told me today was the day. . ." Bea let her words trail off.

Peg closed her eyes. "Me and my big mouth." She plopped the pillow over her face and rolled back under the covers.

"Hush now. I'm going to the kitchen and make us something to eat. Then we'll talk."

"Bea, honestly, go home. I prefer to be alone."

"I'm sure you do. It's been twenty years, Peg. And trust me, this will be the last time you will respond this way. Today is the day you deal with the past and forgive yourself once and for all." Bea left without waiting for a response.

How dare she come in here and assume she has the cure-all for what ails me. The nerve! Peg huffed. She threw the covers off, marched over to her robe, and put it on.

Stomping down the hallway, she made her way to the kitchen. "Just who do you think you are, Bea? You can't come into a person's house and tell them what they are going to do."

"Oh, so you like living like this? Going through this anguish every year?"

"No, but. . ."

"Exactly. Peg, sit down. Let me get us some tea, and we can discuss it." Bea turned and pulled open the cupboards, looking for the teacups.

"Where's James?"

"In your sitting room. He's fine for awhile. He ate well and fell asleep on our way over."

"Go home, Bea. I can handle this."

"Of course you can. But this year you've got me to help you through it. You don't need to handle this alone. Tell me about being pregnant. Personally, I couldn't wait to give birth to James. This heat and those extra pounds were a killer."

"Thankfully I was in cooler weather for the last months," Peg answered without thinking.

"Did you name him? I mean, while you were expecting, did you call him anything?" Bea poured the water into the kettle.

Peg's voice caught. "Yes. I named him John, God's gift."

"No wonder it hurt so much when he died." Bea stepped up beside her. "I want you to tell me everything, Peg. Who his father was, how you fell in love. How it felt to lose your very heart and soul once he was born. Everything. We'll get you through this, and you'll be able to accept the past, your flaws, and God's grace."

"I don't know, Bea. I pour my heart out to God every year. It's no use."

"Ah, but this year you have me to hear you, to sympathize with you, and to tell you where you're missing the mark."

Peg chuckled. "You're rather sure of yourself."

"Hey, I've been living with Cook for a couple years now. Something has had to wear off on me." Bea grinned.

Peg tossed her head from side to side. Maybe she should try it Bea's way. After all these years, her way wasn't working. "I'll try, Bea. But if I need space you have to promise me to give it to me."

"Fair enough. So, start from the beginning. How'd you meet John's father?"

Peg began slowly to tell Bea about her whirlwind romance with Billy. How handsome he was. How persuasive.

The day wore on. James was a perfect child, eating and sleeping while they talked.

"Billy just ran away, huh?"

"Yes. Daniel says he was in some other trouble. At the time I didn't want to listen. I was so certain he left because I told him I was with child, that we would have to get married right away."

"That could make a man run. On the other hand, he seemed to speak from both sides of his mouth, talking about his great love for you and then running away from you. Seems to me there might be something to what Daniel said he heard about him."

"I think you're right. Daniel told me yesterday that when he went home last year to settle Mother and Father's estate after they died that word was Billy had returned a couple years later only to stir up more trouble. Seems he killed a man and hung for it."

"Oh my," Bea gasped.

"Isn't a pretty image, is it? What's worse is that Danny said he showed no remorse for anything he'd done, knowing he was about to die. He stood there, proud as a peacock."

"Lord, have mercy. How can a man be so hard?"

"I don't know. I don't recall much of that Billy. He only showed me that side of himself the night I told him about John."

Bea reached out and took Peg's hand.

"Did your parents ever soften?"

"Eventually they saw I changed. Mother said she used to place flowers on John's grave. They really did forgive me."

"Then you can forgive yourself, Peg. Face it, you're human, and we humans make mistakes. Lots of them. Some are big, and some are not so big. Some we can hide and keep in secret. Others show themselves in time. Thankfully, we have a Savior who died for those sins and covers them with His blood."

"I know God forgives. I suppose I know I should forgive myself."

"Of course you know it. The question is, are you strong enough to release yourself from the guilt, to allow God's grace to perform a miracle in your life? To accept a gift for the future?"

"What gift?"

"Oh, I don't know. A husband, perhaps?"

"Not you too?"

"*Moi?* Surely you jest." Bea feigned a hand to her chest.

Peg rolled her eyes.

"Seriously, Peg. I don't know if there is or isn't a man in your future. I'm just saying, being bound to the past can't allow you to go forward. You're limiting what God can and wants to do through you. You, more than anyone, know there are many who have gone through what you have. Those women could use a gentle hand, a kind word, to help them come to our heavenly Father. And someone who's been through it, like yourself, can help."

Peg thought of Julie in New York and how she was able to help Nate understand what had happened to her. Julie's most recent letter to Nate confessed the rape, how much shame she felt, and how her family tried to help her. And yet, somehow they weren't sure she did everything possible to prevent the rape from happening. Nate had run off to New York on the next ship heading north. *Maybe Bea's right, Lord. Maybe I can be of help to some women.*

"Peg, you know Grace Perez, right?"

Peg nodded.

"Well, she's expecting. It's all hush-hush, but one of my husband's employees is the father. He ran off to Cuba as soon as he found out. She's scared, and she's alone."

"But. . ." If she started helping folks, her own shame would be known. Hadn't she and Daniel left Savannah so they wouldn't have to live in shame?

"I'm not telling you to do or say anything. I'm just pointing out there are people who could use the wise words of someone like you."

"Wise? You can't be serious. I still feel like a flounder flopping on the deck of a ship. I even have dreams that my son is alive and well."

"Well, that's just your mother's heart having a hard time accepting the loss. I don't know if you'll ever get over that."

"No, I suppose you're right. I don't think I'll ever get over it."

"Did you see him after he was born?"

"No. The doctor just whisked him off to another room, then came back in and told me."

Bea closed her eyes, then opened them slowly. "That doctor deserves a good swift kick in the backside. Who did he think he was, telling you it was all your fault for having relations outside of marriage? I swear, he cursed you."

"Cursed me?"

"I guess that's the wrong word. But it seems to me that those words of his are the ones that have rambled around in your head for all these twenty years. The words that haven't allowed you to forgive yourself. You know as well as I that God doesn't kill every child that is conceived out of wedlock. In fact, He's taken sinners and those who are the result of sin and included them in His own heritage. Look at Rahab, the harlot. Who would have thought God would have used her to be a great-great-great-grandmother to Jesus? Well, more than three greats back—many greats—but you get my meaning."

Peg rubbed her hands over her face. Had she let the doctor's words bind her to the past? Was that why she couldn't forgive herself? Was it his unkind words that brought judgment and self-condemnation?

"I see I've got you pondering."

Peg groaned.

"Tell me, is the word on the street true? Are you and Matthew Bower seeing each other socially?"

Matt pushed down his inner thoughts today. He would not visit Peg Martin. As curious as he was to see her, and see how she was handling the past, he knew he didn't want to see her in anguish. He didn't want to see eyes painted red from salty tears. No, she closed the store for a reason, and that reason was alive and well and living in Savannah. How much longer could he keep the secret? *Should* he keep it?

"Stop it, Bower. Enough is enough," he barked at the half-shaven face in the bathroom mirror. His straightedge razor slid down the left side of his jaw with ease. He'd tried growing a beard years ago, but found it was just as much work, if not more, to keep a beard groomed properly as it was to shave every morning. Besides, Esther always enjoyed his clean-shaven look. A slight grin made the lather rise on his cheek. He finished shaving and dressed for the day.

He had several meetings before him this morning. First, he'd need to find an architect to decide if tearing down the present building and restarting from scratch was a better option. He felt confident that tearing down the present structure was his only real choice, since sections of the dock were rotting, but he'd be prudent to examine the various possibilities.

He placed his reply letter to Micah in his pocket. Hopefully there would be a ship heading north that would be entering the Savannah River before going further. Matt thought back on Micah's letter and a certain Miss Anna. He wondered what she was like, what his son found so compelling about her. Was she the one the good Lord had designed to be the perfect helpmate for Micah?

Matt knew he had a multitude of questions. He could hardly wait for his son's arrival as he worked his way down the ground coral streets.

"Good morning, Mr. Hewitt, how are you this morning?" he said as he entered an office building.

"Fine, fine. I heard you bought Jefferson Scott's place." The balding middle-aged man extended his hand.

"You heard right. I also was told that you might be the man to help me expand the dock and possibly the building." Matt stepped farther into the man's office.

Hewitt's grin broadened. "I heard you got William Horton working on it."

"True, but I'm a businessman, and I expect bids. William will give me his by the end of the week. Are you interested?"

"Does a turtle have a shell?"

Matt chuckled. "Great." He went on to explain the specifications he had in mind for the work, then left Hewitt to his own devices.

So far, William Horton seemed to be the better man. His work spoke for itself. However, Matt knew business demanded estimates, and he'd be foolish not to look at every one.

Now to speak with Ellis Southard about shipping schedules. Matt headed toward Ellis's dock. He found Ellis and Mo working on the new building at the landside edge of his dock. " 'Morning, gentlemen."

" 'Morning," Ellis called down from the slight peak of a roof.

"I was wondering if I could have a word with you about the shipping of your product."

"Sure, give me a minute to secure this beam." Ellis pounded the nails into the carrying beam, then climbed down the ladder. "What kinds of questions do you have?"

"I'm wondering if you have an exclusive contract with the various ships that come to port?"

"Not really. I've gotten to know several of the captains, and when they have extra space I'm able to place some of my wares on the vessel. Most of the time this works well, since sponges don't take up weight and can be wedged into many nooks and crannies onboard a ship."

"I see. Would you be interested in working out a schedule with my ships?"

"You own your own vessels?"

"Yes, Sir. I found it to be profitable in the long run. At first there wasn't much profit. But once I paid off the debt on the vessels, they soon paid for themselves."

"Interesting. I'd been thinking about purchasing my own ship for that very reason. We'll have to talk more."

Chapter 11

The next week Matt found himself driven to see Peg Martin. Thoughts of her and her suffering were beginning to plague him. He knew the truth; she would no longer suffer once she knew. But then again, it was always possible she'd suffer even more knowing the last twenty years had been robbed from her. Unable to determine what was best, he decided that the only course of action was to befriend her, get a feel for how she really thought. Then he could determine whether it was best to keep the secret or to tell her. Micah would be arriving in a matter of weeks. Matt had to settle this issue before his son arrived.

"Good morning, Peg." He smiled upon entering her store. "How are you?"

"Fine. Thought I'd seen the last of you. You know I keep men at a distance, but you're something else. All I did was place my hand upon yours at a point in which you had shared your heart about your wife. I certainly wasn't interested in something more, as you so obviously insinuated from the touch."

What was she talking about? The moment in the restaurant flew back into his mind. "A simple touch was not the problem. Forgive me for giving you that impression."

"Seems to me you've been avoiding me."

"I reckon there might be some truth to that, but it wasn't because you reached out and placed your hand upon my forearm."

"The rumors?" Peg inquired.

"In part. Heard we were engaged and planning to have a handful of children. Personally, I'm not sure I'm young enough to have more children." He smiled.

"Children? Just how many are we supposed to have?" Peg flowed right in with the gentle teasing.

"Last count, I think we were up to three."

"Three's not too bad. But a woman my age. . .and running around after young 'uns. . .I don't know. We might have to curb that rumor."

"How?"

"Oh, I don't know. Let's adopt some pets or something. Children take a lot of time."

She's not too interested in having children, Matt mused. How would she have been as the mother of Micah?

"On second thought, let's have a baker's dozen. I mean, if were going to have them, we might as well go all out," she teased.

"Thirteen? Woman, you'd bury me in an early grave."

"Ah, but just think how many wonderful memories I'd have of you by looking into the delightful faces of your children." She winked.

Matt's stomach fluttered. He swallowed hard. Perhaps this game of one-upping the local gossips wasn't really such a good idea. "Have mercy, dear lady. I have only fathered one. I'm ill prepared for a house full of little ones under foot."

Peg chuckled. "You know, I don't know if I could handle a pack of young 'uns. I love children. Don't get me wrong. But I'm old enough now where I like things quiet and simple."

Matt smiled. "Trust me, I understand. When my younger sister brings her children over to the house for a visit, it takes all the patience I can muster. I was spoiled having only a single child, I suspect."

Peg looked down to the floor. *Oh, that was brilliant,* he chided himself. She obviously loved children. So why had she not gotten married after she had her child and had some more? She had admitted keeping men at a distance. *Has she not made peace with the past? Is that why she takes the day off on Micah's birthday?*

"Seriously, I've been rather busy getting some bids and working out the time schedules for relocating the business. I'm thinking I might keep a smaller operation going in Savannah. But I'm not sure I could handle the two locations. Micah's been working hard trying to keep things running, but I'm uncertain whether he'll want to stay in Savannah or come and work here with me."

"Ah, you're like my father, deciding for your son what his future should be."

"No. Micah's gone to the university. He's doing what he wants."

"Is he? Have you given him the options or have you just assumed?"

Had he given Micah the option? Had he listened to the desires of his son's heart and not just assumed he would want to follow in his father's footsteps with the family business? Matt sighed. "I believe I gave him the choice."

"What does he love?"

Matt stepped up to the counter. "At the moment he seems fascinated with a young lady." Matt chuckled.

"Oh, do tell."

"Apparently she works at a restaurant he's been taking his meals at. He says her father has a past the family might not be pleased with."

"Ooh, a touch of scandal for Savannah. I like that," Peg teased.

"I'm not so concerned about the young lady's father as much as I am concerned about whether or not she loves Micah. But he is aware of how certain women are attracted to him because of his family wealth. Ever since he was sixteen, he's had certain women swooning at his feet. He's a handsome young man, which makes him a very desirable catch."

"If he looks as fine as his father, I'm certain the ladies find him irresistible." *Is she flirting with me?*

"Now don't read something into what I just said," she said quickly, as though reading his thoughts. "I was merely commenting on your handsome features. A woman notices a handsome man, you know. We just aren't like the men who hoot and holler when a fine specimen walks past."

Matt roared. "My dear Peg, in my neighborhood a man does not hoot and holler over a woman. He simply takes an appraising glance at her fine assets."

Peg broke out in a hearty laugh.

Tears of laughter poured down Peg's face. It was good to laugh, to enjoy life. And she had to admit it, Matthew Bower brought humor and joy back into her life.

Matt collapsed on the stool in front of the counter. Their game of tempting the gossips was really quite fun. He pulled out a white handkerchief and handed it to her.

Peg retrieved it and dabbed the tears from her eyes and cheek. His musky scent on the handkerchief filled her nostrils. A flutter of awareness that she was drawn to this man in a way she'd not been drawn to another in so many years coursed through her veins like a riptide. "We shouldn't tease the gossips."

"But it's so much fun," Matt snickered.

"True, but how many do you suppose might take our teasing humor and run with it?"

"Let 'em run. You and I know the truth. That's all that should matter."

"I suppose you're right, and it is fun playing like this. I don't know when I've laughed this hard in years."

"Me either. I guess Esther's death took a part of myself."

Peg sobered. "I would imagine it would. You said you'd been married for twenty years, and you said you had a good marriage."

"Yes. We had a good marriage."

Peg stepped back behind the counter and pulled her needlework out from behind it.

"What are you working on now?" he asked.

"Oh, something for a special family member."

"May I see?" Matt reached out.

Peg held it up for him.

"John, God's gift," Matt read.

"It's a pillow."

"You really have quite a talent there. Names can be so powerful. Micah means 'who is like the Lord.' "

She smiled, her eyes on her work. Since the twenty-eighth, she had felt the burden lifted from her shoulders. Bea was right; that day had marked the end of her sorrow. It had been time to forgive herself. Actually, she should have forgiven herself years ago but. . .what did it matter? It was done. She was at peace with the past.

"As much as I enjoy your fine company, I must get back to work. Would you be free this evening to join me for dinner?" Matt stood, his eyes fixed on her for an answer.

"What, and have them up the number of children we'll have to four?" Peg teased.

Matt raised his hands. "Don't start that again. I'll not be able to keep a straight face when I meet some of the folks on the street."

"Trust me, you're going to have a hard time with it anyway. I'll be happy to join you tonight, though. But how about if I fix us up something special? Could you use a home-cooked meal?"

"Woman, don't tempt me." Matt grinned. His green eyes sparkled with excitement. Maybe inviting him to her house wasn't such a good idea, she realized. "If you're offering a home-cooked meal, how could a man turn that down? When should I arrive?"

"Better make it six. I don't close the shop until five."

"Sounds wonderful. Can I bring some fresh bread or rolls from the bakery?"

"That would be fine."

Matt nodded and proceeded toward the door. "Thanks, Peg. You're a breath of fresh air."

"So are you, Friend." Peg waved him off. Perhaps they could be just friends. Not all men and women had to get romantically involved in order to have a relationship, right? She rehearsed the morning conversation through her mind once again. What would it be like to have a child with such a handsome man?

"Child?" Peg groaned. She didn't even want to entertain that thought.

"Miss Martin?" A slender Hispanic girl stood in her doorway.

"Hello, Grace. Come in." Peg started to shake. Could she go through with this?

🛴

Matt continued to chuckle as he walked toward the center of the business district. The town was relatively quiet this morning. People hard at work, he presumed. He marched over to the baker's and ordered a loaf of rye with raisins and chopped walnuts.

"I can make that. But you might have to buy the second loaf. Ain't a normal order down here." The baker stood with a white apron decorated with patches of flour and crumbs.

"I understand."

"I'll try and sell it to another customer but. . ."

Matt raised his hand. "No bother. I just haven't had that bread for awhile. I'm willing to pay for both loaves."

"You said you like it the way the French cook it?" The baker raised his furry gray eyebrows.

"Yes, is that a problem?"

"No, no. It's a hard crust. Simple, really. You just brush on some water to the outside of the bread before it cooks. Do you want a thick crust or thin, hard crust?"

"Thin, if you don't mind."

The baker grinned. "No problem. I can make it. You come by my store later.

I'll fix you your bread. You see, Mario can bake anything."

"I'm sure you can. Thank you."

"You're welcome, Mr. Bower."

Matt supposed everyone knew his name, but he was certain he didn't know Mario's—other than the fact that the outside sign to the bakery shop said "Mario the baker." And he sounded Italian, which seemed odd. "I'm afraid I don't know your name, Mr.—"

"Mario Falluchi."

"Pleasure to meet you, Mr. Falluchi."

"Call me Mario. Everyone does."

Matt nodded his head. "Mario it is then. When should I come back?"

Mario glanced up at the wall clock. "Four o'clock."

"Perfect, I'll see you then." Matt stepped out into the balmy tropical sun. He really needed to get some cooler clothing if he was going to make his home here. He walked over to a small shop where men's attire hung in the front window. In between the baker's and this shop, he counted at least three vacant storefronts. Perhaps Peg was right; finding a place to rent wasn't going to be a problem for her.

"May I help you?" A short, well-rounded Hispanic woman came from the back room upon his entrance.

"I was looking for something a bit more comfortable in this heat."

"*Sí,* you need a Guayoubera"

"What's a Guayoubera?"

"A Cuban male's shirt. It's light and gives a man relief. You don't tuck it into your trousers like you wear your business shirts."

"Could you show me one?"

The friendly woman walked over to a row of shirts and pulled a white, short-sleeved boat of a shirt off the rack. He would have to be out of his mind to dress in that.

"Come, try it on."

"I—"

"*Señor,* try. If you don't like, no problem."

Matt removed his vest, tie, and then his dress shirt.

"*Hijo!* No wonder you're so uncomfortable."

Matt tried the strange shirt. He'd seen a few men dressed in these around the island. Even businessmen wore them in their offices. A tie was totally inappropriate for such a shirt. Perhaps he could adjust to them. They appeared comfortable.

"The shirt, it blocks the sun, but it's loose so the body heat can escape, *sí?*"

"Hmm, are they supposed to hang so loosely over the shoulders?" Matt lifted the shirt on the top of the shoulders and let it drop back down.

"*Sí.*"

"*Gracías.* How much?"

"Five dollars."

"Five dollars?" *How could a simple shirt cost so much?*

"Four?"

Hmm, he'd forgotten that some folks liked to barter and work their way down in price. He scanned the store and decided not to press the woman further. It seemed full of items and few customers. "I'll take five shirts then."

"*Gracías*, Mr. Bower."

Her eyes sparkled. He examined the shirt more closely. It was well tailored, and he suspected the saleswoman had made it. "Did you make these?"

"*Sí*. Do you want all white?"

"Let's add a little color—that light blue and pale yellow—the rest will be fine in white."

"No problem." She hesitated, then asked, "Do you need anything else?"

"Can you give me another Guayoubera in a smaller size, one for my son. His shoulders are not as broad as mine."

"*Sí*, I have just the Guayoubera for a young man."

She pulled another off the rack. It looked identical to the one he had on. "Thank you. It will make a fine Christmas present."

She nodded. Her smile stretched across her face and touched her eyes. Times had been tough on this island. Perhaps his company would help bring some welcome relief. The question was, how could he turn down an applicant? More would apply than he had jobs for. Matt sighed. *I guess I'll deal with that when the time comes, Lord.*

He paid for his Guayouberas and brought them to the small cottage. At home he fixed a light lunch for himself and determined his afternoon schedule. A trip to Mobile to check on shipping from there might have to be planned soon. His recent letters had come back unanswered. His business depended on the farmers being able to ship their cotton to him as well. He penned another letter and prayed this one would be answered.

A rap at his door made him slip with his pen.

"Mr. Bower, come quick!"

Chapter 12

Peg groaned. The gentle lull of the waves lapping the pilings confused her anguished mind. The throbbing pain made her open her eyes once again. She needed to focus.

"The pain!" she cried out.

"Hang on, Miz Martin. Help is on the way."

Who called to her? Where was she? Her fingers grasped the wooden planks around her. She tried to move her right leg.

A cry of pain ripped through her throat. "Oh, God, help me."

"Relax, Miss Martin. You're going to be all right."

Peg tried to focus. Who had spoken?

"Miz Martin, relax. I'll take care of you." Mo's familiar voice called out to her. Someone she recognized. At least a voice she recognized. When she opened her eyes, she saw several figures with no definite shape or size. Mo, on the other hand, was a large man. She figured he was the dark blob kneeling down in front of her.

Peg moaned.

"Give us some space!" called another voice she thought belonged to Ellis Southard. "Relax, Peg, Mo and I will get you out of here."

Out of where? Where was she? And why did it hurt so much? Why was she half standing, half lying face down? Wooden splinters bit into her cheek.

"Everyone move back. There's no telling how rotten some of these other boards are," Ellis ordered.

Peg heard various gasps from the crowd.

Water splashed below her.

"She's bleedin' bad. We've got to get her out, Mr. Ellis." Mo now lay beside her. "I can see below. She's pinned by a two-by-six that's cut into her right thigh."

Peg now understood. She'd fallen through a piece of rotten decking on the dock behind her store. She'd gone out there with Grace Perez to talk about private matters. Parts of that dock were unstable. She knew better. Peg mumbled, "I mustn't have been paying attention."

"Doc's on his way," someone yelled from some place off to her left.

Tears burned down her cheeks. "Oh, God, please help."

"Can you lift your body, Peg?" Ellis asked.

Peg pushed the boards with her hands. The pain increased. She screamed.

"Miz Martin, listen to me. I'm goin' to lift this here board, and Mr. Ellis, he'll pull ye out. If'n you feel too much pain, grab my arm. We'll stop. All right?"

Peg nodded and placed her hand on Mo's large muscular forearm.

Words were mumbled. She felt Ellis reach his arms under her own. "Hang on, Peg."

Mo lifted.

"Stop!" she screamed, clawing her nails into Mo's arm.

"Get me a saw!" Mo hollered.

"And some clean rags," Ellis added.

"I'm gonna cut the board, then when we lift it off you, it won't be pressing in on ye," Mo advised.

Peg licked her lips. Her stomach heaved. She closed her eyes and fought the onslaught of fresh pain. She couldn't feel her leg below the board in her thigh.

"What happened?" Matt gasped. "Get her out of there," he demanded.

"We're working on it," Ellis groaned.

Matt lay down on the boards beside Peg opposite Mo. "Hang on, Peg."

"I'm trying," she groaned through her teeth.

Matt reached in below the boards and held her thigh. She'd seen a flash of white linens in his hand but didn't dare ask where they came from. The pressure added slightly to her discomfort at first, then seemed to be helping.

Peg heard the sawing of the wood. With each thrust the board jiggled in her leg. "Oh, God, help!"

"Almost through, Miz Martin," Mo announced.

Almost wasn't good enough. She wanted him to stop, and she wanted him to stop *now*. The wood cracked beneath her, and she started to slide down. Another strangled scream tore its way past her lips. "Dear Jesus, this hurts. Please help me, Lord," she cried.

"Clean rags," Matt demanded. He lifted his hand off her thigh and tossed the now bloodstained rags aside. "Now, Mo."

Mo pulled the board free from her leg. Ellis held on to her as she felt her body hang below the dock. Mo helped lift her as Matt continued to press the linens against her thigh.

"Bring her to my office. I'll need to operate," Doc Hansen ordered.

Peg blinked at the crowd. Blurred images of people standing there with horror on their faces slowly focused. Mo cradled her in his arms. Matt continued to press the rags on her thigh.

"Peg!" Daniel cried.

"Daniel," she whispered.

"She's goin' to be all right, Mr. Daniel. I need to take her to the doctor's office." Mo continued to hustle her in that direction.

"What happened?" Daniel asked.

Someone filled him in, or at least she thought she heard someone mumbling something about rotten boards. Her body chilled and heated at the same moment. She floated away from the pain, away from Mo's arms, into the deep recesses of her mind.

Matt paced the length of Dr. Hanson's front parlor. Daniel sat in a chair, huddled over in prayer. Ellis and Mo left, with stern words to fetch them when there was news. They insisted on going down to the dock to repair the damage in case small children would be curious. Matt had to agree with them on that score.

Dark woodwork framed white plaster walls. Various pieces of Queen Anne furniture were neatly placed around the room. Every few minutes someone would pop into the doctor's parlor and ask how Peg was doing. Did she have any idea how many people genuinely cared for her? Matt wondered.

"Mr. Bower, please sit down," Daniel pleaded. "Your pacing is making me more nervous."

"Sorry." Matt plopped down on the nearest chair.

"Do you think she'll be able to walk again?" Daniel asked, without really looking for an answer.

"I couldn't say. I pray she will."

"What was she doing back there on that dock anyway?" Daniel clutched his fist.

"I'm sorry. I was at home when it happened. I–I. . . ," Matt mumbled.

"I'm sorry. I know you don't have the answers. I guess no one does but Peg." Daniel closed his eyes. "Lord, she has to be all right."

Matt heard Daniel's voice crack. He swallowed his own bitter tears. *It's my dock. I'm responsible. I saw the condition of some of the wood. I should have roped it off. I should have done something, Lord.* Hindsight was always perfect. Matt folded his hands and kneaded the tension out of them.

He removed his pocket watch for the hundredth time. It had been three hours since he helped lay Peg's motionless body on the table.

The dark oak door creaked as it opened. Dr. Hansen dried his hands off with a fresh white towel. Blood stained his apron. Matt's stomach rolled. There was so much blood.

"Daniel," the doctor called.

Daniel's head popped up from prayer. "How is she, Doc?"

"She lost a lot of blood, but she's going to be fine. I want her to spend the night here, possibly another. It all depends on how quickly she responds."

Daniel nodded his head. "Whatever it takes."

"How badly was her leg injured?" Matt asked.

"There's a lot of damage to the quadriceps muscle. With God's grace, she won't lose her limb. But it will take some time before she can use it. We have to monitor the limb, watch for any signs of gangrene. I might have to remove it in order to save her life."

"No," Daniel gasped.

"What can we do to help prevent that?" Matt stepped closer to the doctor. There had to be something he could do.

"Change the dressing regularly. Massage the limb, encourage the blood to flow back and forth in the limb."

Matt held his tongue. These were private matters for family, and he wasn't family. He'd only been raising her son for the past twenty years.

"I'll see to her care, Doctor." Daniel raised his shoulders and strengthened his resolve.

"Gentlemen, if you'll excuse me, I have a patient to attend to." Doc Hansen stepped back toward his inner office. "Daniel, might I suggest you find a couple of women to take care of her. She'll need around the clock attention for a few days."

Daniel's face flamed as brightly as Matt's felt. "Yes, Sir," they mumbled in unison.

"Now go home and let me care for my patient. I don't have time for dealing with brothers and lovers."

"Lovers?" Matt and Daniel harmonized, looking at each other. "What?"

"You heard me. Now shoo, the both of you."

"Can I see her?" Daniel asked.

"No, I've not cleaned up in there, and I don't need another patient passing out on me. The nurse and I will have things cleaned up, and Peg should be awake by morning. Good day, gentlemen."

The doctor stepped back into his office, not waiting for a response.

"I'll see you in the morning, Daniel." Matt took a single step toward the door.

"No, Sir. You're going to tell me what's going on with you and my sister," Daniel demanded, his right hand fisted.

"Nothing, Daniel. Peg and I are friends. We haven't so much as even held hands. It's just this island and its silly rumors. In fact, Peg and I were joking about it this morning. Apparently, according to the gossip, we're engaged and going to have three children." Matt smiled.

Daniel relaxed his fist. "On your honor, it isn't true?"

"I swear. We're just friends."

Daniel nodded and made his way through the front door.

Matt sighed. *Of all the times to have to deal with small-town gossip, now is not it.*

Matt walked back to Southern Treasures and examined the repair job Mo and Ellis had done. The walkway was boarded off and a small sign read UNSAFE. He went to the door of the store and found it open. On the counter, folks had placed notes of get-well wishes and prayers. Matt grinned. *There are certain advantages to living in small towns.*

⚓

Peg groaned, her mind foggy. Pain coursed through her body. She blinked. The room seemed dark, her bed stiff. Opening her eyes, she tried to focus on something in the room, but everything seemed out of place.

She closed her heavy lids again and tried to think. She fought to reopen her eyes again. Her lids were unresponsive. A dark room means nighttime, she reasoned. *I'll just go back to sleep.*

"Miss Martin, how are you feeling?"

Peg grasped the edges of her bed. *Who was in her room?* Fear gave her eyelids the strength she needed. She shot them open. The room appeared brighter. Everything was not as it should be. "Where am I?"

"Relax, Miss Martin, you're at Doc Hansen's house."

Peg groaned. Memories of the accident, the pain, all flooded back. It all made sense now. She tried to bring into focus the darkened silhouette of the woman now sitting beside her. Peg smiled as Mary Hansen leaned closer to the light. The doctor's wife often worked side by side with her husband. She was his nurse, secretary, and anything else that needed doing in the office. "Mrs. Hansen."

"Yes, Dear. You've given us quite a scare. How are you?"

"Hot and sore. What happened to me?" Peg tried to roll onto her right side to face Mary. Pain surged anew up her right leg to her lungs. A cry of pain eased past her lips.

"Stay still, Peg. You don't want to undo my husband's fine work." Gray wisps of Mary's hair fell out of her bonnet.

Peg glanced under the sheet toward her right leg. It seemed to be braced with something.

"You fell through the dock."

"Yes, I can remember that. But what damage did I do?"

"A board pierced your right thigh. There was damage to your leg muscles. You've been in and out for a couple of days due to a high fever brought on by infection, although my husband did give you something for the pain, which aided your sleep."

"A couple days?" Peg whispered. "What about my store? Christmas is only a few weeks away."

"I believe Mr. Bower has been taking care of your store. Your brother has been checking in as often as possible. In fact, half the island's been in here. Greg finally put a message on the slate informing them of your condition." Mary smiled. "My husband, as fine a doctor as he is, doesn't like answering the same question over and over again."

Peg relaxed against the bed. *Matt Bower is working in my store? Why?* "Two days?"

"Yes, Dear. Let me check your fever."

"What time is it?" Peg asked when Mary took the thermometer from her mouth.

"Close to midnight. I'm not certain." Mary lifted the sheet over Peg's right leg. Peg looked down and saw the swelling and discoloration. "Will it heal?"

"We hope so. You're fighting the infection well."

"Will—will I have to lose my leg if the infection doesn't heal?"

"Oh, Peg, don't go frettin' about things before it's time. One thing is certain with medicine, no one knows too much before it happens. Some folks have lost their limbs from less of an injury, others have lost use of them, and still others recover quite well, and you'd never know they had been hurt. Just do as you're told, and I'm certain the good Lord will take care of the rest."

Was that supposed to encourage me? Peg wondered. *I could lose my leg, I could be lame, or I might possibly walk again. Oh, joy.* She bit down her sarcastic thoughts.

Mary glanced at her face. "I'm sorry, Peg. I should have kept my mouth shut. Relax. You're healing well. Can you see this?" Mary pointed to the outer side of Peg's right leg.

Peg lifted herself up on her elbows. "A little."

"Well, yesterday that area was bright pink. Today it's half the shade, much paler. A very good sign."

"Really?"

"Yes. I forget some folks don't want, or even need, to know all the possible problems they could be facing."

"No, don't apologize. I think I prefer knowing." Peg collapsed back on the bed. It was too difficult to hold herself up on her elbows. "I feel dizzy."

"You lost a lot of blood. But you're young, healthy."

"I'm not that young."

Mary grinned. "When you reach my age, you'll remember just how young thirty-eight is."

Peg chuckled. Her ribs hurt. "My sides hurt when I laugh."

"You cracked a rib. Not much the doctor can do but bind it. It shouldn't give you too much trouble."

Peg lay there wondering how many other injuries she sustained from her fall.

"Grace Perez has been coming by checking on you. She even sat for a spell, giving Greg and me some time to rest."

Peg nodded. Their private conversation had barely begun when she fell through the dock.

Mary continued to change the bandages.

"Rumor has it that you and Mr. Bower are planning on getting married after his son arrives." Mary sat back down into her rocking chair.

Peg rolled her eyes and groaned. This time it wasn't from the pain.

"Another island legend, I see." Mary winked.

"Yes," Peg whispered.

"Normally, I'm not one to give ear to such conversation, but with the way he's been checking in on you and filling in at your store. . .I just thought it might be true." Mary picked up a small needlepoint.

"Matt probably feels somehow responsible for the accident since he bought the place. He isn't. It wasn't his fault. I knew better. I shouldn't have been out there."

"Why did you go out there?"

"Grace and I had some private matters to discuss. I didn't want anyone walking in on our conversation."

"Makes sense. I had no idea that wharf was in such bad repair."

"Most of it is solid. There are just a few spots. I forgot to watch where I was going." Her mind had been on helping Grace by sharing her own story.

"I'm forever forgetting to watch. I've sprained my ankle more times than I can remember. Did you know that's how I met Greg?"

"No." Peg smiled. Mary was great at stirring a conversation. "Do tell."

Mary put down her needlework, placed a cool cloth on Peg's forehead, and rocked back. "I'd been walking around the pond at the university, and I wasn't watching where I was going. Apparently, a gopher had burrowed a tunnel across the pathway. I stepped in, fell down, and proceeded to hobble to the school's treatment center. Greg was the student doctor on call."

Peg listened to the older woman ramble on about her husband's exquisite hands and something about his eyes. Peg's own eyes were falling quickly. Soon Mary's words seemed to disappear.

When she opened her eyes, Matt Bower towered over her bed. "Ready for me to take you home?"

Chapter 13

Peg's complexion had returned to normal. Matt couldn't help but be pleased with her progress. Dr. Hansen had filled him in that morning, letting him know that she'd awoken during the night and that they seemed to be winning the battle over the infection.

"Huh?" Peg blinked her vivid blue eyes.

"I'm here to take you home. Dr. Hansen said you could sleep at home just as easily, perhaps even better, in your own bed." Matt pulled the rocker up beside her bed.

"Where's Daniel?"

"He'll be here shortly. Grace Perez has volunteered to care for you. I'll come by in the evening and report to you the day's events at Southern Treasures."

Her gaze darted back and forth. "That isn't necessary, Matt," she whispered. *Yes, it is.* "Isn't a problem. I'm happy to help. Your niece, the militant guard—"

"Mariella?"

"Yes, that's the one. . .will also be sleeping in your apartment."

"Daniel can take me home," she insisted.

"He and I just reasoned, and Daniel saw the wisdom in my helping to take you home. If you're uncomfortable with my presence, I understand, and I'm certain we could find another volunteer."

Peg lay motionless before him.

"It's no bother to lend a hand, and my work does not require a nine-to-five work day."

"True."

"Your sister-in-law, Carmen, has the younger children she needs to be fresh for. Grace Perez has no children to watch over. And she seems quite skilled in caring for another in discomfort. I want to help you, Peg."

"But what about the rumors?" Peg pulled the covers up to her chin.

"Ahh, well, they already have us married and having children. How much worse can they get? You fell through my dock, Peg. It's the least I could do to help."

Peg mumbled something he couldn't quite make out.

"What?" he asked.

"Nothing. Tell me why you've been working at the store?"

"Well, you've been a tad laid up, wouldn't you say?"

"A simple note on the door would have told folks where I was—not that anyone doesn't know." Peg grinned.

"True, you made the front page of the paper." Matt enjoyed their playful banter. It felt good. It felt healthy. Too many images of Esther being laid up and the pain she suffered had visited his dreams since Peg's accident.

"Tell me it isn't true."

"Afraid it is. You were and still are the big news this week."

"Great," she moaned and closed her eyes.

"Peg, it can't be any worse than the questions I'm being asked all day. For example, 'When are you and Miss Martin getting married?' Or even bolder yet, 'I didn't know you and Peg were already married. How come you didn't invite me to the wedding?'"

Peg's body started to shake with laughter. She grasped her ribs.

"Sorry, didn't mean to make you laugh." Matt held back his own merriment. "How is the store?"

"Busy. Everyone and their brother has been in to buy just one more item for Christmas. The special orders have been the hardest to track down. Vivian Matlin has been quite helpful on that score. Seems the woman has been in your store a fair amount."

"She has. If it weren't for Vivian, I'm not sure the store would have ever gotten off the ground."

Matt eased back the rocker and crossed his legs at the ankles. "I've kept track of all items sold, and the bank has graciously accepted each day's income to deposit in your account even though I'm not you. I guess the rumors have come in handy also. Or perhaps it's because it's a small, secluded place where everyone knows everybody, and they know I'm not trying to set myself up to rob your account. On the other hand, the amount of cash I deposited in the same bank upon my arrival should give me some liberties."

"You've been on this island for such a short time, and you've gotten yourself quite respected. I'm impressed."

"Don't be. It's just the money talking."

Peg knitted her eyebrows. "No, I don't think so. I think it's the man. Folks are seeing you as someone they can trust. Someone they can bank on."

Matt took a deep breath and let it out slowly. *Once she knows the truth of why I've come, she won't be thinking that way.*

"Hi." Daniel beamed as he walked into the room.

Grateful for the distraction, Matt relinquished the rocker and stepped away from Peg's bed.

"Doc says you can come home. Matt borrowed a wagon, and Grace is setting up your apartment. I didn't know you and Grace were such good friends."

"I imagine she feels guilty since she was with me at the time of the accident. But she can use the distraction of helping to take care of me. Not to mention the income. We are paying her, aren't we?"

"If you can get her to take some income, you're a better man than I," Daniel teased. Matt crossed his arms and watched the loving relationship between brother and sister.

Peg grinned. "I'll work on it. So when do I leave?"

"As soon as you're ready to go," Matt responded. "But Doc said he wanted to examine you once more before you leave. I'll be back. Someone asked to pick up an order this morning from your store." Matt waved. "Just have the doctor send someone to fetch me when you're ready."

"Thank you, Matt." Daniel extended his hand.

"Nothing anyone else wouldn't have done. I understand there's been quite a list of volunteers."

Daniel chuckled. "I believe it's given old Doc Hansen the motivation to release her early."

Matt grinned. "Your assumption is probably correct." He left Daniel on the steps of the doctor's house and headed toward the harbor. His grin slipped as the words from Peg echoed in his mind. *Folks are seeing you as someone they can trust.* But he knew the truth: He wasn't worthy of her trust. But could he reveal his secret? Would it be fair? To her? To Micah? To himself?

⚓

Peg slid between the covers of her freshly made bed, enjoying the familiarity of the soft feather mattress. Someone had placed poinsettia plants around her room. Their brilliant reds cheered the place.

"Grace, sit down, please. I'm exhausted just watching you."

Grace silently sat beside her on the small oak chair.

Peg felt more like herself every day. Matt's thoughtful attention and ability to make her relax in her own home had been a tremendous help. She also found Grace had been blaming herself for Peg's accident. Over the past few days, Peg had revealed little about her own past, but she thought she had helped Grace understand her own future. Ironically, last night Juan had returned and decided marriage was the answer for him and Grace. Grace, on the other hand, was so nervous she fussed with everything in the house.

"Grace, tell me what you're thinking."

"I don't know, Miss Peg. I want to believe Juan. I know my parents would be much happier when we married. I don't know if I can trust him. Does that make sense?"

"Yes, he ran out on you once. So you're afraid he could do it again."

"*Sí.*"

"Did he explain why he ran?" Peg fluffed up her pillow.

"Something about being afraid."

Peg rolled to her left side. The wounded right leg could easily rest on the lower left one. "Give him a chance, Grace. I'm not saying you should marry him, but if he's serious, he'll wait. He might be able to help you with your own fears. Weren't you afraid when you found out?"

"Terribly."

"But a woman can't run away from it like a man." Peg smiled. "If she runs, the baby comes right along with her."

"*Sí*." Grace giggled.

"You and Juan are young. You've made some bad choices. That doesn't mean they can't be corrected. We serve a God of forgiveness. He takes our mistakes and fixes them."

"I not so sure about Juan and whether he believes in Jesus."

"Hmm, you might want to ask him." *Juan's lack of faith would definitely be another hardship on this couple, Lord. Give her wisdom,* Peg silently prayed.

Grace fidgeted with a cloth she'd been using as a dust rag.

"What is it?" Peg asked.

"Why are you being so kind to me, knowing. . .knowing. . ." Grace looked down at her feet.

"Because people sin, and I'm no exception. What's the good Lord say about taking that log out of our own eye before we try and take a splinter out of someone else's? We've all made bad choices in our lives, Grace. Thankfully, God's mercy covers them all."

A smile rose on Grace's pink lips. Her dark black hair and dark eyes glimmered with relief. Was it necessary to tell her the rest? That Peg too had been in the same situation at nearly the same age? *No, Grace seems to have gotten the message without the confession.*

"Shall we try and see if I can stand with those crutches?"

"You know the doctor said not for another day."

Peg flopped back down into her pillows. "I feel so helpless."

Grace giggled. "You are."

"I should be working."

"How?"

"I could at least do some embroidery. Surely that isn't going to reopen the wound."

Grace rolled her eyes heavenward. "It's a good thing Mr. Bower is selling everything in your store."

"What? What do you mean?" Peg rose quickly and her sides ached. *Cracked ribs,* she silently reminded herself.

Grace tossed her head from side to side. "Did you hear the word 'selling,' as in people are buying?"

"Oh."

"You like to control, don't you?" Grace grinned.

"Possibly. I am the older sibling, you know."

Grace wandered off toward the sitting room. Peg hoped she would bring her needlepoint. Sitting did cause some pressure on her thigh, but she figured if she angled herself just right she might be able to do a couple stitches.

If she were honest with herself, her inability to just lie around was due more to the fact that she missed Matt. She liked Grace, but she felt a constant need to be a mentor for the young woman. Grace was young, while Matt was only a few years older than herself. They even found a few safe things from Savannah to talk about. Peg found herself more and more comfortable with him. She felt a sense of harmony in the house when they were together. And for the first time in more years than she cared to think about, she was considering the possibility of courting. *Courting, at my age. Ridiculous.*

"Here, Peg. I think you should stay down, though, give that leg some more time to heal," Grace suggested, handing her the needlepoint Peg hadn't touched in nearly a week.

"What smells so good?" Peg hoped Grace would be distracted so she wouldn't see the strain on her face as she shifted her battered body enough to sit up in a reclined position.

"Chicken and dumplings. Cook gave me the recipe."

Peg's mouth watered. If Cook told Grace how to make the dish, it was guaranteed to be good. Peg always liked Cook. Cook was far more vocal then Peg had ever been, but they both loved control and organization. "Smells wonderful."

"Mr. Bower asked for it. Seems he's been missing some of what he calls Southern cooking. Never heard him complain before about the beans and rice, or any of the other dishes I've made."

"I'm surprised he didn't ask for grits."

"Grits?"

"It's a corn dish." How could you describe grits, at least so they sounded edible?

"Never heard of it." Grace sat down beside her and watched Peg weave the needle through the fabric.

"Do you sew?"

"Some, nothing fancy like you."

"Would you like me to show you some stitches?"

"Would you?"

Peg smiled; at last she had found a purpose in being laid up. She'd take on the responsibility of teaching Grace how to do needlework.

⚓

"Hello, anyone home?" Matt called as he plopped his attaché on the small table in the sitting room. As much as he hated to admit it, he was behind on some of his own affairs.

Micah had written another letter to confirm his ship and anticipated arrival on Key West. Ten days and his son would be here, the day before Christmas. The question was, would Matt tell him the truth? Would he tell Peg? Every time their discussions revolved around children in general, she was fairly talkative. But once they got to more specifics, to why she never married, she'd claim to be tired and needed to rest. He didn't doubt the need, but it became far too convenient.

"We're in the bedroom, Mr. Bower," Grace called out.

"I'll be right there." Matt pumped some water and washed his hands and face. His nostrils took in the sweet aroma. "Chicken and. . ." He lifted the lid. "Dumplings!" He grabbed a spoon and stirred the pot, sampling a small dose of the broth. His stomach rumbled.

Grace broke out in laughter. "You should see him, Peg. He's like a hungry dog hovering over his dish."

Matt plopped the lid back over the pot. "I was merely sampling your fine cooking."

"Yes, yes. I have to leave for awhile, Mr. Bower. Are you all set for serving dinner?"

"We'll be fine, Grace. How is she?"

"Getting ready to jump up from that bed and hop around the island."

"I heard that," Peg called out from her room.

Matt smiled at Grace and winked. They both understood just how difficult it was for Peg to be a good patient. To be patient, period. "Thanks for your help." Matt escorted Grace to the front door.

"*Buenos noches*, Peg."

"*Adios, hasta mañana,*" Peg responded.

Matt now understood various greetings and salutations in Spanish. He wasn't certain he'd ever become fluent in the language, especially when he'd heard Peg on more than one occasion rattling off in Spanish to Grace.

"Hungry, Peg?" Matt closed the door behind Grace and walked to the bedroom doorway.

"Starving. I've smelled it cooking all afternoon and not once was I able to steal a taste. I take it Grace caught you scooping out of the pot?"

"Possibly." Matt grinned.

"Well, how was it?" She lifted her body into a sitting position. Her jaw tightened, and her eyelids closed. Pain shouted from her body, but her lips remained silent.

"Wonderful. We'll feast tonight. It's been ages since I've had homemade chicken and dumplings. How about yourself?" Matt stepped back toward the kitchen, lifting a couple of large bowls off a tray Grace had obviously set out earlier.

"Be ready for a real treat. That's Cook's recipe. No one on Key West can cook chicken and dumplings like that woman."

"Cook, Ellis Southard's servant?"

"Housekeeper and cook. Some folks don't like the term servant when referring to their employees."

"Thanks, I'm still making that adjustment. Please note, I didn't call her a slave. There's something about that woman. I can't picture her ever being anyone's slave."

"Her family was freed when she was a baby. She and her husband, George, came here from the Bahamas to make a life for themselves."

Matt entered the room with two very full bowls on the tray.

"I'm so hungry my stomach is floppin' like a flounder."

Matt chuckled and placed the tray over Peg's lap. "Where'd you get that expression?"

"My father."

"Oh, right, he was a fisherman."

"Yes."

"Do you miss him?"

"Some, but Dan and I have lived apart from them for so many years it's hard to feel the same loss as if I'd seen them every day."

Matt removed his bowl and sat down in the small oak chair. Definitely a woman's chair. Actually, it felt more like a child's chair. He couldn't picture Peg sitting on it for long periods of time. "Shall we pray?"

They said a brief prayer, then the room silenced. The gentle ting of silver spoons clinking the china bowl lulled him back to Georgia, to Savannah, and to a time when he was a small boy enjoying his first hearty bowl of chicken and dumplings.

"Where were you?" Peg whispered.

"My childhood home, six years old and eating my first bowl of chicken and dumplings. My father loved the meal until he discovered it was common food. It was never served at our table again. Bessy, she was one of our house slaves, would save me a bowl from time to time. And I'd have a real feast. Don't know what it is about this dish, but I sure do love it." He scooped another hearty spoonful.

"Chicken was a treat in our household. We grew up eating tons of fish. Now, don't get me wrong, I enjoy most fish. But when it's your steady diet. . ."

"Say no more, I truly understand."

Peg smiled.

"Do you know you have the most adorable smile. I love it." Matt dropped his spoon in his bowl. Had he really spoken those words? He gave her a sideways glance. Yup, he'd spoken the words. His heart hammered in his chest. He'd been thinking about Peg more and more lately. Not about her injuries, not about her business, and not too much about the fact that she was Micah's mother. But as a woman. Was he really ready to think about another relationship in his life?

Chapter 14

Peg swallowed the thickest hunk of dumpling imaginable. Had he really commented about her looks? He seemed nervous and as ill prepared as herself. "Matt?"

"I'm sorry, Peg. I didn't mean to be so forward."

"I think we ought to talk about this."

Matt shifted on the chair. Granted, it was a stiff and uncomfortable chair, but that wasn't his problem. "I was merely commenting about your looks. You are a beautiful woman, Peg."

"I see. So the fact that you're squirming like a four year old who needs to use the privy has nothing to do with any feelings you might have."

"Are you sure *you* want to discuss this?"

"What is that supposed to mean?" Peg fought to stay still on the bed and not tip the bowl of chicken and dumplings.

He raised his voice slightly. "You're as afraid of your feelings as I am of mine."

Peg silently counted to three before she answered. "What feelings?"

"Try being honest, Peg. You react every time I walk into the room."

If there ever was a problem with pale skin, that was it. The slightest sign of embarrassment and she'd blush brighter than a beacon. Her face flamed. She grasped her spoon. "I'm sorry I brought it up."

Matt nodded and went back to his dinner. The two of them ate in silence until their bowls were finished. "Would you like some more?" he asked.

"No, thank you. I've been sitting for awhile. I should lie down."

He removed the tray and silently slipped into the kitchen. They weren't ready to discuss a relationship. They weren't ready to have a relationship, were they?

"I'm sorry, Peg."

Peg jumped, then groaned.

"Oh, Peg, I'm sorry. I didn't mean to scare you. Are you all right?"

Her leg throbbed. "I'm okay. I'm sorry too."

"I know we both agreed we weren't looking for a relationship, but I think one is developing. I mean, something more than just friendship."

"I know." Peg felt her face brighten yet again.

"I also think we're mature enough to handle this. If the Lord is bringing us together, should we fight it?"

"I don't know, Matt. I don't know that I'd ever be suitable as a wife for anyone."

"What kind of nonsense is that?" His voice raised slightly.

"I'm too old and set in my ways. As Grace put it earlier, I like to be in charge."

"Ah, so submission to a husband is out?"

"Husband? Don't you think you're pushing things?" Peg raised the covers up over her chest.

Matt chuckled. "I wasn't suggesting. I merely was thinking about what you've obviously thought about all these years to remain single."

"Oh. Yes. I guess I decided that would definitely be a hardship on myself and my husband."

Matt sat down beside her on the small chair she used to put on her boots for social occasions. The rest of the time she wore sandals, which she just slipped on.

"Esther had a hard time with that for awhile. She, like you, was the oldest. And the good Lord gave her an incredible brain. Most men would have run away screaming from a woman like that. She said that most men didn't call on her more than once."

Peg laughed. "I think I like your wife."

"Good. You probably would have gotten along really well. But then again, you might have bumped heads too. Hard to say." Matt rose. "I best be going."

"No, Matt. Mariella isn't here."

"I'll go fetch her. Do you need Carmen's help?"

"Yes, thanks."

After Matt returned with Carmen and Mariella and private matters were taken care of, Peg lay down while Carmen changed her dressing. "How's it look?"

Mariella scrunched her nose. "Like fish guts."

"Mariella!" Carmen scolded.

"That bad, huh?" Peg joked back.

Mariella nodded her head up and down and didn't say another word.

"Actually, it's looking much better. The scabs are healing on some of the minor cuts," Carmen offered. "Doc Hansen will be pleased."

"Do you think he'll let me start walking soon?"

"It would be foolish for me to even hazard a guess," Matt said from the doorway.

Carmen looked at Matt, then at Peg. "You two all right?"

"Fine," they both chimed too quickly.

Carmen hid her smile well, but Peg caught a glimpse of it. The leg dressed, Carmen worked on it. Doc Hansen said it would help the blood circulation. What he didn't know was that Matt's gentle and loving ways were dissolving her defenses. If given a chance, she would never mind submitting her authority to this man.

⚓

Peg's fondness for Matt was growing day by day. Each day they opened themselves a bit more to each other. Affectionate glances and an occasional caress of each other's hands brought a deeper and deeper intimacy. Conversations about marriage were discussed more freely between them. But if this continued, soon she would have to confess the truth to Matt. It wouldn't be fair for him to enter a relationship with her not knowing the truth. However, finding the right time in which to tell him was hopeless. Their visits were shared with a chaperone. Peg had never been so grateful for the easy distraction of children. She could send them off looking for something, or give them a dollar and ask them to run to town for her. Either way, it provided her only stolen moments alone with Matt.

Peg limped with her crutches to the small sofa. "Mariella went to town for us."

Matt grinned. "Micah arrives tomorrow."

"I can't wait to meet him. The doctor says I can go back to work tomorrow if I'm careful. Mariella said she wouldn't mind spending the day in the store with me."

"Hope you can find everything." Matt winked.

"What have you done?"

He reached out and held her hand. "Peg, we need to talk."

"Peg, are you in there?" Daniel called out, then her front door creaked open.

"So much for a private moment," she mumbled. "Yes," she hollered.

Daniel marched in through the front door.

"What's the matter, Daniel?"

He looked around the room. "Where's Mariella?"

"She ran to town for me." Peg blushed.

Matt released her hand.

Anger rose in Daniel's face.

"Daniel, why were you looking for me?"

"I was going to ask you to help me surprise Carmen for Christmas, but I guess it's a good thing I came in when I did." The anger and disappointment in his voice boomed through the house.

"Daniel." Peg blushed. "You have no right."

"No, Peg. You have no right."

"Daniel." Matt cleared his throat. "Nothing inappropriate has happened. We're both mature adults."

"Nonsense. You know this island and its rumors. Peg's reputation could be soiled. . . ." His words trailed off. He stomped out of the house.

"I'm sorry, Matt. Daniel's right. You should go." Peg rubbed her hands together. Why had she allowed herself to steal private moments with Matt?

"That's ridiculous, Peg. We've done nothing wrong." He stood.

"Please, Matt. You wouldn't understand."

"Try me."

"Please," Peg pleaded. What could she say? This wasn't the way to tell him the truth about herself and her past, something she and Daniel had fought long and hard to protect. Something for which he'd given up his life—to help her re-build her future. And she had. They had. And in one foolish moment of wanting to be alone with Matthew, she might have ruined twenty years of restoration.

How could she have been so foolish?

Matt lifted her chin with his finger and caressed her lips with his thumb. "Since I've already soiled your pristine reputation, then I guess you won't mind this."

He captured her lips with his. Peg found herself looping her arms around his neck. Her whole world crumbled around her feet as tears ran down her cheek. He released her and boldly stepped away.

"Good day, Miss Martin. If you can't trust me, then we have no relationship."

Matt stormed through town. They'd come so close to confessing their love for one another. But how could he truly give her his heart when she hid such a dark secret from him? He couldn't. He wouldn't. It wasn't worth the risk.

He marched to his dock and walked out to the farthest point. Ships sailed gently in and out of the harbor. It had been a mistake to come to Key West. He should have buried the information Dr. Baker had given him so many months ago. Why had he bothered to seek the mother of Micah? To tell her the truth? To tell her that her son did not die?

Her pristine identity in Key West would never welcome the knowledge that her son was alive. Micah would never be accepted. People would always consider him illegitimate. How could a man cope with that information, never having known his entire life that he wasn't his parents' child?

No, it wasn't fair to Micah. He'd been foolish to even think it might be a good thing. Thankfully, Micah knew nothing about Dr. Baker's confession. With everything that was in him, Matt determined he would never tell Micah the truth. He was better off not knowing. While his birth mother had some charming aspects, her heart was hard as stone. She was determined to be something she wasn't, determined to live a life alone. *Well, she can live it alone. I don't need to be here any longer.* It wouldn't be too difficult to move his business back to Savannah. It hadn't really left there yet anyway.

What was he going to do when Micah arrived?

A pelican swooped down in front of him and captured a fish dinner. Matt took in a deep breath and let it out slowly.

A small ship passed and the man at the helm waved. Matt thought he'd met the man before and waved back. Fact was everyone waved as ships passed. A common courtesy of the sea.

A sail—perfect. He and Micah could sail to Key Visca. Spend Christmas together, alone and safe.

Matt headed back from the end of the pier and set about renting a sailboat for the next week.

Peg fought her troubled emotions all night. She had been looking forward to going back to work yesterday. Today the mere thought of it was pure agony. Her leg throbbed. Her concentration was off. The thought of even half a day on crutches made her back stiffen.

She still couldn't figure out why Matt had reacted as he had. Granted, Daniel had too, but that was correctable. Daniel not only apologized, he even went to Matt's home to apologize. Matt had even accepted his apology, but then he said it didn't change the real issue, the real problem.

All night Peg tried to figure out what the "real" problem was. All night she came up blank. She knew she had to tell Matt about her past, but he didn't know that. So she reasoned that couldn't be the problem. But what was their problem? How did he dare say that honesty was the issue? Hadn't she always been honest? Had she ever deceived him about anything?

He never even asked for details concerning her past relationships. He talked freely about himself and Esther, but he never asked about anyone from her past. Why was that?

Daniel knocked on her door bright and early to give her a ride to town. It was hard to believe—she still wasn't strong enough to walk the short distance from her house down to the harbor on her own.

At work, she marveled at the nearly empty shelves. Moving to her new location wouldn't be as difficult as she had anticipated. Matt must be some kind of salesman.

Peg bit her lower lip. Well, that was true. He sold her his heart, and she accepted it. "Why can't we work this out, Lord? I really don't understand the problem."

She rested on the stool and read through all of Matt's entries. He'd been very detailed in every record he kept. She could never question the man's honesty.

"Honesty. Have I been less than honest with him, Lord?" Peg glanced at the harbor. A two-masted schooner was sailing in. She wondered if Micah were on board.

She went back to work, going over Matt's figures. The cries of a ship arriving soon filled the streets. Folks hurried to the harbor in anticipation of packages, guests, and returning family members. Peg looked over the crowd. Matt was nowhere to be found.

The ship slid up along the end of the pier. The seamen jumped on the dock and secured the lines. How many times had she seen ships docking over the years? She couldn't wager a guess. But each time brought her a certain fascination. Most captains were highly skilled, and the ships came to a gentle stop. Once in awhile you'd get a newer captain, and he'd bang into the pier. Even fewer times she'd seen some damage done to the vessels. But those events were less than a handful.

Today's captain was an expert seaman. His ship kissed the dock with such a tender touch there was hardly a whisper of the lines going taut. Peg smiled.

Soon the passengers started to depart. Some wobbled, but most found their legs quickly. Probably from Savannah, she thought. She watched for Matt's son.

One by one, the passengers departed and were greeted by those awaiting their arrivals.

Peg's smile broadened. Nathaniel waved with his arms draped over a young woman. She watched him point toward her window. Peg stood closer and waved in return. Julie must be Mrs. Nathaniel Farris by now. *Won't the island be buzzing?* Peg quickly scanned the locals watching the passengers disembark. Sure enough, women were already smiling and whispering one to another.

Peg chuckled and glanced back at the ship.

A young man with golden waves jumped off the ship. He searched the crowd, looking for his family. Peg took a closer look. Her hands clasped the sill. "Lord, it can't be," she gasped. "Billy."

Chapter 15

Matt worked his way through the crowd. He'd been late getting up this morning, having spent most of the night packing and making the boat ready for his trip to Key Visca. When word reached his door that a ship was docking, he was only half dressed and hadn't shaved.

"Micah!" he shouted.

His son turned his head toward him. "Excuse me," Matt said, stepping past another man.

"Father!" Micah hollered back.

Matt fought the tears that filled his eyes. Both men ran up to each other and wrapped their arms around each other, giving each other a couple of good solid slaps.

"It's good to see you, Son." Matt pulled back and scanned his son from head to toe. Then Matt's stomach flipped. Beyond his son's shoulder, he could see Peg staring at them.

"It's great seeing you. The house is so lonely without you." Micah beamed, then scanned the area.

"I'll be returning with you, I think."

"What? I thought Key West was the answer for the business."

Because your mother is here, and I've fallen in love with her. But he held his inner thoughts at bay. "We'll discuss it later. Where are your bags?"

"A seaman said he'd bring them."

Matt grinned. "I think you're thicker around the middle."

"Too many meals at Anna's restaurant."

"She owns the place?" *Nice change of subject.* Micah's love life seemed far more appealing to discuss.

"No, she just works there. But she fed me well."

"How's that relationship going?"

"It's not. I mean, I like her and all, but I don't feel the sparks. You know, like you and Mother had."

Matt grinned and fussed with his son's hair. "I know. You'll have to tell me all about her and school. How did your final examinations go?"

"Well, my grades were all in the upper percentiles."

"Wonderful. I knew you could do it, Son. I'm so proud of you."

"Thanks. I had my moments."

Matt chuckled. "Don't we all. Advanced studies can drive a man crazy. Your mother really helped pull me through. She was the distraction I needed."

"Work did that for me. Don't let me forget to tell you about some interesting developments."

"Oh?"

"I may have made some good contacts for us."

"Do tell!"

Micah chuckled. "Later. We have plenty of time."

"True. So how was the voyage?"

"Fine. The weather was calm, no storms." Micah turned his head to the left. Something behind Matt had caught his attention. Silently, Matt prayed it wasn't Peg Martin.

"Hello, Mr. Bower, is this your son?"

Thank You, Lord. "Hello, Ben. Yes. Let me introduce you. Micah, this fine young man is Ben Hunte, and he's very industrious. Ben, this is my son, Micah."

Micah extended his hand. Ben took it, then leaned into Matt and whispered, "Did he own slaves?"

"No, Ben. Micah has never owned a slave."

Ben beamed. "Pleased ta meet ya, Mr. Micah."

"Pleasure meeting you, Ben." Micah caught Matt's eye and raised his eyebrows.

"Later," Matt mouthed.

Micah grinned.

Micah's bags arrived.

"Need help bringing 'em to your house, Mr. Bower?"

"No, thank you, Ben. I think we can handle it."

Ben stepped back. "All right. Have a merry Christmas, if I don't see ya again."

"You too, Ben." Matt reached into his pocket and pulled out a silver dollar. "Merry Christmas."

"Thanks."

"You're welcome. You've been a big help to me while I've been on Key West."

Ben shuffled his feet in the dirt. "I was hoping to get a job from your warehouse, once you built it."

Matt didn't have the heart to tell the child on Christmas Eve that he probably wouldn't be building the warehouse. "We'll see, Son."

Ben ran off after saying good-bye. "What's this about owning slaves?" Micah asked.

⚓

Peg grabbed her crutches and headed toward the door. Billy, or rather his look-alike, was Micah, Matt's son. Had Esther been a relative of Billy's? Was Matt a cousin of Billy's? Peg couldn't remember Billy ever talking about having rich cousins. He was as poor as her family had been. Which wasn't as poor as some folks, but certainly not as well off as others.

She had watched as Ben Hunte was introduced to Micah. Surely, Matt would bring Micah here. But was that the "truth" that Matt had mentioned yesterday? Did he know she and Billy had an affair? Could he have just told Matt or his family that he'd had his way with her?

It was all so confusing, and yet it strangely made sense of yesterday's conversation. If Matt had known. . .then he would have known she hadn't told him everything about her past.

Mariella walked into the store. "Is that Mr. Bower's son?"

"I believe so." Peg shifted on her crutches.

"Where's all your stuff?" Mariella demanded with her hands on her hips.

"Appears Mr. Bower's been selling it. And probably told folks to not bring in anything new until after I move."

"Makes sense. Whatcha want me to do?" Mariella scanned the nearly barren room.

"Your father insisted that you come to the store with me. If I didn't expect to hear from him when I returned later in the day, I'd let you go."

"Yes, I hear you. Daniel can be. . .'"

"When did you start calling him Daniel?"

"Momma said I don't have to call him Father if'n I don't want to. It's not that I don't love him or nothing. It's just that he isn't my father."

"I understand. I imagine Daniel does too, but don't you think it might be wise to call him, oh, I don't know, something like Uncle Dan, or some other name like Papa, or at the very least, Father Martin or Mr. Daniel?"

Mariella shrugged.

"Showing Daniel respect by giving him the special honor of a special name would make him very proud. I do know he loves you very much."

"Yes, he's a good man, and he's wonderful with my mom. He treats her like she's special. When my father would come home he always made Momma work. Momma said it was the Spanish way. A wife showed honor to her husband by doing everything for him and treating him like a king. Personally, I like Mr. Daniel's way better."

Peg grinned. She turned back to see Micah and Matt heading toward town. Her heart sank that he wasn't bringing his son to meet her. But then again, did she really want to be confronted about her past in front of Mariella or Micah?

No, she would just have to wait until a more appropriate time. After all, Matthew Bower would be staying in Key West for quite awhile. There was plenty of time for them to heal the differences between them. Even if they didn't become anything more than friends, Peg hungered to have their relationship right.

Peg waved as Matt turned back and saw her standing in the doorway.

"Who's that?" Micah asked.

"A friend. Her name is Peg Martin. She and her brother were born in Savannah."

"Really, what happened to her? I mean, why is she on crutches?"

Matt waved back at Peg. As angry as he was with her, he wasn't about to show it in front of his son. Peg nodded and hopped back inside her store.

"She fell through the dock we just purchased."

Micah's jaw dropped. "You bought a rotting dock?"

"In places, yes. It's behind that building she's in."

"That doesn't sound like you, Father. I've never known you to make an unwise business purchase. Is there something between you two that I ought to know about?"

"No. We're friends, nothing more." Matt coughed.

Micah's blue eyes pierced his own.

"Sure."

"Seriously, Son. After her accident I helped her out with her business, and I visited her most evenings."

"You visited her?" Micah turned and headed toward Peg's store. "This woman I've got to meet. Come on, you've got approximately two minutes to tell me everything before I ask the lady myself."

"I owned the dock at the time she had the accident. I felt guilty. After all, I knew the condition of the dock but didn't rope it off, and I didn't put up a no trespassing sign. Legally, I was responsible for her injuries."

"Now that sounds like my father." Micah grinned. "I still want to meet her. I suspect there might be other emotions at work here besides guilt."

"If there were, and I do mean if, there's no room for anything to develop between us. We look at life differently." A hint of bitterness rolled off his tongue.

"Ouch."

"Micah," Matt groaned.

"All right, all right. You win this time. But trust me, Father, this conversation isn't over. Besides, if you've found someone, I'm sure Mother would be pleased. I know she didn't want you to remain single. She and I talked about it many times before she died."

"You what?" Matt raised his voice. "Why on earth would you and your mother be discussing such matters?"

"I believe she wanted me to be comfortable with the idea if you should ever find someone."

Micah placed his arm around his shoulders. "Your mother was something."

"Yes, she was. I really miss her. With you being gone for the past two months, I've realized just how lonely life is without her and you around."

Matt took a step toward his house, leaving Southern Treasures a step farther behind him and Micah. "I rented a boat, Micah. I thought we could sail to Key Visca and have a quiet holiday on the sea."

"I just got off a boat and you want me back on one?"

"I suspect it would be quite conducive for private conversation." Matt leaned closer to his son's ear. "This island has the fastest gossip chain I've ever seen. A lightning strike during dry season hitting the beach grass can't burn faster than this island news. Never seen anything like it before."

"Interesting. I've been hearing a bit more gossip lately from Anna than I ever knew existed between people. That girl can talk. Nothing is safe around her. I learned quickly to guard my tongue. I heard more news about folks I never met than I heard in a lifetime of sitting around talking with my cousins and their servants."

Matt chuckled. "Sounds like she'd love Key West."

"Obviously, we have private matters to discuss, and if an ocean voyage with the two of us is the answer, I'm willing. When do we leave?"

"I hoped tonight, with the evening tide."

"Would the morning one be all right? I'd really like to spend one night in a bed that doesn't move." Micah grinned.

Matt chuckled. "Tomorrow it is then."

"So, where do you live?"

"Couple more houses up on the left." Matt could make out the whitewashed fence in front of the cottage he'd rented. "There," he pointed.

"Not too far from the harbor," Micah commented. "What's all that?"

Matt noticed bundles and packages piled next to his front door. "I have no idea."

The sun began to sink in the sky. Mariella turned the OPEN sign in the door window to read CLOSED. "I can't wait to go home."

"Thank you for helping me today. I know we didn't have too many customers, but I'm not as strong as I hoped I'd be."

"I don't mind." Mariella fingered a small stuffed animal. "*Tía* Peg?"

Mariella didn't call her aunt too often, and rarely in Spanish. "What do you need, Child?"

"I know I said I'd help you but. . ."

"The day is done. It's time to go home and start preparing for our holiday dinner."

"No, I mean, well, I don't want to sound awful, it's just that I have a friend I'd like to give a gift to, but I don't have any money. And I didn't want to ask Daniel, I mean, Papa Dan. . ."

"I like Papa Dan. I think Daniel will like it too."

"Thanks." Mariella looked down at her feet.

"There isn't much left in the store, but pick whatever gift you think would suit your friend. You earned it."

"Really?"

"Yes, Dear. Go ahead." Peg wasn't surprised to see her pick up the small stuffed animal. She'd seen Mariella return to it several times. In fact, Peg had thought she herself might sneak it home as another gift for Mariella. It pleased her to see Mariella picking a gift for a friend instead of something for herself—a definite sign of maturity.

"Thank you, *Tía* Peg."

"Shall we wrap it?"

"You make such pretty packages. It's hard to open them they are so pretty."

Peg smiled and sat on her stool. "Is this friend a boy or a girl?"

"A girl. Her momma works real hard but. . .well, her father also died in the war. They don't have much."

"Hmm, why don't you pick out a couple other things then. Something for her mother. Does she have any brothers or sisters?"

"No, it's just her and her mother. She's only five."

"Would she like one of those dolls over there?" Peg pointed to a couple of rag dolls she still had left.

"Oh, yes." Mariella's face lit up.

"Come on, we have some work to do. Let's put these gifts together as a surprise. If you wish, we could have them delivered to her house, and she wouldn't know who gave them the gifts."

"Is that better?"

"Depends on why you want to give. The Bible talks about us giving to others so that one hand doesn't know what the other is doing. In other words, doing our good deeds in secret. This could be our little secret. Only God will know."

Mariella placed the rag doll and stuffed animal on the counter. "Jesus' birthday is a good time to show people God's love. I think we should do this in secret. Who can we get to deliver our package?"

"I'll find someone. Let's wrap these items up. Under that counter over there I have special squares of fabric just for wrapping gifts. You'll also find some ribbons. Pick some bright reds and greens. Perhaps some ivory too."

Peg gathered a couple items she felt a woman might appreciate and placed them on the counter as well. "Anything else?" she asked Mariella.

"Some of these items you didn't make. You'll have to pay for them."

"True, but I only pay a part of the price. Besides, Mr. Bower made quite a few sales this month. Perhaps I should be laid up more often. I don't think I've ever sold as much merchandise in a month as Mr. Bower sold in the past couple weeks."

Mariella grabbed another small trinket suitable for a child.

"Now let me show you how to wrap this so that it makes unwrapping it just as much fun as receiving the presents."

Her eager student sat down beside her.

The door rattled in its hinges, and they both jumped. Peg looked up at the storefront window and saw Bea Southard frantically waving. "Mariella, open the door for Mrs. Southard."

Mariella obeyed, and Bea pushed into the room. "I'm so glad I caught you. Is it true?"

Chapter 16

I s what true?" Peg stood up too quickly on her bad leg.

"That Grace is returning to Cuba with Juan?" Bea sat down at the counter.

"Yes, she told me the other day that she and Juan were going to marry and move to Cuba. He found a job there." Peg looked over at Mariella. She wasn't sure what she knew or didn't know of Grace's condition, and she hoped Bea would catch the movement of her eyes.

"Then I am truly happy for them. What do you have here?"

Mariella chirped, "They are some gifts for a friend of mine."

"They are quite nice. May I help wrap them?" Bea asked.

"Of course. An extra set of hands is always helpful. We're wrapping each item first, then gathering them all together in this cloth."

Bea raised her eyebrows but didn't comment. The three women made short work of it, and Peg gathered the larger cloth around the smaller items and wrapped the edges like a bowl. "Now a delivery man." Peg scanned the street. "Mariella, there's Ben Hunte. Grab him."

Mariella hurried out the front door.

"Okay, what's really the matter, Bea?" Peg quickly asked.

Bea's smile slipped. "Later. Can Mariella go home before you?"

"Yes. I can send her on another errand."

Mariella and Ben returned promptly. "Ben, Mariella knows where this needs to be delivered. We don't want the folks to know where it came from. Just tell them that God loves them."

"I can do that."

Peg reached into her purse and pulled out a silver dollar, handing it to Ben. "Thanks, Ben."

"Nope, it's Christmas. You keep the money. My part of the gift will be the delivery." Ben winked.

"You're growing up too fast, Mr. Hunte," Bea praised. Peg placed the coin back in her purse.

A bright white grin appeared on his chestnut brown face. He scooped up the package. "Lead the way, Mariella."

"What's that gift about?" Bea settled on the stool opposite Peg's.

"Mariella has a young friend whose father died in the war. Her mother and she are all alone. I gather they have no other family in the area. I don't know for sure, just my gut instinct. The war's been over for a couple years now. But this

344

young mother appears to have no one else around. Anyway, Mariella kept eying this stuffed animal in the store. Naturally, I thought she liked it and I was going to bring it home for her, in secret, of course." Peg winked. "But it turns out it was for this friend. We just went shopping in the store and gathered a few more items to go with the stuffed animal."

"A few, huh?" Bea chuckled.

"What really brought you in here huffing and puffing?" Peg rubbed her leg.

"Juan and Grace. The way I heard the rumor was that he was forcing her to return to Cuba with him."

Peg laughed and gathered the leftover pieces of fabric and ribbon and put them away under the counter. "This island."

"They were half right. But I wanted to make sure he wasn't forcing her to do anything she didn't want to do."

"Grace is beginning to show. Juan did find a job working on a tobacco farm in Cuba. If they return to Cuba together, they will face less shame. They married a couple days ago but will be staying through the holiday with her family."

"I'm happy for Grace if this is what she wants."

"She and Juan talked many times. You'd be proud of Grace. She held her own. Juan definitely had to prove his love before she agreed. She didn't want to go to Cuba only to have her husband run off on her again. Her parents gave her a small gift. Juan sees it as a small jewelry case. There's a secret panel in the box that, once removed, reveals some silver and gold coins."

"What?"

"It's for the just-in-case scenario. If Juan should take off on Grace, she has the money to return home to Key West."

"That's not showing much confidence in Juan."

Peg folded her arms around her chest. "It's the money her parents set aside for her wedding. Juan left her once. Grace's father isn't confident the man will stay by her. Personally, I think he will, but her father has a point."

"As a parent, I guess I can understand Grace's father's actions. If I had a daughter I'd want her to be safe."

Peg agreed.

"Is Matt coming to your house for Christmas dinner?"

Peg's heart hammered in her chest. Tears began to pool in her eyes. "No, I don't think I'll be seeing Matthew Bower again. At least, not on a personal level."

"What happened?"

Peg took in short gasps of air. How could she explain? "I think Matt knows about Billy Ingles and our having a baby."

"How? Did you tell him?"

"No, I didn't tell him. Although I was about to. Our relationship was beginning to develop to a point that if we were to go further I would have no choice but to tell him about my past. But just as we were about to share our first kiss, Daniel came storming into the house, saw that the two of us were alone, and hit the ceiling. It was horrible, Bea. I've never seen Daniel behave in such a way before. Granted, I'd never given him the opportunity to be so upset with me. But we're grown adults. Matt and I can have a moment or two alone, can't we?"

"Yes, you can. But I don't understand why that is enough to prevent you and Matt from seeing each other again."

"Micah, Matt's son, is the spitting image of Billy Ingles. I just about fell off my feet when I saw him. Of course, I'm a tad bit unstable on this leg," Peg added, feigning humor.

"How can Matthew Bower's son look like Billy Ingles?"

"He's not an exact copy, and granted I didn't see him up close. He's just familiar enough that I don't doubt that Matt or his wife must have been a relative of Billy's. Somehow Matt must know the truth about my past, and doesn't trust me."

⚓

Matt fought the need to run, to remove Micah from harm's way all afternoon. The battle waging inside himself was only compounded by the loving gifts that had been brought to his door. Island residents blessed him with home-baked goods for his and Micah's Christmas dinner. He had been given more dinner invitations then he recalled ever having received for all the social occasions he and his wife attended while living in Savannah.

"Reconsidering?" Micah asked, stepping out of the bedroom.

"No, not really. But it will be hard on the folks here when they discover we're not going to move the business to Key West."

"You haven't explained why. What's happened since our last correspondence?"

Micah sat down across from him. His son's blue eyes were so like Peg's. The set of those eyes, and the bridge of his nose. . . Would he ever be able to look at his son and not see Peg Martin, his birth mother? The same woman he had fallen in love with. *God, help me. I can't believe I have such strong feelings for her. If I tell her and Micah. . .* He hesitated. *What would they do?*

"Father?"

"I'm not satisfied with the property. The size of the warehouse I'd be able to build wouldn't suffice. We'd need an additional location, which would mean additional transportation of the goods to and from the harbor."

"But I thought you said you could build upon the present structure."

"True, but I've been reconsidering."

"Would you mind terribly showing me the property? Perhaps I could come up with an alternative. That isn't to say I don't think you've explored all the options but. . ."

"No, I don't mind." Matt pulled out his pocket watch. Peg would have left the store hours ago. It was safe to go there. "Why don't we go now before the sun sets?"

Micah gave him a lopsided grin. "Sounds good."

The two of them headed toward the harbor, back toward Southern

Treasures. The sign on the door said CLOSED. Matt breathed a sign of relief.

Micah placed an arm across his father's shoulder. "Is she someone I should meet?"

Matt blinked back the honest question from his son. Yes, he should. But if he did, their lives would be forever altered. "I think it's best that we not pursue a relationship."

"So, you *did* find someone?" Micah grinned. "Mother would be pleased, you know."

"What?" Matt walked around to the backside of Peg's store. The fresh boards reminded him of the horrid scene when he came upon Peg twisted between the rotting boards.

"Look, I'm not the one to give you advice about love and relationships. I'm still learning that for myself. But like I said, Mother and I spoke on the matter before she died. We both agreed a good wife would be best for you."

"You two decided, huh?" Matt teased.

"Come on, Father, you like her, don't you?"

"Yes, I like her. But we come from different backgrounds. Our values are not the same."

"She's not a believer?"

"No, she's a believer. Has a healthy relationship with the Lord. It's not that." How much longer could he skirt around the real issue?

"Anna isn't a believer, which is one of the reasons I know she's not the right one for me. At first I wondered if God would use our friendship to help bring her to salvation. I still hope He might. But I know it's wrong to set one's heart on an unbeliever. So I kept my guard up. Slowly, I began to see that, while we had some similar interests, we looked at life totally differently. In a way, she thinks the world owes her something, I guess because her father was hung for murder when she was a tiny baby. She doesn't see a need to give something back to society."

"Ah, I've met a few of those in my lifetime. It's one of the things we need to guard ourselves against with our employees. Some feel they don't need to work for their wages. Just their showing up should be enough."

Micah chuckled. "You wouldn't believe how many assumed, because you were gone, that I would be an easy touch. You've taught me well, Father. Hard work is to be rewarded. Sloths can find the door."

Matt grinned. "I'm proud of you, Son. But tell me, is this what you want to do with your life? Peg made me realize that I'd done the same with you as my father had done with me. I've assumed you would want to take over the business one day. You don't have to; the choice is yours. You can use your education and pursue any career you'd like."

"Now I'm definitely going to have to meet this Peg Martin."

Matt's stomach tightened.

"What's the matter, Father? What happened between the two of you?"

Chapter 17

Matt sat down on the end of the dock and patted the board beside him. Taking in a deep breath he let it out slowly. "Micah, I have something to tell you. But before you hear it, I need to hear you say that you know that I love you."

"Father, I know you love me. I've never doubted that love for a moment."

"Good, because what I'm about to tell you will shake the very foundations of that love."

"What?"

"Bear with me, Son. This is difficult."

Micah nodded and clenched the end of the dock, rocking slightly.

"About three months ago, I was called to a man's bedside because he was dying, and he felt he needed to tell me something about his past."

Micah nodded, his face sharp with interest.

"His name was Dr. Baker."

"Our old doctor?"

Micah gave a single nod. "Doc Baker said he needed to tell me something. I had no idea what it was. I thought a pastor would be the more appropriate person, but a man doesn't turn aside a dying man's request."

Micah's golden brown eyebrows knitted.

Matt took in another deep breath and eased it out slowly. *Oh, Lord, help me do this right.* "He told me that he had taken a newborn baby from a young mother and replaced it with an infant that had died during childbirth."

"What? Who did he think he was, God?"

"Apparently. He reasoned that this young mother, who wasn't married, wouldn't be able to raise the child. And the couple whose child had died would be good parents."

"But that's unethical." Micah's sense of justice and the idealism of youth brought out his zeal for what was right.

"Exactly."

"Why was he telling you this? Why are you telling me?"

Matt paused. "Because, Micah, my dear, dear son—" Matt choked back the tears.

"No!" Micah blurted. "No, Father. It can't be true. I'm your son."

"Yes, you are my son. Nothing will ever change that." Tears streamed down Matt's face. "I love you. You're as much a part of me as life itself. I didn't want to believe it either. But as some time passed, I started putting some things together."

"Such as?" Micah's knuckles were white from holding the deck so tightly.

"Your hair and skin coloring. No one in my family or your mother's has blond hair."

"But. . ." Micah's eyes brimmed with tears.

"It doesn't change the fact that I love you, Micah. I loved you as my son and you are my son. I've raised you. You're a part of me and your mother. Nothing will ever change that."

"Did he tell you who I really am?" Micah looked out at the sea.

"Yes," Matt whispered.

"And?" Micah demanded.

"I don't know who your father is, but he gave me the name of the girl who gave birth to you."

"And?" Micah raised his voice, his gaze now firmly planted on Matt's own.

Please, Lord, help him understand. "She moved away from Savannah twenty years ago."

"Who is she? Where is she?"

"I tracked her down, Micah." Matt paused. "I'm so sorry, Son. I thought of not telling you. But I honestly don't know that I could keep it in much longer. The fact is, the girl who gave birth to you lives on Key West."

"That's why you came here? Why didn't you tell me? Why all this secretiveness? We've never kept secrets before. Not about Mother dying—nothing, ever. Why now, Dad?" Micah stood up and paced back and forth on the dock.

"Because I needed to find her. I needed to find out whether I should tell you or not. I wished Dr. Baker had taken his unethical practice to the grave. Our lives were better off not knowing."

"And what of this woman who is my mother? What of her life, Dad? Was it right for her to believe her child was dead all these years? Was it?" Micah's voice mirrored the red fire of the sunset.

"No, Son. It wasn't fair." Matt hung his head. The truth of the matter was out. It wasn't fair. It wasn't fair to anyone.

"Does she know? I mean, did you tell her?"

"No."

Micah stomped farther away down the dock then stopped and faced him. "You're as bad as Dr. Baker was. Who is she, Dad? Who is my mother?"

⚓

Peg finished dressing her presents for Daniel and his family. She set aside the two items she had purchased for Matt and Micah. He wouldn't be coming to Christmas dinner; she could feel it in her bones. He hadn't introduced his son to her.

The memory of his kiss still burned her lips. Peg closed her eyes and quelled her emotions. She wouldn't dwell again on that kiss. When she opened her eyes, the gifts blinked like the twinkle of moonlight dancing on an ocean. She would take them to his doorstep and leave them there. No, she corrected herself, she wouldn't take them. She'd have Daniel do it. She didn't need to see Matt. She just wanted to. But how would she explain her past? A past he obviously knew about? He must think her dishonest.

But why should the entire world know her sin? Peg paced back and forth in her apartment until her leg throbbed. She sat down and raised her leg, massaging it as the doctor had taught her. The wound was healing well, though it looked uglier than sin. Peg caught herself in her thoughts. Sin. . .ugly. . . She closed her eyes and blinked back the tears. Her own sin had scarred her heart as badly as the beam puncturing her thigh. But God's grace covered that sin with the shed blood of the cross. The scar remained; the sin did not.

She knocked on the door joining her apartment to the big house. No one answered. She turned the handle and entered. The kitchen was hot, and the fragrance of fresh baked breads and pastry filled the air. "Hello, anyone home?" she called.

"*Tía* Peg." Mariella came running. "I hid in the bushes. I saw Lisa and her mother find the package on their front step. Ben placed the bundle on the step, rapped the door, then ran, hiding around the corner of the house. Oh, *Tía*, they cried. It was so beautiful."

Peg reached over and embraced her niece. "Yes, it is wonderful to give to others and not expect a reward."

"Yes. Thank you. I would never have been able to give them such fine presents."

"Remember, it wasn't us. It was God working through us. We just happened to be in the right place at the right time."

Mariella nodded in agreement.

"But it still feels good, doesn't it?" Peg encouraged.

"Yes." Mariella beamed.

"Where's Papa Dan?"

"Upstairs with Momma."

Peg listened. Hearing no sounds, she decided not to interrupt them. They were probably taking care of last-minute details for the Christmas holiday. "Would you tell him, when he has a free moment, I need him to run an errand?"

"Sure. Can I do it for you?"

"No, thank you. The sun is set. I think Daniel should be the one to deliver it for me."

"You're right, Papa Dan doesn't want us in town when the sun goes down."

"Wise man, your Papa Dan." Peg smiled. Daniel had been truly blessed with quite a family.

Back in her own apartment, she pulled out some needlework and tried to get back to the calm she'd known before Matthew Bower had come to Key West.

Hours later, Peg found herself alone yet again. Daniel had come and gone. She had enjoyed a meal with his family. Now she faced the empty sounds of a house devoid of hope and love. How she appreciated and missed Matt's presence. Their time together. Their playful banter. Her stomach tightened, and she massaged her throbbing leg.

A sudden knock on her door startled her. "Who is it?" she called out.

"Matt. Peg, open up, please."

Peg worked her way to the door, using furniture for crutches. She found Matt with his hair disheveled, his eyes red. He appeared to have aged ten years since she last saw him. "What's the matter?"

"Is Micah here?" He looked past her into the sitting room.

"No, why would he be? What's wrong, Matt?" Peg fought the desire to reach out and touch him. She remembered all too well his reaction when she'd done that in the past.

"We need to talk." He walked past her and made himself comfortable on her divan. "Come join me, Peg."

She hobbled over to the sofa and sat beside him. "All right, Matthew, what is the problem? Has something happened between you and your son?"

"Yes. No. I don't know. Look, I came to Key West for a reason. I don't know how to say it other than to say it straight out." Matt raked his black hair back with his right hand.

"All right." Peg sucked in a deep breath. He was going to tell her he knew the truth. Her hands trembled. She held them on her lap.

"I came to Key West because of a dying man's confession. This man had done something so unthinkable I had prayed it wasn't true. But now, in the end, I know it is true. I even, at one small moment, hoped and prayed his confession was the result of the disease that was taking his life. But it wasn't. Peg, that man was Dr. Baker. I think you knew him too."

Peg gasped. "I'm sorry, Matt. I would have told you the truth of my past and why I came to Key West if our relationship developed any further. In fact, I was about to tell you that same day of our argument. I didn't know you knew."

"Peg." Matt grasped her hand. "I know. But it's not what you think I know."

"What?" Peg searched his dark green eyes.

"Hear me out, please," he pleaded.

Peg nodded.

"Doc Baker confessed to me that he switched a young woman's baby with another baby. They were both born minutes apart from each other. He delivered them both."

Peg knit her eyebrows in confusion.

"Peg, he switched your son with my dead son."

"What?"

"Micah is your son."

A sob groaned out of her throat, a fury of emotions and no discernible thought. What could she think? Her baby was dead. No, Matt said his son was her son? "But how? Why?" Tears burned a track down her cheek.

"I don't know. He knew my wife could never have another child after she gave birth. He also knew you weren't married. I guess he assumed—"

Peg jumped up and screamed.

Matt leapt to his feet and held her. "Is it your leg?"

"Yes. No. Let go of me!" She pushed him away. "You've known this since you arrived on Key West and you didn't tell me? Were you planning on not telling me the truth? Why did you come looking for me? So you could shame me?"

Daniel came running into the apartment. "What's going on in here?"

"Matt says John isn't dead. That his son, Micah, is my son."

"What?" Daniel stood toe to toe with Matt. "Are you daft?"

"Doc Baker confessed he switched our babies."

"What?" Daniel plopped down onto the sofa. "This is ridiculous. Doctors don't do that."

"Apparently, Doc Baker thought he had the perfect solution," Matt groaned. "I can't deny that I am glad he switched the babies. I love Micah. He's such a part of me and my wife. I never would have thought in a million years that he wasn't my son. But he is my son. I've raised him."

"So, where does that leave me?" Peg cried. "I've mourned the death of my baby for twenty years. I've stayed away from relationships bound and determined that God kept me single because of my past. And that still may be the case. But I have a son, a son who's alive and breathing, who doesn't know me."

Peg collapsed on the rocking chair. "When I saw Micah get off the ship I nearly fainted. He's the spitting image of Billy."

"Not really. I never met Billy, but I know my son, and he has your eyes, and your hair coloring, although his hair is wavy."

Peg held her sides and rocked. *My son is alive? My son is Matt's son, Micah.*

"Peg?" Matt knelt in front of her. "I'm sorry. I should have told you sooner but—"

"But you couldn't decide if I was worthy," Peg fired back. "Get out of my house, Matt. I need to be alone."

"Peg, please. I need your help. We need to find Micah. He's been gone for hours. He wasn't pleased with me either."

Daniel got up. "He looks like Billy?"

Peg nodded.

"I'll go find him. Just let me tell Carmen first."

"Thank you," Matt offered. "With all of us looking, we should be able to find him."

"To think I almost gave my heart to you," Peg hissed. "I can't believe you would keep something so important from me."

"Peg, try and understand. I had to think of Micah too. What's it going to be like for him to learn the truth? Would it be fair to him to have him labeled as illegitimate? I thought Key West might provide the place for him to live with no shame, but this place is so gossip infected no one could have a chance here."

"Well, we may have a problem with gossip, but we're island folk, and island folk stick together. I'm not saying it wouldn't have been rough for awhile. Goodness, no one here even knows about my past. Well, except Daniel and Bea Southard. No one would believe it. But then they would remember who I am. They know me, they trust me. They'd understand, in time. At least my friends would."

"I'm sorry. You're probably right. But it's just as much of a shock for me as it was for you. I never would have thought my son wasn't my son. Just saying it doesn't make it seem plausible."

As much as she wanted to be angry with Matt, he did make sense in a strange sort of way. He did love his son. He couldn't stop talking about his son. To all of a sudden find out Micah wasn't his biological son must have sent the man spinning like an eddy during the change of tides.

"We'd best get started," Peg decided and grabbed her crutches. She couldn't go far, but she'd go as far as her legs would allow.

"I'll go to town and check out the taverns," Matt replied. "Micah isn't a drinker, but this kind of news could cause the strongest of men to drink."

"I'll check the waterfront," Daniel volunteered.

"I'll work my way through the streets closer to this side of the island."

With great effort, Peg limped her way through the various streets between her home and Matt's cottage. Minute by minute, hour by hour, her leg throbbed. She needed to take a break. Her heart ached. Her mind was confused; she was a mixture of emotions—anger toward Dr. Baker, resentment at Matt for keeping this information to himself. In some small way, she understood his confusion. But it didn't dull her anger. Or, as she thought about it, perhaps it did. A little.

The same judgmental attitude that Doc Baker showed was the very reason she had moved to Key West to start fresh. Now she discovered the pain and agony of losing her child had been false. Her son wasn't dead. He was alive, alive and well. But he belonged to another. She would never know what it was to watch him grow up. To see him take his first steps, speak his first words. Nothing. All of it snatched away because of some self-righteous old man. Peg's nostrils flared.

She rarely got this angry. She needed to calm down. She worked her way down a street that ended at a small inlet. Her mourning place. The small stretch of beach where she sought God out year after year to try to understand why things had happened as they had.

She needed to rest. Peg sat down on a fallen palm tree and rubbed her leg. The moonlight glistened on the water. "Father, comfort Micah."

The long leaves of a nearby bush rattled in the wind. Peg glanced over to see a man stand up and march over toward her.

"You're my mother, aren't you?"

Chapter 18

Matt was frantic. Hours of searching and nothing. Not only could he not find Micah, he'd lost track of Peg as well. Daniel had returned home unable to find Micah at the waterfront. The two men decided that time was what Micah needed. So Matt wandered down another street looking for Peg. She couldn't have gone too far on those crutches. But then again, he couldn't imagine what was going on in her mind at the moment.

Matt rubbed the back of his neck. Time was what everyone needed. Time to heal and time to understand just what had happened to all of them because of one man's tragic lack of judgment.

Coming to a dead end, Matt turned around and retraced his steps. He plunged farther back from the harbor trying to find Peg. He needed to talk with her. No, he *wanted* to talk with her. To try to explain his heart.

Peg had to be somewhere. He pushed his way up another narrow street. The darkness of night, the covering of the trees, brought out the fear he'd buried deep inside. *Lord, let her be all right.*

Several times he'd backtracked to her apartment. He'd even gone back to his own. She was still out there, somewhere. *Where could she be, Lord?*

🌴

"Yes, Micah. I guess I am."

Micah sat down beside her. She silently thanked the Lord for a full moon, so she could see his face. She reached out to touch him. He didn't pull away. Her fingers shook as they caressed her son's features. "You look a lot like your father."

"Who is he?"

Peg turned away from her son. She had to confess the truth. He of all people deserved to know the truth. She swallowed hard. "At the time, I loved him very much. We were going to get married. At least that's what I thought. Turns out it was just another case of Billy's smooth tongue. My brother Daniel tried to warn me. But he was several years younger, and I thought I knew it all."

"Tell me, tell me everything," Micah pleaded.

"Oh, Micah, I've mourned you terribly." Peg wiped a tear from her face. "I was just about eighteen when I met Billy. He seemed so exciting. So unlike the other boys in town. He didn't work on the fishing boats, and he didn't smell like fish." Peg paused. "At the time, that was quite an advantage."

Micah chuckled.

"Anyway, he was a bit wild, and I was a bit rebellious. I fell madly in love with him, or rather, with the idea of being wild and free. I overlooked Billy's bad habits, his ability to have money without working hard. That should have put up a warning flag, but it didn't. Anyway, he promised we'd get married when I was eighteen. I turned eighteen and found out I was expecting you. I was scared at first, but then I thought how wonderful to have a product of our love growing inside of me.

"Billy didn't see it that way. He thought it was all my fault and said he wasn't raising no brat. He left, and I had to go home and tell my parents the truth. They sent me away to have the baby. But as the time to deliver came close, my mother wanted me near her. So I lived the last days of my pregnancy at a rooming house near Dr. Baker's office." She sighed. "The rest I figure you've heard from your father."

"He's not my father."

Peg reached out and held his hand. Micah wrapped his fingers around hers. "Oh, Micah. He is your father. Billy Ingles would have ruined your life."

"Billy Ingles is my father?" Micah's voice was high with disbelief. *How does he know Billy?* "Yes, do you know him?"

"No, not really. I met his daughter. Oh, no!" Micah grabbed his stomach.

"Are you all right?" Peg draped her arm over his shoulder.

"I met his daughter, Anna Ingles."

Billy had another child? Peg calmed herself by taking in a deep breath.

"I almost courted her. Can you imagine? My own sister?"

If Peg ever wanted to curse someone right now, it was Dr. Baker. "No, I can't imagine. I'm sorry, Micah. It's all my fault."

"All your fault? Dad said Doc Baker did this."

"True, but if I hadn't sinned with Billy, none of this would have happened."

"But then I never would have existed." Micah reached down and picked up a handful of sand and let it run through his fingers. "How long have you been here?"

"I moved to Key West with my brother Daniel shortly after we buried the baby."

"It's a good thing Doc Baker isn't alive. I'd have a mind to—"

"Micah, your parents didn't raise you to behave that way," Peg scolded.

"I know. I'm just so angry. It's horribly unfair. I don't know what to feel. I think of the word mother, and I think of my mother. Now, I look at you and see I am a part of you. I just don't know what to think."

"Why don't we just take it one step at a time? Matt and Esther were your parents. They raised you. They went through every sleepless night a parent goes through for a child. I, on the other hand, mourned a child I never knew. I want to get to know you, Micah. But you're not a child; you're a man. The most we could ever hope to have is a close friendship, one adult to another."

"I suppose you're right. I can't separate who I am from who I was supposed to be."

Peg grinned. "God says if we wait on Him, He'll make our paths straight. This is one of those times when the paths are not very straight, where people have gotten in and messed with God's plan. I messed with it by getting involved with Billy in an inappropriate way. Doc Baker messed with it by trying to correct a wrong. Somehow, I know if we give God enough time, He will work this all out."

"Tell me about yourself," Micah pleaded. "I want to know you."

"Only if you tell me all about yourself." Could it be this easy? Could they become friends? She looked at Micah and saw herself and Billy. Always Billy. He would permanently be a part of her past, a part she'd blocked out for many years. She waited for Micah's response.

"Fair enough. You start."

"All right, my name is Margaret Elizabeth Martin, but everyone calls me Peg. My father was a fisherman. . . ."

Matt listened in the distance. He'd come upon Peg sitting on the log when he heard Micah approach her. They were talking. His first instinct, to come to Key West and correct a wrong, had been correct. He had lost his son, but it was the right thing in the end.

Matt walked back toward the cottage, leaving mother and son to their discovery. They needed time. He grabbed his duffel bag and loaded up some provisions for his sail. His trip was in order as well. It would give Peg and Micah a chance to get to know one another. Maybe someday they would forgive him for his deceit.

With the boat loaded, he trekked back to the cottage and penned a letter to Micah.

> *Dear Son,*
>   *I've decided to take that trip and give all of us a chance to calm down. Peg Martin is a wonderful woman. You were correct when you sensed we had feelings for one another. But the past will probably prevent us from having a future. I'll return in a few days and we can talk.*
>   *Know this one thing, Son. I love you. I always have, and I always will.*
>   *Your father forever*

Matt swallowed hard. He'd done enough crying for a grown man in two lifetimes. He'd always seen himself as a strong man, but Esther's death, Doc Baker's deception, and the loss of his son were more than one man should be asked to bear in his lifetime.

He closed the door to the cottage as a predawn glow gave a surreal feel to the day. The yellow and white light dancing on the waves cast an orange tone to his skin. Palm trees were dark silhouettes against the eastern sky.

" 'Mornin', Mr. Bower. Heard your son came in yesterday." A local fisherman stepped from his boat to the dock with such an easy stride anyone observing would know he'd grown up along the water.

"Yes, Sir." What else could he say? It was Micah and Peg's choice to reveal the truth of their relationship, not his.

"Where ya headin'?"

"Key Visca. Thought a short sail would be nice."

"Just the two of you, or are you bringin' Miss Martin along?"

Matt groaned.

"Sorry, didn't mean nothin'. Just heard you two were getting married."

Matt pulled the line to bring the boat closer to the dock. "We're just friends." He almost threw in they had never even kissed, but then he remembered his actions in Peg's home the other day.

"Sorry, guess a man ought to ask before he assumes. Have a good sail. Wind's coming up from the southwest, should have a nice tropical breeze pushing up the coast."

"Thanks." Matt waved as the man boarded his boat. He cast off the bowline and gave the vessel a slight push away from the dock as the fisherman stepped on board. Odd, Matt thought, that he was going out on Christmas morning.

Matt boarded his sailboat, made the mainsail ready, and went below to retrieve the jib. In the ship's hold, he rummaged through the bow looking for the right sack that contained the jib. Finally he spotted it and neatly placed everything that wasn't needed back into the bow.

As he poked his head out of the hold, Peg stood before him with her hands on her hips. Her crutches lay on the dock. "And just where do you think you're going?"

⚓

Peg braced herself. The leap to the boat had put a lot of strain on her leg.

"Key Visca." Matt pushed past her.

"And for what purpose?"

"Peg, you and Micah deserve time to get to know one another. I need to give you and him time to absorb the full ramifications of what has happened."

Peg struggled to grasp something as her leg lost its strength. Matt caught her in his arms and lifted her up off her feet. "Sit down before you damage that leg some more. It's swollen, Peg. You've been on it too long."

"I know." Peg smiled as Matt worked his hands down her leg.

"Lie down and lift your leg," Matt ordered. "Have you been up all night?"

"Yes. Same as you; same as Micah. Matt, don't go. We need to talk." Peg reached out and placed her hand on his shoulder.

"What is there to talk about? Doc Baker took Micah away from you."

She could feel his body tense below her fingers. "Yes, but. . ."

"No buts, Peg. It was wrong. You know it. I know it. Micah knows it. And before too long, everyone will know it."

Peg looked along the shore. No one was in sight. Due to the Christmas holiday, most folks were still snug in their beds. "Probably. I can't hide the truth any longer. But, Matt, I want you to hear from me what happened, who Micah's father is, why a foolish girl of seventeen—nearly eighteen—found herself in such a predicament."

"I think I understand the process, Peg. Where's Micah?"

"At the house. I told him I would stop you from setting sail if you hadn't already left. He's lying down. It was quite a shock for him."

Matt frowned and looked out to sea.

"Matt, please. I think you and I. . .well, I think we started to have rather strong feelings for one another, but we're both too scared to admit it. I've got nothing to hide now. You know everything about me. Well, almost everything. Am I such a terrible person that you wouldn't want to have a relationship with me?"

"Goodness no, Peg. I enjoy talking with you, spending time with you. I knew from the first moment I stepped on the island who you were. But that didn't stop me from—"

"From what, Matt? Say it."

"From falling in love with you," Matt whispered. He knelt down beside the seat where she was lying down with her leg propped up on the outer rail.

"Oh, Matt. I love you too. I've fought it, but when you kissed me I couldn't deny it any longer."

"What about the past? What about Esther and me raising your son?"

"Our son. You and Esther will always be his parents. The best I can hope for is a close adult relationship with Micah. Maybe, in time, a special bond. I love him with all the passion I felt for my child when I thought he was dead. But it doesn't erase the fact that I had no hand in raising him. He's a lot like me, you know."

"Yes, I know." Matt grinned.

"Oh, I suppose you do."

"How's Micah with all of this?" Matt asked.

"Wondering when you're going to be a man and kiss the woman," Micah piped in from the dock.

"Micah," Matt and Peg called out. There he stood, with his arms crossed over his chest and a foolish grin on his face. The past hours had not been wasted. Peg had been able to share some of a parent's heart with Micah, helping him understand Matt's actions, and convincing herself in the process of why Matt had done what he had. Why he had kept the secret so long.

"Well, are you going to kiss this woman and begin our new lives?" Micah demanded.

"Hmm." Matt wiggled his eyebrows.

Peg giggled.

"Should we seal our future with a kiss, Miss Martin?" Matt brushed the top of her lips ever so lightly with his finger.

Peg groaned and felt her face flush.

"Micah, would you please turn around?" Matt motioned with his finger.

"Father, you can't be serious," he said, but he obeyed his father.

"Now, where was I?"

Peg felt her face grow hotter still.

"May I?" he whispered.

She blinked her agreement and relished the sweet surrender of their lips connecting, of becoming vulnerable one to the other. Her life verse flooded back in her mind, Isaiah 40:31: *But they that wait upon the Lord shall renew their strength; they shall mount up with wings as eagles; they shall run, and not be weary; and they shall walk, and not faint.*

God had turned her painful mistake into a long-awaited blessing.

Micah coughed, then tapped his foot loudly. "Folks are gathering, you two."

Matt pulled away. Peg tried to draw him back. His finger touched her lip. "Not now, my sweet, my southern treasure. What a wonderful Christmas gift you are. Merry Christmas, Peg."

"Merry Christmas, Matt." She smiled, her heart spilling over with joy. God had given her a special gift this year—a new family of her very own.

One Man's Honor

To Jonathan and Joshua, my twin grandsons,
who were the original inspiration behind Richie in A Time to Embrace.
May you two grow up to be strong and honorable men for God.
This is my prayer.
Love, Grandma

Chapter 1

Key West, April 1, 1886

"Fire! Fire!"

Richard Southard jumped from his bed and ran down the stairs, rushing to answer the pounding fist on his front door.

"Your dock's on fire!" The young man's eyes bulged. "And your warehouse." He gasped for breath.

Richard sniffed the air. "Thanks." His dock was on fire? *Lord, have mercy.* "I'll get some buckets," he mumbled.

"Don't think they'll do much good. Half the town's on fire." The man turned and leapt off the porch.

"Would you go tell Mo Greene for me?" Richard didn't wait for an answer and rushed up the stairs two at a time.

"What's all the hootin' and hollerin' for?" Cook grumbled, tightening the old bathrobe around her.

"Town's on fire, Cook. You better stay here. Get some buckets of water ready to dampen some rags for breathing through."

"Lord protect us," Cook groaned. She'd been with the family since before he arrived on Key West, as the housekeeper and cook for his uncle. But, in point of fact, she'd been the closest person he ever had to a grandparent.

"Amen." Richard finished his hike up the stairs, removing his robe before entering his room. No time to undress and dress. He slipped his clothes on over his nightshirt, shoved his feet into his boots, then ran toward the family dock and business. His uncle Ellis had developed a healthy sponge fishing industry on Key West. Richard had returned to Key West last fall to work the family business while Ellis and his family returned to New York.

Thick smoke drove Richard from his thoughts. The warehouse glowed in the early morning hour. The wind continued to whip the flames up as they licked the leaves of palm trees. Drying sponges became soft cannonballs of flame.

The single fire truck could never handle this.

Richard coughed. The acrid taste of smoke burned his throat and eyes. He tore off the bottom of his nightshirt and fashioned a mask to breathe through.

He scanned the long dock that worked its way into the harbor. Fire on the ocean—what an incredible sight! Dry season was not the time for the island to have a fire. They hadn't had rain on Key West for weeks, perhaps months.

Richard pulled off his outer shirt and soaked it with ocean water. At least he could try and stop the balls of fire that were being spread by the sponges blowing off his roof. He ran after a sponge fireball and slapped it several times with his drenched shirt.

"What happened?" Mo Greene called out.

Richard jumped hearing Mo's voice. He turned to see the tall black man's stride slow down. "I don't know. I found the place like this. But look up Duval Street; everything is on fire. There are five docks on fire counting ours," Richard informed him.

"Ain't seen nothin' like this in all my days."

"Won't have many days if you don't put something over your nose and mouth." Mo stood head and shoulders above most men. He had worked for Richard's uncle since Richard was a small boy. Mo and Lizzy's children had been his playmates. Now Richard was Mo's boss. Somehow it seemed odd, telling Mo what to do, especially when Mo had had a hand in correcting him a time or two when he was a young boy growing up on the island.

Mo removed a handkerchief and wet it with ocean water, draping it over his nose and mouth. "Want me to try and save the dock?" he yelled. The roar of the wind and flames made his normal voice a hoarse whisper.

Richard shook his head no. "We need to stop the sponges from starting more fires. The dock should burn itself out."

Mo removed his shirt. Dampening it, he filled a couple buckets he'd brought along with him. They each took a bucket and proceeded to chase the sponge fireballs.

Hours later, they sat exhausted, breathing in fresher air as the sun crested the horizon. The winds had shifted. The stale smell of burned wood hung in the air, but it was more breathable.

Hundreds of men had come out to battle the flames, but their efforts did little good. Ironically, the town had decided not to upgrade the fire department the previous year. Richard knew that would change immediately. "Day late and a dollar short," he mumbled.

"Huh?" Mo asked.

"Sorry, was thinking about the single fire engine. The town will need another. Our population is nearly as large as Jacksonville. One fire engine isn't enough."

"I helped your uncle build this building. Hard to believe it could be destroyed so easily."

"Buildings can be rebuilt. It's the people I'm worried about. I pray no lives were lost tonight."

"Amen. I'm going home to freshen up. I'll be back in a few hours to help clean up."

"Thanks, Mo."

Mo lifted his massive dark frame and slowly walked away. Richard could not help but be amazed all over again at the man's depth, how hard he'd worked to educate himself and improve his speech.

Richard turned and looked at the smoldering remains of the family business. Should they rebuild? The last letter from Nanna and Ellis said they were reconsidering staying in New York and using the house on Key West as a winter home.

There was no question his uncle was beginning to slow down. That would leave Richard and his cousin James in charge of the family business. Richard gnawed his lower lip. The question was whether he wanted to run this business, go west and explore the new territories, or return to the farmstead. He'd been working the land for five years. He enjoyed it. He had a natural talent for farming, like his father before him. So what was he doing in Key West? Why had it seemed so important to stay here and keep the sponge business going? His uncle had plenty of offers to buy the business. Richard looked at the rubble and sighed.

"Richard." Micah Bower worked his lean body through the charred remains. "You've been hit hard."

"How'd your place fare?"

"We're fine. The fire didn't get that far east. Glad we purchased the new location five years ago." Micah sat down beside him, his clothes streaked with smoke. Richard gazed down at his own clothing. The soot and smoke had stained his nightshirt.

"Have you been up Duval Street?"

"Nope. How bad is it?"

"Looks like fifty buildings and five docks went up. The fire spread down to Greene Street."

"Fifty?" Richard sighed. "How'd it start?"

"No one knows, but they're looking into it."

"Are you going to rebuild?" Micah scanned the debris.

"Yes, James is planning on returning to Key West after his education. I'll need to reestablish the business so he has something to come home to."

Micah nodded. "It's going to take some time to rebuild. I can't imagine how long."

"Or how many shipments of supplies. Thankfully, there are a few docks still standing."

"There are some drawbacks to living on an island."

"Why did you stay on Key West?" Richard knew Micah was around his own age when he'd come to the island.

"At first I wanted, and needed, time to get to know my mother, to reconcile what had transpired in our lives. But after a few years I found the island and its people growing on me. Although I must say, there are far more folks living here now, almost too many."

Richard smiled and acknowledged he had similar thoughts.

"After I met Catherine there was no question. I was staying for awhile longer." Micah grinned.

"Ah, a woman will do that to ya."

"And what do you know of women?" Micah challenged.

Richard raised his hands. "Not a thing. Trust me, I've kept myself away from them. I have too many demands on my time; I don't need a woman messing up my life."

Micah roared. "That, my friend, is simply because you haven't met the right one yet."

Richard examined the soot on his friend. "You might want to jump in the ocean before you return home to Catherine and the children. They'll never recognize you."

"Cook might have trouble recognizing you when you get home too."

"Oh no, I forgot about Cook." Richard jumped up. "She's eighty now, not that you'd know it by looking at her. This air had to be difficult on her breathing."

"Take care, Richard. I'll lend a hand when I can."

Richard watched Micah wave as he rounded the corner and headed down Front Street. Thankfully, his house was east of the fire. Richard coughed as his lungs fought to recover from the smoke he'd inhaled. "Lord, please let her be okay."

"Cook!" he hollered as he ran through the front door.

No response. "Cook!" he yelled louder. Frantic, he ran to the back bedroom. He paused and tried to calm himself before opening the door. *If she died. . .*

He steeled himself and pushed it open. A sigh of relief passed his lips as he saw her empty bed and room.

"Richie," Cook called.

Her voice carried from the back yard. Richard ran down the hall, skidding on the throw rug on the well-polished oak floor. How many times had his uncle and nanna scolded him about running in the hallway? A wicked grin creased his face. *Too many,* he answered himself.

"Cook, are you all right?"

He saw her bent over, carrying a bucket of water from the cistern. Her natural brown color seemed paler this morning—or could it be a contrast to the black charred remains of the fire? "Let me get that for you."

"You're a mess. Take them clothes off, what's left of 'em, and get yourself cleaned up," she ordered.

Richard chuckled and scooped up her bucket. "Yes, Ma'am."

"Have ya seen yourself?" She applied a loving hand on his elbow. He could feel the unsteady gait as she walked beside him. She claimed bones just had a way of stiffening up, getting ready to lie down for eternity.

"No, but I've seen others. Couldn't imagine how Mo could look darker than he is naturally. But he sure was black."

Cook chuckled. "He's a dark one, all right. You're just about his equal with all that soot on ya."

"Closest I'll ever get, I imagine." Richard's pale complexion never really tanned. He did have a tan, though most wouldn't know it. Blond hair, blue eyes, and pale skin weren't exactly tropical colors for a body.

"Well, ya stink too, so go wash up."

"Yes, Ma'am." The woman could scold him from sun up to sun down if she wanted. She was safe, and that's all that mattered.

He put the bucket in the kitchen and went behind the house to the outside shower. *No sense getting this soot in a tub. I'd only have to clean it out later.*

Cook lifted the window above him. "Catch."

She tossed him a clean washrag and a bar of soap.

"Thanks."

"How bad was the fire?" she asked. He could hear her dragging a chair to the window.

"Bad, real bad." He lathered his skin, amazed at the gray mounds of soap bubbles coming off him. "Micah Bower says pretty near fifty buildings went up and five docks. We lost the dock and the building. Everything will have to be rebuilt."

"God protect us! How many folks you suppose'll be outta work?"

"Quite a few, but I imagine they'll be hired to help rebuild. I know I'll have our men doing that." He poured some water over his head and lathered his hair with the soap.

"Anyone hurt?"

"Don't know. I can't imagine folks not getting injured with that much destruction. I had to wear a mask most of the time I was down there. The air was so thick."

"Mercy." In his mind's eye, he could see the old woman folding her hands and offering another prayer.

Cook was not a person to try and pull the wool over someone's eyes, but she was also one of the strongest prayer warriors going. Maybe he should tell her his dilemma. He could use the extra prayer support. He opened his mouth, then clamped it shut. Nope, he was a man now, and a man needed to make certain decisions on his own.

"What are you going to do, Richie?"

"First I'll need to clean up the mess. Then I'll need to rebuild. The business needs to be in order for James's return."

"I'm sure Mo will be happy to hear you're going to rebuild."

Mo—he'd almost forgotten. Six men and their families depended on his family business. *Lord, I feel so ill equipped. I know I've had the book learning about running a business, but that's not enough. Uncle Ellis always said that if you were good to your employees, they would work well for you. You couldn't just give them everything; they'd have to earn it. But being generous, whenever possible, would produce loyal workers.*

I can't dispute that, Lord. Mo's been working for the company for nearly twenty years. Help me, Lord. I don't know where to begin.

"Richie?"

"Yes, Cook." Richard rinsed his body off one last time.

"If'n ya don't mind, I'm goin' to lie down. I've been up since you left."

"No problem. I'll be in town most of the day myself. Don't bother to cook for me. I'll find something."

"There're a couple loaves of Cuban bread in the bread box. You might want to take one and some cheese. Drink plenty of water too. Cleaning up from a fire isn't easy work."

"Yes, Ma'am." Richard wrapped a towel around his waist and dumped his clothes into a barrel, then filled it with some water and lye soap. Cook would have his hide because he washed his own clothes, but she didn't need the extra work. Besides, he knew the fresh clothing he'd put on later would be just as filthy, if not more so, after working at the shop.

Digging through the debris certainly proved he would be black again. He salvaged a few knives, sponge hooks, and various pieces from the shop, but basically the entire business was lost. The schooner, the *Sea Dove*, and half a dozen of the spongers' skiffs were safe, along with the tools from the boat.

A trip to Cuba might be in order. He'd certainly get the building supplies he needed sooner. Richard sat down on the edge of the seawall in front of the burned-out building. Reaching into his sack, he pulled out the Cuban bread.

"I'm a fish out of water, Lord." Richard tossed a piece of his Cuban roll into the water, then bit off a piece for himself. The soft white bread with a thin crust had been a food item he'd missed. "Who am I, Lord? The farmer or a businessman?"

Richard tossed another chunk of the bread into the water and watched a small school of fish fight for the tasty morsel. The brightly colored parrotfish jumped out of the water, chasing the elusive crumb. Although Key West was in turmoil after the fire, the fish under the sea seemed free from such hardships. He'd heard four people had died.

The gentle lull of a feminine voice teased his ears. "Cast thy bread upon the waters: for thou shalt find it after many days."

Richard turned and caught a glimpse of her as she headed away from him into town, a lily among the ruins. Her wavy black hair draped over a clean, crisp, white blouse. Her golden skin was vibrant among the mounds of charred debris. The familiar passage from Ecclesiastes echoed in his mind. He looked down at the loaf of bread, pulled off another chunk, and tossed it in the waters below.

"Could it be that simple, Lord?"

Chapter 2

Isabela turned, sneaking another glimpse of Richie Southard, or at least she thought it was him. He'd returned to Key West after being gone for five years. She'd been on the island for six. She had been all of fourteen when she first spotted him working with his uncle at the dock. He was handsome then, but now. . .well, she wouldn't allow her thoughts to drift in that direction.

He seemed so alone. She knew she shouldn't have spoken to him. It wasn't proper, but. . . *I just couldn't help myself.*

She scanned the ruins from the great fire. The town was decimated. Her father's cigar factory was gone. In fact, several cigar factories were gone.

She needed to get a job. She'd been trying for what seemed like eternity but hadn't found work to her liking. Oh, she'd cleaned houses and done other simple tasks, but a desire stirred deep within her to do something more, to be something more. But what?

Now the town would be set on rebuilding, and construction wasn't something she felt skilled at or inclined to do. Not that any man would hire her even if she applied. With her head for numbers, she'd hoped to get a job at a bank. With her bilingual abilities, she figured she would be welcomed. Instead, she found no job openings anywhere. Not even a sales clerk opportunity had presented itself. Every day she'd come to town, and every day she'd returned home without a job.

Should she be trusting God with the same passage of Scripture she'd tossed out to Richie Southard?

Isabela took in a deep breath and practically gagged from the ash-laden air. Small patches of debris still had fine trails of smoke floating upward. "Lord, what am I going to do? There'll be no work for my father, and I haven't found a job. What's the family going to do?"

A thought flickered through her mind that she should trust the Lord and leave the concerns of the family in His care, not hers. But she fought off the idea. She had to do something, anything. Her family depended upon her. Her father had not been blessed with a son, and she was the only child. She had little to offer, other than marrying well. . . . Richie Southard's blue-gray eyes, crowned with a riot of golden curls, passed in front of her mind's eye. *No, I couldn't do that,* she reprimanded herself.

She couldn't even get a job at the cigar factory where her father worked. He had been most adamant that his daughter not work with the tobacco. He did it because it paid the bills. "No, you shall marry a good husband, and God will provide for you," he'd always say. Which is why, at age twenty and still not married, she desperately needed employment. If she didn't find a job soon, Papá would find her a husband.

"Isabela."

She turned to find Mariella carrying her young son Miguel and pulling her daughter Rosetta along with her. "Isn't this such a horrible disaster?"

"*Sí.*" Mariella still spoke Spanish, but she primarily used English now. "What are you doing down here with the children?"

"My curiosity got the best of me. I couldn't stand it waiting at home." Mariella pushed her long dark hair behind her shoulders.

Isabela smiled. "Me too. Have you heard how it started?"

"No, just rumors. Some say it was Cuban businessmen who wanted to stop the production of the cigars here."

"But didn't they move up to Tampa?"

"*Sí,* but they also don't like competition. Who knows if it was them or some of the other wild rumors floating around. Everything is so dry here. The buildings were all wood, with wooden roofs. . . . It just spread so fast."

"It's amazing no one was injured."

Mariella reached out and placed her hand on her forearm. "You haven't heard? Four men lost their lives."

"Oh, no. Who?"

"I don't know. I guess they're waiting to have a positive identification before they say anything to anyone."

"Dear Jesus, be with their families," Isabela prayed out loud.

"Amen." Mariella adjusted Miguel on her hip.

"How's your aunt Peg's business? Did it get burned?" Peg Bower owned a small shop of various items crafted by islanders. Her own specialty was beautiful embroidery work.

"Her store is fine. Uncle Matt's dock and buildings are fine too. Micah came by early this morning and let us know. Miguel is happy he still has a job."

"I can imagine. The Southards' dock and building are destroyed."

"I wonder how Richie is going to handle this. He's come back with all that college learning, and I haven't seen a change in the business. Don't get me wrong, Ellis Southard built up a fine business, but to put it in Richie's hands and just leave the island like that. . . . The man must have been crazy. But Mo Greene still works for him, so that's a blessing."

Isabela had heard the gossip before about folks not expecting much from Richie and his fancy college education. She'd often thought people's concerns were more about his age rather than his abilities. "Seems to me he managed his farmstead just fine for five years."

"I don't know. Why did Ellis have to go to New York if it hadn't been for some mismanagement on Richie's part? After all, he let Richie go there by himself for his education. Why not let James do the same?"

This was the foundation for the gossip. "I'd prefer to give Richie the benefit of the doubt. Besides, what are the other businessmen going to do now that their businesses have been destroyed?"

"You know, you're probably right. After all, Richie's been running the business for eight months now and kept everyone gainfully employed, plus hired a couple more hands."

See, Isabela wanted to boast but bit her tongue. It had to be difficult on Richard to have the whole town thinking he was inept at running the business, even though he'd proved himself over the past eight months. This fire would definitely be another test for him to endure. She shot another prayer heavenward for Richard Southard. *Give him strength, Lord.* She picked up a charred board.

"Put that down," Mariella scolded. "I better get these *niños* home before they are as black as some of the men working in the rubble. Good to see you, Isabela. Come over for tea sometime."

🌴

"Mo, I'm going to take the *Sea Dove* to Cuba and load her up with supplies." Richard glanced over at the white-hulled two-masted schooner glistening in the harbor. He turned his gaze back on the remains of the warehouse. "Will you take care of the cleanup?"

"Whatever you need, Richard."

"Thanks. I'll take a couple of men with me to help sail and load the vessel. I'm not sure how much she can handle, but we'll load her as full as we can."

"You be careful. Two trips are better than one if you and the ship end up lying on the bottom," Mo warned.

"Don't worry. I'm impulsive but not stupid."

"Never said you were, Son. Just don't push it. I know you're under a lot of pressure to prove yourself, and this here fire ain't gonna help none. Just remember, God doesn't give us more than we can handle."

Richard reached up and grabbed Mo's shoulder. "Thanks, Mo. I appreciate that. Will you keep an eye out for your mother-in-law for me? I'm sure you would anyway, but she's getting on now."

"Of course. Lizzy and I will take care of her. Tried to get her to move in with us, but she wouldn't hear of it. And with my mother having a small room to herself, I'm sure Francine would feel she was imposing. She wouldn't be, but she'd feel that way. Heard even George asked her to move in with them." Mo grinned. "But she insists she needs to take care of you."

"She's always been there as long as I can remember. The house would definitely not be the same if she were to move out. I could manage just fine on my own, but you won't catch me telling her that."

Mo laughed. "What would be the point?"

"Exactly." Richard chuckled.

"You've been doing a fine job, Richard. Don't let what the island gossips say get ya none." Mo placed his hand on Richard's shoulder this time.

"Thanks, I try not to listen to them but. . ."

"They're like the constant buzz of a mosquito you can't swat fast enough." Mo chuckled and swatted an invisible bug swarming around his head.

"Yeah."

"I know. Lizzy and I had to deal with them a time or two. Not much a man can do other than to do his best before God. Everyone else really doesn't matter."

"I'll keep that in mind. Now, I better get a move on so I can set sail with the tide."

Richard hadn't been too surprised to see no one show up this morning to work. Yet there really wasn't any reason why they couldn't go sponging. But where would he dry the sponges if they had collected them? He worked his way through town and found some of his men helping to remove the debris. He gave them orders to report to Mo or himself in the morning. At home, he washed and packed for his ocean voyage. Back in the office, he sat at his uncle's desk and worked out the materials he would need to rebuild the warehouse and dock.

A gentle knock on the door broke his thoughts. "Come in, Cook."

"I brought ya some hot coffee, Richie."

"Thanks. Have a seat."

Cook slowly settled her aging body in the chair opposite him. She'd always been so active; it hurt to see her less than agile.

"Don't you go frettin' 'bout my old bones, Boy. I may take a little more time doin' this or that, but I'm still getting around on my own steam, which is more than I can say 'bout some my age."

"Cook, you'll never change. How'd you know I was thinking that?"

"I've known you since you were less than three feet high. I suspect I know ya pretty well."

"I suspect you're right." Richard leaned back in the office chair behind his desk.

"Whatcha workin' on?"

"The figures for the materials needed to rebuild the warehouse. I'm going to order brick and mortar. If there's a fire again, I don't want the whole building going up."

"Wise decision."

"I'm tempted to put in more windows for better ventilation, but that gives more room for someone to break in. Not that stealing a ton of sponges wouldn't be hard to get away with."

"What would your uncle Ellis do?"

"I don't know."

"Well then, I guess it's up to you. He trusts ya, Richie. He knows you'll make the right decision."

Richard tapped his pen on the papers he'd been working on. "It's just that—"
A knock at the front door broke his ramblings.

"Wonder who that is?"

"Stay right there, Cook. I'll get it." Richard hurried to the front door. "Yes, may I help you?"

A group of five men stood on his front porch. Some were men he recognized; others he didn't.

"Mr. Southard, we heard you were going to Havana to purchase some building materials. We'd like to secure passage on your schooner. We need to do the same."

"Come in, Gentlemen. The schooner has been stripped of any cabins. It's strictly a boat for hauling."

"We don't care," a thin man with a razor-straight nose said as they walked past him into the hallway.

"The thing is, Mr. Southard, we all need supplies," Ben Greely piped in.

"True. Take a seat in the parlor, Gentlemen. Let's see what we can work out. Make yourselves comfortable. I'll be right in."

The men streamed into the front room, and Richard went back to his office. "Who was it?" Cook asked.

"Some men from town wanting to book passage on the *Sea Dove*. Can you make us some coffee, Cook?"

"Certainly."

"Thanks." Richard took some fresh pieces of paper, plus some pens and ink out to the front parlor. "All right, Gentlemen, let's see what we can do."

All six looked at him with amazement. One older man with white hair and a balding top rolled his eyes. Obviously, paper and pens reminded him of Richard's fancy college education.

"Here's the situation. My ship is small. I can handle a very limited amount of weight. However, the suppliers in Havana have their own shipping vessels. I can take your purchase orders just as easily."

David Zachary leaned forward and took a sheet of paper. "Sounds good to me."

Another knock jarred the front door. "Excuse me, Gentlemen."

"I heard you were going to Havana?" a Hispanic gentleman asked.

"Yes."

"May I come? I have family in Cuba I haven't seen in a long time. I would be deeply in your debt if you would let me travel with you."

"Come in. I'm working on the details of the trip with others. Take a seat in the front parlor."

Richard noticed a stream of people making its way toward his house or front door. "Just come on in," he hollered and joined the men in the parlor.

"Looks like you folks aren't the only ones. If you trust me, I'll bring your orders to the suppliers. But I only have limited room for passengers."

Each man took a sheet of paper and began to write his list.

"Before you write your lists, let me tell you my plans. I'm going to rebuild the warehouse with brick. This will help protect against a future fire."

"Hmm, you might be on to something there." Ben tapped the end of the pen against his chin. "I think I'll do the same."

The rest of the evening was filled with other guests making similar requests. Most gave their orders to Richard; a few wanted to travel to see family. But when they found out he was only staying for one day in Cuba, they decided not to go at this time. By the time he went to bed, he had twenty orders and two extra passengers.

He penned a letter to his uncle and explained about the fire and his plans to rebuild.

Later, as his mind drifted off to sleep, the memory of the lily of the ruins brought a smile to his face.

"You're going to Cuba?" Isabela couldn't believe her ears.

"*Sí*, I must visit your grandmother."

"But, Papá, what about work? The fire?"

"It doesn't matter. There's no work right now, and I can visit your grandmother."

"But, Papá, what about rebuilding the factory? There will be work, *sí*?"

"*Sí*, but Mr. Southard is ordering the supplies for the men. If I go with him, I will return with the supplies. Then I can work when I return."

That made sense. "May I go, Papá? I would love to see Grandmother."

"I don't know, *Niña*. A boat with a bunch of sailors is not the place for a beautiful woman such as yourself."

"Oh, Papá, I don't care about the sailors. I only wish to see Grandmother."

Her father looked over to her mother. His silver-streaked sideburns made him more handsome in his later years. Isabela fought down a grin; she knew she was getting to him. Whenever he looked to her mother, Isabela knew she'd convinced her father. Her mother wasn't as easy to sway. "Oh, please, Mima. It's been so long since we've seen Grandmother."

"I don't know, Isabela. Your father makes a point about the sailors."

"But, Mima, are they really sailors or just some of Mr. Southard's employees? I mean, it is his boat."

The idea of traveling with Richard Southard to Cuba excited and frightened Isabela all at the same time. Would he say anything about her speaking to him earlier today?

Her mother put down her sewing. Her dark brown eyes examined Isabela's. "How do you know Mr. Southard?"

"I pass his warehouse every day I go into town. It's not hard to miss a man with yellow ringlets of hair." *And the most incredible blue-gray eyes I've ever seen,* she added silently.

"You have spoken with Mr. Southard?"

Ah, the real issue. Should she lie? Should she tell the truth and face certain punishment? "Not really, Mima."

"And what is that supposed to mean?" She saw her father stiffen.

"I merely quoted a verse of Scripture as I passed by this morning. He was tossing pieces of bread into the water and I quoted Ecclesiastes to him. He seemed so tired. The fire destroyed everything of his business. Even his dock."

"I see. And you've not addressed him other than this?"

"No, Mima."

"Yolanda, what is the harm in quoting Scripture to a man?" her father asked.

"Nothing." Her mother's eyes narrowed.

She knows, Isabela thought.

"May I go, Mima?"

"*Sí*, but you must not speak with Mr. Southard if you are alone. Only when your father is around."

"*Sí*, Mima, I promise."

Chapter 3

Richard tossed his satchel in the captain's quarters and stepped out onto the deck. He'd packed all his cash from the safe to order his supplies; hopefully, it would be enough. The galley was loaded with fresh water and provisions for the small crew. Emile Fernandez approached him with a barrel of what Richard assumed was fresh water.

"*Buenos días, Señor Southard, como está?*"

"*Bien,* and you?"

"*Bien,* thank you for asking."

"I wish to ask an additional favor from you. My daughter would like to travel with us to visit her grandmother. If you see it in your heart to let her go, I shall pay for her."

"Mr. Fernandez, the *Sea Dove* is not a place for *niñas.*"

"Isabela is a young woman."

Richard could not allow a woman to travel on such a ship as this. He opened his mouth to protest.

"My daughter, she knows this is not a pleasure cruise. She understands. I shall be with her whenever she is on deck. I know I am asking a tremendous favor, but her grandmother, she is old and we don't know—"

"All right, all right." Richard raised his hands in surrender. "But tell her I want no complaints about her lack of comfort."

"*Sí, muchas gracias, Señor.*"

"*De nada.*"

Just what he needed, a spoiled young lady on board. Richard went forward to check the rigging.

"Richard, the food's stored below. You should have plenty, even with your extra guests." Mo smirked.

"You heard?"

"Yessa, and I'm sure glad I'm not the captain of this here trip." Mo looped his thumbs around the waistband of his trousers.

"You know, Mo, I don't see any reason why you couldn't take the trip. I could manage the men on shore."

"Sorry, Richard, my wife would have my hide if'n I didn't return for several days. Come now, I know you'll find Isabela's a fine young lady."

"Fine spoiled young lady."

"Perhaps." Mo smirked again and quickly went over the edge, slipping down into the skiff below.

"Chicken."

Mo simply roared with laughter.

Who is this Isabela Fernandez, anyway? He'd never spoken with Emile before last night, and there were so many people on Key West now that he couldn't possibly know everyone.

Richard climbed the mast to the yardarm and examined the rigging. A hooded creature in a skirt scurried on board and went down below. *Perhaps a woman to cook the meals wouldn't be such a bad thing after all,* he mused.

He climbed down the rigging and, having thoroughly examined the boat, he ordered, "Raise the mainsail." The massive sail fluttered in the wind. "Hoist the anchor."

Richard grabbed the wheel and nudged it until the wind caught the sail. He navigated the ship out of the harbor as if he were walking down the street. He knew the waters and the reefs around the small island like the trees in the garden behind his house. Once out of the harbor, he looked at his compass and set a course for Havana. Ninety miles due south or there about. Richard enjoyed the rush of wind to welcome him back to the open sea. Sailing would definitely be one of the things he'd miss if he moved back to New York.

"Take the helm, Ben. I'm going to my cabin to work on the various orders." Ben Greely had been one of the two who decided to join him on his trip.

"With pleasure, Captain." A grin quirked Richard's lips as he headed toward the captain's quarters. He wasn't sure how necessary it really was for Ben to travel to Cuba, but the man seemed to genuinely love the sea.

Before entering his cabin, he paused. *Should I check on our other guests? Nope, this isn't a pleasure cruise, and I'm not their host.* He opened the door to his small quarters and pulled out the attaché with each man's orders. Some of the men had given him contacts in Cuba, folks with whom they'd done business before. Others had given him deposits for their orders, while still others had promised their word was as good as gold. Richard checked and rechecked the figures, making a master list of items needed and a secondary list of who had ordered what.

Hours later, he worked the crick out of his neck, massaging it. The gentle whiff of something cooking made his stomach gurgle. Yes, allowing a woman on board wasn't a bad decision, he mused.

He dropped his pen into its holder and gathered his papers, putting them back into the waterproof attaché. He couldn't afford to have these papers destroyed by water. He placed the attaché in the secret safe with his money and followed his nose to the galley.

"Smelling mighty fine, isn't it, Captain?" Ben smiled.

"Sure is. Whoever said a woman wasn't welcome on a ship ought to have their heads examined."

Ben chuckled. "Miss Isabela ain't too bad on the eyes either."

"What?"

"You haven't met her?" Ben raised his eyebrows and strained to keep a smile from his face.

"No, Emile asked this morning. I was up on the yardarm when she came on board."

"You're in for a treat, my friend."

Just great. He didn't need a beautiful woman on board stirring his men's thoughts in the wrong direction. Then again, most of his crew were family men. He had to keep reminding himself he wasn't on a ship with a bunch of earthy seamen. These were just his employees and a couple businessmen from Key West. Besides, with Emile on board, a man would be foolish to bring on a father's wrath. If the hood over her head was any indication, Miss Isabela had been raised in a very strict and old-fashioned Spanish home.

"Personally, I don't care what she looks like. I'm more interested in that heavenly aroma coming from the galley. I've never smelled anything so fine coming from down there."

Ben chuckled. "Never brought Cook along?"

"Nope. She always said if the good Lord wanted us on the water, He'd have given us fins. Of course, she likes to sail every once in awhile. She just isn't partial to long sea voyages."

"Ah, well, no one could ever make Cook do anything she didn't want to," Ben quipped.

"You're telling me? I grew up under that woman's hand. Trust me, I know."

Ben chuckled again. "Keep forgetting that she lives in your place."

"Shall I bring you something up or would you like me to relieve you for a spell?" Richard asked.

"I'm fine, had a big breakfast. After you've eaten, I'll go down."

"Okay, I'll be back shortly."

"Don't rush. I love sailing." With a feather touch, Ben guided the helm.

"I can tell. You know, I might be in need of a captain for a spell to ship my orders. You interested?"

"I'll think on it. Generally, my business keeps me in port."

Richard nodded and headed toward the galley.

"What smells so good. . . ?" His voice trailed off. The lily of the ruins was aboard the *Sea Dove.*

Lord, help me.

⚓

"Mr. Southard, this is my daughter, Isabela."

Isabela watched Richard slowly close his lips, turn inquiringly to her father, then back to her.

"Buenos días, Isabela, como está?"

"*Bien, muchas gracías* for letting me travel with you. I promise to stay out of the way. Father suggested I help out by making the meals. Is that a problem?"

"No, no, not at all, unless you consider the fact that the good smells will have my crew's stomachs rumbling for hours before they can eat." Richard smiled. His blue-gray eyes darkened a touch. "And what did you make that smells so good?"

"*Asopado de mariscos.*"

"Smells great. May I have some?"

Isabela fumbled for a bowl and scooped out a healthy portion of the fish and rice stew. *Lord, help me not pay him too much attention.*

"When do you expect to arrive in Havana?" her father asked Richard as he sat down at the small table.

The men's hammocks hung behind the galley. She'd examined the ship, discovering there wasn't a private room for herself and her father. She would have to hang a canvas or blanket to create some privacy.

"If the winds hold, I'm hoping to arrive late tonight. Mr. Fernandez—"

"Emile," her father corrected.

"Emile, I'm afraid we're going to have to change the sleeping arrangements. There isn't a private room on ship, except for the captain's quarters, and I insist that Isabela stay in there. I'll bunk below with the men."

"No, Señor Southard, we cannot impose."

Oh, Father, why do you insist on. . . No, he was right. They were not passengers; they were simply glorified stowaways.

"No, Señor Fernandez, I insist. I can't put your daughter in such a compromising situation. You may not be aware, but there is no privacy for her. I thought perhaps you and your daughter could stay in the bow, and I'd have the men move the sails, but I think my quarters are the better choice and easier all the way around."

Isabela handed him the bowl of *asopado de mariscos.*

"*Muchas gracías.*"

Isabela nodded and sat down beside her father. "I wouldn't want to impose."

"No imposition. I will have to use the desk a time or two before we arrive, but I'll try and do that while you're on deck or cooking down below. That is, if you wish to continue cooking. This is wonderful."

"Thank you." She folded her hands in her lap, hiding her sweaty palms. Why did this golden-haired man affect her so?

"You're very kind, Mr. Southard. . . ."

"Richard," he corrected her father with a smile.

Lord, You made him with such a wonderful smile. Isabela blinked away her wayward thoughts as her fingers fumbled along the edge of her apron.

A grin raised the furrowed lines of her father's face. "Richard, have you figured out how much material you're ordering?"

"Some. I need to finalize the figures. Are you familiar with some good men to do business with in Havana?"

"I'd be honored to help you. I shall ask around. And my cousin Manuel—he sells building supplies."

"Thank you. The men gave me several contacts with whom they've done business before."

"*Sí*, that is good."

Richard lifted his bowl to spoon out the remaining stew. "Exquisite *asopado de mariscos*, thank you." He sliced off a hunk of bread and cheese. "I'll have my quarters ready in an hour."

"*Muchas gracias*, Mr. Southard."

She watched him climb the ladder.

"He's a good man," her father whispered.

"*Sí.*"

Isabela cleaned up Richard's dishes and fed the other men as they came down. Staying in the captain's quarters would make this trip much more pleasurable, and the view from the stern windows would be wonderful.

"Isabela?"

"*Sí*, Padre?"

"I'm going to carry your baggage up to the captain's quarters. Do you wish to come up on deck with me?"

"*Sí.*" She couldn't wait to breathe in the fresh air. The galley wasn't bad, but the heat from the small stove and poor ventilation from the small window didn't provide much comfort.

The bright sun danced on the deep blue ocean. They were several hours south of Key West now. The sun arced high in the sky, and the brush of the wind on her face caused her to stretch her arms out to cool down her body.

"Isabela," her father spoke sharply under his breath.

"I'm sorry, Papá, I wasn't thinking." A woman did not flaunt herself in such a way. She followed behind him as he made his way to the captain's quarters. It was a small room set in the stern. Her father knocked before entering.

The room was empty; the bed, freshly made. A small brown leather pouch sat on the desk, *which also serves as a table*, she surmised.

"Where would you like these?" her father asked.

"Put them on the bed, Papá. I'll unpack a dress for tomorrow and leave the rest for our visit with Grandmother."

"*Sí*, that is wise. Do you wish for me to sleep in here?"

Isabela looked around the small cabin. He'd have to sleep on the floor, unless there was a hammock she didn't know about. "No, Papá, I'll be safe. There's a lock on the door."

"I'll stay with you until it's time to retire this evening."

"I would like your company. Maybe Mr. Southard has a chess board or something for us to pass the time."

"I shall ask him while you unpack."

Isabela went right to work. She removed a long cotton skirt and a white cotton blouse for tomorrow. She hung them in the small closet, where she found what she presumed were Richard's clothes. A quick glance over her shoulder told her she was alone, and then she reached for his dark blue suit coat and smelled it. *Oh, Lord, help me. I'm attracted to this man in a way that would not be pleasing to my parents or to our customs.* She dropped the coat sleeve as if it singed her fingers. For her own personal sanity, she would have to find ways to limit her contact with one Richard Southard. *But how can I do that on a ship?*

Richard stood at the helm and sailed the ship into Havana Harbor. The trip had been uneventful. Having arrived late in the evening, he'd anchored just outside the harbor. Isabela's fine cooking made the journey all the more pleasurable. He'd thanked the Lord on more than one occasion that she'd stayed out of the way. Last evening he'd almost gone to her when he saw her standing on the bow, but something stopped him. He prayed it was good common sense. Emile Fernandez guarded his daughter like a hawk. A man would be foolish to attempt a one-on-one meeting with her. Growing up in Key West had allowed him to learn of some of the strong Hispanic customs some of the families practiced. Emile was no exception.

Richard had watched Isabela keep her eyes focused on the ground, anywhere besides looking directly at him, unless he spoke to her within her father's presence. Then, and only then, would she look at him. Her deep brown eyes sparkled with fiery passion. Given the right environment, she would be a force to contend with.

He'd been up most of the night fighting his attraction to her. How could a man be so attracted to a woman he barely knew? He didn't have an answer but knew if he were ever to win her affections, it would take time. Lots and lots of time.

The sails fluttered in the breeze as he fell off on his approach. "Drop anchor," he called out to his men. The rapid *ching-ching-ching* of the chains as they went through their guides in the bow was quickly followed by the splash of the anchor hitting the water.

While Isabela cleaned up the evening meal, he'd finished figuring the amount of supplies needed. Ordering the material would take a day, perhaps two.

In his brown leather satchel, he had all of his cash and the cash of the others. Truthfully, he'd been surprised at how little some of the men had given him. Many claimed they had standing credit with several of the area businesses.

Richard hollered out the orders, and the ship creaked to a halt. Isabela and Emile stood ready at the side of the ship. He waved to them and they returned the gesture.

"Ben, see the Fernandezes have a skiff to take them to shore. Mike, Pete, you two will stay on board. The rest of you can come to town with me. I'll need some hands to get these orders back to the ship. Mike, can you navigate the *Sea Dove* to the dock?"

"Yes, Sir, Captain. Ain't a woman I can't handle," he replied, his grin creasing his weather-beaten face.

"Great, watch for my signal."

Mike nodded and went back to his work. "Gentlemen, it's time; the skiff has returned."

The men worked their way over the side and down the rope ladder. At shore they jumped out of the skiff and headed up the beach. "Take her back, John. I'll send the others to relieve the three of you after we've filled our orders."

"Thanks, Captain."

Richard pulled out his list. "Let's see. Let's start with the bricks."

"Sounds good," Ben offered, and the small group made their way into town. It didn't take long before Richard had given each of the men a different task.

After a short time of searching, they found the brickyard. *"Buenos días, Señor, como está?"*

"Bien. May I help you?"

"Sí. My name is Richard Southard and I'm from Key West."

The deeply tanned man nodded.

"We've come to place an order."

"We heard the island burned up."

"We had a fire, yes. That is why we are here."

"I'd be happy to help you, Señor Southard. You have money?"

"Sí."

The man then broke into a smile. "Come to my office, Señor."

Richard soon learned in their discussion that he would ship only the bricks for which he could pay cash. The man would not extend any credit to anyone from Key West. No amount of arguing with the man could persuade him.

"Thank you, Señor. I'll need to check with the other merchants."

"Sí, I understand, Señor. But the news of the great fire has spread across the island quickly. I don't believe anyone will give credit to a man from Key West."

"Thank you, Señor." Richard nodded and headed out of the small office. "Come along, men, we've run into a problem." After a brief explanation, each man was given the task of contacting one of the businesses that had been recommended by someone on the island. The money Richard had with him was not nearly enough to satisfy the owner of the brickyard, and Richard was quickly suspecting that it would not satisfy any of the businessmen in Cuba.

"Señor Southard, I heard you were in town. I'm sorry, I cannot extend credit." The thin man with wiry gray hair looked down at the floor.

"Why? You've done business with the men on Key West before. They've always paid their bills, haven't they?"

"Sí, Señor. But how can a man pay without a business to run? Can you guarantee everyone will pay their bills within the month?"

And that was the problem. Richard could not guarantee what he did not know to be true or not true. *Lord, what am I to do?*

Chapter 4

Richard paced the deck of his ship. *What should I do, Lord? Folks back home are counting on me. I've enough money to take care of my own expenses, but what about the others? Some of those businesses need to be up and running immediately for the sake of the rest of the people living on the island.*

"Señor Southard." Richard turned and saw Emile Fernandez climbing up and over the rail of the ship.

"Emile, what's the matter?" Richard hadn't expected Emile or Isabela's return until tomorrow morning.

"We have heard the merchants will not extend credit."

"Yes, it's true." Without thinking, Richard leaned over and reached his hand down for Isabela to latch on to. Her hands were strong, yet soft as delicate rose petals.

"Thank you, Mr. Southard." Isabela straightened her skirt as she stood beside her father.

Richard's gaze shifted to Emile, who was examining Richard for boldly assisting his daughter. "What are you going to do?" Emile asked.

"I'm not sure. I have some money, but it won't meet the island needs."

"No, one man shouldn't have to pay for everyone."

"No, and this man doesn't have that amount of money." Richard leaned on the rail and looked over Havana Harbor, lined with various ships of various styles and sizes. His white two-masted schooner stood out among the darker hulled ships.

"You spoke with my cousin today, *sí?*"

"Honestly, I don't know. I didn't catch the names of most of the men I sought to do business with."

"My cousin, Manuel, he's short, thinly built, and has—how you say, rough gray hair."

"Stringy?" Richard asked.

"*Sí.* Stringy," Emile answered, while Isabela stood quietly by her father.

"Yes, I met with a man fitting that description." He was pleasant enough but, like the rest, he would not extend credit, Richard recalled.

"Manuel, my cousin, he says he'd like to work out a deal with you."

"What kind of a deal?" Richard put his arms across his chest and braced himself.

"He says if you give him your ship, he will hold it until the money is sent from the others."

"The *Sea Dove*?" Richard's raised voice echoed off the water. "He's got to be loco."

"He may be. No one else will do business without the money. He will take your ship as, how you say, collateral?"

"Yes, collateral is the correct word." *Collateral, Lord. What would Uncle Ellis say or do? How can I tell him?* "Oh, by the way, your ship is in Havana until everyone in Key West pays their bills." Richard wagged his head from side to side. "I don't know."

Isabela reached out and touched his arm. "Manuel can be trusted, Richard."

Her rich brown eyes held his gaze. *Lord, help me. I want to believe this woman, but should I do this?* "I will need to bring this matter before the Lord. And I will need to speak further with Manuel. Can he get me all the materials on my list?"

Emile placed his hand on Richard's shoulder. "He said he would try."

Richard nodded. If ever he needed to spend time in prayer, the time was now and here, in a foreign country, all on his own to make a decision that would have a profound effect on many people. Who would fault him for not releasing his ship to the hands of such blackmail? It was ludicrous for the people of Havana to take advantage in this way. He'd been thinking of a trip up the Florida Gulf Coast or directly to Mobile as the best alternatives to this crisis. Now he was presented with an offer that could provide the necessary help but didn't give him much assurance. And, strictly speaking, he could solve his problem by buying only what he needed for himself and returning to Key West. The question was, was this a time when a man put his personal needs aside for the benefit of others?

Father God, give me wisdom, he prayed.

Late into the night, Richard continued to seek God's wisdom. He ran the what-if scenarios so often he felt they had almost become real. Deep in thought, he paced back and forth across the deck. The starry sky shimmered in its peaceful state. The gentle lull of the waves lapping the sides of the ship beat a gentle lullaby of peace. Richard closed his eyes and listened to the stillness of the world. In the distance, some night sounds from Havana played.

He pulled in a deep breath. "Lord, help me, but I see no other way. You call me to do unto others as I'd want done to me. I guess, given the same circumstance, I'd hope someone would come to my aid."

"Richard," Isabela whispered.

"Isabela?" Richard turned to see her standing in the shadows of the forward exterior wall of the captain's quarters. "What are you doing out here?"

"Looking at the moon. Are you really going to let Manuel have your ship?"

"I have no other choice."

"But you do. You don't have to accept." Isabela took a step toward him.

Richard slipped into the shadows to meet her. "A man has to do what's right, even when there appears to be great risk to himself. If I lose the *Sea Dove*, our business will suffer, compounding the damage the fire has already done."

"Then why take the risk?" she whispered.

He shouldn't continue to talk with her in secret like this. What if her father discovered them? Then again, perhaps the Lord had placed her here to help him determine the way he should go. "I don't know if I have any other choice. I've gone over the figures. There are some men in Key West that might not have the resources for months to pay off their bill to Manuel. The damage to their businesses was that extensive. Of course, I don't know their personal financial status, but I think it's safe to assume in some cases they have limited resources. For me to give up the ship would be to put a substantial amount of equity at risk."

"I understand. So why are you seriously considering doing it?" she continued to whisper.

Richard lowered his voice a tad more. "Because I believe God wants me to."

"If that be the case, Señor Southard, then you will be blessed. God will provide." She smiled and walked away.

Richard stayed in the shadows. Her honor dictated that no one know they had spoken. "Father, keep her reputation unsoiled, and thank You for her assurance that I should sacrifice the *Sea Dove*."

Isabela rubbed her arms vigorously. The cool evening breeze washed over her as gooseflesh danced on her arms. She knew she shouldn't have spoken to Richard, but he seemed so lost and alone. And when she'd heard his prayer, she couldn't keep herself from speaking to him. "Lord, forgive me for being alone with him. I just wanted to help."

They had intended to sleep at her grandmother's house, but once Manuel came by and told her father about his proposal, they'd left immediately. They might be stuck on Cuba until they found passage back to Key West if Richard did give up his boat to her cousin.

Her mind drifted back to the argument her father had had with Manuel earlier in the evening. Passions flared between the men. She'd been surprised to see her father give Richard such an honorable recommendation of his cousin. But that was the custom. Families were honest and open with each other—but only with family. It wasn't that her father didn't trust his cousin, Manuel. He was just angered that a man who had worked well with others in previous days would be so concerned about extending the credit at this time.

If there was one thing Isabela understood, it was finances. Working mathematical figures in her head was a talent she possessed and one her father worked to keep well hidden. Many men felt women just didn't have an aptitude for numbers.

Isabela unfastened her skirt and slipped it over the chair so it would be fresh in the morning. She hadn't packed enough clothes for an extended stay. How would they get home and when?

She removed the rest of her clothing and slipped on her nightclothes. Before sliding under the covers, she went to Richard's desk and looked over the figures he'd been working with earlier in the day. Her hands trembled as she realized the amount of money Richard would be sacrificing for others. "Oh, Lord, keep Manuel honest." She let the paper float back to the desk.

Isabela jumped from the gentle knock on the door. "Isabela, it's Richard, are you in there?"

"Yes. Did you need something from your desk?" She spoke behind the closed door, her hand braced against the door, her heart pounding.

"No, it can wait until morning."

Isabela heard her father's voice. "Señor Southard, may I help you?"

Isabela's face grew hot. Her father wouldn't understand. . . .

"Isabela?"

"*Sí*, Papá, I'm fine." She ran to the bed and slipped under the covers.

"Emile, tell me more about Manuel," she heard Richard say. Her father answered, and the two men's voices receded from the door.

Isabela clutched the covers to her chest. She'd disobeyed her parents tonight by seeking out Richard. To have her father discover her talking with him. . . Thankfully the door was closed, not that she would have opened it. "Lord, I care for this man far too much. Mother will see it in my eyes when I return. Help me, Lord. I don't want my heart to go to anyone who isn't the best You have for me."

The next morning Richard woke still upbraiding himself for having been so foolish as to approach the captain's quarters. Emile's fatherly reprimand consisted of a look that would send any sane man running as far away from Isabela Fernandez as he could possibly get. And yet, he found himself even more attracted to her.

Cold ham and biscuits sat heavy in his stomach, a sharp contrast to Isabela's fine cooking the day before. He'd assembled the men early this morning and asked them to gather any of their personal effects on the ship, as well as anything others might have left on board. For some reason, he knew he had to give the *Sea Dove* as a sign of good faith, but he also had the nagging suspicion he might never see the ship again. Richard rubbed his temples and went back to his paperwork, checking and rechecking his figures.

How is it that a man can know what is the right thing to do and yet still have the hardest time trusting it is the best thing? Richard kneaded the tension out of his neck.

"Señor Southard."

Richard found Isabela standing outside the cabin. "Isabela." What could he say? He looked past her to see her father was nowhere in sight.

"I saw your figures last night. I just wanted to say, you've been asked to sacrifice a lot. And thank you for understanding our customs."

"Why are you here now, Isabela? If your father caught you, he'd be very angry." Richard stood up at the desk and assembled his paperwork.

"*Sí*, he would. But I'm out here keeping my distance."

"But you're still speaking with me." Richard slung the leather pouch with his papers and money over his shoulder. He stepped closer to the door. "You know as well as I, your father would not approve."

"True, but I have come to retrieve my belongings. My father can't object to that."

"No, I suppose he can't. Come in."

Isabela stood steadfast outside the cabin. "No, I'll wait until you're through."

"So, if I stay in here and continue to talk with you, your father would not object?" He knew the answer before he asked, but the thought of sneaking a brief conversation with Isabela controlled his better judgment.

"No, he would object. Richard, are your figures correct? Would you be sacrificing thirty-five thousand dollars?"

"Yes. But how did you come up with that? I never put the figure down."

"I'm fairly good with mathematics."

"Ah, Nanna is very good with figures too. She taught me well." Richard opened his hidden panel and pulled out an additional leather pouch.

"What is that?"

"Isabela, has anyone ever told you, you ask too many questions?"

Her brown eyes shimmered. "Some have said as much."

Richard chuckled. "You are an amazing woman, Isabela. Now if you'll excuse me, I need to see your cousin and make arrangements."

She stepped aside for him to pass.

"Richard," she whispered.

He turned to look at her. Her head bowed down. "You're an amazing man," she whispered.

Richard forced every muscle in his body not to reach out and pull her toward him. He'd never met a woman to whom he'd been so attracted. Yes, she was beautiful, but that wasn't the only source of attraction. Every stolen moment together he'd learned another fascinating feature about her. She definitely piqued his interest. A change in subject would help. "Can you and your father afford passage back to Key West?"

"Father will find a way."

"I'm sorry, Isabela; this hasn't been a pleasant trip for you."

She looked at him then. "It is not your fault, Richard."

Richard. She'd said it again. For a young Hispanic woman, she was very daring. To speak to him, to call him by his first name, to understand math. . . Perhaps he should seek her father's permission to court Isabela. *But if I did, Emile might think that something had already happened between Isabela and me.*

Has it, Lord?

Chapter 5

"Papá, I did not tell Señor Southard." Isabela stood defending herself in her grandmother's small home. Thankfully, her grandmother was working in the garden. She could just imagine the scorn she would get from her grandmother for having spoken with Richard Southard.

"Then how did he know?" Confusion and anger played across her father's face.

"Did you pay him for passage to Cuba?"

"No, I offered, but he refused."

"He knows on his own. I swear I did not tell him we didn't have the money to buy passage on another ship."

Isabela rehearsed what she did tell Richard in her mind. Not once did she mention that the money would be a problem. Part of her father's anger with Manuel was that his plan had put them in a difficult place to return to Key West, and Manuel had not offered to help.

Emile paced back and forth in the small front room. Isabela focused on a small table he had refurbished for her grandmother. "We will have to pay Señor Southard back."

"*Sí*, I'm sure he would agree." Isabela thought again about the tremendous sacrifice Richard was making for the folks in Key West. Would anyone ever really know the extent of his benevolence?

"Papá, we must go now. Señor Southard's instructions said the ship would be leaving very soon."

"*Sí.*" Emile grabbed his bag, kissed his mother as she entered the house, and headed for the door.

"Grandma, I love you. *Adiós.*" Isabela hugged the frail woman. Her father had tried to convince his mother to come to Key West and live with them, but she refused. "This is my home," was her reply.

Isabela and her father hurried through Havana's narrow streets, making their way to the harbor. Isabela looked for Richard Southard but could not find him. She couldn't find him on the ship either. He'd purchased passage for them in a large guest room of the captain's. The ship was a four-masted schooner, much larger than Richard Southard's.

"Captain, is Señor Southard on this vessel?"

"No, Miss Fernandez. Mr. Southard had more business in Havana."

"*Gracias.*"

Isabela found the voyage uneventful, boring almost. Thoughts of Richard Southard and the *Sea Dove* seemed more pressing. Admittedly, it wasn't as grand of a ship, a work boat, Richard had called it. But somehow this four-masted schooner with all its glamour and wealthy guests seemed to pale in comparison.

Back in Key West, Isabela tried to find a job. Day after day no employment could be found. If she were a man, there would be plenty of work. But as a woman, there was nothing. Richard had returned to Key West on a cargo ship loaded with most of the materials the islanders had ordered. Some spoke of his having to leave the *Sea Dove* in Havana as collateral, but the urgency of rebuilding the island kept the people from their usual gossip.

Every day she would walk past Richard Southard's property, and every day she was careful not to speak with him. Today she hesitated as she gazed over the ruins of the Southard warehouse.

"Looks pretty bad," a voice said from behind.

Isabela gasped. "Don't scare me like that."

"I'm sorry," Richard apologized. "I thought you would have heard me coming."

"Any word about your ship?" She turned to face him.

"Nothing worth mentioning. There are several who will not be able to pay their debt for at least sixty days."

"Oh, Richard, I'm so sorry. What are you going to do?" Isabela fought the desire to touch him.

"I'm going to do what my uncle used to do. I purchased enough wood to rebuild the dock. I have the men sponging now, and we'll wash and dry the sponges on the dock. I'll barter with every captain who comes to port to haul the sponges. Slowly, we'll get some more money in and I'll be able to purchase the material for the building, unless the others can pay me back sooner."

Isabela scanned the nearly completed rebuilt dock. "You've worked quickly."

"Mo's been a tremendous help. As you can see, we've only rebuilt about half of it. I hope to have the rest of it built by the end of the week, depending upon the manpower that's available."

Yes, plenty of work for men, nothing for a woman.

"Isabela?" Richard perused the area, then settled his gaze back on her. "Is something wrong?"

"What? No. No, nothing."

"You seemed to have drifted far away there for a minute."

"I've been trying to find work, but there's only work for men in Key West right now."

"Oh, I'm sorry. I'm afraid I don't have work for a woman either."

Isabela felt a crimson blush working its way up her neck. She hadn't meant to hint that he. . . "I didn't mean to imply that you should hire me. I know your company has no place for a woman."

"I will pray for you to find a suitable job. What do you do?"

"Nothing. I mean, I could do plenty, but no one will hire me. I tried to get hired in the banks, but no one trusts a woman to handle money."

"Hmm."

"I've tried to get work at the baker's, but he's not hiring. Let's face it, I've tried to find work everywhere, but no one is hiring women. Everyone's too involved with getting the town rebuilt. Not that I blame them, but. . ."

"It would be nice to be employed."

"Exactly." He understood and was not offended. Why was it so easy to speak with him?

Richard sat down on the dock. Isabela started to follow suit, then stopped herself.

Richard jumped up. He'd seen her hesitation. "I'm sorry. I forgot."

She wished she could forget. If it weren't for the large Hispanic population and the fact that everyone on Key West knew her father, she would have loved to sit down beside him to talk, just talk. *What is the harm in that, Lord?*

Richard cleared his throat. He'd felt so comfortable talking with her. "Isabela?"

"*Sí,*" she whispered.

"Isabela!" Emile Fernandez roared. Richard would recognize the man's voice anywhere.

"Over here, Papá."

"Señor Southard," Emile said curtly.

"*Buenos días, Señor Fernandez, como está?*"

"*Bien.*" Emile's voice was curt. "Isabela, why are you here?"

"I was on my way back home."

Richard watched as Isabela's gaze caught her father's. She would be in trouble. Richard knew he had to come up with something. "Emile, your daughter is good with numbers, right?"

"*Sí,* Señor, she has a pretty face but a very keen mind."

Richard wouldn't acknowledge the part about her pretty face, but the mind was neutral territory, he hoped. "Emile, would it be all right with you if I asked your daughter to come and work for me?"

"Pardon?"

"I could use someone to work on my financial records. I'm afraid with all the work I've been doing on the dock, and eventually the building, I haven't time to keep my books. Uncle Ellis would not be pleased. If Isabela feels she could learn the bookkeeping, would you give her your permission to come and work for me?"

"You have no office. Where would she work?" Emile's confusion deepened.

"I have an office at my home. Cook is there most days. I would be here on the dock most of the day. However, I would need to talk with Miss Isabela on occasions in order to conduct business." *Why am I doing this? I don't need a bookkeeper that badly. Admit it, Richard, when it comes to a certain Miss Isabela Fernandez, you do some mighty foolish things. Like paying for her transport back to Key West on a luxury ship while you yourself were snuggled up with the building supplies you were bringing back to the island.*

"It is not proper for a young woman to talk with a young man without a chaperone."

"Papá," Isabela pleaded.

Emile raised his hand in objection. Isabela stood rigid and clutched her hands into fists. Richard could tell she was fighting to obey her father, while her heart rebelled against being treated like a child.

"Yes, but I would be her employer. Isn't that allowed?" *Employers do have to talk with employees,* he reasoned. "And as I said, Cook will be there. I will try to always speak to Isabela when Cook is in earshot. Would that be acceptable?"

"How do you know Isabela has a mind for math?"

Richard swallowed the lump forming in his throat. Emile had him there. "She commented about some figures I had been working on in Havana. Only a skilled person would have come to the right tabulation."

"And how do you know this?" Emile stared at his daughter.

"Papá, Señor Southard behaved properly. He was in his quarters, and I commented from outside the room while we were on board the ship."

Emile turned toward his daughter. He was about to speak to Isabela in Spanish when he stopped himself, Richard guessed. Emile knew that was hopeless since Richard understood the language.

"This does not please me." Emile didn't break his gaze from Isabela.

"Señor Fernandez, would you agree that Isabela needs a job?"

"*Sí.*"

"And would you also agree that your daughter does not have a mind that should be limited to simple tasks such as someone's laundry?"

"*Sí.*" Emile sighed.

"Then let me hire your daughter. I give you my word, I will not behave in an inappropriate manner with her."

"Your honor?"

Richard swallowed hard. He'd been taught his word was his bond. Could he honestly live up to this commitment, especially in light of the fact that he and Isabela had already spoken on two, no, three occasions? "*Sí,* Señor."

"Then she will work for you. When should she begin?"

Isabela smiled and turned her head away from her father's gaze.

If she was as interested in him as he was in her, Richard knew he would have a problem on his hands in future days. *Do not fret about tomorrow. . . .* "She can begin tomorrow. Come to my home around nine o'clock."

He'd have to rearrange his schedule and work on the books tonight. They were in sad shape, not only from the past week because of the fire, but he'd been putting off the bookwork for about a month. He'd been thinking too much about himself and his future to do all that was needed for the business.

"Nine," Emile repeated. "She'll be there. *Gracías,* Señor Southard. I know you are a man of honor and you will treat my daughter with proper respect."

Richard nodded, his throat too tight to speak.

As Emile escorted Isabela away from Richard, she turned and mouthed a silent thank-you. His heart soared. She appreciated the job. She was independent enough to want to have found one on her own, but respectful enough to allow her father the final decision.

"Lord, You're going to have to help me here. Working side by side with Isabela will test my strength in more ways than one. She's so beautiful, Lord. But You know that."

Richard bent down and pulled out a charred stick from the rubble. "Can I really rebuild this business?" He'd sent letters to the companies expecting shipments, telling them of the fire and an approximate date they could expect delivery. Now the only question was, could he come through?

As soon as they entered their home, Isabela regained a measure of composure. "Papá, you embarrassed me in front of Señor Southard."

"Me? What about you, Daughter? Speaking to a man alone, what were you thinking? Do you want everyone to speak of you as being a. . .a. . ."

"Papá, people speak to each other all the time on the island. No one thinks that way anymore. In Cuba, yes. Here, no."

"There are still plenty of our people living here in Key West. They think as I," Emile insisted, folding his arms across his chest.

Her mother walked into the room. "What has Isabela done now?" she asked, rubbing her hands on a dishcloth.

"She was speaking with a young man."

Yolanda turned and faced Isabela. "Who?"

Isabela couldn't face her mother's examination and glanced at the floor. "Señor Southard."

"I see. Emile, what did you do?"

"I contained myself. Richard Southard speaks our language, so I could not speak to Isabela without him understanding everything I said. She is, however, going to work for him."

"Pardon?"

"Now, now, relax, Yolanda. I have it all arranged. She'll be working at his office in his house while he's working on the docks. There will be a time or two when he needs to speak with her, but Cook will be in the house."

Yolanda lifted her daughter's chin. "Do you want to work for Señor Southard?"

"*Sí,* Mima, very much."

Her mother's gaze fixed on Isabela's. "We shall speak later."

"All right. I'm going to my room; excuse me." Isabela stepped back and made her way down the hall, leaving her parents speaking in rapid whispers. How could she keep herself from speaking with Richard Southard? He was so comfortable to talk with. He was a man of honor; perhaps she could depend upon him to keep their relationship purely innocent.

"Hah," Isabela taunted her reflection in the mirror. Richard Southard was as attracted to her as she was to him; she'd seen it in his blue-gray eyes. She removed the pins from her hair and picked up her hairbrush.

She had a job, a real job. One that fit her talents and abilities. She smiled at herself as she worked her hair with the brush, then began to pace in the small path between her bed and the wall.

"Lord, thank You for the job. But can Richard Southard afford to hire me at this time? I saw the figures he worked on in Havana. The risk he was taking, the loan he was making to others—how can he afford it?"

"Isabela, it is not for us to question." Yolanda walked in and sat down on Isabela's bed. "Come, sit with me."

Isabela's hands shook. She folded them on her lap.

"You care for Señor Southard, don't you?" Her mother spoke in loving Spanish. "Sí."

"Does your papá know?"

"No."

"Does Señor Southard know?"

"No. . .I don't know."

"I see." Yolanda reached over and held her daughter's hand. "It's hard to be a woman and respect our ways. It is harder for you having grown up in Key West and not Cuba. But you have to understand how your papá and I feel about such matters."

"Oh, Mima, I do, honest I do. It's just that when I'm near Richard—"

"Richard?"

"Señor Southard."

"I know his name, Darling. I'm surprised you feel comfortable calling him by his given name."

Isabela took in a deep breath. "I know, Mima, I'm surprised at myself too. But that is just it. I feel this connection with this man. He's so incredibly handsome and—"

Yolanda whispered a laugh. "And you expect to be able to keep your mind on your work for him?"

"I will work, and I will do a good job," Isabela affirmed with ardent determination. "I will try not to speak with him unless it relates to our work."

"And what will you do if Richard asks to kiss you?"

Love every minute of it. The heat of embarrassment warmed her cheeks. "Señor Southard would not do that." Oh, but she hoped he would.

"I see, and why do you say that?"

"Because he gave Papá his word."

"What exactly did he promise in his word?"

"That he would not dishonor me."

"I see." Her mother caressed her hand. "Isabela, promise me something."

"What, Mima?"

"Promise me that when these feelings for Señor Southard develop to a point when you think you'll burst inside, that you will tell me." Yolanda pushed Isabela's wayward hair behind her shoulders.

Could she do that? Were her thoughts already to that point? No, she wasn't about to explode. . . . "*Sí*, Mima, I will do that."

"Good, because at that time we will have to speak to your father about your marriage to Richard Southard."

"Marriage? Mima, I'm not going to work for Señor Southard just to marry him."

"No? Then why are you going to work for him?"

Chapter 6

Richard pinched the bridge of his nose after running his fingers across his eyelids. It was nearly midnight and he was still working on the paperwork.

"Richard, what are you doing up so late?" Cook placed her hands on her ample hips.

The sound of her voice sent a sense of peace washing over him. "Working?"

"Whatever for? Didn't ya say you hired Isabela Fernandez to do this work?"

"Yes, but I need to get the books in order before she starts."

"Seems to me she could be doing that. You just need to show her how and let her go to work."

Richard scanned the various ledger sheets. "You might be right, Cook." He tapped the paper covered with scribbles.

"Richie, you told me what happened in Cuba about the ship. But what is goin' on with you and Isabela?" She sat down on a high-backed chair by the door, her voice filled with motherly concern.

"Nothing, really. She needed a job, I know she has the mind for the figures, and I'm behind."

"So, ya don't have feelings for her?" Her gray eyebrows rose into her warm, cocoa forehead.

"Cook," Richard sighed, "she's special, and she's attractive, but I don't have time for romance. I have too much to do, too much to make right before James returns to take his place in the family business."

"So is that what's been on your mind the past few weeks? James?"

"Somewhat. The past week I haven't given it much thought other than the fact that I need to get the business back on its feet and I have a limited amount of time in which to do it." Richard pushed his chair back away from his desk.

"Care for a game a checkers?" Cook winked.

Richard chuckled. When he was a small boy, it had been his favorite game. "Don't you think we should retire for the evening?"

"Sure, but one game won't hurt ya, unless you think you're going to lose."

"You're on. I'll fix us a cup a tea; you set up the board. Would you prefer chess?" he asked, heading toward the kitchen.

"Goodness, no, Child. That takes far more brain power than what I have at this hour."

A game of checkers proved to be the distraction he needed, although it lasted longer than he thought it would. Either he'd gotten rusty or Cook had been practicing.

"Good game, Richie. Now, I think I should retire." Cook rose slowly from the chair.

"You and me both. Morning comes early when you stay up this late. Go to bed, Cook. I'll clean up."

Richard straightened the sitting room and put their cups into the sink. Once Cook would have flatly refused his offer to help. She definitely was getting older. The fact that she had already lived longer than most didn't make it easier to accept the prospect that she might be gone one day. What would he do? He'd experienced losses in his life—his mother, his father—but those events happened when he was so young. "Lord, keep her around a bit longer and keep her healthy." He rinsed the teacups and headed up the stairs to his bedroom.

Dressed for bed, he settled between the sheets after completing his prayers. The lily of the ruins drifted into his mind as he floated off to sleep.

🌴

"Richie, wake up." Cook placed a loving hand across his brow. "Son, are you feelin' all right?"

His eyes flickered open. "Cook?"

"It's well past dawn and you hadn't surfaced, so I thought I better check on you. Are you all right?"

Richard did a hazy check of his senses and determined he felt all right. "I'm fine, just overslept."

"We were up rather late last night," she said with a wink.

"Yes, we were. What time is it?"

"Just about nine. Isn't that the time you said Isabela Fernandez was comin' over this mornin'?"

Richard bolted up out of bed. "Yes. Where are my trousers?"

"Over the chair. I picked them up off the floor."

"Oh, sorry. I guess I was really tired when I went to bed."

"Uh-huh. You get yourself ready; I'll fix ya some breakfast."

"Thanks. If Isabela comes before I'm dressed, sit her in the front room, please."

"Certainly."

Richard poured some water into the basin and washed his face and brushed his teeth. "I can't believe I overslept, Lord." *Admit it, you were having pleasant dreams of Isabela.*

He heard Isabela's voice. "Good morning, Cook."

" 'Mornin', Miz Fernandez. Mr. Southard will be with you shortly. Can I get ya a cup a tea?"

"No, thank you."

"Come this way." Richard glimpsed Cook walking her into the sitting room from the top of the stairs. He slowed his pace. He didn't need to appear as if he were in a rush. The question was, was he rushing because he'd woken up late or because Isabela was in his house? Truthfully, it was probably the latter, he admitted.

Richard took the steps one at a time, slowly descending to give himself time to catch his breath and calm his nerves. He'd promised her father he would be a man of honor. "Lord, give me strength," he whispered before entering the front sitting room. "Good morning, Miss Fernandez."

"Good morning, Señor Southard." Isabela rose from the sofa.

"Sit, sit, I will be with you in a couple of minutes." He turned to Cook. "Can I bring you something from the kitchen?"

"No, Sir, I'm fine." Cook sat with her feet up on the footrest. Seeing her resting like that sent a flicker of worry through his heart.

"Excuse me, ladies."

Isabela couldn't believe the complexity of Richard Southard's financial records. Not only was he tracking the monies from the sponging business, but he also had his own personal finances that he had invested in various businesses in the North. On paper, Richard Southard was a very wealthy man. At the moment, his cash flow was more than most, but the employee salaries would quickly deplete the limited funds. He'd need an infusion of revenue before the month was up, she analyzed.

They'd spent the morning with him showing her the various ledgers and accounts. What had surprised her even more was the total outlay of cash he'd added to the debt for the fire. She had no idea he'd brought that much money with him to Cuba, and she doubted anyone else on the island knew just how deep his sacrifice had been.

Richard did not return to the house by the end of the day. "Cook, I'll be leaving now. I've left a note for Mr. Southard on his desk. Would you see that he gets it?"

"Of course, Child. Did you enjoy the work?"

"Yes, very much. I'm not sure what he'll want me to work on tomorrow, so that's what I asked him in my note."

"I'm sure Richie will have more work for you."

Isabela nodded. Why did people still insist on calling him Richie? "Good night, Cook."

"Good night. I'll see you in the morning."

Isabela walked down the streets and worked her way toward her family home. It felt good to have a job. And yet, at the same time, she found herself even more drawn to Richard Southard. She never would have guessed he had so much wealth. He and his uncle's family lived a conservative lifestyle on Key West. They weren't in the largest home on the island. They didn't go to all the elite social occasions, as best she knew. Not that she or her family went to such events. Her father's job of rolling cigars was not a position that would bring wealth into a household, yet her parents had always managed to feed and clothe the family.

"Papá, Mima, I'm home."

The next week began and ended the same. She'd go off to work, put in a full day, and come home to help with the evening meal. She was more and more comfortable with the Southards' books. Several of the businessmen had sent along notes to say when they could pay their debt in Cuba, and a few of the island men had paid some or part of what they owed Richard. He never commented on it. He simply gave her the receipts for the day and told her what was what and where to file the information.

As the days passed, she found her father's worries about her being in a compromising situation unfounded. Richard left notes; she left notes; they were hardly ever in the same room together.

As she was thinking about Richard, Isabela opened a piece of his correspondence and scanned it. "Oh, no."

She got up and ran from the desk. "Cook," she hollered.

"What's the matter, Miz?"

"Is Richard at the docks?"

"I believe so, but I don't keep track of the boy any longer."

"If he should come home, tell him I went to town to look for him at his dock."

"What's the trouble?"

"Later, Cook. It's important."

Isabela ran out of the house and hurried down to the wharf. "Richard," she called. "Richard!" she called again. No one was there. What should she do now?

"Richard Southard?" Marc Dabny called after him. "Hold on a minute."

Richard turned around. Marc's rounded belly and balding head showed his age. "What can I do for you, Mr. Dabny?"

"Nothing. It's more of what I can do for you."

"What's that?"

"I heard they are holding your ship in Havana as collateral until the residents pay off their debts."

Richard nodded. It wasn't something he wanted spread around the island, but information of this sort was readily shared. "Yes."

"I'm willing to loan you enough to return your vessel."

"Why would you do this?"

Marc grinned. "Call it my generous nature. I can see that you weren't able to buy the materials to rebuild your warehouse."

"I can put that off for awhile."

"The choice is yours. If you'd like the monies, I'd be happy to lend it."

"Lend, as in provide a loan for a certain interest rate?"

Marc reached over and placed his hand on Richard's shoulder. "Minimal profit."

"What percentage rate are we talking, Mr. Dabny?"

"Call me Marc."

"Marc," Richard repeated with a nod of his head.

"I'm thinking ten percent. We could negotiate on that point. It would all depend on the amount of time you'd need the money."

"Put it in writing and I'll give it consideration." What else could he say? He might need to take this loan in order to make payroll.

"Have a good evening. I'll get the proposal put together and have it delivered to your. . . Where would you like to have me deliver the paperwork?"

"My home."

Marc Dabny nodded and waddled down the street.

There had to be a better way. Richard sighed.

A ship had come in from Cuba with a fresh supply of beef today, and he wanted to pick some up for dinner. He headed toward the market, grateful it was still standing.

"Richard."

Richard turned to see Micah coming toward him. "I'm glad I caught up with you. Mo said I'd find you in town."

"What's the matter, Micah?"

"Nothing. My father and I were just talking about your ship being held in Cuba and we wanted to offer you some room on our next ship leaving port—and any others—until you have the *Sea Dove* back."

Richard extended his hand. "Thank you, Micah, I appreciate that. I can't dry as many sponges at the moment, but I do have a shipment that should be ready in a couple of days."

"Excellent. I'll have our skipper come by your dock after he's loaded our supplies. Oh, this ship is heading north. I didn't figure you wanted a shipment going to South America," Micah added.

"No, I don't have any customers down there."

"Heading to the market?" Micah asked with a glint of excitement in his eyes.

"Yup."

"Me too. Fresh beef is more common than when I first moved here, but it still comes in limited quantities."

"That's one thing I miss about living in New York. I had fresh meat regularly, even raised a couple heads for myself and the neighbors. Pigs were easy and less maintenance."

"Don't have that kind of land down here," Micah commented, keeping in step. A line was forming outside the butcher's.

"My farm back home is ten times larger than the entire island and has hardly any people there."

"Do you miss it?"

"Yes and no. I'm uncertain. I like Key West. I grew up here. But there was something very satisfying about working the land. I suspect it's something from my father. Uncle Ellis said his brother loved the land and was a natural farmer."

"Few stay here for long," Micah observed and raked his golden brown hair with his right hand.

"Yeah, I'm wondering what effect it will have on my uncle and his family living back in the old house, working the land. There's a part of me that could just walk away from the sponge business since it went up in flames but another part of me that needs to rebuild. It will be James's one day."

"Is that what James would want?"

"Honestly, I don't know. But it's not my choice to make. It's something he has to decide for himself. I'm responsible to have something left here for him to choose."

"You know my grandfather prearranged my father's career. Dad gave me the option and I still chose to go in the family business. Is your uncle forcing James?"

"Oh, no, not at all. It's part of the reason he brought the family back North, to give the boys the options and show them there is another way of life." Not to mention Richard hadn't been sure if he wanted to sell the property or keep working the land. The next couple years in Key West were to give him that time to decide.

"My father and I have been having the same discussion. With the railroad's expansion, Key West seems an unnecessary port for shipping cotton. Savannah and Mobile are better locations. I met my wife here and our children were born here, though. It could be a tough adjustment moving to either place. My preference would be to go back to Savannah rather than Mobile."

Richard grinned. "Savannah is a beautiful city—been there a few times."

The line moved forward a couple of steps.

Richard lowered his voice and continued their conversation. "Marc Dabny just made me an interesting offer."

"Oh, what was that?"

"He offered to lay out the funds to get my boat back from Havana."

"Interesting." Micah leaned in closer and lowered his voice a fraction more. "Are you inclined to take him up on it?"

"I'll have to do some calculating. For instance, is the interest he'll charge less than the loss of not having the boat?"

"You've got your work cut out for you. Say, that reminds me. I heard Isabela Fernandez has been doing some bookkeeping for you."

"You heard correctly. She's got quite a head for numbers."

Micah stepped inside the threshold of the building. Richard wasn't too surprised that there were half a dozen folks still in front of them in line.

"Do you have enough work to keep Miss Fernandez employed full time?"

"I do at the moment, but it's quite possible that soon I won't have need of full-time help until I have the warehouse rebuilt."

"If she can hold her own with the figures, I might have some part-time work for her also."

"I'll keep it in mind if I have to reduce her hours. She's so efficient I might just run out of work for her."

Micah stood up to the counter. "A four-pound roast, please."

Richard watched as the butcher cut a large hunk of meat for Micah and his family. A steak had been what Richard had wanted, but looking at the roast, he wondered if he should reconsider. His mouth watered in anticipation of a feast.

"Richard." Micah leaned into him and whispered. "Be careful around Marc Dabny."

Chapter 7

Isabela hurried back to the house. Richard was nowhere to be found. She'd have to leave a message for him to read the correspondence she'd opened. *Cook will bring it to his attention right away.*

In the office, she penned a note, folded it, and placed it on top of the opened letter. "Cook," Isabela called as she headed toward the kitchen. "Cook?" she searched farther and headed into the kitchen. The older woman sat on the floor. "What's the matter?"

"I. . .I'm. . ." Cook struggled for the words.

"Shh, can I help you to your bed? To a chair?"

"Doc. . ." The old black woman fell back against the floor.

"Help me, Lord! Help her." Isabela jumped up and ran to the living room. She pulled a small pillow from the sofa and a lap blanket. Back in the kitchen, she placed the blanket over Cook and gently placed her head on the pillow. "I'll get the doctor. Hang on, Cook."

Cook blinked her eyes but did not speak.

"Dear Jesus, be with her." Isabela raced down Front Street toward the center of town.

"Isabela?" Richard hollered from across the street.

"Richard, Cook's ill, she's on the floor in the kitchen."

"I'll get Dr. Miller. Go back and stay with her."

"All right." Isabela turned and hightailed it back to the house. Should she go get Lizzy? Someone should, but someone needed to be with Cook also. Who should she ask? Who was around? Just at that moment Peg Bower stepped out of Vivian Matlin's old house.

Isabela called out, "Mrs. Bower, would you go get Lizzy Greene? Cook's fallen ill."

"I'll go get her," Peg said, waving to her to go on. "Tell Cook I'm praying for her."

Isabela continued to speed through the Southards' yard and into the kitchen. *Lord, tell me what to do.*

"Cook, the doctor's on his way."

Isabela knelt by the fallen woman. Her eyes seemed dim. Isabela reached for Cook's hand and held it. "Cook, answer me, please." Tears pooled, threatening to spill onto her cheeks. She didn't know Cook well, but during the past couple of weeks, she'd come to care deeply for her. She seemed so vibrant. What could have happened to her?

"Cook, Isabela!" Richard hollered. "Where are you?"

"The kitchen."

"Cook, speak to me." Richard bent down and let the tears stream down his face.

Isabela choked back her own. He loved this woman, truly loved her.

"Isabela, help me. I'm going to put her in her bed."

"What can I do?"

"When I lay her down, you can make her comfortable."

"*Sí.*"

Richard hoisted the woman and carried her back to her room. "Hang on, Cook, the doctor will be here in just a couple of minutes."

He turned to Isabela. "What happened?"

"I don't know. I came into the kitchen to give her a message for you and found her holding her chest, sitting on the floor. She didn't speak."

Lizzie rushed through the door and knelt beside the bed. "Momma!"

Lizzy, unlike her mother, had kept her slim figure even after seven children. But Lizzy was now a grandmother, and the white in her well-groomed hair gave her an air of quiet sophistication.

Isabela stood back. Lizzy would care for her mother's needs.

Richard bent over Cook and kissed her cheek. "I love you." His eyes were red with tears.

Dr. Miller came running in with his black leather bag. "What happened?"

Isabela explained what she'd seen.

"Did she hold her arm?"

"Not that I noticed."

"Thank you. Now, if all of you will excuse me while I examine my patient."

"I'd like to stay," Lizzy asked.

"Yes, Lizzy, you can help. The rest of you can leave."

They left Cook's bedroom, and Isabela followed Richard back to the kitchen. He continued out the door into the backyard. Should she follow him? Or did he want to be alone?

Isabela stayed in the kitchen, picked up the blanket and pillow, and returned them to the sitting room. *Sometimes a person just needs to be alone,* she reasoned.

⚓

Richard escaped into the trees' shadows in the back garden. He fell to his knees. "Father God, please don't take her now. I need her. I'm not ready to let her go just yet. I know it's horribly selfish, but she means the world to me. If it's at all possible, please let her stay a bit longer."

Salty tears stung his cheeks. Impatiently, he wiped them away. *A full-grown man and I'm crying like a four year old.*

"Oh, God, please don't take her." He crumpled over in his anguish. "I know she isn't my grandmother, but she certainly is as close as I've ever had to one." His father's parents had died before he was four. His mother's parents had visited a couple of times after he went to live in Key West with his uncle, but they passed on before he'd moved north.

He continued to pour his heart out to God for what seemed like an eternity. Finally, it occurred to him that he should go back in and see what the doctor had to say.

He felt someone gently place a hand on his shoulder. "Richard," Isabela whispered. "Here, place this on your eyes. It will help."

She held out a damp cloth. Richard took it and did as she recommended. She sat down on the ground beside him. "You love her a lot, don't you?"

"Yes, she's lived in my house since I was four. Before Uncle Ellis married Nanna. I've been noticing how much she's slowed down, but I wasn't prepared for this."

"She loves the Lord, Richard."

"Is that supposed to make it all better?" he cut back.

"No, but it helps, doesn't it? Knowing that even if she does. . .well, if she does, you know. . .she'll be going to heaven."

"Yeah, I suppose that does help some. There are just so many different things going on right now that I. . .I. . ." What did he really want? Was his personal need for Cook in his life his only reason for wanting her around? She wouldn't mind going to heaven. She'd been looking forward to it for years. But Cook always reasoned the good Lord kept her around for a reason. Sometimes she'd say she had to keep busy "messin' with people's lives so as they get it right." And that she would. Cook had no trouble telling folks how things really were.

"I guess it's selfish, really. I love her, and she's a stabilizing force in my life. Not having my family with me right now, it's given me solace knowing she was here."

Isabela placed her hand on top of his. "I think I understand that."

Richard looked at her rich chocolate eyes, her high cheekbones, and her silky golden skin, and he wanted to reach out and kiss her. He pushed back her hair and cupped the back of her neck. He gave it the slightest pressure, feeling her body shiver from his touch. "Oh, Isabela, I—"

"Don't, don't say it, Richard. We can't."

Richard shook his head. "I'm sorry." How stupid could he be? Her father would be furious. He'd given his word he wouldn't act in an improper way toward Isabela, and here he was about to kiss her senseless. But she wanted him to. Regret gathered in her eyes.

"I'm sorry, Isabela. It won't happen again."

"But. . ."

"No, Isabela, I need you to work for me. I can't ruin that by allowing my emotions to take control. If I kissed you, your father would never permit you to come and work for me again."

"Unless you married me."

Marriage, for a kiss? No, thank you. "I think we'd better go back inside and see what the doctor has to say."

He got up and extended a hand to Isabela. She refused it, which was probably a good thing. Having that woman's hand in his own would only stir up more desires, desires he couldn't act upon.

"After I find out what the doctor has said about Cook, I'm going home. My parents will be wondering where I am."

Richard nodded. What could he say? He'd taken a private moment and turned it into something they both regretted.

Inside the house, they found Lizzy and the doctor sitting at the kitchen table. "How is she, Dr. Miller?" Richard asked, taking a seat in one of the remaining chairs.

"Her heart is failing."

Richard's own felt like it could burst. "Is she. . . ?"

"She'll be around for a little while if she takes it easy."

Lizzy wiped her tears with a linen napkin. Richard reached out and held her hand. "She's resting now," she said. "I'm going to stay with her, if you don't mind, Richard." Lizzy's voice cracked.

"Of course I don't mind. You know you're more than welcome any time in this home." He squeezed her hand.

"Thanks."

Isabela stood in the doorway. "Mrs. Greene, my family and I will be praying."

"Thank you, Isabela."

"Señor Southard, I'll be back in the morning."

"Señor" again; it was probably best. *"Buenos noches, Isabela."* Richard turned back to the doctor. "What can we do to help Cook, Doctor?"

🌴

Isabela fought her tears the entire walk home. As she suspected, her parents were getting ready to look for her. The thought of them coming upon her and Richard when he was about to kiss her. . . . Thank the good Lord that didn't happen.

"Isabela, what's wrong?"

"Cook has taken ill. The doctor says her heart is failing."

"Oh no, we must pray for her." Yolanda's words quieted Isabela's heart.

"Sí, I told Miss Lizzy we would pray. It's all so sad; she's such a wonderful woman."

"Ah, but each person is given a time to live and a time to die." Her father spoke softly.

"I know, but it doesn't make it easier." Truth was, her tears were not just for Cook—she truly would miss the woman—but her tears were more for herself and Richard and what probably would never happen between them due to her family's ancient traditions. Life could be so unfair sometimes. "I'm not hungry tonight. If you don't mind, I'd like some time alone in my room."

"*Sí*, you do what you need to do, *Niña*." Her mother gave her a tender embrace and Isabela slipped past her. Her room was filled with familiar memories, items from her entire life, a short life when compared to someone like Cook.

"Lord, be with Cook. Strengthen her heart and make her whole again." Memories of the anguish Richard had expressed in private drew her back to the moments in the garden just before she'd let him know she was there.

He loved Cook. She certainly had a personality that won folks over, but Richard's love surpassed that. It was as if his own mother were dying in the house. Cook had told Isabela that his parents died when he was a boy and he had no real memory of his own mother, only the memories his nanna, his name for his aunt Bea, had given him. Bea had become Richard's only real mother. What part did Cook play in his life? His grandmother. . .of course. Isabela should have realized that before. Cook had no problem telling the young man what he should or should not do, and yet she also would step back and let him make his own choices. Yes, she was his grandmother, a woman who unconditionally loved him and didn't have to be the one to always discipline him.

"Oh, Richard, no wonder your heart is breaking." Fresh tears burned the edges of her eyes. She buried her face in a pillow. "Lord, I would have loved to have held Richard in my arms and kissed him." But did he really want to kiss her—or was he seeking consolation because of his anguish over Cook?

"How can I show Richard that I care for him while I still honor my parents, Lord?"

A gentle knock on her door stopped her prayer. Isabela got up and opened it.

"Are you okay, Isabela?"

"I'm fine, Mima." She slipped back into her room, leaving the door open for her mother to follow.

"I wasn't aware that you've become so close to Francine Hunte."

"Francine?"

"Cook's real name." Her mother sat down on the bed beside her.

"Oh, sorry. She's a sweet woman."

"*Sí*, I've heard she has a tremendous heart for others and has never minced words. But that still doesn't explain how you could have such deep feelings, having known her for such a little time."

"I guess I'm more concerned for Richard."

"Richard? I see. Should we be talking about something else?"

"No, Mima, not really." She couldn't tell her parents. They wouldn't understand. They'd insist that Richard marry her for the sake of her virtue. Of course, he hadn't kissed her, so maybe they wouldn't go that far.

"Your feelings for Señor Southard are growing?"

"*Sí*." Isabela folded and unfolded her fingers.

"How often do you see him alone?"

"Very seldom. It's amazing that I can work in his home and work for him, and he's never around. He leaves me messages and I leave him some. I think we've been alone discussing the books maybe three times in the past couple of weeks."

"Then how is it you've come to have stronger feelings for him?"

"I don't know, Mima. I'm fighting them but. . ."

"But your heart has decided differently, yes?"

"Yes, Mima."

"And how does Richard feel about you?"

"I don't know, Mima. Please don't embarrass me and speak to him. I know it is our custom but. . ."

"But you wish not to have us approach him until you are certain about how he feels?"

"*Sí*, Mima, you understand?" Isabela breathed a sigh of relief.

"*Sí*, I understand. I think it's foolish, but if it is as you say, and you do not spend time alone with him, then we can wait for awhile."

"*Gracías*, Mima. His heart is breaking over Cook. I would hate for him to have to speak with you and Papá at this time."

Yolanda reached out and captured her hands. "Tell me the truth, Isabela, have you and Richard spoken about private matters?"

Chapter 8

Richard checked on Cook as she slept. He found Lizzy sitting in a rocker next to her mother's bed. "Lizzy, I made up a bed with fresh linens for you, if you're inclined to sleep."

"Thank you, but I'll probably stay right here for tonight."

"Wherever you're more comfortable. Can I get you a cup of tea or something?"

"No, thank you, I'm fine."

"All right, I'll see you in the morning. I'll be in my office for a bit, then I'm going to try and get some rest."

"Good night, Richard. Thank you."

"Anything for Cook." The words stuck in his throat.

He slipped out of the room and went to his office. Earlier he had penned a letter to his uncle and sent it to town with a courier in the hope it would sail out with the first ship heading north. Somehow, he'd need to focus on work. He sat at his desk and pulled out a sheet of paper to write a note for Isabela. He dipped his pen and poised it over the paper. What should he say? What did he need done? Honestly, he hadn't gone over her work today, not with Cook's emergency. Putting his pen down, he reached for the ledgers. There on top of them lay a single piece of paper and an opened envelope. "What's this?"

Richard opened the folded sheet of paper.

Dear Richard,
    I tried to bring this to your attention earlier, but I couldn't find you at the docks. Please let me know what you would like me to do about it.

                                 Sincerely,
                                 Isabela

Richard found himself tracing her signature with his finger. Why had he almost kissed her earlier today? Whatever possessed him to attempt such a thing?

My emotions regarding Cook must have gotten the best of me, he reasoned. But wasn't she about to kiss him before good common sense got through to her? Or had she simply been in shock that he would even make such an attempt? Would she even come to work tomorrow? With her father's strict code, she might not be allowed to go back to work.

Richard got up and began to pace. What should he do? Should he go to her home and explain? *Explain what?* He turned and paced in the opposite direction.

That I almost impulsively kissed her? He groaned. Would he have to promise marriage in order for her to continue working for him?

No, he could hire others to do his bookwork. Now that he was beginning to have more time, he could do his own books. Didn't Micah mention the possibility of having her work for him a few hours a week? Perhaps there were other businessmen who might be interested in hiring her also. Now that she had the experience of working for him, she'd be more hirable.

Maybe it's for the best. I need to spend more time at home to help watch over Cook, and I can't do that with Isabela there. "Lord, heal Cook, please," he whispered, his hundredth prayer for the day.

A knock on the front door pulled him out of his meandering and brought him back to the present. "Who could it be at this hour?" he wondered aloud.

Lizzy leaned out of her mother's doorway. "Who is it?"

"Don't know. I'll get it. Stay with your mother." Richard approached the front entrance as the second knock rattled the door in its hinges.

A young man, perhaps fourteen, stood at his door with a folder under his arm. "May I help you?"

"Package for Mr. Southard."

"That's me." Richard pulled a fifty-cent piece out of his pants pocket. "Thank you."

The young man jumped off the porch and ran back toward town. Richard closed the door with his foot and opened the sealed file. "What can this be?"

As he thumbed through the pages, he discovered it was Dabney's offer. The paperwork was very detailed and had obviously been drawn up by a lawyer. "I'll have to look at these carefully."

Richard tossed them on the left-hand corner of his desk, where he noticed the letter Isabela had mentioned in her note. He reached for it and pulled out the thin onionskin paper. He scanned the first words and collapsed on his chair.

⚓

Isabela tossed and turned. She'd been so caught up with Cook and the aborted kiss, she'd forgotten about the letter Richard had received earlier today. Should she tell her parents? A letter was a private matter, but maybe they could help. Richard was a proud man and might be offended if her parents interfered. And if she said something, he might lose confidence in her ability to keep private matters confidential.

Unable to sleep, she dressed and decided to take a walk to the beach. The gentle lull of the waves as they rolled up on the shore calmed her haggard nerves. "What a day, Lord. I know I should be able to rest in You and Your peace but. . . I'm just not doing a good job."

Isabela sat down on the sand and let the fine bits of broken coral and shells flow through her hands. The full moon painted the night sky in rich blues. She took in a deep breath and released it slowly. There was something about the ocean that always calmed her.

"Father, I'm so confused."

"Isabela."

"Richard?" When she turned, she saw that his blond curls were like spun gold in the moonlight. "What are you doing here?"

"I followed you. I was outside your home debating about knocking and waking up your family when I saw you slip out. What are you doing out here at this time of night?"

"I. . .I couldn't sleep."

Richard sat down beside her. "We have to talk."

"*Sí.*"

"I'm attracted to you, Isabela, but I can't consider marriage, at least not now. I'm responsible for too many things. A romance, a marriage, would take away from my work."

"I was joking about the marriage."

Richard knitted his eyebrows.

"All right, yes, my father would have insisted you marry me if you kissed me."

A crooked grin lifted his lips.

"You know my family customs very well."

"I grew up here. I've known several Hispanic families. Most were from Cuba, but there are some from other countries."

"With the cigar industry there are many of us here now." She hesitated. "What are you going to do about Manuel's letter? He says he can wait no longer for you to send the money."

Richard picked up a stone and tossed it into the waves. "I don't know. Just today a man offered to give me a loan to get the boat out of Havana. I might have to take him up on it, although the paperwork he sent me looks like a study in legal double-talk."

"I'm so sorry. At the time I thought it unfair of Manuel to offer such a thing to you. My father fought with him for a long time on the matter, but Manuel could not be moved."

"Thank you for telling me that."

"I'm glad you understand our ways."

"We have a few of our own, also. But growing up here, I've learned a lot about the various cultures that exist in the world. Back on the farmstead in upper New York State, we were all the same, our families going back many generations."

"In Cuba, it is that way, also."

Richard picked up a handful of sand and let it stream through his fingers. "What brought your family here from Cuba?"

"Work. Papá got a job rolling cigars. He felt there might be more opportunities for him here. But he does just the same as he did back in Cuba."

"Do you want to return to Cuba?"

"No, I like it here. I like the freedoms."

Richard placed his hand on hers. "Isabela, if someone sees us talking, your father would insist we get engaged."

"I know, but I also enjoy speaking with you."

"And I enjoy speaking with you." He kissed the top of her hand. "Shall I ask permission to escort you to dinner some evening?"

"No, Richard, then Papá would not allow me to work for you."

"Wouldn't you like to see if we could develop a relationship?"

"Yes, very much, but you don't understand. In order for me to not be paired off with someone, I had to get a job. My father is ready to have me married. It's not that I object to marriage—I would like to get married one day. It's just that I want to marry for love. Oh, I know I could eventually fall in love with the man Papá would choose, and he would choose wisely. But I guess I've lived in this country long enough to want what others have."

He released her hand. "I understand, and I will not ask your father. But I can't continue to dishonor your father by talking with you. Mr. Bower has asked me if you might be interested in doing some bookwork for him. And I believe there will be others. Perhaps if you start working for a variety of businesses, we might then be free to explore a relationship."

"Didn't you just say you didn't have time for a romance?" *Why is he trying to find other work for me? Am I not doing a good enough job?*

Richard grabbed another handful of sand. "Okay, so my willpower hasn't caught up to my brain yet. If we continue talking with each other, your parents will not be happy."

"True."

"What's the answer? Do I ask to court you so that we can talk?" Richard well understood the custom; if he asked to court Isabela, that would mean he was also interested in marriage.

"That won't work. We'd have to be chaperoned every minute we were together."

"All right, then we won't talk about anything except business. . .or what's left of my business."

"How are you going to get the money to get your boat back from Manuel? Will you take it from your savings? Manuel said he would take the other man's offer by the end of the month."

"I honestly don't know. I'll have to keep praying and seeking the Lord's wisdom because I'm fresh out."

"Would you like my father to talk with Manuel?"

"No, I don't think that will help. I can't blame Manuel, and since some of the islanders have made it clear that it will be a good sixty days before they have all the debts cleared, I understand his concerns."

"I don't understand," Isabela continued cautiously, "how you could go to

Cuba on good faith and not only leave your ship there for the others but use up your own funds as well, and no one seems to notice."

"Some notice, but I guess I believe in what the Bible says about your right hand not knowing what your left hand is doing."

"Richard, you've put yourself and your uncle's business at risk extending help to others."

"I know, and the Bible also says not to be a lender. I'm not sure where I went wrong or how to balance the needs of everyone and my own."

"I'll pray for you." Isabela covered his hand with hers and gave it a gentle squeeze.

He captured her fingers with his own. "Isabela," he whispered.

She placed her other hand gently across his mouth. "Shh, don't say it."

Richard closed his eyes and nodded. "Let me walk you home." Richard got up and extended his hand.

"Gracías, but I better go on my own."

His fingers slipped through hers, leaving a burning path of desire. How could they obey her parents and still get to know one another?

And how can I fight my growing desires for him? She looked up at the stars and fired off yet another prayer for the Lord to help.

Richard followed Isabela at a distance. While she didn't seem to need his protection, he'd be less of a man if he didn't watch over her. And who was he fooling anyway? He was attracted to her to the point of wanting to pursue a relationship, although a commitment of marriage at this point seemed completely out of the question. The idea of being married to Isabela wasn't a negative prospect, he had to admit, but he wasn't ready to take on the responsibilities of a wife. At least not until he settled what he was going to do with his life. Would Isabela even be interested in moving north if he should decide to stay on the farm? Or would she like the idea of going west and settling the untamed land? All things one would need to talk about long before they fell in love, he hoped.

Isabela slid through her open front door and waved.

Richard stifled a chuckle. She knew he had followed her home. He worked his way back through the streets to his own home.

A light burned dimly in Cook's room. "Hang on, Cook," he whispered as he walked by.

The next morning Richard brought the legal documents to a lawyer. As he suspected, the interest was high; and the slightest delay in payment would not only forfeit the boat to Marc Dabney, but the business could ultimately be lost to him as well. A loan from Marc Dabney on those conditions was totally out of the question. Even if he lost the boat to Manuel, he'd still own the business.

Richard washed the sponges in the vat. The dock was now rebuilt. The debris from his building had been taken away, but there would be no funds for reconstruction for awhile. At least not until the end of the summer, possibly longer.

Richard watched Mo bring in his skiff. "Good haul, Mo."

"Thank ye, Richard." Mo paddled the boat to the dock. "How'd your meeting with the lawyer go?"

"Fine. Unfortunately, I was reading the papers correctly."

"Sorry to hear that. What are you going to do?"

Mo lifted his sponges onto the dock.

"Not much I can do. If I take the loan, I could possibly lose the business and the boat. If I let Manuel sell the boat, then I only lose the *Sea Dove*."

"Doesn't sound like an easy answer."

"Nope, but there are some men who might not be able to pay back their debt in time. Even if everyone who owes me paid me the cash I paid out, instead of ordering my own materials, I'm still taking too large of a risk."

"I wish there was something I could do. I have some savings, but I don't think it will help you much."

"Thanks, Mo, but unless it's more than thirty-five thousand, it won't help. And even then it wouldn't give me the amount I need to rebuild." He did have other assets, but to cash them would quite possibly cause other problems. No, he'd have to take the lesser of the two evils; it was his only realistic option.

"I wish I had the answer, Richard." Mo secured the nets full of sponges to the pilings for drying. "If you don't mind, I'm going to go home and clean up, then relieve my wife."

"No, please go. I wish I could be there with Cook."

"You'll be there tonight. I still have trouble picturing Francine lying in her bed. I can't imagine you'll get much sleep with all of us coming in to take care of her."

"Sleep is the least of my worries."

"I'll see you back at your house later, then." Mo waved good-bye and walked down the dock.

With all his worries about the business, he hadn't been giving Cook much thought this morning. "I suppose that's because Lizzy is taking care of her, Lord."

When Richard finished cleaning up the dock from the day's labor, he headed for home. What he didn't expect to see was a house full of strangers, the kitchen full of food, and Isabela giving orders.

"Thank you, Mrs. Williams. Tell Pastor Williams we appreciate the prayers. I'll give your messages and the food to the family," Isabela said, receiving the pot of food.

"What's going on here?" Richard whispered, standing behind her and giving Mrs. Williams a polite smile.

"People have been coming all day, bringing notes of encouragement, flowers, food. . . . It's absolutely amazing."

George Hunte, Cook's son, leaned up against a wall. "How is she, George?" Richard asked.

"She's doing better. Some color is back, and she's able to talk some." George rubbed his large brown hand over his face.

"Do you think it's all right if I go in?" Richard asked.

"She's been asking for you all day. You best go in," George answered.

"Thanks." Richard stepped closer to Cook's room, took in a deep breath, and twisted the doorknob. "Cook?"

"Richie, come here." His heart beat wildly in his chest when he heard how she slurred her words together. She looked so pale, so ashen, so lifeless. *God, give me strength.*

He knelt down beside her. "I'm here, Cook."

"I love you, Son. Don't fret. I'm going to get out of this bed. The good Lord ain't done with me yet."

A shadow of a laugh buried itself in his throat. "I love you too, Cook. I'm glad you're feeling better.

Chapter 9

Isabela retreated to the office. Where were all these people coming from? It seemed like just about everyone on the island had stopped by to express their concern. Thankfully, Lizzy guarded her mother's need for rest as patiently and tactfully as anyone she'd ever seen. Isabela discovered she harbored an appreciation for the refined schoolteacher. Several of her students had gone on to college.

Isabela checked her figures one last time, then closed the ledgers for the day. Richard's cash balance for salaries was getting mighty low. Perhaps he was concerned about how to pay everyone their salaries and that was why he suggested she work for others. Truth be told, unless he had other work for her, she would be spending a lot of hours doing nothing.

Maybe Richard merely treated her like he did everyone else, kindly and generously, thinking of others before himself.

Lord, it's my emotions getting in the way. He's trying to do what's right and I'm resenting him because of my attraction to him. Isabela's hands shook. Was it time to admit to her mother that her feelings for Richard were getting difficult to control?

"Isabela." Richard stepped into the room and closed the door.

"Richard, the door," Isabela's voice cracked.

He turned and opened it halfway. "Better?"

"Yes, thank you."

"You're welcome. About last night. . ."

"Shh, you mustn't speak of it. Would you contact Señor Bower for me and see when I might be able to start work for him?"

"Will you still work for me?"

"*Sí,* but only one day a week. Perhaps Señor Bower's friends can hire me for other jobs."

"Isabela, you don't have to leave."

"Richard, have you looked at your cash flow lately?"

"Yes. I know it's low, but I should have some payments coming in soon."

"You'll need them. I've got your books up to date, and I think my coming in once a week will keep them in order."

"You're very good, Isabela. I will certainly recommend you to others."

She didn't want his recommendation; she wanted his love. "Thank you. I enjoy working with numbers."

"I do too, but I haven't had much time for it lately." Richard's smile sent a flutter down her spine.

"What are you going to do about Manuel?"

"I reckon he'll be owning a boat at the end of thirty days."

"I'm so sorry, Richard. What about the loan?"

"Unless we can renegotiate another contract, it isn't in my best interest to borrow the monies."

"Again, I am sorry. I somehow feel responsible because Manuel is my cousin."

Richard stepped closer and placed his hand upon hers. "This isn't your fault."

Isabela wove her fingers with his. She knew she shouldn't, but her love and compassion for this man grew moment by moment. His blue-gray eyes ignited with passion. He stepped closer, behind the desk, beside her.

"Richard," she whispered.

"My sweet Isabela, you—"

"Shh." She pressed her fingers to his lips. "Don't. Not now, not yet."

"How long?"

Her entire body trembled. She turned away. She couldn't resist him and look into his handsome face. "We must be patient; we must wait."

"I will ask your father's permission to court you."

"No, not yet. I. . .I. . ."

"All right, Isabela, I'll wait."

She turned back to him and saw his head bent down, his left hand clutched in a fist, the right clenching the edge of his desk.

"When will you come back to work for me?" he asked, not looking at her.

"How does Thursdays sound? I can do your payroll on Thursday and you can give the men their pay on Friday."

"That will be fine. I'll see you Thursday." He lifted his head and looked at her now. His eyes were dull and unfocused.

"Thank you, Richard. I'm sorry about everything."

"*Buenas noches*, Isabela."

"*Buenos noches.*" She picked up her purse and headed out of the office.

The house bulged with people. Some folks she recognized, others she didn't. Everyone seemed to be talking together in small groups.

"It's a shame," said a thin woman, perhaps in her forties, who stood wagging her head from side to side. "Don't seem right. Cook's been there for so many of us. We ought to be able to do something."

"Ain't that the truth." A young black man shuffled his feet. "But we's can pray. Cook be glad to hear me sayin' that."

"That woman could pray a tortoise out of its shell. But you're right, we can pray for her."

The small group grasped each other's hands and went into prayer.

Lord, be with Cook; give her strength; make her comfortable. Isabela added her own silent prayer. She continued to work her way through the maze of people.

As she opened the door, she turned around and found Richard standing on the stairs watching her. An awkward moment passed between them. She took in a deep breath and walked out of the house.

Richard fought the desire to run after Isabela. She seemed so vulnerable. How could he call himself a man of honor when he continually put her in compromising situations?

He turned and continued his flight up the stairs. His emotions were wreaking havoc with his peaceful existence. He was glad to see Cook determined to fight and live a bit longer, but she still seemed so frail to him. In all the years he'd known her, he only remembered a handful of times when she'd been sick.

He'd scheduled a meeting with Marc Dabny at his office this evening. What he wanted to do was call Marc a thief with his ridiculous offer, but what he needed to do was try to renegotiate the contract. If Marc wouldn't budge, then he'd walk away. He couldn't sacrifice the entire business for a loss of thirty-five thousand dollars.

Richard found a fresh set of clothes on his bed and clean towels in his room. Even with all the people in the house, it somehow seemed cleaner. Lizzy must have been cleaning all day, just trying to keep from worrying about her mother. Nanna was like that too, always cleaning when something was on her mind. Richard grinned, remembering the time Cook forced Nanna to stop cleaning one day. *"You're gonna wear a hole clear through that floor if you don't stop scrubbin' it."*

Nanna sat down in the puddle of water. "I just can't stop thinking about it."

Cook waddled over and sat down in a chair beside her. "Ain't nothin' you can do by frettin' about it. What's done is done. Now, trust the good Lord to make it right."

Richard sat on the edge of his bed. *What is done is done.* Possibly he shouldn't have turned his vessel over to Manuel, but it was done. The men on the island who owed Manuel money for the supplies should be more concerned about paying their debts in a timely manner, but what was done was done. Richard knew the risks when he'd used his boat as collateral. Now he just needed to make wise decisions, and signing Marc Dabny's contract as it was wasn't wise.

He buttoned his shirt and put on his bow tie. He ran a finger through his collar to remove some of the pressure from the foolish contraption. *Who invented these things anyway?* He looked at his image in the mirror. It did make him appear older, more businesslike, but who would wear these things willingly? A final brush of his hair and he stepped out of his room and reentered the sea of humanity filling his home. All these folks were here, not for gossip, but to show their love and appreciation for Cook. Richard's throat tightened. A tear stung the corner of his right eye.

Politely, he greeted several folks and made his way out of the house. He took in a deep breath and headed for Marc Dabny's office.

" 'Evening, Richard," Marc greeted him as he walked through the office door. "Did you look over my proposal?"

"Yes, Sir. And, as it is now, I can't accept it. However, if you're willing to make some changes, we might have something to discuss."

"Excellent. Set yourself down there and let's go over it, shall we?" Marc's smile seemed way too friendly. Richard fought the stiffness of his spine and sat down across from Marc's massive mahogany desk.

Marc's round belly pulled some of his shirt buttons tight when he sat down. "So, what are the items you'd like to discuss?"

"The lien you'd put on the business if the payments weren't made in sixty days. In fact, the way you have it worded, it appears that with the slightest delay, you'd own Southard Sponges."

"Hmm, let me look. I had my attorney draw these up. Let's see how he worded it."

Richard watched Marc scan the pages and stop at the appropriate spot. "This is pretty standard, Richard. If I lend you the money, I need to have something to guarantee that if you are unable to pay me back for some reason, I'll have ownership of something to sell and recoup my loss."

"I understand that. But look at the line that says you will own everything relating to the business. That's unacceptable. The business and its property I might be able to see, but our house and our land is above and beyond the value of the loan. Even the waterfront property is worth more than you've valued it at. And the value of the business is four times what you've put on the contract."

"Hmm, perhaps we can remove the house and the land, but the value of the business, I'm not sure. Seems to me, without the boat, the business isn't worth much."

"The boat is an asset to the business, but its value does not exceed the value of the business. I can transport the sponges on other vessels as I've been doing for the past couple weeks. Granted it's easier and a higher profit to ship the shipments myself but—"

Marc raised his hand. "I see. Let me think. I'd really like to help you out here."

"That's not my only concern about the contract, Mr. Dabny. The interest rate is extremely high, and the time to pay off the debt seems awfully short."

Marc drummed his fingers on the desk. "Let's see. . . . What if I give you ninety days?"

"Possibly." Richard eased back in the chair.

"I'd have to increase the interest."

Richard wanted to scream, but the better part of wisdom and self-control took over. He set himself for a long night of negotiations.

After a couple hours, he left Marc's office, none too certain they would work out an acceptable agreement between them. For everything Marc conceded, he would add another stipulation. Richard agreed to see the new contract after it was drawn up, but he wasn't hopeful.

He undid his bow tie and let the ends drape down his shirt. His stomach growled. He hadn't bothered to eat before he went to see Marc. Now he was happy his kitchen overflowed with baked goods.

" 'Evening, Richard. You were out late." Lizzy stood in the doorway of the kitchen.

"Yeah, had a business meeting. What's good here?"

Lizzy chuckled. "Set yourself down and I'll serve you."

"No, you've done quite enough. Sit down and tell me about your day." Richard smiled. "I'm an expert at raiding the kitchen—just ask your mother."

"I have no doubt about that. I couldn't keep Benjamin out of the kitchen for a spell. That boy sure could eat."

Richard grabbed some fried chicken, biscuits, and salad.

"Are you sure you have enough?" Lizzy seated herself in the old oak chair.

"No, I'll probably go back for some of that pie and possibly some guava pastries over there."

"Richie, Mo told me you had an offer from Marc Dabny."

"Yup. Ain't a good one, but he made me an offer."

Lizzy played with the edges of the tablecloth.

"Why do you ask?" Richard put down his chicken and wiped his fingers on a linen napkin.

"I don't know if I should be saying this, but I think you might want to know. Your uncle had an offer from Mr. Dabny years ago. He turned him down."

"Marc said something about that. Didn't appear to be any ill will on his part."

Lizzy bit her lower lip.

"Miss Lizzy, what aren't you telling me?"

Chapter 10

Richard mulled over the information Lizzy had shared with him last night. Marc Dabney's lack of respect for black people certainly said something about his character. A nagging suspicion that Marc Dabney had waited twenty years to get his hands on the sponge business began to form. Illogical or not, Richard couldn't shake his suspicion. Renewed pride for his uncle formed when he heard about Marc Dabney's rude behavior toward Lizzy and how Ellis ended the matter.

"Sin abounds in the world, but each of us must choose how we will live out our own lives." He could almost hear his uncle's words of exhortation, telling him not to be like others, to be himself, his own man, not swayed by other's perceptions. The advice had served him well in college when duties of the farm and studies kept him from raising Cain with the other students.

Richard rubbed the tension from his temples. He'd been doing too much thinking. He decided to check in on Cook as a change of pace.

"Good morning, Cook. How are you feeling today?" He sat down beside her bed in the small rocker Lizzy spent her time in.

"Better." Cook rolled over to her side and faced him, her hair pushed back under a scarf. "Now, what's been keeping you up late these past few nights?"

Richard smiled. "How'd you know? Never mind." Ever since he arrived on Key West, Cook had a way of knowing things most others didn't. She also watched over this house like a hawk protecting its young.

"Richie, it would take a fool not to notice. I may be stuck in this here bed for awhile, but I'm not deaf, at least not yet."

"You know I put the boat up as collateral in Havana."

Cook nodded her silver-crowned head.

"Apparently someone's offering to buy the boat, and the thirty days is nearly up. Several of the men on the island can't pay yet. Which doesn't surprise me, but I thought Manuel and I had an understanding that it could take a few months. In any case, he's of a mind to take up the offer, and Marc Dabney is offering a loan to allow me to get the boat back. But the loan is certain death to the business if I can't pay in time."

"Never trusted that man. Not from the first moment he stepped in this yard trying to court Bea."

"Nanna?"

"Yup. He decided she'd make him a good wife. What he had in mind for a wife was a maid, to put it nicely."

"Lizzy shared with me another incident."

Cook chuckled, then coughed.

Richard placed his hand on her shoulder. "Are you okay?"

"I'm fine. Can't laugh too well, yet. And it's as you say, I was never more proud of your uncle than that day."

"I've pretty much ruled out Marc Dabney's offer, which means I'll lose the boat."

"I'm sorry to hear that, Richie. Seems to me those men who owe ought to help out somehow."

"I spent hours talking with them. Some wished they could help. Others just about said it was my own fault for putting the boat up, which is probably true; but shouldn't they at least be appreciating the fact that I put my business at risk to help theirs?"

"Would be nice, but we aren't always rewarded here on earth."

"True. Anyway, that's what has been on my mind."

"Oh, I thought perhaps it had something to do with a certain pretty young lady who's been working in your office every day."

Richard sent his gaze heavenward.

Cook grasped his hand. "Richie, I know their customs, and I know you aren't being disrespectful, but there's been a certain look in those blue-gray eyes of yours, something very similar to your uncle's eyes when he first met your nanna."

Richard groaned.

"Tell me it ain't so and I'll leave it be."

Richard gazed at the small oriental rug below his feet.

"Thought so. I might be getting close to leaving this here place, but I'm not losing my touch."

"Cook, I can't. I gave my word, and if I were to ask to court her, I'd lose her as an employee. Not that she'll be working much for me now, but still, Isabela says it's not the right time to ask."

"She'd know. Respect her wishes, Richard. Honor the Lord and He'll work it out."

"Yes, Ma'am."

Cook rolled onto her back. "Can I get you anything?" he asked.

"No. I'm just not as strong as I thought. Son, I love you as if you were my own, you know that."

Richard nodded. "I love you too."

Cook's smile tugged at his heart. He fought the thought of her leaving him. She continued. "You're stuck like a conch in his shell. You may lose the boat, you might even lose the business, but God always takes care of His children. All we can do is walk with our heads high and know we are doing what is right. You do that and you'll be fine."

"Thanks, Cook. I won't refuse any prayers you think to send my way."

"Already sent, but I'll send some more. Now, leave me, Son. I need to rest if'n I'm gettin' out of this bed before I meet the good Lord."

Richard bent over Cook and kissed her on the forehead. The delicate mahogany of her skin tone had returned. She might be tired, but she was better than she had been. "I'll check in on you later."

Cook blinked and closed her eyes again. Sleep was good, he reassured himself as he slipped out of the room. He closed the door to his office and knelt down on the floor. "Father, give me strength. Help Cook, and lead me down the right path with the business."

He paused and listened to the silence of the house, his eyes closed, and he focused on images of heaven with God seated upon His throne and the crystal stream flowing from underneath it. "Help me, Lord."

Isabela didn't bother to knock any longer. With Cook sick and Richard always at the dock, there didn't seem to be a need. She opened the office door. "Richard? Oh. . .sorry." She closed the door. Wasn't he supposed to be at the docks, not bent over in prayer in the middle of the office? Not that praying was a bad thing—she just didn't expect to see him there. "Cook?"

Isabela rushed to Cook's room. Lizzy sat peacefully rocking beside her mother's bed. Cook appeared to be sleeping. "How is she?" Isabela whispered.

"Fine, she's been sitting up this morning. She's taking a nap now. How are you?"

"Fine." But was she? She'd spent the entire night awake, pacing back and forth. Was it right for her not to tell her mother of the growing awareness between herself and Richard? She had promised. Of course, she only promised to say something when the emotions became hard to handle. But was she handling them?

Feeling awkward, she stepped back into the hallway.

Richard stood in the doorway of his office, his arms crossed over his chest. His silky golden curls and blue-gray eyes made her shiver in appreciation. "Good morning," she stuttered.

"Buenos días. Como estás?"

"Bien. I'm sorry, Richard, I had no idea you were in there."

"Nonsense, nothing wrong with walking in on a man praying." Richard moved aside so she could enter the office. "I've decided not to take the loan from Marc Dabney."

"All right." She sat behind the desk and sorted through a stack of papers on which Mo had scribbled the men's hauls for the past week. "Does this mean you'll lose the ship?"

"Most likely, unless the Lord has a miracle I'm unaware of."

"I'm sorry. I don't understand Manuel."

"He's a businessman. He might be taking advantage of an unfortunate event, but he's not being totally unreasonable."

"He should never have asked you to use your boat. He's done enough business with people from Key West to know they will pay their bills eventually."

"True, but we don't know what kind of strains his business might have been under. He might not have had the financial backing to float the credit for as long as some obviously needed."

"I hadn't thought about that."

Richard smiled, and Isabela felt gooseflesh rise from her toes to the top of her head. She broke their gaze and looked back at the sheets of paper.

He stepped closer and placed his hand on hers. "My Bella. . ."

"Mr. Southard, come quick," she heard someone calling from the yard.

Richard bolted and left her quivering from his closeness. *How could I have fallen so quickly for this man?*

Isabela stepped up to the window and brushed the sheer curtains aside to glimpse the stranger. Richard's golden curls bobbed as he ran with the man back toward town. What could have happened? she wondered.

She sat back down behind the desk. A gentle knock on the door caused her to look up. "Yes, Lizzy?"

"What was that all about?"

"I don't know. Richard ran toward town with some man."

Lizzy grasped the doorway. "Mo," she whispered.

"Oh, I don't think it was about your husband. Don't you think Richard would have come in if it were about him?"

Lizzy sighed. "You're right." She sat down in one of the office chairs. "Ever since Mother collapsed, I've been overly concerned about everything."

"Seems only natural." Isabela put down the payroll papers. "I can't keep my mind on work. Care for a cup of tea?"

"Sounds wonderful. Let me tell Mother, and I'll join you in the kitchen."

"Great."

"Oh, and pick out some of those fancy pastries the folks have been bringing by. It's horrible for my waistline, but they are delicious." Lizzy winked.

Isabela wouldn't mind having another guava roll herself. She'd walk home a bit faster tonight and work it off. In the kitchen she set the kettle on the stove and prepared the table with some bone china teacups. Bea Southard's collection of fine china was more than she'd ever seen before. Each was hand painted and of the finest workmanship.

"Pretty, aren't they?" Lizzy commented as she took her seat at the table.

"Very. Where'd she get them all?"

"Several were wedding gifts, the rest are a collection she had started as a child. Her father would indulge her on her birthdays."

"Do you know Mrs. Southard well?"

"Yes. She's possibly my closest friend. We've been friends for twenty years.

I wish she and Ellis hadn't moved back to New York, even if it is temporary."

"Why did they move back?"

"For James's education. Ellis had cared for the property until Richard became of age. Now that it's been in Richard's care, I wonder if it wasn't to check up on how the poor boy would handle the business. Of course, there were never prouder parents. Richard had increased the farm's profit considerably. I guess Richard has to decide if he wants to stay in Key West and work the family business or go back to New York and work the farmstead."

Richard in New York. . .oh dear. Isabela's knees weakened. She flopped into the other chair. "I didn't know he was planning on returning to New York."

"It won't be for awhile. Of course, Ellis and Bea should be returning early in the fall. Bea doesn't want to go back to those cold winters after living down here for so long. One winter is enough."

"Is this her first time back in New York?"

"Oh, mercy, no, Child. They've been back several times. My Daniel would watch over their business, and they would enjoy themselves for a long vacation."

The kettle whistled. Lizzy retrieved it and poured out the steaming water. Isabela stared, focusing on nothing. If she married Richard, would she have to move to New York? Away from her family? To a place so foreign it had snow? Isabela shook at the mere thought of weather that cold.

"Are you all right, Dear?"

"Fine, fine." Isabela sipped the piping hot brew. "I could never live in snow," she mumbled.

Lizzy sat up tall and set a piercing gaze at Isabela. "What?"

⬥

Richard gasped for air as he tried to catch his wind. "What's wrong, Mo?" It didn't appear he was injured, something that had run through his mind as he ran to the dock.

"Ye better have a look at this, Richard." Mo leaned over the newly built dock and pulled up the lines that held the skiffs. Each of them was cut clean through.

"What?"

"Appears someone took off with all your skiffs last night."

"Did you call for the sheriff?"

"Yes, Sir, then ye."

"Thanks." Richard leaned against a piling and raked his unruly curls with his fingers, pushing the wayward strands off his face. "Why would anyone steal our skiffs? They aren't worth much, and you certainly can't go too far in them."

"Beats me. But some folks ain't thinkin' like they should since the fire. Most have come together and worked for each other, but there seems to be a small group of folks just set on bemoaning their woes."

"That's true enough." Richard had observed the same reactions in some of the islanders.

The sheriff soon arrived, and after taking a brief description of the stolen skiffs, he offered little hope. He figured whoever had stolen them would have sailed out of port with them in tow. He'd put the word out to the captains to be on the lookout, but he didn't expect much help from them.

Okay, Lord, I must be missing something here. First, I get word that the Sea Dove *will be sold in Havana unless I can offer to pay the debt in full. Now this? What else could go wrong? Should I merely give up and go back to New York? Is that what You want?* Richard pinched the bridge of his nose and tried to concentrate. He knew God wasn't a vengeful God, but events like the past couple weeks were trying his faith.

Mo went home; after all, there was no work. Without the skiffs, Mo couldn't bring in more sponges, and if he couldn't bring in more sponges, Richard didn't have any revenue; without revenue, the business would fail. Richard slowly made his way around the waterfront, looking for any boats he'd be able to possibly buy. Even one would help some.

"Ahoy, Pete, how was the fishing today?" Richard asked a local fisherman unloading his haul of lobsters.

"Not bad." Pete rubbed the stubble on his chin and squinted as he looked up at Richard on the dock. "Heard your boats were stolen last night. Is it true?"

"Afraid so."

"I have an old dingy at the house. Ain't much, has a leak I never got around to fixin', but you're welcome to borrow it if you think it will help."

"Thanks, I may just take you up on it." Richard looked down the docks. So many ships. . . Some moored out in the harbor, others bound to the docks, and not another one had been stolen. If he didn't know better, he'd swear someone was out to ruin him.

"Ain't much, as I said, but it's something. Ellis helped me out a time or two. I'd be happy to tow the dingy out in the morning to save you some time. You might be able to get two runs in that way."

"That's a generous offer. I appreciate it. Thanks."

"Like I said, Ellis was kind to me on more than one occasion."

Richard shook Pete's tanned, leathery hand and continued his search.

As he walked closer toward the naval base, he saw Emile Fernandez marching toward him. His determined strides and the tight set to his jaw made Richard brace for a frontal assault. Had Emile heard about his moments with Isabela?

"Señor Richard, I need a word with you."

"*Buenos días,* Señor Fernandez, *como está?*"

"*Bien.* . . No, I'm not good. I'm angry. My blood is—how you say—boiling red?" The short man seemed taller.

"Just boiling."

"*Sí,* boiling."

"What is the matter?" As if he didn't know. He'd nearly kissed Isabela, he'd spoken with her privately on more than one occasion, and he'd touched her hand

Chapter 11

"Mima, what do you mean, Papá ran out of the house looking for Señor Southard?"

"What have you done, *Niña?*"

"Nothing, I swear. We spoke privately, but no one saw us, I'm sure of it." Isabela's entire body started to shake. She'd seen her father this angry once before. She'd never known what happened that time. He and her mother never spoke about it again, at least not in front of her.

"When?"

"The other night. I couldn't sleep, so I took a walk. He found me at the beach."

Yolanda pulled Isabela down to sit beside her. "I asked you to tell me if you started to feel—"

"I know, Mima," Isabela broke in. "But I can control my feelings. They aren't at the place where I cannot."

"If your father has heard about you and Señor Southard, you do realize you will be engaged?"

"*Sí.*" *Oh, Lord, please let it not be so. If Richard and I are meant to be together, please don't have it happen in this way. I would never know if he truly loved me or was just being an honorable man.*

"I'm not going to be working for Richard more than a single day a week. Señor Bower also has some bookwork that he'd like me to do."

"Have you failed Señor Richard?"

"No, Mima, but I can't talk to you about his personal finances."

"Oh, *sí*, I understand." Yolanda held her daughter's hand. "Do you love him?"

"I don't know. I'm attracted to him, but how can you love a man when you can't even talk to him to get to know him?"

"There are ways." Yolanda winked.

"Mima, what are you saying?"

"That even within our culture there are ways to learn about a man before one is courted by him."

"How? Please tell me. I don't want to bring dishonor to you and to Papá."

Yolanda chuckled. "I suppose I've been remiss from teaching you the ways of learning about men. But you've never seemed interested before. Richard is special, no?"

"*Sí*, Mima, very special." And her feelings for him were growing day by day.

"How do you know this?"

"I've watched him and how he relates to others, how he's conducted his business. He's a very fair man."

"Perhaps you don't need your mother's instructions at all." Yolanda grinned.

"Oh, Mima, please tell me. How can I get to know Señor Richard without bringing dishonor to the family?"

"If you haven't already, you mean."

Isabela's stomach prickled as if she'd swallowed a sea urchin whole.

"If your father is not already upset with Señor Richard, then you should continue to observe him, as you've been doing. How he relates to other people in good and bad situations shows how he will relate to a wife. This is not always the case, of course. There are men who put up a wonderful image in public, but in private would beat their wives or worse. But I don't believe Señor Richard would be this way."

"Oh no, Mima, he's very kind. He waits on Cook as if she were his grandmother. I walked in on him praying for Cook. There were tears in his eyes."

"*Sí*, this is what I mean by observing. How does he react to situations? You've been with him when Manuel insisted his boat be used as collateral; you saw how he responded. You know more than most about his personal finances. How does he handle his money?"

Isabela opened her mouth to tell her mother once again that she could not share such knowledge.

Yolanda raised her hand. "No, Dear, I was not asking you to tell me. Examine for yourself how he handles his money. Where he spends it reveals his heart."

Isabela thought of the generous loans he'd made to some of the men on Key West. Of how well he paid his workers. . .yes, he was a generous man. And seldom did he purchase items for himself. Almost all of his expenses were for the business or his home. "*Sí*, Mima, he has a good heart, a generous heart."

"*Bien*. Now, when you decide this man is the man you would like to court, you need to approach your papá and me. Your papá will decide if he is worthy of your affections."

"But Mima, we live in America now. Can't I decide for myself?"

"Haven't you already? By letting us know you are interested in Señor Richard, haven't you told us your heart?"

"*Sí*, but—"

"Hush, *Niña*. Trust your papá and me. We will pray. I have already begun."

"Oh, Mima, I don't know. I'm so confused. To have Richard near me. . .my bones soften like a jellyfish."

"Ah, then I suggest you decide quickly. Courtship takes time."

"But Señor Richard—he isn't ready for courtship. He's a busy man."

Yolanda raised her right eyebrow. Her rich black hair, pulled back, accented her hazelnut complexion. "You have spoken with Señor Richard about such matters?"

"Señor Richard, what do you have to be sorry for? It is my cousin Manuel I am angry with. I have heard he wants to sell your ship, is it true?"

"He has a buyer, yes." Richard relaxed his stance. *I guess I won't be getting married today*, he silently thanked the Lord. Although the idea of having someone as warm and passionate as Isabela for a wife was not a discomforting thought.

"I will go to Cuba and I will speak with my cousin." Emile planted his hands firmly on his hips. The man was ready for war. Richard couldn't help but be pleased that Emile wanted to fight for him and not against him.

"No, it isn't necessary. Manuel won't sell the boat until the thirty days are up. He assured me in his letter he wouldn't be doing that."

"He should not hold you responsible for other men's debts. It is not fair."

"I signed the paper knowing the risk. Unfortunately, some of the men who owe the money do not have the cash to pay their bills in full within that thirty days." Not to mention the debts some owed him.

"Is it true that your fleet of sponge boats was stolen last night?"

"Yes."

Emile wagged his head. "I've never understood stealing."

"It isn't something I could imagine doing either." Except for that time when he was six years old and stole a pocket full of penny candy from Old Man Bennett's store. Richard unconsciously rubbed his backside from the memory. Uncle Ellis made certain he would never steal again.

"I shall ask my friends and see if anyone has some boats to sell."

"I'm afraid I don't have the funds to purchase any additional skiffs at the moment. Perhaps after I get a shipment of sponges off to market, then I will be able to."

"Was your money in the bank that burned down?"

"No." Thank the Lord for that blessing. "But the cost of the building supplies has stretched my resources."

Emile rubbed the day's growth on his chin. "Perhaps some of my friends can loan you a boat."

"I won't be turning down an offer like that. If you find someone, have them come to my house and we will make arrangements."

"*Sí*, I can do that. It's the least I can do for the way my family has treated you."

Without waiting for a response from Richard, Emile marched back toward town with the same determined steps.

Richard blew out a relieved breath. *That was close.* He would have to be more careful with Isabela. His business was on the brink of failure; meanwhile, he was spending his free moments remembering the lily of the ruins, her long wavy black hair cascading down her shoulders and back.

Stop it. He didn't have time for daydreaming.

"Richard," Mo called. The huge black man came toward him with giant strides. Mo was head and shoulders taller than most men, but he also had the most tender heart Richard had ever seen in a man.

"Mo, what brings you here?"

"I've been lookin' for you. I brought my boat to your dock; it's fully loaded with some sponges. I went out and brought in a haul. Benjamin came out with me and lent me a hand. I'm hopin' we have enough time to go out again."

"You went out and brought in a haul?" He didn't know why this should surprise him. Mo had always been a valuable employee.

"Just did what a man ought to, given the situation. If we get these sponges soakin', we might be able to have a good haul to go out with Bower's ship first part of next week."

"I hope so. We need the money."

"I figured you'd be hard pressed soon. Don't understand why those folks who owe you aren't borrowin' the money from the banks and payin' ye back. Don't make sense."

"I didn't ask them to."

"Ye shouldn't have to. A man should just do it." Mo nodded his head once for emphasis, and Richard knew that was the end of the matter.

"Let's get to the docks and unload your skiff."

"I'm sure Ben has it all done by now. But he and I need to be gettin' out there if we're going to take in another haul today."

Richard looked at the placement of the sun. They had about four hours until sunset. "Tell you what, if you go out again, promise me you'll be back before sunset whether your nets are full or not."

"That won't be a problem. Ben's wife, Edith, would be none to pleased if we weren't back before then."

Richard chuckled. There were advantages to being single. A man was his own man. He could do what he wanted, when he wanted it, and didn't have to fret over being home at a certain time or not.

"I'll have these rinsed and ready for drying by the time you get back."

Mo waved as he stepped down into the small sailing skiff. With the late afternoon breeze, Mo and Ben would be out to the harvesting area in a much shorter time. Richard rubbed the kinks out of the back of his neck. Perhaps he should consider changing the type of vessels he used to gather the sponges. The small steam engines they were making now could enhance a craft's ability to get the workers out to the gathering area each day.

"Enough dreaming," he muttered. "If you don't get to work, you aren't going to have the money to buy anything."

Several hours later, he pulled at the net heavily laden with damp sea sponges. Placing it on the center of the dock, he began to squeeze the seawater out in order to put them in the fresh water tanks.

"Lord, help me. I don't know what to do regarding the business. Should I sell it while there is something to sell?"

Isabela worked her fingers over the dress she'd been trying to sew all afternoon. Anything to try and keep herself busy and her mind not on her father's anger. "How could he have found out?" she murmured.

She nibbled her lower lip. Did she know enough about Richard to want to pursue a relationship with him? She'd skirted around her mother's question. But her mother was a wise woman; she knew Isabela had talked with Richard about such personal matters. The hurt she saw in her mother's eyes bothered her. At the time, speaking with Richard didn't feel wrong, but she now knew she had injured her parents. "Oh, Lord, if Papá finds out, we'll be married before nightfall."

She pushed the needle through the delicate lace she was attaching to the collar of her new dress. This would be a dress for church and social occasions; it was far too feminine for work. If she wore it to work, her mother would be convinced she was hunting for a husband.

But do I really want a husband now? She put the dress down and began to pace back and forth beside her bed. Richard's handsome face, his golden curls, and his blue-gray eyes came into focus in her mind. She sighed. To be married to Richard wouldn't be a chore. It would be a blessing, an honor.

But he's not ready for romance. He's too busy working for his family. And would he be moving back to New York once his family returned? *Is that why he doesn't want to get involved, because he knows he's not going to stay in the area?* Isabela twisted her hands.

"Isabela," her father called.

She stepped toward her bedroom door and opened it. *"Sí,* Papá. I'm here." She braced herself, holding the knob. Her knees started to shake. "What do you need?"

"Come here, please," he called from the front room.

Isabela took in a deep breath and eased it out slowly. Her moment of truth had arrived. With great effort she forced herself to move forward, one foot at a time. She rounded the corner of the hallway to find only her father sitting on the sofa. He seemed calmer. And Richard was nowhere to be seen. Tentatively, she stepped into the front room.

"Sí, Papá."

"Come, sit with me. I have something I need to discuss with you." He patted the cushion on the sofa next to him.

Lord, help me. Give me the right words to speak. She sat down beside her father. He cupped her hand in his. "I have to ask you something."

His rich, dark brown eyes scanned her own. *"Sí,* Papá?"

Yolanda came into the room, wiping her hands on her apron.

"It concerns Señor Southard."

Isabela swallowed hard and looked to her mother for support. Yolanda put her hand to her chest and sat down on the rocker. "Emile," she whispered.

Her father's gaze shifted to her mother's, then back again to Isabela, and slowly back to his wife. "What are you not telling me, Yolanda?"

"Nothing." Yolanda looked to the floor.

"I'm worried for Señor Southard," Emile continued. "Manuel has told him he is selling the boat at the end of the month, that he has a buyer for it. Did you know this?"

"*Sí*, Papá, but I couldn't tell you about Señor Richard's business affairs."

"I understand that. . .Richard? You call Señor Southard Richard?" His voice rose a fraction.

"*Sí*, Papá. He asked us to on his ship." She prayed that was answer enough for her father. Yolanda rocked back in her chair.

"Is Manuel selling Richard's boat what got you so upset earlier?" Isabela nervously asked.

"*Sí*, I cannot believe he would do such a thing." Emile turned back to Isabela. "This is what I wanted to speak with you about. Richard mentioned his finances were tight. How bad is it?"

"Oh, Papá, I don't believe I should say."

He held his hands up. "No, no, not the dollar amount, but is he in trouble?"

"I should not say. But I will say I will only be working for him one day a week now." There, she hadn't exposed Richard's finances but merely stated the truth of her current job status.

"I figured he was in trouble. He has not started to rebuild his warehouse. What of all the monies he brought to Cuba?"

"Oh, Papá, he's a generous man. Do not ask me such information." Isabela bit her lips. Her father shouldn't be putting her in this position.

He tapped her knee. "I only ask to see if I can lend a hand. I feel responsible for my cousin's actions. How he conducts his business affects the entire family. I will not share Señor Southard's financial situation with anyone. I did hear someone has offered him a loan to get his boat back."

"Offer? Huh! I would not call that an offer—more like a businessman's thievery." Isabela had read Marc Dabny's offer. There was much she didn't understand, but when she did the math, the interest was horrendous.

"I'm not surprised, if it is the man I have heard made the offer."

Yolanda leaned forward in the rocker. "What can we do?"

Chapter 12

Richard stretched the kinks out of his back. Morning came all too early today. No word had surfaced about his fleet of sponge boats. The sheriff suspected they went out with another ship during the night. No one in Key West would be able to hide the boats.

He spent a few moments with Cook before heading off to work and found her in better spirits. Her color was returning and her overall health improving.

At the dock he found Pete's old skiff turned over and a fresh patch on the hull drying in the sun. Richard smiled. Pete must have worked on it last night. *Amazing,* he mused.

" 'Morning, Richard." Mo waved.

" 'Morning, Mo." Following Mo up the dock was his son William. " 'Morning, Will."

"Good to see you, Richie. Been awhile." The two men shook hands. Will and Richard used to play together, having grown up close in age. But Will had married young and was the father of two boys. "So, Mo dragged you out to help him this morning, huh?"

Will's broad smile spread across his deep chocolate face. "You might say that. But I'd like to believe it was more the idea of helping a friend in a time of need."

Richard slapped Will on the back. "Thanks, Will, I really appreciate that."

"My pleasure."

"All this yappin' ain't gonna get our work done. We'll be in before noon with our first load, Richard. Have the vats ready."

"Yes, Sir." Richard smiled. In a way, he seemed more at home taking orders from Mo than giving them. He'd worked many summers for his uncle, and Mo had always been his boss. He'd never been quite able to look at Mo as an employee, but more as a partner. Times like this he was more certain of it. If the family didn't want to return to Key West, Richard was inclined to suggest that he just give the business to Mo. Except Mo was getting close to retirement age; perhaps he wouldn't want it.

He waved to Mo and Will as they went aboard Mo's boat.

"Richard?" a voice called from behind him. He turned to see Micah Bower heading toward him. "Heard about the robbery. What can I do to help?"

"Do you have a boat going north soon?"

"Yup, leaves tonight. Have some sponges?"

Richard pointed to the large mound of dry sponges on the beach above the high-water mark. "That pile there is ready."

"Great, I'll have my men come over with a wagon and load 'em up. Who should they be shipped to?"

Richard gave him the name and address of his distributor in New York City. "This will help. Thanks, Micah."

"Pleasure to lend a hand. Who do you suppose stole your boats? Never heard of anyone ever doing a thing like that before."

"If I didn't know better, I'd say someone was out to ruin me. But fact is, the fire had nothing to do with me or my business."

"No, it didn't, but someone might be trying to take advantage." Micah leaned against a piling. His blond hair had now become sandy brown. There weren't many on Key West with blond hair, and because Micah had the same color hair as Richard's, he'd always felt a kindred spirit with the man. Now, as a man himself, it seemed pretty foolish; but as a child, looking so very different from most of the people he played with, it had meant a lot.

"Word on the street has gotten around about Marc Dabny making an offer to lend you the money. Personally, I wouldn't be surprised if the rumor came from Dabny himself. He always seemed to want to make more of himself, and I think he thought this was a good horn to blow."

"Perhaps. I don't know the man all that well. His proposal was no real offer."

"You alluded to that the other day. What's the deal he offered, if you don't mind me asking?"

"He basically was charging about twenty percent interest, and I think it was compounded. I didn't take the time to do the figures on that. Then he had clauses in there that if I was as much as a day late with any portion of the payment, he'd essentially own the business."

Micah crossed his arms over his chest and groaned. "You didn't take him up on it, right?"

"Of course not. I'd rather lose the business than have it stolen from me legally."

"You're a wise man for someone so young. Who taught you about contracts?"

"School. Of course, my nanna had a hand in making me wise about my money when I was no taller than a sea turtle. She used to talk about 'seed money.' I think she called it 'corn money' when I was really small. Anyway, she let me know if I spent it all, I'd have nothing to grow with the following year."

"Wise woman, your nanna. A bit unorthodox for her time, I'd say."

Richard chuckled. "I think that's why she loved it so much down here. Back home she'd have to conform to strict society. Here she didn't have to worry about social rules. Although more of that has come to town in recent days, I've seen."

"Afraid so. As a town matures, social etiquette does develop along with it. Can't believe this little island has the second largest city in the entire state of Florida. Been exciting watching it develop, though."

"Heard several families were pulling out because of the fire," Richard commented.

"Such a shame. But I guess it's the way things are. Are you going to survive?"

"Honestly, I don't know. If some of the men don't start paying me back soon, I'll be in real hot water. I didn't expect them to not pay me back right away."

"Risky business loaning a man money when he ain't asked for it."

"True, but I thought they would have understood and appreciated that I went out of the way to lend them a hand."

Micah readjusted his stance. "I think most feel they are in your debt and will pay you back."

"Oh, I'm not saying they won't pay me back, just that I wasn't expecting them to tell me it might take months before they could."

"Months?" Micah whistled. "No wonder you're concerned."

"I'll be lucky if I get the warehouse rebuilt by the end of the summer."

"What about your ship?"

"Nothing I can do there. I figure it's lost, and what the men owe Manuel they will owe me."

"Listen, I'll do whatever I can do to lend a hand. I've got some funds set aside. Would you like to borrow some to purchase some more skiffs?"

"Actually, I was thinking about waiting on them and buying a motorized vessel or a sailing vessel like Mo has."

"Going modern, huh?"

"If it will save me money and allow me to make a profit, you betcha."

"That attitude, Son, will keep you in business. I've got to run. I'll take care of that order of sponges for you. Do you have a letter that needs to go north?"

"No, I sent one the other day when Cook collapsed. Wish we had a telegraph down here."

"Would be nice. Have a good day, and don't work too hard." Micah winked and left him there with his sponges.

Should he write his folks and let them know about the boat, the skiffs, and the problem with the loans? It would certainly let them know he wasn't quite the businessman he'd hoped to be. *Vanity, all is vanity,* he reminded himself. Perhaps he should write a letter. Perhaps Uncle Ellis could save the business. Richard certainly was running out of ideas. And there was always the possibility of cashing in some of his trust funds. But if he understood banking, they were being used at the moment.

"Señor Richard," Emile Fernandez called out.

"And here comes my other problem," Richard mumbled to himself.

⚓

Isabela felt like a five year old being dragged around by her father. She hadn't been allowed to say a word, and why he needed her to come with him this morning still eluded her.

Richard's shoulders squared after her father called out to him, Isabela noticed. His shirtsleeves were rolled up past his elbows and he stood beside a mound of smelly sponges.

"*Buenos días*, Señor Fernandez, *Señorita, como están?*" Richard smiled, but his stance reflected concern and caution. He glanced at Isabela for a fraction of a second.

"*Bien.* I've come with good news."

Isabela wasn't too sure how good her father's news was. He'd been bending every man's ear he knew this morning asking for favors. Richard was a proud man, or at least she thought him to be a proud man. She hoped he would not be offended by her father's zealous behavior.

"What news do you have?" Richard asked cautiously.

Isabela observed the tiny dimple in Richard's chin when he was concerned. Normally, it was barely noticeable. When he smiled it was very pronounced.

"I have spoken with some men. This evening after work they are going to go sponging for you. They will be using their own boats, or they will go with another who has a boat."

"What?"

"They wish to help you. They have heard of your troubles and want to help."

"But why?"

Isabela knew why, and Richard would not be happy with the strong-arm tactics her father had used. He had pleaded with the men's sense of justice, their sense of honor, and their sense of national pride—all because Manuel was Cuban and had treated Richard poorly.

"It is a matter of honor. I am here to work for you for the day and I will go with the men this evening."

"Señor Fernandez—"

"Emile," her father interrupted.

"Emile, I really appreciate your offer, but there is little to be done at the moment. I have these sponges to wash and soak, but that is about all."

"You need more vats?" Emile surmised.

"I lost most of them in the fire."

"I can help you build vats. You can work with your sponges and I can build vats."

Isabela closed her eyes and sighed. Once her father determined to do something, there was little that could prevent him from completing his task.

"Emile, you need to support your family. I can't pay you."

"You insult me, Señor. I do not ask for money. I merely wish to repay a debt my family has caused you."

Richard folded his arms across his chest. The dimple in his chin nearly disappeared. "Then I accept your offer. I did not mean to insult you."

"*Sí*, much better."

"Isabela, what can I do for you?" Richard asked. "Please don't tell me you are here to work also?"

"No, Papá asked me to accompany him."

"I see." His forehead knit with confusion. Isabela looked down at the dock.

Emile cleared his throat. "Isabela tells me she is to work only one day a week for you."

"She is very good at her job. I will only need her one day a week until I can rebuild the warehouse. Then I will have more need with inventory."

"I see. She says Señor Bower wishes to hire her."

"That's right." Unfolding his arms, he relaxed them against his sides.

"He is a good man, no?"

"He is a good man." The dimple in Richard's chin returned.

"Then I should speak with him before Isabela goes to work for him."

"Papá!" She hated being talked about as if she weren't there.

"Señor Fernandez." Richard cleared his throat.

"Emile. . ."

Richard held up a hand to stop her father's protest. "No, Sir, for this I need to speak with you with respect."

"Oh?"

Isabela looked into Richard's wonderful blue-gray eyes and knew what he was about to ask. Should she stop him? Did she really want to stop him? No, she would like to be courted by Richard.

"I would like to speak with you about your daughter, Isabela."

"*Sí.*" Emile's voice strained.

Isabela shook her head, no, ever so slightly, and she saw Richard's eyes flicker. He swallowed.

"I wanted you to know just how gifted she is working with numbers. I have been extremely pleased with her work. This is why I mentioned her to Señor Bower. You should be very proud."

"Richard, I am very proud. Now, if she would get this foolish nonsense out of her head to work and find a handsome man like yourself to settle down with, that would make me very proud."

Isabela felt heat crawl up her neck.

"With someone as beautiful as Isabela, I'm sure the right man will come around any day now." Richard winked.

At least now she would have time to think about him and whether she truly wanted to marry him and move so far away. Coming with her father this morning had not seemed necessary, but who can refuse a father? What was he really after? Had he suspected more was going on between Richard and she than would be allowed by their culture? If so, why wasn't he demanding that Richard begin courting her?

Too many questions, and she felt like a flounder flopping on the ground trying desperately to gather some oxygen to live.

"Times a-wastin'. I need to get back to work. If you'll excuse me." Richard reached down and grabbed some damp sponges and placed them in a vat.

"No problem, I will get to work on some vats."

Richard had some wood that could be used for that purpose, but not nearly what he needed to keep this business pulling in a profit. Thankfully, the other sponge fishermen had taken employment in town rebuilding some of the businesses. *With my money.* He bit back the aggravation he felt toward the men who owed him the most. He couldn't hold resentment toward them. It wouldn't be right.

Isabela caught his attention with the gentle swish of her skirts. Why hadn't she wanted him to ask her father's permission to court her? Emile was walking toward the shore. "Isabela?" he whispered.

"Shh," she whispered back and handed him a folded piece of paper from out of the pocket of her skirt.

He slipped his hand over the paper and traced the delicate skin of her palm. "My Bella, why?"

"Read," she whispered. "Señor Richard, which day do you wish me to work for you this coming week?"

Formalities, for her father's sake. "Thursday would be fine."

Isabela nodded and left him standing there. He planted his feet firmly on the decking of the dock. She didn't want him to chase after her. She didn't want. . . *No, wait until you can read the letter.* Richard sighed and slipped it in his pants pocket. *If only Emile wasn't helping me today.*

Richard pushed the weight of his body down on the sponges in the vat, releasing the remaining seawater so they could soak up the fresh water. After placing the remaining sponges in the vats, he set out hanging the sponges to dry. He strung them on strings and hung them off the pilings. Strings of half a dozen sponges drastically changed the appearance of the pilings, turning them into furry, brown-tipped poles.

Richard turned around to see Emile unexpectedly walking off. *Just let the man be. He's probably got something on his mind,* he thought, reminding himself it wasn't his place to dictate the schedule of a volunteer.

"Mr. Southard," Mo's fourteen-year-old son, Joseph, came running up.

"Hi, Joe, what can I do for you?"

"Tell Dad Momma needs him at your house when he comes in."

"All right. Is something wrong?"

"Grandma's asked to see him."

"Cook!" Richard dropped the sponges in his hand and ran.

Chapter 13

Not Grandma Cook, my other grandma," Joe yelled.

Richard stopped abruptly. Having only grown up with one set of grandparents and having seen them so very seldom, he often overlooked that most folks had two sets. Mo had found his mother a couple years after he and Lizzy had married. Ever since that time, she'd been living with them. Mo had built her her own single-room house in the backyard. It took many years for the former slave to get used to freedom, but slowly she settled into her own.

"Of course, I'll tell him. So, how come you aren't in school today?"

"No school today." Joe's wide grin reached his mahogany eyes, his father's eyes.

Richard scanned the harbor. "There's your dad now. Why don't you wait and tell him?"

The urge to go home and check on Cook still pulsed through his veins. . .and what was Mo's mother doing at his house? He hadn't brought a lunch—it would make sense to go home. Richard slipped his hands in his pockets as they waited for Mo and Will to pull up to the dock. He could wait no longer. He pulled it out and read:

Dear Richard,
Please forgive my father. I'm not certain what he has in mind to do tomorrow morning; just know that his sense of family honor is at stake. My mother is going to your house tomorrow morning to help Cook. I'll be there after I run the errands with my father.

Your Bella

Isabela was at his house? What was going on? "Leave the sponges, Mo, I'll take care of them after lunch."

The four men marched toward Richard's house.

"Joe, what's your grandma doing over at the Southards'?" Mo asked.

"I don't know. The house is full of women. I only came by to get something to eat, and they sent me to fetch you."

As they approached the house, Richard saw half his rugs hanging over the railing on the front porch. Others, he later discovered, were hanging in the back. Curtains were on the clothesline. The house was swarming with cleaning women.

Richard stopped dead in his tracks. Something about a woman cleaning meant more work. Did he dare go in?

"Oh boy," Mo mumbled.

Will spoke up. "Dad, I'll see ya back at the boat after lunch." He turned to leave.

"Chicken," Mo muttered.

"Got that right. My wife did her spring cleaning two weeks ago and I still haven't recovered."

"Face it like a man, Son."

"Nope, she called for you, not me. *Adíos.*" Will chuckled and hustled out of the yard.

Richard had wanted to see Isabela; now he wasn't so sure. "Do you think I could sneak in and get some food without being noticed?" he asked.

"Not likely," Joe spoke up. "There's a mess of food in the kitchen, but also three or four ladies in there."

"Why didn't you warn me, Son?" Mo sighed.

"I told you there was a house full of women."

Richard rubbed the back of his neck. "Guess we best face it head on. They can't ask us to do too much. They know we need to get those sponges in."

"We can hope." Mo stepped forward first.

Isabela appeared on the front porch. "Richard, Señor Mo," she beamed.

"What's going on, Isabela?"

"Several ladies wanted to help Cook out and give the place a good spring cleaning. Everyone knows she won't be up for awhile. They just want to do something for her. She's always lent a hand to so many."

That was true enough, and ever since Cook got sick, people had been coming that he hadn't really seen in years, everyone wanting to do something for Cook. But knowing Cook, Lizzy probably had to tie her to the bed with all these ladies here. "How's Cook taking the invasion?" Richard slowly climbed the front steps.

"Okay. Lizzy has a way with her mother." Isabela winked.

"Where's my mother?" Mo asked. "She sent Joe here to fetch me."

"Last I knew, she was out back by the old kitchen."

Another Hispanic woman came out on the front porch. "Señor Southard."

"*Buenos días, Señora, como está?*"

"*Bien.*" The regal-looking woman stood beside Isabela.

The similar set of her cheekbones and nose reminded him of Isabela's. "Your mother?" he asked her.

"*Sí,*" the woman answered. "I am Isabela's mother. Are you speaking of matters of business?"

"I was inquiring about the invasion of the island womenfolk on my home."

"*Me llamo Yolanda*, Señor Richard." She extended her hand with a chuckle.

"A lovely name for a lovely woman." Richard bowed his head slightly in her direction.

"You are a silver-tongued devil, no?"

Richard paled. "No, no. I. . .I meant it as a compliment."

"You can speak with me in front of my mother," Isabela offered as her mother took a few steps backward, allowing them privacy to talk.

"Thank you." Richard nodded at Yolanda Fernandez. This is why she came out on the porch, to protect her daughter's honor and to allow them to speak. "Does she. . ."

"Mima is aware that we have spoken."

"And?"

"We need to be careful to always have someone with us when we speak." Isabela looked down at her feet. She didn't agree with her family customs, but she wasn't going to outright defy them either.

"This morning you would not allow me to—"

"Richard," Isabela interrupted him again, "are you planning on moving back to New York?"

So she knew about that. Was that why she didn't want him to ask permission to court her? Perhaps she was right; it would only complicate matters between them. He could be leaving as soon as three or four months from now. "I am uncertain of where I will make my home."

Isabela nodded. The gold flecks in her deep brown eyes sparkled. Did he want to leave this woman? They knew so little of each other, and yet, admittedly, they were both attracted to one another.

Yolanda picked up a broom and started to slap the rug to Richard's left. "My Bella," he whispered. "Is this what you wish, that we no longer speak with each other?"

"No, but if you move to New York, what point is there in pursuing a relationship?"

Attraction wasn't enough to build a relationship on. She was right: They shouldn't complicate their lives.

"Very well, I shall not ask your father's permission to court you. And I shall be your friend, nothing more."

Tears filled Isabela's eyes. Neither one of them wanted this, but it was best, wasn't it? Richard fought the knot developing in his stomach.

⚓

Unwilling to deal with her own emotions, Isabela avoided her mother for days, certain she had heard her whispered conversation with Richard. Isabela had seen him working on his dock, but kept herself in the shadows. If she didn't want to develop a relationship with him, why had she signed her note "Your Bella"? she asked herself. And why was she bothering to check up on him every chance she could? It was like the days before the fire, when she hadn't yet spoken to him, admiring him from afar.

"Isabela," Micah Bower called to her.

Startled, she looked up from the desk and focused on Señor Bower. She'd been daydreaming again. "Yes?"

"Would you be so kind as to pull together the operating expenses for this time last year and throughout the remainder of the summer? Then go back and do a comparison of two years prior. I think I'm seeing a pattern and I'd like to check on it."

"Yes, Sir."

Isabela blew the ink dry on the ledger where she'd been working and safely closed it. Señor Bower had a larger business than Richard's, and its operating expenses were much higher. That probably had more to do with the products the Bowers imported and exported, she assumed. Sponges didn't take special crating or careful storage.

Over the next hour she worked on the figures for Micah. He'd been right; there was a definite pattern in the expenses during those months. She opened the daily ledgers for each of those months to try to discover where these extra expenses were coming from.

Her mind focused, she jumped when she heard Micah ask, "Find anything?"

She took a deep breath. "Yes, I was just starting to look at the daily ledger sheets to try and find the source of the increase."

"Don't bother. I think I know where to look. Tell me if the amount of the increase adds up because of payments made to Arcny Transport?"

Isabela slid her index finger up and down the pages, scratching the totals on a separate sheet of paper. If she subtracted the normal transport fee from non-summer months, she found the difference to be the exact amount of the increase. "Yes, that is the increase."

"I suspected as much." Micah locked his hands behind his back.

"Why do you use them in the summer months?"

"Because the rest of the year Ed Flanigan works here on the island. During the summers, he returns to Boston and spends the summers with his family."

"What are you going to do?" She closed the ledgers and put them back in their proper places.

"Not much I can do until I find another man willing and able to do the work." Micah stepped back toward the door. "Great job, Isabela, thank you."

She'd never heard of Arcny Transport before, hadn't even seen a sign in town for them. So why would they jeopardize steady income by overcharging every summer? Some business matters she didn't understand. However, she saw Micah was determined to stop the overcharging.

She reopened the daily ledger and continued with the figures she'd been given earlier. Her hands trembled after reading the name Southard Sponges upon a receipt. The captain had received five hundred dollars, and she was to deduct the expenses of the transport. Isabela thumbed through the pages.

Frustrated, she went through the pile once again—still nothing. She went through the completed file—still nothing. After searching for fifteen minutes, she decided she'd better speak with Micah Bower. She lightly tapped the closed door to his office.

"Come in."

⚓

Richard thankfully deposited the five hundred dollars Micah had given him for his last shipment of sponges. He couldn't help but believe that Micah hadn't taken off for his own expenses, but at this point in time, he decided not to argue the point. If Micah wished to be generous, he would accept it.

He grinned at his bank account, which now boasted three thousand dollars. Some of the men had paid back smaller loans. He still prayed daily for a miracle. He had two days to raise the thirty-five thousand in order to have his boat released. The probability was slim that the money would come in, but he wouldn't rule out a miracle. God's grace was the only thing getting him by these days.

Cook was feeling better. For that, Richard felt especially grateful. She'd even begun to sit in the front parlor for small portions of the day. Lizzy had moved back home with Mo, which Mo appreciated. After nineteen years of marriage, he'd grown accustomed to his wife's home cooking. Lizzy still spent most of the day with her mother, but Cook was reaching her limit for constant companionship. Richard grinned and headed out of the bank and toward the rebuilding of the city.

Most of the debris had been carted away. Fancy new brick buildings in various stages of completion lined the streets. "Lord, if You see Your way fit to let me build a brick building for the new warehouse, I sure would appreciate it." Richard mumbled his prayer as he stood at the area where Southern Treasures had once stood. For years, Matt and Micah Bower had run their business from that dock, but when the area continued to expand, they purchased some waterfront property on the south side of the island, outside of the harbor.

Richard scanned to his left and saw the bits of remaining foundation of his warehouse and his new dock heavily laden with drying sponges. On the dock he saw a man and a woman. He stepped closer. Who would take a woman out on such a messy dock? he wondered. Having left hooks and knives all over, he decided he better get over there before the people hurt themselves.

As he got closer, a familiar profile came into focus. "Uncle Ellis, Nanna!" he called and ran toward them.

"Richard," they called back in unison.

Richard leaped to Bea Southard and lifted her off the ground. "It's so good to see you, Nanna. I've missed you."

Her gentle hazel eyes smiled. "I've missed you too, Son."

"Put your nanna down and give me a hug." Ellis grinned. "We came as soon as we got word about Cook."

"Have you seen her? She's doing much better." Richard was clasped against his uncle's barrel chest and slapped him on the back.

"Yes, we came in on the morning tide. You weren't about, and we headed straight to the house. You built a strong dock, Son. I'm proud of you."

Richard looked down at his feet. "After you see the books, I don't think you'll be all that proud." The books. . .Isabela had come in last Thursday. He'd left her a note. She'd done her job. She didn't leave him another note. He hadn't realized how much he'd been counting on seeing her for some kind of explanation.

"Nonsense, you did the best you could. I'm certain the good Lord will work it all out."

Richard's spirit brightened some, knowing his uncle wasn't disappointed in him. "But I've lost the *Sea Dove*."

"Cook told me. I would have done the same thing. Many of the men you lent money to have written me and praised your generosity to them at such a horrible time. They are also aware of what this has cost our business. They are good men; they'll pay us back."

"Not before the deadline in Havana, I'm afraid."

Ellis grabbed Richard in a playful headlock and rubbed his knuckles on the top of his head. He'd been doing that to him since Richard first came to live with his uncle. "If we lose the *Sea Dove*, we lose it. Not everything a man has to do is for profit. Sometimes our greatest tasks cost us more than others, and yet our profit is in the good will we've created. Besides, I might have some possible solutions to get the *Sea Dove* out of hock."

Nanna snuggled into Ellis. "Honey, let's take this boy home. His brothers and sisters ought to be settled into their rooms by now."

"James is still in New York continuing his studies, isn't he?"

"Yes, but it was hard on him to not come back and see Cook." Bea placed her hand in the crook of Richard's arm.

"I've been cleaning sponges all morning, Nanna. You wouldn't want to soil that pretty new dress."

"Nonsense, I've hugged your uncle when he was in far worse shape over the years. It's just a little saltwater."

"That stinks to high heaven from all the mud and small pieces of seaweed attached to the sponges."

"True, but I'm not going to allow a little smell to get in the way of being near my son whom I haven't spent any time with in months." Bea grinned and pushed them forward to their house.

"So, what's this about Marc Dabny offering you a loan?" Ellis asked.

Chapter 14

Another restless night of sleep plagued Isabela. The mere thought of going to work for Richard in the morning kept her tossing and turning. She didn't dare go to the beach to let the gentle roll of the waves soothe her, for fear she'd meet up with Richard once again.

Micah Bower had not charged Richard for the expenses of the shipment, and he'd asked her to keep that knowledge private. Richard had said Micah was a good and fair man; now she knew it for herself.

Isabela dressed for work in her most conservative outfit. She'd suffer from the heat, but it seemed wise to have a high-collar dress and long sleeves. She didn't need to tempt Richard any further, not that she'd been trying to. Maybe she *had* been trying to get the man's attention. But now that she had it, she'd been keeping him at bay. He had respected her request and hadn't come by. Today would be their second time working together since she'd asked him not to come around. Last week worked out perfectly. They hadn't seen each other, just passed notes concerning work to be done and work that had been done. Would he be in the office today? she wondered.

She greeted her mother as she left her room.

"Did you sleep well, *Niña?*"

"No, Mima." Isabela sat down at the breakfast table and ate the wonderful meal her mother had made.

"Ah, this is because you are working for Señor Southard today, *sí?*"

"*Sí,* Mima."

"Let your heart lead you, *Niña,* not your head." Yolanda went to the sink and plunged her hands into the water.

"Would you want us to marry and move to New York?"

"No, but I will trust the Lord. I believe He dictates our steps. If they are the right ones for us to follow, He will help us."

"But it snows up there. I'd be very cold."

Yolanda laughed, then sobered. "Ah, but do you want to be cold at night by sleeping alone the rest of your life? Even here the single life is cold and lonely, unless the good Lord is calling you to be single. I cannot say, but—"

"No, Mima, don't say it."

"*Sí,* I will honor your wish. Just remember, your Señor Richard wanted to court you and you pushed him away, not the other way round."

"*Sí,* I know this, Mima." Isabela finished the last of her coffee and carried her dishes to the sink. *"Muchas gracías* for the breakfast, Mima."

"You're welcome, *Niña.* Have a good day at work."

In no time at all, she'd walked from her home to Richard's. The house seemed different. She couldn't place what was out of order.

The rich scent of bacon filled her nostrils. Richard must have cooked this morning, she thought. She went on to the office and opened the closed door. Papers and ledgers littered the desk. *What has the man been doing?*

She dropped her purse on the chair by the door and immediately started going over the papers to put them in their right order, filed in the appropriate places. Her hands trembled seeing a list of income and expenses for Richard's land in New York. She placed it in the file and moved on to the next. "What are Bea's personal papers from her trust fund doing out?" she mumbled. This was quite odd. Richard would have no need to go over his aunt's papers. She tucked the paper in its designated file and again found private trust funds for each of his brothers and sisters scattered on the large desk.

Perhaps Cook would know what was going on, but she didn't want to wake her. She'd been instructed by Lizzy that Cook needed her rest.

With the papers placed back in their appropriate places, she started working on the invoices and salaries for Southard Sponges. Richard had taken no salary, as usual. She went to the cash box to count out Mo's salary for the week. "Where'd all this come from?" she asked.

"And who are you?" a deep booming voice responded.

Startled, she jumped up and faced "Señor Ellis!"

"Now that we've established my name, I will ask again, who are you?"

"I'm sorry. Isabela Fernandez. Richard hired me to do the bookwork for him."

"Ah, he did mention that. Forgive my rude greeting." Ellis bowed slightly.

"When did you return?" She fumbled with the cash in her hands, glad that Richard had told her uncle about her, or else he would have thought her a thief.

"My family and I returned yesterday. You cleaned up the desk."

"I'm sorry, I—"

Ellis raised his hand to halt her words. "No apologies. It is my mistake to have left the place a shambles. We worked late into the night and simply retired for the evening. I thank you for taking care of it for me. Please, sit and relax."

"Thank you." Isabela sat back at the desk and placed the money on top of it. "Is Richard still here, or has he gone to the dock already this morning?"

"He set sail for Cuba."

"You raised the money to get the ship back?"

"No, I'm afraid the *Sea Dove* is lost. He's bringing some important papers for Manuel to sign that will at least transfer the debt the others owe him to us for the payment of the ship."

"I'm so sorry. My father is quite upset with his cousin for doing this to you."

"Tell your father it is the way of business. A good businessman can't fault another when he is doing what he needs to do to protect his business from ruin. So, how is it you love working with numbers?" Ellis sat down in a chair, placing his elbow on the arm and folding his hands together.

"I've always been good with numbers, ever since I can remember."

"Richard has always been good with them as well. How he managed to keep the business running while all these other things were happening surprises even me. Who is your father?" Ellis asked.

"Emile Fernandez. He works in one of the cigar factories."

"I believe I may have met your father, though I'm not certain." Ellis sat back, making Isabela more comfortable.

"Yes, my father says he has met you before."

Ellis nodded. "I won't keep you from your work. When you have finished with the books for the day, would you mind showing me what you've done?"

"Yes. Where will I find you? I don't think this will take me more than the morning. I'm supposed to work the entire day, but I don't see enough work to hold me here."

"Hmm, join us for lunch and you can show me the accounts afterward."

"*Gracías, Señor.*"

Ellis got up to leave. She eased out a deep breath she'd been holding since Ellis walked into the room. Did Richard also tell him of his attraction to her? Is that why he wanted to socialize with her?

She wouldn't be seeing Richard today. Wasn't not seeing him what she wanted? So why was she sad? Isabela gnawed her lower lip and looked at Mo's ledger of the men's worksheets. Only one man had worked for a couple of days. Perhaps she didn't even have a morning's worth of work here.

She sighed deeply. "Lord, keep Richard safe."

⚓

No matter how encouraging Ellis had been, Richard still felt like a failure. Meeting with Manuel in Havana had been one of the hardest jobs he'd ever had to do. Hearing that the company that wanted to buy the ship had canceled their bid gave him some breathing room. As of this morning, when he left Havana Harbor to go back to Key West, the *Sea Dove* was officially on the market. They had a slim hope that the men of Key West would be able to pay their debts fast enough, and they might not lose the vessel. Admittedly, it was a very slim reprieve.

Manuel had been shocked by Richard's appearance with the title of ownership made out to him, and he agreeably gave the debt of the others to Richard. Once the debts were repaid, Ellis would buy another vessel. He'd reminded Richard that he ran the business quite successfully for many years without his own ship, and they could do that again.

Richard stood on deck as he watched the island come into view. Taking in a deep breath, he eased it out slowly, allowing the rhythm of the waves to calm his anxious heart. He wasn't perfect; he'd make more mistakes in his life, but he had wanted to do a far better job than this for his uncle.

Isabela's sweet face and ebony hair came into his mind's eye. He'd ruined his chances with her as well, although he wasn't exactly sure how he had messed up with Isabela. Perhaps their stolen moments alone—but if those had been revealed to Emile, he'd be a married man by now, or at the very least, engaged.

A wicked thought crossed his mind. If he let word get out that he and Isabela had talked privately, Emile was certain to demand an engagement. Then Isabela would have to spend time with him. But he didn't want to force a woman to be with him, and if he played that card, wouldn't that be exactly what he'd be doing?

"Lord, give me some direction here. I'm feeling rather disjointed."

"Mr. Southard!"

Richard turned to see Captain Daggett heading toward him. "Captain." Richard nodded.

"Does the end of your dock have deep water?"

Richard smiled. He'd hoped to persuade the captain to take a delivery of sponges up to New York. "Eight feet during low tide. How deep do you need?"

"That'd be pushing it a bit; she draws eight."

Richard scanned the pilings to see the placement of the tides. "It's about midtide now and going out. I can have the sponges loaded in thirty minutes tops, perhaps ten, if they are ready for transport."

"All right, point out your dock; I'll risk it."

"Thanks."

"I'll have a couple of my men go ashore and help you."

"I appreciate that as well."

"Join me at the helm. You can warn me of any problems on our approach."

Richard advised the captain as they passed his dock and turned the ship around for clear and easy sailing out of the harbor later.

"Amazing the damage that fire caused. I can see you were hit hard," Captain Daggett observed.

"Lost the warehouse and the dock. I hope to have the warehouse rebuilt by fall."

"Who's waving us on at the dock?"

"That's my uncle Ellis."

"Ellis Southard! I used to run sponges for him years ago. I should have recognized your last name. Sorry about that, Boy."

"Nothing to fret over. Of course, we're not the only spongers on the island now." Richard waved to Ellis. Looking down the dock, he was pleased to see bundles of sponges ready for shipment.

"True." The captain leaned down and shouted, "Ahoy, Ellis, been longer than a man paddling across a flat ocean. How've ya been?"

"Fine, fine. Been up north for awhile. Richard here has been minding the business. He's done a fair job of it too."

"You're still afloat after the fire. All things considered, that's better than some." Captain Daggett jumped onto the dock. "Richard says he has some sponges he'd like me to haul up north for him. Don't have time to chew the fat with the tide going out. I've got a couple men ready to help them for shipping."

"I'm way ahead of you. Everything on this end of the dock is all set. I hoped Richard might find a ship willing to take a load." Ellis winked.

Captain Daggett smiled. "Can see he learned well. Load 'em up, men."

In five minutes the sponges were loaded. "I'll stop by in the next few months when I'm heading north and see if you have any stock ready for shipping, Richard." The captain extended his hand.

Richard clasped his hand around the captain's. "Thanks. We'll be needing your help for awhile."

"Good day, Ellis, see ya next time." Captain Daggett leaped on his boat and hollered, "Cast off. Ready those sheets."

Ellis slapped Richard on the back. "Good job, Son. I'm proud of you."

"How'd you know to have a shipment ready?"

"Figured that's what I would have done." Ellis chuckled. "So, tell me, how'd things go in Havana?"

"Isabela."

She turned. "Mariella, what brings you to town today?"

"Miguel was into everything at the house so I'm hoping a trip to town will wear the child out. What about you? I heard you've been working for my cousin. Are you enjoying it?" Little Rosetta sat down on the curb beside her mother. Isabela fought a smile. The young girl knew her mother.

"*Sí*, very much. Working with numbers has always been a pleasure for me."

"Thank the Lord I don't have to do any of the household finances. My husband does them. My interest lies in reading. Have you read the newest book by Mark Twain, *Huckleberry Finn*?"

"No, I don't think I've read anything by Mark Twain."

"Oh, you must. He writes so differently. The first book I read of his was *Tom Sawyer*. Came out in seventy-seven. I guess it kinda appealed to the tomboy in me. Anyway, it's great to see you again." Mariella tossed Miguel up on her hip. "Need to wear out the children before I have to get dinner ready."

"*Adíos,* my friend." Isabela smiled.

"*Adíos,*" Mariella replied, and so did little Rosetta and Miguel.

They were so adorable with their dark hair and large brown eyes, Isabela mused. She wouldn't mind having a couple of children to raise. A fleeting image of a child with blond curls and her own peanut butter complexion flashed before her. Was it a boy? A girl? Only one man could father that child. Well, only one man she knew, she amended. She glanced back at the harbor. Had he returned from Cuba?

She headed toward the cigar factory. "Papá," she called, as he emerged from the building, his shoulders slumped over. "Papá, what's the matter?"

"The company is moving to Tampa."

"Why?" To move again. . . Hadn't they moved to Key West because of the company? Why did they have to move again? She'd never get a job in Tampa like the one she had now. If only she could find a way for her family to stay in Key West.

"I believe it is because of the union. In Tampa, there would be no union."

"So, you would be paid less?"

"*Sí*. Come, let's give the bad news to your madre."

"Papá, what about finding another job, one that would allow us to stay in Key West?"

"I know of no such job. I learned only one trade as a boy growing up in Cuba. I could try and find work with other cigar factories in the area, but I do not think I would be the only man doing such a thing. I don't know of a single man who is happy to hear about the move."

"No, I don't suppose any man would want to work for less pay doing the same work."

"*Sí*, that is the problem. Come, your mother awaits."

Tradition or not, she knew only one man well enough to ask for help.

Chapter 15

Richard answered the knock on the door. " 'Evening, Micah, what can we do for you?"

"I'd like to have a word with you and Ellis, if you've got a few minutes." Micah ran his hand through his hair.

"Sure, come on in. Uncle Ellis is upstairs. Make yourself comfortable in the front parlor." Richard stepped back and opened the door farther.

"Thank you."

Richard climbed the stairs two at a time and knocked at his aunt and uncle's room. "Uncle Ellis, Micah Bower is here and he'd like to have a word with us."

"Tell him I'll be right down," Ellis called from behind the closed door.

Richard worked his way down the stairs a bit more slowly, then entered the front sitting room. Micah was admiring some of the collections his family had gathered over the years. "Can I get you something to wet your whistle?" Richard asked.

"No thanks. These are very delicate pieces of art. Where'd you get them?" Micah placed a small jade figurine back on the shelf.

"All over the place. Uncle Ellis started the collection before Nanna and I arrived. Since then everyone in the family has added to it from time to time."

"They're fascinating." Micah moved toward the high-backed sitting chair.

"Uncle Ellis said he'd be right down. Go ahead and make yourself comfortable."

"Thanks. How's Cook? Haven't heard a word about her in awhile."

"She's doing just fine, thank ya for askin'," Cook said with a wave as she walked by.

Micah and Richard chuckled.

"She's a bit slower on her feet—but I wouldn't want to test that theory," Richard teased.

"I heard that," Cook called back.

" 'Evening, Micah," Ellis said as he entered the room. "You picking on Cook again, Son?"

"Possibly."

Ellis leaned toward him and lowered his voice. "Good, I think it keeps her going."

"Speak up, Mr. Ellis, I didn't quite hear ya."

"Good." Ellis sat on the sofa with Micah. "So, what can we do for you this evening?"

"Have you ever used a company called Arcny Transport on the island?"

"Can't say that I have. Don't recall even hearing of the business. Why do you ask?" Ellis sat back in his chair.

"What did you say the name was?" Richard asked.

"Arcny. Have you heard of them?"

"Not sure. Manuel Fernandez, in Havana, mentioned an Arce Transport was interested in purchasing the ship, but decided at the last minute not to purchase."

"Arce and Arcny are pretty different sounding, Son," Ellis offered.

"You're probably right. Why do you ask about Arcny Transport, Micah?"

"I've been trying to track them down for a couple of days. I've gotten nowhere. Even the man who works for the company doesn't know where the business is centered. He says his pay is delivered to him at his home every Friday evening."

"That's a rather peculiar way of doing business," Ellis suggested.

"It gets worse. They charge me double what I pay the rest of the year to Ed Flanigan. Ed's been going back to Boston for the past few years, and he recommended Arcny Transport during the time he's gone. I figured it was an island company, they delivered on time, never had a problem with them. But I was doing some audits and I realized my summer expenses went up every year, then come fall they would return to where they were. By the way, Richard, thanks for recommending Isabela. I'd never have had the time to do these audits; I've been so swamped since Father retired."

Micah sat back. "I'm a fair man, and I wouldn't mind paying a little extra knowing I'm only using that company during the summer months, but double, well, that's plain old ridiculous."

His uncle rubbed his hand over his face. "How do you get in touch with this company to let them know you have work?"

"I don't. Jesse Ryan just comes over the day after Ed Flanigan leaves for Boston. I always assumed Ed knew who to contact, never asked any questions. It's just some minor transportation needs from the warehouse to the wharf and some supplies for the warehouse. Ed's been doing the job for near twenty years now."

"Is there a postmark on the bill?" Richard inquired.

"Never looked. I'll do that when the bill comes in this month."

"You could send a post up to Ed Flanigan in Boston and ask him who Arcny is and how he heard about them," Richard added.

"I might just do that."

Ellis leaned back and draped an arm across the back of the sofa. "So how's the wife and kids, Micah?"

"Wonderful. . ." Micah went into an update on his family, and Richard's mind focused back on his conversation with Manuel. Wouldn't that be interesting if a Key West company was after the *Sea Dove*?

"Excuse me," Richard interrupted. "Uncle Ellis, what if someone in Key West is deliberately trying to ruin Southard Sponges?"

"What are you saying, Richard?" Ellis leaned forward and braced himself with his elbows on his knees. Micah did the same.

"Let me ramble for a bit. It might be nothing, but here's what I'm thinking. Someone had to know the ship was being held in Cuba."

"Just about everyone on the island," Micah interjected.

"True, but someone on the island also knew that I was managing to keep the business running without the *Sea Dove*."

"Go on," Ellis urged.

"Because after I had the offer from Marc Dabny. . ."

"Wait." Micah reached in his pocket for a pencil. "I need a piece of paper." Ellis reached in the small writing box and pulled out a single sheet of Aunt Bea's finest stationery. Micah scribbled down Marc Dabny's name. "Look at this." He scratched out the M from Marc and the Dab from Dabny.

"Can it be?" Ellis and Richard asked in unison.

"Hold on a second." Richard jumped up, left the room, and ran into the office. He thumbed through the files for Marc's offer. He pulled out the thick document and hurried back into the parlor. "I knew I'd seen or heard that name before, but I couldn't place it. Look here, on page eleven, three-quarters of the way down the page."

"He's still up to his old tricks, I see," Ellis sighed and handed the document to Micah.

"Okay, so we know Marc Dabney is the man behind the Arcny Transport, and we know he overcharges me, but I don't see how we can connect him to trying to ruin your business."

"I'm not saying Dabny's the one behind ruining the business, just that it's got to be someone local. Someone who didn't like me starting to pull the business together even without the *Sea Dove*, because that's when the fleet of skiffs was stolen."

Ellis sat back and brushed his beard. "And knowing that we can't come up with the funds to buy back the *Sea Dove*, he withdrew his offer to Manuel."

"Exactly."

"And I thought I had problems," Micah chimed in.

The front door rattled in its hinges. "Who could that be at this hour?" Ellis muttered.

"I'll get it," Richard offered. When he opened the door, he found a young man with a note.

"Richard Southard?" he asked. "Got a message for ya." He handed Richard a tightly folded square of paper with sealing wax on top.

"Thank you." He pulled out a coin, handed it to the young man, and closed the door. He wandered back into the parlor, wondering who could have sent him such an odd note.

"Who was it?" Ellis asked.

"I don't know. Someone delivering this strange note for me."

"Well, you going to open it, Boy?" Cook now stood in the hallway with her hands on her ample hips.

Richard slipped it into his pocket. "Later." He winked.

"Ain't good for my heart to be teasin' an old woman, you know," Cook replied. The room erupted in laughter.

Isabela paced back and forth at the edge of the shore. Why hadn't Richard come? Did he get her note? Or had he decided not to come? Hopefully her parents were none the wiser that she had slipped out of the house. Perhaps she should have gone directly to his house and not worried about the social consequences of her actions.

She sat on the fallen palm tree that formed a natural bench and removed her sandals. Unconsciously, she dug the sand with her toes. "Lord, please bring Richard here. I know he can help my father. I don't know why I've been so afraid of Richard courting me. I guess it's the rebel in me."

"Or that independent streak," a voice whispered from behind.

"Richard."

He gathered her in his arms. "You will let me ask your father's permission to court you now, won't you?"

"I'd be lying if I said I didn't want you to."

"Good. Is this what you wanted to see me about?" Richard released her and she sat back on the log.

"No. My father's company is moving to Tampa."

"Union?"

"*Sí.* They won't have to pay union wages up there."

"I've heard that's why most of the companies have been moving up there. So, what do you need my help with?"

"I don't want to move. I like my jobs. I know it's selfish but—"

He grasped her hand. "Is it only the jobs that you don't want to leave?" he whispered.

"No," she responded in the tiniest voice she could squeeze out.

"Good, because I can't stop thinking about you." He wrapped her in his protective arms once again. "I know your customs, and I know if your father should see us now, we'd be married by morning. But, honestly, I don't care. I wouldn't mind being caught if you'd become my wife." He grinned.

"How can you be so sure? You don't really know me. We've spent so little time together."

"My Bella, my sweet Bella, of course I know you. You're kind and considerate, a diligent worker, and you have a passion for life that goes beyond most. Besides, you've haunted my dreams day and night since you first spoke to me the day after the fire."

"And you've plagued mine," she confessed.

"I've prayed and asked the Lord if you're the woman He means for me to marry. I believe my feelings have continued to grow stronger with each passing day. Bella, tell me you feel the same."

"I feel it too. But what about New York? Will you be moving back there?"

Richard released her and clasped his hands in front of him. "That's something I still don't have an answer for. I enjoyed working the land, overseeing the property. Uncle Ellis says I get that from my father and his father before him. I feel it is in my bones and I can't shake it. I love Key West as well, but a man can't plant miles of corn and wheat here. He's fortunate to have a small garden plot in his backyard."

"True." She paused. "I've heard the snow is very, very cold."

"Ah, but, Bella, it blankets the land with a pure, fresh covering. I often think it's like the covering we'll receive when we go to heaven. Light and airy, covering our sins."

"You did not mind the cold?"

"No, my Bella, you can always dress warmer. Here you can only take off so many layers of clothing to get cooler."

"My other concern is my parents. I wouldn't see them often. I've always wanted them to be close to their grandchildren."

"Hmm, there is no easy answer for that. I suppose we could try and make a yearly voyage back to the island."

"We are getting ahead of ourselves here, aren't we?" she asked and prayed he wouldn't say it was so, because at this very minute, she knew she wanted to be married to Richard, to bear his children and live wherever he lived.

"Perhaps I do need to ask your father's permission to court you. He might not find me suitable."

Isabela giggled. "My father is very proud of you. He cannot believe that you've treated Manuel with honor in spite of what he's done to you."

"The Bible gives very good direction on that. 'Do unto others. . . .' "

" 'As you'd have them do unto you.' "

"Exactly. I'm not a great man, Isabela. I'm a sinner; I have my moments when I'd like to strike out, but God wouldn't be honored by such behavior. If I were truly honorable, I would not be holding you as I have this evening. I know your customs, and I have not honored them. It doesn't matter if I agree or disagree with them. I should have more self-control."

"Set your mind at ease. I am the first to dishonor them by asking you to meet me here."

"I will do what I can to find a new job for your father. Does he have any skills besides rolling the cigars?"

"No. But he is a smart man and learns quickly. He's repaired broken chairs, tables, and such, and refinished them. I think he has a talent. But he says he just does what any poor man would do in his situation."

"Okay, I'll keep that in mind."

"Thank you, Richard. I knew I could count on you."

"Let me escort you home before your parents find you have snuck out once again. Tell me, once we are married, you won't be sneaking out in the middle of the night, right?"

"No, I would have no need. The man I've come to see will be home with me."

"I long for that day, my Bella." He kissed the top of her head and led her home. They spoke not another word to each other and parted with the slightest squeeze of the hands. Her heart fluttered like a butterfly; everything would be all right. Richard would find a job for her father. They would begin courting. She silently slipped into her house.

"Isabela!" her father's voice boomed.

Chapter 16

Richard halted his steps upon hearing Isabela's father bellow once she stepped inside the house. Should he knock on the door? Or should he leave and let Isabela handle it? No, he should take the lead, and he returned to the house. "Father, help me, I need Your patience and grace here." He raised his hand to the door and knocked.

"*Buenas noches*, Señor Fernandez." Richard purred the formal greeting, hoping to placate the man.

Emile Fernandez relaxed his stance. "Señor Richard, why are you at my door at such an hour?"

"May I come in?"

"*Sí*, come in." Isabela stood behind her father. Her cheeks shimmered with fresh tears.

"I've come for two reasons. One is a business matter; the other is a personal one."

"*Sí*, you are the reason my Isabela was out in the middle of the night, no?"

"Yes. She sent me a message to meet her. She's concerned about your move to Tampa and hoped I could help find a job for you in Key West."

"Isabela, is this true?" Emile asked.

"*Sí*, Papá. I didn't want you to be angry with me. I just wanted to help."

"You foolish *niña*. A woman should not be out alone in the middle of the night, no matter what the reason."

"*Sí*, Papá."

Her father turned back to Richard, his anger clearly appeased. "Can you help me find a job here on Key West?" Emile asked.

"I can do my best. Do you know how to swim?"

Emile chuckled. "No, I could not dive for sponges. That is young man's work."

"Isabela mentioned you are quite skilled at repairing furniture."

"I can repair some, but always out of necessity."

"This is not true, Papá. Show Richard your work." Isabela pointed to a rocker in the corner.

"May I?" Richard stepped toward it.

"*Sí*." Emile came up beside him and pointed out the various things he had done to the chair.

"Señor Fernandez, you should consider repairing furniture as a trade. You are quite good."

"A man such as yourself would accept such work?" Emile asked.

Richard knew that Emile wondered whether or not a well-to-do man would pay for such work. "Skilled craftsmanship is a fine art. As best I know, there isn't a man doing this on Key West, and you've probably found some of these furnishings being cast out by their former owners."

"*Sí*, I did not steal them." Emile's chest swelled with pride.

"I would not suggest such a thing. I merely say this to point out that many have need of the services you can provide. Perhaps you have a whole new business you could conduct here on Key West."

Emile sat down in the rocker and rocked back. "It would be satisfying work, no?"

"Very satisfying." A trade in furniture repair would take skill that Emile obviously had.

"I will give the matter prayer. Thank you for bringing it to my attention. Now, what is this second matter you wished to speak with me about?"

Yolanda Fernandez walked into the room. "As if you did not know, Emile. The boy's in love."

Emile looked at Isabela, then back to Richard. Richard felt as if he had been put under a microscope. "Is what my wife says true?"

"Yes. I love Isabela and would like very much to start courting her."

Emile's face reddened and he looked to his daughter. "You have shamed me."

"No, Papá," Isabela cried.

"Señor, Isabela has not shamed you. She is an honorable woman and tries very hard to follow your customs."

"Then how do you know you love her?"

Richard sat down on the sofa, and Isabela joined him after her mother gave her a slight nudge in his direction. "Besides being the most beautiful woman I've ever laid eyes on, she has a heart that exceeds her beauty. She's thought often of her family before her own needs. A man looks for a woman who will love him and his children with such conviction."

Emile nodded.

"I have to confess, I wish not to merely court your daughter, but I want us to be engaged immediately. Señor Fernandez, my intentions are honorable. I want everyone to know Isabela is to be my wife. I know some of your customs, but, I must confess, I don't know the process for an engagement."

Emile seemed too stunned to speak. Yolanda chimed in. "First you must begin by courtship. I would accompany you on every date as a chaperone. If I am unavailable, an aunt or grandmother would then accompany you and Isabela. You would be expected to buy the chaperone's dinners and any other expense of the evening."

Richard nodded.

"After a period of courtship, you would have to ask permission to marry Isabela from Emile. Then the time of the engagement is set by the father and

Isabela's family. During this time you will also continue to be chaperoned. Isabela would begin working on her wedding dress and assembling necessities to set up a home. You, of course, would be locating or building your new home for your bride."

Richard coughed. "What if I already have the home?"

"This would be taken into consideration as to the length of time for your engagement. And, of course, we would host a large party to announce your engagement. That is, if Emile decides if you would make a good husband for Isabela."

"I understand."

"Papá, say something. You are scaring me." Isabela sighed.

Richard looked at Emile and wondered what was going on behind those dark eyes. "You should know that I might take my wife to New York, where I own a large farmstead."

Emile blinked and mumbled, "New York?"

⚓

Isabela trembled. She wanted Richard to wrap his arms around her again and make her feel safe but knew he wouldn't do something so forward in front of her parents. Would Father let them marry? Would he require a full year's engagement?

"Yes, New York. I have not decided what to do with my property there."

"What of your business here?" her father asked.

"Southard Sponges is my uncle's business and will one day be my cousin's. Since I have the property up north and trust funds my parents set up for me before they died, I felt I didn't need a share of the sponge business."

Isabela watched her father become speechless. He had no idea how wealthy Richard was. How could he understand Richard's funds were not fluid, but property and other assets that could be cashed in but would bring great financial loss if he did.

"But your ship?"

"Señor Fernandez, the hour is late. If you will forgive me, I shall return tomorrow and we can discuss my financial situation and how I can take care of your daughter. And I will try and clarify how I could not just loan myself or my uncle the thirty-five thousand Manuel needed."

"Sí, I would like to speak with Isabela privately." Emile rose from the rocker.

Richard turned to Isabela. "My Bella, forgive me for seeking your hand in marriage without proposing to you first." Richard took her hand and tenderly kissed the top of it.

She didn't want him to leave. She wanted to jump in his arms and stay there. But the time was not right, and she would wait and honor her parents. "Buenas noches, Richard."

He nodded and removed himself from the room, but not without having given her parents their proper salutation. She gnawed her lower lip and waited for her parents' chastisement.

"Emile, can this wait until morning?" Yolanda asked.

"No, I must know one thing. The rest can wait."

Isabela folded her hands in her lap.

"Do you love him?"

"*Sí*, Papá, very much."

Emile knitted his eyebrows and stepped back into the shadows of the hallway leading to his room. Isabela's heart beat rapidly in her chest. Yolanda whispered, "You should not have gone to Richard this evening. You've made this very difficult for your father. The only thing that has helped ease this situation is the fact that Richard has asked for your hand. Your father would have demanded that."

"*Sí*, I know, Mima. But I also know that Richard loves me, and even if Papá forced him to marry me right away, he would do it for love, not because he was forced."

"That is a good thing to know. But Isabela, you have shamed us."

"I know, Mima. I tried not to, but he was the only one who I felt I could ask."

"I understand. I don't agree with your actions, but I understand, and I will try and smooth things over with your father. Go to bed, *Niña*, and get some rest. Tomorrow will be a hard day for everyone."

"*Sí. Gracías, mi madre.*"

Yolanda slipped down the hallway and Isabela blew out the lamps. Tonight she was happy to know Richard loved her, that he wanted to marry her. This knowledge would help her face her parents in the morning. "Dear, Jesus, I have made a mess of everything. Please, help me make peace with my family."

Isabela removed her clothes and slipped into her nightdress. She lit the lamp beside her bed and pulled out her Bible. Sleep would be in short supply tonight. She would need a healthy dose of Scripture and time with the Lord before she faced her parents.

"Lord, thank You for having Richard come in. He helped Papá get control before he got really angry with me. Richard is such a kindhearted man. Please help me to be a good wife for him when that day should come. If that day should come," she amended.

It was still possible her father would move the family to Tampa. If he wanted to save face, he might just move them all up there with no one the wiser. "Oh, Lord, please don't let Papá move to Tampa."

Richard walked through the dark streets to his home. How was he going to tell his uncle and aunt that he had gotten himself engaged without having spent any time in a courtship? Thankfully, it could wait until morning. By then he should have figured a way to tell them.

He crept into the house, removing his shoes before he entered, praying he didn't wake anyone.

A groan came from Cook's room. He dropped his shoes and ran to her bedside. "Cook, Cook, are you all right?"

"Richie! Good heavens, Child, what are you doing in here? What time is it?" Cook raised her head off the pillow.

"Are you all right?"

"I'm fine. What's the matter?"

"I swear I heard you groaning in pain. I came in to check on you."

"Ain't no pain I'm feeling now. Maybe I was dreaming."

Relief washed over him. She'd been doing so well, almost back to her old self again.

"Are you just getting in?"

"Afraid so." Richard stood to leave.

"What on earth kept you out so late? If you don't mind me askin'." Cook smiled.

If he told her what had happened tonight, he'd be up for another hour explaining himself. "Cook, I'm exhausted. I need to get up in a couple of hours. I promise to tell you after I return from work in the morning."

"Fair enough. If I didn't know better, I'd say you've hooked up with a woman." Richard chuckled. "Good night, Cook."

" 'Night, Son. We'll talk in the morning." She pulled her covers up and rolled over.

Richard found his way to his room in the dark. The house was utterly still. In his room he undressed and slipped between the covers of his freshly made bed. A grin creased his face. It was nice having Nanna back home. His mind floated back to the images of him and Isabela on the beach earlier in the evening. There was a sense of peace or calmness that stirred within him when he embraced her, a sense of completeness. "Lord, be with her tonight; give her this same peace. I know that to her family this is a horrible shock, but please help the Fernandezes understand. And let me know if I should move back to New York or simply sell the land."

Richard completed his prayers for his various family members and let the lateness of the hour overtake him.

⚓

At the sound of the rooster's first crow, Richard pulled down the covers and swung his legs over the edge of the bed, his eyes still closed. He braced the edge of the bed with both hands and waited a moment before rising. He needed to wake up. He needed. . . He sniffed the air, and the fresh scent of coffee infused his body. "Coffee," he moaned.

Dressing quickly, he found himself in front of a large mug of deep, rich Cuban coffee. The warmth of his first sip coursed through his veins, reviving his weary body. He took another.

"Up late?" Bea asked.

"Very," he answered, not pulling too far back from this life-giving nectar. He swallowed another gulp.

"Thought I heard you come in around two and figured you might need some coffee this morning." She poured herself a cup and sat beside him. She placed a loving hand on his forearm and asked, "What's the matter, Son?"

"Another cigar factory is closing down and moving to Tampa. Isabela asked me to meet her. She is hoping I'll be able to help her father find a job that would allow them to stay on Key West."

"Isabela Fernandez?"

"Yes." He put the cup down on the table. Now was as good a time as any to explain his actions last night. "Nanna, she's a special woman."

"Richard, do you know what you've done, meeting her in private?" Bea's eyes widened.

"Yes, I'm well aware of the strict Cuban custom. And I had been intending to ask her father's permission to court her, but she didn't want me to ask him."

"Why? That doesn't make sense, unless she doesn't care for you."

"No, she cares, but she heard that I might be moving back to New York. She had to decide for herself whether or not to even get involved with courting me, knowing she might have to leave her family."

"Ah, so has she changed her mind about that?"

"Yes, and I've asked her father's permission to court her, but they caught her sneaking back in the house last night. So, before he insisted, I asked permission to marry her."

"Oh my." Bea sat up straight in her chair. "Do you love her?"

"With all my heart. There's a lot we don't know about each other, but I'm certain the Lord is directing our paths. It's just a matter of whether or not Señor Fernandez will accept me as a possible suitor for his daughter."

"I think you forced his hand on that by meeting her in private." Bea fumbled with her napkin.

"True, but I could not allow her to face her father alone."

"I understand, Son. Will they insist on a long engagement or a short one?"

"I don't know. I'm willing to marry her right away, but I'm hoping she and I will have some time getting to know one another first. I think her mother will help smooth things over. She was very helpful in explaining what they would expect from me. Did you know courting a woman involved paying for the chaperone, or chaperones, to come to dinner with you as well?"

Bea chuckled. "I'd heard that. I've seen a time or two where a young couple would be at one table and three older women at another."

"Three?" Richard groaned. "I think I might go to the bank today and remove some money from one of my trusts."

Bea continued to laugh. "And what about the engagement ring?"

"Engagement ring?" Ellis asked as he entered through the back door.

"Your son got himself engaged last night."

🛉

Isabela stayed in bed longer than normal. She didn't want to face her parents yet.

They were not pleased with her behavior last night, and while it was noble to try and find her father some work, it didn't excuse the fact that she and Richard had met alone and talked about courting and marriage. Isabela had shamed them. They knew it and she knew it; even if no one else on the island was aware, they were.

Hearing her father leave for the factory, she got out of bed and readied herself for work.

Her mother waited for her in the kitchen. "Your father is very aware of why you stayed in bed so long this morning."

Isabela hung her head, looking at her feet. "I'm sorry, Mima. I did not mean to shame you."

"Sit, Isabela. We need to speak."

"*Sí.*" She sat beside her mother at the table, and her mother poured her a cup of tea and handed her a guava-filled pastry.

"Your father is going to speak with Richard and Ellis Southard today, if he can locate them after work. He agrees you and Richard should be engaged and that some time should pass before you marry. But, with the transfer to Tampa, your engagement period would be hard. He is scheduled to leave for Tampa by the end of the month."

"No, Mima, please don't go. Won't Papá at least look for work in Key West?"

"He will look, but you've put your father in a tough position. He is a proud man, Isabela. You should have known he wouldn't take well to the knowledge that you spoke to someone outside of the family about his employment."

"*Sí,* but. . ."

"No 'buts,' Isabela. You were wrong. You should have come to me and I would have suggested your father speak with Señor Richard about possible employment. He's not ashamed to look for work, just that you spoke on his behalf, as if he were unable to."

"I know; I'm sorry. I was more concerned about myself and not you or Papá."

"This is true. Now tell me, what private matters did you and Richard speak about last night. Did you kiss him?"

"No, Mima. I wanted to kiss him, but we did not." Should she confess the kiss upon her head? "Richard held me in his arms—it was wonderful. I felt so at peace from his embrace, Mima. Does that make sense?"

"*Sí,* it makes sense."

"He did kiss the top of my head ever so gently, at least I think it was a kiss."

Yolanda grinned. "Then it was a kiss. Papá will arrange a schedule with Richard for you to go out with him. He is free to come to the house and visit as long as either one of us is home. If you go to his house, one of us must accompany you. You understand, if you sneak out again to meet Señor Richard, your father will be very angry with you."

"Sí, Mima, I understand. I will not sneak out."

"*Bien.* Now, we need to start work on a wedding dress. I have no sewing machine, so we will need to stitch it by hand. I also don't have your grandmothers here to help me. We will need to work hard."

"How soon is Papá planning the wedding?"

"I don't know, *Niña*. It all depends on when Richard will have a house ready for you and how long an engagement he feels is necessary for you and Richard to get to know one another before marriage."

Isabela sipped her tea. How long would Papá insist on? And if he moved to Tampa in less than a month, that would mean she and Richard would have to court long distance. They might not even see each other before the wedding. One good thing about that, if there could be a good thing about the long separation—letters would be private. "Mima, could you and I stay on Key West if Papá goes to Tampa?"

"No, I will go with my husband. And you cannot stay here alone. We have no relatives for you to live with here."

Isabela's heart quivered. *Lord, please find Papá a job here on Key West. I know I'm being selfish, but I don't want to leave Richard. Please find a way, Lord.*

Chapter 17

Richard changed from his work shirt to a dress shirt and headed toward the center of town. All things considered, his uncle and aunt had taken the news fairly well. He knew he wouldn't need to tell Cook. If she hadn't heard him explaining to them, she would hear it before he returned home.

He stopped briefly at the bank and gave a note to the manager, saying he would return in an hour to pick up the requested information. Nathaniel Farris's jewelry shop hadn't survived the fire. However, many of the items had been locked in the safe the night before the fire hit. He'd heard Nathaniel was working out of his home until the shop could be rebuilt.

Richard knocked on Nathaniel Farris's door, and a gangly ten-year-old girl with red hair and freckles answered it. "Is your daddy home?" Richard asked.

"He's working," she answered and started to close the door.

"Would you tell him Richard Southard would like to speak with him."

She shrugged her shoulders and yelled, "Daddy, a man wants to see you."

Richard held back a chuckle. He'd done the same thing on more than one occasion when he was that age.

"Richard, what can I do for you?" Nathaniel asked.

"I need an engagement ring." He grinned.

"Come on in. Who's the lucky gal?" Nathaniel stepped aside, opening the door farther.

"Isabela Fernandez." Richard entered the roomy two-story house and followed Nathaniel to a front study converted into a small jeweler's shop.

"I don't have much, but let's see what you like first."

"I know nothing of women's jewelry. Nanna wore a few pieces, but by and large I haven't been around a lot of feminine jewelry. What is appropriate?"

"A solitary diamond is a traditional gift. But I've seen pearls, emeralds. . .anything that seemed special to the couple."

"Her family is very traditional." A smile curled his lips at the thought of how untraditional Isabela was. "However, she's more unique."

"Hmm, do you like diamonds?"

"They sparkle pretty enough; but I'm not the one who should like it, she should." Richard released a nervous chuckle.

"Ah, but a ring should reflect the beauty you see in her. Here, let's look at some stones, then I'll show you some settings."

Nathaniel gave Richard an abbreviated course in gemology. He soon knew more about clarity and carets than he ever wanted to know. In the end, he picked out a three-quarter caret white diamond with two small amber stones. Nathaniel said he could have the ring finished by the evening and delivered to his home. They guessed on the ring size, and Nathaniel agreed to change the size to fit if they'd gotten it wrong. Thankfully, Nathaniel's wife Julie's fingers were long and slender like Isabela's.

The engagement ring and matching wedding band out of the way, he went back to the bank.

"Welcome, Mr. Southard," Nick Farley said as he entered the bank. The short balding man sat behind his desk. "I have the figures ready that you asked for."

"Thank you."

"This is such an odd request from you. You've always known exactly where your accounts stood."

"True, and I still do." Richard examined the financial statement. "But I needed a statement from the bank for a certain matter."

"Ah, yes, I've heard of that mess in Havana. I had hoped you wouldn't have to pull out such a large sum. The penalty payment will be so high."

"True, and I'm not withdrawing any money to secure the ship."

Farley's eyebrows rose.

"I also know if I pulled out such a large amount of capital, the bank could be put in a tough situation. I'm assuming these funds were used to secure the loans to the islanders?"

"Yes. You understand the banking business well. Many don't. They think we keep everyone's money in the safe at all times."

"I was taught that great wealth came with a great responsibility to others. My funds here are only some of my funds, as you well know. I would never compromise the security of your other loans. The truth of the matter is, while the *Sea Dove* is a fine ship, she's not the only ship; and once the funds are returned, we can purchase another vessel. And the value of one man's business does not exceed the needs of the community. At least not this family's business."

"Thank you. Now, what else can I help you with?"

"I do need to withdraw some money from this fund." Richard pointed to a small fund he had with the least penalties on it. "I would like you to put five thousand dollars into my personal savings account."

"Very well, you do understand—"

"About the penalties, I know. Do what you must." This fund was the balance of all his earnings over the years working for his uncle. He'd saved most of the money and used some for schooling. It was perhaps the money he was most proud of because he'd earned it himself. *What better fund to use to purchase your fiancée's engagement ring?*

On his way out of the bank, he ran into Marc Dabny. "Hi, Richard, how are you today?"

"Fine, Mr. Dabny, and you?"

"Fine, fine. Life couldn't be better."

Richard resisted the urge to question the man about Arcny Transport.

"You're just the man I was looking to find. I heard about your skiffs being lost. And a friend of mine has some used skiffs. He's pulling out of the sponging business. I was wondering if you might be interested in purchasing them?"

"Be glad to look at them. Where are they located?"

"Key Visca. I'm about to meet up with him. He's here in Key West for the day."

"Sure, what's he asking for the skiffs?"

"Says he's willing to let them go for a couple hundred."

"A piece?" Richard halted.

"No, no, for the whole lot of them."

"Lead the way." Richard followed as Marc Dabny waddled down the street toward one of the taverns. "What's the name of your friend's sponging business? Perhaps I know it?"

"Arcny Sponges."

Isabela couldn't keep her mind on her work, and she left the Bowers' office early, her mind flooded with bridal gowns, white satin, and lace. Adding and subtracting numbers were buried somewhere in the midst of all that lace, but where she couldn't figure out. The additional worries of not having spoken with her father this morning only added to her concerns. She should have faced him. Then she would have known how he was feeling, if he still loved her in spite of her having shamed them.

"Mima, I'm home," she called and dropped her purse on a table in the hallway.

"Isabela, come in the sitting room. We have guests."

Isabela walked in to see Bea Southard, Peg Bower, and Lizzy Greene. "Hello." She found a seat and sat down, looking to her mother for an answer.

"These ladies are here to help us with the wedding dress and anything else we have need of."

Isabela looked at Bea Southard and flushed. "How—how soon is the wedding?"

"We still don't know, *Niña.*" Yolanda reached over and placed her hand on Isabela's.

"Isabela, we know your family is alone on Key West. Each of us has a good hand for stitching, although no one compares with Peg here." Bea winked at Peg. "We're only offering to help. Richard is special to each of us, and since you are special to him, you are also special to us. However, we do not want to impose on any plans you and your mother are making. We are the laborers; you and your mother are the designers."

"Mima?"

"*Sí,* Isabela, this is good. We spoke this morning about how long it would take us."

"*Sí.*" She turned to the women. "Thank you, it's a very kind offer."

Lizzy spoke up. "We're here to help in any way we can. The wedding dress is one thing, but if you need help with anything else, don't hesitate to ask."

Peg Bower, brushing back strands of her light brown hair, added, "I also would like to make something special for your wedding gift. What do you have in the way of linens in your wedding trunk?"

"Mima?" She looked to her mother. She hadn't put anything in the trunk. Her mother might have been putting in things, but she hadn't been planning on marriage, hadn't even been thinking about it until she met Richard. And since then there hadn't been any time.

Yolanda stood up. "Follow me." All three of the ladies followed her mother down the hall. Isabela sat stunned. Her future mother-in-law, or aunt-in-law. . . *How does that work in our situation?* A warm thought fluttered through her mind. *Our.* She was thinking in terms of Richard and herself together.

Isabela got up and followed the ladies' murmurs. She was surprised by the contents of her trunk. When had her mother gathered those items? After the women left, she sat with her mother and asked, "Mima, when did you have the time or money to gather all those things?"

"*Niña,* I've been collecting since you were first born."

"I never knew."

"*Sí,* it is something I wanted to do. Your papá allowed me to save and collect."

Isabela looked over the matching silver service for eight. She picked up a spoon and looked at the design. A small rose had been stamped on the handle. "They are beautiful, Mima. *Muchas gracías.*"

"You're welcome, *Niña.*" Yolanda placed the items back in the trunk.

"I want to tell Richard about these and the women coming to help, everything."

"All in good time, *Niña,* all in good time."

"*Sí,* Mima. I will wait."

"*Bien.* Now, why did you come home early from work?"

⚓

Meeting Marc Dabny hadn't been providence. Richard suspected the man had been waiting for him, as if he'd been aware of all his actions. The mention of his visit to Nathaniel Farris's house triggered additional caution.

"Yes, I was looking to purchase some jewelry." Richard sipped his now cool coffee.

"Perhaps you truly did not need my offer." Marc wiped his mouth with his napkin. "I don't understand where Raphael could be."

"You'll have to tell him that I couldn't wait any longer. I have other family matters I need to take care of."

Marc grabbed his wrist. "Give him another minute."

Richard looked down at his wrist, and Marc released his hold. "All right, just another minute, but then I must go. Are you making a profit on the sale?"

Richard couldn't help but ask. The fact was, he knew Marc Dabny had to be the owner of Arcny Sponges, just as he was the owner of Arcny Transport.

"A small finder's fee for locating a buyer. Only a trifle."

Richard scanned the dimly lit room. Seeing no one new enter, he rose. "I'm sorry, Mr. Dabny, I really must go. Tell your friend to bring the skiffs by my wharf in the morning and I'll give them a look over. If they're in fair condition I'll buy 'em. If not, you know the answer to that."

"Very well. Saw you coming out of the bank. Did you secure a loan to get your ship back?"

"Nope, brought the papers to Manuel a couple days ago. The ship belongs to him."

"That's rough. How you going to keep the business afloat?"

"With the Lord's help, we'll find a way. Good day, Mr. Dabny." Richard didn't hang around for an additional comment. Dabny was fishing for something. There probably wasn't another man representing Arcny Sponges. He didn't know how he knew, but he firmly believed Marc Dabny owned the other business.

At the house, he found his uncle and a room filled with the men to whom he'd lent money. "Come in, Richard, these men are here to see you, not me."

The men nodded and waited for Richard to sit down. The spokesman of the group, David Zachary, cleared his throat. "Richard, we heard about the loss of the *Sea Dove* and we've dug up what we could, but I'm afraid it still won't cover the debt."

Richard looked at the itemized list of names and numbers. Each man had put down his debt and how much he had paid.

"We feel bad that you extended yourself so far on our accounts and lost the ship," David continued. "We can't do much, but anything we can do to help rebuild your warehouse, stock it, whatever, we're ready, willing, and able."

Richard didn't know what to say. "Thank you. Don't feel badly about the ship, not that I won't be taking all of you up on your offers, mind you."

The tension in the room broke and the men started laughing. Ellis tapped him on the back and whispered, "Well done, Son."

"I could use a favor, though." The room hushed. "What do all of you know of Marc Dabny's businesses and Arcny Transport?"

"You borrow from him, he'll own you for life," Ben Greely offered.

"Thankfully, I noticed it on the contract long before I signed," Richard added.

"You know, I ain't never done business with the man. Avoided him actually, but I did find it odd he went to Cuba a week after the fire and didn't bring anything back with him. I thought for sure he'd have filled the ship and charged folks triple the asking price for it. Guess I might be wrong about the man."

A week after the fire? About the time Manuel got the offer from Arce Transport. "Has anyone known any of his businesses' names?"

"Afraid not," David put in. "He's one you need to watch yourself with. Something about a man who owns a business that no one sees. He's got an office and all, but nothing else."

"Interesting." Ellis rubbed his beard. "Why are you asking, Son?"

"I ran into him when I was leaving the bank today, saying he had a friend with some sponging skiffs for sale. His friend never showed, and his friend's business is Arcny Sponges."

"Arcny, that's the name I heard once," Ben offered.

"Arcny Transport was the name in real fine print on the contract Marc offered me."

"If we hear anything, we'll let you know." David rose to leave and extended his hand to Richard. "Pleasure doing business with you, Richard. If you need anything, don't hesitate to call on me."

"Thank you."

Each man gave his salutation, and when the dust settled behind them, Ellis walked back into the room and asked, "What was all of that about Marc Dabny?"

"I have a feeling he's behind the offer in Cuba, and I don't trust him about the skiffs. Here's the real interesting thing, Uncle Ellis. He knew I'd been to visit Nathaniel Farris. How could he? Nathaniel lives out from the center of town, and yet Dabny knew it right after I visited him. Granted, island gossip spreads faster than rain but. . ."

"But he may have had someone watching you," Ellis finished.

"Yeah, how'd you know?"

Chapter 18

I've had similar thoughts in the past." Ellis sat down on the sofa. "Never any proof. I also wouldn't be surprised if some of the problems I've encountered over the years could be traced back to him. For the most part, nothing was substantial enough to warrant an investigation, mostly just annoying incidents."

"Do you suppose he stole the skiffs?"

"Possibly. But it might be more like him to mention to someone in need of cash the suggestion to steal the skiffs."

"Ah, so he never does his own dirty work?"

"Precisely."

"How can we catch him?"

"Other than catching him with the stolen skiffs, I doubt we can."

"He was real curious about why I was in the bank. Even Farley was concerned that I'd pull out the thirty-five thousand from my trust fund to secure the *Sea Dove*."

"I imagine he used it to loan the money to others." Ellis sat back.

"Right." Richard rolled his shoulders and stretched his neck from side to side. "I'm expecting Emile Fernandez this evening. He needs to speak with me about my ability to care for his daughter."

Ellis stifled a chuckle. "Is that why you were in the bank?"

"Yeah, I had them prepare a statement for me of my accounts there. I figure the monies there are more than enough. I shouldn't need to go into my other funds."

A knock on the door got Ellis on his feet. "Aptly spoken, Son. I believe you have a visitor."

Richard anxiously waited for his future father-in-law to enter.

"Thank you," Ellis responded to the unseen guest. "Relax," he called back. "It's a delivery from Nathaniel."

Cook, Bea, and his cousin Grace stepped from various rooms to see. "Well, ain't ya goin' to open it, Boy, and show us?" Cook asked.

Richard took the small box from his uncle and grinned. "I believe the receiver of the gift is the one to show you the ring."

"Oh, phooey, you're no fun," Grace pouted.

"All right, come here." Richard opened the box and carefully removed the rings. Nathaniel had outdone himself. The rings were beautiful. He'd even carved a curl in the wedding band to match the gentle twist to the engagement ring.

"Oh my, Richard, they are beautiful."

"Thanks, Nanna."

The women chattered about the rings until the door rattled again in its hinges. Richard braced himself. If Emile knocked that hard, then maybe he wasn't too happy about Isabela and him getting together.

"*Buenas noches,* Señor and Señorita Fernandez, *como están?*" Ellis greeted.

"*Bien,* Señor Southard," Emile answered. Isabela stood looking down at her feet. Richard fought every urge in his body to sweep her into his arms and hold her tight to reassure her everything would be all right.

"Come, sit in the front room, Señor Fernandez," Richard encouraged.

"*Gracías,* Richard."

He called me Richard. . .that's a start.

Isabela followed her father into the sitting room. Richard reached for her hand and squeezed it. It was the best he could offer. She turned to him, and he whispered, "I love you, my Bella."

"I love you too," she replied in a hoarse whisper.

"Richard, I've come to see if you can provide for my daughter," Emile announced.

Richard pulled out the envelope from his shirt pocket. "I went to the bank this morning and had them prepare this statement of my assets in their bank." He handed Emile the paper. "Forgive me for asking, but do you read English?"

"Not very well; that is why I've brought Isabela. This would normally be done without her present so as not to embarrass the child."

Richard nodded. *She is not a child.* Nanna stepped up beside him and handed him the ring box, which he promptly put in his trousers pocket. "The numbers will be the same, but to understand the terms, Isabela is very capable. She is also well aware of these statements."

Emile opened the envelope and looked over the figures. His eyes widened. Richard was certain the poor man had never earned in his entire life the balance of just one of his funds and never dreamed of their combined balance. Emile cleared his throat. "Am I understanding this is how much you have in the bank?"

"Yes, Sir, in this bank."

He handed the sheet of paper to his daughter. She looked over the numbers. "Sí, Papá, these are true figures."

In Spanish, Emile asked his daughter why she did not tell him, and she replied it wasn't her position to speak of another man's private financial matters. Reluctantly, Emile agreed. "I see you can care for my daughter financially more than I could ever give her, and you've shared your heart last night about your feelings for her. As she has shared with me also. I cannot turn down your request to marry my daughter, but I am not happy with how this came about."

Richard cleared his throat. "I ask your forgiveness in the forward manner in which I approached your daughter."

Isabela's heart was breaking to see Richard so contrite and taking on her sin as his own. She wanted to protest. But her father would never understand that she was the one who had been forward.

"I am responsible for this dishonor I have caused your family. I know of no way to correct that wrong. I do love your daughter and would never compromise her, but my customs and yours differ so on this point."

Emile raised his gaze to face Richard one-on-one. "I have always respected you as a man of honor. To have spoken with Isabela on more than one occasion about private matters of the heart without a chaperone has taken some respect away. But to face me like a man, admit your wrong, and ask my forgiveness has shown me respect. I accept your apology, and I wonder when you would like to marry my daughter?"

Isabela stood breathless.

"I trust your judgment on that decision, Señor Fernandez. But may I ask that I be able to share a custom of mine with your daughter before we decide on the date?"

Emile tilted his head. Isabela wondered what custom Richard was speaking of.

"*Sí,* I will have to learn to be gracious with your American customs since you are to be my son."

"*Gracías.*" Richard turned to Isabela and took her hand. He bent down on one knee and faced her. He rubbed the top of her hand ever so gently with the ball of his thumb. Her heart pounded with anticipation. "My Bella, would you do me the honor of becoming my wife? I love you so much, I can't imagine life without you by my side."

"Oh, Richard, I love you too. Yes," she answered and wanted to jump in his arms.

He reached into his pocket. "Then please accept this ring as a symbol of my commitment to you and a sign to the rest of the world that you belong to me."

Her hands trembled as he placed the ring on her finger and kissed the top of her hand. She opened her arms to him and he embraced her, kissing the small of her neck, sending shivers down her spine. Maybe it was best there was a room full of people to keep their passion in check.

"I love you, Bella, my sweet Bella."

Emile cleared his throat. Ellis Southard coughed. Richard reluctantly released her.

"I think a short engagement period would be in order," Emile offered.

Isabela flushed and saw the same crimson stain on Richard's face.

"Where will you live, Richard? You mentioned a farm in New York?"

"For now, I think Isabela and I should remain in Key West. When she is ready and we have the Lord's peace about it, we'll probably return to New York."

As much as Isabela shuddered at the thought of the cold, harsh winters in

New York, she remembered the warmth of Richard's embrace and kiss. A slight smile crept up her cheek. She'd be staying warm in the winter.

"Señor Fernandez, is it proper for me to hold your daughter's hands and to kiss her?"

"*Sí*, you are engaged now. It is acceptable."

Richard grasped her hand and held her firmly. "Isabela, may I kiss you?"

She couldn't speak. Desire fluttered through her body. *Thank You, Lord, that Papá has agreed to a short engagement.* She nodded her head. Richard's sweet lips captured her own as she wrapped her arms around him, pulling him closer. He held the distance between them. He was right; there was a room full of people, and a time and a place would come when they could embrace more intimately.

Richard needed every ounce of his willpower to pull away from Isabela and to refrain from pulling her into his chest, where she so clearly wanted to be.

Richard held her hand. "When. . ." He cleared his throat. "When would you like to set the date, Señor?"

Ellis and Bea were holding each other's hands on the sofa. Richard noticed the approval in their eyes.

"Three months. I should think that will be enough time for the women to get the dress made and for you to find a home for your bride."

"Three months it is." Admittedly, he had hoped for tomorrow. But three months would give him time to put things in order. One thing was certain: He'd have to find his future father-in-law a job in order to keep them in Key West. "Señor Fernandez, are you moving with your company to Tampa?"

"I have little choice." Emile sat back in his chair.

Richard encouraged Isabela to sit down in hers. "Then perhaps a wedding in one month would be more in order."

"One month?" Emile squeaked.

Richard's eyes widened. He hadn't meant to speak, but he'd spoken his thoughts out loud. His face flamed red with embarrassment. "Ah, yes, this way Isabela wouldn't have to leave with you and your wife. But are you willing to stay in the area if we can find work for you?"

"Certainly, if it's work I can do and be proud of."

"What if we do this? We'll plan on the wedding in three months. But if you haven't found a new job in a week, we could move the wedding date up to just before you leave," Richard suggested.

Emile rubbed his chin. "I don't know; seems very quick. But you might have a point. To move Isabela up to Tampa only to have her move back in a couple months doesn't seem logical."

A few other matters surrounding wedding plans were discussed by everyone. Even Cook came into the room to add to the discussion. Richard pulled Isabela to a corner of the room. "Are you happy with this?"

"Yes. I'd like more time, but we don't have it. Even if I were to move to Tampa, we would not see each other very often."

"Oh, don't be too sure of that. I would move to Tampa and wait. I don't want you out of my sight." He watched her smile brighten. "Do you know how much I love you?"

"I'm learning." She winked.

"May you never stop." Richard pushed back the dark strands of her hair from her face. "Do you like the ring? Does it fit?"

"It is beautiful. When did you have time?"

"I saw Nathaniel Farris this morning and ordered it. He had the setting made, so it was just a matter of putting in the stones that I selected."

"It is wonderful. I will cherish it always. I have nothing to give you."

"You silly woman, you've given me everything by agreeing to marry me."

"Richard, the day I first spoke with you, the day after the fire, what were you thinking about? You seemed so distant, almost lost."

"I was trying to decide what to do with my life. I'm not cut out to be a sponge fisherman. I don't mind the work, but the smell. . ."

Isabela giggled.

"I really do want to return to New York and start building up the farmstead. Industry is changing. So many opportunities are up there, but most important is the soil. I'm happy with my hands buried deep in the dirt. I suppose this was the problem. I knew where my heart lay, and yet I had responsibilities to fulfill here. And I truly do love the island. It's a great place to grow up. But I'm more like my dad than my uncle in that respect. I love the land."

"Oh, Richard, I will go happily. I only need to be with you. I don't even need to work."

Richard chuckled. "As my wife, you do not need to work. Tell me, would your father think it rude of me to invite him to come work on the farmstead with us?"

"You'd want your in-laws about?" Isabela raised an eyebrow.

"I was thinking they would have their own wing of the house to live in. Isabela, this house is not even the size of the wing I would let your parents live in."

"Oh my. How did your family come to have all this money?"

"My mother was wealthy before she married my father. Her estate was put in my name when she was dying. My father inherited the farmstead and any other monies his parents had when they died. My uncle Ellis had to make his own way in the world. Once I was old enough to understand the details of my inheritance and came of age, I put a trust together of half of my father's inheritance and gave it to my uncle to be divided up for himself and his children. Uncle Ellis had not only taken care of everything, he'd continued to have the farmstead make a profit."

"Your uncle is a wise businessman, and you are very kindhearted."

"I try to be fair. Uncle Ellis and Aunt Bea have taught me a lot about the responsibilities wealth brings to a family. Aunt Bea comes from a wealthy family herself."

"You'd never know your family was this wealthy. You don't act rich."

Richard chuckled. "That is probably the best compliment you could ever give me. Do you understand why I couldn't just rescue the boat?"

"Yes, it would have caused a terrible loss in your interest rates."

"More than that, Bella, the bank here wouldn't have had that money to lend others."

"Oh, my." She placed her hand lovingly on his shoulder. "I see what you mean. I hadn't thought of that before."

"Sometimes it is better for us to go without for awhile in order for the community as a whole to stay afloat. I don't think I can move our money immediately out of Key West. And if your parents decide to stay on the island, we will need to have some spending cash when we travel down here during the winter."

"What, and miss the snow?" she teased.

"You mentioned a verse of Scripture that first day. I've seen it played out in several ways over the past few weeks. First in Cook's life. As she lay on death's doorstep, everyone whom she had touched came to lend a hand, say a prayer, extend their love back to her. Tonight before your father came, the men on the island came over and gave what they could, hoping it would help us buy back the *Sea Dove*. It can't, but it will give us the much-needed money to rebuild the warehouse. They gave from their heart, not from duty."

Isabela added, "And just as you cast your bread upon the waters, it has returned to you."

"Yes, and even more. How was I to know I would marry the lily of the ruins," he murmured into her ear. "You captured my heart that day. You stole it with just your presence. Now, it's returned to me fuller, richer, and wanting so much more. I love you, Isabela, my Bella."

"And I love you. Do you know your name means dominant ruler? How fittingly you were named, and how noble and honorable you have lived."

"Oh, Bella, my sweet, sweet Bella." He captured her lips once again and savored the sweet nectar. He could live off of those kisses for the rest of his days, and thankfully the Lord above had seen fit to give him such a sweet gift. *Thank You, Lord.*

Epilogue

One year later

Richard held Isabela's hand as they stood beside Cook's grave. "I will miss her," Isabela whispered.

Tears burned his eyelids. "As will I. But over the past year she'd spoken with me a lot of her departure from this earth. She was looking forward to heaven; and I know it was her time to go."

"Yes, she was special."

A single tear slid down his cheek. "Yes, she was. I'm glad she was here long enough to see justice come to Marc Dabny."

"Who'd have thought he'd be so foolish as to try and sell you your own boats back?" Isabela snuggled into his chest.

"I think he'd gotten his mind so clouded by his sins, he no longer could see straight. It's a good thing we stopped him when we did or else he would have stolen Cook's family home as well. Thankfully, Cook was still alive and had the original paperwork on her property in Ellis's safe. I can't believe the forgeries the sheriff found in Dabny's files."

Richard placed his hand upon his wife's swollen belly. A child, their child, was growing within her. "Have I told you today how beautiful you are?"

"Only twice." She winked. They had said their good-byes to the island residents last night. Today they would sail for their new home in New York. Emile and Yolanda would soon be joining them.

Richard led her a step back from the grave and looked toward heaven, his throat thick with emotion. "Good-bye, Cook. We'll see you again in heaven, but not for a little while."

A Letter to Our Readers

Dear Readers:

In order that we might better contribute to your reading enjoyment, we would appreciate you taking a few minutes to respond to the following questions. When completed, please return to the following: Fiction Editor, Barbour Publishing, Inc., P.O. Box 719, Uhrichsville, OH 44683.

1. Did you enjoy reading *Key West?*
   - ❑ Very much—I would like to see more books like this.
   - ❑ Moderately—I would have enjoyed it more if _____
   _____
   _____

2. What influenced your decision to purchase this book? (Check those that apply.)
   - ❑ Cover   ❑ Back cover copy   ❑ Title   ❑ Price
   - ❑ Friends   ❑ Publicity   ❑ Other

3. Which story was your favorite?
   - ❑ *A Time to Embrace*   ❑ *Southern Treasures*
   - ❑ *Lizzy's Hope*   ❑ *One Man's Honor*

4. Please check your age range:
   - ❑ Under 18   ❑ 18–24   ❑ 25–34
   - ❑ 35–45   ❑ 46–55   ❑ Over 55

5. How many hours per week do you read? _____

Name _____

Occupation _____

Address _____

City _____ State _____ Zip _____